THE GIRL FROM THE TEMPLE RUINS

SIMEON DESILAS

The Girl from the Temple Ruins
Simeon DeSilas
This edition Copyright © 2017 by Oxford eBooks Ltd.
Story Copyright © 2017 by Simeon DeSilas

ISBN 978-1-910779-41-5(Paperback)

Book design and typesetting by
Oxford eBooks Ltd.
www.oxford-ebooks.com

Part 1

The Destruction of the temple of the goddess

1

THE HIGH PRIEST, KHAUR

THE HIGH-CEILINGED BEDROOM was in almost complete darkness when Khaur, the High Priest of the Amalishah Temple, awakened with a loud cry. Sunrise was no more than a hope and the only illumination was a feeble yellow light from the small, finely carved oil lamp on the low table beside the bed. The lamp gave out an oily smell because the wick had almost burned out.

Khaur tried to overcome the sense of dread that his dream had left behind, but there was nothing in the dark bedroom on which he could focus his mind and anchor his thoughts. He pushed the goatswool blankets to one side and sat up in his bed, exposing his chest and bare arms. The icy tendrils of the night air caressed his shoulders and he shivered: *I'm trembling... but it's not just the cold...* There was no wind and the cold night was oppressively silent. Even the sacrificial captives in their cells were quiet. Khaur remembered that the wretched captives sometimes moaned in the night. But not this night. On this night they were quiet. He was awake because of his dream.

As full consciousness trickled slowly into his mind, Khaur became aware of a throbbing pain behind his eyeballs. Unthinkingly he rubbed his eyes and realised that his forehead was wet with perspiration. The realisation increased his sense of dread and the darkness suddenly seemed threatening, full of menace: *My Goddess, protect me from the demons of the night!* His whispered prayer to the Goddess calmed him slightly and he rubbed his eyes again. The movement, though small, made him aware of a constriction in his chest. He unwittingly sighed and the young wife who lay beside him murmured in her sleep and turned to look at him uncomprehendingly through half-open eyes. He patted her on the shoulder to let her know he was all right. She closed her eyes and smiled wanly before returning to her slumber.

Khaur's dream had started innocuously enough. He was standing alone in the *lair of the goddess*, the vast cavern-temple deep beneath

4

the hill. Even in the dream he felt his age and leaned, as though from exhaustion, against one of the gigantic pillars that stood along the sides of the wide aisle that led to the sacrificial altar. The pillars, immense rock structures hewn from solid rock, helped support the roof that was almost as high above him as an arrow could reach. As he stood against the pillar, Khaur's attention was drawn to the altar at the far end of the cavern, a massive blackstone slab, longer than the length of a tall man, that lay at the far end of the aisle, exactly halfway between the rows of pillars. And as he dreamed he thought: *That altar is holy. It is where my goddess kills and feeds!* A few paces beyond the altar was a broad dais, almost as high as the eyes of a kneeling man, at the centre of which was the goddess's throne. The goddess always sat on the throne, with two or more priestesses by her side, when she addressed her supplicants. In the dream the throne was empty and the dais deserted.

The vast cavern-temple was usually in semi-darkness, for it was too large to be fully lit by the torches that were firmly attached to the pillars. But in the dream the cavern-temple was resplendent with light. Not only were there brilliant flames on all the torches on the pillars, but there was also torchlight – as bright as sunlight! – from behind the pillars and from the arched ceiling high above, a huge concavity festooned with long stalactites. The dazzling light emanated from all directions and permitted no shadows, so that the uneven floor seemed smooth and the rough walls of the temple reflected the light like clear water in an earthenware bowl. But as Khaur watched in his dream, unaware that he was dreaming, the sacrificial altar and the goddess's throne suddenly vanished and Khaur was left contemplating the vacant dais. Even though he was dreaming, he felt anxious, dismayed and empty.

As happens in dreams, when some things vanish other things take their place. In place of the altar there appeared a mound of human bones, and it seemed to Khaur that the goddess lay asleep on the mound, wearing no jewellery and almost naked except for a white diaphanous gown that completely covered her torso and legs. As she lay on the mound of bones the goddess whispered Khaur's name and he responded eagerly to her summons, more curious than afraid, for even in his dream he knew that no living man had ever seen the goddess while she slept. But as he approached the Goddess there was a deafening sound like the reverberating thunderclaps that terrify travellers on the peaks of mountains. Still in his dream, Khaur stopped some ten paces from the goddess and closed his eyes tightly, covering his ears with his hands: *I must not approach my goddess while she sleeps!* With that thought the punishing sound ceased abruptly and, still in his dream, Khaur opened his eyes. The mound of bones was gone and in its place the tall goddess towered before him, standing straight with her arms by her sides and her enormous black eyes flashing like jewels around a fire. Her white diaphanous gown billowed as though driven by a strong wind from somewhere behind him. She looked straight at him in silent accusation, probing deep into his psyche, yet more in sadness than in anger. He tried to speak but could not, and he tried to kneel in supplication, but could not. He could only stare back, fascinated and paralysed, like a mouse that looks helplessly into the eyes of a stalking snake. And then, as he stood helplessly before the Goddess, she reached out to him with her hand open and the palm facing upwards. He desperately yearned to respond, to do something, anything, that would let her know that his life was devoted to her, that he was her slave as long as he lived, but he was unable to react to her gesture, and as he watched in that state of total physical paralysis that occurs only in dreams, the goddess burst into flames and burned with a fire that was as bright as the sun at midday. He could only watch in horror, unable to move or speak, and even as he watched his goddess burn he suddenly realised, still in his dream, that he did not know whether her gesture had been a gesture of indictment or a plea for help. With this thought everything went black and Khaur cried out, awakening with a sense of soul-wrenching dread.

2

The dream had felt so *real*. Although he was now fully awake, Khaur thought he could still feel the heat from the flames. There was no point in trying to sleep again and with a long sigh he laboriously got off the bed and stood ungainly by the little table. His chest ached from the pounding of his heart but the throbbing pain at the back of his eyeballs was gradually becoming more bearable. The oil lamp on the table continued to burn softly without sputtering, casting a quavering mellow glow upon the heavy rugs that hung on the walls to protect the air in the room from the cold stone. He looked lovingly at the lithe, curled-up body of the sleeping wife to check whether she was well covered, then inspected the wick of the lamp and noted that the oil was almost depleted: *So it's almost daybreak!* he mused, *And what new worries will this day bring?*

Khaur was a small, lightly built man whose body suffered from all the ailments that came to those who were well past middle age. His complexion was unusually dark for an Assyrian and his long unkempt beard was grey and as thick as his hair, which fell in a tangled mass of black and white down his shoulders. His eyes were small but piercing, black as night, and closely set on either side of a thin aquiline nose that was disproportionally large. He sighed once more and covered his bare shoulders with his tunic as he shuffled towards one of the curtainless windows at the end of his bedroom. The two wooden shutters, carved in a fine filigree pattern, permitted coolth but not the hot sunshine to enter the room during the day. Because it was not the cold season, the shutters were open and attached with a small thong to the wall on either side of the aperture. The window appeared to Khaur as a blurred rectangle of darkness, for there was no moon. Had his eyesight permitted, he would have been able to see a multitude of stars, for Khaur's bedroom was on the highest floor of the senior priests' living quarters and the window had an unimpeded view of the Eastern part of the temple; but the High Priest was old and his eyes could no longer see anything clearly. By the starlight he could just make out the outline of the *Palace of the Goddess*, which was the largest building in the temple. Between the living quarters of the High Priest and the *Palace of the Goddess* was a small courtyard ringed by trees that were almost always leafless and needed constant care.

The *Palace of the Goddess* was a circular building constructed partly of locally made bricks and partly of wood that had been brought from distant forests at great cost. There were carved and painted wooden columns all around its outer perimeter and the roof was wooden, as were all the supports that held the structure together. The *Palace of the Goddess* enclosed a large circular room, the *Sacred Chamber*, whose walls were decorated with intricate multicoloured patterns inlaid with semi-precious stones. All around the interior of the Sacred Chamber, about two paces from the circular walls, was a concentric ring of wooden columns, likewise intricately decorated. The floor of the chamber was of polished rock, no different from the rock of the flat-topped hill upon which stood the Amalishah Temple, and at the centre of the Sacred Chamber was a wide pit into which descended a winding spiral staircase without a central column. The winding staircase, cut out from the rock around a natural chimney, led down to the Holy of Holies, the cavern-temple deep beneath the surface, the *lair of the goddess.*

Khaur leaned against the windowsill and breathed in the cold early-morning air. As his brain cleared, he went over all the points of his dream so as not to forget any detail. The review of the dream left Khaur confused and anxious and he turned his attention to the life-size statue of the goddess that stood to the left of the window. The statue, which had stood in that place for centuries, towered over the High Priest, for the goddess was unusually tall and the low pedestal beneath her feet made her seem taller still. The statue was carved from a single piece of translucent milk-white stone and was as near to perfection as human expertise could produce. When the sun shone through the window in the late morning, the sunlight diffused and scattered through the translucent folds of her dress so that the statue glowed like a candle in an alabaster vase. The stone was uncoloured except for the carving of a diadem of golden leaves that encircled her head and of a large red jewel that hung around her neck. The statue showed the goddess standing on a low pedestal, with her legs close together and her left arm by her side. Her right arm was slightly raised, the open hand holding a small owl in its palm. The goddess's expression was serene and wise, her look ageless. The owl was a reminder that the goddess was a creature of the night.

Haunted by his dream and impelled by a sudden overpowering fear that his goddess might be in danger, Khaur fell upon his knees before the statue and raised his arms in supplication: "Oh my goddess", he prayed in a low voice, "You who are immortal, you who understand beyond all understanding, you who know all that is in your servant's mind better than he, make me understand, *please make me understand,* what my dream means lest your servant unwittingly offends you through his foolishness!" He clasped the statue's cold knees tightly, as he had done many times before when his burdens had seemed too onerous to bear. The statue did not respond, and after a while Khaur sank limply to the floor, staring at her feet. The statue continued to gaze benignly across the room, her generous lips hinting at the shadow of a smile.

Khaur yearned to see his goddess and tell her of his dream, but without being invited to her lair even the High Priest of the Amalishah Temple was only allowed to call upon the goddess during emergencies or on the few nights when the moon was full and the goddess had fed.

3

Later in the day Khaur consulted each of the temple's three soothsayers separately, as he always did, and told his dream to each of them as accurately as he could. He was very perturbed by what they advised him, and for the rest of the day he walked wearily and leaned heavily upon his stick. All three soothsayers had warned of unexpected events and possible calamities. But nothing unexpected happened that day, and when the day was over he went to bed tormented by the memory of his dream and by the words of the soothsayers. He slept badly and alone, for he had no wish to be with any of his wives when his mind was unsettled.

In the early afternoon of the second day after the High Priest's dream, the temple's routine was shattered by a commotion at the First Gate, which lay roughly to the North-East of the temple. The guardian priests on the tower that overlooked the gate waved their bows frantically and shouted that there were 'armed foreigners' within view of the tower. Both the First and Second gates were hurriedly closed and the alarm spread quickly throughout the temple compound, not least by a number of hysterical pilgrim women who ran through the narrow alleys pulling their hair and screaming that the temple was under attack.

While the senior priests assumed responsibility for maintaining order, the lesser priests saw the hubbub as an opportunity to escape from the tedium of their lives. They gathered in small groups to argue about what this unheard-of event might mean. Outside the quarters of the minor priests and acolytes two young priests were trying to stop a group of curious children from rushing to the First Gate to see what *foreigners* looked like: "You must not let the foreigners cast their eyes on you!" one of the young priests advised the children, "Foreigners have *the Evil Eye!*" The children became frightened and subdued.

A group of priests armed with spears and bows ran to the Second Gate to forestall a possible attack at the rear of the temple. In almost no time at all the news was carried even to the most isolated of shrines, with their sleepy and life-weary attendants, and even to the living quarters of the menials and neophyte priests. No one had ever heard of *armed foreigners* coming to the Amalishah Temple and the unfamiliar excitement evolved into something akin to panic. Amid the hubbub and near chaos a slim priestess with green eyes, not quite so young but not yet middle-aged, sought out the senior guard of the First Gate, a priest of middle rank. After speaking to him quietly for a short time, she walked calmly but purposefully towards the *palace of the Goddess*. Like all the priestesses, her head was covered so as to partly conceal her long hair, but the veil that covered her hair was white and of very fine cloth, which showed that she was one of the seven priestesses who lived in the underground temple with the goddess herself.

"So what is all this shouting about *foreigners*?" Khaur asked the young priest who had rushed to tell him the news but was too excited to speak intelligibly.

"Foreigners!" replied the man, and he bowed repeatedly as though the word itself was a sacrilege that needed to be expunged.

"I know that!" exclaimed Khaur impatiently. "Are we under attack? How many are they?"

"Nine foreigners, Oh High Priest" said the man subserviently after he had finally stopped bowing. "They are armed!"

"Could they be pilgrims?" Khaur asked hopefully.

"They are *foreigners*," repeated the neophyte, as though this settled the issue.

"Do they bear gifts?" persisted Khaur. There was a time, long before he was born, when foreigners used to visit the temple bearing gifts.

"It would appear not, Oh High Priest. They carry leather bags like poor travellers, and they have curved swords hanging from their waists. But they carry no shields or spears."

So they cannot be dangerous! thought Khaur.

The High Priest hurried to the First Gate, closely followed by the young priest who had brought the news. Khaur was perturbed; no foreigners had ever come willingly to the Amalishah Temple in his lifetime nor, as far as he knew, in the lifetimes of the last two High Priests before him, his father and grandfather. As long as he could remember, the only visitors to the temple had been pious pilgrims carrying gifts and, more recently, parties of well-armed soldiers bringing captives to be sacrificed to the goddess. The temple was far from human habitation and the surrounding wilderness, the *wastelands*, was much too inhospitable for casual visitors to cross.

Yet despite the isolation there were always pilgrims and supplicants before the nights when the moon was full. The goddess was popular, especially among the old, and pilgrims from all walks of life came to worship and ask for small favours. There had been poor shepherds and princes, artisans and wealthy merchants, soldiers and courtesans. All brought the goddess and her priests and priestesses such gifts as they could afford: goats, pulses, gold ornaments, cereals, precious metals, jars of oil, copper and bronze utensils. Pilgrims were the temple's source of income and news from the outside world.

"I think they are Hittites," said the young priest as he followed Khaur.

The young man's words broke Khaur's train of thought. "Hittites? What makes you think they are Hittites?"

"Their skins are lighter and redder than ours, Holy One. They are certainly fairer than the Sumerians we know. They look like some of the Hittite boys that are brought to the temple as gifts to the goddess."

"We shall soon find out what they want. Now run ahead!"

The man ran ahead and Khaur returned to his thoughts. What would the goddess expect him to do? There were nine *foreigners* at the First Gate, and they bore no gifts.

4

The foreigners had brought their own interpreter with them, a dour man whose home lay near the border between Assyria and the land from whence the foreigners had come. With some difficulty the interpreter managed to explain to the temple guards on the tower that he and his fellow travellers were Hittites, that their leader was a Hittite prince whose name was Artaxias, and that the Prince Artaxias wished to speak to the High Priest of the temple on a matter of importance. The information was conveyed to Khaur by a succession of excited priests and priestesses of lower rank who ran up to him as he approached the First Gate.

The High Priest tried to decide in advance what should be done but was unable to make a decision. He found the novelty of the situation confusing, and such was the power of this new experience that all conscious memory of his dream and of the warnings of the soothsayers was driven from his mind, although some of the anxiety remained and served to further obfuscate his thinking. Khaur had been High Priest for over thirty years but he had never had to face the *unexpected* before: the temple was like a water wheel that turned predictably without stopping and whose buckets, though individually distinguishable, were in practice impossible to tell apart. Khaur's task, as he saw it, was to preserve continuity and to ensure that the goddess was worshipped according to age-hallowed traditions. He always looked to the past for guidance on how to deal with the present, but now he sought in vain for something that would show him the proper way to deal with armed foreigners at the main gate of his goddess's temple.

When Khaur reached the First Gate he found a small crowd milling about the entrance to the Greater Audience Chamber, which was close to the First Gate. The proximity of the Greater Audience chamber to the First Gate enabled the High Priest to greet important visitors immediately after they entered the temple. The goddess spoke to visitors only in her underground cavern deep beneath the *Sacred Chamber*.

Everybody respectfully made way for the High Priest. Khaur stopped for a moment to catch his breath and then spoke a few curt words to the middle-rank priest who was in charge of the First Gate. The man nodded and shouted to the guard priests at the top of the stone tower which guarded the gate: "Prepare to receive the High Priest! The Holy One will be coming up the ladder!"

"We gratefully await his presence!" came the reply.

Assured that someone would help him climb off the ladder and onto the platform at the top of the tower, Khaur took hold of the sides of the ladder and started to climb laboriously. Some of the pilgrims muttered prayers to the goddess for his safety. It was not an easy climb, especially for an old man, for the rungs were far apart and the tower was three times the height of a man. When he reached the platform Khaur was diffidently helped off the ladder by the guard-priests at the top of the tower. After pausing long enough to recover from his climb, Khaur leaned over the parapet and glared down at the unwelcome visitors.

The visitors were not impressive. They were of medium stature, though muscular and broad-shouldered. Unlike the many dignitaries who had visited the temple, these foreigners wore no ornaments and appeared too poor to bring gifts. They were all dressed similarly in warm but unadorned clothes and the shapeless travelling bags they carried loosely on their backs had no adornments and looked merely functional. Even their long capes were all of the same colour, light brown, and their upturned boots were sturdy but without decoration. Three wore metal helmets and two wore tall hats like truncated cones.

The others were bare-headed, and the only distinguishing feature of the prince, who wore neither hat nor helmet, was a thin silver ring around his head that held his long hair away from his eyes. None carried shields or spears. *So these are the redoubtable Hittites!* Khaur thought. *They are but stout men with round beardless faces!*

5

Khaur found it hard to take the title of their leader seriously: *Even the servants of our princes dress better than that!* Yet, although the visitors cut a poor figure in Khaur's view, he was anxious to impress them with the grandeur of the Amalishah Temple and the importance of his position. The only Hittites Khaur had seen – at a distance – were prisoners captured by Assyrian raiding parties on their ever-more-frequent forays into neighbouring lands. Those were gifts for the goddess and were invariably young but half-starved specimens with broken arms and, not infrequently, without eyes. Their captors were keen to ensure that the prisoners would not give any trouble. Once at the Amalishah Temple they would be fattened before being offered to the goddess, but Khaur would not see them when they were ready to be sacrificed. Only certain priests and the inner circle of the temple priestesses would attend to the sacrificial victims, and even they would never see the goddess feed.

As Khaur glared at them mutely, the Hittites took off their travelling bags and, after a brief consultation, turned to face the massive portals of the First Gate. They stood patiently and silently, without expression, in a semi-circle some seven paces from the wooden portals. But their hands were on the pommels of their scythe-swords, and their eyes were most often on the spot where the wide wooden portals, if opened, would first reveal what lay behind them. If the priests were to prove hostile the Hittites' deployment offered the best defence against a surprise *sortie*. To someone who knew about armed fighting their stance would have said: Beware! These men are not strangers to violence! But to Khaur they appeared no better than beggars, and as he looked down at them contemptuously his gaze met that of the Hittite prince.

Their eyes locked and Khaur was suddenly struck by an unexplainable unease, as though the anxieties brought up by his dream had been awakened, but the novelty of the moment had made him forget his dream or what the soothsayers had told him. The Hittite prince, unaware that the old man who was glaring down at him was the High Priest of the temple, showed no emotion. Then Khaur abruptly turned away and cautiously began to climb down the wooden ladder. Only when he was half way down did he realise that the Hittite prince's unperturbed gaze had somehow reminded him of the frustration and helplessness he had experienced in his dream. The memory, complex though it was, carried a sensation of alarm in its wake, but Khaur's inability to cope with novel situations did not allow him to translate these feelings into anything deeper than the simple question: *Should I turn them away or let them in?* Khaur was inclined to turn them away, or perhaps have them killed, but the goddess herself had told him never to decline information, and these unwelcome visitors would not have travelled so far if they had nothing to say.

Khaur ordered the guards to allow the foreigners to enter, on condition that they were escorted by armed priests at all times. Khaur reasoned that the foreigners were exhausted and, anyway, were too few and poorly armed to cause trouble. However, he made it very clear that they were not to be offered shelter, food, or even water. Khaur was too set in the temple's isolationist mentality to attach any importance to what the prince might have to say, but he was idly curious about these strangers and, besides, it could do no harm to change the temple's routine just a little and for a short time. Khaur decided to see the prince and his companions in the Lesser Audience Chamber, which was at the other side of the temple, near the Second Gate, at the South-West of the temple compound. The Lesser Audience Chamber was no more than a large room, bleakly decorated, used for audiences with visitors of low status. In Khaur's eyes all foreigners were unimportant or, at best, of minor importance.

6

When the strangers were brought before Khaur, the Lesser Audience Chamber was crowded with armed priests, pilgrims, and curious onlookers, including some women and children. At close quarters the Hittites looked anything but threatening. They were covered in dust and obviously exhausted, and if one looked carefully one would notice that their capes were torn in many places. The temple priests who escorted the Hittites into the Lesser Audience Chamber watched the strangers with ill-concealed hostility. The priests carried shields and long spears with sharp bronze tips, which they held at the level of the *foreigners'* chests in readiness for any eventuality, although they kept themselves at a safe distance. Khaur and two senior priests sat on comfortable seats at the far end of the Lesser Audience Chamber, opposite the entrance, and scowled at the visitors who stood silently in a line before them.

The Hittite prince stood proudly erect with his hands at his sides, waiting for permission to speak, for good manners dictated that, in a temple, a High Priest had seniority even over a Royal Prince. Eventually Khaur nodded in the direction of the Hittites, indicating that whoever was to be their spokesman had permission to speak.

The prince spoke calmly, although he was weary from his travels and surprised by the rudeness of his hosts: "Our King, my uncle," said the prince through the interpreter, "Sends greetings to you, Oh High Priest. We have come a long way to ask something of you."

Khaur scowled haughtily but made no answer and the prince continued: "Our king, the king of the Hittites whose land is far from here, is displeased by what he hears happens to his subjects who are abducted from their villages by Assyrian raiding parties. We understand the desire of your king to extend his borders, that is the privilege of all rulers, but our king is gravely displeased to hear that Assyrian excursions onto our lands are solely for the purpose of capturing young men to bring them to this temple for your goddess, who lives beneath the ground, to feed on their blood. Our king cannot accept such a fate for his kindred."

"So why don't you take the matter up with *our* king?" replied Khaur mockingly. He was not used to being addressed without long and humble preliminaries; the *foreigner* was being much too direct.

"This is too small a matter for dialogue between kings," replied the prince. "It is only what happens here, in this temple, that concerns us."

"What happens here should not concern you at all," said Khaur, and the two senior priests beside him laughed. "When I saw you at our gates I knew that you were nothing if not a beggar, wanting something. And I was right."

The Hittite prince had never been insulted before, yet despite his tiredness he managed to control his anger. "We are representatives of the Hittite king," said the prince, "What my uncle, the king of the Hittites, is asking of you, and what I, a Hittite prince of the highest rank, am asking of you, is not unreasonable."

Khaur spoke with ill-concealed contempt: "And what does your king, of whom I have never heard, wish us to do?" Khaur had certainly heard of the Hittite king, but he could not resist the temptation to insult the visitors.

"Our king, my uncle, only asks that you henceforth refuse to accept our kindred as gifts to her that lives beneath the ground, whom you call a goddess. It is a small thing to ask."

"It is a great thing for *you* or *your king* to ask," said Khaur, and his scowl grew darker. "All prisoners brought here are gifts from our king, who is a King of Kings, to our goddess, and it is the King of Kings' wish that she feed on them, or else do with them as she pleases."

The prince nodded, as though accepting that a gift from the Assyrian ruler to the goddess was beyond the authority of the High Priest to refuse: *But there must be a way I can ask this man to put a stop to this. Surely there is some way he can stop this without displeasing his king!* The prince continued: "We know very little of your goddess except that she feeds on blood. We also know that the blood need not be the blood of men. Again I ask you, I beg you, please refuse to accept our kindred as gifts to your goddess. We Hittites have always been willing to worship new gods and goddesses, that is why we are sometimes called 'the people of a thousand gods'. If you grant us this small thing you may rest assured that many Hittites will soon join the Assyrian pilgrims to the Amalishah temple, laden with gifts. Our king himself shall thank you with gifts of great value."

Khaur laughed loudly, and almost everyone in the Hall joined in the laughter. Only the Hittites and their interpreter did not laugh; they and the slim, veiled woman with green eyes who stood silently at the back of the Lesser Audience Chamber, concealed by the crowd.

7

When he stopped laughing Khaur spoke disdainfully to his visitors: "Hittite pilgrims to the Amalishah temple? More beggars at our gates? Gifts from your king? You have nothing to give that we would find desirable, foreign beggar. The blood of your kindred is all we want, and we shall offer it to our goddess even if your king himself comes here to beg for favours!"

"Even as you stand here before us," added the senior priest who sat to the right of Khaur, "We have some of your kindred with broken arms languishing in our dungeons, waiting to be fed to our goddess!" He gave a cackling laugh.

This was too much for the Hittite prince. Unable to hold his anger and his horror, words escaped from his mouth as though squeezed out of his lungs: "Your goddess who feeds on human blood," he said to himself through clenched teeth, "Is known as *a monster* everywhere outside Assyria!" Perhaps because he was so tired, or perhaps because he had been provoked more than he could bear, the prince had spoken louder than he had intended. He had spoken in Hittite and the translator had not translated, but someone among the audience shouted: "He called our goddess a monster!"

Khaur stared unbelievingly at the prince as all activity in the Lesser Audience Chamber stopped. The whispers among the throng suddenly became silent, the shuffle of standing bodies abruptly ceased. The priests seemed to freeze almost immediately, then the pilgrims, and finally the children. Everyone looked to the High Priest expecting him to order the immediate death of the visitors but, to everyone's surprise, Khaur raised his hands and laughed again: "You are playing with your life, Hittite, but because you amuse me I shall forgive your bad manners. I could have you all killed now, or I could have you flayed alive, or I could give you and your companions to our goddess with your eyes gouged out and your arms broken. But, this once, just this once, I will tolerate your blasphemy because you are a foreigner and ignorant of civilised ways. So go back from whence you came, and tell your uncle, whose name I neither know nor wish to know, that our king does whatever he pleases, wherever he pleases." The interpreter translated Khaur's words accurately but mechanically.

After a long pause, the prince said to his companions: "Let us go, brethren, but we'll be back!" The interpreter did not translate.

"Just go!" said Khaur, as though he had understood what the prince had said. With a dismissive wave of his hand he seemed to lose all interest in the visitors. He turned to the senior priest to his left and asked him to have the Lesser Audience Chamber vacated.

The Hittite prince was going to say more, but the armed priests were already prodding his companions with their spears and ushering them out.

"Is that all that we get to say, my prince?" asked one of the Hittites, a younger man, "Is this all we get to say after the long journey we have made?"

"We said what we came to say, Norr," replied the prince, and he was about to turn to leave when the interpreter, thinking that he might be called upon to translate what the prince had said, hesitated and turned to face one of the armed priests. The priest jokingly jabbed him in the arm with his spear. The thrust was stronger than the priest had intended and the sharp bronze tip of the spear pierced the skin. The interpreter shouted in pain and a small stream of blood dripped from the wound onto the stone floor. Some of the onlookers would have started laughing again had the Hittite prince not pulled out his scythe-sword and struck, with a lightning sweep, at the spear of the offending priest. The sword cut through the wooden shaft as though it were made of straw and the priest, in a state of shock, was left holding part of the shaft. The remainder, with the bronze tip, flew a short distance before clattering onto the floor.

The armed priests shouted loudly in outrage. It might well have been the end of the Hittite *mission* to the Amalishah Temple had Khaur not stood up and raised his arms, commanding silence. The Hittites swiftly gathered together back to back with their swords drawn, retreating slowly towards the exit of the chamber.

"Let them go!" ordered the High Priest. "We want nothing of this band of beggars, not even their blood!"

There was a lot of muttering among the priests, as this was the second time that Khaur, against all expectations, had refrained from ordering the massacre of the visitors. But no one dared openly question the High Priest, and the visitors were escorted without further incident out of the Lesser Audience Chamber and out of the Amalishah Temple through the Second Gate.

Khaur was not too interested in military matters, so he did not notice the ease with which the Hittite's sword had cut through the heavy wooden shaft of the spear, nor did he notice that it was made of a black metal that had never been seen in the temple before. But the slim veiled woman with green eyes took note of everything, just as she had heard and understood every word that had been said. She withdrew from the Lesser Audience Chamber immediately after the strangers left, and walked swiftly towards the *Palace of the Goddess*.

8

If Khaur could have had his way he would have had the *foreigners* killed on the spot for daring to insult the goddess, or for raising a weapon against a priest of the temple, but the goddess herself had decreed that anyone who came willingly to the temple without hostile intentions should be allowed to leave unmolested. Even a High Priest could not contravene a decree by the goddess. *Still*, he thought, *they were offered neither food nor water, and they were unceremoniously sent out of the Second Gate, like beggars, even though it will be dark soon!* Khaur cursed them and hoped that something terrible would befall them once they were far from the temple. He felt sure that he had acted correctly, though perhaps overleniently, and that whatever threat to his goddess these *foreigners* might have posed was safely eliminated. *After all*, he thought, *the man had nothing of real importance to say.* Yet Khaur could not reconcile his apparently successful handling of the situation with the feelings brought up by his dream, which still haunted him.

By the next day the temple had returned to its normal routine and Khaur, with two priests and two acolytes, was conducting a ritual in one of the temple's many shrines. The ritual was on behalf of some wealthy pilgrims who had travelled a long way and brought many rich gifts. As the priests chanted in the language peculiar to the Amalishah Temple, an old but imposingly tall priestess entered the shrine and made her way to where Khaur was conducting the ceremony. The priestess walked slowly, leaning on a staff and taking each step with the calm deliberation of those for whom every movement of the hips brings pain. But she moved with the quiet dignity that comes from spending most of a long life in a position of authority, and when it was apparent that she wished to speak to Khaur the ceremony stopped. When all eyes were turned to her she beckoned to Khaur and he hastened to her side.

"Yes, Neera? To what do I owe the honour of your visit?" Khaur managed to sound diffident without being servile. Neera was the goddess's oldest and most senior priestess, a daunting woman. She spoke curtly to Khaur: "The goddess wishes to speak to you!"

"Now?"

"Now!"

"Yes, of course!" Khaur instructed one of the priests to proceed with the ceremony without him. The High Priest was too pleased at the invitation to notice that Neera's curtness might be an indication that the goddess was displeased with him. He followed the priestess as fast as her slow gait allowed but his excitement at the prospect of telling the goddess about his dream had dulled his usual sensitivity to the tone with which messages from the goddess were delivered. At the door of the *Palace of the Goddess* the old priestess turned to him and said: "You shall continue alone. The goddess is expecting you."

9

The goddess lived in her *lair* with her seven 'white' priestesses who served her and provided for her needs. These women formed the inner circle of the Amalishah temple and were distinguished by the right to wear milk-white veils in addition to the distinctive necklace that distinguished priestesses from the other women in the temple. All the women who became priestesses had been *gifts* to the goddess while still children, to be her willing and total slaves for the rest of their lives. Of the many young girls brought to the temple, many were rejected; of those that were accepted the majority became normal priestesses, and the few that were distinguished by their intelligence and loyalty to the goddess were chosen to become 'white' priestesses and live underground with the goddess herself. The 'white' priestesses had free access to the surface and would occasionally run errands for the goddess, both within and outside the temple. The purpose of the outside errands was almost never disclosed, but it was rumoured that the goddess exchanged information with the High Priests of other temples and even with the king himself. The excursions of the 'white' priestesses outside the temple often lasted several moons.

One of the duties of the 'white' priestesses was to bring the *sacrifice* to the goddess. This always happened two or three days before the moon was at its fullest, so that the goddess would not be hungry during the lunar-monthly ceremony when the pilgrims and her priests were allowed to see her. However, during the twelve years when the goddess was given only human sacrifice she had fed ever more rarely. It was now several moons since a prisoner had been brought to her and Khaur had frequently wondered how long she could subsist without feeding.

Khaur remembered the time when the goddess would sometimes visit the surface at night. At that time the goddess had fed only on the blood of goats and fowl, though then, as now, no one was allowed to see her feed. Human sacrifice had started with the present King, who had insisted that she feed only on prisoners from his frequent campaigns or captives brought to the temple by his raiding parties.

It was understood that the King would punish the priests and priestesses with unspeakable cruelty if his wishes were not obeyed, and so the goddess had been forced to acquiesce. The Assyrian King had delivered his *request* in person, during the only visit he had ever paid to the Amalishah Temple, and he had spoken to the goddess alone and in private. Khaur knew that the goddess found human sacrifice repugnant and he suspected that she fed secretly on animals that were secreted into her temple by her priestesses, but for reasons that the High Priest never understood, the goddess had never visited the surface again after the King's insistent demand that she feed on human blood alone.

10

To Khaur, the long winding flight of steps that led down to the cavern-temple seemed endless and he was tired and out of breath when he reached the small hemispherical cavern at the bottom of the steps. He expected to make his way through the long, low tunnel that led from the small cavern to the lair of the goddess unimpeded, and was surprised and worried when, halfway through the tunnel, his way was barred by two priestesses who told him to wait. This was a sure sign that the goddess was displeased with him. The realisation disturbed him.

Eventually he was admitted into the huge underground cavern-temple. He could not help remembering his dream and was relieved to see that nothing had changed. The giant pillars on either side still formed an aisle more than a hundred paces long and more than forty paces wide, and at the end of the aisle the monolithic altar still stood some seven paces before the low dais upon which stood the goddess's throne. Despite his tiredness, Khaur hurried past the altar as fast as he could manage, and when he reached the end of the aisle he prostrated himself on the cold stone floor between the altar and the dais, with his arms spread out, waiting to be acknowledged by the goddess.

She sat straight-backed on her throne of black stone, her exceptionally large eyes half closed and focused on the farthest point of the cavern. Behind the throne stood two 'white' priestesses. They avoided looking at Khaur.

"Tell me of the visitors!" she ordered.

Khaur told her of the Hittite delegation in his usual circuitous way, although he knew that she was well aware of all that had happened. He told her everything, even the small detail that, according to someone at the Lesser Audience Chamber, the Hittite prince had referred to her as a *monster*.

The goddess listened patiently until Khaur had finished. When she spoke there was a slight irritation in her voice:

"The temple defences must be repaired and, if possible, strengthened. See to it."

"Yes, my goddess. It shall be done as you say. I shall..."

The goddess interrupted him: "You will send a courier with a message to the king at once. You will ask for troops to help defend the temple. Finally, you will collect all provisions in the storerooms and put them under guard. The goats and fowl that are outside the temple must be brought within and kept, also under guard, in the courtyards."

Khaur raised his head in disbelief as he lay prostrated on the floor before the dais: "Surely, my goddess," he said imploringly, "You do not believe that the Hittites, or anyone else, would dare attack your temple? It is under your protection, and the protection of the king!"

The goddess did not answer.

"My goddess," continued Khaur. "Your temple is impregnable! There are well over two hundred and fifty armed priests, and almost as many armed acolytes. Your temple is on a hill with steep sides, and the defensive wall is higher than a standing man!"

The goddess seemed not to have heard him, then after a long pause she answered in a low voice: "The Hittite king's nephew was not blind, Khaur," she said, finally looking down at the old man. "As he crossed the temple, from the First Gate to the Lesser Audience Chamber and then to the Second Gate, he saw our defences and estimated the number of our fighting men. For any competent general, that is enough. You will send the request for reinforcements and see to the defences and provisions."

"I shall send a courier to our king at once!" Khaur spoke as grudgingly as he dared. "He will send an army that will crush any invaders and bring you enough prisoners for ten years!"

"Do not speak of that!"

"Forgive me, my goddess. But the thought of any threat to you, no matter how empty, or how ignorantly made, makes me hot with anger!"

Again there was a pause before the goddess answered him: "I know your feelings, Khaur." She smiled at him; a weak smile tinged

22

with sadness. "I do not doubt your loyalty, or the fervour of your love for me. Go now and do what I told you. Send the courier to the king at once, and pray that if reinforcements come they will be adequate and not too late."

Khaur decided that this was not a good time to tell the goddess of his dream

1 1

Instead of reinforcements the king sent a batch of prisoners for the goddess. Seven terrified young men, five of whom were Hittites, arrived under escort some eight weeks after the Hittite delegation had left the temple. Most had their arms broken but none had been blinded. They were put with the rest of the temple prisoners in the windowless prison close to the *Palace of the Goddess*. Khaur was not surprised when a minor priestess brought a message saying that the goddess wished to see him and the leader of the prisoners' escort immediately.

As required, Khaur and the officer prostrated themselves before the dais and waited to be spoken to. The officer was in full ceremonial dress, armed with a bronze sword and a short bone-hilted knife. Khaur had hurriedly changed clothes and removed all his jewellery except for a small amulet. He wished to be as self-effacing as possible.

The goddess was sitting rigidly on her throne with one young and very pretty 'white' priestess standing by her side. The goddess rarely showed any emotion, but from the way her eyes flashed Khaur guessed that she was clearly displeased, perhaps even angry. Only two of the torches were lit so that most of the cavern-temple was dark, and this usually meant that the goddess was about to feed. With a pang of fear Khaur suddenly remembered that the goddess had not fed for a long time. He cast a sidelong glance at the officer who was lying face down beside him: *If you must feed, my goddess, please feed on him!* The man was not unattractive although his beard was flecked with grey. He was also muscular with many scars that spoke of experience in the field of battle, but Khaur knew that he would be no match for the goddess despite his weapons. The goddess was said to have supernatural strength and could move faster than a striking snake. But the altar had not been prepared for sacrifice: there were no aromatic herbs or fragrant flowers upon the flat top of the monolith, and the incense burners were empty. Still, Khaur had never known the goddess so displeased, and he could not forget that she had not fed for some time. The unprepared altar did not reassure him.

The goddess ignored Khaur and spoke to the officer with unusual coldness: "And what message does the king send?"

The man raised his head and recited what he had been ordered to say: "The king sends you, our living and immortal goddess, his warmest greetings. He asks you, who will live forever, to accept his small gift of seven young men in the prime of life and the king hopes that they will prove..."

But the goddess interrupted him: "How many armed men have you brought with you?" She spoke in a calm voice that, nonetheless, cut like a knife. The goddess's voice was uncommonly deep for a woman, and in the silence of the underground temple she sounded ominous and threatening.

"Twenty armed men," stammered the officer, "To accompany the seven prisoners who are our king's gift to you. They have been made harmless, as usual."

"Are you going to remain in the temple?" she asked.

"No, goddess. We must return to the main party the day after we deliver the captives."

"Where are the reinforcements I asked for?"

"I know of no reinforcements," replied the man in a low voice, as though he was afraid to say what he had to. "I and my men are part of a large raiding party that was ordered to raid villages outside our borders and capture healthy young men to bring as gifts to you from our king. After delivering the prisoners we are to spend one night in the temple and then rejoin the raiding party and return home."

"Where is the raiding party now?"

"Waiting for us, one day's travel from the temple."

"How many men are in the raiding party?"

"Eighty-six, my goddess, including me and my twenty. It is a large raiding party."

"You alone will return to the raiding party. You will tell your leader to come to the temple at once with all his men."

The officer covered his face with his hands. "I cannot do that, my goddess," he said. He was trembling visibly. "We were explicitly ordered to keep the main force away from the temple and to send only the prisoners with an escort, as many men as we deemed necessary. The escort was to stay in the temple for no more than one night. The seal on the order was from the king himself. To disobey is to die."

The goddess nodded and said nothing, but Khaur was outraged: "You dare disobey the goddess?" But before the officer could answer the goddess rose from her throne, forcing the men to silence.

"Khaur, make sure that this man and his brave companions spend the night comfortably. Tomorrow they shall leave the temple with gifts of food and water. Now go, both of you!"

Because the goddess was standing the two men had to leave the cavern-temple backwards on all fours, a task that was both painful and very slow for Khaur. After they were gone, the Goddess turned to the young priestess who was standing beside her.

"The temple shall have to stand alone, Hasha," she said quietly.

"I do not understand," said the young priestess. "Why would the armed men not come? Does the king think that the Hittite prince spoke empty words when he said he would be back?"

"No, Hasha" said the goddess. "The king does not think so. But when an empire has two heads one of them is bound to sacrifice the other."

"I still do not understand, my goddess. Forgive me."

The Goddess smiled sadly at the young priestess. "That is because you have led most of your short life in the temple, Hasha, and do not understand the ways of the world outside. Now I want you to bring all the other 'white' priestesses to me."

When the young priestess was gone the goddess wept.

1 2

"What do you mean 'they are gone'?" exclaimed Khaur to the acolyte who was serving his breakfast of goat's milk, eggs and hard bread. "Gone where?"

"I do not know, Holy One," said the acolyte. "But one of my wives tells me that early this morning all but two of the 'white' priestesses were seen leaving the temple through the Second Gate. They took the children and many of the mothers with them. All the pilgrims who were in the temple left also."

Khaur rose from his table without taking his meal. "I must see the goddess!" he exclaimed. The acolyte bowed down and spoke in a halting voice: "May I remind the Holy One that only yesterday one of the priestesses said that the goddess does not wish to speak to anyone but her 'white' priestesses?"

"That was yesterday," muttered Khaur as he waved the acolyte away: "When things were still normal!"

Khaur did not go far before others confirmed the unbelievable news. Only two 'white' priestesses remained in the cavern-temple, the others had taken all the children and left. To his questions: 'Why did they flee?' and 'Where did they go?' Khaur was offered no explanation. When Khaur asked why he had not been consulted, or why the mothers had consented to allow their children to be taken away, the answer was always the same: 'We thought you knew. It was the wish of the goddess!'

At first Khaur was as angry as he dared be with the goddess: *Does she not trust me any more? Am I to be sidestepped now?* But his anger turned to fear and then to terror as he descended the long winding staircase to the underground temple: *If the goddess does not trust me she will kill me!* He fumbled with the little amulet that hung around his neck; it had been a gift from the goddess to his great-grandfather. Khaur suddenly wished that he had other gods to pray to, but all his life he had prayed only to the goddess of the temple, and the disloyal thought made him feel guilty and increased his terror. It was not inconceivable that the goddess would feed on him if he came to her alone and if she were sufficiently displeased. But Khaur was not quite sure why the goddess was displeased with him.

As Khaur walked hurriedly along the long aisle that separated the dais from the entrance to the cavern-temple he observed that although all the torches were lit some were already sputtering, ready to burn out at any moment. The thought of being alone with the goddess in total darkness almost made him faint with terror.

She received him courteously enough, sitting regally on her throne with only Hasha and the aged Neera standing beside her. Khaur was not surprised to see that the fanatically loyal Neera had stayed behind; Neera was too old and in too much pain to walk long distances. However, the presence of the young and innocent Hasha surprised him: *Perhaps Hasha is too young to leave! Outside the temple a pretty girl like her would need a permanent male escort!*

As always, Khaur prostrated himself before the dais. The floor was cold and hard, and he fervently hoped that the goddess would allow him to stand. For many years she had allowed him to stand when there was no one about but her 'white' priestesses. But this time she kept him lying uncomfortably on the cold hard floor.

"Speak Khaur!"

"My goddess is displeased with me."

"Have you seen to the temple defences as I told you to?"

"All is as you ordered."

"Have you seen to the stores and animals?"

"All is as you ordered."

"You came because some of my 'white' priestesses left with all the children."

"Yes, my goddess. I was wondering who will bring you your sacrifice now that most of the 'white' priestesses are gone."

"*You* will, Khaur, with two priests."

"Yes, my goddess. But may I remind you that I, who have served you faithfully all my life, like my father and his father before him … we have never had to do this task?"

"Things change. How many prisoners are there in the temple?"

"Thirty-two, my goddess."

"How many of them are Hittites?"

"I think nineteen or twenty, my goddess."

"Have all but one of the Hittites killed and bury the bodies where they cannot be found."

"Yes, my goddess."

Khaur cleared his throat. "There is another matter. One of the 'white' priestesses also acted as your, er... Eyes and Ears, my goddess. I hear that she is gone too. Who will fulfil her duties now?"

"You, Khaur. In the temple, just you."

"I do not have her skills, my goddess. How will I manage to fulfil her tasks?"

The goddess did not answer.

"I understand." Khaur remembered again that the goddess must be very hungry, but perhaps this was not the time to speak of human sacrifice. "Would the goddess like a goat or some other animal, perhaps?" Khaur was acutely aware that the king had demanded that only human sacrifice be offered to the goddess, but perhaps this was a good time to show that he obeyed none but his goddess.

"The animals may be needed on the surface, Khaur. When the Hittites come there may be a siege. Until then, I will feed only on prisoners."

"Yes, my goddess. But are you so sure the Hittites will come?"

"They sent a Royal Prince, Khaur. He came a very long way and made his request in the humblest tone. If their king is as old and as

27

wise as travellers say, that could only be his final plea before a reluctant but inevitable use of force."

The old man bowed his head. He could not but regret how he had insulted the man: *If any harm comes to my goddess it would be because of me!*

"And there is something you must tell the armed priests and acolytes," continued the goddess. "When the Hittites attack the temple, they must not fight them hand to hand. Do you understand me? They may shoot at them with arrows, throw spears and stones at them, do anything they can but they must not get close enough for the Hittites to use their swords!"

"Yes, my goddess," Khaur agreed, too stunned to ask why.

"Tonight you and two priests will bring me the Hittite that was not killed. And you will bring your own torches, for the cavern-temple will henceforth be in darkness."

2

The Hittite prince, Artaxias

1

"I can see the Sharan pass," said Norr excitedly. He pointed to a barely visible cleft in the mist-shrouded mountains ahead of them: "There, beyond the clump of dead trees! Between the two peaks on the horizon!" Norr was the navigator and youngest member of the *mission* to the Amalishah Temple. A square-jawed young man with a pronounced sense of humour, his proclivity to embrace ideas enthusiastically made him the perfect counterweight to the thoughtful and restrained Artaxias.

The return journey was through the Sharan pass because it offered the shortest route from the Amalishah Temple to Hattusas, the Hittite capital. The outward journey from Hattusas had taken a different, longer, route because the objective then was secrecy, not speed.

"I see it," said Artaxias, squinting. "If we walk with few rest periods we shall sleep among our own people tonight!" He adjusted the silver headband that held his hair away from his eyes.

The navigator groaned. "I agree, my prince, but it is past midday and we have been walking since dawn. I dread the thought of more walking through the afternoon and into the night!"

The prince smiled. "It's either that or sleeping in the wastelands one more night!"

"I'm getting used to it!"

"Think of those big hairy spiders that love to crawl under our blankets!"

"Akh! I had forgotten about the spiders!" Norr pretended to shiver with revulsion but Artaxias was already thinking of other things. "If we reach the pass some time after nightfall," he said slowly, "and if we are very careful, then anyone sent to waylay us will not see us approach."

Norr was not ready to turn his mind to the possibility of new dangers. He scratched vigorously under his cape and said: "I am *so* looking forward to sitting in a tub full of hot water! How I relish the idea of drowning all those little bugs that have been eating me since we entered the wastelands!"

The interpreter nodded understandingly but Artaxias only gave a polite smile.

The party was having a rest, and the prince, Norr and the interpreter had stopped slightly ahead of the others. Artaxias raised his arm to signal that the rest-time was over. As they waited for the others to catch up, Norr commented: "You know, my prince, now that we're near our own land, I can confess that the constant fear of being followed by murderous priests, or of accidentally crossing the path of an Assyrian raiding party, has worn me down."

"It's worn us all down," replied Artaxias with a grim smile. "And you forgot to mention the possibility of being ambushed by bandits."

"Oh, we can deal with any bandits!"

"On half-empty stomachs?"

"You're right!" said Norr. "I'm also tired of being perpetually hungry!"

While in Assyrian territory the nine Hittites had avoided any contact with the local inhabitants. This had not been difficult as the territory they had to traverse was almost uninhabited, but it had presented serious difficulties in getting provisions, notably water. Hence the presence of Norr, who knew where they could find water and where they could place their night-traps so as to catch the elusive little animals that lived in the wastelands. Norr had no combat experience, but despite his young age he had travelled extensively and had the gift of remembering even the most minute geographical details.

"Let's just hope that an Assyrian raiding party isn't having a rest in Sharan!" said the prince.

"Sharan is too important to be raided," said the interpreter, whose home was on the outskirts of the small town that had grown around the pass. The interpreter had rarely volunteered information before and the prince wondered whether this sudden talkativeness was due to the proximity of his home. Although Artaxias knew practically all there was to know about the little border town on the pass, he decided, on a whim, to encourage the man to talk more.

"Why is Sharan so important to the Assyrians?" he asked, although he knew the answer to his question.

"It is a meeting place for caravans, my prince, not only from Assyria but also from many distant lands. Rich caravans from the East and South prefer to pass through Sharan on their way to our cities, and many caravans from our cities have to pass through Sharan on their way to their destinations in the East and South."

"And this makes Sharan immune to Assyrian raids?" asked the prince, amazed at how talkative the interpreter had suddenly become.

"Yes, my prince. An attack on the town would inconvenience far too many wealthy merchants. Some of the Assyrian merchants whose caravans pass through Sharan know the Assyrian king personally."

"And pay him handsomely for the privilege of knowing him," interjected Norr. The Assyrian king's 'friendships' with wealthy merchants invariably involved privileges and other favouritisms in exchange for generous contributions to the king's personal coffers. As no one answered him, Norr added: "Well, let us hope that there are no Assyrians in Sharan enjoying the local girls over their husbands' dead bodies."

The interpreter flinched at Norr's words and then turned away, scowling. *Norr should not have said that!* thought the prince. *The interpreter's family lives in Sharan! Now the man will again be as talkative as a wine jar!*

Artaxias was going to make a mild rebuke but the rest of the party caught up and he thought it best to make a reassuring comment for the benefit of all: "We are not at war with the Assyrians," he said, "And the town of Sharan is on Hittite land."

"And you think that all Assyrian field officers will observe such niceties?" said Norr.

"The commanders of the raiding parties know that the game they play requires circumspection," answered the prince, speaking to all with what he hoped was a reassuring smile. "They won't raid an important town, even if it is small."

Before the present Assyrian king the town on the Sharan pass had indeed been popular with the long caravans that travelled between the rich cities of the Assyrians and the mountain strongholds of the Hittites. There were few caravans from Assyria now, though many caravans from the East and South continued to travel along the northern border of the wastelands so as to enter Hittite territory through the pass. Sharan boasted a sizeable and unusually good *caravanserai*, or traveller's inn, and a number of reliable and clean wells. For the poorer wayfarers there were small shelters for rent. Close to the caravanserai were stalls that sold provisions and other things that caravaners and other regular travellers could find useful. Sharan had grown around the caravanserai, and had relations between the two superpowers whose border it straddled been better, the town would have had much more than the caravanserai to offer. But when the Assyrian raids destabilised the borders many of the craftsmen, artisans and farmers left, and they were replaced by the kind of people who could pack their belongings at a moment's notice. Such folk do not make towns blossom.

2

Although the night was dark, with a cold wind and a thin crescent moon that seemed to enjoy hiding behind the clouds that raced across the sky, the Hittites approached the border town warily, stealthily walking half way round the scattered houses so as to enter it from a direction that no-one could foresee. When it was decided that there was no danger the interpreter asked to be paid so that he could go home.

"It would be safer for you if you stayed with us," whispered Artaxias, "At least for a little while longer."

"When the moon shines I can see my home from here," the man whispered back, "It's just there, outside the town on the little hill. My wife and children are there!"

He pointed at a small house that was just visible in the light of the crescent moon. It stood alone on a slope, far from the other houses, as though nobody wanted to live next to the interpreter.

"I cannot hold you," said the prince, "for your task with us is done. But Sharan lies on the border and we do not know who could be waiting for us in the darkness. It would be safer for you if you stayed with us at least until we reach the inn."

"I need to go home, my prince. I cannot wait."

Artaxias hesitated: *Is the man really so anxious to see his wife and children?*

"You *must* let me go home!" insisted the interpreter, raising his voice. "Please, my prince, I beg you!"

The man's expression was so earnest that Artaxias paid him and let him go. The man ran noiselessly towards the house he had pointed out and quickly vanished in the darkness. For a moment Artaxias wondered whether the man had somehow betrayed them: *Is he so anxious to reach the safety of his home because we are walking into a trap?* Artaxias reviewed the interpreter's behaviour during the *mission*. The man was not a pleasant fellow but there was no deviousness in his manner. *Perhaps he really did miss his wife and children!* The prince felt a pang of longing as he remembered his own wife and his little daughter, Melapenna. He could not suppress a sigh as he recalled the large black eyes and the small perfectly oval face. Melapenna was a happy child and her father doted on her.

When they finally entered Sharan and were cautiously making their way to the caravanserai they passed some twenty paces from a large mud-and-stone enclosure. The enclosing wall was thick and almost as high as a man's shoulders.

"Where's the gate?" asked Norr in a normal voice.

"It must be on one of the other sides," whispered the prince, making the point that voices had to be kept low.

Artaxias had dismissed the enclosure as a possible source of trouble because the walls were too high for any attackers to jump over. His attention was on the empty stalls and carts that lay between him and the caravanserai, which was about two hundred paces away. But Norr's curiosity got the better of him and he left the group and strayed over to investigate the enclosure.

"*Norr!!*" exclaimed Artaxias in a stage whisper.

"I just want to see what's in there, my prince, behind the wall!" the navigator stage-whispered back. He quickly reached the enclosure and climbed up onto the thick wall, using the rough stones as handholds. When he reached the top he crouched low so as not to present a silhouette against the starlit sky. "By all the gods and goddesses!" he exclaimed as he balanced precariously on all fours, "It's full of sleeping camels!"

The creatures were asleep, crouched down in the sleeping posture peculiar to camels that have travelled long and far. But when Norr inadvertently pushed a stone off the wall one of the beasts opened its eyes. Norr cursed eloquently and assumed a squatting position, the better to see the effect of his carelessness. But at the sight of Norr squatting on the wall in the weak moonlight the camel squealed and rose to its feet with a loud grunt, somewhere between a moan and a growl. Other camels immediately sprang to their feet, uttering loud grunts and squeals. The prince ran over to the stupefied Norr and was on the point of pulling him down roughly when he noticed, behind the complaining animals, a number of horseless Hittite war chariots parked at the opposite side of the enclosure, near the closed enclosure gate. Ignoring the animals' loud noises, Artaxias climbed over the wall and went to investigate the chariots more closely. Two of his companions, who had experience with camels, followed the prince and quickly pacified the animals with soothing whistles.

Hittite war chariots in Sharan? thought Artaxias as he approached the vehicles. He counted the chariots; there were ten of them. *Has there been trouble in these parts?* But the thin moon happened to peep from behind the clouds at that moment and the prince just managed to recognise, on one side of each chariot and just beneath the place where the lead charioteer rests his hand, a thin sheet of copper showing a two-headed eagle with its wings half open and holding a hare in each of its talons. *The Royal Insignia! These chariots are from the king's personal guard!* Artaxias' heart raced with the sudden hope that his uncle had sent them to Sharan to provide him and his companions with transport and an escort

There were no horses with the camels, which probably meant that the horses were in the stables at the back of the inn. Still, the chariots could have been captured and hidden here! Artaxias instructed five of his companions to spread out and reconnoitre the area around the inn: "Be wary and look for concealed Assyrian chariots or war-horses. We shall be at the caravanserai!"

"Don't you think you are being unnecessarily cautious?" complained Norr, who did not like the idea of the prince remaining with only two men.

"Perhaps," admitted Artaxias, "But we *walked* back from the temple. A mounted messenger from the High Priest could have come here before us and prepared an unpleasant surprise. There are men in Sharan who would do anything for money!" Artaxias did not wish to communicate his suspicions about the interpreter. Norr grudgingly agreed; the prince was known for his extreme caution. Artaxias, Norr and the remaining man made their way to the inn.

3

The inn was a sprawling structure of many parts that had been extended and built upon over several centuries. The main structure was a large two-storey building known simply as the *dwelling*. There were eight small rooms on the upper floor, two of which were used by the innkeeper and his family while the remaining six were used as bedrooms for rent. The *dwelling* had no doors or windows on the outside and was built around a substantial courtyard that contained small patches of fragrant herbs for use in the kitchens. On the upper floor and all around the courtyard was a narrow wooden balcony that could only be accessed from the upstairs rooms. On the ground floor was the main kitchen with its enormous ovens and a well, a large hall that was used as a communal sleeping place by guests who could not afford an upstairs bedroom, and a small room that held shrines for some of the many gods worshipped by the innkeeper and the guests. The stone walls that surrounded the courtyard as well as the wooden frame of the upper floor balcony were covered by climbing jasmine whose fragrance in the early evening sometimes competed with the odours of cooking.

A massive door to the east of the *dwelling* led from the main kitchen to a large, high-walled and partly roofed enclosure known as the *eating place*, where food and drink were served. The only access to the *dwelling* was from the *eating place* through the main kitchen. The roofed part of the *eating place* extended no more than about twenty-five paces, and at the centre of the unroofed part was a secondary kitchen built around a single oven and a second well. At the eastmost part of the *eating place*, at about thirty paces from the secondary kitchen, were small roofless cubicles that served as toilets. The only entrance to the inn was a massive wooden door that was built into the high wall of the enclosure. It led into the roofed part of the *eating place*, which was adjacent to, but not part of, the *dwelling*. The stables were in a separate building some sixty paces from the main entrance. The defensive possibilities of the inn did not escape the prince as he approached the entrance, whose imposing wooden door was flanked by two brightly shining bitumen torches.

With his hand on the hilt of his sword, Artaxias cautiously pushed open the wooden door and entered the sheltered part of the *eating place*. Although it was only partly roofed, the *eating place* was hot, very crowded, noisy and smelled of cooking and perspiration. There was also an oily smoke from the numerous but dim oil lamps that hung from the rafters and the walls. Artaxias was surprised to see many people still eating so late into the night: *Does this place never sleep? But I suppose caravans and travellers arrive at all hours.*

From where he stood, Artaxias could see, seated or milling about around the tables and benches, traders, merchants, merchants' messengers on trade errands, some heavily made-up women with charcoal-blackened eyelashes, and sundry travellers. Two Asiatics with yellow skin and slanted eyes sat alone, their backs to a corner, enjoying a meal. Not too far from them sat a group of colourfully dressed Indian merchants, laughing noisily while they waited for their meals. To the right of the door sat two ostentatiously rich and very fat Phoenicians with their armed escorts. The caravaners, the tough professional travellers who looked after the camels and donkeys as well as the animals' burdens, tended to congregate in the roofless part of the *eating place*, which was larger than the roofed section.

All the women were local. Some were busily serving the customers while others, with heavy make-up and clothing that revealed more than they concealed, walked languidly among the tables, offering their bodies to whoever might be interested enough to pay the price.

"It looks normal!" said the prince.

"I agree," said Norr. "But I don't see any empty places."

"There may be some empty places at the far end, behind all these busy travellers," commented the prince, "Let's go!"

The three men looked around carefully before stepping away from the door and pushing their way through the motley collection of people. Because of the crowd, it was not possible to see very far and they had elbowed their way almost halfway through when Artaxias noticed some armed Hittites sitting at a very long rectangular table eating and drinking. They were sitting on both sides of the table, which lay almost at the edge of the roofed part of the *eating place*. They saw the prince the moment he approached and rose joyfully to greet him. Relieved, the prince strode boldly towards them.

4

"Hail Varousht!" said Artaxias to the eldest of the group. The others bowed low and clasped their hands together in respectful greeting.

"Hail prince!" replied the middle-aged senior charioteer whom Artaxias had greeted personally. A short but heavily built man, he met Artaxias halfway and took hold of the prince's elbows with his large, calloused hands. "The gods have been kind to my old eyes, my prince! They have been yearning to see you for many days." The prince smiled cordially and they made their way to the rectangular table. The senior charioteer ordered food and wine before introducing his comrades.

"It is good to see you, old friend," said the prince after the introductions were over, "What news from Hattusas?"

"Your family are all well," said Varousht, "And the king is anxious to see you. We are to take you to him as soon as possible."

"That's wonderful," exclaimed the prince, "But something is bothering me, Varousht. Our interpreter left us in something of a hurry just outside the town."

The senior charioteer looked at him and frowned. "We were told before we left Hattusas that your interpreter was Yura, the grumpy fellow."

"That's him. Do you know him?"

"I met him in Hattusas many winters ago. He is from Sharan."

"Yes. He seemed unaccountably anxious to see his family."

"He is well known here in Sharan, and he has recently been the subject of some of the local gossip."

"What does this have to do with him being in such a hurry to leave us?"

"Well, my prince, according to local gossip, his wife was embroiled with one of the caravaners for some time. She is gone now, with the children, and he shall find his home empty."

"I see," said the prince. "Poor man, no wonder he was so anxious to get home. But I am relieved to know that it was not treachery that drove him home in such a hurry."

"The men around here are not prone to treachery," said the senior charioteer. "In border towns such as Sharan people have to trust each other. Treachery of any sort brings sudden death!"

"That is good to know." The prince changed the subject: "Any serious trouble in these parts?"

"Some time ago a large Assyrian raiding party attacked some villages not too far from here."

"They took prisoners?"

"Many boys."

Artaxias' face darkened "Curses on their goddess. When did this happen?"

"I don't know. News travels erratically near the border. The boys are probably in the clutches of the monster as we speak."

"May the gods help them. When can we leave?"

"The rest of my men are scattered but should be easy to find. This place has only simple pleasures to offer, and those are mostly for the younger men without wives. We should be able to leave at dawn. Where are your other companions?"

"I expect them to join us soon." The prince sighed: "What's the wine like in this place?"

"Abysmal!"

"Pity, but it's just as well. My men and I are too tired to be finicky about our drinks. We shall spend the night here and leave tomorrow soon after dawn."

"From the looks of you, you will also want baths!"

"Indeed! Are baths expensive here?"

"Very! But I trust you are equipped to handle such things?"

"Don't worry, Varousht. I am, as you say, well equipped for all emergencies."

At that moment they were joined by the rest of Artaxias' party. The men had nothing to report and sat, with their backs to the wall, at a table next to that of the prince.

It was not long before the innkeeper, an old and portly Sumerian, came over to find out about this strange group of raggedly dressed men whom the heavily armed soldiers treated so respectfully.

"You have just crossed over from the land of the Assyrians?" he asked the travellers, not quite sure who the leader was.

"What makes you think so?" replied the prince.

"You are covered in wasteland dust!"

"Is wasteland dust different from other dust?"

"For those who have travelled in the wastelands, yes."

"Have *you* travelled in the wastelands recently?"

"I am an old man," said the Sumerian. "There is no more travelling for me. Now all I do is collect news and gossip." The Sumerian had quickly recognised an opportunity to sell information.

"And what news do you have that could be of interest to us?"

"That depends on who you are and why you are here."

Artaxias put a small piece of silver on the table. It was more than the innkeeper's average weekly earnings. The Sumerian picked it up smoothly and said: "Ah! You are a man of means despite the dust and your ragged clothing. I will make sure that you and your men are given the best accommodation my humble inn can provide. And you will want hot baths, of course?"

"Thank you."

"Would it also interest you, my lord, to know that there is a small party of Egyptian priests staying at my inn, that they seem wise and knowledgeable, and that they are on their way from Nineveh to a very important place? One of them speaks very good Hittite."

Artaxias put another piece of silver on the table. The old man picked it up and bowed low: "They are originally from Thebes and are on their way to the oracular centre at Metsamor. Would my lord like to meet them? I feel sure they have information from Nineveh that my lord shall find interesting. A private meeting can be arranged."

Artaxias put a third piece of silver on the table. The innkeeper bowed low again and said: "The Egyptians go to bed at sundown and rise with the sun. Would it be to your convenience for them to visit you in your quarters shortly after dawn tomorrow?"

The prince nodded.

"It shall be so, then. I am sure the Egyptians would be as honoured to meet you as I am." The innkeeper bowed one more time and then, as though as an afterthought, he said: "Our very best food and drink, my lord, shall be served to you in a short while by my own daughters." He bowed again and left. Not much later an excellent meal was served by three pleasant but plain-looking girls who set the food on the table without raising their eyes. The prince and his companions fell to with relish.

Artaxias had finished his meal and was on his third cup of wine when a sound of loud grunting and squealing could be heard above the hubbub of the inn.

"There go the camels again!" muttered Varousht, the senior charioteer, "It's the second time tonight!"

"The first time was us," said Norr. "I wonder who it could be this time!"

"Someone who does not understand camels," said the prince. "Perhaps someone who is used to travelling by chariot! It may be a good idea to go slow on the wine."

5

The noise of the inn suddenly subsided and all who were standing either sat down or quietly moved away from the entrance to the *eating place*. From where he sat Artaxias could now see the door and the three tall armed men who stood rigidly just within. They had straight black hair that reached down to their shoulders and thick short beards that were richly decorated with shiny ornaments. All three wore ornate armour under their black capes, but the armour of the one who stood in the middle was by far the more resplendent.

Artaxias instinctively pushed the table away in readiness for possible action: *A high-ranking Assyrian officer and his bodyguards! By what strange whim of the gods do we meet here tonight?* The inn remained completely silent while the Assyrians cast their eyes sternly this way and that across the *eating place*. The silence was unexpectedly shattered by the innkeeper, who bustled over to the Assyrians.

"Welcome, welcome, my lords!" he said jovially in Hittite. "It is such an honour to have Assyrian visitors of your standing in my humble inn!"

"We would like good food and clean beds for the night," replied the taller of the two bodyguards in a deep guttural voice. Although he glared at the innkeeper with the expression of a hawk he spoke in Hittite, which was a courtesy, of sorts. The high-ranking officer remained silent and did not deign to look straight at anyone, but his piercing grey eyes missed nothing.

"Yes, of course, come in, come in!" continued the innkeeper. The Assyrians seemed to relax slightly but they kept their hands on the hilts of their weapons as they stepped forward.

"We do not see any suitable place for our lord to sit," said the bodyguard. "We do not wish our lord to sit with just anybody, least of all with merchants!"

The innkeeper turned around and looked pleadingly at Artaxias, who nodded discreetly.

"We have other distinguished visitors here tonight," said the relieved innkeeper. He moved out of the way so that the officer could see Artaxias and his party. An experienced host, he left it to his patrons to sort out protocol.

"We would consider it an honour if you would sit with us," said Artaxias evenly, his voice just loud enough to be heard across the now silent *eating place*. His eyes were on the senior officer: *This man reminds me of someone! By the gods! It's Uri!*

The tall Assyrian looked down at the seated prince and scowled as he took note of the Hittite's shabby attire. He was about to decline contemptuously when he realised that the man was not cowed by his presence and had spoken with the calm authority of someone who was used to being obeyed. It was a known fact that Hittites of high rank often dressed shabbily for no apparent reason, and his father had often said: 'You cannot always tell a Hittite's status by his dress!' The Assyrian's eyes narrowed as he weighed the shabby attire against the Hittite's calm expression and authoritative voice: *Perhaps this is an important person, after all...* He made up his mind instantly but only answered after a suitable delay. "We gratefully accept your kind invitation," he said in perfect Hittite. His voice was a beautifully modulated baritone.

6

The men around Artaxias got up and stood with their backs to the wall, and after two serving girls had cleared the table the Assyrian took the seat opposite the prince. He sat rigidly and neither moved nor spoke while one of the bodyguards ordered food and wine. The two bodyguards remained standing behind the officer.

"It is unusual for an Assyrian officer of high rank to be seen in Sharan in full regalia," said Artaxias conversationally.

"I am sure it is," replied the Assyrian curtly.

"Was your trip here over dangerous land?"

"There is danger everywhere these days."

"All the more on Hittite land," said Artaxias mildly.

"I am here on official business with the Hittite king's full knowledge," snapped the Assyrian. "I am the new Assyrian envoy to the court of the Hittite king!" This was expected to impress the men across the table and discourage further conversation, but Artaxias continued calmly: "And you are here with only two bodyguards?"

"There are thirty more outside!"

"That's very thoughtful," said Artaxias. "You will find our king an interesting man."

"Oh?" said the officer haughtily, as though saying 'How dare you talk of a king in familiar terms!' The food and drink were brought to the table by a young girl and the Assyrian started to eat.

"What kind of expertise does one require," asked Artaxias pleasantly, "To become the Assyrian king's envoy to the Hittite king's court? I mean apart from speaking our language so well."

"My father was the envoy of our previous king!" replied the Assyrian brusquely. He was irritated at being talked to while he was having his meal.

"So you knew the Hittite king," persisted Artaxias.

The Assyrian looked up from his food and glared at the prince. "He was like a father to me! Who are you to ask me questions?"

"My name is Artaxias."

There was a pause during which the Assyrian chewed mechanically while continuing to glare at the Hittite. "The *prince* Artaxias?" he finally asked after he had swallowed what was in his mouth.

"Yes, Uri, and I remember you from the time when we were children playing in the gardens of my uncle's palace."

The Assyrian's face lit up with the warmest of smiles: "Arte!" he cried, and he reached out to grasp the prince's hand but then suddenly pulled it back.

"Arte, we are not children any more," he said solemnly. "We have loyalties that may bring us against each other!"

"I know," replied the prince. "Our loyalties to our kings transcend even brotherhood. But as long as we understand each other's loyalties we should not get in each other's way."

"I hope so, and we may even help each other while we serve our kings."

Artaxias smiled: "Friendship and loyalty are gifts from the gods. If the gods are well disposed towards us they shall not make us choose between friendship and loyalty!"

This time the Assyrian reached out with both hands.

7

After talking for some time as only childhood friends can, Artaxias suddenly asked: "Uri, why did you leave so suddenly?"

"As you know, our previous king died," replied the Assyrian carefully, "And the new king recalled all Assyrian envoys. He wanted no envoys until he could decide on the policies he would pursue towards each of his neighbours."

"And now he sends us you. After more than, what, twenty winters? I can arrange that you get the same house your father had when he was the envoy to my uncle's court. Would that please you?"

"That would bring back very pleasant memories!"

"Then think of it as done, old friend. Do you have a family?"

"Of course, but they shall come to Hattusas after I am settled."

"You are now on your way to Hattusas?"

"Yes, but not directly. Your uncle's officials arranged for us to get to Hattusas by the most circuitous of routes and my king's officials agreed. We are to wait for a Hittite escort here in Sharan, to guide us to Hattusas by the approved route."

"And to make sure you are not mistaken for a raiding party," added Artaxias.

"That too, of course." The Assyrian smiled. "I think that both our rulers want your people to see that relations between the Hittites and the Assyrians are good."

"That part of your brief may be harder than you have been led to believe, old friend."

"I am aware of the problems." The Assyrian grew quiet, thinking of what he should say next. "I know that my people are hated in many places, Arte, but I *have* to believe that my king spoke sincerely when he said he wants good relations with your uncle. I *must* believe it if I am to persuade your uncle."

"I hear your sincerity, Uri. I would hate it if you were deceived. If there is war, 'Uri the envoy' would quickly become 'Uri the hostage.'"

"That possibility is at the back of my mind." The Assyrian looked down at the table, chewing thoughtfully.

The prince sighed, as though there was something he was reluctant to say. Uri looked at him expectantly. The prince spoke slowly. "You may not wish to answer this, Uri, but what is your own view of the goddess who drinks human blood? Do you know that your king has personally decreed that she feeds only on prisoners? And do you know that these prisoners are often abducted from our villages?"

Uri looked away and Artaxias noticed that the two bodyguards had suddenly tensed. "I know about the prisoners," said the Envoy, his voice strained, "But I cannot speak against the wishes of my king. I can only express my regrets from the deepest part of my heart."

"Yet you are the envoy who has to persuade my uncle of your king's good intentions."

The Assyrian pondered long on how best to answer. Then he said: "I can only say that I do not understand why my king has compelled the goddess to do this yet has given me the task of persuading your king that he has no hostile intentions."

Artaxias nodded, he did not wish to put his friend in a difficult position. "We shall not talk of this again."

"Thank you."

"How old is the goddess, Uri?"

"Nobody knows. But she is very old, though she does not appear to be, if I remember correctly."

"You've *seen* her?"

"Yes. My father and I visited the Amalishah Temple when we were on our way to Hattusas. I was a very young boy then and only remember that she was unusually tall, taller than my father. I do not remember her face at all. My father wished to hear her counsel before taking up his post as envoy to the Hittite court. But please don't ask me any more questions about the goddess, Arte. The king does not want her discussed."

"Not even between friends?"

"Not even between Assyrians! Our King wants her out of the minds and hearts of his people."

"Uri, we have just returned from the temple of the goddess."

"*What?*"

The prince recounted the story of the *mission* to the Amalishah temple, leaving out small details but emphasising that it had failed. The Assyrian raised his hands as though to say: 'That is how it is, but it has nothing to do with me!'

"I know, Uri, but you can see how your goddess casts a dark shadow over my people."

"Then please, Arte, in the name of friendship, speak no more of the goddess."

3

THE PRINCE AND THE KING

1

THE CHARIOT HORSES were being watered beside a stream when the prince was approached by an old Hittite peasant accompanied by a very young girl child. Their clothes were tattered and torn and the old man was bent with age. He took off his battered hat and introduced himself in a hesitant voice, speaking very slowly and sometimes slurring over the words. He did not introduce the child, who said nothing but stared at the ground morosely.

The prince had just washed his face in the stream. He nodded in acknowledgment but the peasant did not speak at once. He stared ahead of him while his fingers weaved compulsively in and out of his grey-white beard. The prince wondered whether the old peasant was blind, but then he reached out and took the young girl's hand in his and the prince thought: 'The old man is not blind, he is like some men after their first battle. His thinking is muddled because painful memories get in the way!'

The prince waited patiently for the old man to speak, and eventually the old man said: "The raids against our villages are making the people of the lowlands afraid and very angry, my prince."

The prince said quietly: "I know."

The old man pointed a gnarled finger towards the direction from which the sun rises.

"Four days walk from where you stand, my prince, was once my village. Five families lived there, and they had eight boys and seven girls between them. We worked our soil and the gods were generous. One night, we were awakened by the frantic barking of the village dogs and we thought that a bear had come for our goats. Then the barking stopped and we thought the bear was gone. We had almost gone back to sleep when bearded men with swords and spears pushed down our doors and

45

climbed in through our windows." The old man stopped speaking and closed his eyes. Then he took a deep breath and started again: "We had never seen men like that before and we were afraid. We did not know what to do. None of us had fought armed men and we had no weapons. Even so, our men and some of the boys fought as best they could but the bearded men killed those who fought them. What were those bearded men, my prince?"

"They were Assyrian raiders," replied the prince, surprised at the question. Surely the old man knew?

"That is what I was told," the old man murmured, speaking even more slowly. "These Assyrian raiders killed our dogs, then all the men and boys who fought, and when all who fought were dead or dying they raped our young women."

The old man stopped speaking and his shoulders suddenly hunched. His wrinkled face seemed to crumple inwards and the prince thought the old man was going to weep. But the old man held back his tears and spoke in a surprisingly firm voice: "When the Assyrians left they took six of our boys. Why did they take our boys, my prince?"

"They took them to feed to a monster that lives in a cave!" replied the prince, hating the answer.

"That is what I was told," the old man murmured again. "They have a goddess who feeds on human blood!"

"What became of the other two boys?" asked the prince, hoping they had escaped.

"The boys the Assyrians did not take were old enough to fight beside their fathers, my prince. They were killed in their own homes and their mothers watched them die!"

The old man stopped speaking again and drew a deep breath. Then in a louder voice he said: "I ask you, my prince, how long will these raids be allowed to continue?"

The prince's reply was almost inaudible: "I do not know."

The old man nodded as though everything was clear to him, but then he repeated what he had said before: "These raids on our villages are making the people of the lowlands afraid and very angry, my prince!"

The prince remained silent and the old man lowered his eyes. He then walked away without saying farewell, holding the young girl by the hand. When he was at some distance from the prince he started singing a children's lullaby in a faltering voice.

2

The terrain between the Sharan pass and Hattusas was mountainous and rugged, and the ten Hittite war chariots passed through many villages on the way. In almost every village Artaxias was assailed by tales of cruelty and horror, and almost every time he was asked the questions: "Why isn't something done about the Assyrian raids? Is our king too old?" Everywhere among the villagers there was doubt about the king's decisiveness. The prince felt subdued and helpless: *It is perhaps good that the mission to the Amalishah temple was kept secret. The mission failed miserably, and if that were known it would only strengthen the suspicion that our king is weak and not feared by the Assyrians! Yet what can my uncle do? Nobody knows where a raid will strike. How can he stop the raids without starting a war?*

The prince shared a chariot with the senior charioteer. Although Varousht was quite short he had enormously broad shoulders and occupied more than his fair share of the restricted space on the chariot. He was, however, an informed and loquacious man, and the prince learned much concerning the thoughts of the army officers in the field. Varousht did not have an analytic mind but he conveyed information adequately through tales mixed with gossip, parables and old proverbs. The prince was not surprised to learn that there was anger among the field officers at the lack of a military response, and he was disturbed when told that the unpredictable Assyrian raids had started a slow migration from the southern villages to the cities. As the border garrisons were dependent on the local villagers for provisions, this migration implied a gradual weakening of the Hittite army *presence* and could, in time, entail the effective withdrawal of the Hittite borders.

When they finally reached Hattusas, Varousht insisted, in the name of tradition, that they enter the city via the West Gate: "We must be welcomed by the lions!" he said.

He was referring to the stone lions that stood on either side of the main city gate. Although entering the city via the West Gate required a slight detour and a small delay, the prince did not object because he knew how highly men like Varousht regarded tradition. The senior charioteer was an old soldier, and like most men whose lives had been moulded by the battlefield he had his own personal blend of tradition and religion, which consisted mostly of simple directives for pleasing the gods and the other supernatural beings who were believed to rule over human lives. Artaxias knew that Varousht *expected* him to concur because age was of greater import than titles, and the charioteer was considerably older than the prince.

The ten war chariots entered Hattusas together but, once within the city, the chariot carrying the prince separated from the others and thundered purposefully through the narrow streets towards the king's palace. When Artaxias dismounted at the steps of the Royal Palace he bade farewell to Varousht and made his way as swiftly as he could through the labyrinthine corridors to the throne room. His back ached and his knees felt wobbly. On the way to the throne room he had to pass the Palace Library and the Archives, which were always guarded. He paused only long enough to commandeer two Royal Guardsmen, for despite his ragged clothes a Royal Prince could not walk through the palace without an escort.

Unlike the Assyrian royal court, whose imposing dimensions and magnificent decorations spoke vividly of glorifying the gods through conquest, the Hittite throne room was a modest hall whose design was ultimately functional. The furniture was simple but comfortable and the only decorations were coloured patterns on the walls and large empty vases on squat pedestals. The few windows were tall and barred and the oil lamps around the walls were of simple but heavy bronze. These were the spartan halls of a king whose ancestry lay in the wild mountains. When the prince reached the throne room he dismissed the two Royal Guardsmen and entered, still carrying his travel bag.

King Aleshanr was sitting on his throne conversing with the envoy from India when his nephew was ushered in. "Forgive me," said the king, laying his hand apologetically on the elbow of the Indian dignitary, "but I see that my nephew has returned!" The envoy bowed before withdrawing, and the old king watched impatiently as the prince walked stiffly across the room. Artaxias had only walked a few steps when the king rose impulsively from his throne and rushed to hug his nephew. As they embraced the king whispered in his ear: "Do not speak of your mission to the monster's temple." Much more loudly he said: "I am happy to greet you, nephew. I see that you have come a long way! It seems that your knees can hardly hold you!"

"I have yet to decide which is worse," laughed the prince. "Walking long distances with a heavy bag or riding a speeding war chariot through the bumpy streets of Hattusas!"

The lavishly dressed men and women who comprised the royal

entourage smiled, made welcoming noises, and clasped their hands together.

The king gave a short speech of welcome, saying all kinds of pleasant things about his nephew but not mentioning from whence Artaxias had returned. When the ritual platitudes for the benefit of the court were over, the king took his nephew aside and quietly said: "Let's go somewhere where we can talk without being heard!"

The king and his nephew bowed politely to the courtiers and left, followed by the two Royal Bodyguards who always accompanied the king.

3

The palace was a labyrinth of twisted shadow-haunted passageways with uneven floors. "Where are you taking me?" asked the prince after following his uncle through seemingly endless corridors, "I have never been to this part of the palace before!"

"To my *thinking room*," answered Aleshanr, "I had a little room appointed specially for solitude and safety. It's at the top of one of the towers."

"Safety? In your own palace?"

The king did not answer.

Aleshanr finally turned off a main corridor and passed through a low door that led to a narrow and poorly illuminated flight of steps. One of the Royal Guards positioned himself at the foot of the stairs while the second ran up ahead. The steps were worn but very steep and wound round a massive central pillar whose diameter was at least three paces. After rising a short distance, the stairs were illuminated by narrow slit-like windows at every seventh step. The sunshine that came through the slits was reflected off airborne dust to form golden shafts that made it difficult to see clearly.

"The tower and the chamber are old but the changes are new," said the king as he made his way up. Artaxias followed a few steps behind his uncle. The Royal Guard who had run up ahead was nowhere to be seen.

The prince had gone round the central pillar several times when he saw, at the top of the flight of steps before him, a narrow landing on which stood a young guard with a sword and quiver at his hip and a bow in his hand. The moment the tower-guard saw the prince he brought an arrow to the bow and was on the point of pulling it back when the king said: "It's all right!" The guard relaxed and returned the arrow to its quiver. Only when the king reached the landing did the tower-guard step back and stand next to a little wooden cupboard on the landing.

"This is my *thinking room!*" said the king pleasantly as he passed the tower-guard and entered a narrow open door immediately opposite the stairs. The prince reached the top of the flight of steps and had almost passed the guard with the bow when he realised that the Royal Bodyguard who had run up the stairs ahead of the king had disappeared: The Bodyguard was not supposed to follow the king into the *thinking room!* He immediately gripped the hilt of his sword and called to the king: "Uncle, where is your bodyguard?"

"Look behind you!" answered the voice of the king from behind the open door.

When the prince looked down from the vantage point of the bowman he understood the sudden disappearance of the Royal Bodyguard. Not far below the landing the massive central pillar had been hollowed out into a small alcove. The Bodyguard who had run up the stairs was sitting within the hollow. *Very clever,* thought the prince, *an assassin climbing hurriedly up the stairs would be looking ahead and would only see the guard with the bow on the landing!* He would not see the guard in the alcove and would be attacked from the rear as well as the front! Although someone climbing the stairs in a hurry was unlikely to see the Royal Bodyguard in the alcove, the stairs, the landing and the alcove were so designed that the bowman at the top of the stairs and the Royal Bodyguard in the alcove could keep an eye on each other at all times.

Artaxias entered the little room at the top of the stairs and stood before the king, who had already made himself comfortable on a goatskin-covered divan. The tower-guard with the bow remained in his place at the top of the stairs.

4

"Well, here we are," said the king, motioning to Artaxias to sit beside him. "We are alone and can talk freely!" The room at the top of the tower was surprisingly large, roughly semicircular, and contained only the divan, a few chairs, and a small low table. The walls were bare and had large unlit oil lamps hanging at regular intervals. There were three narrow windows, through one of which the sunshine poured in.

"Very clever that trick with the alcove," said the prince. He stood before the king, looking around the room.

"I think so. Now relax, sit down beside me."

The prince sat on the divan. "And that tower-guard outside is rather quick with his bow."

"He is. He is a good man but if I am not careful he will shoot one of my guests."

"Have there been attempts on your life, uncle?"

"No. But I am old and can no longer wield my scythe-sword as in the days when I led my armies along the Euphrates. And you, who would be king one day if the Council of Elders agrees, are rarely here to protect me. These are good days for assassins, don't you think?"

Artaxias nodded. "I see no reason to leave Hattusas in the near future."

The king nodded back slowly, showing that he understood what his nephew had said but did not actually agree. "We live in dangerous times, Arte, and you may be called upon to leave sooner than you think."

"Has there been trouble with the villagers in the southern regions?"

"No serious trouble yet, but those accursed Assyrian raids have made many people unhappy. And it is not only the villagers who are unhappy, even the vassal kings and governors are becoming nervous. Discontent in the villages breeds insecurity in the palaces; it offers opportunities to those who would settle scores or try to seize power."

"Have the vassal kings shown signs of rebellion since I left?" asked the prince.

"The short answer is 'No,'" replied the king thoughtfully, "But something may happen if we continue to do nothing."

"You know that many of the border villagers are moving into the towns and cities."

"When did you find that out?"

"I learned that from Varousht, the charioteer who brought me here."

"That's been going on for many planting seasons. I tried to stop it by increasing the number of garrisons and patrols, but that was not enough to reassure the villagers. The raiders are very good at avoiding our armed men."

The prince sighed. *So the king is aware of the discontent caused by his lack of action against the Assyrian raids.* "This is a cosy little place," he said, trying to conceal his thoughts.

"It gets very cold in the winter and my joints start to hurt."

"I take it you have something very important to tell me."

"Yes, but tell me first about your little trip to the temple of the monster."

The prince narrated the main events of his *mission* to the Temple of Amalishah and the king listened attentively, interrupting often to ask for more detail or to change the direction of the narrative. Although the prince wished to dwell on the hostile attitude of the High Priest and the events in the temple the king seemed more interested in the Assyrian envoy and in what the Egyptian priests had to say about the goings-on in Assyria. The king was also very interested in what Varousht had said regarding the mood of the field officers.

When the prince finished, the old man did not appear surprised at his nephew's failure to dissuade the High Priest from accepting Hittite prisoners for the goddess.

"Do not take the failure wholly upon yourself, nephew," said the king. "Our neighbours are arrogant and unreasonably resistant to reasonable requests." The prince nodded but remained silent.

"I think we have talked enough about the *mission* and the unpleasantness of the High Priest," said the king with an eloquent shrug. "The question is: what shall we do now?" From the king's tone of voice, the prince realised that the question was rhetorical and that his uncle had already made a decision. The prince said nothing but looked gravely at the old king.

The king continued: "Did you know that, before sending you on your *mission* to the Amalishah Temple, I had sent several formal protests to the Assyrian ruler?"

"No uncle, I did not," said the prince.

"I must have forgotten to tell you, as you were very busy with other affairs. I am growing old, you know."

The prince smiled. His uncle was old, yes, but he rarely forgot to say something that he considered important. He must have had his reasons for not telling him.

"And what came of these formal protests, uncle?"

"Oh, they were either ignored or answered with the usual oily politeness that promises nothing."

"Would the High Priest have known about your protests when my men and I got to the temple of the monster?"

"Possibly, if only by hearsay. My protests go back three winters."

"Three winters!"

"Three winters. Before that the raids were very infrequent and could have been due to the ambitions of field commanders who like adventure. But after my first protest the Assyrian raids grew ever more frequent. This suggested orders from the Assyrian king."

"Are you saying, uncle, that you *expected* the High Priest to dismiss my plea as unworthy of consideration because he probably knew of the Assyrian king's replies to your protests?"

"Ummm... yes. It is not what I hoped for, of course, but I did expect it." The king sounded contrite.

"So why did you send us on this mission?"

"Because, nephew, we had to try *all* peaceful means to stop the feeding of our brethren to the abomination that lives beneath the ground."

"I see. But we were badly humiliated and could even have been killed!"

"Perhaps. But as you know, Arte, you may be king some day." The king put his hand on his nephew's shoulder and smiled. "An occasional humiliation is a good thing for someone who would be king; it teaches the humility that all good kings must have. As for being killed, if you could not handle a bunch of silly priests you don't deserve to be king."

5

The prince took a deep breath. "So what is left to do now, uncle?"

The king sighed. "We must understand the overall situation as best we can. High-level decisions are rarely made on absolute evidence. Kings and princes must often make decisions by guessing what other kings and princes are thinking. Let us look at some facts. Here is one fact: during the reign of the previous Assyrian king, priestesses were constantly coming and going between the monster's temple and the Assyrian royal court. It is even said that the monster offered counsel to the previous kings during her long life and that this counsel was gratefully accepted. Now, the priestesses of the Temple of Amalishah never visit the king."

"Forgive me for asking, uncle, but how do you know that?"

"Oh I have spies and paid traitors in the Assyrian court, just as the Assyrian king has spies and paid traitors in mine!"

"Assyrian spies here in Hattusas?"

"In this very palace, nephew. I see that you have been too busy with your campaigns to pay attention to what goes on in royal courts."

"That is true."

"Then the first thing you should learn is that communication between kings does not always rely on official messengers and envoys."

Artaxias remained silent and the king, wishing to give his nephew time to digest what he had just been told, called to the guard outside the entrance and asked for wine and biscuits. Artaxias was pleasantly surprised to learn that the wooden cupboard on the landing contained cups, sealed wine jars and hard oatmeal cakes. The prince waited patiently for the king to continue but the king said nothing until the wine was brought, mixed and served. When the guard left, Aleshanr said: "You will agree that this is very good wine?"

"Yes, uncle. It is excellent wine."

"And won't you try the biscuits?"

"I've had enough of hard biscuits during my trip."

The old king smiled. "Akh! What was I saying? Oh yes. It would appear then that relations between the temple of the monster and the Assyrian ruler are not very good."

"But the present king *did* order the monster to feed only on prisoners."

"Yes nephew, we know that only too well. That was a direct order from the king to the monster, delivered personally, and from what I have heard the monster had no choice in the matter."

"Or perhaps the Assyrian king wants us to *think* that relations are not very good."

"Too much caution leads to inaction, nephew. The facts suggest that the Assyrian king would not be unduly dismayed if we destroy the temple and kill the monster."

The prince was taken aback. "That could start a war, uncle!"

"Perhaps not," said the king mildly, "Although it would increase the risk."

"But is it possible to kill the monster? It is claimed that she is a goddess."

"Just because she has lived much longer than a normal woman does not mean she cannot be killed."

"You have been thinking about this for some time, haven't you, uncle?"

"Of course. I am understandably reluctant to obliterate a sacred temple within the territory of our belligerent neighbour. But do you see any alternative? Our young boys are being abducted and horribly murdered! And remember the effects these raids are having on our border populations, quite apart from their effect on our reputation as a people not to be trifled with."

"How have our more friendly neighbours reacted?"

"So far, with extreme caution. They do not wish to be singled out by the Assyrians. But they have lost young men too, you know, and they are looking to us for leadership."

"There seems to be no alternative then. But you said risking a war, not starting one..."

"Oh no! Not starting a war," exclaimed the king, "We cannot afford a war for such a small issue. But what would you say about a *secret* little campaign? One that would erase the temple and remove the reason for the Assyrian incursions whose only purpose is to collect sacrificial victims? If the job is done properly the Assyrians may not even be sure it's us!"

"A little campaign *could* start a war."

"Of course, of course. But did the Egyptian priests whom you met in Sharan not say that they did not see any large scale military preparations?"

"Um... yes."

"And let me try to recall what you quoted the Egyptians as saying: *'The Assyrian king did not wish to speak of the Amalishah temple. For him it does not exist any more'*. Is that not what you said were their exact words?"

"Yes, uncle."

"And did your friend Uri not say much the same thing?"

"He said nothing about it not existing any more. But, yes, uncle, he did say that the king did not want the goddess discussed, even among his own people."

"And how long did you say the Egyptians were in Assyria?"

"More than two planting seasons."

"Yet they were not allowed to visit the monster's temple."

"Yes, uncle, they were not."

"Did they not *ask* to be allowed to visit the temple?"

"They told me they did, but their requests to visit the Amalishah temple were categorically denied."

"But they *were* allowed to visit other temples."

"Of course."

"Is that not surprising? After all, the Amalishah Temple is the only place in our neighbour's land that claims a real, living goddess! To my knowledge, it is the only place *anywhere* that can boast a living goddess. A woman who does not die! Even the Egyptians have nothing like that! Now if *we* had a temple with a living goddess we would have proudly shown her off to everyone, would we not?"

"I suppose we would."

"But the Assyrians, who are not too different from us in many ways, prevented even Egyptian priests from seeing her."

"Yes."

"Then would you not think that the Assyrian king is trying to um… sideline the goddess? Make her seem unimportant to important visitors?"

"It would seem so, uncle."

"And what does that suggest to you? The Assyrian raids for the purpose of collecting prisoners started at about the time when the Assyrian king ordered the monster to feed exclusively on human blood, and the raids became more frequent after my protests."

6

"Are you telling me, uncle, that the Assyrian king is *inviting* us to attack the temple?"

"It is a very strange idea, but it could be so. At least insofar as a provocation can be taken to be an invitation. The sending of an envoy lends further support to the idea that the Assyrians shall not go to war if we destroyed the Amalishah temple."

"Why doesn't he abolish the temple himself if he wishes it removed?"

"Was the temple rich?" asked the king.

"It seemed so to me. There were lots of foodstuffs in jars and baskets. These were obviously gifts, and from the little we were allowed to see it appeared that there was no shortage of precious metals and valuable artefacts."

"That shows that the monster is popular with the people, or was. So even the Assyrian King cannot dismantle her temple without a very good excuse!"

"But why would he want to dismantle the monster's temple?"

"I really do not know."

"So we are going to play his game without knowing his reasons?"

"Do we have a choice?"

"It seems not, though I wish it were not so. But the Egyptian priests could have been duped," said Artaxias thoughtfully. "They are wise but not infallible. And your spies could be wrong. And the sending of an envoy could be a ruse to mislead us into doing something foolish."

"True. But I have met Egyptian priests before; we have quite a few of them in Hattusas, and if the priests you met are like the ones we have here, I am sure they kept their eyes open and are not easy to fool. The Assyrian king's intentions are of great interest to the Egyptians, for even mighty Egypt is not wholly outside his ambitions."

Artaxias nodded thoughtfully. The king raised his cup and drained his wine in one go.

The possibility of an attack on the temple had occurred to Artaxias while he was still exchanging words with the High Priest. Yet the prince had dismissed it immediately. Although the Assyrians could afford to be permanently in a state of war-readiness, because they lived in comparative ease on fertile lands, the Hittites could not. The Hittite lands were mostly inhospitable mountains where life was hard and surpluses scarce. Moreover, the Hittite lands were sparsely populated because a harsh environment does not encourage large concentrations of people. For the Hittites, therefore, the prospect of all-out war entailed serious organisational and economic problems.

After a long pause Artaxias said: "Uncle, a secret little campaign *could* start a full-fledged war if it isolates us from our allies."

"I know," replied the king, "That is why, before deciding to destroy the temple, I asked our allies for assurances of economic and, if necessary, military support in the event that the Assyrians waged war against us. I did not, of course, mention the possibility of a Hittite attack on the temple of the monster."

"Do these inquiries also go back three years?"

The king smiled. "No," he replied. "And the assurances only reached me recently, shortly before your return."

"Can we depend on these assurances?"

"We cannot *depend* on them," said Aleshanr, "But the Assyrian ruler will, no doubt, hear about them also, and *he* will not be able to depend on these assurances *not* being implemented. The assurances we received might stay his hand from starting a war for the loss of a temple that he wants um… sidelined."

"That depends on how much he values the temple, sidelined or not."

"Yes, of course," said the king. "That is why I am not depending on the assurances of our allies to stay his hand, for although their territories are also being raided to feed the monster we cannot be absolutely sure of their help against a foe as powerful and vindictive as the Assyrians."

The prince nodded and smiled. He gently prompted his uncle to say more: "Yes uncle?"

"All my spies in the Assyrian court," continued the king, "Even though they do not know of each other, have stated that it is *very* unlikely that the Assyrians would resort to military retaliation if some foreign power brought a calamity to the Amalishah temple."

"The High Priest seemed unaware of a rift between his goddess and the king…"

"The High Priest doesn't know everything," interrupted Aleshanr. "And he is old; he may have failed to recognise changes in the Assyrian court that bode ill for his temple."

The prince finished the wine in his cup.

7

"Would you like some more?" asked the king, "It is very good wine."

"No, thank you uncle. So when do we begin preparations?"

"They have already begun," said the king, "Secretly and thus slowly. You will be told everything after you have rested. For the present go to your comfortable home. I know that you did not stop to see your lovely wife and gorgeous daughter on your way here."

Under normal circumstances Aleshanr would have scrupulously avoided getting involved in Assyrian domestic politics. As a wise Hittite king had once said, such an action would be like taking sides in a conflict within a wasps' nest. Not only would it be very difficult to decide which side to support, but there was also the risk of the whole nest turning abruptly against you. However, under the circumstances, Aleshanr felt that if the Assyrian raids were to be stopped the temple had to be destroyed, even if this meant playing the Assyrian king's game. Even so, Aleshanr had not made the final decision to invade Assyrian territory until he had consulted the oracle at Metsamor. The reply was broadly affirmative but advised caution. It had said:

The gods shall look favourably on those
who do their bidding in the night

Even if the Assyrian king had not intended the Hittites to destroy the temple of Amalishah, Aleshanr and his nephew were reasonably sure that he would not start a war if the destruction of the temple were presented to him as a *fait accompli,* especially if nobody, least of all the Hittites, claimed responsibility. However, the Assyrian king was clever, politically astute and well-informed. He was aware of everything of political or strategic importance that was known to his vassal kings and princes, and through them and his spies he was also aware of much that was known to the vassal kings and princes of the Hittite king. If any of the Assyrian king's vassals harboured the least suspicion that the Hittites were planning to destroy the temple they would let him know at once. When Aleshanr had asked for reassurances of support from his friends and allies he had therefore been very careful not to even hint at the possibility of the Hittites initiating hostilities against anything in Assyrian territory.

It was also necessary to consider the monster's apparent popularity among the Assyrian rank and file. Despite the evidence and the reassurances of his spies, Aleshanr knew that the slightest *rumour* of an impending attack against the temple of Amalishah could inflame Assyrian public opinion and compel the Assyrian king to publicly proclaim his support for the goddess. At the very least he would have to reinforce the defences of the temple and threaten war. The Assyrian king would have no choice but to respond robustly and aggressively to any rumour of a foreign aggression, no matter how insubstantial the evidence, as anything less would be construed as weakness, and it was well known that many a hapless Assyrian ruler had been deposed because he had appeared weak.

Preparations for the attack on the temple were therefore carried out in the greatest possible secrecy. Only the supreme commanders of the task force would know the target of the campaign until the task force was well into Assyrian territory. But a Hittite army on the march, no matter how small, was sure to be seen. The news would spread among the villages. A vague story was therefore spread among the Hittite populace that an Eastern vassal of the Hittite king was thinking of defecting and needed some military *persuasion* to toe the line.

The one eventuality that could not be guarded against was that the commander of some roaming Assyrian raiding party, hearing that a Hittite army was on the move, would guess that its target was the Amalishah temple. The Assyrian commander would almost certainly call for reinforcements and intervene without waiting for permission from his king. There was thus no question of a long campaign; the Hittites would have to move fast and the Amalishah Temple would have to be destroyed in one fell swoop.

"Once you reach there, the temple has to be destroyed in three days or less," Aleshanr had said to his nephew during one of their many meetings.

"That would require a considerable force, Uncle. The temple is built like a fortress. And the larger the force, the harder it would be to keep its mustering a secret."

"You have to weigh the alternatives very carefully, Arte. I would say that secrecy is the primary consideration."

"So the force would have to be small but effective, and able to move fast."

"It would seem so. Choose your men and any ordnance you wish to take carefully."

8

Artaxias had made a quick but expert study of the temple defences while being led from the First Gate to the Lesser Audience Chamber and then from there to the Second Gate. The journey had traversed the width of the temple. Although he was a comparatively young man, he was very cautious by nature and caution was a trait approved of by his uncle. But the king also knew that too much caution could lead to prevarication, so he chose the customary two advisors to Artaxias very carefully. He decided that the subordinate commanders should be Her-unt and Norr. Her-unt was old and an expert on chariot warfare, a skill that might not be considered very useful against an Assyrian stronghold, but he was a veteran of many campaigns and renowned for his perception and level-headedness. He was also known to have no small measure of the *field commander's art*, namely the instinctive skill of knowing when to act and when to abstain from action. Norr was a younger man who had been with the *mission* to the Amalishah temple. He was an excellent navigator with a detailed knowledge of the terrain between the Hittite border and the target. It was imperative to choose a way that avoided all contact with Assyrian settlements.

Norr had no battle experience, but in a hit-and-run campaign such as this it was essential to know one's way at all times. Many military expeditions had ended in disaster because the army had lost its way or taken an inappropriate route.

Artaxias was to avoid engaging any Assyrian force, no matter how small, before destroying the temple. If engagement were unavoidable he was to destroy the enemy utterly to make sure that no one would report the presence of the task force. He was also to take no prisoners from the temple except children too young to remember their origins. The task force was to consist of fourteen *action groups* of heavy infantry, with twenty men in each group, and twenty-one two-man war chariots, not including the personal chariots and charioteers of the three commanding officers. Siege engines were dispensed with on the grounds that they would reduce the mobility of the force. Unlike the usual practice, all provisions except water would not be collected along the way from towns and villages but would be carried along from the start. The expedition would carry its own supplies of food and water in small carts drawn by horses too old to be used in war chariots.

Mustering and preparing an expeditionary force takes time. The small Hittite army set off some four moons after the *mission* to the Amalishah temple had returned to Hattusas. They left just before dawn, through the East Gate as tradition decreed, in almost total silence.

Unbeknown to the prince or his companions, a slim woman with green eyes left Hattusas almost immediately after the departure of the Hittite force. She was accompanied by a huge heavily-built man. They were both warmly dressed and hooded, and they rode a small cart laden with provisions as though for a long journey.

9

"Must you leave tomorrow, Arte? Must you?" It was almost the end of the night, and she had been kept awake by her fears.

"You know I must, heart-of-my-heart."

"You are a Royal Prince, my husband. Can't someone else go in your place?"

"It is because I am a Royal Prince that I must go."

"What if you don't come back?"

"Why shouldn't I come back?"

"Although you haven't told me where you are going, I feel it in my heart that you are going back to those Children of Darkness. These Assyrians are dangerous, Arte!"

"So am I, heart-of-my-heart!"

"No man is braver than you, Arte. Nor a kinder husband. Nor a more loving father. But what if you don't come back?"

"Why shouldn't I come back?"

"I feel a heavy weight in my breast, my husband. I have never felt like this before!"

"It is almost daybreak. Go back to sleep, heart-of-my-heart!"

"If you must go then I have something for you. I made it myself."

She got off the bed and brought back something small, which she held in the palm of her hand. "I made it from my own hair and the hair of our daughter. It is something for you to wear around your neck."

"What is it?" He could not see very well in the soft light of a single oil lamp.

"It is a necklace with a little blue stone to ward off evil. Promise me you shall wear it until you return!"

"I promise to wear it, heart-of-my-heart, until I return."

"What if you don't come back?"

"Then the king shall find you a less unfortunate husband."

"I shall never have another husband, Arte."

"Then know that if I die I shall think fervently of you and our daughter even as I leave this body, so that my soul shall love you both forever."

She wept, and he comforted her as best he could.

4

DEPARTURE FROM HATTUSAS, AND THE TEMPLE OF ASHTARTE

1

HITTITE ARMIES NORMALLY left the cities with appropriate fanfare. At the fore would be the drummers and the bagpipe players, behind them would come the bulk of the chariots in long parallel lines, with the commanders' chariots in the lead. The pace was set by the heavy infantry, who followed the chariots and were themselves followed by the light infantry and the bowmen. Behind the bowmen rumbled the siege engines, which were normally pulled by teams of oxen. The physicians with their specialised tools came next, travelling in horse-drawn carts, as did the cooks and general handymen who were responsible for sundry maintenance chores and the care of goats, fowl, and other provisions. Reserve weapons, war drums and bagpipes, and the equipment for tents and other shelters also travelled by cart but had no particular place in the column. At the end of the column would be the remainder of the chariots, for a Hittite army on the move would always have chariots at both the front and the rear.

The task force that set out for the Amalishah temple left Hattusas before dawn. As tradition decreed, it left the Hittite capital via the East Gate, so that the men would face the rising sun, but it left in secret, in silence and in haste. The bagpipes and the drums were silent. The commanders' chariots were in the fore and there were chariots at the rear of the column, but there were no siege engines and the foot-soldiers comprised only heavy infantry; there was no light infantry and no bowmen.

The long column pushed forward as fast as the heavy infantry could go. It was essential to skirt villages and studiously avoid caravan routes. The Hittite villages, with their distinctive closely huddled houses and flat roofs, were particularly difficult to avoid because much of the terrain was mountainous and the villages were often built on the only routes available. Nonetheless, with Norr's expert guidance, the Hittites made good progress without being seen except, perhaps, by the occasional farm labourer in his field. The wastelands were almost within sight before the moon had time to complete one cycle.

It was early afternoon and the column was only two days march from the wastelands when Norr, the navigator and one of the three commanders, raised his arm to give the signal to stop.

"Why are we stopping?" asked the prince.

"There is a village ahead of us, less than a day away," said Norr, "It lies on the shortest route, but the villagers are sure to see us and tell everyone that a small army passed their homes travelling towards the wastelands." He sounded as though he were facing a difficult decision.

"So we avoid it like we avoided all those other villages on our way," said the prince.

"We cannot avoid this particular village so easily," said Norr, "To do so we would need to make a long detour to the East, which would take us to the Sharan Pass and make us cross the caravan routes!"

The prince understood why Norr was unwilling to make the decision on his own. "So we must decide whether to pass by the village, and be seen by the villagers," said the prince thoughtfully, "or go past the Sharan Pass and risk being seen by a caravan, possibly even an Assyrian caravan on the way home." He stopped speaking and then said "I think we should go past the village."

"The villagers are sure to see us whereas it is possible that we shall not be seen by a caravan near the Sharan Pass," argued Norr, "We could travel at some distance from the town of Sharan, and if the gods are well disposed there shall be no caravans in our way."

"We cannot depend on the whimsical gods!" said Artaxias impatiently, "I say we go past the village!"

"But neither the caravans nor their scouts travel at night," persisted Norr, "If we cross the caravan routes in the dark we are unlikely to be seen."

"I insist we take the shorter route past the village," said the prince, "The caravan routes are busy at this time of year. If only *one* traveller or caravaner catches a glimpse of us, within a few days everyone shall know that a small Hittite army is marching southwards."

"If we travel at night only the wild animals are likely to see us," argued Norr, "while it is certain that the villagers shall see us if we pass close to their village!"

"Even if some of the villagers see us it is doubtful whether they shall tell anybody for some time," said the prince, "Peasants do not travel far from their homes and they are not as talkative with strangers as the people of the road."

Her-unt, the third commander of the task force, was perturbed by the clash of wills between Artaxias and Norr. Her-unt privately agreed with the prince, that they should go past the village, but during a campaign all decisions pertaining to the choice of routes were traditionally made by the navigator. The prince was pulling rank. If the navigator's decision were overruled it would set a precedent that would undermine Norr's confidence when making future decisions. The Chariot Leader decided to intervene: "Too much is at stake here," he said placatingly. "If we are seen by the wrong people then word of our presence shall spread and all northern Assyrian strongholds, perhaps even the monster's temple, may be put on alert…"

"Yes, and if we are seen marching southwards towards the border," interrupted Artaxias, "we might provide cause for the Assyrians to start a war even if we turn back!" He could not suppress his annoyance at Norr's inability to assess the risks.

"Precisely, my prince," continued Her-unt, "As I said, too much is at stake here. We must therefore not have to choose between two conflicting but equally worthy opinions. So why not find out more about this village before we decide anything? For all we know it is full of old men and women who never leave their village and are unlikely to tell anyone anything."

"I agree," said Artaxias, who was secretly unhappy at having to impose his will against that of the navigator, "That is the best thing to do!"

"You are right, Chariot Leader," said Norr, visibly relieved.

The prince ordered an unscheduled halt and a chariot was sent ahead to have a look at the village. Because a chariot travels much faster than heavy infantry it would take no more than half a day for the scout-chariot to inspect the village and return. The prince decided to wait alone, away from Norr and Her-unt: *Something is the matter with Norr!* he thought, *Surely he could see that a long detour which crosses the caravan routes greatly increases the risk of being seen by unfriendly eyes, not to speak of the time lost!* His thoughts explored several possibilities and he was startled by the most likely conclusion: *Does part of Norr's heart wish this expedition to turn back?*

When the scout-chariot returned the men reported that the village was empty. All three commanders were surprised.

"Empty?" exclaimed the prince, "Why is it empty?"

"Because there is nobody there," replied one of the scouts. He was not trying to be facetious, but he was young and always spoke the first thing that came to his mind. Norr burst out laughing and only stopped when the prince gave him a stern look.

"We don't know why it is empty," said the other scout quickly.

"Well, it's settled then," said the prince, "We pass by the village. Do you agree, Norr?"

"Yes, my prince."

"Chariot leader?"

Her-unt nodded: "Of course, my prince."

2

The village consisted of five houses and was indeed deserted, although the water in the well was fresh and the buildings were undamaged. The mud ovens had been cleaned and the storage jars were standing, empty, in neat rows within the houses.

"The villagers must have left voluntarily," said Artaxias, "There is no evidence of violence."

"And some of the roofs had been repaired and are still weatherproof," commented Her-unt, "The villagers could not have left more than two planting seasons ago."

"They obviously hoped to return," said Artaxias.

"But why would they leave a perfectly good village?" said Norr.

"Most probably because it is too close to the border," replied Her-unt, "We must be within striking distance of Assyrian raiders."

"Ha!" shouted Norr, "If the gods are playful we might play host to an Assyrian raiding party tonight!"

"We shall not camp in the village or anywhere near it," said the prince, "And if a raiding party decides to pay this village a visit it shall be allowed to leave as it came, unaware of our existence."

"To attack another village tomorrow? Why not catch them and teach them to leave our villages alone?" Norr was aghast but the prince looked away.

"Because, Norr," said Her-unt, "Much as we would like to come face to face with an Assyrian raiding party on Hittite soil, we cannot be sure that we shall catch *all* of them. They shall almost certainly have chariots, and in the darkness one or more could manage to escape and tell others about us."

"I understand," said Norr, visibly abashed. "We cannot risk that."

They stopped in the village long enough to take fresh water from the well and then pushed on as fast as they could to make up for lost time. Later that night they camped far from the village and well away from any of the routes that an Assyrian raiding party was likely to use.

3

Three days later they entered the wastelands. The terrain became dry, flat and featureless, and according to Norr it stretched all the way to the Amalishah temple and beyond. The few trees that could be seen were stunted and carried no leaves, and even the shrubs and dry bushes that dotted the landscape seemed to avoid each other, as though each guarded its territory jealously.

"Norr, are we still on Hittite land?" asked Her-unt. His chariot was ahead of Norr's.

"A Hittite would say 'Yes' but an Assyrian would say 'No,'" replied Norr.

"So this is where one of our patrols is most likely to meet a raiding party," said Her-unt.

"Why is that?" asked Norr conversationally, he had not given much thought to how the leader of an Assyrian raiding party would plan his route.

"Oh, because both sides would believe they are on their own territory and not bother to conceal themselves too well."

"What would we do if *we* come across one of our patrols?" asked Norr.

Artaxias, whose chariot was in the lead said: "They would have to join us. They cannot be allowed to return home. But until we left Hattusas, none of our patrols had reported intercepting a raiding party. This could have been due to the light-heartedness of the gods," he paused and turned around to face Norr, "but it is much more likely that the Assyrians have orders to scrupulously avoid…**BY THE NAMES OF ALL THE GODS!**"

The prince pointed to the back of the column.

The earth of the wastelands was dry and fine, so that despite the best efforts of the charioteers the chariots produced a conspicuous plume of brown dust that rose high above the men. Artaxias raised his shield-arm in a crisp motion and the column stopped dead.

"Let us hope that nobody saw that dust cloud!" exclaimed Norr.

Her-unt could not get his eyes off the plume of dust. He looked very worried.

"From now on we shall have to travel during the night and rest during the day," said the prince, "Also, henceforth the infantry shall march ahead of the chariots and the carts. We don't want our men to breathe dust while they march!"

"But if you are at the back of the column," said Norr, "How will the men see your signals?"

"They won't be able to see us in the dark anyway," said the prince, "We shall use one of the chariots to pass on instructions."

"Shall I order the column to rest because we shall henceforth be moving only during the night?" asked Her-unt.

"Yes," said the prince, "And please let the infantry know that from now on it is to march in front of the chariots."

"What about the scout-chariots that are ahead of us?" asked Norr, "They may be several thousand paces away and will not know that we shall travel only at night."

"We shall let them know of the change when they return to report," said the prince, "They are unlikely to be seen, even during the day." The scout-chariots were deployed ahead and on both sides of the column and returned to report roughly every quarter day. Their horses as well as the carriages were covered with goatskins soiled with the local brownish earth and were almost invisible from a distance.

4

The speed of the small force was limited by the walking speed of the heavy infantry. These men marched in three lines carrying their personal provisions and their war spears, shields, mattocks, bows and quivers on their backs. Their scythe-swords were attached to their belts. The distance between the lines was dictated by the length of the war spears, which were attached diagonally to the backpacks at an angle that would not impede walking but lessened the risk of inadvertently stabbing someone in an adjacent line. The risk was very real while the infantry travelled at night.

Because war spears could not be used to assist walking, as the rough ground would wear away the spear butts, most of the infantry carried stout wooden staffs that they had brought with them or picked up along the wooded pathways of the Hittite mountains. But some of the infantry held nothing in their hands, for they believed that when one has to walk long distances the freedom to swing one's arms is preferable to using a staff.

The heavy infantry was composed of muscular young men whose habitual expression of grim determination derived partly from their heavy backpacks and partly from living in a society that had to struggle perpetually against the elements. The Hittite lands were strewn with rugged mountains, and the winters in some places were so cold that the trunks of the fruit trees needed to be covered in animal skins to prevent them from freezing and dying. In other places there were frequent earthquakes so violent that they would bring down the sturdiest fortifications. Despite their heavy backpacks the Hittites travelled fast.

There was only desolation as far as the eye could see in the moonlight. The wastelands were inhospitable and exuded an atmosphere of sullen hostility. Norr decided to move his chariot forward among the infantry to gauge the mood of the men.

"This is a terrible place," he said to an *action group* leader, "Not at all like our mountains, which are covered in beautiful flowers in summer and pure white snow in winter."

"It makes us march all the faster," replied the man, "To finish this affair and get back home!"

"I agree with you," said Norr, "We all want to kill the monster and get home as soon as we can."

"Even the trees resent us!" said another infantryman, "Their branches are like the bony fingers of witches who have suddenly been turned to wood!"

"Yes!" said the man who had first spoken to Norr, "Witches turned to wood while in the act of cursing all living things around them!"

Norr turned his chariot around and returned to the rear of the column. While the chariot rumbled back he thought: *The monotonous marching in the moonlight through this dreary place is having a depressing effect on the men. I must tell the prince about this, though he probably knows. As for the other thing which is eating into my heart, should I tell him about that too? Better not. It will do no good and could weaken his resolve!*

As the column travelled into the wastelands the trees became fewer and there started to appear large clumps of boulders that became more common the deeper they entered into Assyrian territory. The ground often showed rock through the loose sun-baked earth. The fine earth would turn to slippery mud if it rained.

On the fifth night of travelling in the wastelands, the stars shone like tiny jewels and some small clouds played hide-and-seek with the moon. Her-unt brought his chariot alongside that of the prince.

"My mother used to say that gossip travels faster than the wind. I would add that if we are seen here the news of our coming would travel even faster across the Assyrian lands."

"You've said that several times already," said Artaxias, and he smiled at the older man. Only after he had spoken did he realise that his friend might not be able to see his smile in the capricious moonlight. So he said: "Don't worry, Chariot Leader, the men knew that they were not to talk about the expedition to anyone before we left and on our way we gave all the villages and travellers' routes a wide berth."

"It is not what we did or did not do back in our own territory that preys on my mind," said Her-unt, "It is this bleak and desolate land. At night it is much worse than during the day. I feel that the stones and even the soft earth hate us. They would reveal us to our enemies yet hide our enemies from us."

"I know there is peril here, old friend," said the prince, "But the stones and the brown earth are impartial. They care little about the affairs of men. As for being seen, that is why we have chariots scouting the land ahead of us and to our left and right. Our scouts are well-trained and aware of the danger."

Her-unt did not reply but brooded grimly, absorbed by his thoughts.

The prince's heart felt suddenly heavy: *Her-unt is not just worried about Assyrians seeing us. Since we entered the wastelands something deeper is troubling him. Could it be the same thing that is troubling Norr?* After they had entered the wastelands Norr and Her-unt had often spoken together furtively when they were alone, as though they shared a secret.

5

The prince noticed that Her-unt became more restless and short-tempered as they travelled in the dark and even Norr, who could put up a happy face at the worst of times, seemed to be more affected than he should be by the emptiness around them. Although Artaxias was aware of his friends' worries he kept silent. The circumstances discouraged inessential talk.

Late one night, when the moon had long set and the army was progressing wearily across the wastelands, one of the scout-chariots returned in haste. It hastened straight to the commanders, who were travelling almost at the rear of the column. Artaxias was dismayed to hear how much noise a fast-travelling chariot made on the earth-covered rock. Even with the axles heavily greased and the hooves of the horses enclosed in goatskin its approach could be heard long before it became visible in the starlight. The First Charioteer hailed him and the prince grunted a curt greeting.

"There is some kind of habitation ahead of us," reported the charioteer, "It appears too small to be a village. It is difficult to be sure because there is no moon and there are large rocks all around it."

"That is the empty ruin we saw from a distance during our first trip to the temple," said Norr, "It is empty and poses no threat."

"Are you sure there is no one there?" Her-unt asked Norr.

"Quite sure," replied the navigator, "It's been abandoned for a very long time."

"What were these ruins?" asked Artaxias.

"A small settlement built around a shrine," said Norr. "I was told about it by an old Assyrian who lived in Hattusas. He had been on a pilgrimage to the temple of the monster when he was a child. He mentioned passing a derelict shrine as he travelled with his grandfather."

The prince spoke to the scout-charioteer. "How close to the ruins did you get?"

"Two hundred paces," said the First Charioteer, "We did not dismount and investigate on foot because we thought we should come back quickly."

"It is now not much more than two thousand paces ahead of the column," added the Second Charioteer.

"You were right to come back as quickly as you could," said the prince, "You may now have something to eat and join the other chariots. Your scout duties have been taken up by another chariot."

The column had not stopped while the scout made his report but soon after the chariot had taken its place in the column Artaxias raised his shield-arm. One of the chariots behind him immediately rushed forwards to the infantry lines to give the signal to stop. The message was conveyed soundlessly.

"Why are we stopping?" asked Norr.

"To rest," replied the prince, "Tomorrow morning we shall pay homage to the god or goddess of the shrine."

Her-unt nodded in approval but Norr exclaimed: "A ceremony will cost us a whole day, my prince!"

"I know," said Artaxias, "But we cannot afford to offend any of the gods. We shall rest now and conduct a short ceremony tomorrow, in the daytime. The men have been marching for almost the whole night and can do with an early rest." The prince alighted from his chariot and the word was passed down the column that there was to be a respite from the gruelling walk in the darkness.

6

The three commanders pulled up their cloaks and squatted on the hard ground. It was bitterly cold but no fires were lit. Norr pulled out some smoked meat and started to chew.

"You're always eating," said Her-unt.

"I'm always hungry when I'm worried!"

"Why are you worried?"

"We are going somewhere to kill a goddess and you ask me why I am worried?"

Although Norr and Her-unt had spoken in a low voice Artaxias' attention was immediately directed to the exchange between his fellow commanders.

"She is a demon, not a goddess," said Her-unt quietly. He did not sound very sure of what he was saying. "One might be able to plead or reason with a goddess, but not with a demon!"

"We have *our* gods on our side," said Artaxias, but he thought: *Or so we hope! Who knows what the gods shall decide to do?*

"How can we be sure that the gods shall not protect their own?" asked an unfamiliar voice. Two infantrymen stood by in the gloom, barely visible; they had silently come up to where the commanders were sitting.

"We are sure because the king consulted the oracle at Metsamor," replied Artaxias reassuringly. "Why are you here and not with the rest of the infantry?"

"Most of the men can sleep when they please," replied the young man, "We are not able to do that." The young man seemed ill-at-ease speaking to the prince.

"What are your names?" asked Artaxias.

"My comrade's name is Vosher. He is my mother's brother's son and we come from the same village. My name is Ovanne."

"And who is your group leader, Ovanne?" asked Norr.

"The leader of our action group is Urdzhe."

"Urdzhe is an experienced soldier," said Artaxias. "I am sure he has trained you well."

"He has indeed trained us well," said Ovanne. "But we only know how to fight men, not goddesses or demons!"

"You *will* fight only men," said Artaxias. "It is *my* duty to fight and kill the monster."

"Are you not afraid?" asked the young man quietly.

"Afraid?" exclaimed Her-unt gruffly. "What kind of men are you to think that a war prince is afraid? Pull yourselves together and go get some sleep!"

"No wait!" said Artaxias. "How old are you, Ovanne?"

"My mother tells me I've seen sixteen winters. My comrade is older but I do not know his age."

The prince looked them up and down: *Despite their size, they're just boys on their first campaign. And there must be many others like them. This has to be handled carefully.*

"Why can't you sleep easily?" asked the prince.

"The men say that the goddess of the temple is immortal," said Ovanne. "Some even say that she is a sister to the gods who rule the wastelands."

"That is not true," said Artaxias, "She is not a goddess. She is a monster who kills our brethren to drink their blood. The Assyrians call her a goddess, but we call her a monster. The gods are on our side because they do not favour monsters. Least of all monsters that drink human blood."

"So we have been told many times," said Ovanne, "We are not afraid to fight, my prince, we are afraid of being punished by the gods because we are on our way to kill a goddess!"

"She is *not* a goddess," repeated the prince, "She is just a woman who somehow became a monster and managed to live for a very long time. She feeds on human blood and the gods are as angry with her as we are. Do not fear any reprisals from the gods."

The other young man, Vosher, stammered: "I m-must admit that our fear of the g-gods is mixed with the fear of b-battle, my prince. We cannot s-suppress the fear of not returning to our families, and this fear is m-mixed with the fear of angering the g-gods."

Ah! He lets his cousin do most of the talking because of his stammer. "You must separate your fear of the gods from the fear of not returning home," said the prince, "Our gods stand behind us in this venture. You can be sure of that."

"And the f-fear of battle, m-my prince?"

"It is natural to be afraid on the way to battle," said Artaxias, "And let me tell you a little secret. Even when you get as old as we are, you shall never lose that fear. You shall merely forget it during the fighting. When you are fighting you don't have time to think of anything except the enemy who is standing in front of you and is trying to kill you!"

"I th-thought officers were n-never afraid," almost whispered the boy, his stammer getting worse.

"We are all afraid of something when on campaign," replied Artaxias, his voice soft. "I left a wife and a tiny little girl, the kind that loves to cuddle her father. Do you think I am not afraid of never seeing my little girl again?"

"What if the monster *is* a goddess?" said Ovanne, "If we kill her… if *you* kill her, won't the gods be angry?"

"They won't be angry with you," said Her-unt abruptly, and he seemed to be irritated by something other than what the boy had said. "The decision to kill the goddess and her priests was not yours! If the gods decide to curse anyone it will be the officers, not the infantrymen and the charioteers."

Aah! thought Artaxias, *so that is what is bothering Her-unt! He is not just worried about the Assyrians finding out about us, he is also afraid of committing sacrilege! Is this what is bothering Norr too?*

The prince spoke softly: "If the gods did not approve they would have shown it before we entered the wastelands! Remember the words of the oracle at Metsamor. Look how the weather has been kind to us. Look how the village we could not bypass turned out to be empty. Look how easily we reached here, unseen and unheard!"

"I think you are right, my prince," said Ovanne. "I am sure we have nothing to fear from the gods." The two boys withdrew.

When Artaxias was sure the boys could no longer hear him he turned to Her-unt and said: "Vosher and Ovanne are almost convinced of the rightness of our cause. But have I convinced *you* old friend?"

"What makes you think I need to be convinced?" asked Her-unt.

"We *all* need to be sure that we shall not anger the gods by killing the monster," said the prince, "This expedition makes heavy demands on our bodies. Because of that we need to remove the burden of any doubts we may have within our hearts."

"*I* also need to be convinced," said Norr quietly, "How can we be sure that the monster is not a goddess?"

"The oracle was quite explicit!" said the prince firmly. "The gods approve of this expedition. Is your superstitious fear of the monster stronger than your faith in the oracle of Metsamor?"

"Oracles are never so explicit as to remove all doubts," said Her-unt.

"What you say is true," admitted the prince, "But I don't think there is more than one way to interpret the oracle. We can only look at how the gods have treated us so far, for it is by such signs that the gods speak to us. And if we do not destroy the monster, think of how many more of our brethren it shall kill!"

"You do not need to remind me of that," said Her-unt. "And I know that we have little choice. Nevertheless I fear to kill someone, or something, that is believed by many to be an immortal goddess. If the gods thought her evil, they would have destroyed her or let her die of old age like the rest of us!"

"Perhaps the gods need our help," said Artaxias, "The monster is not alone. She is surrounded by priests who might continue their evil ways if she were to die of natural causes. The gods may wish not only to destroy the monster, but also those who might perpetuate her evil."

"I was brought up to respect priests," said Norr. "All priests, be they Hittite or Assyrian or Egyptian or Sumerian. They have secret knowledge that we cannot possess. They are also closer to the gods than the rest of us!"

"That is what all priests wish us to believe. Yet not all priests are good," said Artaxias, "And religion is often an excuse for bad men to do evil things! Let us rest now."

Her-unt and Norr lay down and wrapped themselves in their cloaks. Within minutes Her-unt was snoring loudly.

But the prince could not drift off to sleep. *An army cannot fight bravely if it doubts the goodwill of the gods. Despite my own doubts I must find a way to convince my men that the gods are fully on our side! That way, only I shall carry doubts, for I am able to conceal my doubts within my heart as in an iron box.* He sighed audibly. *That is the price of being in command, I must carry the heaviest burdens alone!*

7

When the Hittites awoke the sun had just risen and its rosy light reflected eerily off the soil of the wastelands, which was damp with the moisture that had settled during the night. Elsewhere the effect would have been quite beautiful.

"How can there be a shrine here, in the middle of nowhere?" said Her-unt as the chariots took up their positions behind the infantry.

"The shrine is probably much older than the temple of the monster," replied the prince, "I have heard that the wastelands were not always empty and that many people lived near the place where the monster's temple now stands."

"What happened to them?" asked Her-unt.

"I was told that they were all pushed out when the temple of the monster was built."

"Were they Hittites?" asked Her-unt.

"No," said the prince, "As far as I know this was always Assyrian land."

"So why were they pushed out?"

"I don't know."

"Perhaps the monster did not wish to have neighbours," said Norr.

The column moved forward towards the shrine.

It was not long before they could see, almost hidden by boulders and small clumps of stunted trees, the remains of what had once been a few small mud-brick huts and a larger semicircular structure. At a signal from the prince three *action groups* rushed forward quietly and formed a wide ring around the place. The ring contracted slowly as the men closed in on the ruins.

"The shrine is deserted, my prince," said Norr, "Why are we bothering to surround it?"

"The shrine might have been deserted for a very long time," said Artaxias, "But we cannot be sure there is no-one there now."

"Anyone living in such a place would be insane!" said Norr.

"Even the insane can recognise a foreign army on Assyrian soil."

Norr was about to show his exasperation when one of the men who had surrounded the settlement shouted: "Hai!" He appeared to be struggling with something that squirmed near the ground. It was a small half-starved dog.

The prince leaned over the front of his chariot and shouted: "Spread out and find its owners!"

Its owners, or rather what was left of them, were found almost immediately. There were human bones within the ruins of one of the smaller huts; the bones had been gnawed and scattered by animals but had not yet been covered by soil. The men who had found the remains withdrew as the three commanders went over to investigate.

"Three adults and a child," said Her-unt, "It is not many moons since they died."

"They must have died of thirst," said Artaxias, "But what were they doing here at this ancient shrine?"

"They were probably pilgrims," said Her-unt. "They probably got lost after they left the temple of the monster. When they saw the shrine, they probably came in the hope of finding water."

"Or perhaps they got lost while seeking the temple of the monster," said Norr.

"Whatever the reason for their being here," said Her-unt impatiently, "The question we should ask is: What do their deaths mean for us? Is their failure to escape the wastelands a good omen or a bad omen?"

"It could be a warning by the gods!" exclaimed Norr. It had not occurred to him that finding the human bones could be an omen.

"Yes, we could have done with a soothsayer," murmured Her-unt.

"The message of this tragedy is quite clear," said Artaxis, "The gods are not on the side of those who believe in the monster. If she were a true goddess she would have protected her worshippers, whether they were on the way to the temple or after they left!"

Her-unt shook his head thoughtfully. "That argument might convince Norr and me but it may not convince all of our men, my prince."

"Nonetheless that is what they shall be told," said Artaxias. "Please see to it, Chariot Leader. Norr, please make sure that the dog is fed and the bones properly buried."

"The dog died, said Norr, "The excitement must have been too much for it."

"Then have it buried too."

The shrine proper was no more than a thick, semicircular wall whose fire-baked bricks had almost survived the weather of the wastelands, though its roof had long-since vanished. On either side of the shrine were the weather-worn remains of mud-brick huts and, about twenty paces from the shrine, was a mound that must have once been a communal oven. The apertures of the oven had caved in and the mound was covered by thick almost-dry bushes that clung to its sides tenaciously.

At the centre of the semicircular wall stood a stone idol. Although the details of the idol were badly eroded by the wind and the rain, it still showed a lithe young woman holding what might once have been a bow. At the back of the idol was an irregular shape that might have once represented a quiver full of arrows. The statue stood on a low pedestal but was no more than shoulder-high.

"This is a shrine to the goddess Ashtarte!" exclaimed Norr, "The goddess of the Evening Star!"

To the Hittites, Ashtarte represented love and fertility, the caring motherhood that was in the spirit of the land beneath their feet. As the supreme mother-goddess, it was to her that the Hittites prayed for the wheat and barley to grow without mishap, for the trees to bear fruit, for the cattle and goats to multiply. To the Assyrians, Ashtarte was also the goddess of hunting and war.

Artaxias entered the semicircle and stood before the statue. Turning to his men, who had hesitated to enter the shrine, he said: "This is our goddess Ashtarte, whom the Assyrians worship also though for different reasons. It is not right that we find her shrine without paying homage. The Sun Goddess shall be high in the sky soon, and when our shadows are shortest we shall perform a ritual that will ensure the blessings of Ashtarte on our campaign. After that we shall sleep, and in the night we shall continue our march to the temple of the monster!"

The men took this as an indication that they were to prepare for a ceremony. They scattered to see to the horses and chariots and then cleansed themselves ritually with the dry earth that lay within the shrine.

8

The sun was at its highest point when the Hittites prepared for the ceremony. Although Artaxias was not a priest, he was a royal prince, and royal princes, like kings, had the right to don the mantle of priesthood on special occasions when they were on campaign.

A goat was sacrificed and its body laid ceremoniously at the foot of the statue. The prince, wearing his helmet and in full battle armour, stood before the statue while the others, holding only their swords and shields, stood respectfully in a silent throng outside the entrance to the semicircular shrine. The prince raised his arms and called in a vibrant voice:

"In the name of the thousand gods I call upon thee, my goddess!
I call upon thee to bless this expedition, Oh Blessed Ashtarte,
I call upon thee to offer us your helping hanh, for our cause is just.

The prince lowered his arms:

The Sun Goddess, who travels across the sky,
And the Earth, our mother who cares for her children,
they can still hear the cries of those who died in the darkness
to feed the monster, Amalishah!
I call upon thee to help us, my goddess, for our cause is just!"

The prince drew his sword and continued:

"The mothers and the fathers of those who were killed to feed the
monster still weep and call upon the gods for vengeance!
And so I call upon thee, Oh Ashtarte, as a mother to us all,
I beg you to hear my plea! And the plea of those who still mourn,
Help us destroy this demon who has deluded those who are blind and
those who are evil!
Help us destroy this monster
who has tricked the evil and the gullible into calling it a goddess
in blasphemy before the gods, among whom you are queen.

Oh Ashtarte
Help us destroy this demon,
whose blood-nourished shape is as nothing
when compared with your glory!

I beseech you, oh goddess Ashtarte
Stand beside us when we remove this living affront to the heavens,
She who has brought tears and pain
to the mothers, fathers, wives, brothers and sisters
of those who were given to it in blasphemous sacrifice!
Hear my prayer, Oh Ashtarte,
For our cause is just
And I pray to you as a humble worshipper!"

Her-unt and Norr entered the temple and butchered the carcase of the goat with their scythe-swords. Parts of the animal were then ritually burned on a makeshift altar in front of the statue. The wind, as though in tune with the ceremony, wafted the smoke in the direction of the idol.

When the ritual burning was over, Artaxias walked the short distance to the mound that had once been an earthen oven. Throwing back his cloak and raising his sword, he climbed to the top of the mound and, turning to face the general direction of the Amalishah Temple, cried out in a voice that all could hear:

"I beseech you, Oh Ashtarte, give us a sign.
Give us a sign that you look favourably upon our plea!"

And he brought the sword to his chest in salute. The men responded by striking their swords against their shields. There was a loud sound like the breaking of many branches and, as though in divine response, from beneath the prince's right hand a solitary bird flew skyward from the bushes that surrounded the mound.

There was a loud murmur of awe from the men. "Our goddess Ashtarte has shown us her approval!" shouted the prince. "She sent us a bird that flew to my right"

He sheathed his sword and turned once again towards the statue in the temple.

"Please accept my thanks, Oh Ashtarte!
I thank you and my men thank you,
We shall worship you with all the strength in our hearts
for as long as we live!"

The prince descended from the mound. The ceremony was over.

9

The men withdrew from the site and prepared to rest for the remainder of the day. There was much laughter, and even Her-unt seemed very pleased. Only the prince was pensive as he settled down to rest, *Forgive me, my goddess,* he thought as sleep overtook him, *for knowing about the bird in its nest, and turning to face my men so that the clatter of their shields would cause it to fly to my right! But I have a task to do, and my men must have no doubts about the righteousness of our cause!*

5

THE EYES AND EARS OF THE GODDESS

1

IT HAD STARTED cordially enough, but the visit of the green-eyed priestess to the Assyrian Envoy in Hattusas had developed into a less-than-polite exchange:

"I tell you that these creatures are preparing an assault on the temple of our goddess and you choose to do nothing?"

"I must choose to do nothing, Lady, unless you tell me more about why you believe that the Hittites are going to attack the temple of your goddess." The baritone voice was smooth and beautifully modulated.

Despite her anger, the priestess spoke with icy control: "I told you that the goddess herself expects these creatures to attack her temple. I told you that I was sent to spy on the creatures and return when I had seen and heard all that I needed to know. What more can I tell you?"

"You can tell me why you think the Hittites are going to attack your temple."

"Envoy, I am merely asking for two or three chariots and an escort. It is not much to ask of someone in your position!"

"It is indeed not much to ask, Lady. But you still have not told me why you believe the Hittites are intending to attack the temple of your goddess."

The priestess was unaccustomed to giving explanations. She waved her hand in a gesture of impatience: "I was there when our High Priest spoke to the creatures. I heard the words of the so-called prince before he left. He said 'We shall return' and there was the threat of many deaths in his voice!"

The Envoy sat back in his chair: "The goddess did not speak to the Hittites?"

"Of course not! How could the High Priest allow such a thing?"

"So you believe that the Hittites are intending to attack your temple because of the words of an angry man, and your goddess came to believe that her temple will be attacked because of what you told her."

"Our goddess makes her own decisions, Envoy. What I told her was exactly what happened in the Lesser Audience Chamber. No more and no less!"

"But you did tell her of the supposed threat of many deaths in the prince's voice."

"That was part of what happened in the Lesser Audience Chamber."

"Did you make allowances for the fact that the prince had been treated very badly?"

"You are not talking to an ordinary priestess, Envoy. I am the Eyes and Ears of the goddess! I am trained to read a man's thoughts in his speech and to make whatever allowances are necessary!"

"I am sure you are very well trained, priestess. But is it not true, nonetheless, that your goddess came to believe that the Hittites are planning to attack her temple only because of what you told her?"

"I tell you again, Envoy: I am the Eyes and Ears of the goddess. I report to the goddess accurately and do not make empty conjectures!" The priestess did not like the way the Envoy kept redirecting the conversation; in all her dealings with men she had always been in control.

"Be that as it may, Lady, although you might have persuaded your goddess of a coming attack on her temple, you have yet to persuade me."

The eyes of the priestess half closed and she was silent as she thought: 'Why does he keep saying 'your goddess'? His words and manner imply a need to distance himself from our goddess. Why would he feel a need to distance himself? I must find the reasons for this but now is not the time.' The priestess smiled engagingly: "You are not easy to persuade Uri, and that is a good trait in an Envoy. So I shall tell you more. Here in Hattusas I asked questions and found that our goddess was right. The creatures are mustering a small army whose target is kept secret. It is your duty to help me warn the temple of our goddess."

"I know my duties, Lady. They do not include providing a priestess of the Amalishah temple with the means to do mischief!"

The priestess's smile vanished and she leaned forward: "Do you call warning our temple of an attack by these creatures 'doing mischief'?"

"You shall do much more than warn your temple, priestess. If I let you have what you want you shall not only warn the priests of your goddess but every Assyrian you meet. You would start rumours that could lead to war!"

"What do I care about that? Why should you care about that?"

"Perhaps you are assuming, Lady, that we shall necessarily win. Yet even now all the little kings and princes – even those who pay tribute to the King of Kings – are preparing to descend upon us like vultures in the event that there is a war and the Hittites defeat us!"

"Bah! Crows and petty scavengers hoping that the goose will overcome the eagle!"

The envoy rose from his chair and paced the room like a lion in a cage. He could not tell the priestess that his king had forbidden him to discuss the goddess, nor could he tell her that his king would strongly disapprove if he became involved in any way with the temple of Amalishah. Yet neither could he dismiss this woman or her allegations. This was a priestess of rank and, yes, she would not make empty conjectures. What she was saying was probably true, and she would persist in her demands. He had to pacify her, reach some compromise. He turned to face her and said: "You must tell me more of what you have discovered in Hattusas. I cannot allow you to spread fear and hostility merely because you heard an angry prince say 'We shall return'!"

She smiled again and said: "My suspicions may have begun with what I heard the so-called prince say, Envoy, and our goddess came to the same conclusion as I, but I told you that our goddess's words were confirmed by what I saw and heard in Hattusas. The temple of our goddess will be attacked because the so-called prince was humiliated."

"A decision to attack an Assyrian temple is not for a prince to make, Lady. Not even a Royal Prince."

"So he managed to persuade his uncle. From the way he said 'the king, my uncle' the king of these creatures and his nephew are very close."

"Perhaps they are, but a Hittite king would not wage war against us because his nephew was insulted!"

"Perhaps not war, Envoy. But he could try to destroy the Amalishah temple because that is where his nephew made an impudent request that brought him nothing but humiliation. And there is, of course, another reason for the creatures to destroy the temple of our goddess.."

"And what is this other reason?"

The priestess's eyebrows rose in feigned surprise: "Why, Envoy, is it not obvious?' – she paused for the briefest of moments – "To stop our goddess from feasting on the blood of boys caught in Hittite land!"

The Envoy looked away and was clearly uncomfortable with what he had heard. In a low voice he said: "You skilfully avoid telling me

84

what you claim to have seen and heard in Hattusas, Lady. But if I am to help you I need something more substantial than the anger of a prince who has been treated very badly. And even the reason that cannot be mentioned does not persuade me that the Hittites will attack your temple."

She glared at him, her green eyes afire with indignation at being doubted. Would nothing convince this man? She had even mentioned the unmentionable! But the priestess **had** to warn her temple and to do that she needed the help of the Envoy. She had to understand why the Envoy stubbornly refused to accept that, for whatever reasons, the temple of her goddess was in imminent danger. This was the only reality: a Hittite task force was being mustered to destroy the Amalishah temple! The reasons behind the creatures' impending attack were irrelevant, not worthy of discussion. With an effort of will she suppressed her anger and forced her training and intuition to fuse into a sharply analytic tool that probed into all that the Envoy had said. Silently she reviewed the words he had used, the expressions which accompanied the words, the unconscious movements of his hands, the varying tension in his shoulders as he spoke. There were several possible explanations for her inability to convince him; all but one were considered and rejected, and the one that remained surprised her: The Envoy would not accept what she was saying because he was **certain** that the Hittite king could not have been swayed by his nephew! She had not considered this possibility! 'Could the Envoy be right? After all, the Envoy knew the king of the creatures personally!' Her glare softened until her face lost all expression. 'He must be right! He knows enough about the creatures not to be wrong in such matters!' Her heart started pounding as she followed her new insight to its logical conclusion: 'But if the nephew did not persuade the uncle then the decision to attack the temple must have been taken **by the king himself!** Since the king could not foresee what the nephew would say upon his return, or even whether his nephew would return at all, the preparations for the attack must have begun **before** the return of the nephew!' The priestess's eyes widened as she realised that a Hittite force could set out for the Amalishah temple sooner than she expected!

She managed to suppress a surge of panic and said evenly: "Very well, Envoy. I need your help and shall overlook the insult in your refusal to be satisfied with what I have already told you. Let us say, then, that in Hattusas I learnt all that I needed to know from a war-horse."

"Are you saying that you have informants in the Hittite war-stables while I have yet to organise my spy network?"

"I am not criticising your competence, Envoy. I know that you are new here. I am simply asking for your help."

"Can you tell me more of what you have seen and heard in Hattusas?" The question was asked tentatively, without the Envoy's earlier robust confidence.

"I cannot tell you more without revealing secrets that are not mine to reveal." And she thought: 'I've got him! He is wavering!'

"I understand," said the Envoy, and there was a subtle note of capitulation in his voice. The goddess had lived long enough to have spies everywhere. In time, there would be spies even on him! He returned to his chair and spoke without emotion: "If I decide to help you, Lady, you could put me in a very difficult position."

"I am merely asking for a few chariots and a bodyguard. The priests I came with have returned to the temple and I cannot travel on my own."

"And if I provided you with chariots and a bodyguard, how far do you think you would get through Hittite lands?"

"You are the Envoy of the King of Kings. You could make it appear to be official business. The creatures would not dare interfere with an official communication from you to our king!" She was pleased with the way she said 'our king'.

"That is out of the question. I cannot be seen doing anything outside my brief."

"I have no wish to jeopardise your position, Uri. But the fact remains that the creatures are preparing an army to destroy an Assyrian temple, and you must help me to ensure that the temple is warned."

"Who is to lead this supposed expedition?"

"The creature who visited the temple dressed like a beggar, the Hittite king's nephew!"

The Envoy rose from his seat again and stood pensively in front of the window. The Assyrian king had given him no guidelines regarding the temple of Amalishah; the subject was taboo even in the confidential instructions of a king to his envoy. 'Do I hold your life in my hands, Arte?' he thought. 'Does the loyalty to my king extend to the temple of Amalishah?' He tried to remember the face of the goddess as he had seen her when he was a child, but his memory failed him and he could only recall the smiling face of a fair-haired Hittite boy playing in a flower-strewn garden. He took a deep breath and thought: 'I shall give you a chance, Arte, and leave the unravelling of this story to the gods.'

He turned to the priestess. Her green eyes were studying him closely but there was a faint smile of satisfaction on her lips.

"I shall help you return to your temple, Lady," he said with some reluctance, "But I shall make two conditions."

She spoke coldly: "Name your conditions!"

"My first condition is that you shall not leave Hattusas before the Hittite expedition, assuming that an expedition against your temple is ever mounted."

"Oh there is certainly going to be an expedition, Envoy. But why can't I leave before the creatures?"

"Because, priestess, you have yet to convince me that your temple is in danger. The Hittite army you claim is being prepared may be against someone else. There is talk of trouble with one of the Shaamite princes. If you are wrong, and the Hittites have no hostile intentions regarding your temple, you would do endless damage if your warnings are false."

"What damage could I do?" Her voice was innocent, childlike.

"Many kinds of damage. My king ordered me to do everything in my power to reassure King Aleshanr that he has no hostile intentions. Aleshanr will become suspicious of our king's motives if he hears that someone is telling our people that the Hittites will attack an Assyrian temple!"

"And how will Aleshanr hear of that?"

"Kings have ways, Lady, especially in troubled times."

"Does our king really care about what this Aleshanr believes?"

"He told me personally that he does. You shall also make my job much harder if Assyrian officials turn against the Hittite merchants who are trying to re-establish trade relations."

"Huh!" The priestess spoke with disgust. "Trade relations! Of what importance could they be?"

"I assure you, priestess, they are very important."

"Very well, I accept your first condition. What is the other?"

"You shall travel by cart and take only one man for your escort."

The priestess almost rose from her seat in outrage: "A cart, Envoy? Am I the fat wife of a peasant to travel by cart?"

"A cart would be safer for you than an Assyrian chariot. You speak Hittite perfectly and so does the man I have in mind. You can pass as a Hittite woman with her husband. The lands near the border are full of people who are wandering around looking for new places to settle."

The priestess shook her head in disapproval. "But if I leave after the creatures and if I travel by cart, how am I to reach our temple before the creatures?"

"I shall give you a good horse and you can follow the shortest route

87

once you are certain of their destination. If a Hittite war party does set out for your temple it will have to make many detours to avoid being seen. It will also travel more slowly than a cart with a good horse because it must include heavy infantry and siege engines."

"They are not taking any siege engines."

"Then it is unlikely that they are intending to attack a fortified temple."

The priestess ignored the Envoy's remark. "I really would very much prefer to leave before the creatures, Uri."

"You can leave as soon after the supposed expedition as you please, but not before. Find a place to stay somewhere near the East Gate. All Hittite military expeditions leave Hattusas by the East Gate, usually at dawn."

"Perhaps you are right. For a moment I doubted your loyalty to our goddess. And who shall be my escort?"

"The former fighting champion, Baalshe. I shall tell him to join you soon. But lest you intend to persuade him to leave before the supposed expedition, I should warn you that he is completely loyal to me, and he shall remain so until you both leave Hattusas – if you leave Hattusas!"

The priestess smiled again, just managing to suppress the scowl that threatened to reveal her true feelings towards the Envoy.

2

The priestess was deep in thought as her cart clattered over the tracks left by the Hittite chariot-wheels. They were still in Hittite territory and the ground was soft enough for her and her companion to be able to follow the Hittites without the need to keep them in sight. But soon they would be harder to follow and, in the wastelands, where the ground was flat, dry and featureless, they would have to be extraordinarily vigilant, for they would have to balance the need to know the Hittites' whereabouts against the possibility of being seen.

As the cart rolled drearily on, the priestess went over all that had happened since the arrival of the Hittite delegation at the temple, her thoughts punctuated by a repetitive squeak from one of the cart's axles. Foremost in her thoughts was her last meeting with the goddess. The Hittite delegation had barely left the temple when the priestess had stood before the goddess and recited all that had transpired in the Lesser Audience Chamber. The goddess had sat passively and said nothing while the priestess spoke, but when the account was finished she had asked: "The prince made no overt threats at any time?" The priestess had replied: "No. Although he called you a monster when our priests' taunts became unbearable and he was otherwise as polite as a prince who has been insulted can be." The goddess had nodded, indicating that she had heard and understood all that the priestess had said. After a long pause, she said: "Go immediately to Hattusas. In a little while the Hittites shall come to destroy the temple. Find out when the Hittites will be here and the strength of their force. When you know all that we need to know, come back and warn us."

The goddess had always spoken with a quiet confidence that made it impossible for anyone to read her thoughts, but her last words to the priestess were spoken with a sadness that the priestess had found surprising, and the priestess had wondered whether there was also a tinge of resignation in the goddess's voice.

The priestess's thoughts turned to the Envoy, and the more she thought about their meeting the less she trusted him. Why did he feel a need to distance himself from the goddess? It could not be because he disapproved of the goddess feeding on prisoners; it was the king himself who had asked this of the goddess. Could the Envoy have somehow developed sympathies towards the creatures? His reaction when she had named the commander of the Hittite expedition particularly disturbed her. Even while she spoke the words 'The creature who visited the temple dressed like a beggar, the Hittite king's nephew!' his behaviour had changed. He had become more pensive, seemingly more aware of factors that had not been brought up in their conversation. For a moment she had even feared that he would betray her to the Hittites. The memory of that fear transferred her suspicions onto her escort, the giant Baalshe.

How trustworthy was the man? The thought of killing him and continuing her journey alone floated past in her mind, but it was left to pass ungrasped. Without an escort she would be prey to any vagabond she might meet; far from human habitation a lone woman was fair game. Anyway, this man would not be easy to kill. Even while he slept, he appeared to sense every movement within ten paces. On the second night from Hattusas he had killed a prowling rat seemingly in his sleep. The animal had soundlessly strayed within range of Baalshe's knife and had been immediately skewered.

3

It was many days since the priestess and her escort had stealthily followed the tracks of the small Hittite army out of Hattusas. They paced their speed so as to always keep the rearguard just out of sight. During this period the woman had hardly spoken a word to her companion; for hours on end she had stared vacantly ahead of her, as though deeply preoccupied by overwhelming concerns. Baalshe wondered if this was because she was thinking of the difficulties of her task, or could it be because she thought him unworthy of sharing her thoughts? The man was a warrior of renown, but he was not particularly endowed with intellect and he had little interest in the kind of issues that senior priestesses were wont to think about. Yet Baalshe was wise enough to know his limitations and his place.

But men of action tend to become confused and sullen when not spoken to for some time. When the wastelands were almost in sight and the priestess had ordered a brief halt, he felt a need to be reassured by the sound of her voice or, at least, by her attention. After thinking of, and dismissing, several opening phrases, he finally blurted in a timid tone: "The Assyrian family you stayed with in Hattusas were very hospitable, my lady."

The priestess was pulled out of her reverie.

"Yes." she replied laconically.

"When I came to pick you up," he said with more confidence, "I enjoyed playing with the children."

The priestess did not answer and he realised that this subject led nowhere.

"I think there is no doubt that the Hittites are heading for the temple," he persisted, unwilling to let the conversation, such as it was, die out.

"We must be sure."

Her statement surprised him. Was she not certain that the Hittites were on their way to her temple? "What shall we do if they are not going to the temple?" he asked.

"I'll tell you when I am sure of their destination," she snapped.

The man bit into his smoked meat and tore his loaf of dried bread viciously before stuffing a piece into his mouth. Sensing his frustration, and aware of how much she depended on him, the priestess tried to make her voice sound kind: "Don't be too anxious, Baalshe. It is important that we be sure of where these creatures are heading before we make any decisions." *I must test this man's loyalty to me. The Envoy may have ordered him to kill me if he thought I would warn the temple needlessly.*

"All decisions are yours to make, my lady. I am here to protect you and be your guide."

Again the priestess did not answer, but she thought: *There is no guile in his voice. Perhaps he is one of those supremely violent men who always speak the truth.*

They had entered the wastelands when the priestess condescended to speak to Baalshe again: "I think there is no doubt that they are making for the temple."

Baalshe, who was holding the reins, looked away from the priestess. "Their way is not straight," he said sullenly. She had ignored him for too long and he was not in the mood to agree easily with anything she said.

"Of course it's not straight! They are taking the route that will avoid meeting anyone!"

"Yes, priestess."

She let the tone of familiarity pass: *He can call me 'priestess' if he likes, I must expect lack of manners from this lout!* "It is time to break away from their tracks and travel as quickly as we can to the temple." *If he is to attempt to kill me it would be now!* The priestess pretended to yawn and stretch, and her hands slipped beneath her long hair behind her neck as though by accident. They stayed there, toying with something behind her neck, as she watched what Baalshe would do.

"There are many ways we can take," said Baalshe, unaware of what was passing through her mind.

"We shall choose the fastest." *So he does not have orders to kill me! He is not devious enough to try and kill me later.*

"The fastest route will take us on a course that shall eventually meet with that of the Hittites," said Baalshe, grateful that he had her attention, "even if they do not travel on a straight path."

"No matter! We must take the fastest route. This cart is too slow as it is."

Baalshe stole a quick look at the priestess. He had not seen her so pleased since they had left Hattusas. They were now on Assyrian soil and Baalshe decided that it was time they stopped pretending to be a Hittite couple. He would pay some attention to his appearance. His beard had been allowed to look scraggy, like the beard of a wandering

4

"It is always a shock when you pierce a man for the first time," said the middle-aged charioteer to his son. "You don't expect human skin to be so resistant to the metal. That is why so many men die in their first battle – they strike too softly to make a telling wound and are then killed by the counterstroke!"

"So should I strike as hard as I can?"

"No. That could make you lose your balance and compromise your defence. The trick is to move fast but not so fast that you are not in control of your balance, then just before the tip of your metal makes contact, push as hard as you can! That would make your jabs shorter, but more controlled."

"When do I use the cutting edge?"

"At close quarters. If you are grappling with your enemy and cannot pierce him, cut him if you can. But remember that the tip can do more damage than the edge!"

The lesson in the tiny courtyard of a Hittite home was interrupted by the appearance of a stocky woman whose long auburn hair was liberally flecked with grey. Beneath her loose dress her breasts hung limply above her generous stomach, but the large brown eyes and delicate arch of her nose suggested that she had once been beautiful. "Husband, you are too old for this sort of thing and he is too young!" she said loudly.

"A boy is never too young to be trained in the fighting skills."

"I don't like all the mystery about where you are taking him," she said, lowering her voice, "all the charioteers' wives I know are very worried. They don't know where their husbands will be going."

"That is just empty talk."

"Some say there will be war with the Assyrians."

"Your friends don't know what they are talking about! I told you there is no danger involved. It's probably just a routine expedition against Shaamite rebels in the East."

"Oh? If it is just a routine expedition then why will it be led by the war-prince Artaxias?"

"My dear Ani, that is only loose talk among charioteers' wives! We don't know who will lead the expedition."

"So why don't you know if it's only a routine expedition?"

"*Because it's such an unimportant expedition that the leaders shall be chosen at the last moment!*"

"*Husband, we have known each other since we were children. Don't try to fool me! If it is so routine why have you been training our boy so rigorously?*"

"*Because it will be our boy's first taste of a campaign!*" he said with exasperation.

"*Well, it's time to come in. Lunch is ready!*"

"*Yes, wife.*"

The boy put away his sword. "*Yes, mother.*"

5

After entering Assyrian territory, Artaxias had assigned two more chariots to scout duty and, moreover, had ordered the scout-chariots to fan out both ahead and to the sides of the main force. In their haste to reach the temple well ahead of the Hittites, the priestess and Baalshe had veered away from the route the Hittites were taking and had failed to observe this change of deployment. They had also failed to observe that in the wastelands the Hittites slept during the day and travelled by night. And so it was that in the morning of the fifth day after the priestess had decided to stray from the tracks of the main Hittite force, she and Baalshe unwittingly came upon one of the scout-chariots.

It was only a short time since the sun had risen and the day was cloudy with a light mist that reduced visibility to a few hundred paces. The chariot was concealed between two boulders surrounded by short trees whose shadows fell across it, obscuring its outline. Both charioteers were sleeping under the chariot when they were alerted by the distant creak and rumble of the cart. They groggily climbed onto their vehicle and turned it so that it would face whatever was coming towards them, unsure of whether they should fight or run to warn the main force. Then for a brief moment a gust of wind dispelled some of the mist and the charioteers saw the cart and its occupants clearly.

"Assyrians!" exclaimed the First Charioteer, a middle-aged man. "A man and a woman!"

Assyrian men were recognizable by their heavy beards, and Baalshe's beard was now not only well groomed but was also pleated and adorned with tiny coloured ribbons.

"Ai!" said the much younger Second Charioteer who stood nervously to the right of his companion. "What should we do, father?"

The young man had never faced an enemy before.

"Kill them, of course. We cannot let them spread news of our coming!"

"But one is a woman! They're probably just travellers!"

"There are no travellers here, boy! They must be going to the temple!"

"Ah! I see! They'll tell the priests they saw a Hittite war chariot!"

"Yes, son. That is why we must kill them!"

"May the Weather God help us!" The boy muttered some prayers under his breath.

Baalshe had stopped the cart even before the war chariot emerged from between the boulders to turn and face them, some two hundred and fifty paces away. He and the priestess had been travelling without rest since dawn and were both tired, which was the main reason why he had failed to discern the chariot earlier, almost hidden as it was by the mist and the shadows of the trees. As the chariot turned, Baalshe jumped off the cart and threw off his coat, revealing an ornate battle armour that spoke of his reputation as a warrior. The priestess did not move, but sat in the cart, regal and immobile, watching the Hittite war chariot through half-closed eyes.

At sight of the armour the First Charioteer took hold of his spear and whispered to his son: "Hold on, boy! This man is a warrior and may be very dangerous!" Then he pulled up the reins and shouted at the horses to charge. He intended to hurl the spear when the horses were almost level with the Assyrian. The boy took hold of his bow, preparing to shoot the Assyrian if the spear missed.

Reading the charioteer's intentions, Baalshe slowly moved seven paces to the right of the cart and waited with his sword in his right hand, inviting the charging chariot to pass on his left, away from his sword arm and between him and the cart.

"Goddess help us!" hissed the priestess as the chariot accelerated towards them. "*You* brought us into this, Baalshe!"

For once, Baalshe did not answer the priestess but frowned darkly, glaring at his enemy from beneath bushy eyebrows that were knotted in a frown of intense concentration. As Baalshe expected, the charioteer aimed the chariot between him and the cart.

The chariot accelerated furiously and reached its full speed when it was less than thirty paces away from the Assyrian and slightly to his left. As it thundered towards him, Baalshe seemed to freeze, his eyes riveted on the horses that were bearing down upon him. The First Charioteer tightened his grip on the reins and prepared to hurl his spear. His young companion bent forward with his eyes wide open, clutching his bow and fumbling with an arrow. He was anticipating with excitement but also with some horror the drama he was now certain would unfold before him.

But then, to the consternation of both men on the chariot, at the last moment the Assyrian sprang to his left towards the cart, dashing across the path of the galloping horses. So close did the animals pass that their wind brought Baalshe the smell of their acrid sweat, but his eyes were now no longer on the horses but on the suddenly pale face of the young man who was clumsily toying with his bow and arrow as he approached the Assyrian at dizzying speed. In the split second that it took the chariot to thunder past him the Assyrian reached outwards and swung his sword at the face of the young man. The boy made a gurgling noise as his skull shattered. He crumpled to his knees and fell off the chariot, taking his bow and arrows with him. The First Charioteer was unable to hurl his spear because the horses were in the way

The Assyrian's expression became blank as he stepped back and the chariot continued past him, leaving the body of the boy in the dust with his bow and arrows by his side. The body writhed for the time of two heartbeats, then became still.

"By the thousand gods!" exclaimed the First Charioteer loudly as he realised how wrong he had been to drive the horses so close to the foe. His mistake had cost the life of his son! Too furious to feel the pain of his loss, he slowed the horses and, desperately trying to control the reins, tried to turn the chariot in as small a circle as he could so as to face the Assyrian again.

The First Charioteer was now aware that this was no ordinary fighter. Even as he swung the chariot round and raised his spear for a second run his blood ran cold when he saw that the Assyrian had picked up the bow and arrows and was already pulling the bow. The man cursed his bad judgement and decided that a charge against a competent bowman would be suicidal. Crouching to gain what cover he could from the sides of the chariot, the charioteer turned the chariot again and sped as fast as he could away from Baalshe.

"Kill one of the horses!" screamed the priestess.

But the order came too late – Baalshe had already released the arrow. As the chariot rolled away the Assyrian's arrow hit the charioteer in the side, just beneath his ribs. The man jerked backwards and let go of the spear before collapsing slowly to his knees, but he did not fall off the chariot. The chariot sped away with the charioteer kneeling in pain as he desperately clutched the reins with one hand and the front of the chariot with the other.

Baalshe quietly inspected the young man's body and took the man's sword and cape to the priestess.

"May I keep the sword?" he asked. "I have never had one like it."

"Keep the cape too," replied the priestess disdainfully. "That wounded charioteer shall soon be with the other creatures. You should have aimed at the horses!"

"I did what I could, priestess. I hoped that we would be able to use the chariot!"

"That was the wrong choice. Now they shall hunt us!"

"I did what I could," repeated the man.

"Enough backtalk!" snapped the priestess. "Remember that you speak to the Eyes and Ears of the goddess! Conceal the body and hide all traces of the killing!"

6

The charioteer was dead before he reached the Hittite camp. In his agony he had taken several wrong turns so that it was late afternoon before the horses padded softly among the sleeping men. Some further time was lost before one of the maintenance men noticed the scout chariot with its dead passenger. The man awakened the prince and the other commanders. A physician was called immediately and the body was laid on the ground.

"Does anyone know what happened?" said Artaxias as he squatted, bleary eyed, beside the body of the middle-aged Charioteer. The camp was now fully awake and a small group of men stood silently by the corpse.

"He died from loss of blood due to an arrow wound in his side," said the physician. "Here is the arrow." Someone handed the bloodstained arrow to Artaxias.

"That is one of *our* arrows!" exclaimed the prince. He could not help blinking repeatedly.

"Could he have quarrelled with the Second Charioteer?" one of the men asked.

"Was there any known enmity between the two men?" asked Norr.

"Charioteer pairs are not chosen at random," replied Her-unt gruffly. "The men have to trust each other completely. There could not have been any enmity."

"I knew them," said an infantryman. "They came from my village. They were father and son."

"Akh!" exclaimed the prince, and sighed. His head was beginning to clear. "So what message does our dead companion bring?"

"Many possible messages," said Her-unt, "All equally disquieting."

"That is a dreadful message!" said Artaxias. "We must assume that at least some Assyrians know of our presence."

"But can they guess the size of our force?" asked one of the men.

"A single chariot could only be a scout," replied the prince. "That implies the presence of a larger force. But can we assume that they also know where we are headed?" The question was directed at Norr.

"Even if the other charioteer died before he could tell them anything," replied Norr, "our destination would be easy to guess. Where would a Hittite force in these parts be headed if not the Amalishah temple?"

"Since we know nothing we must assume the worse!" agreed Her-unt.

Artaxias nodded. "Are there any arrows or arrow marks on the chariot?"

"None," said one of the men, "Just a lot of blood."

"So only one arrow was shot," said the physician, "And it fatally wounded the First Charioteer. There must have been only one bowman, a very good one."

"There could have been more than one bowman!" growled Her-unt, "If the others were just too slow!"

"The arrow is one of ours," said Artaxias. "Perhaps this is an important clue. What do *you* think happened, Her-unt?"

"I think one or more Assyrians came upon our men as they slept," replied Her-unt slowly, "Perhaps they killed the bowman and tried to capture the First Charioteer, who then escaped but was shot with his son's bow."

"What do you think, Norr?" asked the prince.

"I would agree with Her-unt. But I should draw attention to the fact that the First Charioteer bled to death as he tried to reach us. He died *some time* after he was shot."

"So?" said Her-unt.

"Well," said Artaxias, catching the direction of Norr's thoughts. "Whoever shot the arrow would have known that the charioteer was wounded but not killed. So why didn't they hunt him down to stop him reaching his fellows? With a chariot they could have caught up with him easily."

"A man with this kind of wound cannot drive a chariot too well," agreed the physician.

"Exactly," said Norr. "I think that this man's killers have no chariots! If they had, they would not have let him get away!"

"So it was not a raiding party!" said Artaxias, "That means there is hope if we don't waste time!"

"But what if the companion is a prisoner?" said one of the men, a young man with red hair, "We can't just leave him! The Assyrians do terrible things to prisoners!"

"Was the second charioteer a friend of yours?" asked Artaxias.

"Both charioteers were my friends!"

"Then I am truly sorry. But whatever they may have done to him, they would not waste time. He is probably dead by now."

The red-haired man suddenly had tears in his eyes.

"Behave like a man!" said Artaxias sternly. "Whoever did this is probably rushing to warn the temple of our coming. We must intercept them. If your friend is still alive, he would be with them. If he is not... well, pray to the gods that you shall have the chance to avenge him!"

The red-haired man bit his lip and managed a smile. Some of his companions escorted him away.

Artaxias turned to his officers: "It is safest to assume that some Assyrians in the wastelands know where we are going. We must hurry. If they manage to warn the temple, only the gods know how many of us shall die!"

"I would tend to agree with you," said Norr, "Our first priority is now speed, not concealment. I shall plan the changes in our route."

"Thank you, Norr."

Artaxias stood up and ordered that the dead man be buried with only the minimum of funeral rites. "I was wrong to spread out the scouts so thinly," he said.

"You could not have foreseen this," said Her-unt.

"Perhaps not," said the prince, "But we shall have to change deployment." He turned to the *action group* leaders who had gathered around him. "Her-Unt and I shall take all but two of the chariots that are here and move ahead. Norr you shall stay behind with the heavy infantry and the carts and follow us as fast as you can. As the scout-chariots return to change shifts you shall send them on to catch up with us. I hope this will give us a good chance of intercepting whoever, at this very moment, may be speeding towards the Amalishah temple with word of our coming."

"Where shall you and the chariots wait for us?" asked Norr.

"We are close enough to our target to relinquish caution and move in as straight a line as we can," said the prince. "After we deal with whoever killed the charioteers we shall wait for you at the small circle of boulders where we stopped to rest when we were on the *mission*. We cannot meet much farther because the guards on the towers of the temple might see us. Not far from the boulders there is a grove of little trees that would hide us from anyone who might come out from the temple for whatever reason."

"I shall find the place," said Norr, "As you say, it is in a straight line from here to the temple and you have a good chance of catching whoever killed our charioteer and his son if they are on foot."

"Let us hope that whoever we are chasing will also travel along this straight line, if they don't have chariots that would be the logical course if they are trying to warn the temple as quickly as possible."

Her-unt and Norr turned away to give the necessary orders for the new deployment. Artaxias put his hand to his forehead. *'We must no longer take for granted that this land is as unpopulated as it appears,'* he thought. *'But we must henceforth face the danger, not avoid it. May the gods help us, for our cause is just.'* He unconsciously touched the small blue stone that hung from his neck. It was attached to a leather thong by locks of hair that were skilfully interweaved.

7

"What's that?" said the priestess, pointing at a small dark spot not too far below the horizon.

Baalshe was already looking in that direction.

"It is too far to see in the haze," he said. It was early morning, and the sun had not yet evaporated the early morning mist.

"They may not have seen us," said the priestess as she bent forward as though to see better. She frowned: "We can get around them!"

"They may be Assyrians," said Baalshe, "This would be a likely place to come across a raiding party on its way to capture prisoners."

"What if it's more of the creatures?"

"I cannot say yet, but if it's one of our raiding parties they would have chariots."

The priestess nodded. With a two-horse chariot they could more than treble the speed at which they travelled. Moreover, an Assyrian raiding party was sure to provide them with an escort. "The risk is worth taking," she said. "We shall approach them cautiously, using whatever trees and boulders lie on our way for cover. Remember, if they are Hittites we are man and wife. We got lost whilst looking for a new home. Take those silly ribbons off your beard and try to make yourself look like a peasant!"

Baalshe obediently removed the ribbons and ruffled his beard and hair. He showed no emotion as he directed the cart towards the dark spot.

It was not long before Baalshe exclaimed triumphantly: "They are our own people! It's a soldiers' camp!"

Indeed, the Assyrians were camped in the open without any attempt at concealment.

"Do you see any chariots?" asked the priestess as the features of the camp became discernible. Her eyesight was not as good as his.

"Yes, my lady. I see at least three."

"Come on then!" said the priestess impatiently, "Get us there as fast as you can! Let the horse die of fatigue if necessary; we shall not need the cart if we have a chariot!"

Baalshe urged the animal into a trot. They were soon close enough to the camp to see some of the soldiers running towards them.

The soldiers reached them when they were two hundred paces from the camp. Baalshe stopped the cart and sat passively, waiting for the priestess to speak. She looked down at them haughtily and said: "Watch what you do or say! I am a priestess of the Amalishah temple and this is my bodyguard!"

"A priestess eh?" said one of the men, an uncouth young fellow with a luxurious beard. He looked at her hungrily: "And what are you doing here?"

"Take us to your commander, my good man," said Baalshe quietly. "We have come a long way and have important news."

The soldiers spoke to each other excitedly as they escorted the cart and its two occupants into the camp. They had not expected to meet any wanderers in the wastelands. When they reached the camp everybody stared at the priestess and her escort suspiciously. Baalshe and the priestess got off the cart and were ushered wordlessly to the tent of the commanding officer. The flap was open and the priestess noticed that the man was resting on a rough cot drinking something from a wooden cup. When Baalshe and the priestess stood expectantly in front of the tent he got up and stepped out. One of the men who had escorted the cart said: "Raish, we bring two prisoners!"

"Prisoners eh?" exclaimed the officer, eyeing the priestess quickly up and down. He gave a quick look at Baalshe before turning to stare at the priestess again. Her green eyes intrigued him. Soldiers from all parts of the camp strolled over casually to watch. It was very unusual to capture prisoners on Assyrian soil.

"Who are you?" the officer asked the priestess gruffly.

"I am a priestess of the Amalishah temple and this is my companion," said the priestess, "We need your assistance urgently!"

"You are obviously of our own people," replied the man, not too pleased with her tone of voice. "But even our own people have been known to be spies."

"What is there to spy around here?" asked the priestess. She was on the point of saying more but the officer cut her short.

"Perhaps you can tell us."

Some of the men laughed.

"Listen to me," said the priestess trying to control her voice. "There is a Hittite army heading at this very moment towards the Amalishah temple!"

"Are they going to worship the goddess?" This time all the men who heard the officer laughed.

Although the officer was considerably taller than the priestess she looked him in the eye and said: "This is not a joking matter. The creatures are intending to destroy the temple of our goddess!"

"Oh?" The man shrugged. "That is of no concern to me now. I want to know more about *you!*"

The priestess was shocked by the officer's indifference: *This is an animal who does not care about the fate of the temple and will not accept my authority as a priestess! I have to use the right words or he will not help us.* "I and my companion have followed the creatures out of Hattusas," she said soothingly, "They are on their way to destroy the Amalishah temple and we are on our way to warn the priests. If the temple is not warned it could be in dire peril. We urgently need your help to get there as quickly as possible."

There was a subtle flattery in her last sentence and her change of tone made the officer pay more attention to what she was saying. After a short pause he nodded gravely and said: "I don't see how I can help you, priestess. I have only forty-odd men and four chariots, one of which is having a wheel repaired. If there is a Hittite army in the wastelands all we can do is keep out of its way and hope that their scouts don't see us!"

"My brave man, all I ask of you is *one* chariot. With a chariot I and my companion can reach the temple ahead of the invaders. With enough warning our priests will catch and kill the foreigners like fish in a net!"

The officer turned his attention to the giant Baalshe: "And who are you?" he asked. He pointedly ignored the priestess.

Baalshe opened his cloak, displaying his finely decorated armour. "I am Baalshe," he growled. "Perhaps you have heard of me!"

"I have heard of *a* Baalshe," replied the officer, admiring the armour. "And perhaps you are that man. But your word is not enough."

"Look!" said the giant. "I have my sword and this is the scythe-sword of a Hittite I killed. Is this not proof?"

"If you are a Hittite spy you would naturally carry a Hittite sword. The weapon speaks against you!"

Baalshe looked confused and once again the men laughed. Two captured spies could provide good entertainment while the chariot wheel was repaired.

"I shall tell you again," the priestess said angrily, "There is a Hittite army on its way to destroy the Amalishah temple. I ask you to give us a chariot so that we can warn the temple priests. Time is very short, and you are wasting it with stupid questions!"

"I like neither your tone nor your words, woman!" said the officer casually. He turned and shouted to someone behind the tent: "Has that wheel been repaired?"

'Not yet!' came a muffled reply. The officer stroked his beard and his eyes roamed over the body of the priestess. "I *could* lend you a chariot," he said softly, "But it would cause us no end of trouble. Our task is to catch some young Hittites for the goddess, and it leads us *away* from the temple." The priestess was attractive and the officer had never met a woman with green eyes before. "If I lent you one chariot how would I get it back?"

"So lend us two," said the priestess, "with two men. Then after we reach the temple they can come back to you."

The officer shook his head. "No," he said flatly. "If I lent you two chariots and two men how would they find us after you reach the temple? We shall be travelling all the time. Anyway, I shall need all my chariots when I am hunting for captives on Hittite land." His eyes wandered to her breasts and then down to her groin.

"What could I do to persuade you to help us?" asked the priestess in a much softer tone of voice. She was fully aware of the officer's thoughts.

"We could talk it over in my tent."

"And if I come to your tent, do I have your word that you shall help us? By the goddess?"

"Not by the goddess," laughed the officer, confident in the strength of his position, "If what you say is true, then she is in peril even as we speak." All the men around them laughed; only Baalshe did not laugh. He felt an anger growing inside him.

"By which god, then?" asked the priestess.

"Look woman, do you want that chariot or not? If you come into my tent I *might* decide to help you. If you don't, well... I won't!"

This was too much for Baalshe. He surged forward and took hold of the officer by the throat, lifted him bodily off the ground with one hand. The man's face went red and his feet kicked weakly.

"Watch how you speak to my lady!" Baalshe growled. The soldiers around them reached for whatever weapons they were carrying but the officer signalled them to keep away. The tip of Baalshe's Hittite sword was pressing against the soft spot beneath his chin.

Slowly, Baalshe lowered the officer but did not pull away the upward-pointing sword. "We want a chariot with two horses," he said mildly, "And fresh provisions!"

Nursing his neck, the officer said boldly: "You have yet to convince me that you are not spies!"

To everyone's surprise Baalshe laughed. "You are a brave man," he bellowed. He lowered his sword and put it back into its scabbard. "And I have no doubt that your men are just as brave. So why don't you all come with us to the temple? If we are spies you shall find out soon enough and you can kill us, but if we are telling the truth then you would help an Assyrian temple and the gods shall smile on you!"

The officer noticed that the priestess's attention was on the chariot whose wheel was being repaired. He lowered his head and whispered: "My orders are to have no dealings with the temple other than to deliver the captives. If you are the Baalshe who is famous as a fighter, you will understand the meaning of orders!"

For a moment Baalshe looked puzzled. He was suddenly torn by conflicting loyalties and did not know what to say. The priestess felt the silence and turned to the officer: "You said you are on your way to capture prisoners for our goddess." She moved closer to him and laid her hand on his shoulder, making sure her hand touched his neck softly. "But if the temple is destroyed what would you do with your prisoners? You would have put yourself and your brave men in danger for nothing! Come, let us go to your tent before we decide what to do."

6

THE ASSYRIAN RAIDING PARTY

1

THE FLAPS OF Raish's tent were closed and the priestess lay panting on the cot with her eyes shut. She was naked except for delicate anklets of crimson crystals on her ankles and a necklace of similar crystals around her neck. The jewellery complemented and highlighted the milky pallor of her skin. Her arms hung limply by the sides of the cot and her long legs, slightly apart, were bent at the knees. Her panting caused her chest to rise and fall like the bellows of a forge and her necklace, rising and falling in tune, enhanced the heaving of her breasts. Raish stood by the cot, leaning against the tent pole. Although he was completely satiated he could not take his eyes off her.

The officer had agreed that the whole of the raiding party would escort the priestess to the temple, and he had also agreed to urge his men to travel as fast as they could. In return, the priestess would share his tent every night of the journey. After sampling the priestess's sexual skills Raish would have agreed to anything. He had never imagined that a woman could know so *perfectly* how to please him, and as he stood by the cot, he could only think of how he might delay the moment when he would have to relinquish her. What of his men? Well, they would have to dream of blue-eyed Hittite girls for a little while longer. In due course those who were destined to become officers would have their turn at self-indulgence. Meanwhile, the men would have no *formal* grounds to complain if he dawdled a little before crossing into Hittite territory, as long as he did not actually enter the temple without prisoners. Just before the raiding party left its base his regional commander had reminded Raish that his orders carried the royal seal and stated:

'You must only enter the Amalishah temple to deliver your captives.

You must only take enough men into the temple to guard the captives.
You and your men must not stay in the temple longer than necessary.'

Although she lay with her eyes closed, the priestess was fully aware of
Raish standing by the cot and eyeing her lasciviously. Little of what
the priestess did was not deliberate, and her slightly open legs, the
bending of her knees, and even the implied passion in her heaving
bosom were intended to direct Raish's thoughts in one direction, and
one direction only. Raish had evidently not been with a woman for
some time and his needs were intense and simple to read. Putting on
a good performance had been easy. Several times she had inflamed
his desire to heights he had never imagined possible, and each time
she assuaged his boiling passion she had left just enough for him to
crave another round. Only when she had decided that the man had
been sufficiently *conditioned* did she put an end to it. She left him
exhausted and satiated, yet looking forward to more. The priestess
was rapacious in her sexual needs and always enjoyed applying her
skills, but in this instance her task was to addict Raish with dazzling,
sublime levels of pleasure that would make him completely dependent
on her. She had to be able to control him during the duration of the
trip, for the survival of the temple depended on her ability to egg him
on relentlessly.

2

Raish did not believe that the Hittites intended to destroy the
Amalishah temple. He suspected that the Hittite force was a large
patrol sent out to intercept any raiding parties it could find. This
made it all the more dangerous, of course, for its scouts would prowl
along the routes that raiding parties were likely to take, but Raish
was confident that he could evade the Hittites with the use of his wits
and the help of the gods. The wastelands were vast and, if what the
priestess had told him were true, the Hittites were lumbered with
heavy infantry and carts. Their inability to move fast would limit the
terrain they were able to scour.

It was early afternoon when the chariot wheel was finally repaired
and the raiding party prepared to break camp. Raish and the priestess
stood hand-in-hand in front of his tent: "You are sure the Hittites
are going to the Amalishah Temple?" he asked conversationally. He

knew what she was going to say, but he wanted her to remember that whether the temple would be warned on time was completely up to him.

"*Of course* I'm sure!" Her words were uttered with mellifluous sweetness.

Raish smiled knowingly. "How can you be sure? You said that they were not taking a direct route."

"I knew their destination before they set out!" More mellifluous sweetness.

"I see!" He frowned: *If the Hittites are a large patrol they would naturally be going towards the temple because that would increase their chances of ambushing a raiding party bringing captives!* "Can you tell me, priestess," he asked, "how far the Hittites are from the temple?"

"They must be at least two days ahead of us!" she answered, sounding earnest.

"That is not possible," retorted the officer, letting go of her hand. "From what you told me, you followed them closely until you were sure of their destination and then you took a direct route."

"What of it?"

"Well, you said they frequently made detours so as not to be seen; that would slow them down. You also said they had carts and heavy infantry; that would slow them down further. Finally, since the Hittites don't want to risk being seen, they probably travel only at night. That would slow them down further still!"

The priestess pretended to be petulant: "I don't understand these things!"

"Priestess," said Raish patiently, "At this moment we should be closer to the Amalishah temple than they are!"

"Perhaps," she said, and she sensuously caressed his bare arm with her fingers.

He was not in the mood for caresses just yet, and particularly not in front of his men. He pulled his arm away: "You must not lie to me, priestess!"

"I am merely trying to stress the urgency of our task," she said, sounding innocent and sincere.

He grunted and gave out a set of orders to his men.

"Remember your promise to get me to the temple as soon as you can!" she cooed.

"Enough, woman!"

3

She shrank away from him: *I was told that this kind of man is driven by his sexual urges when he is not fighting. That may be true, but his interest in me dies so abruptly after his lust is extinguished!* The priestess considered whether she had been too generous with her favours to soon. The man was evidently recalcitrant by nature and his mood changed quickly. He was also, she decided, unaccustomed to taking women seriously. She should not be too persistent before he was properly conditioned. The priestess accepted the fact that despite her training she still had much to learn about men. And there was another factor: *At the Temple, all the priests except Khaur are subordinate to the senior priestesses and never question what they're told. That makes us think all men are stupid. This Raish is crude but he is no fool and I must not underestimate him!*

During her training as the *Eyes and Ears* of the goddess, the priestess had been taught how to use sex as one of the means of extracting information from men. She had been told that the desires of stupid men do not rise above the level of their loins, but that intelligent men often have deep emotional needs that they hold as closely guarded secrets or may even not be aware of. 'This means,' her teacher had told her, 'that intelligent men are best enmeshed by the *emotions* that accompany sexual acts. Hence the value of *roles*. When you are with a man always try to assume the role that he secretly wants you to play, even if he doesn't know what it is!' At first the priestess found the idea of Raish harbouring secret emotional needs laughable, but upon reflection she concluded that it was not impossible: *He is crude and violent, but he is intelligent enough to – perhaps – have emotional needs behind his animal passions!* Emotional needs were more dependable than brute sexual desire and any emotional addiction she could instil in him could be harnessed to her wishes. Identifying his emotional needs, or creating them if necessary, was an avenue to be explored. What kinds of emotional needs could someone like Raish possibly have?

Men in positions of authority were *expected* to dominate their women but, sometimes, particularly if they were troubled, they needed to be sexually dominated. Being dominated provided a temporary relief from the worries and responsibilities that burdened their minds: *Raish has postponed fulfilling his duties and is risking censure when he returns. He is under pressure to keep his men in line. He is in constant fear of being detected and hunted by the creatures. He knows that a single wrong decision could be the end of him!* She puckered her lips and quickly went over all that had transpired between her and Raish: *He could be ripe for playing the role of slave! As my slave he could forget his worries! If that is what he secretly wants I can make his need of me like an arrow chasing a fleeing man, pushing him to run ever faster!* Satisfied with her decision, she turned her attention to what was going on in the camp.

4

The four chariots were manned and ready. The infantry stood in a broad line facing the chariots while Raish gave orders regarding their new destination. He spoke with absolute authority, and if the men were surprised at being told that they were going to the Amalishah temple they dared not show it. The priestess smiled to herself: *Your men are terrified of you and you act like a little king! But tonight you shall be forced to act as my slave! If I dissolve your worries in a bowl of pleasure then your need of me shall not vanish so quickly!* Raish invited the priestess to ride with him in his personal chariot. She accepted gracefully but would not allow him to hold her hand.

It was getting dark when she noticed that his eyes were more often on her body than on the road ahead. Although the temperature was decidedly cool, she said: "It is quite warm. Would you mind if I remove some of my clothes?"

"Do as you wish," he answered, unwittingly staring at the region below her waist, "but don't show too much, my chariots and infantry are right behind us."

"Do we really need the infantry?" she asked, pitching her voice so as to sound warm and intimate, "They are slowing us down. Why don't we push ahead and wait for the others at the temple? If we push ahead we would be alone longer." Her green eyes glowed with passion.

"I have already told you it would be dangerous to leave the others behind!" His tone was brusque and his voice hoarse.

"Oh, I meant you to leave only the infantry behind. Your chariots would accompany us, of course."

"I am the only one who knows the way, priestess!" Raish was sorely tempted to leave the infantry behind, but it was necessary to appear strong in front of his men. Those within earshot would listen to everything he said to the priestess and they had to be reassured that their safety took precedence over her wishes.

"I was only hoping that we would be alone sooner," she said.

"I know that, priestess. But if my infantry travel separately they might get lost and blunder into the path of a Hittite scout. The scout shall summon other Hittites and that would be the end of my infantry, and perhaps the end of us too."

The priestess did not care at all what happened to Raish or his men, but she was no less anxious to avoid meeting the Hittites. Where were the creatures? How much closer would they get to the temple while she wasted time pleasing this Raish every night? The Hittite force was definitely slower than the raiding party and Raish had probably been right in saying that they would have to travel at night. A moving column of chariots and infantry, accompanied by carts, would be far too noticeable in the wastelands during the day. She recalled the incident with the Hittite charioteers: When she and Baalshe had first seen the scout-chariot it had been stationary and almost hidden, which implied that the charioteers were sleeping. They would not have been sleeping while the main force was on the march. *Although I was preoccupied with the escape of the wounded charioteer, I should have realised that the creatures had decided to travel only during the night!* The priestess reprimanded herself for the uncharacteristic oversight.

There was some consolation in the fact that, if the Hittites only travelled when it was dark, they would move *considerably* more slowly than the much lighter raiding party. The Assyrians were not encumbered with carts and their infantry did not carry heavy backpacks because they expected to get food and water from the Hittite villages they plundered. The Assyrians were also on the shortest route to the temple. The priestess did some mental calculations and was very pleased at the outcome: *I could reach the temple as much as five days before the creatures and certainly not less than two days!* The thought lessened her anxiety and she felt more inclined to resume her titillation of Raish. Very slowly, she took off the outer layers of her garments. She left only enough to cover but not conceal the narrowness of her waist and the alluring curve of her bottom. A quick sidelong glance showed that the charioteers behind Raish's chariot were eyeing her hungrily, and she was gratified to see that Raish had reacted to his men's attention in the way she expected:

he was frowning and his tense facial muscles showed the almost-rage of the jealous and possessive male. The priestess was pleased at Raish's behaviour: *Stare at my bottom all you want, but my favours shall not come cheaply tonight! You shall be forced to beg and every time you get pleasure I shall exact a promise of speed!*

Raish knew that, despite their detours, the route of the Hittites would eventually cross that of his raiding party. Moreover, if the Hittites were on the lookout for Assyrian raiders their chariot-scouts could spread far ahead of the main force. It was essential that he know the distance of the main force from the temple relative to that of his raiding party. "Priestess," he growled, "You know the Hittites' speed and you know the direction they were heading when you left them. It is important that you tell me how far ahead of them we are."

She did not answer at once. How she replied would determine his alternatives, and she did not yet control him as well as she wished. "I think they are a little farther from the temple than we are," she answered.

"Can you estimate how much?"

"No," she lied, although she knew that if the Hittites travelled at the normal speed of their heavy infantry they could not reach the temple less than two days after the raiding party. Two days would give the temple more than enough warning.

Raish was not satisfied. "Then I shall have to ask Baalshe."

"No, wait!" she exclaimed, unwilling to let Baalshe dilute her influence over the officer, "Let me think for a moment."

"Take your time, priestess."

She pretended to think carefully: "They might reach the temple less than two days after us. Unless they speed up!"

"Good. And from what you may have seen, how often did their scouts come back to report?" How often the scouts returned to report would allow Raish to estimate how far ahead of the main force they normally ventured.

"I don't know. I was never close enough to see the scouts return."

Raish nodded: *She probably doesn't know. But as the Hittites get closer to the temple they will send their scouts farther in search of raiding parties. Perhaps as much as three days farther. If the main force is two days behind us their scouts might see us!*

"Thank you, priestess."

5

Travelling by chariot is monotonous. Speed was limited by the pace of the infantry and the only sounds were the repetitive creaks of the axles and the short rumbles of the chariot wheels when they passed over some unevenness in the ground. Raish's thoughts wandered widely, but he thought of the orgiastic nights he had enjoyed much more often than he thought of the Hittites. The priestess had assumed a dominant role and had controlled their sexual games with an imagination that he found awesome and pleasurable beyond his wildest fantasies. It was as though she could read his mind. But she had not won his trust, and Raish was a strong-willed man who could manage his passions when he needed to. Eventually he thought: *I must stop thinking of her all the time!* The priestess noticed the small and barely perceptible changes in his behaviour and read his feelings: *He is starting to rebel against his need of me! I must promise rewards other than sex – but my promises must be given at the right time!*

Her opportunity came soon enouggh. At the end of a long day, one of the chariots moved forward and the senior charioteer said respectfully: "Raish, you should know that the men are grumbling about the hardship they have to endure while you indulge yourself with the woman!"

The statement was given as a fact that required no reply, and the chariot withdrew immediately after the message was delivered. Raish was taken aback by the boldness of the charioteer, but he did not feel anger because he took the complaint seriously. Such an accusation would cause him a lot of trouble if it were reported to his regional commander. The accusation was made out of loyalty, out of concern for him. He turned to the priestess: "Because of your incessant demands for more speed my men are suffering and blaming *me!*"

"The comfort of your men was not part of our agreement!"

"We must slow down. My men must not suffer while I get all the rewards, priestess!"

"Don't they know of the gold that is waiting for them at the temple?" she asked, as though Raish and his men should have known all along.

"What gold?" Raish growled.

"The gold they shall be given to your men if we warn the temple on time, of course!" replied the priestess, as though stating the obvious.

"The temple of the goddess has more gold than you have ever seen!"

"What about *me?*" asked Raish.

The priestess smiled disarmingly: "Why Raish, if we reach the temple well before the creatures then, in addition to the many rewards I have given you, when you and I enter the temple I shall reward you further and also give you enough gold to make you wealthy for the remainder of your life!"

"How much gold can you give?" Raish asked.

"I am the Eyes and Ears of the goddess," she replied haughtily, "when we pass the Main Gate I shall order the priests to give you all the gold you deserve for saving the temple from the creatures!"

The offer of gold was interesting but frustrating to Raish. He could not enter the temple without captives. Would she remember her promise to give him and his men gold when they returned to the temple after capturing young Hittites for the goddess? It could be longer than two moons before the raiding party returned to the temple with prisoners, so probably not. The women Raish had known did not take their promises seriously, but to stop his men complaining he told them that the temple would reward them with gold. Their reaction was subdued, but they ceased to complain about the pace at which they were forced to travel.

6

The raiding party travelled in the wastelands with the four chariots in front and the infantry about sixty paces behind to avoid breathing the dust thrown up by the chariot wheels. Every night the priestess entertained Raish with consummate skill, but the raiding party did not travel as fast as the priestess would have wished even though they travelled as fast as the infantry could go. As Raish's chariot lumbered over the uneven ground, the priestess regularly held him by the arm and used the swaying of the chariot as a pretext to rub her hips against him. More than once she let him catch a glimpse of her breasts, as though by accident: *I must not let him forget the delights that await him at night. He must keep his ruffians moving as fast as they can!* Nor did she miss any opportunities to remind Raish that his nightly delights were but a small part of his reward for warning the temple as early as possible. She talked often about the vast treasure that was stored in the temple, and described at length some of the gifts that rich pilgrims had brought over the years. But every time the priestess spoke of the gold that awaited him, Raish's frustration increased.

Two days before they expected to reach the temple she casually mentioned that he would get his gold soon after they passed the First Gate, even before she took him to her quarters to reward him the way he liked best. She thought that her words would goad him to push his men harder now that they were close to the temple, but Raish knew that he could not pass the First Gate, or any other gate of the temple, without captives, and as his frustration flared up he spoke to her brusquely without thinking: "I'm not forgetting the gold you promised woman, but I cannot make my men move any faster!" Almost immediately he remembered that he needed to hide his annoyance, for this priestess could perhaps read minds and might wonder why he was annoyed at the mention of his rewards after they entered the temple. She might be able to reason that he could not enter the temple without captives! He put his arm around her: "It shall be dark soon and we shall be alone again!"

"I am greatly looking forward to that!" She placed her head against his shoulder and caressed his bare arm. "But let us go on a little more. The closer we are to the temple the more I shall please you!"

He smiled lewdly: "Very well. But your body beckons to me like cool water to a thirsty camel!" She smiled back, not because she appreciated the compliment but because she found his choice of words apt: *How right he is to compare himself to a camel. Camels are ugly and smell vile!*

He misunderstood her smile and said: "My men need to rest but my need to feel you throbbing with pleasure is greater!"

"You know that your men do not exist for me, Raish," she murmured as she took his hand in hers. "For me, you are the only man here." *I'll have to be careful tonight! Treating this animal as my sex slave is working well, but I must not overdo it or he shall find reasons to waste time!* On his part, Raish was thankful that the priestess would not condescend to speak to his men. She must not get to know about the orders from his commander and of how inflexible they were.

After they had travelled some distance one of the charioteers said: "Raish, the infantrymen are very tired and it is almost dark."

Raish replied: "We shall stop soon, but not yet." He looked at the priestess and grinned, showing a mouthful of crooked yellow teeth: "We have travelled as fast as we can so that you remember to reward me in your special ways?" *I have two more nights left! Nothing must spoil that!*

"I promised, did I not? And after we warn the temple and you get all your gold you shall come to my quarters and I shall give you more pleasure than ever before!" The priestess smiled broadly to hide her revulsion of the man, yet even as she smiled she thought: *But once the temple has been warned and you are in my quarters I shall kill you as you grovel between my legs. You will not boast to anyone about what I did for your pleasure!*

7

Raish smiled contentedly and squeezed her hand: *She really believes that her temple is in danger, but the Hittites won't be able to take the temple whether she warns the priests or not!* If Raish had believed that the Hittites could destroy the temple he would have taken the urgency of warning the priests more seriously. He would not have tolerated the destruction of an Assyrian temple by foreigners. But the priestess had purposely avoided telling him how large the Hittite force really was in case he decided to turn back to report the presence of a *significant* Hittite army in the Assyrian wastelands. When pressed for more information she had told him that the Hittite force had some heavy infantry and about twenty chariots but no siege engines. This had strengthened Raish's suspicion that the Hittite force was just a large patrol: *How could they hope to take a fortified temple without siege engines?* The Hittites were to be avoided by all possible means, but Raish saw no reason to worry about the safety of the temple. Like most Assyrian rank and file, he believed that the temple of the goddess was impregnable. That night the priestess gave an exceptional performance.

It was mid-afternoon on the day before they expected to arrive at the temple when they reached an unusual collection of clumps of boulders. Clumps of boulders were common in the wastelands but, thus far, they had been little more than randomly scattered squat and solitary heaps of rock. Here, curiously, many of the boulders stood taller than a man and the more prominent rocks formed a rough ellipse that was large enough to enclose a small village. Within the ellipse there were a few small trees and a profusion of bushes in various stages of dryness, but there were no large rocks and the soil was soft. To one side of the ellipse was a grove of ancient but healthy trees. Although the grove indicated the presence of water, the wind had piled up large amounts of dry branches and dead bushes against the larger stones. Raish gave the order for the raiding party to stop.

"Why are we stopping?" asked the priestess. "It is still early and the temple is not far beyond the horizon! If we continue a little way we shall see the guard towers!"

"I know."

The priestess was tired and very sleepy. Every night of the journey Raish had awakened her repeatedly with his unsavoury demands and, now that they were close to the temple, he had kept her awake almost the whole of the night: *Does he want me **now?*** she thought in alarm, *I must not give myself to him here!* With a revulsion she could barely conceal she remembered the persistent groping of his unwashed hands and the stench of his breath.

"Let us go on," she urged warmly, "And at the temple I shall reward you with a performance you shall never forget! And remember that you shall get enough gold to make you rich for the rest of your life!"

He pushed her away. "I'm not in the mood to think of such things now," he said.

"So why are we stopping?" she persisted, and the pitch of her voice rose. "If we hurry, the chariots at least could be at the temple before the night is over!"

Raish pretended not to hear. "If we continue we shall reach open ground and might be seen by Hittite scouts, even if they travel only at night." He was speaking not so much to the priestess as to his charioteers who were within earshot. "This is a good place for us to stop and hide from any scouts."

"The creatures are not far behind us!" exclaimed the priestess. "We must go on!"

"You told me the Hittites could not reach the temple less than two days after us, priestess," said Raish, "So this is a good place to stop. I was told that it is called the Teeth of the Jackal because of the way the rocks stand in a ring around us." The raiding party stopped near the centre of the ellipse of rocks.

8

The priestess did not care about what the place was called. "You have not explained why you want to stop here!"

Raish's main reason for wanting to stop was because he was concerned about Hittite scouts who might be roaming well ahead of the main force, but he also hoped that his last night with the priestess would be the longest. He tried to pacify her by adopting a conciliatory tone: "Here, priestess, we shall be concealed by the large rocks and the ground is soft enough to half-bury and hide the chariots. Also, near the trees there is water not too far beneath the surface."

"You promised to help me warn the temple as soon as possible!" she reminded him angrily.

"All in good time, priestess!" Her anger awakened his passion: *And I'll have one more night of your delectable body!* The priestess had not washed since she had left Hattusas, but such were the officer's tastes that he found the odour of her body irresistible.

"You promised to help me warn the temple as soon as possible!" she repeated, this time shouting loudly enough for his men to hear.

Raish was not an even-tempered man and his rising anger quenched his passion. No woman could talk to him like that in front of his men! *Where is that Baalshe?* He swivelled round to see where the giant warrior was. Baalshe was some eighty paces behind with the rearmost infantry. After having travelled for many days with the supercilious priestess, the fighting champion had sorely missed the banter of his own kind and had fraternized freely with the Assyrian infantry. When the raiding party stopped he was laughing and joking with the men of the infantry.

The priestess started to shout at Raish again. Aware of his distance from Baalshe he turned and cuffed her viciously across the mouth. The frail woman reeled and fell off the back of the chariot. When she recovered she found herself lying on the soft ground with her head spinning. She rose slowly to her feet, her lips and left cheek throbbing with pain, and steadied herself by holding onto the sloping side of the chariot. Her face was deathly pale except for the flush caused by the blow.

"Why won't you hurry?" she asked poignantly, her voice shaking. "Why won't you keep your promise? I've kept mine every night!"

Raish ignored her. The men of the infantry were close enough to hear him clearly: "We shall camp here," he called out, "The main force of the Hittites is at least two days behind us but now that they are close to the temple their scouts might be three days ahead of them. Don't light any fires and make sure that nothing of us can be seen if they pass us in the night!"

At the words 'if they pass us in the night' the priestess almost swooned. Something in her brain exploded with the sudden, cataclysmic realisation that Raish had no plans at all to warn the temple as early as possible. He did not – would not – grasp the urgency of the situation. What if she had miscalculated how far the creatures were? What if the creatures had somehow speeded up? She stood beside the chariot with her knees barely able to sustain her, overcome by hysterical weeping while her mouth, seemingly endowed with a will of its own, muttered threats and promises in turn.

The raiding party set down to work. Baalshe pretended not to notice the priestess's distress; he gave brisk orders to the men who were digging the trenches in which the chariots were to be lowered and covered with dead bushes. Dead bushes were everywhere and were ideal for covering and concealing the camp. While some men dug trenches, others collected dead bushes and dry wood to make low, well-camouflaged shelters. There would be no tents in this camp. All the horses except those of Raish's chariot were led away to be concealed in the grove of trees outside the ring of boulders. They were tethered and given water and food. Raish stayed on his chariot to supervise the arrangements and ignored the priestess.

Raish's plan was to conceal his men and chariots within the ring of boulders during the night, when the Hittite scouts were expected to be on the move. Once the camp arrangements were over he would pacify the priestess and get one more night of her delicious charms. Early the next day his raiding party would resume their march to Hittite land to capture boys and young men. A slight detour would bring them close enough to the temple for the priestess and Baalshe to be able to walk the short distance on their own. They would accompanied by a chariot that could collect any gold the temple was willing to give. Even if the Hittites foolishly intended to attack the temple, the bulk of their war party would not reach the temple before the priestess so she would have no reason to invoke the gods against him. Meanwhile, it was imperative that the raiding party remain concealed from Hittite scouts. Close to the temple the Hittite scout chariots could be travelling in battle-ready groups, and if the raiding party were detected by even a single scout group it might be able to summon enough other groups to pose a serious threat. During the night Raish's men would have no chariots, for the horses would be in the grove, and although they were equipped to deal with unarmed villagers his men would be hard pressed if required to confront the redoubtable Hittite war-chariots.

9

Raish did not regret postponing his incursion into Hittite land. The pleasures he had enjoyed had been well worth the time lost and, had he not met the priestess, he would have been unaware of the Hittite patrol and might have had a very unpleasant surprise on the way to the temple after he had acquired some captives. He hoped to enjoy the priestess one more night, but if she continued to annoy him he would turn her over to his men and have Baalshe killed. He did not deign to look down at her while she begged and pleaded beside his chariot, and he failed to notice when she became grim and silent. The acts she had performed in his tent had made him lose the awe he would normally have felt for a high-ranking priestess, and even close to the temple he did not fear her wrath.

But the goddess had not chosen the green-eyed priestess as her *Eyes and Ears* only for her loyalty and extraordinary skills. Behind her ruthlessly analytic mind lay a predisposition for violence. The conviction that she could fail her goddess because of this repugnant man magnified the memory of the goddess's parting words until they were like the clanging of a huge bell within her skull:

Come back and warn us!
Come back and warn us!

She made her decision. With a cold smile she arched her back coyly and passed her hands behind her neck, keeping them beneath her long black hair. At the back of her necklace, concealed by her hair, hung a jewelled scabbard with a small curved knife. Raish was not looking at her as he stood on his chariot; his attention was fully on his men as he supervised the preparations for the night. With her hair covering her hands she carefully slid the knife from its sheath and moved casually to the back of Raish's chariot. Raish continued to ignore her. She judged the distance to him carefully, for speed was essential, and she only paused for the space of a heartbeat to make sure that none of the men was looking in her direction. Then with the fluidity of a cat she sprang onto the chariot and pushed and twisted the short but very sharp bronze blade into the side of Raish's neck. The knife cut through and severed the artery as well as the muscles at the side of his neck and his head lolled sideways as he collapsed soundlessly. His blood was still spurting over her feet as she kicked his trembling body off the chariot and, taking the reins in both hands, frantically urged the horses forward: "Haiahh!" she shouted, as she had heard Raish shout at the horses, **"Haiahh!"**

But this was Raish's *personal* chariot and the highly trained warhorses would only respond to the voice of their master. They fidgeted but did not move forward. The priestess froze with horror as she realised her predicament. Her mind went numb as she watched the events that unfolded around her as though in slow motion. She saw Baalshe pull out his Hittite sword and run to protect her, only to be overcome and slaughtered by the furious soldiers. A man prized the Hittite sword out of Baalshe's dead hand and waved it in the air. Another tried to remove Baalshe's armour while struggling with others who also wanted a share of the spoils. Then the men converged upon the priestess and she could only stare at them expressionless.

10

Just before they reached her she closed her eyes, expecting to be torn to pieces. Instead, there was silence. Then she heard a young voice say: "Stop! We cannot kill a priestess! The curse of the gods shall be upon us!" She opened her eyes. A tall young man stood beside the chariot, his arms spread wide to prevent the others from reaching her. As her eyes met his, he repeated softly: "We cannot kill a priestess!"

She looked at him blankly as a faint glimmer of hope made her mind seek frantically for a way to turn his beliefs to her advantage. But she could not think clearly, her mind was too numb. She could only stare mutely at the youth. The other men had now surrounded the chariot and were arguing noisily among themselves about what they should do with her. The young man said: "Priestess, forgive us but we cannot let the murder of our officer pass unnoticed. Your fate will be decided tomorrow, when the enemy is sleeping. Now we are in danger. You must come off the chariot and hide with us." He held out his hand to help her get off the chariot.

She accepted the proffered hand and got off the chariot to stand before the tall young man. Without saying anything two men carried away the body of Raish. During the silence that followed, someone came over and took Raish's horses to the grove. Then the silence was shattered by a shout from one of the men: "So what do we do now?" Another shouted: "We have no leader!" And as though they had all been harshly awakened from heavy slumber they started arguing loudly again, but the question that preoccupied them now was: What had Raish planned to do?

The officer had not shared his plans with anyone for fear that someone might inadvertently say something that would make the priestess or Baalshe suspicious.

"Why not just go and bring some prisoners to the goddess?" asked one.

"Do you know your way in Hittite country?" asked a man who had been digging and was naked to the waist. "Only Raish knew the way!"

"Let us go to the temple!" shouted another of the men.

"That is forbidden!"

"We cannot enter the temple without prisoners!"

The priestess followed the argument as though in a nightmare. She could not understand why they thought it was *forbidden* to enter the temple without prisoners. *By whose orders? Surely not the king's? Was the betrayal of Raish just a small part of a much larger betrayal?* The priestess pushed these questions away because she had to confront the present. She had to convince these men that their only option was to go to the temple because the priests had to be warned. As the men argued noisily around her she knew she had to intervene and sway the argument. She would offer gold, or sex, *anything*, but her mind was paralysed by the enormity of what she suspected: *The king is behind this! I was right to suspect the king when I was with the Envoy! But if the king has turned against the goddess I have to be sure!*

The priestess could only listen and watch, as in a stupor, while the argument among the men about what they should do raged loudly and aimlessly. Some argued that they should return home because they had no leader. Others argued that it was safest to go to the temple. Then she heard someone say: "The order that we stay away from the temple carried the king's seal!" and her worst fears were confirmed. This new information *had* to get to the goddess. It was almost as important as the impending Hittite threat! The additional pressure to get to the temple stimulated her resolve and cleared her mind. "Stop arguing like silly children!" she shouted. "Listen to me. I am the Eyes and Ears of the goddess!"

It is doubtful whether most of the men fully understood what that meant, but she spoke with authority and they were used to bowing to authority. They stopped arguing and listened.

"You cannot go to the land of the Hittites because you do not

121

have a leader who knows the way!" There were grunts of assent and murmurs of 'We know that!'

"You cannot go back to your homes because you would fall into the arms of the enemy. You will get killed and you shall never see your wives and children again!"

The men looked at each other and the priestess read their expressions easily: they agreed with her and were afraid.

"If you are to live," she said solemnly, "if you want to see your loved ones again, you must go to the temple..."

The priestess was going to continue but someone interrupted her: "And who are you to make us ignore our king's orders?"

The priestess looked steadily at the man who had spoken and said: "You will not ignore our king's orders if you enter the temple to save your lives. The king does not want brave men like you to die. And if you go to the temple you shall help our priests catch these vile Hittites like game birds in a hunting net. The Hittites are here to attack the temple! So look! If some young Hittites survive you will be able to carry out our king's orders because you would provide our goddess with more young captives than you could ever bring back from a raid!"

The argument was won. The men shuffled but they were now fully convinced.

"So what do you want us to do, holy one?" a man asked.

"Bring out the chariots that you buried. Bring back the horses. Prepare to run to the temple as you have never run before!"

"What if we are seen by a Hittite scout as we run?"

"We have enough chariots to deal with any scout. You have nothing to fear, for the main force shall not reach you before you reach the temple!"

The priestess pointed a finger at the tall young man who had saved her life. "Are you a charioteer?"

"Yes, my priestess."

"You will supervise the preparations for the dash to the temple. After that you will ride with me."

The men moved away to their respective tasks. They had a leader again, and like busy shadows in the falling gloom some began to remove the bushes that covered the chariots while others hastily decided what should be taken and what should be left behind. It would be a long run in the dark and they would have to carry as little as possible.

The priestess felt elated and triumphant. The temple would be warned. Her goddess would be told about the Hittite war party and the king's betrayal. The priests would set up the temple's defences. But her hopes were suddenly destroyed when someone shouted: "The Hittites! The Hittites are upon us!"

11

Not the full force, but the twenty-one chariots that had sped ahead of the heavy infantry and the carts. They had not sent out any scouts as their aim was to catch whoever had killed the two charioteers and knew of their presence. It was an unfortunate accident for the priestess as well as the raiding party that the place at which Raish had chosen to camp was also the distinctive spot at which Artaxias and the chariots were to wait for Norr and the infantry to catch up.

The Hittites had known that those who had killed their charioteers were ahead of them and had driven their chariots as fast as they could. They had travelled speedily in the daytime, with only short stops at night. The Assyrians, confident of their lead and expecting the Hittites to travel only in the dark, had not realised that the dust raised by their four chariots would betray their location to the enemy.

The raiding party could not have been worse prepared. Three of the chariots were still half-buried in their trenches and the horses were hidden among the trees. Some of the men had left their weapons because they had been working feverishly to cover the chariots with dead bushes that the wind had piled up against the rocks.

The Assyrians watched in terror as the twenty-one chariots separated into two lines that rumbled slowly on either side of the camp. As the Assyrians pulled back the Hittite chariots moved just beyond the boulders, staying outside the range of the Assyrian bows.

"They are going to encircle us!" shouted the young man who had saved the priestess's life. "Take cover! Prepare your bows for a chariot charge!"

"Use the bushes to build a wall around us!" shouted a charioteer, "Quickly! We must prevent their chariots from charging through the camp!"

The priestess pressed her hands against the sides of her head to suppress the pounding of her wildly beating heart: *The temple is beyond the horizon but the priests have to be told that the creatures are coming! The goddess **has** to be told about the king's betrayal! The*

Hittites had come from the direction opposite to that of the temple and there was still a gap between the closing lines. Perhaps the Hittites would allow one solitary woman to escape? Without weighing her chances, the priestess broke into a desperate burst of speed and ran as fast as she could towards the temple between the closing lines of the Hittite chariots. Something in the priestess had snapped and all she could think of was to reach the temple before the Hittites.

But someone at the head of one of the lines of Hittite chariots barked an order and two chariots broke off and converged upon her, the leather-armoured horses accelerating rapidly to a gallop. In the dwindling light the priestess could see that the charioteers were crouching so as to present the smallest possible target to the Assyrian bowmen. She just managed to catch the eye of the First Charioteer when one of the horses hit her. Her feet left the ground and she spun once before she was hit by the second horse and fell, like a loose-jointed doll, to be trampled beneath the flailing hooves and run over by one of the chariot wheels. Having brought the woman down, the chariot veered sharply to return to its place in the encircling line just as the second chariot ran over her. Then it, too, turned sharply, but before it could return to its place a train of arrows flew from the Assyrian bowmen, but the arrows flew too late. With a few arrows stuck to its side the second chariot returned to the now almost completed line of chariots that encircled the camp. Some of the Assyrians continued to release their arrows until someone shouted: "They're too far! Don't waste your arrows!"

The priestess, her body mangled by the hooves of the horses and the wheels of the chariots, lay still. But she was still alive. Her soul struggled to wrench itself from her body but was held back by her guilt at having failed her goddess. When the circle of chariots finally closed, the faint thudding of the horses' hooves and the creaking of the wooden vehicles died out. The only sound in the silence was the voice of the dying priestess as she repeated faintly: "My goddess, forgive me... forgive me!" Then she fell quiet.

12

A Hittite in one of the leading chariots raised his arm and then brought it down to point towards the Assyrian camp. It was the signal for the chariots to turn and face the foe. With creaks and groans that were ominously audible in the silence of the wastelands the chariots turned in the semi-darkness to face the encircled Assyrians.

The men of the raiding party were hoping for some kind of frontal attack and were poised, standing or kneeling among piles of bushes and dead branches, with arrows fitted to their bowstrings and bows ready to be drawn. They saw that they had almost twice as many bowmen as the Hittites and felt that they could repel a chariot charge even if it came from all directions at once. But they also knew that they could not move from their position while the Hittites could come and go at will: any man making a dash for the horses in the grove would be picked off by the Hittite archers on the chariots. A concerted run for the horses would be crushed by a chariot charge.

The Hittite who had given the signal shouted an order and, almost immediately, the small light of a fire-carrier appeared in one of the chariots. Within seconds, the golden light of what might have been a torch lit up the two-man crew. While the Assyrians watched in horror the light spread from chariot to chariot until all the charioteers were lit up by the radiance of flaming tar-dipped arrows.

The Hittites' intentions were all too obvious.

"They are going to burn us!"

"Be quiet! Let us die like men. In silence!"

The Hittite commander, knowing that his bowmen were outnumbered, was not going to risk a frontal assault or an exchange of arrows. There was a sharp order and one of the chariots suddenly sprang towards the Assyrians, closely followed by four others from points that were evenly spaced around the circle. The Assyrian bowmen, lacking a centralised command, released their arrows before all the chariots had come within lethal range. As the Hittite commander had hoped, most of the arrows were aimed at the chariot that had sped ahead of its fellows. The charioteers were crouching and were not hit, but both horses were hit and the chariot overturned, hurling its occupants high into the air and over the horses. There was a loud cheer from the Assyrians but it was quickly cut short when they realised that they had wasted most of their arrows on a single chariot. Before they could draw their bows again the Hittite bowmen on the four remaining chariots released their fire-arrows and the chariots quickly turned to gallop back towards their places in the circle. As each chariot swung round the second charioteer put down his bow and raised his shield behind him to protect his back and that of his companion. The Hittite fire-arrows were aimed indiscriminately, not so much at the men as at the piles of bushes and dry wood that littered the Assyrian camp. Within moments, the bewildered men of the raiding party were standing among blazing tongues of flame. The four Hittite chariots had barely returned to their positions when five other chariots surged forward and released their fire-arrows when they came within range. The Hittites repeated this tactic until the only movement in the Assyrian camp was in the leaping flames or the frantic groping of smoke-blinded men.

The Assyrians were unable to shoot straight because of the smoke. They shot their arrows in haste and terror without bothering to wait for clear targets. The circle of chariots gradually closed in, and whenever an Assyrian was silhouetted against the fire the Hittite bowmen fired a salvo of arrows and brought him down.

1 3

The night was at its darkest when the last man of the raiding party fell. Sparkling embers rose high into the air as though to greet the stars that embellished the black sky. The Hittite commander got off his chariot and approached what was left of the Assyrian camp. There was no one left alive.

"Casualties?" he asked.

There was a short silence. Then: "Only three wounded charioteers and five dead horses, my prince. One of our chariots is smashed beyond repair."

"No matter," said the prince. "We have enough chariots and we have the Assyrian horses. Are the charioteers seriously wounded?"

"No, my prince."

"It's a pity that the Assyrian chariots are burning," said Her-unt.

"We don't need more chariots." The prince turned to the men: "Do what you can for the wounded until the physicians arrive with Norr."

The men got off their chariots and began to clear away the Assyrian dead. Someone kicked one of the corpses but the prince rebuked him: "These men fought bravely!" he ordered, "Bury them with the respect brave men deserve!" The men close to the prince nodded in acknowledgement. "And bring me the body of the woman who tried to escape," the prince continued.

"Who was she?" someone asked.

"I don't know," said Artaxias. "But I want to see her." The body of the priestess was brought over and laid gently upon the ground before him. Her white veil was lost and her clothes were soaked with blood, but her face and hands had been wiped clean. She looked beautiful, as though asleep. The crimson necklace glittered in the light of the fires.

"I recognise the necklace!" said the prince, "Such necklaces were worn by the priestesses at the temple of the monster! What was a priestess doing here?"

"The raiding party had no prisoners," said Her-unt, "perhaps it was escorting the priestess to the temple before continuing into our land to capture boys for the monster."

"That is possible," said the prince, "but the men of this raiding party must have known of our whereabouts. They would not have tried to conceal themselves if they did not believe they were in danger. The raiding party could only have been going to the temple to warn them of our coming."

"But the temple is not far," said Her-unt. "Why would they stop here and not make straight for the temple?"

"Perhaps they thought that in this place they could hide from us," said the prince, "Perhaps they feared that they could not escape if they were seen by a scout and our chariots chased them over the open space between here and the temple."

"They had no reason to expect our chariots to be so close behind them," said Her-unt.

"I do not profess to understand what happened here," said the prince. He recalled the conversation with his uncle. "Perhaps they *had* to stop here," he added quietly, "Why we shall never know." What his uncle had said regarding the Assyrian king's intentions towards the temple seemed far in the past.

There was silence. Then a Senior Charioteer said: "If this woman was a priestess and the Assyrians knew of our coming then that would explain why she tried to run between our chariots. She must have desperately wanted to warn her temple!"

"Yes," said Her-unt, "And her soul would now be in torment. She must not be buried with those who failed to take her to the temple on time."

The prince nodded: "Do not bury her, but place her sitting against one of the large rocks at some distance from here, facing her temple. Chariot Leader, is there anything else we can do to placate her spirit?"

Her-unt shook his head. "No, my prince. Except pray to the gods to escort her spirit to a place of rest."

127

There was no rejoicing at the thought that the temple could have been warned but had not been, for the men were superstitious and feared that the death of the priestess would anger the gods. Later, Artaxias would tell his men that the failure of the priestess to warn her temple was a clear sign that the gods were on their side, but for the moment the men could not overcome their guilt at having killed a priestess without the absolution rituals that had to precede the killing of a *kahanah*.

7

RITUALS AND THE START OF THE ASSAULT

1

HITTITE ETHICS DEMANDED that the body of a dead woman be touched as little as possible by adult men, and so the priestess was carried to her final resting place on a makeshift bier composed of spears and shields. Had there been any women in the Hittite force, the priestess would have been washed and her clothes changed, and because she was a lady of rank, her body would also have been perfumed with fragrant oils. But there were no women and no suitable fragrant oils, and so all that could be done was to cover her body with a clean sheet of white finely-woven cloth. The cloth left her face and hands exposed.

The moon had not yet risen when the two commanders and fourteen charioteers accompanied the priestess to her final resting place, which was in the direction of the temple and at some distance from the site of the battle. They walked slowly, as befitted a funeral procession, but no torches were lit and there were no mourning drums. The four charioteers who carried the bier led the way, walking cautiously to avoid stumbling over the uneven ground, and behind them came the prince and Her-unt. Last came ten charioteers in single file. All walked pensively and in silence, for after the heat of battle there often comes a time of reflection, and each man wondered in his own way how he could atone for taking part in the killing of a priestess.

Some two hundred paces from the site of the battle, the men collected large stones and built a cradle-shaped cairn against the largest rock they could find. When the cairn was completed they lowered the priestess gently into the hollow, so that she sat with her back to the rock as though in repose, with her hands on her lap and her feet close together. The whiteness of the cloth that covered her body contrasted sharply with the necklace of crimson crystals that hung around her neck, which looked black in the semidarkness. Although the priestess's eyes were shut she had been placed on the cairn so as to face in the direction of her temple, and because she no longer had her veil the night wind made her long hair blow this way and that in gentle waves.

The men stood silently before the priestess, each absorbed by his thoughts, until a thin crescent moon rose unassumingly above the horizon. The silence was broken by the prince: "I wonder who she was," he said softly, "And how she got to be with a raiding party."

"She has taken her secrets with her," said one of the charioteers, "we shall never know."

"I feel that it is not right that a priestess die alone in the wastelands," said the prince, as though speaking to himself, "and that she be laid to rest without ceremony."

"The gods appointed the time she was to die," said Her-Unt, "and brought her here knowing that we had no choice but to end her life. But after doing what had to be done we treated her body with great respect, and now she lies facing her temple, closer to it than she was when she died. We did all we could for her, my prince."

Artaxias remained silent. He did not wish to share the other concerns that were gnawing on his mind: *Does the presence of a temple priestess among the men of a raiding party mean that the Assyrian king is on good terms with the goddess? But then why would he give us reason to attack the temple? Does he seek an excuse to start a war?* The ramifications were alarming: *There might be Assyrian troops at the temple!* The thought brought a shock, but then followed further disturbing thoughts: *The smoke from the battle might have been seen by the guards on the watchtowers. If Assyrian troops come to investigate the smoke they could be here at sunrise!* Preoccupied with his thoughts, he stared at the corpse as though entranced.

Her-unt was concerned by the prince's seeming fascination with the dead priestess and feared that she might be casting a spell on him: "My prince, when the men finish burying the dead perhaps we should go and camp somewhere else."

"Why camp somewhere else?" asked Artaxias blankly, his mind on other matters.

"The spirits of the dead Assyrians are all around us, my prince. They seek the mothers who gave birth to their bodies. Let us wait for our infantry somewhere else."

"We told Norr to meet us at this place, Chariot Leader. If we go somewhere else Norr and the infantry may not find us easily. That would waste time."

"Norr would be able to follow the tracks of our chariot wheels."

"I think we should wait for Norr where we said we would wait."

"My prince, it is not good to camp near the graves of men we killed."

The prince smiled at the older man: "The Assyrians were soldiers like us, old friend. Their spirits bear us no ill-will."

Her-unt did not reply and the prince continued: "Also, if we dig near the grove we should find water. This is a good place to wait." And he thought: *If Assyrian troops from the temple visit us tomorrow it is best to be close to water. Thirsty men and thirsty horses tire easily and do not fight well!* Her-unt nodded and the prince put his hand on the older man's shoulder: "With the help of the gods we did well today. We destroyed a raiding party and avenged the killing of our scouts. Let us rest until Norr and the infantry catch up." *The questions that trouble me shall be answered soon enough!*

"Couldn't our scout charioteers have been killed by someone else?"

"Did you not see the Hittite sword among the weapons of the slain? That could only have been the sword of one of our charioteers!"

"I'm very tired, my prince. I'm becoming forgetful."

"We are all tired, old friend. You and the men go back and help set up camp for the night. I wish to wait here alone for a while."

"Alone, my prince?"

"I'll be quite safe."

"Very well, my prince." Her-unt was reluctant to leave but he was too tired to think of any compelling reasons why he should not leave the prince alone. He and the men returned to the site of the battle, leaving Artaxias with the dead priestess.

2

In the weak light of the crescent moon the landscape looked eerie and mysterious, and the grove of trees just beyond the camp was a dark mass, its features hidden by the darkness. Perhaps it was the home of minor gods and demons who resented intruders. But gods and demons tended to mind their own business, and Artaxias wondered what more substantial dangers might be lurking behind the scattered rocks that dotted the landscape. Were there dangerous animals in the wastelands? Would they try to feed upon a prince who was foolish enough to remain alone? For a brief moment Artaxias entertained the thought of confronting some large animal, perhaps of a kind he had never seen before, with only his scythe-sword. The thought was enjoyable and exciting but he quickly suppressed it: *Akh! I am indulging my fantasies like a little boy!* If a large animal had come down from the mountains it would have starved to death long before reaching this far into the wastelands! The only danger was from humans, for this was Assyrian territory: *But Assyrians billeted at the temple would not patrol this far, and Assyrians arriving to reinforce the temple would not pass this way!* What about a raiding party returning with prisoners? They could come from any direction: *But raiders are not sent out to capture prisoners more than once a planting season, so a second raiding party near this place is very unlikely!*

The prince felt that something important had somehow slipped his mind. It could not be the thought of wild animals or marauding Assyrians. Was it the possibility of collusion between the temple and the Assyrian king? The thought increased his unease but he pushed it aside: *There is nothing I can do about that now!* What if there were Assyrian troops at the temple and some were sent out to investigate the smoke? *They would not be sent at night and would not reach us before tomorrow!* He inhaled deeply and suddenly remembered the real cause of his disquiet: *Why did the Assyrians stop so close to the temple?* It was not an urgent question, but somehow the presence of the dead priestess made it seem important: *The Assyrians were undoubtedly a raiding party sent to capture prisoners; they were too lightly armed to be reinforcements. But a raiding party without prisoners should have been going towards our villages, not towards the temple! They must therefore have been on their way to warn the priests! That would explain why the priestess panicked and ran desperately towards the temple rather than to some place where she could hide! But then, why did the raiders stop here?* He sighed: *Perhaps they questioned our scout-charioteers before one of them escaped, and they were made to believe that we are not a serious threat to the temple!* For reasons he could not explain he felt that the answers to his questions were held, somehow, by the dead priestess.

His attention turned to the corpse with renewed awareness. She looked very beautiful in the pale light of the moon and the stars. Her expression was calm, beyond all cares, oblivious to the strands of black hair that the wind sometimes blew across her face. Yet her generous lips were tense, taut, almost stretched into a thin line, and the prince sensed a lingering anger in her, a deep malevolence that death could not erase. "*Why* were you among the men of a raiding party?" he asked, "*Why* did they stop here? If only you could talk to me!"

It could have been the night wind pulling at her hair, but the head of the priestess suddenly tilted forward as though she were nodding in answer. Artaxias felt icy fingers at the back of his head and the muscles beneath his long hair tensed: *Her cold spirit touched me! She is still here and is tormented by something she wants me to know!* He unconsciously grasped the necklace with the little blue stone that hung around his neck. The string was woven from the hair of his wife and daughter, a small part of home he had brought with him: *Perhaps she wants to remind me that I am the reason why she did not warn the temple!*

Had the priestess been killed in the temple the prince would have felt differently, for that would have been after the absolution rituals; but the priestess had died in the wilderness, burdened with the urgency of her task, alone in spirit like any commander in the field. Alone like himself. The prince had often felt the loneliness of absolute authority, and he had learned to control it although he had never managed to eliminate it completely. The wind whistled and moaned mournfully as it blew around the rocks, and Artaxias thought of the spirits of the dead Assyrians, condemned to roam this world for forty days, perhaps not knowing how to move on to the next. He muttered a prayer to the Weather God: *Be not harsh on them, Taru. Some had mothers and fathers who shall grieve for them, and some would have had wives and children... and they all died in this desolate place because of the monster who feeds on human blood!*

But when he looked again at the dead priestess he felt that her anger was still there, directed personally at him: *Maybe the kahanah die like the rest of us, maybe they don't rise to join the gods and leave all worldly cares behind! Maybe they die and take their last feelings with them, like we do!* He bowed his head and clasped his hands together in respect. Without knowing why he sang tunelessly to the corpse in a low voice:

"Oh you who were so beautiful
Bear us no ill will!

It is the murder of our young brethren that brings us here
With the blessing of Taru, the Weather God
And of the all-powerful sun-goddess of Arinna,
And of the benevolent Ashtarte
And the blessing of the other gods also
Because the goddess whom you served
Is false!

Oh you who were so beautiful
Be happy and content in the Other World
Where you can comprehend more things
Than you ever comprehended in this world of toil and tears
And where your understanding
Is nourished by the gods and goddesses
Who know all that was and all that is to be.
Be content with the will of the gods, Oh priestess,
And bear us no ill-will."

He did not unclasp his hands when he ended his song but stood in contemplation, assessing his emotions.

His apology to the dead priestess partly washed away his guilt and he felt free to be elated at the thought that the gods had favoured his cause: *If the Assyrians had not stopped here, whatever their reasons, we might not have caught up with them before we came within sight of the temple! The priests would have seen us and prepared themselves before the heavy infantry arrived!* Yet the feeling that the priestess had not forgiven him did not subside. *I stand here and pray for her forgiveness although I know that the night creatures shall eat her flesh and scatter her bones. Yet to leave her unburied, facing her home, was all I could do. It is the wish of the gods that the temple remains unwarned, and her body lies broken before me only because her duties did not agree with the wishes of the gods!* The prince took a deep breath and the night air of the wastelands almost froze his lungs. He returned to the camp, still thinking of the priestess and of the many questions raised by her presence among the men of a raiding party.

3

Early the next morning Artaxias prepared his chariots in case Assyrian troops stationed at the temple came to investigate the smoke from the previous night's battle. The dry wood and bushes were not smouldering and there was no more smoke, but the smoke and the light from the fires of the previous night would have been visible from the temple's guard towers. If there were Assyrian troops at the temple their commander would want to know what had happened so close to the temple and he would almost certainly send some chariots to investigate. What if there were no Assyrian troops at the temple, would any priests come to investigate? Probably not; the priests would not consider the smoke as indicative of a threat. It was very unlikely but not impossible that some priests would come, but Artaxias did not consider the chariotless priests to pose a threat.

It was only when a full day had passed that the prince felt sure that no Assyrian troops or temple priests would come to investigate. Did this mean that there were no Assyrian troops at the temple? Perhaps it only meant that they had no chariots and hated walking long distances! But Artaxias could not afford to spend too much time waiting, he had to prepare for the assault on the temple. He arranged rotas for nine scout-chariots to stealthily patrol the surrounding area while keeping out of sight of the temple guard towers. The scouts were in groups of three and they were ordered to destroy any pilgrims or troops they came across. Anyone leaving the temple might become aware of the Hittite presence and would report it upon arrival at their destination; anyone travelling to the temple would strengthen its defences. It was imperative to destroy any Assyrians in the vicinity. If three chariots were not enough for the job, they could call the other scout-chariots or even the main force for help. But, as Artaxias and the main force waited for Norr and the heavy infantry, every time a group of chariots returned they reported that they had met no one.

4

Norr arrived in the late afternoon five days after the battle, accompanied by the heavy infantry and the two chariots that had stayed with him. The carts followed some hundred paces behind. The men of the heavy infantry had marched as fast as they could and were exhausted, even the horses that pulled the carts looked tired. In the early hours of the night, while most of the heavy infantry were still resting, the three commanders and the *action group* leaders sat around a small fire to eat and discuss the final plans for the attack on the temple. The meal was simple: smoked meat, cheese, raisins and hard flat bread. The fire was in a deep hole in the ground so that its light could not be seen from a distance. It gave very little warmth.

"I wonder if the old High Priest is still alive," said Artaxias, "He was a singularly arrogant man. It would have cost him nothing to have shown us some civility!" The broad details of the *mission* were known to all the men around him.

"It may be written that you shall be the one who takes his life," said Her-unt with his mouth full. Her-unt lacked several teeth and was having a hard time with the smoked meat. "The gods sometimes prepare a man for a particular task. Perhaps the gods were kind to you and purposely made him so unpleasant. You would have found it difficult to kill an old man who had treated you courteously."

"You are right," said the prince, "The decision to destroy the temple might have been cancelled if the High Priest had agreed to stop feeding our brethren to the monster. Nothing less would have prevented this expedition. If he had treated us courteously and yet rejected our request the expedition would not have been cancelled and I would have found it very hard to kill him!"

Her-unt smiled as he remembered the stories he had heard about the confrontation between his prince and the temple priests. Artaxias had been grossly insulted but he had lost his temper only at the end, when he had been severely provoked. "From what I heard, my prince, you called their goddess a monster!" he said, "That was unwise!" Despite the difference in rank, Her-unt was considerably older than the prince and had the right to reprove him, albeit mildly.

"That is true," admitted Artaxias. "I lost control when one of the senior priests said that there were Hittite prisoners in the temple waiting to be fed to their goddess! I called her a monster in our tongue but someone understood and told the priests."

"You could have had us all killed!" muttered Norr.

"Come to think of it, why didn't they try to kill you all?" asked Her-unt.

"Our King asked precisely that question," said Artaxias. "As did I, when we left the temple and I had the chance to think clearly. It is all the more strange given that I drew my sword in front of the High Priest and broke the spear of one of his priests!"

There was a pause, as everyone thought about this while they chewed.

"That was unwise too," said Her-unt eventually, and then changed the subject: "But this talk leads nowhere. From what you told us, the defenders are not too numerous but the temple defences are formidable. Can you tell us more about the temple, my prince?"

5

The prince chewed quickly and swallowed what was in his mouth. "As you know," he said, "The temple is on a broad flat hill. It is roughly oval, I estimated that it is about five hundred paces long and three hundred and fifty paces wide. The sides of the hill are high and steep and the temple can only be reached by two ramps that lead to well-built gates."

"There are only two gates," added Norr, "we checked that."

"How wide are the ramps?" asked Her-unt.

"Five or six chariots wide at the bottom, much narrower at the top. The ground on the ramps is quite soft and the chariot wheels would get stuck even if the horses pulled them up the ramps with the charioteers on foot beside them."

"So no chariots," said Her-Unt. "The defenders are all priests?"

"There might be Assyrian troops at the temple now, but we only saw armed priests and acolytes. We could not tell whether they were trained in the fighting skills or not." Artaxias stopped speaking as he remembered being ushered along the short journey from the Lesser Audience Chamber to the Second Gate. He had expected a sudden attack by the younger priests once they were out of sight of the pilgrims. But there had been no attack, which seemed to suggest that the priests had been *ordered* not to kill them: *Who could have ordered them not to kill us? Not the High Priest!*

His thoughts were interrupted by Her-unt: "Please continue, my prince."

"We estimated that there could not be much more than two hundred and fifty armed priests, perhaps four hundred armed men in all if we include older priests and young acolytes. As seen from within the temple, the defensive wall that surrounds the temple grounds is at least as high as a man's shoulder. From outside the temple, the defensive wall merges with the sides of the hill and becomes an extension of the precipice, which is steep everywhere except at the ramps."

"In short," said a Senior Charioteer, "we cannot climb the sides of the hill and clamber over the encircling wall."

"That is correct, replied the prince.

"The height of the flat-topped hill is many times the height of a man," said Norr, "but I do not know how many times."

"What is the encircling wall made of?" asked Her-unt.

"Mud bricks," answered Norr. "So it won't burn. And it is wide enough for bowmen to stand on it."

"What are the gates made of?" asked Her-unt.

"Both gates are made of wood," said Artaxias, "They have massive wooden portals supported by an equally massive wooden frame. When we saw them many moons ago the gates were not covered with metal sheets. If they are still not covered with metal sheets they could be set on fire. However, the gates open outwards and cannot be rammed."

"Ramming the gates is not an option," added Norr, "It would be impossible for our men to run up the soft earth of the ramp with a battering ram heavy enough to knock down the portals."

"That is immaterial because we don't have a battering ram," said an *action group* leader.

"Let us first decide whether we should focus our attack on the gates," said Artaxias, "I see no other weakness in the temple's defences."

"Yes," said Her-unt, "It must be the gates since we cannot climb the sides of the hill and then clamber over the encircling wall."

"I see no alternative but the gates," said Norr. The other men agreed.

Her-unt cleared his throat: "Then we must decide which gate to attack. Or are you thinking of attacking both gates at once, my prince?"

"I think it would be best if we do not divide the infantry that shall spearhead the attack," said Artaxias. "If we attack both gates the priests shall guess that we have a sizeable force even if they do not see all of us. That might make them organise better. Besides, our force should not fight in two places at once. There aren't enough of us."

"I agree," said Her-unt, "If they underestimate our strength they may not organise their defence too well." All the others nodded.

"So which gate shall we attack?" asked Norr.

"The southern ramp is shorter but much steeper," said Artaxias. "The heavy infantry won't be able to run up swiftly on the soft ground and would make easy targets for bowmen standing on the walls. I suggest we attack the northern gate, although its ramp is longer. The men would run faster and make poor targets."

"We'll have to think about that carefully," said Her-unt, "Are the defences the same at both gates?"

"Yes," said Artaxias, "There is a tall guard tower to the left of each gate, as seen by someone coming up the ramps."

"Apart from the darkness, my prince, is there anything that could conceal our men before they climb the ramp?"

"The temple is surrounded by boulders that are larger but otherwise not too different from those we have here. In the dark, our men could approach stealthily to about two or three hundred paces of the gate without being seen. There is a particularly large clump of rocks just before the northern ramp, to the right of someone facing the ramp. To the left as one climbs the ramp, reaching to about eighty paces from the gate, the hill extends outwards and there is a thick grove of trees. The grove starts from about half way up the ramp."

"Then we should attack the northern gate," said Her-unt, "the men will be able to move quickly and, if necessary, some could hide in the grove."

"So we attack the northern gate," said Artaxias. The men nodded in agreement.

"It's just as well we did not bring any heavy equipment," said Norr, in case any of the men had misgivings about the lack of siege engines.

"Yes," said Artaxias. "Siege engines would not be of much use given the height and steepness of the hill and, on top of that, the enclosing wall. They would have slowed us down without providing any benefits."

"Could the heavy infantry muster behind the rocks without being seen by the tower guards?" asked another *action group* leader, returning to the previous point.

"If it is dark enough," said the prince. "But the rocks could also conceal enemy troops and possibly a few enemy chariots."

"Do the priests have chariots?" Her-unt was suddenly alert. Chariots were instruments of attack. If there were chariots in the temple then the priests might not be novices in the skills of war.

"We did not see any," said Norr, "Anyhow, what would temple priests do with chariots?"

"I was thinking of chariots sent by the Assyrian king to supplement the temple's defences," said Artaxias, "If there are chariots in the temple they would charge out against the men climbing the ramp and cause a lot of trouble. The soft ground may not impede chariots coming down the hill."

"Assyrian chariots would present us with a problem," admitted

Norr, "We would not be able to use the infantry until we dispensed with the chariots. That would give the priests time to prepare the temple's defences."

"It is now more than four moons since your return from the temple," said another *action group* leader. "How likely is it that the Assyrian king would have reinforced the temple with troops and perhaps war chariots during that time?"

6

Artaxias had not told anyone that his uncle suspected the Assyrian ruler of secretly wanting the temple to be destroyed. The subject was not irrelevant to the discussion, but the presence of the priestess among the men of the raiding party would have complicated the issue and detracted from the main topics of the discussion. The prince thought carefully before answering the *action group* leader's question: "The Assyrian king *would* have sent regular troops," he said, "only if he had reason to believe that the temple would be attacked or if the temple expected an attack and asked for help."

"Let us hope that neither the Assyrian king nor the priests expected us to attack the temple," said Norr quietly.

"Please continue with your description of the temple, my prince," said Her-unt.

"The two gates, each with a tall guard tower to guard it, are on the north-eastern and south-western flanks. The temple has two large buildings, one of which is rectangular and the other circular. The rectangular building is almost certainly the living quarters of the senior priests. Because it is beautifully decorated, we guessed that the round building houses the monster. There are also many smaller buildings, some of which are probably shrines to minor gods if the temple of the monster is like other Assyrian temples. There is a courtyard between the two large buildings and the smaller buildings and shrines are connected by narrow streets. Skilled bowmen hiding within the buildings can pose a serious threat to our men."

"So the main battle should be away from the buildings," said Her-unt. The men of the heavy infantry would not be very effective at dodging arrows from concealed bowmen.

"Yes," said Artaxias, "If at all possible the defence should be broken before we reach the temple buildings."

"The buildings are mostly of mud brick and wood?" asked the *action group* leader.

"We think so," replied the prince, "At least the smaller ones we saw. The larger ones may be of wood and stone but I am sure they are all held together by wood. The Lesser Audience Chamber was built of stone held together by wood."

"So we set fire as we fight," said Norr. "The buildings should burn in this dry weather!"

"That is why we brought so many torches and fire-carriers," said Artaxias.

"Could we entice the garrison to leave the protection of the temple?" Norr asked.

"We should try," replied Artaxias. "But whether we succeed would depend on the calibre of whoever commands the garrison."

Her-unt said: "If the king has sent reinforcements they would be under the command of an experienced officer. He is likely to be of good calibre."

"I think it is unlikely that the king would have sent anything but a token force," said Norr.

"Why is that?" asked Her-unt.

"Oh, because a serious force, stationed for an indefinite time and needing to be fed as well as housed, would be a drain on the temple's resources. It is more than four moons since the *mission* returned. If reinforcements had been sent, they would have arrived about two moons ago and probably left by now."

"Unless they arrived more recently," said the *action group* leader, "The Assyrians could not have sent reinforcements immediately after they heard of the *mission*."

"We must leave the question of reinforcements to the gods," said the prince, "And assume that the temple is as we left it."

The men around the prince nodded, but their worries had not been put to rest. Norr decided to change the subject: "The assault on the Northern gate," he said, "Should it be in silence or with the full banging of the drums and the wailing of the bagpipes?"

"A good question," replied Artaxias, "What do you think, Her-unt?"

"The advantages of silence will wear out quickly. If we want the priests to get out of their hiding-holes we should make all the noise we can but without showing our full strength. Hopefully, it would bring them to the gate and lessen the chances of their waiting for us in the narrow streets with bows and arrows."

Norr agreed: "Yes! And if we awe them with noise they shall be all the readier to rush out of the gate if we make them think they're winning."

"I have two more questions," said Her-unt. "What does the monster look like, and where does she live?"

"It is said that she is very old and very tall," answered Norr. "So I guess she looks like a very tall old hag, although she is supposed to be extremely strong and dangerous."

Artaxias shrugged. "We don't know how dangerous, and she is supposed to be immortal. I hope this only means that she would live forever unless she is killed."

Her-unt nodded thoughtfully, digesting the information. Norr said: "The interpreter managed to find out that the monster lives within the circular building, at the bottom of a deep pit. That is the second of the two large buildings and the taller of the two. It has columns all around it."

"Are the columns made of wood?" asked Her-unt.

"We could not be sure," said Norr.

"If the monster can be reached only through the circular building we should leave it for last," said Artaxias. "We deal with the monster when we are sure no one will attack us from the rear."

The discussion continued into the night. It was agreed that the temple had only one weakness: its gates. Though each gate was strongly built, the massive portals of the gates were old and wooden, and it had not rained for some time. It was also decided that, later that same night, the war chariots that were not already out would scatter along a wide circle around the temple, keeping out of sight of the temple guards. The chariots were to join up with those that were out on forays and patrol in groups of three or four. As much as possible they were to keep in contact with one another in case they needed to join together to form a fighting unit. Their immediate task was to prevent anyone from reaching the temple or leaving it. They were to be particularly alert for Assyrian reinforcements, in which case they would attack and destroy them or, if that were not possible, stay out of their way and inform the prince of their strength and whereabouts. Any Assyrian scouts were to be killed and their positions reported at once.

7

Not long after the commanders and the infantry were asleep, all but the commanders' chariots left the Hittite camp to encircle the temple. Their purpose was to eliminate anyone, including pilgrims, who could reinforce the temple's defences or interfere with the assault. If the chariots could not eliminate any incoming Assyrian forces they would inform the commanders and there would be a change of plan. As matters stood the chariots encircling the hill would not play an active role in the assault itself.

However, the senior officers and the heavy infantry were to attack a sacred place. Even though the goddess of the Amalishah temple was acknowledged by all Hittites to be false, her priests and priestesses were *kahanah*, or servants of the divine powers. Despite having lived all their lives in the service of the monster, they were entitled to participate in the performance of sacred rituals in all temples. The Hittites, who shared many gods with the Assyrians, could therefore not kill the temple priests and priestesses before the proper absolution rituals were performed. The unabsolved killing of priests and priestesses, irrespective of which deity they served, was sure to bring down the wrath of the heavens.

8

There was only starlight and a crescent moon when Artaxias awoke. Close to the grove there was water beneath the surface, and while all but the guards were still asleep Artaxias got up and ritually washed his whole body with water before rubbing it with oil that had been brought from the temple of Arinna in Hattusas. The solitary purification rite was accompanied by an ancient repetitive incantation, sung in a subdued voice, whose purpose was to set the timing for each part of the ritual as much as to prepare his mind for the role of *celebrant priest* during the coming ceremony. It was to be a long ritual, and all the men in the camp were up before he had finished and donned his full formal dress, with helmet, scythe-sword, armour and cape. The sky was a dull red when the horses were brought to the three chariots of the commanders and everyone got into place for the coming ceremony.

The heavy infantry stood silently in a circular ring facing inwards while the prince and the two commanders waited on foot beside their chariots outside the circle. The infantry wore their helmets but their shields and weapons lay on the ground before them. All who would accompany the commanders and the infantry to the temple but would not take part in the fighting, including the physicians, the drummers and the bagpipe players, stood passively outside the circle. Within the circle, at each point of the compass, North, South, East and West, stood an *action group* leader holding a tall bronze battle standard topped with two gilded swastikas. To the Hittites, swastikas represented the rising or setting sun, depending on the orientation of the tines, and to anyone within the ring the swastikas on the battle standards all showed the sun rising.

Shortly before the sun was due to rise the prince entered the circle and the battle standards were lowered in deference. As the prince reached the centre of the circle the battle-standards were raised aloft once more. The sky was streaked with pink and blue and everybody stood silently without moving as they waited for the sun. The prince waited at the centre of the circle with his sword sheathed.

When the sun rose in a blazing glory of golden-pink light the men bowed low and stretched their arms towards the sun. Artaxias also bowed, facing the sun, but he did not stretch out his arms. An *action group* leader brought a large white ram and held the fidgeting animal in place before the prince. The men straightened as the prince took hold of the ram by one of its horns with his left hand. After a short pause the prince began to chant in a voice that rose and fell at regular intervals:

"Oh Sun Goddess of Arinna,
Look favourably upon us!
Look favourably upon your children who worship you
And help us in this hour of uncertainty!"

He unsheathed his sword and all the men bowed low:

"We ask you, we beseech you,
Do not turn your fearsome eyes away from us!
Do not look away
But look down upon us
With a benevolent gaze.

The men straightened and Artaxias continued:

"By the names of all the gods in the Heavens
And on the Earth
And in the Air
And in the Rivers and Lakes,
We implore you
Oh Sun Goddess of Arinna,
To grant us your favour.
We beseech you to intercede on our behalf,
With Taru the Weather God
And to ask, on our behalf, your brothers and sisters
The gods and goddesses of the night
To help us in the perilous task
That lies before us and from which we cannot retreat
And which we are duty-bound to perform
While we honour all the gods in the Heavens
And on the Earth
And in the Air
And in the Rivers and Lakes.

The men picked up their swords and shields. Artaxias raised his sword:

"In token of our servitude
We offer you this ram
Whose blood shall be sacred to you
And with which we shall cleanse our weapons in your name
So that we might have your strength and your blessing
In the difficult task before us
Where the enemy
Are holy priests and priestesses"

The battle standards were lowered towards the sun as the prince's scythe-sword fell and almost decapitated the ram. The animal shuddered once, then collapsed and lay still. The men who stood in a circle as well as the *action group* leaders who held the battle-standards began to chant the *Hymn of Praise to the Sun*.

With his sword still dripping, Artaxias cut off a lock of hair from his forehead and placed it on the carcase, then knelt and thrust the curved blade of the sword into the dark red blood that gushed from the animal's severed neck. The Hymn of Praise grew louder. Artaxias pulled out his sword and turned to face his men as he straightened and stepped back two paces.

One by one the men came over to the ram, starting with Her-unt and then Norr, followed by the men of the heavy infantry. Each man solemnly cut a lock of his hair and placed it on the carcase before bowing and ritually cleansing his sword in the blood. When all the men had come and returned to their place, with last of all the *action group* leaders who held the battle-standards, the prince stood alone once more. The chanting of the *Hymn of Praise* stopped. Artaxias raised his sword up high and said:

> *"Our swords are now sacred to you, Oh Sun Goddess!*
> *They shall not be used for any purpose*
> *Until we complete our task which is now sacred*
> *To you, Oh Sun Goddess.*
> *And we shall forever praise your name*
> *And the name of the Weather God*
> *And the names of your brothers and sisters*
> *The gods and goddesses of the Night*
> *And the names of the gods in the Heavens*
> *And on the Earth*
> *And in the Air*
> *And in the Rivers and Lakes*
> *We shall praise you and them, Oh Sun Goddess*
> *With every beat of our hearts*
> *And with all the strength of our arms.*
> *And as we perform our task*
> *We shall praise you above all, Oh Sun Goddess*
> *And we shall praise the Weather God*
> *And the gods and goddesses of the Night*
> *We shall praise you all, with all the strength of our hearts*
> *We shall praise you with our mouths and tongues*
> *Though they are of mere flesh*
> *But we shall praise you with words that burn like fire."*

The ritual was over. The prince removed his helmet and the men returned to the camp, to rest as long as they could before the final stage of the journey to the temple. The body of the ram, covered in locks of hair, was left in the sunlight.

9

It was late afternoon when the army began its march towards the temple. They marched silently in triple columns behind the three chariots of the commanders. The non-combatants and carts followed the troops. They marched with only short breaks until it was almost dark and the tops of the temple's guard towers were just visible above the horizon. Artaxias gave the signal for the force to stop.

"We cannot get closer without being seen," he said as he alighted from his chariot. "Let the men rest."

"It is a good place to stop," said Her-unt. "It is far enough for the priests on the guard towers not to notice us, yet close enough to the temple for the men to be fresh for battle when we reach there tonight."

Norr was impatient and wanted to get closer to the temple before stopping, but the prince overruled him.

"We are sure to be seen if we get any closer," he said. "And the men will fight better if they sleep without worry before their last march to the temple. It will be a difficult night and we cannot tell how long the battle will last."

Norr nodded with a grunt. It was his way of conceding agreement.

The carts were emptied and overturned, the old horses that pulled the carts were carefully tethered, some of the supplies for the return journey were buried, guards were chosen from among the non-combatants and their rotas arranged. The force settled down to rest, but no fires were lit and all talk was in subdued tones. Although he was no less weary than his men, Artaxias could not sleep but sat on the ground with his back against one of the wheels of his chariot. The strategy for the attack itself had been decided in detail and there was no more to be said. But he knew that, without the protection of the chariots, the last leg of the journey would be the most dangerous. The area around the temple hill was strewn with large boulders that could easily conceal an enemy, and though most of the infantry carried bows and were well trained in the use of spear, sword and mattock, the men would be hard put if they faced an Assyrian force supported by war chariots. The prince hoped fervently that his uncle had interpreted the intentions of the Assyrian king correctly and that the temple's defences had not been reinforced by troops with chariots.

None of the patrols returned to report the arrival of pilgrims or Assyrian forces, but Artaxias could not tell whether this was just his good fortune or whether it meant that the Hittite attack on the temple was *expected*. Eventually he lay on the ground and drifted off into sleep. But his sleep was not peaceful; he turned frequently and sometimes spoke terse words as though he were addressing his men during a difficult battle.

10

Soon after midnight Artaxias awoke to give the order for the final march to the temple. The commanders left their chariots and walked at the front of the infantry columns. The non-combatants remained behind, with the overturned carts and the three empty chariots. The army marched in silence, for the human voice travels far in the still night air, and all signals were passed silently from man to man. The moon was a thin crescent that had sunk low in the sky and most of the stars were covered by small clouds when the men reached the first of the large clumps of boulders that surrounded the hill. The hill and the temple that crowned it formed a long black silhouette against the stars that shone between the clouds, and in the faint light of the low crescent moon the guard tower of the North Gate stood like a faintly phosphorescent sentinel above the dark mass. Artaxias whispered something to the *action group* leader who marched behind him and the man put his fingers to his mouth and gave a high-pitched whistle, like the two-tone piping of a night bird. It was the signal for the force to stop and it was repeated several times along the column. After a few moments the whistle sounded a second time, slightly differently, and five men broke silently away from the main body and moved ahead to reconnoitre. They vanished silently. Artaxias and his men stood and waited, hardly daring to move lest they made a noise that might alert anyone concealed behind the rocks that lay between them and the temple hill. Only when all five scouts returned and indicated to the commanders that all was well did Artaxias give the signal for his troops to take up their attack positions.

In the light of the dying moon, the commanders and the infantry moved stealthily forward like dark, silent shadows. When they were a hundred paces from the temple hill, the Hittite force quietly separated into two parts. The commanders and nine action groups, roughly one hundred and eighty men, made straight for the ramp in front of the First Gate and took up their positions behind any cover they could find. The remaining five moved on in total silence to encircle the hill and cover the Second Gate. Of the nine action groups concealed before the First Gate, the two that were closest to the ramp placed their backpacks on the ground. These forty men were the *preliminary attack force*, and they were under the command of a veteran of many battles, a powerful man called Urdzhe. They would be the first to assault the gate. They stood in silence, each man carrying only his shield and two or three unlit bitumen torches. Their swords hung from wide belts at their waists. Three men, each carrying a small flame concealed within a clay pot, hid behind a large boulder close to the foot of the ramp.

So far, everything had worked out well. The temple seemed quiet and isolated from the outside world. The only sign of life were the two guards on the tower, barely visible forms in the faint light of the thin moon. The guards spoke to each other in the harsh, staccato tones of the Assyrians, and in the stillness of the night Artaxias could sometimes hear the words distinctly though he could not understand what was said. Some of the temple residents might have been awake: there was a weak yellow light in the upper window of one of the taller buildings that was close to the wall. A dog started barking and, as though this was its cue, the moon hid behind some clouds. When Artaxias was sure that the encircling of the temple had been completed, the high-pitched whistle sounded again: once, twice. This time it was answered by the thunderous booming of five enormous battle-drums which began beating the *battle cadence*. After three beats the battery of bagpipes joined in. The men of the *preliminary attack force* lit their torches from the flames in the clay pots and converged upon the North Gate, swiftly climbing the incline and chanting their war song to the rhythm of the drums. The bagpipes made an unearthly strident wail like cats in agony while the huge battle-drums beat a slow, monotonous rhythm. The resulting sound was intentionally unnerving.

8

THE ASSAULT ON THE TEMPLE

1

A STATE OF vigilance is difficult to maintain for long periods of time, and it was more than five moons since the goddess had ordered Khaur to put the temple in a state of alert. Like the other residents of the temple, the guards on the tower had sunk back into the security of their routine-driven lives and ceased to expect an attack. When the predawn silence was shattered by the wailing of the bagpipes and the booming of the battle-drums it was like a forgotten nightmare that had suddenly become real:

"**Ayah! What is that noise?**"

"**It's from the darkness beyond the ramp!**"

The guards all rushed to the side of the tower that overlooked the ramp:

"**Look! Foreigners with torches!**"

"They are coming to the gate!" Almost a whisper.

"**We are under attack!**"

The men of the *preliminary attack force*, chanting their war song and holding only burning torches and shields, were running up the ramp in twos and threes so as not to present concentrated targets to any bowmen on the tower.

"**They will climb the gate!**"

"**No, it is too high!**"

"**What are we to do?**"

"**Let us wait and see!**"

And so precious time was wasted, and the foremost infantrymen had almost reached the portals of the First Gate when the priests on the guard tower loosed a few ill-aimed arrows and raised the alarm by blowing on a ram's horn.

The blast on the ram's horn was still echoing when some twenty priests, rudely awakened by the clamour of the drums and bagpipes, arrived half-naked and climbed onto the defensive wall on either side of the portals to see what was happening. Unaware of the nature of the threat, they had not brought bows or spears and could only shake their fists and shout insults and execrations at the invaders. They realised the futility of their actions soon enough and most returned to their sleeping quarters to collect their weapons, but before the priests on the walls could pose a serious threat almost all the men of the two *action groups* had reached the top of the incline, hurled their torches at the base of the wooden portals, and turned to run back down the ramp.

"**The foreigners are trying to set fire to the gate!**" cried a guard on the tower.

"**May the gods burn their homes!**" answered an acolyte on the wall.

"**We'll catch them all and flay them alive!**"

"*The gate is burning!*"

The blowing of the horn became more strident and one of the tower guards hastily climbed down the ladder and ran frantically towards the quarters of the senior priests. The attention of the priests and acolytes was so fixed on the attackers that none thought of calling for water to douse the flames:

"When there are enough of us we'll get out and chase them!"

"We'll catch them and teach them a lesson!"

"Ayah! Let the gate burn! It's old anyway!"

The horn on the tower was answered by horns in other parts of the temple. Here and there, the hollow blackness of the temple's windows was dispelled by the flickering light of oil lamps. From all directions came hoarse rallying cries and the narrow streets resounded to the slap-thud of sandaled feet running hurriedly between the buildings. Even the temple dogs sensed that something was amiss and barked furiously. The news of the attack spread so rapidly that for a short time most of the priests did not know where the attack was taking place. By the time a small crowd of armed priests had gathered to defend the First Gate the huge wooden portals were standing in a bed of flames.

The Hittite commanders, previously almost invisible in the weak light of the cloud-concealed moon, were now illuminated by the burning gate. The prince stood rigidly on the highest point of a clump of boulders about thirty paces from the foot of the ramp. Her-unt and Norr stood to his right and left, on slightly lower rocks. All three wore helmets and had their swords at their sides, but although Her-unt and Norr carried their shields the prince carried only a long broad-headed spear, which he held rigidly with its tip pointing vertically upwards. Tradition demanded that, during a battle, if the commanding officer were not actively engaged in the fighting he would stand in a prominent place and hold only a spear. The direction of the spearhead determined the phase of the battle, and the commander would stand straight-backed and immobile so as to ensure that no unintended signals were sent to the troops by casual gestures or accidental movements. The upwards-pointing spear indicated that the battle was still in its initial phase.

2

The number of angry priests at the top of the tower, as well as behind the gate and on the walls on either side, swelled rapidly. The booming of the battle-drums and the wailing of the bagpipes pulled in the priests from all over the temple much like the carcase of a dead goat attracts hungry vermin within range of its stench. But the priests were so seething with fury at the thought that foreigners had come to defile their temple that no organised response was possible. A few priests on the wall threw spears at the invaders, but they were too frantic to aim properly, and before any arrows from the agitated priests on the tower and along the walls could find their targets most of the *preliminary attack force* had thrown their torches at the foot of the gate and ran back, to melt away into the little grove or disappear behind the boulders beyond the ramp. The rapidly increasing throng of angry priests grew frustrated and impatient and several arguments broke out as to whether they should wait for orders or push open the burning gate and pursue the attackers down the ramp:

"Let's catch them before they get away!"

"We must wait for Khaur!"

"We can't wait for Khaur – the foreigners will escape!"

"We *must* wait for Khaur."

"That noise is driving me insane! I want to kill the men who are banging on the drums!"

"Me too, but we must wait for Khaur!"

The arguments were replaced by cries of dismay when the flames that licked their way up the exterior of the gate reached the narrow gap between the portals and the top of the supporting frame.

When he was satisfied that the fire would do its work Artaxias pointed his spear towards the ground with a crisp movement. The drums and bagpipes stopped abruptly and in the sudden silence the few men of the *preliminary attack force* who were still on the ramp slid down the sides and disappeared into the darkness.

Khaur had reluctantly accepted the goddess's warning of an impending Hittite attack – the goddess was *never* wrong – but he had not lost his conviction that the temple was impregnable. Was the future not like the past? No invader had ever set foot within the Amalishah temple, so why should things change now? The missive he sent the king asking for troops to help defend the temple had been half-hearted and unduly apologetic, and although he had ordered the storing of provisions – like the goddess had ordered – he had not seen any need to reinforce the gates. At the urging of other senior priests he had agreed to have piles of swords, spears and arrows placed at strategic locations around the temple and, as an afterthought, the younger priests had been told to carry their weapons at all times. But Khaur had considered these preparations to be unnecessary disruptions of the temple's routine, and after two moons he had decided that the *foreigners* must have changed their minds. Perhaps they had come to know that Khaur had asked the king to send troops to strengthen the temple's defences, or perhaps they had come to understand that the temple was invincible.

The lesser priests and priestesses were not so sure that the temple was invincible and the goddess's warning had given them, for the first time, a taste of fear. They had all heard gruesome tales of isolated temples that had fallen prey to wild nomadic tribes or foreign adventurers. But the sense of fear, although acute, was novel and unfamiliar, and a fear that is not constantly fed sits loosely on the human psyche and can be reasoned away: *Surely* the High Priest was right when he said that the foreigners had changed their minds? *Surely* foreigners would not cross the wastelands to attack a temple that was famous for its fortifications? *Surely* the king had ignored Khaur's request for reinforcements because he knew that no attack was forthcoming? And so the *fear* of an attack, the *terror* of being annihilated in a wilderness so remote that no help was likely to arrive, had gradually died away as the cycles of the moon passed and no attack came. Three moons after the goddess's warning the younger priests stopped carrying their weapons because the sight of temple officials carrying spears and swords unsettled the pilgrims; the provisions that had been stored were scattered; the animals that had been kept in their pens were released and left to roam freely because this made it easier for the priests to feed them. The spears and arrows that had been stashed in strategic locations found their way back to the temple's arsenal or the private quarters of the priests.

3

When Khaur was told that the First Gate was under attack his first concern was to ensure that the temple treasures were systematically collected and concealed. All the young priests he could find were ordered to empty the shrines and living quarters of all that was valuable and even the life-size statue of the goddess in Khaur's bedroom was removed and hidden. In the panic the statue suffered a small scratch on the right ankle. Khaur's fatal error was not to have any large water containers placed near the wooden gates, or indeed anywhere else, so that very little could be done about the fires which were destined to consume everything that was combustible in the temple. As the gate burned, a few men and women frantically pulled water from the wells to quench the fire, but the water that was thrown onto the portals from the adjacent walls was too little and came too late.

Before long the gate was burning uncontrollably and the top of the guard tower was enveloped in black fumes. The priests on the tower could not abide the smoke and climbed down, coughing convulsively. When they reached the ground most of them abandoned their bows and took to their spears as they joined the priests who stood or crouched menacingly behind the burning gate. Meanwhile, without a thought of a possible attack at the Second Gate, panic-stricken priests from all over the temple took hold of their weapons and rushed to support those who waited behind the burning gate for any attackers foolish enough to enter. They waited with swords drawn and spears pointing at the gate, ready to face the invaders in hand-to-hand combat. This was what Khaur, at the command of the goddess, had specifically told them not to do, but such was their zeal that they believed they could stop any number of attackers, no matter what their weapons or fighting skills. The lesson of the blackmetal sword had not been learnt, and the possibility that the forty men who attacked the gate was not the whole of the invading force did not occur to anyone in authority.

The sky was starting to show the orange-and-pink harbingers of dawn when the fire had so weakened the massive wooden frame that it could no longer sustain the bulk of the portals. With a groan of tortured wood the frame gave way and the whole structure crashed down, scattering the priests. The portals and their supporting frame became a pile of burning timber from which rose a plume of tiny embers that engulfed the tower like a cloud of fireflies. The priests behind the gate quickly recovered from the shock and rallied to roar in defiance, daring the invaders to pass through the flames and face their swords, but the invaders did not respond to the challenge. They seemed to have dissolved in the semi-darkness of the predawn light and only the tiny figures of the three commanders could be seen standing on their rocks, lit by the glare of the fire, like statues on their pedestals, indifferent to the events at the top of the ramp.

"Where is Khaur?" shouted one of the senior priests who had joined the throng. He felt the fury and frustration of those around him but did not have the authority to order the men to push the burning gate aside and rush out to destroy the invaders. His cry was taken up by others:

"Where is Khaur?"

"Where is our High Priest?"

"Is Khaur with the goddess?" asked the senior priest.

"No. I heard she is alone with Neera and young Hasha!"

The senior priest looked away and shook his head.

"The foreigners will escape if we don't chase them now!" said a muscular acolyte.

"There is nothing I can do," said the senior priest.

The frustration of the mob of priests grew apace.

"The accursed foreigners are gone!"

"Ayah! They've done their mischief and left!"

"What were they?" someone asked.

"They were Hittites!" someone answered, "like the wretches who came to the temple a few moons ago!"

"They're not gone," said an acolyte who stood at the front, close to the pile of blazing wood, "the three who were standing on the rocks are still there!"

"Where are the others?"

"The cowards are hiding somewhere!"

"No, they're waiting for something!"

"What are they waiting for?"

"**They are waiting for the fire to burn itself out!**" answered an authoritative voice behind them. It was the High Priest himself, who had finally come to take command of the defence at the gate now that the temple treasures had been safely hidden. The priests who had been waiting noisily were suddenly hushed. Khaur pushed through the crowd and stopped less than a dozen paces from the burning pile. The priests backed away respectfully and waited in awe for him to speak.

"**They cannot get in and we cannot get out easily while the fire burns,**" shouted Khaur in a voice loud enough to be heard above the roar of the fire. "**We vastly outnumber them, and if they dare enter we shall kill them all except for the youngest, whom we shall take alive as gifts for our goddess!**"

There were enthusiastic cries of approval. The priests liked the idea of capturing sacrificial victims themselves rather than having to wait for prisoners to be delivered by the king's raiding parties. They grinned at each other and exchanged encouraging words:

"My spear is thirsty for Hittite blood!"

"My sword has long been waiting for a time like this!"

Perhaps because he had been unceremoniously awakened from his sleep, or perhaps because he had become emotionally part of the bloodthirsty mob that surrounded him, Khaur decided to ignore the advice of the goddess and let the priests fight the invaders any way they pleased. After all, his priests did not have the opportunity to kill *foreigners* very often. But he had not forgotten what the goddess had said: "*When the Hittites attack the temple, my priests must not fight them hand to hand... They may shoot at them with arrows, throw spears and stones at them, do anything they can but they must not get close enough for the Hittites to use their swords!*" The memory of the goddess's words brought Khaur a sense of foreboding, but he managed to suppress it: *I feel that way because I have never disobeyed my goddess. But my priests will deal effortlessly with this small number of foreigners, and after we kill them we shall talk about our victory for a long time. I shall order the construction of a new gate and have it decorated with the heads of their leaders!* Khaur's faith in the temple's defensive capabilities had not been shaken, yet the remains of the gate continued to burn, although less fiercely than before.

The mob, with Khaur and some other senior priests standing among them, waited with barely controlled impatience as the fire relentlessly consumed what remained of the gate. But as the fire slowly

their men massacre the invaders shouted enthusiastically in support. The priests who were closest to the Hittites threw spears, axes and even their swords at the retreating enemy, expecting to retrieve them and use them again. The priests who were further behind and could not grapple with the attackers gleefully trampled any Hittite bodies that lay in their path, or else stabbed them repeatedly with whatever weapons they carried. The Hittite retreat appeared to be a complete rout as the survivors fought in disarray and apparent desperation against the priests who erupted in growing numbers from what had been the First Gate. Over a hundred and sixty priests pressed the remnants of the *preliminary attack force* back down the ramp.

"Urdzhe and his men performed their task well," said Artaxias grimly, "This is when we shall see whether the priests have chariots or other reinforcements from their king."

"Yes my prince," said Her-unt, "If there are regular troops or chariots in the temple now would be the time to bring them out, to slaughter our men before they can scatter!"

But no chariots or Assyrian troops appeared, and when the retreating Hittites with the pursuing priests had almost reached the foot of the ramp Artaxias raised his spear and held it horizontally above his head with both hands. The big drums and the bagpipes started again and what was left of the *preliminary attack force* turned viciously upon their pursuers. The priests were surprised but they did not slow down and they shouted all the louder but then, with a sound like that of a multitude of frightened birds rising into the air, a volley of arrows flew from the grove in a high arc that passed over the Hittite infantry and descended upon the rearmost priests. The priests in the forefront, who had been so confident of catching and slaughtering their fleeing enemy, looked behind them and then at the grove in consternation.

"There are bowmen in the grove!" shouted a priest from the front, almost at the foot of the ramp.

The cry was taken up by others just as a second volley of arrows was unleashed at those behind them:

"They are trying to cut us off!"

The second volley had barely done its work when the grove and boulders came alive with heavily armed and armoured men. The seven *action groups* of heavy infantry that had lain in hiding surged forward to join what was left of the *preliminary attack force* and engage the confused and panic-stricken defenders. The priests, most of whom had no armour other than breastplates, were suddenly confronted with experienced soldiers whose numbers were comparable to their own. Even so, they fought bravely with fanaticism and panic-induced ferocity, but they were no match for the trained and disciplined heavy infantry. They fought and died, and their bronze swords and bronze-tipped spears bent or broke whenever they clashed with the blackmetal weapons of the attackers. The *preliminary attack force* had suffered heavy casualties, but the fresh heavy infantry that had been concealed in the grove and behind the rocks ensured that less than thirty priests managed to escape and pass back through the gate they had so unwisely cleared.

7

It was late afternoon when Urdzhe and some of the other *action group* leaders came to ask Artaxias for instructions. The prince and the two commanders were inspecting the remains of the gate and the now empty fortifications at the base of the guard tower.

"The temple is ours," said Urdzhe. "All the buildings are burning except for the large round one. The priests who survived the fighting are in there and our men are searching for anyone who may be hiding in the ruins. We have lost over seventy men and many have been wounded. Some of the wounds are serious."

"Did any of the priests try to surrender?"

"Nobody tried to surrender, and we killed all we could find, including old men and women. It was not pleasant, but we released all of the temple prisoners."

"What state are they in?"

"They appear to have been well fed and some tried to join us in the fighting. There are no Hittites among them, and none of the young men we found understand our language. Three have broken arms and two are without eyes; they could not help us."

"Are you sure there were none of our people among the captives?"

"There were no Hittites, my prince."

The prince's face hardened. After a deep breath he asked: "Are the physicians tending the wounded?"

"Yes my prince. Our dead have all been brought out and are ready for burial."

"How many young children did you find?"

Urdzhe shook his head and one of the *action group* leaders who had come with him said: "We found not a single child!"

"That is strange," said Her-unt.

"They may be with the priests who retreated into the palace of the monster," said Norr.

"You must be right," said the prince, "There were many children in the temple when we first came here."

The thought of killing children was repugnant to Artaxias, who had a child of his own, but he knew that it was necessary to leave no survivors except children who were too young to remember the destruction of their homes and families. These would be taken back to Hattusas to be allocated homes and brought up as Hittites. The prince spoke bitterly: "Three of the *action groups* will bury our dead far beyond the ramp, in the direction from which we came, putting no markers on the graves. When that is done these three *action groups* will join the rest of the force who are now in the temple."

"Will there be no ceremony for the burial of our dead?" asked the *action group* leader.

"No," replied the prince, "Ceremonies take time and we must leave as soon as our task is done. Appropriate ceremonies to remember the dead will be performed when we return home, but none of us must be here if anyone comes, be they Assyrian troops or unarmed pilgrims. And we must make sure that we leave nothing behind that would tell who destroyed the temple."

"Do the orders regarding children still stand, my prince?" asked Urdzhe. Despite his long experience as a soldier he shared Artaxias' feelings regarding the killing of innocents.

"Yes. If there are children, spare only those who are too young to remember this day. And if you find it hard to carry out such orders remember your flayed comrade! Remember the rags stuffed into his mouth!"

"What about any food and drink that we find?"

"Help yourselves to anything you find but waste no time looking for things!"

The *action group* leaders returned to their men, who were busy setting fire to or pulling down what remained of the temple buildings. Only the *Palace of the Goddess* was left untouched. The mud-brick huts and small shrines that were scattered about the temple were easy to pull down, and their draperies and rugs burned fiercely. The more solid temple structures were not so easy to dismantle, for they were made of cut stone or baked brick, but they were held together by wood that burned readily and, once the fires had weakened the wooden frames, the supporting beams buckled and the buildings collapsed. The crackling of the fire was like the sound of a storm, interrupted only by the occasional crash of a collapsing building. The Hittites did not bother to pull down the defensive walls, nor did they spend time looking for treasure. There was, after all, the possibility that an Assyrian relief army was on its way, and in the waning afternoon light the smoke of the burning temple would be visible from a great distance.

8

There were no defenders left in the streets or in the ruins of the buildings and the smell of burning wood was everywhere. Women and old men had been hacked down as they ran down the streets or stood at bay, pathetically wielding what weapons they had, trying to defend their homes. As the prince looked down at the dead who lay scattered everywhere he thought: *I feel more like a butcher than a soldier! The monster is the cause of all this, and the blindness of these people who did her bidding!* His hatred for the goddess was like a sharp knife in his stomach.

When he reached the *Palace of the Goddess* he found that it was already surrounded by his troops, as the three *action groups* who had buried the dead had returned. Some of the men were holding goats and terrified oxen that lowed mournfully. Among his men Artaxias noticed a small number of armourless wide-eyed youths with bewildered expressions, as though they had awakened from a bad dream into a situation they did not fully comprehend: *These must be the released prisoners, I wonder what their mothers will say when they see them again – assuming their mothers are still alive!* The youths stayed together and seemed reluctant to mingle with the Hittite infantry. Artaxias nodded at them and they nodded back, unaware of who he was.

Isolated from the rest of the buildings, the *Palace of the Goddess* was untouched by the flames and stood majestically above the invaders, beautiful and awe-inspiring in the light of the late afternoon and the red glare of the fires.

"Are you sure all resistance around the temple has been dealt with?" Artaxias asked some *action group* leaders who had come to report on the last stages of the fighting.

"There are no survivors outside this large building," replied one of the men.

"Did anyone try to leave by the South Gate or over the walls?"

"Yes, my prince, but none escaped."

"And we have had relatively few casualties," continued another, an old campaigner, "this is the easiest battle I have ever been in!"

"This battle is not over yet!" snapped the prince, "The monster is still alive!"

"It would be a pity to destroy such a fine building," said Norr as he looked with evident admiration at the *Palace of the Goddess*, which towered above them.

"How many priests are inside?" Artaxias asked the *action group* leaders, too concerned with the demands of the moment to appreciate the beauty of the *Palace of the Goddess*.

"We don't know, but we chased no more than thirty or forty, though there might have been others already inside. All the surviving priests are in there. Some women and children may be in there too, but we cannot know for sure. We have seen many women, including many priestesses, but we have not seen any children yet."

Artaxias nodded grimly and said: "Bring an interpreter to call out a priest."

The interpreters were somewhere at the back, with the physicians and other non-combatants, but one was eventually found and brought to the *Palace of the Goddess*.

9

The setting sun was almost down to the horizon when Khaur himself came out of the small door of the *Palace of the Goddess*. He looked dazed and exhausted beyond words. Artaxias felt a pang of pity, but it was quickly dispelled by the memory of the flayed infantryman.

"We meet again, High Priest," said Artaxias solemnly through the interpreter.

"As you say," replied the High Priest, "We meet again." He spoke mechanically, without emotion.

"Your King has not protected you, and your goddess shall die soon!"

"Your success, so far, is only because *I* have failed her," replied the old man, "*you* deserve no credit for this and she is blameless!"

"I wish to strike a bargain with you," said Artaxias. "I cannot promise you or your priests and priestesses your lives because of all the evil deeds you have allowed, but if you deliver us your goddess I shall spare all the very young children who are with you. They will live among us and I promise you, by all the gods and by my honour as a prince of my people, that they shall be loved and cared for no differently from our own children. We have not come here to bring carnage, but to put an end to your goddess."

"There are no women or children with us, foreigner," replied the High Priest, and he sneered as he said foreigner. "You have nothing to bargain with!" Despite the circumstances Khaur managed to regain some of his arrogance.

"Old man," said the prince patiently, "To lie at a time like this would displease the gods. I myself have seen many children the last time I was here. Since my men have not found any children they can only be with your priests, and therefore in danger. I shall therefore repeat my offer to you: If you bring out your very young children we shall spare them without exception provided you deliver your goddess to us. We shall take the children to our homes and care for them like our own. Otherwise, some young children who stay with your priests may inadvertently die during the fighting. Know that we shall not return to our homes as long as the monster Amalishah still lives!"

"The last time I saw you," replied Khaur, "you were dressed like a beggar. This time you are acting like those men who speak nonsense to make people laugh. I told you, foreigner, that there are no children among us. And what makes you think you will return to your homes? Even as we speak a large army from our king is on its way to the temple! You will die soon, Hittite, though I may die first. As for our goddess, whose name when spoken by your foul mouth is an insult to all the gods, she shall shatter you and your men like clay dolls!"

The prince paid no attention to the insults. "So be it," he said, "Go back inside and get ready to defend your goddess."

Khaur bowed mockingly and withdrew into the *Palace of the Goddess*.

10

Artaxias turned to Her-unt and Norr. "It has been easy so far," he said, "But it will be harder now. This huge building has many windows but they are too small and too high to climb through. The only entrance is the one door, which is too narrow to allow more than two or three men to enter at a time."

"It is even too narrow to shoot arrows through," added Norr, "especially as it is too dark inside to see anything."

"Anyone who goes past the door," said Her-unt, "will not go far. The priests are waiting in there like spiders on their webs!"

"Why don't we just set fire to the building?" said Norr.

"That is a coward's way!" exclaimed one of the *action group* leaders who stood beside the commanders. He did not mean to be disrespectful to Norr, but he was flushed with the excitement of the easy victory. The prince could not ignore Norr's comment.

"Setting fire to the building may not kill the monster," he said, speaking to Norr, "remember that she lives at the bottom of a pit."

"You are right, my prince," said Norr.

"What pit?" asked the *action group* leader.

"You have not listened while we debated the attack!" admonished the prince curtly.

"So listen carefully now," said Her-unt, "The monster lives at the bottom of a deep hole that is supposed to lead down from this building. We don't know how deep the hole is. If we set fire to the round building the heat from the flames may not reach her and she may survive and come out unharmed after we are gone."

"And if the building is set on fire the flames shall take a long time to subside," said Norr. "That will delay our entrance. So what should we do, my prince?"

"We must get in *somehow*," replied the prince, "and fight our way until we reach her. We shall only be sure she is dead when we hold her head in our hands!"

"Let us wait until tomorrow then," said Her-unt. "I don't like fighting when the night is upon us. Neither do the men. I don't believe this talk of a rescuing army."

"I don't believe that an Assyrian army is on its way either," said the prince after the briefest of pauses, "but tomorrow *could* bring a relief force, if there is one, closer to us. We should go down into the pit as soon as possible and kill the monster. It does not matter if the night is upon us, as it will be dark in the pit anyway. The men shall fight better while they are still hot with the excitement of battle. We cannot wait. Let the bowmen fire their arrows through the narrow door."

The assault on the *Palace of the Goddess* began with a hail of arrows aimed at the darkness behind the door.

There was no response.

"Where are the priests?" exclaimed Norr.

"On either side of the door, of course!" replied Her-unt.

11

"The first man to enter that dark entrance will die," said one of the bowmen.

Artaxias knew that the man was right: *And the second, and the third and many more of the men who shall pass through that narrow opening shall die. How can we take a building with a narrow door without destroying the building?* The prince turned to Her-unt, who was busy studying the structure of the *Palace of the Goddess*.

"As we suspected, shooting arrows at the darkness is useless. Do you have any ideas, Chariot Leader?"

"This is a very tall building," said Her-unt, "with stone walls all the way to the top. I think that the ring of columns that surrounds the building is to help support the weight of the upper part."

"They are made of wood but are too thick to be purely decorative," said the prince, "Is that important?"

Her-unt nodded. "From what I can see through the door the walls are too thin to carry all the weight. I suspect there is another ring of columns inside. So if we leave the columns alone we can enlarge the entrance without having the top of the building fall on our heads!"

"Yes! We need a battering ram!" exclaimed the prince.

Artaxias ordered his men to search the collapsed buildings for a heavy wooden beam to be used as a battering ram. This was not hard to find, for although most of the structures had collapsed as they burned, the smoke and dust of the falling masonry had extinguished some of the flames before they had consumed all the wood. There were plenty of massive wooden beams amidst the ruins of what had once been the living quarters of the senior priests.

Before long a makeshift battering ram smashed repeatedly into the mud-brick walls on either side of the door and the aperture became wide enough to allow many men to enter together. As Her-unt had predicted, the building stood firm. The fading rays of the setting sun could not illuminate the interior, but through the enlarged aperture the Hittites could just see the inside of the building by the light of the fires behind them. It was a large round hall with an inner ring of wooden columns. At the back of the hall, opposite the aperture, huddled the priests. Some were standing and some were kneeling. Those who stood held their spears pointed at the enemy and those who knelt held bows with arrows ready to be loosed. Between the priests and the Hittites, at the exact centre of the round floor of the building, was a circle of blackness.

"That black hole must be the pit of the monster!" exclaimed Norr.

"It would seem so," said Her-unt.

Artaxias remained silent. There could not be more than sixty priests left alive, less than that according to the reports of the men who had chased them here. Yet they remained defiant although they knew that their lives would be ended soon. *This will be an execution, not a battle,* he thought, *an execution of brave men!* At the sight of the priests the Hittite troops started talking among themselves but Artaxias signalled them to be quiet. Somehow, the occasion demanded silence. The priests must have shared the feeling for they made no sound as they waited.

"Why don't they shoot their arrows?" asked Norr. "Some of our men are within range!"

"They will," replied Her-unt, "Once we get inside."

"I won't sacrifice any more of our men," said Artaxias. He turned to his troops: "Infantrymen, use your bows. Fifty bowmen. Two volleys."

As the bowmen took up their positions the priests quickly realised what was going to happen. Before the Hittite bowmen could release their bows some two dozen arrows flew out of the building's enlarged aperture. The arrows were fired haphazardly and none found a living target; most were caught on the Hittites' shields. Almost immediately fifty Hittite bows twanged in response, followed by another fifty a few moments later. Some of the priests fell and the remainder vanished down the pit.

"Send in five bowmen with two torch-carriers," said Artaxias to Her-unt. "I want to know what lies inside that black hole!" The priests had carried no torches.

12

The seven men rushed off to enter the *Palace of the Goddess*. They were soon back.

"Well?" said the prince.

"The steps are very steep and the light of our torches could not show us how deep the pit is! The priests are somewhere far below. We could not see them or hear them."

"Tell me about the pit!"

"There are winding steps leading down into the blackness. They wind round and round many times, around an open shaft that is wide enough for a man to fall through. Each step can hold two men, maybe three. The steps are very steep and narrow. Our bows would not be very effective down there because an armed man may assault a bowman ere he has time to pull his bow a second time."

"How far down do the steps go?" asked Artaxias.

"I don't know!"

"Then go back alone and drop a torch down the shaft. Find out how deep the pit is!"

The man nodded and obeyed, the other six rejoined the others who now stood behind their officers, waiting impatiently.

Soon the man returned. "What did you find?" asked the prince.

"I dropped my torch down the shaft and it was a long time before it hit the ground."

"So the pit is very deep," muttered Her-unt. The prince was silent.

"We can smoke them out," said Norr.

"No," said Artaxias. "The smoke shall impede us more than it will discomfort them. I want the head of that monster quickly. An Assyrian relief army could be on its way!"

"Surely you do not believe what the High Priest said?" asked Her-unt incredulously.

"I do not believe it, but although a relief force is unlikely it is not impossible."

Her-unt murmured something inaudible, but before any action could be taken, the *Palace of the Goddess* suddenly began to spout thick jets of black smoke.

"Akh!" exclaimed Norr, "The priests have decided to burn themselves!"

"Not necessarily!" said the prince, suddenly worried. This

development was unexpected. "We don't know what lies at the bottom of the pit. There may be a place for them to shelter from the fire. I think we should…" But then the smoke suddenly grew thicker and there arose a deep lugubrious moan, like the bellow of a distressed colossal bull beneath the ground. The sound rose to a muffled roar only to fall for a short time before growing louder again, and so it went on, rising and falling, and each time the volume of the roar reached its peak the *Palace of the Goddess* exuded huge billows of foul-smelling smoke.

9

THE ASSAULT ON THE LAIR OF THE GODDESS

1

LIKE THE TORTURED exhalations of a gargantuan beast in agony, the monstrous bellow rose and fell in tune with the brown-black smoke that gushed rhythmically from every orifice of the *Palace of the Goddess*. The sound was at its loudest just before the jets of smoke reached their peak, but then it declined to rise again at the next cycle. The smoke gathered above the *Palace of the Goddess* and spiralled upwards in a twisted column that glowed red and black in the fading light of the late afternoon.

Her-unt and Norr were standing next to the prince, subdued and mesmerised by the billowing smoke and thunderous sound. "I see smoke but no flames," said Her-unt, as though speaking to himself.

"This dreadful sound is making the ground shake as though with fear," whimpered Norr, "What is it?"

"I don't know," replied Her-unt, "But the sound is not coming from within the round building, it is coming from somewhere deep beneath it!" The *Palace of the Goddess* was plainly not on fire, unlike the living quarters of the senior priests, the ruins of which were burning furiously.

"The noise is affecting our men," remarked the prince grimly. The infantrymen who had so confidently closed in on the *Palace of the Goddess* a short while earlier were now pulling back and shrinking within themselves in terror. Some had dropped their weapons and shields so as to cover their ears with their hands. There were furtive whispers of: "It must be the goddess!", "She is angry!", "May our gods help us!" The men were patently in danger of panicking. "It is the ghosts of the dead priests!" said a bald man who was standing close

172

to the three commanders, "They howl together because they have gathered to defend their goddess!"

"What? What did you say?" Norr asked, "I cannot hear you!" Norr was not sure he had heard correctly because he was unable to see the logic in the man's statement. The bald man waved his hand to show that what he had said was not worth repeating.

Artaxias looked at his men in dismay. They had pulled back not only from the circular building but also from their leaders. Artaxias interpreted the withdrawal as a sign that discipline was about to dissolve: *An army without discipline is an armed mob!* Unable to think clearly because of the deafening bellow, he stared at the *Palace of the Goddess* and, as in a dream, relived an episode from his youth:

He was a young officer-in-training, part of the garrison in a prosperous seaside town far to the South-West. Early in the morning the townspeople had awakened to find a large band of renegade soldiers outside the town's main gate. The renegades were banging on the panels of the gates with the hilts of their weapons and loudly demanding that the gates be opened. They were from several nations and their raucous shouts were in different languages. The town's authorities were soon notified and, not much later, a timid little man from the town council arrived and politely asked the renegades what they wanted.

The renegades demanded the surrender of the communally-owned gold and jewels that was stored for safekeeping in the palace of the governor. They promised to kill all the men in the town and inflict the direst punishments on the women and children if the gold and jewels were not handed over within two days.

The governor and the town council, which was composed mostly of wealthy merchants, could not agree on how to respond but eventually they hired some priests to conduct a public prayer to the god Kumarbis, the father of the gods, to implore him to save the town. However, the commander of the town's garrison, a grizzled man of some fifty years, climbed the wall beside the main gate and curtly told the renegades to go away, adding that he might have taken their demands more seriously if they bathed more often.

Early the next day, two young girls who had unwisely stepped outside the town's defensive wall to do their washing in the stream were beaten and raped. Some of the townspeople blamed the commander of the garrison for what happened to the girls and that evening a mob of angry townsmen gathered in the square before the governor's palace. They carried knives and woodmen's axes and threatened to burn down the palace if the governor did not agree immediately to deliver the gold and jewels to the renegades.

Eventually the great door of the governor's palace opened and the mob fell silent, expecting to see the governor come out and tell them that the treasure was ready to be handed over. But it was not the governor who stepped out, it was the commander of the garrison, and the mob shook their fists and howled with renewed fury. Men who only a week earlier had offered the men of the garrison fruit and honeycakes were now swearing that they would kill the commander and everyone in the palace if the renegades were not given the gold and the jewels. The commander spoke to them calmly: "Good friends," he said, "I understand your anger and I promise you that our girls shall be avenged. The renegades shall not enter the town. So please go home." His words were greeted with the accusation that he valued gold above the lives of their women and children. The commander explained that if the town handed over the gold and the jewels the renegades would only escalate their demands, but the angry townspeople threatened to kill him if he did not get out of the way. Seeing that the mob was not to be placated the garrison commander issued a final warning, as humbly as he could, but his words only incensed the mob further and they surged towards him with their weapons raised.

The commander stood his ground, hoping that the mob would relent, but they did not stop and at the last moment he drew his sword. His action was the signal for two action groups of heavy infantry to emerge from behind the governor's palace and stand behind him in battle formation. The mob hesitated, but when they saw that they greatly outnumbered the infantrymen they surged forward again. The garrison met the mob head on, and Artaxias found himself swinging his scythe-sword against people he knew. Yet as the townspeople smashed repeatedly into the phalanx of heavy infantry he felt neither remorse nor regrets: the presence of his comrades beside him in ordered ranks quelled all emotion. Almost unconsciously he hacked at the body of a blacksmith or a baker or a weaver or street vendor, only to see a look of surprise and recognition flit past the man's features when the realisation of impending death washed away his fury. The mob was dispersed without difficulty, with the garrison suffering no casualties, and that night a surprise sortie led by the commander himself killed the renegades' leaders and scattered the rest. The brief scuffle with the townsmen and the skirmish with the renegades taught Artaxias a lesson he would never forget: Although the men of the garrison were heavily outnumbered in both encounters they *had carried the day because of their **discipline!***

2

Yet now his men were on the verge of forgetting that they were soldiers. They stood stupefied by the demonic sound that issued from the *Palace of the Goddess*, awed by what they believed to be a supernatural manifestation. Norr was visibly shaking while Her-unt looked preoccupied and thoughtful. Artaxias stepped forward: *I must show my men that I am not afraid!* Facing his men he shouted: "This is just a trick by the priests to frighten us! There is nothing in that round building that could hurt us. Remember who you are and why you are here!"

The thunderous noise made it unlikely that any but the closest of his men could hear him, but they could see the confidence with which he spoke and some of those who had dropped their weapons and shields picked them up. However, most of them continued to stare at the pillar of smoke that rose above the *Palace of the Goddess*, terrified by the repetitive subterranean bellow. Artaxias was about to resume his exhortations when the sound suddenly stopped. The smoke jets vanished and were replaced by idle wisps that floated gently upwards.

"That didn't last long!" said Artaxias with relief. "A thirsty horse drinks its fill in less time than that!"

"But what living thing makes such a sound?" said Norr. He was still trembling.

"Perhaps it was not a living thing," said Artaxias. "Earthquakes sometimes make sounds that are almost as loud!"

The men started to move back towards the *Palace of the Goddess*. "They are becoming men again," said Artaxias to Her-unt and Norr. But Her-unt had observed how the loudness of the bellow had varied with the intensity of the smoke. While they all stood staring, half expecting the baleful sound to start again, he said quietly to the prince: "I think I know what that was!"

"It was not their goddess?" murmured Norr.

"Will it start again?" asked Artaxias.

"No it won't," said Her-unt. "The fire in the pit has run out of fuel!"

"So *what* was that noise?" asked Artaxias, his curiosity taking over.

Her-unt half-laughed. "I was once at a blackmetal foundry," he said. "To melt the ore it is necessary to make it very hot and sometimes there is a very tall chimney above the fire to suck up the air. If the chimney is not properly built it sometimes shakes and rumbles like the breathing of a monster when the fire is lit. The priests lit a fire at the bottom of the pit and the shaft acted like a badly built chimney!"

"I have never heard of a chimney that makes a sound like *that!*" said Norr.

"Only very tall chimneys can make a rumbling sound," replied Her-unt, "and only if they are not properly built. The pit that leads to the goddess must be very deep."

"Why would a chimney sound like that?" asked Norr.

"What is a flute but a small chimney with air flowing through it?" said Her-unt, "If the pit that leads to the monster has the right shape, and if the fire at the bottom can bring in air fast enough, it would make a sound like that!"

"But a flute makes a high-pitched sound," said Norr.

"A giant flute could well bellow!" replied Her-unt with a smile.

"Akh! So the pit became a giant flute!" Norr thought the idea was funny and his amusement helped steady his nerves.

Artaxias put his hand on Her-unt's shoulder. "If you are right, Chariot Leader, then the priests had a very hot time down there. They must have cooked both themselves and the monster!"

"Perhaps not," said Her-unt. "The smoke was coming up and out of the pit. Air must be coming in from somewhere else to whatever is down there. The priests would have been safe if they stood between the fire and the place where the air came in."

"Then there must be another entrance!" exclaimed Norr. "The priests and the monster may have escaped while the pit rumbled!"

The prince muttered something very rude but then quickly said to Norr: "Any priests who escaped from the temple would be stopped by the *action groups* waiting around the hill!" He turned once again to the men. "That was not the voice of their goddess!" he shouted. "The priests must have lit a great fire and the fire pushed air up the pit. It was air rushing up the pit that made the noise. The dreadful bellow will not return!"

Most of the men seemed relieved and a few started to drift towards their officers, but some still had doubts in their eyes.

"We can no longer ignore the call of our sacrificed brethren for vengeance!" continued Artaxias, "I am going down into the pit to kill the monster." The men seemed unsure, the unearthly bellow had been beyond anything they had experienced before.

176

"I wish to come with you," said Norr, "although I am as frightened as a little girl in the dark!"

"Thank you Norr," said Artaxias, "Only the brave man acknowledges his fear yet manages to push it aside. But you must stay behind. We don't know what is waiting for us down there, and you will be needed to navigate on the return trip!"

"May I come with you, my prince?" asked Her-unt, although he knew that he was not as agile with his sword as he used to be. Artaxias looked at him steadily and said: "Old friend, if your understanding of this is wrong then it is best you stay behind too. If I don't return, Norr will need a wise companion. If your understanding is right then we have nothing to fear but the smoke and the heat!"

"Don't forget the evil priests!" said Her-unt sharply.

"I am not forgetting the priests," said Artaxias with a smile, "And I will also remember that they will fight with great zeal when we get close to the monster!"

Artaxias turned again to his men: "If the goddess can be killed, we shall kill her! Who will come with me? The monster who drank the blood of your brethren is down there! Shall we let her laugh at our fear? I need no more than *one action group*!"

"Just *one action group* against all the priests?" someone asked.

"One should be enough," answered the prince. "The fighting space down the pit is probably narrow and if we are too many we shall get in each other's way!" Some of the men nodded and Artaxias singled out an *action group* leader.

"You!" he called, "How many men have you got?"

"Only fourteen, my prince. I lost three men during the attack on the gate and two in the temple."

"Your name is Berek, is it not?"

"Yes, my prince."

"Well, Berek, choose six good men to supplement your fourteen and come with me!"

Berek was grim and humourless, but he was a good fighter and completely reliable.

When the twenty men had assembled, the prince said: "Leave your spears behind and take only your swords, your shields, and your bows and arrows. Four of you shall be torchbearers and will carry several torches. It will be very dark down there! We shall go down the steps in a 'caterpillar'!"

"Eh… what is that, my prince?" asked one of the men timidly.

177

He was young and knew little of battle terminology. Artaxias smiled at him: "For those who don't know what a 'caterpillar' is, let me tell you… it is the best way to fight when going down a narrow incline, like a staircase! We form rows of men with bows and arrows but with their swords sheathed; as many men in each row as can fit on one step. As they go down the steps they hold only their bows, but they drop their bows if they need to use their swords. Among every three or four rows of men there is a torchbearer, who will bring light to make the darkness flee! When we see the enemy the first row of bowmen will release their arrows together, then they step aside to allow the next row to step down and release their arrows together, and so on. This way no bowman stays exposed while he is fitting an arrow to his bow, and we move down quickly! Do you all understand?"

One of the men said: "We were told that the stairs of the pit are narrow and winding. Shields take a lot of room and yet more room is needed to draw a bow. What if each step can take only two men? That would be only two arrows in each volley."

"We adapt to the circumstances. If there are only two men on each step then the first *two* rows of bowmen may loose their arrows together," said the prince, "If the steps are narrow we only need to make sure that the man on the inside is not pushed down the shaft!" The men laughed without enthusiasm.

Each torchbearer carried five unlit torches in addition to his sword and shield, but his sword was sheathed and his bow was slung across his back, with his arrows. The rest of the men attached their shields to their lower arms so as to leave their hands free to hold a bow. Their quivers and swords dangled by their sides. The prince and the *action group* were ready to enter the *Palace of the Goddess* when Her-unt said: "Let us exchange swords, my prince. Yours is good but mine has seen many battles and has never failed me!"

A *lucky* sword was a precious gift, and the prince accepted the exchange gratefully. As he was given the weapon he said in a low voice: "If I do not return…" Her-unt interrupted him: "I know, my prince. I shall tell your uncle that his nephew died bravely!" Artaxias nodded and the old charioteer looked away, for he did not want the prince to see the tears in his eyes.

Artaxias entered the *Palace of the Goddess*, followed by twenty men. At the edge of the pit, each torchbearer lit one of his torches and held it in the hand that carried the shield. The unlit torches were pushed through their belts behind them so that they would not get in their way. "I shall descend the winding steps first!" said the prince.

3

Artaxias led the small party carefully down into the pit. Only two men at a time could descend the treacherous steps, encumbered as they were with their shields, torches and bows. All the surfaces were covered in black, sticky soot and the floor was slippery. As they descended the air became thick with acrid smoke and the men coughed uncontrollably.

"My eyes are full of smoke and I can hardly see!" said one of the men behind Artaxias.

"Be quiet!" ordered the prince sternly. "We must depend on our ears as well as our eyes!" The light of the torches extended only a short distance because of the winding steps that spiralled down the pit. As he carefully made his way down, Artaxias wondered at the strange writing that covered the curved wall of the pit. It was quite different from the usual Assyrian cuneiform, and the symbols were interspersed with little drawings, like the writing of the Egyptians.

The descent continued. There was no sign of the priests.

"Will these steps never end?" asked the man again.

"You talk too much!" someone said.

After what seemed an eternity the winding staircase opened up into a small hemispherical cavern at the bottom of the steps. The cavern was no more than twenty or twenty-five paces across, and the whole of its floor was covered with a high pile of ashes and burning embers. The priests had burnt every item of furniture and cloth they could find, and amongst the ashes and other detritus one could discern the charred remains of chairs, cabinets, even wooden ceremonial torches. The pile was still smouldering and several thin columns of smoke rose languidly up the shaft. Like the wall of the stairway, the wall and ceiling of the cavern were covered in oily soot.

On the other side of the ashes was the entrance to what seemed to be a low, narrow tunnel and here, illuminated by the glowing embers and the torches of the Hittites, waited the priests. Only five priests could be seen, standing close together, the rest stood behind them in the darkness of the tunnel. For some reason the priests carried no bows and were armed only with swords, shields and spears. *They must have left their bows behind!* thought Artaxias, *They are singularly inept fighters to bring spears to this narrow place!*

The Hittites were dazed from the smoke and their winding descent down the steep steps, but Artaxias was relieved to find that the priests had not escaped. "The enemy is before us!" he said, "Don't worry about the burning embers and the hot ashes: your boots can take the heat!" He was about to run over the hot pile when one of the priests hurled his spear. Because his eyes were smarting from the smoke and because the distance was so short, the prince was unable to dodge the missile. It went past his shield and struck him in the side. The prince dropped his sword and pulled out the spear with a grunt of pain. He threw the spear back at the priests before he collapsed on the steps but the throw was weak and the heavy spear fell into the glowing pile.

When the prince was struck the priests howled in glee, but before they could throw any more spears six bowmen released their arrows. Three of the priests who were at the entrance of the tunnel collapsed but before any others could come forward the Hittites swarmed down the steps and, in their fury, almost flew over the smouldering embers. The men in the vanguard were wielding their swords among the priests less than a heartbeat after the prince had fallen.

Only a few men could engage at a time due to the narrowness of the passage, and the long heavy spears of the priests were unsuited for fighting within the narrow confines of the tunnel. The priests fought bravely with the zeal of desperation, but they lacked the fighting skill of the men of the *action group* and were pushed back relentlessly down the tunnel, leaving a trail of dead and dying priests. All fought silently: only the clash of metal against metal could be heard, and the groans of dying men.

When the priests no longer posed a threat to the prince, two of the men returned to help him. Artaxias was half-lying on the bottom steps, clutching his side and coughing from the smoke. They carried him across the smouldering embers into the tunnel, where there was no smoke and only a gentle breeze of fresh air that flowed outwards. But Artaxias would not rest while his task remained undone.

"We must find the monster," he gasped, "She must not escape!"

One of the men looked at Artaxias' wound and said: "My prince, you need a physician urgently to close the wound and stem the blood!"

"I'm all right for now," gasped the prince. "Finish off the priests!"

The man looked back into the tunnel. "Almost all the priests in the tunnel have been dealt with," he said, "they are brave but they don't know how to fight and we are driving them back easily."

"Help me up then," husked Artaxias. The men helped him up and he staggered to his feet just as three more men came out of the tunnel. One of them said: "It is over, my prince."

"And the High Priest?" asked Artaxias, "Is he dead?" The pain in his side was excruciating and a stream of blood flowed down his leg.

"Yes, my prince. He did not fight but stood behind those who fought. He took his own life when the last defending priest fell."

"Casualties?"

"Only you, my prince. The priests knew little of fighting."

4

Protocol required that the leader walk ahead of his men when they entered a new place after a battle. Although the pain in his side almost made him lose consciousness, Artaxias managed to walk unassisted while his men stood respectfully out of his way. The prince knew he was losing a lot of blood, but with his jaw tightly clenched he managed to smile weakly as he took the lead. The men followed him silently, holding their swords in one hand and their shields and torches with the other. Their bows hung behind their backs, for they did not expect to use them. The 'caterpillar' had served its purpose and the torchbearers handed out lit torches to some of the men. Each torchbearer kept only one unlit torch in reserve.

The tunnel was strewn with the bodies of the priests. In the torchlight their skin looked pale and their blood looked black. Artaxias walked painfully around them, not wishing to touch them with his foot, for even in death priests commanded his respect. A short distance beyond the last of the priests he came upon the body of Khaur. The old man sat alone with his back against the wall of the tunnel, as though asleep. He had pushed his own dagger so deep into his solar plexus that only the hilt showed. The prince's anger towards the High Priest vanished as he bent forward to look down at the corpse. "Poor old man!" he said, and he thought: *You devoted your whole life to the monster and in the end she brought you only this!* But the most important task remained to be done. With great effort Artaxias straightened himself up. The movement caused the pain in his side to almost overwhelm him and he limped down the tunnel clutching his wound in an effort to stem the flow of blood. He did not see the end of the passage until he had almost reached it, but then he stopped short in awe. The men behind him stopped also, astonished at what they saw.

The tunnel opened onto a vast blackness that could only be a huge cavern: *How appropriate that the monster waits for me in darkness!* For a moment the pain made him forget where he was and he seemed to be somewhere else: in his thoughts he saw his wife, shaking her head: "My love, do not enter..." With an effort he brought himself back to the present: *My wound makes me weary but I must go on!* The prince stepped resolutely into the darkness of the cavern and his men followed, waiting for the order to spread out with their torches.

As his eyes grew accustomed to the darkness that the torches could not fully dispel, Artaxias looked in wonder at the rows of gigantic pillars that tapered towards the roof, one row on either side. The bases of the pillars were almost two paces wide, and the roof of the cavern was covered in stalactites, some longer than the height of a man. At its highest the concave roof that spanned the vast cavern was higher than the height of many men and the light of the torches could barely reach it. Just beyond the torchlight, between the two rows of columns, he could discern a squat dark mass, as high as a man's waist but longer than the length of a tall man. As he looked its shape became clearer and he could see that it was a rectangular block of dark stone with a flat, polished top. At each of its corners was a tall bronze torch-holder.

"That must be the altar," he said, trying to make his voice sound firm. "That is where our brethren were killed by the monster who feasted on their blood!"

"And that must be the monster's seat," said a man behind him. Enough torches had been brought into the cavern for their light to reach the farther end. Beyond the sacrificial altar they could see a dais, and on the dais a massive throne that seemed to be made of the same black stone as the altar.

Artaxias gave the order for his men to fan out, but before the men could step further into the cavern a furtive movement behind one of the pillars caught the prince's attention. "There is someone behind the pillars," he said, his voice weakening as he spoke, "Behind the third pillar on the right!" He pointed with his sword towards the spot where he had seen the movement. The men immediately started to converge stealthily towards where he was pointing.

Aware that it had been seen, a tall hunched figure emerged slowly from behind a pillar and moved warily towards the prince. The light of the torches revealed a very tall old woman with piercing black eyes and snow-white hair. She was dressed in a finely woven white gown richly decorated with gold and silver thread, and on her head was a magnificent jewel-encrusted diadem from which hung delicate golden pendants that reached down to her shoulders. At the end of each pendant was a glittering green stone. Despite her bent shoulders, the old woman's bearing spoke of authority and calm dignity, and at sight of her Artaxias almost forgot the pain: *The monster! At last I meet her!* The men advanced to accost her but the prince husked: "Let her be! She is mine!" *I must speak to the monster before I kill her!*

The men did not intercept the tall figure as it approached Artaxias but they stepped around it, moving closer to their wounded leader, swords at the ready. As though she sensed that there was nothing to fear from the men, the old woman moved faster and now half walked, half stumbled, towards the prince. She seemed to be grinning. Ten paces from the prince she stopped and glared at the prince. *Will she speak to me?* thought the prince, *What can she say? She must know that we are here to kill her!* As the old woman glared at him malevolently, the prince realised that she was not grinning at all: her expression was one of pain: *An old pain, one she has lived with for many years!* In her hand the old woman held a long curved knife whose ruby pommel was as large as an eagle's egg.

As Artaxias watched her his heart beat wildly, like the wings of a small bird behind his ribs, and the pain in his side almost made him swoon. But the thought that he was on the verge of accomplishing that for which many of his men had died gave him strength: *The monster is within my reach! My task is almost finished!* Yet he could not bring himself to kill without warning what appeared to be no more than a frail old woman.

"Aged one," he said, "I have come to take your life in the name of my brethren, and others, whom you have killed. Prepare to die. If you wish you may pray to your gods to help you in the netherworld. But please do it quickly for I am short of time!"

He did not expect her to understand him for he had spoken in Hittite, but she answered him coldly in his own tongue, her words coming slowly and ungrammatically for she had not been to the land of the Hittites for a long time: "May your wound fester, Hittite," she hissed, "And when you die may the demons carry away your spirit screaming in agony!" And she lunged forward with her knife held high.

Her movements were agonised and clumsy. Artaxias easily avoided the rapidly descending knife and forgot his pain as he swung his heavy scythe-sword with all the strength he was capable of. The sharp blade struck its target and the old woman's head flew off her body. The diadem fell onto the hard floor of the cavern with a loud metallic clang and rolled away, but the headless body did not collapse at once. As though the old woman's will resisted the pull of the ground, she continued to move forward and passed by the prince before dropping, slowly, to her knees. There she knelt motionless for the time of a long breath before falling sideways, still clutching the knife. Blood spurted from her severed neck as her heart beat a few more times.

There was complete silence, for the men waited for something dramatic and unexpected to happen. Would the headless woman rise and resume her attack on the prince? Would the head that lay on the ground screech at them in fury? But the head remained mute where it had fallen and the dead woman continued to lie motionless on the hard ground with her arms twisted by her sides. The blood from her severed neck spread slowly to form a small pool that stained the upper part of her white gown.

"The monster is dead!" cried one of the men, breaking the silence. The rest cheered half-heartedly. Artaxias remained quiet, almost unconscious with pain. There was little accomplishment in killing a monster who had proved to be no more dangerous than an angry old woman.

Artaxias leaned against a pillar and gave orders that the body be straightened and turned on its back. Although she had been a false goddess, she was, after all, a *kahanah* and could not be left in a crumpled heap. *We have done what we came to do. This is where the butchery ends!* The prince could hardly think as his pain had become almost unbearable. *There have been too many easy killings on this campaign!* He momentarily lost consciousness but two men held him up and stopped him from falling. A third picked up the severed head and held it up triumphantly by its white hair for all to see. They all stared at it, and the dead woman's head stared back, its malevolence hardly extinguished by death.

"May we take the monster's head to the surface?" asked one of the soldiers who was helping the prince. The prince spoke very faintly "Yes, two of you take it to the surface," and he indicated that they were also to take the old woman's knife and crown.

"Shall we see if there are any more priests or priestesses down here?" someone asked.

"This is a big place!" said another, "There may still be priests or priestesses hiding in the dark!"

But before Artaxias could give his permission for the men to search the cavern, they heard a young female voice say, in perfect Hittite: "There is no need to look for others. Only I am left. There is no one else."

They all looked up and saw, standing very straight in the shadows between the pillars on the left side of the cavern, a very tall young girl dressed wholly in white. Even her sandals were white. She wore neither crown nor veil, and her only ornament was a slim necklace decorated with a single red stone that glittered in the torchlight.

"A young priestess!"

"She must have been hiding in the shadows until we killed her goddess!"

"Kill her!"

"Wait!" ordered the prince. He walked slowly over to the girl. She could not have been much more than eighteen winters old, and though she stood very straight and looked down at the stocky Hittites with calm dignity, her eyes were wet with tears.

"What a beautiful girl!" someone whispered.

"Yet we must kill her!" said Berek, the leader of the *action group* who had followed the prince. The prince was undecided. He remained silent, his sword in his hand, looking at the extraordinarily beautiful girl who stood passively before him. The men waited for the order to kill the young woman if the prince was too weak to perform the task himself. But the prince hesitated and took a deep breath. Expecting the sudden thrust of his sword, the girl closed her eyes and stood even straighter.

The prince shook his head: "Let her live," he said, "We have brought enough carnage to this place!"

"My prince, we are not to take prisoners!" said Berek.

"We shall not take her prisoner," answered the prince. "We shall leave her behind. Let her die from lack of food or from grief, or manage to survive if that is the will of the gods. We have enough blood on our swords." And he fainted from the pain.

Berek ignored the girl and, pointing with his finger at his men, said: "You three carry the prince to the surface and see that he is seen by a physician immediately!"

The men carried the prince back through the tunnel and the rest of the men followed. The *action group* leader went last. When they were almost at the end of the tunnel they heard a loud cry, like the agonised wail of a mother whose dead child is lowered into its grave. Some of the men touched the little amulets that were meant to protect them from evil spirits

"The girl is grieving for her goddess!"

Berek addressed the last three men who were about to enter the small cavern at the bottom of the pit. "You three come back to the cavern with me!" he ordered.

"What for?" said one of the three. They were reluctant to go back.

"To kill that girl! No-one is to remain alive!"

"But the prince said…"

"I know! But the prince is badly wounded and may have forgotten the king's orders!"

The four men ran back to the temple to search for the girl. But although they looked everywhere in the vast cavern she was nowhere to be found; it was as though she had turned into a pillar, or become one of the stalactites. The search was called off when the torches began to burn out.

The returning army entered Hattusas via the West Gate, like all victorious armies, but no crowds came to greet it, just as no crowds had followed it to the East Gate to bid it farewell. The head, together with the crown and dagger, were brought back and ceremonially presented to King Aleshanr and the Council of Elders.

POSTSCRIPT

All Assyrian raids on Hittite land ceased after the destruction of the temple, as did the raids on the other neighbours of Assyria. The task of Uri the Envoy became easier and it is said that he became a firm and trusted friend of the Hittite king. But the joy of the king at the stabilization of his borders was tempered by the loss of his nephew, the war-prince Artaxias, who died from his wound during the long trip back to Hattusas. To the last Her-unt would not leave his side and the prince's last words were to him: "Dear friend, I leave the care of my wife and little daughter to you." The prince was buried in the wastelands, with his shield and Her-unt's sword by his side, in a grave without markings.

Her-unt retired from all military activities and became a loving grandfather to little Melapenna in all but name. Artaxias' wife moved to the king's palace in Hattusas but did not marry again. The navigator

Norr became a great traveller and merchant, and grew rich, as did many other merchants after the shadow of war lifted and peace finally allowed trade to flourish between the Hittites and the Assyrians.

PART 2

THE ARCHAEOLOGIST AND THE LAMIA

1

THE ARCHAEOLOGICAL
EXPEDITION

1

On the British Televised News:

BBC newsreader: *An ancient Assyrian temple believed to have been lost for almost four thousand years may soon be rediscovered by an international archaeological expedition. The expedition is sponsored by several European, American and Middle Eastern institutions and will include teams of experts from a number of universities. Our Ingrid Lamplugh has interviewed the leader of the British team, Professor Michael Townsend of University College, London.*

The scene changes to show an attractive and immaculately dressed young woman sitting across a low table from a boyish-looking man with short curly auburn hair in his early forties. The man is clean-shaven and is wearing a beige turtleneck jumper. His glasses are on the low table and behind him are tall bookshelves stocked with books. At one end of the low table stands a small statue of an Assyrian king.

Ms Lamplugh: *Is it realistic, Professor Townsend, to expect to find a 'lost' ancient temple in this day and age? After all, commercial flights pass over Syria, Iraq and Turkey several times a day and satellites must have photographed the area innumerable times.*

Prof. Townsend: *That is true, but neither the crew nor the passengers of an airliner are likely to notice that what might appear as a tiny splodge* on the ground is actually an ancient temple that is not on the tourist map. As for photographs, because the region is politically sensitive any aerial or satellite photographs would be for military and not scientific purposes. So the proposition that the particular temple we are looking for remains undiscovered, at least from an archaeological point of view, is not implausible.

Ms Lamplugh: What about the local people? Wouldn't they know about the temple?

Prof. Townsend: The local people would know their area very well, but although they may be familiar with the ruins of the temple they are unlikely to know its history, or even its name, and they would have little reason to believe that its ruins are any different from the multitude of ruins that are scattered over that region. I should add that the area we intend to study is largely unpopulated except for a few scattered villages whose inhabitants have little direct contact with the outside world.

Ms Lamplugh: Is it not unusual to make such a concerted international effort just to find a single temple?

Prof. Townsend: I should stress that we would not just be looking for a particular temple. We intend to make an archaeological survey of the whole area, if possible, although the temple of the goddess Amalishah is our main target. Or perhaps I should say that it is my main target, for I have been interested in this temple and its goddess for many years.

Ms Lamplugh: Could you tell us something about the goddess and her temple, Professor?

Prof. Townsend: The goddess Amalishah was a very early Assyrian goddess who was no longer part of the orthodox Assyrian pantheon in the middle and late Assyrian periods. For reasons we do no know, her temple was remote and virtually inaccessible but despite that, from the very little factual evidence that we have, it seems to have done quite well until it was destroyed by the Hittites. After its destruction the Assyrians tried to remove all references to the temple and its goddess from their chronicles, much like the names of unpopular pharaohs were deleted from Egyptian records.

Ms Lamplugh: *Do we know anything specific about the goddess?*

Prof. Townsend: *Most of what we know about Amalishah comes from the writings of the Hittites, who hated her and called her a monster. She lived in the temple and was alleged to be very tall.*

Ms Lamplugh: *Are you saying that the temple had a live resident goddess?*

Prof. Townsend: *Apparently so. She was alive, that is, until she was killed by the Hittites. The temple did not survive her.*

Ms Lamplugh: *So the temple could not have functioned for very long. Not much longer than the lifetime of the goddess.*

Prof. Townsend: *According to the few records we have, the temple existed for several centuries.*

Ms Lamplugh: *Do you have any ideas about that, Professor? I mean about a goddess who lived such a long time?*

Prof. Townsend: *Her worshippers claimed she was immortal, so we can only suppose that the role of 'goddess' was assumed by a succession of extraordinary priestesses. I say 'extraordinary' because whoever assumed the role of 'goddess' must have been a remarkable person. There is evidence that she had considerable influence over some Assyrian kings, at least early in the temple's history.*

Ms Lamplugh: *Do we know why the Hittites destroyed the temple?*

Prof. Townsend: *Not really, although there are several theories. By all accounts the Hittite attack was directed specifically against the temple of the goddess and not against the Assyrians in general, which makes it difficult to explain because the Hittites were normally very tolerant of other peoples' religions.*

Ms Lamplugh: *Do we know why the Assyrians tried to delete all references to the goddess and her temple?*

Prof. Townsend: *I suspect that there might have been some rivalry between the worshippers of the goddess and the worshippers of other gods. Such rivalry wasn't unusual in those days. When the temple was destroyed the opposing teams would have been the only players left and they naturally tried to erase all traces of their former competitor.*

Ms Lamplugh: *So we really know little about the temple and its goddess.*

Prof. Townsend: *That is correct. But we do know that although the temple was destroyed by a foreign power the Assyrians took no retaliatory action. The most likely explanation is that the Assyrians had other troubles at the time. If we find the temple it is our hope that it shall contain records that would tell us something about what those troubles might have been. Such records could fill some of the gaps in our knowledge of early Assyrian history – and possibly also of Hittite history!*

Ms Lamplugh: *I understand that considerable funds were made available by universities and museums in the United States and other countries. Is it just the possibility of finding ancient records that prompts such generosity?*

Prof. Townsend: *According to the Hittites the temple was destroyed but not looted, and other records imply that the site was never reoccupied nor the temple rebuilt. There is therefore a strong possibility that the ruins might still contain valuable artefacts in addition to written records.*

Ms Lamplugh: *You mean there could be treasure waiting to be discovered?*

Prof. Townsend: *Perhaps, although I would not call what we might find 'treasure'. Let us simply say 'valuable artefacts'. Valuable from an archaeological point of view, of course.*

Ms Lamplugh: *What about looters from the more recent past?*

Prof. Townsend: *That is always a problem with ancient sites, but we are optimistic.*

Ms Lamplugh: Thank you for giving us some of your time, Professor.

Prof. Townsend: Thank you.

2

The Land Rover had only two passengers as it sped across the wastelands. One passenger was British and the other was from the Southern United States.

"Well, Mike," said Dr. Leonard Ehrlich in his best Southern drawl, "according to my compass, the map and this photo, the hill should be just about *there!*" He pointed from a set of large black-and-white photographs on his lap to a distant spot on the horizon.

"I believe you're right!" said Michael Townsend. He brought the Land Rover to a halt so that he could devote all his attention to the horizon. "I've been too busy driving to look at the landscape. Yes, that must be the hill over there!"

"Doesn't look like much," said Leonard without enthusiasm.

"The outline isn't very clear in this light, but it's definitely a hill!"

The visible cause of Mike Townsend's excitement was a flat-topped prominence whose silhouette, in the slowly fading light of the late afternoon, was just discernible as a thick grey line on the horizon. From the elevated position of the front seats in the Land Rover, the view as far as the eye could see was a featureless landscape, dotted here and there with clumps of large boulders, stunted trees, and the kind of bushes that grow in places where the soil is poor and water scarce. The prominence stood alone, like a long and very low rock at the end of a choppy grey-brown sea that had somehow frozen into immobility. There was no sign of human habitation anywhere in sight and none was expected. Mike put the Land Rover into gear and pressed on the accelerator:

"Mike!" cried Leonard as the engine revved and the vehicle surged towards the hill, "don't go too fast!"

"With some luck we might reach it before it's too dark to see anything!" Mike did not slow down and the Land Rover bucked and heaved as it sped over the uneven ground.

After ten minutes of clinging to the handhold, Leonard decided that he had had enough: "Mike," he said, "Please slow down! Remember that everyone believes that the Amalishah temple was on

194

the plain. Only *you* believe that it was on a hill!"

"I know."

"Well, it could be somewhere behind those rocks over there! Or there!" Leonard pointed in different directions. "If you drive like a maniac we could pass within fifty feet of what's left of it and not see it in this bad light!"

"So keep your eyes open, just in case. I'll keep mine on my driving."

"That's probably just an old hill, Mike."

"A temple in such a desolate place should have been easy to see from afar. It's therefore most likely to have been on a hill, and that's the only hill in these parts!"

"The Hittite records say nothing of a hill."

"That's true, but then they don't describe the temple at all. They only say that it was heavily fortified."

"OK Mike. But *please* slow down."

Mike eased off the throttle slightly, but the Land Rover continued to buck and heave.

Three days earlier, the head of the archaeological expedition, Professor Nasser ElKureishi of the University of Baghdad, had sent out five exploratory teams from the base camp. They were expected to be away for about a week and the boundaries of the territory each team was to explore had been carefully and precisely assigned. Each of the teams had a Land Rover and a small tent, a set of maps, a set of aerial black-and-white photographs and a radio transmitter-receiver whose frequency was tuned to the main transmitter-receiver in the base camp. The exploratory teams could communicate via radio with each other. In addition to a plentiful supply of fuel, the teams also had portable ovens and a two-week supply of food.

Although the aerial photographs were remarkably clear, they showed nothing that could be confidently interpreted as the ruins of ancient towns or temples. The object of the exploratory teams was to locate and, if possible, identify things of archaeological interest. Each exploratory team was to explore a slice of territory within a sixty-kilometre radius from the base camp and contact ElKureishi the moment they found anything promising. Right on the edge of one of the photographs Mike had noticed a curved shadow that suggested the presence of a hill, and he had asked ElKureishi to be assigned the area that included the curved shadow. The photographs had been taken years earlier as part of a military survey and did not overlap, so that no photograph showed what lay beyond the curved shadow.

There might have been a hill there, and then again there might not.

Now the hill loomed ahead of them; a large grey mass.

"Well, Mike, it's a hill all right!" Leonard's expression conveyed the thought: 'We're on a wild goose chase!'

"Of course!" said Mike, pretending not to notice the good-natured sarcasm.

"Why are you slowing down?"

"There's something wrong with the Land Rover!"

The engine sputtered and died. Leonard looked down at the dials. "Yeah! We're out of gas! Half a mile from the hill."

"That's impossible!" said Mike, "the tank was full less than an hour ago!"

"You must have damaged the gas tank, or one of the pipes, or something. That's what comes from driving over these rocks like a lunatic!" Leonard had no idea about the inner workings of a Land Rover. All he could grasp of its mechanical intricacies was that the Land Rover was supposed to run.

Mike frowned: "If that's the case, I suppose there's not much point in filling the tank." Much of the space at the back of the Land Rover was taken up by petrol cans.

"Nope," said Leonard resignedly, "We'll radio back and tell them to send a repair gang,"

"Um… no. Let's explore the hill first. It's quite close."

"Not tonight, Mike. Please. It'll be dark soon. Let's make camp. We can hike up to the hill first thing tomorrow."

"I suppose you're right." Mike could not get his eyes off the hill. "It's like the stump of a giant low-cut tree!" His excitement was not contagious enough to affect his companion.

"Yeah, it's a bit like a long low *mesa*. Not very likely to've had a temple on its top, is it? In the middle of nowhere and with almost vertical sides!"

"The Amalishah temple was supposed to be *fortified*. A hill with steep sides would be a natural place for it."

"Why would they fortify a temple that's on a steep hill in the middle of nowhere?"

"I could say that the Assyrians were congenitally paranoid, but actually I haven't the faintest idea!"

"OK. Let's prepare to spend the night here."

They set up their small two-man tent beside the Land Rover and had a frugal supper. Mike was too excited to eat much and he was soon sitting on a thick mat smoking his pipe. Leonard sat beside him and lit a cigarette.

"Can't get that hill outta your mind, can you?" said Leonard after a few puffs of his cigarette. Mike did not answer, and for a long time they both stared at the long dark silhouette that dominated the skyline. Not much later they were sleeping soundly.

3

It was a cold, sunless morning when the two men walked briskly towards the hill, approaching it from the South. It was just past 7 am and the sky was covered by small grey clouds that persistently obscured the sun. The hill rose imposingly before them, its flat top high above the surrounding plain.

"Mike, we ain't got a chance of climbing that thing!"

"There seems to be something like a ramp towards the West!"

"If you say so."

It did not take them long to find that the gradient on the south-western side was quite manageable. It was as though that part of the hill had once boasted a small peak that had melted down and flowed down the side. Mike virtually ran to the slope and immediately started to climb it.

"Mike, wait for me! I'm not as athletic as you are!"

"There are trees on the hilltop! That means water not too far below!"

"That still doesn't mean the hill was ever occupied... **Mike, wait!**"

With his head bent forward Mike raced ahead and reached the top of the hill fifteen metres ahead of Leonard. Just as he reached the top he stopped short and looked around. When he looked back at Leonard he was out of breath but appeared sublimely pleased and showed it with a boyish grin. Leonard stood beside him a few moments later.

"Well, Mike, we made it! **Oh my God!**"

The top of the hill was densely covered with short trees and bushes that looked only slightly healthier than their cousins on the surrounding plain. But scattered beneath the trees and bushes lay half-concealed piles of roughly cut stones and broken mud bricks. Here and there, lying on their sides and almost sunken into the ground, lay the broken segments of narrow columns and what seemed like the eroded foundations of what had once been significant structures.

Towards the centre of the almost flat hilltop, rising above the bushes and the stunted trees, was a wide circular mound.

"We didn't see *that* from the ground!" exclaimed Leonard, pointing at the mound.

"We couldn't," said Mike, "the sides of the hill are too steep and there's a lip around the edge."

"There was *something* on this hill, all right!"

Mike didn't answer but he removed his rucksack and took out his binoculars. He climbed to the top of a pile of rubble and turned his binoculars to the furthest points of the hilltop. The pile of rubble lay to the left of the ramp and was almost two metres high; it offered an excellent view of the hilltop. Leonard walked about and examined some of the fragments of brick that were scattered among the bushes. He had no intention of joining Mike atop the pile of rubble.

"Mike, these mud bricks are eroded enough to be from the time of the temple!"

"It would seem so."

"Could this be it?" asked Leonard incredulously.

"You mean the Amalishah temple?" Mike did not lower the binoculars. "I'm not sure."

"What else can it be?"

"It looks like the remains of a small hilltop town; an ancient village wouldn't have been more than a few scattered huts. Whatever this was, it was a substantial settlement, but nothing I can see shows the characteristic features of an Assyrian temple." Mike sounded very disappointed.

"I can't see much from down here. Tell me why you think we haven't found what you're looking for."

At that moment the clouds moved away from the sun and everything was covered in bright sunlight.

"Ah! That's much better!" exclaimed Mike.

"Mike?" Leonard expected an answer to his question.

"Oh do climb up and join me! But take off your rucksack. The pile of dried mud and stones I'm standing on isn't very stable."

Leonard put down his rucksack and reluctantly climbed up the pile to stand next to Mike. "You're right. It was definitely a small town, or something like that, but what was the reason for its existence here? It would have had to sustain itself, which couldn't have been easy even if they managed to cultivate the land around the hill. Only a temple with food-bringing pilgrims would justify a small town!"

"Yes!" Mike said impatiently. "But where is the temple? I don't see the outline of a temple anywhere. If there had been a temple on this hill where are the plinths of large columns? If not columns then where are the remains of thick walls? The walls at least should have formed a distinctive shape that would be discernible from this height!"

"It's been what, four thousand years?"

"Give or take a few centuries. But look, you can see that the structures on the hill were surrounded by a mud-brick wall. That's what made the lip around the edge. All around the perimeter the ground is higher and the soil under the bushes is of a slightly different colour. The same discoloration gives the outlines of some of the buildings. If buildings and the surrounding wall left a trace surely a temple would have too."

"Not if it were an open-air temple without columns or thick walls."

"Len, in all your studies of Assyro-Babylonian history, have you ever heard of the Assyrians building temples without some kind of substantial structure?"

"Nope. But that doesn't mean they never did. Unimportant temples might have been no more than glorified shrines."

"True. But the Amalishah temple was well known in its time, and probably wealthy. The sanctum *must* have had a roof and therefore thick walls even if it didn't have columns!"

"You're the archaeologist, Mike. I'm just a historian. And Assyrian architecture ain't my field."

"Dammit Len! Why can't there be *something* set out in a nice large rectangle?"

The question was rhetorical but Leonard said in his best American accent: "Well, there certainly ain't nothing like that 'round 'ere!"

"Damn!"

"So do we report that we found the remains of a town?"

"Not yet. I want to have a look at that large circular mound first. It's wide enough to conceal something."

"A circular temple on a hilltop? That's even more unlikely."

"I know. But let's go and look anyway."

They climbed cautiously down the pile of rubble and walked towards the mound, looking carefully at the ground as they passed.

"Look," said Leonard, pulling at a small bush to show some cut stones beneath. On the sides of one of the half-concealed stones were faded black stains. "That's what could be the marks of a fire."

"I noticed," replied Mike thoughtfully, "But so what? Town fires were endemic in those days. Even London burned down not too long ago."

"London burned because the houses were mostly of wood. And speaking of wood, I wish we could find some ancient wood or bones under these stones. Then the lab boys would give us a proper date for this place!"

Mike shook his head: "It's unlikely that we'll find any contemporary organic material on or near the surface."

"Yeah!"

Mike thought: *If this were the Amalishah temple, and if the temple were as old as it is supposed to be, then any wood or bone near the surface would have rotted to dust centuries before Christ was born. But archaeologists on the hunt live in hope. What am I hoping to find? The temple? No. I am hoping to find something that would speak to me of Amalishah!*

4

They explored the area around the mound for more than an hour, carrying their rucksacks and looking down at the ground with great care. Occasionally, Mike knelt or squatted to see better at what lay on the ground, or scrutinised with a small pocket lens something he picked up. The circular pile was over thirty metres in diameter and about four metres high. It was composed mostly of the remains of heavily eroded baked-mud bricks that had lost their shape by exposure to wind and rain. There were also several large stone blocks, some of which had once been rectangular.

"How long are we going to monkey around this thing, Mike?" The sun now shone without breaks and the temperature had risen to an uncomfortable level. Both men were glad they had remembered to bring their hats.

"There's nothing like a temple here, is there?" Mike asked despondently.

"Nope. Let's see what we can find elsewhere."

"Whatever this was, it was once very big," said Mike. He was unwilling to move away from the mound.

"Large but the wrong shape to have been a temple," remarked Leonard, "perhaps the temple was somewhere away from the hill. Like on the plain below, like everyone but you believe!"

"I wouldn't have thought so."

Knowing that Mike's frustration could erupt at any moment, Leonard said: "Are you still hoping to find some evidence of columns?" Mike was digging into the sides of the mound at random with the small foldable shovel he had brought with him.

"No. If the temple had columns they would have been quite sizeable and some would have protruded from the sides of the mound. I'm hoping to find fragments of small artefacts, the sort that casual visitors would ignore but which might tell us something about this place."

"You mean things that visiting locals wouldn't have bothered to take."

"I suppose so. I'm not expecting to find anything sellable. The locals must have known about this place and taken whatever they pleased every time they came here. Whatever these ruins had once been, they've been around for a very long time. Lots of people must have visited the place."

They continued to explore around the base of the mound but found nothing of interest.

"We'll get to know much more about the mound when ElKureishi and a work gang get here," said Leonard, "a cut into the mound would reveal everything there is to know."

"I agree, but let's look around some more before calling the others."

"I think this was just a big round building made of stone and mud brick," said Leonard, "maybe someone who was important for a while lived here."

"A round house?" said Mike, "that's not likely."

"Why not? Rich people can afford to be eccentric. Or maybe it was the town's meeting place."

"I'm perplexed at the total lack of pottery," said Mike. "We saw shards almost everywhere we passed on the surface of the hill, but there are none near the mound."

"Yeah. Let's go back to the vehicle and report what we've found and what we haven't."

"I'm first going to climb this mound and see what's on the top!"

"What's the point of that? Any artefacts would be down here, at the base. The top of the mound would have been the roof!"

"You're probably right, but you never know."

"Mike, there's nothing we two can do here on our own! If there's anything worth investigating, old Kureishi will send a properly equipped team!" As an afterthought he added: "And he'll also send some guys to repair the Land Rover."

Mike said nothing. He removed his rucksack and carefully began to climb the circular pile. It was not easy, for although the mound was not much more than four metres high, its sides were steep and it was not as solid as it looked. Several times Mike inadvertently started a small avalanche that threatened to topple him over.

"Watch out for things that crawl under stones and love to bite!" Leonard warned.

Leonard was genuinely concerned about Mike. Mike's hiking boots only reached up to his ankles and if his feet sank into the rubble a sting by even a tiny scorpion could have serious repercussions so far from medical help. Leonard sighed with exasperation: *And there could be things worse than scorpions hiding under these loose stones!* But as he could do nothing to stop his companion. He sat down on the side of the mound and lit a cigarette just as Mike managed to look over the top.

"I'll be damned!"

"What is it?" Leonard got up.

"Len, the mound's like a huge bomb crater!" Mike had almost reached the top of the mound.

"What do you mean?"

Mike was now at the top. "Len, there's something very strange here!"

"What?" Leonard snuffed out his cigarette.

"There's a hole in the middle of this thing!"

"A bunged-up well?"

"No. It's too wide to be a well. There's a lot of debris and the hole seems to have swallowed a lot of rubble but it's not bunged up, it's still a hole!"

"Just make sure it doesn't swallow you too!"

"Len, I'm going down to have a look. Could you please bring me my torch from my rucksack?"

"The hell I am!"

"Oh, and bring my camera too, please!"

"Mike, I'm pretty scared already that something might happen to you!"

"Come on, Len! This could be important! The stuff is quite solid if you're careful!" That was not quite true. The rubble on the slope that led down to the hole was balanced precariously and seemed poised to slide.

"You can't go down that well without proper safeguards, Mike. It's against all regulations."

"To hell with regulations!"

"If you think that well could be important let's tell Kureishi and wait until he sends an excavation team with proper equipment."

"I tell you, it's not a well!"

"How can you be sure?"

"I estimate an initial diameter of about five meters and there are winding steps around a metre-wide shaft." He paused as though he could not believe his eyes. "And if I'm not mistaken, there's what looks like writing on the wall around the steps!"

"OK. I'm getting your torch!" Leonard finally showed signs of enthusiasm.

He climbed up very cautiously, carrying Mike's torch and camera. When he stood gingerly on the rim of the circular mound he cried: **"Wow!"**

"I thought you'd find it interesting!"

Leonard was astounded: "The mound is like a funnel!"

Beneath the rubble that had made its way into the whole the bright sunlight revealed steep steps winding down around a central shaft. Leonard handed over the torch and the camera to Mike.

"Thanks!"

"Oh lord, I think you're right. That looks like writing! But it's in shadow and hard to tell at this distance!"

"Yes!" Mike was almost dizzy with excitement.

"What do you think this was?"

"The hole?" said Mike absent-mindedly.

"No, I mean the whole darn thing!"

"As you said, it was a largish stone and mud-brick building of some kind. Obviously circular and with its upper parts mostly of wood. The roof must have been wooden too; it's completely gone!" He photographed the hole and its surroundings.

"So the wood rotted away and all we see are the remains of the baked mud-brick walls," said Leonard.

"Quite. That's why the hole is not bunged up with debris. The collapsed wooden superstructure kept the melting bricks away long enough for the larger bits and the mud to spread outwards, away from the hole."

Leonard smiled and shook his head. "Gosh, won't you ever stop talking like an engineer?"

Mike smiled: "I can't. I was an engineer before I became an archaeologist!"

Leonard suddenly became very serious. "Yeah, but what you're saying, Mike, is that the circular building was built around the hole."

"It seems that way!"

"I think we should go back to the vehicle and call Kureishi. They'll be here as soon as they can."

"After I have a look down that hole."

Leonard looked very concerned. "Mike, you're my boss and I can't stop you from going down into the pit, but it could be very dangerous!"

"I know, Len. I'll be careful."

"And you will keep your eyes open for things that crawl and bite?"

"Of course!"

Mike clambered cautiously down towards the aperture. Before reaching the yawning mouth he started a small avalanche of loose stones and quickly made his way up again.

"See?" cried Leonard, "You could easily slide down that funnel and fall straight down the shaft!"

"I'm pretty certain that's writing on the wall!" exclaimed Mike, as though the observation made any risk worth taking.

Leonard had seen him excited before, but never this much. However, Mike was one of those rare people who could get very excited about something and still keep a cool head. Leonard tried to reason with him: "Mike, even if you reach the hole in one piece the steps are pretty steep and could be very dangerous! They could collapse under your weight. Let's call Kureishi!"

"If this turns out to be an archaeological dead-end we'll call Kureishi and tell him we found the ruins of a small hilltop town which had a protective wall at the top of a precipice. He'll then have to decide what to do about that. But if we have found something important Kureishi will want to be here at once, with all his *entourage*. So we have to find out whether this hole is important before the whole mob gets here. I've got to go down that hole!"

"I've got a funny feeling about this, Mike."

"I'll be careful. When I return we'll do everything by the book, I promise!"

While Mike checked the torch and the camera; Leonard looked at his watch. It was after 10 a.m. They had reached the hill from their makeshift camp near the Land Rover over two hours earlier. He could understand Mike's burning curiosity, but whom could they appeal to for help if something happened to him down there?

Leonard had a premonition of something momentous and frightening. Although not an archaeologist, he had been Mike's partner at many archaeological digs and, like many archaeologists, he had become just a little superstitious: *The few writings that spoke of the Amalishah temple described it as evil, but there was never anything specific, never anything tangible. The Hittite king who destroyed it had ordered that there were to be no survivors and, for that, he had been called a saviour!*

A cold wind blew away Leonard's hat just as he about to squat on the rim of the mound. He picked up his hat and thought: *At least there won't be any wind down the hole.* Then he realised how silly the thought was. The wind would be the least of Mike's problems.

Mike finished toying with his equipment and was finally ready to venture down the funnel of dried mud and loose stones. Leonard looked at him earnestly: "Mike, I can't stop you from going down that hole because you're my team leader. But the rules say we can't go exploring into holes without proper backup. I think the rules are right."

"There's something more, isn't there? You've never called upon the rules before and we've been to much trickier places than this."

Leonard nodded and stared at his hiking boots before lighting another cigarette. "Yeah. I have a funny feeling that something could happen here!"

"I'm going down, if only a little way. I want to know where those steps lead to. *What* they lead to. The writing on the wall around the stairs is very promising!"

"For all you know, the writing says 'Abandon Hope All Ye Who Enter Here.'"

"Hmm… Perhaps."

Leonard shrugged his shoulders resignedly. "There's probably just water down there."

"No, not water. Not much anyway! It hasn't rained seriously for months."

"Can't I persuade you not to go down that hole?"

"Dammit Len, if that pit were to cave in, it would have caved in centuries ago. It's perfectly safe!"

"I'm not really worried that it will cave in. I just have a bad feeling about that pit!"

"We've had bad feelings before, haven't we? And everything turned out all right. I've *got* to go down into the pit, Len."

"You will be careful, won't you?"

Mike nodded and cautiously clambered down the funnel towards the mouth of the pit. Leonard watched him anxiously, sucking at his cigarette. His thoughts were sombre: *The pit must have swallowed a lot of rubble and yet hasn't filled up! I wonder how deep it is! But Mike's right, the steps and the writing strongly suggest that it was not a well. So what in Heaven's name was it?*

5

It was ten minutes since Mike had disappeared into the hole. Leonard turned away from the pit and looked pensively at the ruins around him. Beneath the stunted trees and the bushes the remains of various structures stretched almost to the perimeter of the flat hilltop. Although he had been with archaeologists for more than twenty years he was still unable to suppress a sense of melancholia whenever he first beheld unexplored ruins. The sight of scattered stones and fallen columns between the trees and bushes reminded him of pictures he had seen of corpses on a battlefield. He hastily banished the thought from his mind.

Mike went down the steps very carefully; his excitement sharpening his senses. Going down the steep steps by the light of his torch was not easy, there were loose stones that could trip him on every step, and there was also the danger that the stairs themselves would collapse under his weight. He hugged the wall closely while he counted the steps as he descended. The writing on the wall, for writing it certainly was, was part Assyrian, part something else. Mike had never seen anything like it. Although it was eroded by the weather, he could tell that it was partly cuneiform, but there were also oval and square shapes with tiny pictograms that were vaguely reminiscent of Egyptian hieroglyphics. He could not decipher it: *I'll work on the inscriptions later with Ohanian, who would decipher them if anyone can. But why did people four thousand years ago go to all the trouble of carving a circular staircase deep into solid rock? And why write on the wall, practically out of sight? People must have gone up and down those steps frequently. There must be something down there!* He photographed the writing every seven steps, making sure the pictures overlapped at the edges.

The deeper he descended, the blacker the walls became. He rubbed his finger against a wall. The blackness felt dry but with a trace of oiliness. *This was once soot! There must have been a tremendous fire at the bottom of this thing! The rain has washed away the soot only at the upper levels.* But he was only down to the fifty-third step when the torch showed signs that the battery was running out. Its light flickered and he stumbled over some rubble on the steps. He almost dropped his glasses and just managed to stop himself from falling down the shaft. *Damn! The spare batteries are in the Land Rover! I've got to go back! And Len won't stop badgering me until I tell old Kureishi about this!*

6

Professor Nasser ElKureishi sat near the communications equipment reserved for maintaining contact with the outside world. The radio transmitter-receiver had its own tent and was now used mainly to keep in touch with the out-teams. He put down the microphone and turned to all who were standing respectfully around him.

"Townsend and his American partner have found something interesting," he said with an air of importance. "It could be the Amalishah temple but Townsend is not sure." ElKureishi was disappointed that it was not someone from his own university who had discovered the interesting ruins.

"Why isn't he sure?" asked Jehan, one of the postdocs, a pretty woman in her middle twenties.

"Townsend says that it looks like the remains of a small fortified town at the top of a flat hill. There is apparently nothing that looks like a temple. He says, however, that the less exposed remains show scorch marks compatible with the Hittite holocaust."

"What do you think he found, Professor?" asked Jehan.

"I think he's found the Amalishah temple, because it is unlikely that there would be two burnt settlements in this area. We shall have to confirm the age of the settlement, of course, assuming that we find some original organic material."

"So why didn't the aerial photographs show the settlement?" asked Jehan.

"The photographs don't show everything, and there are apparently lots of little trees and bushes on the hilltop that cover the tell-tale signs!"

The professor rose ponderously from his seat near the communications equipment. "We have to get there as quickly as possible. And we must take some caving equipment!"

"*Caving equipment?*" asked a young Turkish doctoral student. He was very surprised.

"Oh yes," replied ElKureishi, "Townsend said there is a pit of some kind between the centre and the eastern end of the ruins; a large hole with steps leading down. He also said there is what appears to be writing on the wall of the pit. Townsend said he could not recognise it."

"That is a very unusual thing for Professor Townsend to admit," said Jehan.

"The pit is probably just an old well," said the Turkish student, "We don't need caving equipment for that. The equipment we have is quite adequate for excavating a well if we think it necessary."

ElKureishi bowed his head in thought. "I would agree with you, young man, but *Professor* Townsend said that he was reasonably sure it was not a well."

"What else could it be?" asked Jehan.

"I don't know," said ElKureishi, "But if Townsend thinks it's not a well then I am perfectly willing to go along with that, at least for the moment. And if he thinks that the pit is interesting, he'll try to explore it before we arrive. We must get there as soon as we can in case he... uh gets himself into trouble."

Jehan was not unduly worried about Mike. She considered him a middle-aged, and hence uninteresting, man who behaved as though he were twenty years younger than his age. She did, however, have a vast respect for his competence as an archaeologist.

"So where can we get caving equipment?" she said.

"I'll call Baghdad," replied the professor. "We'll have what is needed airlifted here. It's now 3:20 pm and I am to contact the university at 4:00. I'll make the arrangements personally to expedite things. Now let's go for coffee!"

On the way to the refectory tent ElKureishi had to answer many questions from his assistants and postdocs. As happens in all base camps where everyone waits for reports from the out-teams, news of interesting developments spreads almost instantaneously. ElKureishi was bombarded with questions as he sipped his coffee. "Yes," he said to everyone who questioned him. "Townsend said that there are the remains of something like a small town on a hill. There is also a pit with steps leading down into the hill with what looks like writing on its walls."

"Writing?" said Ohanian, the cryptographer and palaeography expert who never missed an opportunity for a chat over coffee. He had just joined the group in the refectory and was suddenly very interested: "But why did he say it *looks* like writing? It's either writing or it isn't!"

"I suppose Townsend said that because he could not read it. It's probably so eroded that it's hard to tell."

"What else did Professor Townsend say about the pit?" asked Ohanian.

"He said that it was surrounded by a large amount of rubble. This suggests that the pit was once inside a very large structure."

"Perhaps it was a sacred well," said the Turkish doctoral student, "that could explain the writing."

"Perhaps," said ElKureishi. "We know nothing yet for sure, except that if there's something interesting at the bottom of that hole *we* should be there when it's found!" He shrugged in a highly expressive Middle-Eastern way and added: "And if there isn't, we should be there anyway."

7

The authorities promised ElKureishi that the caving equipment would be brought over by Army helicopter in three days. He notified Mike immediately. Mike did not sound too disappointed at having to wait and ElKureishi was also, to some extent, grateful for the delay. He needed time to decide whether Mike's discovery warranted moving the base camp to the hill, and there were other things he had to think through.

As the elderly professor sat alone in his tent that night, he carefully re-read his notes on the Amalishah temple by the light of his favourite gaslamp. None of the ancient chroniclers who referred to the Amalishah temple mentioned a pit of any kind. Nor did they say anything about the temple being on a flat hill. Could Mike and Leonard have found something other than the temple? ElKureishi shook his head: *The ruins **have** to be those of the temple. Mike carefully* *avoided committing himself one way or the other, but he mentioned that the settlement had once been fortified and he also mentioned finding evidence of scorch marks on some of the ancient stones. If a fortified settlement other than the temple had also been put to the torch, the chronicles would have said so.* But what about the pit? If Mike were correct about its depth and the size of the structure that had once enclosed it then it must have played a central role in the settlement's activities. *But if the ruins were those of the Amalishah temple why did none of the records mention anything like a pit?* The Hittite records specifically stated that the temple was burned *'and all the defenders slain so as to destroy the evil within'*. What could have been the nature of this 'evil'? Could it have been related to the pit in some way?

There were many unanswered questions associated with the temple, and in his search for answers ElKureishi let his mind wander. The ancient texts were incomplete and sometimes difficult to understand. In the few better-preserved Hittite texts that referred to the Amalishah temple there were words that appeared to be significant but which nobody could translate. The word that might have sounded like *hur-riah*, for instance, appeared nowhere in the Hittite records except those that referred to the Amalishah temple, and in these it always appeared in the convoluted sentences that referred to the 'evil' within the temple. But hur-riah was not a Hittite word; could it have been borrowed from the Assyrian to describe something that had to do with the 'evil' in the temple? Could *hur-riah* have referred to the pit? Long after the Assyrians and the Hittites an ancient Greek traveller had written:

ηλαμιατουναου

and it was conventionally assumed that the ναοσ referred to was the Amalishah temple. But the reference was oblique and nothing was sure, the only point of contact with the Amalishah temple being that the temple was roughly in the right area and had been burned by the Hittites. Many modern archaeologists and historians dismissed the Greek traveller's writings as useless because, they maintained, the writings contained much that was obviously borrowed from garbled oral traditions. The professor, a man well past his prime and in some ways humbled by ill health, was willing to give the Greek the benefit of the doubt.

But although ElKureishi had a good knowledge of ancient Greek, he was not sure whether the original meaning of the word λαμια had the same meaning as it had in much more recent Greek. If it did, then the Amalishah temple would have been very peculiar indeed. Translated loosely, the Greek phrase said

the (female) vampire of the temple

ElKureishi pondered over the question of how, if the reference were indeed to the temple whose ruins Mike had discovered, the Greek traveller's writings could shed some light on the purpose of the deep hole. *Perhaps the temple priests sacrificed to their goddess by throwing people down that pit. If that was one of the ways the priests worshipped their 'goddess' the Hittites would have had good reason to describe the temple as 'evil'! If the memory of the practice had survived to the time of the Greeks, the hole could have acquired the reputation of being a 'blood-drinker' of sorts. The Greek word for 'hole' is of female gender. A female blood-drinking hole could easily become anthropomorphised into a female vampire. The word 'hur-riah', which was invariably associated with the 'evil' of the temple, could then perhaps have meant 'a pit used for human sacrifice'.*

Professor ElKureishi did not believe in vampires and he felt quite satisfied with his explanation of the Greek phrase and of how, most probably, it related to the deep hole. If he were correct about the mysterious word *hur-riah* then that would also explain why the Hittites did not mention a pit explicitly: they would not have needed to because the word *hur-riah* contained all that needed to be said. ElKureishi extinguished the gas lamp and went to bed.

11

THE BANDITS

Jawad

HE WAS CALLED Jawad, and he was tall and broad and handsome, with golden locks and blue-grey eyes flecked with brown. Eyes such as his are greatly admired in that part of the world, where they are known as 'chakir' eyes.

He spent his early childhood in a Kurdish village not far from where the Tigris and the Euphrates are born, and for the first six years of his life he lived with loving parents and two older sisters who doted on him. But soon after his sixth year his father became embroiled in local politics and fell foul of a group of fanatical militia. Jawad's parents and sisters were murdered and the golden-haired little boy with chakir eyes was allowed to live only because one of the militiamen liked pretty little boys for his personal pleasure.

Jawad lived with the man, nominally as a servant, until he was twelve, when he managed to escape and flee south. He then lived in many households as a servant or, when driven by necessity, as a minion for whoever was willing to provide food and shelter in exchange for sexual liberties. Jawad learned to exploit his good looks and became adept at singling out well-to-do middle-aged men who would pay handsomely for the sexual favours of a golden-haired boy. During these years he taught himself to read and write, but not too well.

Jawad killed his first man when he was fifteen. At that time he was living with one Ali, a sixty-year-old butcher, when he contemplated leaving Ali for a better prospect. Ali learned of his plans and beat the boy until he lay unconscious and convulsing in a pool of blood. That night, despite his aching body, Jawad crawled to Ali's bedroom and cut the man's throat with a kitchen knife. The act forced him to change the way he earned his livelihood. He became a petty thief and, in time, acquired a reputation for violence and ruthlessness that earned him the respect and fear of his peers.

When Jawad was in his early twenties he joined a small gang of bandits led by the wily Attila. Attila's gang lived mostly in the mountains but they occasionally visited the cities or the ill-frequented roads that traversed the flatlands. They preyed on isolated tourists and vulnerable travellers, especially the heavily laden lorries that carried anything from household goods to electronic equipment to sacks of wheat and oats. The bandits were guided primarily by rumour and gossip, and sometimes by reports of rich pickings that waited to be plucked.

With Attila's brigands lived an ever-changing collection of young women. There were no children in the band, as it was an unwritten rule that all pregnancies were to be terminated. And so it was that when Jawad disposed of Attila he inherited not only the man's job but also his woman. This was the fiery Circassian, Aisha, a young woman whose beauty and wit were renowned across the underworld. Not yet twenty when she became Jawad's woman, Aisha had had a life almost as full of vicissitudes as his. Her intelligence and down-to-earth attitude made her the ideal mate for the impulsive and often reckless Jawad.

With the support and guidance of Aisha, Jawad proved an unusually competent leader and his band increased in number until they were more than forty, not including the women. With such a large band it was necessary to split into separate groups that specialised in different activities. Some specialised in robbing tourists and unwary families that dared to brave the mountains in their cars or caravans; others concentrated on single lorries that travelled along deserted roads. It was Jawad's prerogative to decide when and where the attacks would take place, and he was careful not to let his forays display a pattern that would lead the authorities to him. When foreign tourists lost their passports or other valuables the thefts appeared random and unconnected, and when a well-stocked lorry with its crew disappeared the circumstances always suggested accident rather than foul play. It was a lucrative and not very difficult business, and Jawad had the sense not to overdo his activities.

As the years passed and Jawad entered his thirties he developed a dream. The territory he had staked out was vast and had more than its share of ancient ruins. The inhabitants – Arabs, Turkomans, Kurds, some Circassians and a few Armenians and Greeks – had lived there since time immemorial. Not surprisingly, they had inherited a rich lore that spoke of ancient treasure buried in the ruins of palaces and temples. If Jawad could lay his hands on just one such treasure it would bring him boundless wealth from rich collectors and some of the less scrupulous museums.

But although Jawad had occasionally peddled in illicitly discovered pottery and some artefacts, he had never come across ancient gold. The few archaeological expeditions that ventured into the desolate flatlands to excavate ancient sites were always protected by army units, and Jawad felt that he was not quite ready to pit his men against adequately trained soldiers. Not quite ready, that is, unless there was a major find.

And so it was that Jawad was very interested indeed when his informants brought news that some agents were recruiting workers for a very large expedition into the wastelands. The expedition was to be a joint venture from several countries, using funds from the authorities in Baghdad and Ankara as well as foreign universities and museums. The involvement of Europeans and Americans meant practically unlimited financial backing and, to someone like Jawad who would never invest in anything without the promise of high rewards, this meant that they expected to find treasure.

Several of the workers who had been recruited by the expedition's agents were intimidated into withdrawing and were quickly replaced by men chosen by Jawad. They lost no time in letting him know that the main target of the expedition was an unidentified and as yet undiscovered ancient temple. This temple was supposed to be unplundered, having been destroyed by invaders who were alleged to have been more anxious to return home than to search for booty.

12

THE MEETING AT THE BATHS

1

Jawad entered the opulent 'Saleem Pasha' Turkish baths with two trusted bodyguards, burly men with short beards and cold eyes. He pushed back his blonde hair and took a deep breath. Despite the high domed ceiling above the cold-water pool the air was steamy and smelt of aromatic oils. Jawad knew the place well, having been to these baths many times before. *But that was for pleasure*, he thought, *this time it's for very important business!* The bright daylight that streamed through the large stained-glass windows had a slightly bluish tinge that mixed well with the artificial light from the crystal-laden chandeliers. The effect spoke of lavish Eastern sumptuousness, which Jawad found very pleasing.

After paying the exclusively high entrance fee, the three men were taken to an extravagantly furnished *salon* where an attendant, an older man of small stature, provided them with scented bathrobes, towels and the thick-soled wooden clogs peculiar to traditional Turkish baths. Another attendant, an obsequious young man in fine livery, helped Jawad change into his bathrobe. The men left their clothes with the attendants and proceeded silently to one of the little private steam rooms off the main bath. They wore only loose bathrobes and carried clean towels, but beneath his towel each man carried a pistol with a silencer. The young attendant who had helped Jawad change had momentarily raised his eyebrows when he became aware of the weapons, but Jawad only had to look coldly at the man for him to quickly turn the other way. Jawad was well known at the baths not only as a generous client but also as a *very dangerous man* who should never be crossed.

It was common knowledge that, a few years previously, a new local police chief had decided to give chase to some of Jawad's lads. The police chief was young, idealistic and inexperienced, and had been outraged by the murder of a family of tourists who had strayed into the mountains. The officer had vowed publicly that he would bring the criminals responsible to justice, and he and his policemen had been led a merry chase by Jawad's men across uncharted mountain paths. When the policemen eventually returned to their station empty handed, they found it burned to the ground and decorated with the heads of the handful of men who had been left to guard it. The young police chief went insane and his successor avoided all contact with Jawad or his men. Jawad had wanted to have the heads stuffed with straw in the old Ottoman way, but he was unable to find anyone with the stomach to do it.

2

The three men made themselves comfortable in a private steam room suffused with aromatic mist. Fine mosaics covered the walls and the intricately coloured ceiling was bordered by special tiles with hand-coloured *bas-reliefs*. On three sides of the room were oval recesses that provided seats for as many as nine men, and at each corner was a large glazed earthenware pot with a broad-leaved plant. A delicately woven but heavy curtain covered the single entrance, which had no door. There were no windows. Jawad had come to meet the notorious bandit leader Tewfiq Arroussi, a man who had terrorised the people in his 'territory' for over thirty years. Jawad had never met Arroussi before, and had arrived almost an hour before the appointed time in case Arroussi had thought of preparing an unpleasant surprise.

While they waited in silence, their ears alert to any unexpected sound, Jawad pondered over the proposition he was going to make to Arroussi. It was almost certain that the old bandit knew about the international archaeological expedition, and it was very probable that he had his own plans about how to relieve the archaeologists of any treasure they might find. But Jawad had some aces up his sleeve that he hoped would make his proposition irresistible and himself indispensable. In the very polite and long-winded note he had sent to Arroussi via a string of intermediaries, since Arroussi had no fixed address, Jawad had written after the customary courteous preliminaries:

'It is the possibility of a mutually highly lucrative venture that *prompts me to respectfully write to you. For a long time I have lived in the hope that your excellent men would, one day, work alongside mine for our joint profit. The venture I hope to have the honour of proposing to you promises very high rewards with very little risk because I have already taken preliminary steps that will ensure its success, Allah willing. I am confident that the measures I have taken shall prove worthy of the support and cooperation of someone as famous and exalted as you. I beg you to agree to a potentially very fruitful meeting at the Saleem Pasha baths at a time that is convenient to both of us.'*

There followed alternative suggestions as to how the proposed appointment could be arranged via intermediaries. The letter contained spelling mistakes and grammatical errors but ended with the elaborate signature that Jawad had practised for years.

Jawad hoped that the older bandit had not thought of infiltrating his men into the expedition's workforce. That was not his way according to all accounts. Arroussi was reputed to be a bandit of the old school who believed in storm and slaughter, and Jawad was fairly certain that if Arroussi intended to lay his hands on any gold that the archaeologists might find then his policy would be to prepare for all eventualities and then strike at the first opportune moment. However, it was impossible to predict how Arroussi would react to the information that Jawad's men had already infiltrated the expedition's workforce, and Jawad could only pray that Arroussi would see the advantages without being tempted to eliminate him altogether as a dangerous rival. There was not much honour between bandits, and the odd fraternal murder now and then was considered an acceptable means of ensuring the high quality of the stock.

Tewfiq Arroussi arrived punctually. He was accompanied only by his son, a man in his late twenties. The veteran bandit was a huge thick-set man with grey hair, almost two metres tall, with piercing brown eyes and two vertical strips of pure white in his grey beard, one on either side of his mouth. His son was no less tall but was beardless and wore glasses. He was much slimmer than his father. Both men had to stoop as they parted the heavy curtain and entered the small private room.

3

Unlike Jawad, who spent his money on banqueting, women and *Arak*, Tewfiq Arroussi was a man of means who had invested most of his ill-gained wealth wisely, or at least legitimately. It was even said that Arroussi's son had been educated in some foreign university. So Jawad had a certain resentful respect for the older man, although he knew him only by reputation. He rose cordially to his feet and bowed low before greeting the veteran bandit leader with a broad smile.

There were none of the customary handshakes or traditional embracings. Arroussi did not return Jawad's smile and replied to all the formal salutations tersely, not bothering to hide his impatience. For all Tewfiq Arroussi's wealth, he and his son had never been to a Turkish bath before and, like Jawad, the old bandit was very suspicious of unfamiliar environments. Also like Jawad, Arroussi and his son were fully aware of the possibility that an invitation to a *potentially very fruitful meeting* could easily turn out to be an invitation to a quick death. Jawad was known to be impulsive and not always to think things through, and he could well have decided that the chance to kill Arroussi, who was at the top of the bandit pecking order and whose territory overlapped Jawad's, was not to be missed.

"So why are we here?" asked the older bandit gruffly, getting straight to the point after the minimum obligatory formal greetings. Arroussi was a heavy smoker and spoke in a low-pitched rasping voice. He and his son sat directly across from Jawad. They did not remove their bathrobes and held their neatly folded towels on their knees. Jawad knew that the neatly folded towels concealed weapons.

"There is a new archaeological expedition to the wastelands," said Jawad affably, "And I have reason to believe that their findings are expected to be very valuable indeed."

"What does this have to do with me?"

"The expedition is most likely to find treasure," replied Jawad, and his smile broadened, "a large quantity of gold, at least! Possibly other things as well, like ancient jewellery and precious stones! I respectfully suggest that it would be a sin if we did not try to get our shares."

"You brought me here to tell me this?"

"It would be to our mutual advantage to work together rather than at cross-purposes," said Jawad with the warmest of smiles, "Your expert and well-informed advice would be invaluable and, for my part, I have already taken some preliminary steps of which I am sure you will approve."

"What steps have you taken?" asked Arroussi. He seemed only slightly interested.

"All in good time, we have not agreed on anything yet."

"Where in the wastelands is the expedition heading?"

"That is not yet known. They are looking for a temple. An *unplundered* temple."

Arroussi made a snorting sound. Then he said: "All the sites in the wastelands that are worth excavating have been plundered many years ago."

"Not this one, if my spies are to be believed."

"Your spies?"

"Yes. Although the expedition is still in its very early stages, I have trustworthy men in key positions."

"How do they keep in touch with you?"

"We have ways."

"I suppose putting spies among the expedition workers is one of the 'preliminary steps' you claim to have taken."

"One of them."

Jawad's gambit hinged on whether Arroussi had planted his own men among the expedition workers. Jawad had to be careful not to let Arroussi know how his men had infiltrated the expedition or which 'key positions' they held. This could provide clues to their identity and permit Arroussi to eliminate them.

"You have been clever, that is beyond question," said Arroussi, "But what makes you think the findings of this expedition, if any, may be worth my interest?"

"The expedition has at least three large all-terrain army lorries and at least five cross-country vehicles. It is sponsored by two of our universities and several foreign ones, not to mention a number of museums."

"Your information is correct," said Arroussi, nodding thoughtfully. His manner showed that he had sources of his own.

For Arroussi, as for Jawad, no one invested money in archaeological adventures without expecting a reward *considerably* greater than the investment. The number of vehicles suggested a large expedition and the fact that they included *army* lorries indicated support in high places. Certainly a lot of money had been invested here.

"Please tell us what you know about any armed escort," said

Arroussi's son, who had not been introduced to Jawad.

4

Jawad looked sharply at the younger man who had dared speak in the presence of his superiors. If one of his own men had spoken like this it would have been a sign of insubordination. Still, each bandit group had its own rules, and perhaps Arroussi allowed his son a certain measure of independence.

"There is no escort – yet," replied Jawad, addressing the father. "Although an escort is certain to arrive when a valuable discovery is made."

"Or perhaps sooner," said the son, "If it is thought that valuable discoveries are imminent."

Jawad ignored him.

"If the army can provide lorries for the transport of personnel," rasped Arroussi, "It might be willing to provide military helicopters for the transport of treasure. That would give you very little time to do anything useful."

Jawad thought it wise not to appear to underestimate the risks. "That is possible, of course," he admitted pleasantly. "But with inside information we can be sure that the treasure shall not be there if and when any helicopters arrive."

"Assuming we lay our hands on the gold," said Arroussi with an almost-sarcastic half-smile, "do you propose that we fight army helicopters on the run when they pursue us across the empty wastelands?"

"We shall give ourselves a generous head start," said Jawad, "And we shall scatter."

"So any gold we take will be scattered."

"Not necessarily, and the risks involved in getting away can be dealt with."

"I see," said Arroussi, and he gave a cold grin that displayed the absence of several teeth. Arroussi was clearly interested but cautious: *The real fun will start after we lay our hands on the gold! That is when this young upstart will make his play!*

Jawad fully understood the implications of Arroussi's grin and he grinned back. One wily hyena grinning at another: "We shall naturally take all the precautions necessary!" "Without a doubt," replied Arroussi. "But these are details that we or our representatives can thrash out later if I agree to work with you." He scratched his groin thoughtfully. "Tell me, how do you propose to make sure you have the necessary head start?"

"The plans are laid and my men are in place," replied Jawad smoothly. "The helicopters cannot be expected to hover over the lorries before anything of importance is found and the search for the temple may take months! Even if they find the temple, and they probably will, they will first look around and dig everywhere like they always do. If they find gold, *then* they shall call for reinforcements. Given the usual bureaucracy, it will take at least several days before any escort arrives."

"They may get an escort the moment they find the temple," said Arroussi's son, "If only to deter casual thieves who might be after expensive equipment or the odd truck. For if they find the temple they shall stop moving around in the wastelands."

The father nodded approvingly.

"An escort, yes," replied Jawad, this time addressing the son. He had noticed Arroussi's approval of his son's comment. "But nothing serious like combat helicopters. This simply means that when they start digging there may be a small group of soldiers to protect them." He turned to Arroussi: "My honoured friend, you have not given me the pleasure of introducing this young man to me!"

"This is my son, Mukhtar."

"It is a great pleasure to meet you," said Jawad with the silkiest of smiles, but he did not offer his hand. Mukhtar smiled back, and lowered his head as a sign of respect.

"Your son is young yet speaks as though he knows many things."

"He has much to learn," said the father abruptly. "How do you intend to transport the treasure? If it includes artefacts that can be sold it is likely to be bulky."

"I propose to use the trucks with which our men will get there, and if necessary we can use one or more of the expedition's own trucks," replied Jawad, "I hope this idea meets with your approval."

"I could provide a helicopter or two."

Jawad pretended to give serious consideration to Arroussi's suggestion although he had no intention of accepting the offer: *Any treasure that finds its way into a helicopter provided by Arroussi will be lost to me forever! Even if I provide the helicopters it would be impossible to keep track of them. The most trustworthy of pilots can be bribed or intimidated by this old fox!* "Arrangements to lease a helicopter for a destination that we cannot disclose might arouse suspicion," he said, after pretending to give Arroussi's suggestion serious thought, "The authorities will almost certainly be keeping their eyes open for such things."

Arroussi nodded. "Let me summarise your proposition so far," he said. "You propose to attack the expedition very soon after they discover treasure. You expect to face some armed opposition. You intend to carry off the treasure in one or more trucks. You hope to have escaped with the treasure long before the authorities send in reinforcements of the kind neither of us can deal with, like combat helicopters. Finally, you hope to be able to dispose of the treasure through the usual channels before everybody starts looking for it."

"That is a perceptive summary," said Jawad. "The success of our venture will depend on perfect timing and on attacking with sufficient force to quickly overwhelm any military escort."

"And you shall depend on *me* to provide the overwhelming force," growled Arroussi, "Because only I can provide enough men and appropriate weapons."

Jawad smiled again: "Yes. And you shall depend on *me* to also provide men as well as what is needed for perfect timing."

"You can guarantee that we shall know about the treasure, if any is found, immediately after it is found?"

"On the same day!"

Arroussi shook his head. "I am not happy with this. You are too confident and you take too much for granted!"

5

Mukhtar turned to his father. "If I may say something here, father."

Arroussi nodded, but his eyes remained steadily on Jawad.

Mukhtar said: "*If* the expedition finds the temple and *if* they find treasure then, in my opinion, it would take them some time before anything valuable is shipped out."

"Why is that?" asked Arroussi.

"Because, father, that is the way these expeditions operate. Before anything is sent away it has to be classified, recorded, packed, and so on. Also, if they find treasure they shall not send it off before they are certain that there is no more to be found. I would suggest that it would take at least a week after valuables are found before anything is sent away."

Arroussi spoke to his son without taking his eyes off Jawad: "So if we learn about any gold immediately after its discovery we should have time to organise an attack force?"

"I think so, father, if we start preparations as soon as the temple is located and if we begin the *final stage* as soon as we hear that treasure has been found."

"I am sure we shall have the time to do everything we need," added Jawad.

"What if they radio that they are under attack?" asked Arroussi casually, "Helicopter gunships could be there in a very short time."

"But only if they are ready to fly to the rescue, father," said Mukhtar. "It is very improbable that the authorities will have helicopters on standby, waiting for an attack on the archaeological expedition. The helicopters cannot arrive less than two hours after they radio for help, at the earliest, unless an attack on the archaeologists is expected."

"An attack of some sort is sure to be expected, and two hours is much too short a time to do anything!" said Arroussi. He appeared to lose interest.

"Their radio will be dead ten minutes before our attack," said Jawad quickly, aware that he had been forced to display another of his 'preliminary steps', "Not much earlier and not later."

"Oh? The radio would be guarded."

"Of course, but that has been taken into account."

So this jackal has quite a few of his men in there! Arroussi rubbed his beard. "I see that you are as clever as they say. But I am not convinced that there will be treasure. As I said, the temples in the wastelands have all been plundered."

"By small-time grave-robbers!" said Jawad earnestly, "Or by thieves who take what they find without knowing what they leave behind. Think how much money the foreigners have spent on this expedition! Would they put in so much money if they thought they would find nothing?"

"How many men will you need?" asked Arroussi.

"That is hard to say. We shall have to play it by ear. Perhaps many if the escort is serious."

"And how many will you contribute?"

"About fifty, perhaps more. Some of my men will be working from within."

"Less than two hundred men may not be enough. An expensive expedition will have a strong escort."

"The number of men is a small detail. We shall put together the right number of men with the right weapons once we know the strength of the escort."

Arroussi pondered over Jawad's words. Then he asked: "What exactly do you mean when you say 'the right number of men'?"

"Not too few and not too many. Too few will fail, too many will leave a lot of mouths that could talk to the authorities."

"So part of your plan is to sustain heavy casualties."

"Is it not safer that way?"

Arroussi gave Jawad a cold, calculating look. "Safer," he said, "and cheaper for us. But to plan for heavy casualties is a risky way to do things."

Jawad did not wish to dwell on the issue of casualties. The secret part of his plan included Arroussi's demise soon after the treasure was appropriated, so the more Arroussi's attention was steered away from *casualties* the better. No doubt Arroussi had his suspicions, and no doubt he had his own plans for a similar double-crossing, but Jawad was now sure that if Arroussi's qualms were kept dormant they would not scupper the possibility of his co-operation.

Jawad adopted an earnest conspiratorial tone: "*Naturally* we cannot expect the expedition to remain without an army escort if the temple is found. But the army will not waste a lot of men guarding a few idiots digging in the ground. The trick is to know the strength of the escort well in advance. When treasure is found we attack the camp, wipe out any resistance, and whisk the treasure away before reinforcements arrive."

"You think it would be easy to wipe out the resistance? You are talking about well-armed and well-trained soldiers! Much also depends on how resourceful the commanding officer is."

"That is true, but we shall know precisely what opposition to expect. And my spies are competent enough to gauge the resourcefulness of the commanding officer."

"And what do you propose to do with the workers and the university men and women? The workers are from our own people!"

"Do we ever leave witnesses?"

"I see." Arroussi spoke without any emotion at all. "You are contemplating a massacre."

"Father..."

"No, my son. You must learn to live in the real world. There must be no survivors. Survivors always cause problems and we cannot afford problems!"

The son bit his lip but remained silent. Jawad thought: *There could be trouble from the young dog!*

"Are we agreed to work together, then?" asked Jawad. He was not smiling.

"I cannot make a decision unless I know a lot more about how you shall take care of your side of things. Even if they find the temple, I shall need to know what else they find, if anything. I shall not take any risks for the sake of old pottery or a few statues. The museums are full of such things."

"This is not the time for details," said Jawad, "But if you are interested in us working together all details can be arranged."

Arroussi and his son rose to leave. "I am not sure this is a reasonable venture," the old bandit said slowly, "There are too many *ifs* and unanswered questions."

"When the time is right I shall provide the answers to any reasonable questions you may have," said Jawad.

"I am sure you will," said Arroussi. He was about to turn away when the son asked: "What do you know about the temple they are supposed to look for?"

"I was told that it was once called the Temple of Amalishah," said Jawad, and suddenly wondered if he had said too much. *Could Arroussi know where it is?*

But Arroussi shook his head. "That is said to be a very evil place," he said gravely. "Its location has been forgotten because it is guarded by a demon."

Jawad laughed. "Let the foreigners worry about the demon," he said with a curt laugh, "After all, it is they who will be digging for treasure. When the time comes, we shall only have to deal with the armed escort."

"I will let you know what I have decided," said Arroussi. "You are easy to find."

Before Jawad could say anything the old bandit and his son were gone. They remembered to stoop so as not to hit their heads on the frame of the door.

13

THE PIT

1

MIKE WAITED IMPATIENTLY by the Land Rover for ElKureishi to call back. He fidgeted with his rucksack, then with his hat. When the radio finally bleeped he picked up the receiver immediately: "Mike Townsend!"

Leonard knew that this call was important to Mike. He tried to listen to what ElKureishi was saying but all he could hear was an agitated twittering: *Old Kureishi sure sounds excited!* The monologue continued for some time and Leonard noticed that Mike's eyelids were starting to droop: *I wonder if Mike will get a chance to say anything!* Mike finally did have the chance to speak but by then Leonard was rummaging noisily at the back of the Land Rover and could not hear what he said. When Leonard's attention returned to the conversation he was just in time to hear Mike say in a tone from which all emotion had been sifted out: "Am I to understand that you expect to be here in *three days?*"

The receiver twittered some more.

"All right," said Mike, his voice still flat, "We'll take photographs of the ruins." When he was sure that the radio was turned off he smiled triumphantly and turned to stare at Leonard: "They'll be here in three days!"

"You mean," said Leonard, "They won't be here tomorrow, or the day after – they'll be here the day after that?"

"Yes! It'll take that long to get caving equipment and bring it here. I was hoping it would take longer but three days will have to do..." Mike's voice trailed off and he seemed to be preoccupied with something in the distance.

"Why caving equipment?"

Mike's attention returned to Leonard: "Well, when I first told the old boy about the pit in the mound I told him that it ought to lead to something interesting. The hole was obviously very deep but couldn't be a well!"

"Did you convince him of that?"

"I think so. I emphasised the diameter of the hole and the narrowness of the shaft at the centre of the spiral staircase. He agreed that this wasn't like a well at all. I also told him about the writing on the wall of the pit. Finally, I told him that whatever was down there was probably flooded. I could almost hear the crackle of his ears as they perked up!"

"Um…Why would his ears perk up?"

"Because if the bottom of the pit is full of water then it's unlikely that whatever is down there has been looted! So Kureishi had the brilliant idea that we might need caving equipment, including stuff for underwater exploration!"

"Mike…" Leonard sounded accusatory.

"Yes, I know. Flooding is not very likely. I'm afraid I also made some fairly strong hints that there might be wonderful surprises at the bottom of the pit. I hope that's true."

"You really want to explore that pit by yourself, don't you?"

"I do. I certainly want to explore the pit before the other teams and Kureishi's army of specialists gets here."

"Going down that pit without backup could be dangerous, Mike."

"I know. But if this place is the Amalishah temple I want to get first bite of the apple!" Mike put his hat on. "And if it isn't, then I want to be the one who finds out!"

Leonard nodded. No archaeologist had published more papers on the Amalishah temple than Mike. It was well known in certain archaeological circles that his interest in the Amalishah temple, and especially its 'goddess', bordered on obsession.

"And what did Kureishi say we should do while we wait?"

Mike picked up his rucksack before answering: "He suggested we spend the time taking photographs of the ruins. Let's get going!"

Leonard picked up his own rucksack much less enthusiastically. As they made their way towards the hill Leonard asked: "Does that mean you won't be going down the pit until we've taken pictures of the surface ruins?"

"It means nothing of the sort! I don't think the bottom of the pit is flooded at all!"

2

Leonard did not know what to say. He was brilliant as a historian but his psychology was that of a follower, he tended to follow the rules, or a leader. Although he understood Mike's reasons for wanting to be the first to explore the pit, and to explore the pit alone, he felt ill at ease at the way his friend had manipulated old ElKureishi, the leader of the expedition.

"What about the photographs of the surface ruins?"

"If you wish you can start taking pictures of the ruins while I'm down in the pit. I want to take a new set of photographs of the writing. I've got the new zoom lens on my camera."

"I ain't going to wander around taking pictures while you're alone in the pit," said Leonard. "I'll wait for you on the mound in case something happens and you need help. Do you think you'll have time to photograph all the inscriptions this afternoon?"

"That depends on how deep the pit is. But it's not even two-thirty yet. Look! The sun is shining brightly. If there were any songbirds around here they'd be singing their hearts out! I hope to put in at least three hours of work in the pit!"

"OK," said Leonard resignedly. "At least we've brought spare batteries and things."

"Tonight we'll use my laptop to study the pictures of the inscriptions. Maybe we won't need Ohanian, after all."

Oh Lord! thought Leonard, *He's in one of his all-coming, all-seeing and all-conquering moods!*

They talked about what the inscriptions might contain as they approached the hill. It was very hot and the rucksacks were heavy, but their excitement at the prospect of interesting revelations made the discomforts of the trek to the hill and up the ramp easily bearable. Leonard was surprised to find that talking about the inscriptions made him lose most of his reservations about Mike going down into the pit on his own. What information the inscriptions might contain could be *historically* very interesting. If they waited for the others and the descent was shared with the expedition's specialists the thrill would be lost.

3

Not much later they were at the top of the mound. The sight of the gaping hole brought back Leonard's misgivings but he kept them to himself.

"It's not yet three-thirty," said Mike. "I should be back before seven. There will still be some daylight and, anyway, we've got our torches."

"Remember that darkness falls pretty suddenly around here."

"I know."

"You'll watch out for snakes and scorpions!"

"But of course!"

Leonard tried to suppress his unease: *I wish he wouldn't be so flippant! This hole could conceal all sorts of dangers other than snakes and scorpions! The stone steps might not take his weight!*

Mike tried out the batteries of his torch and then checked his camera and the built-in flashgun. The camera was fitted with a zoom lens that could take both wide-angle and close-up. While Mike made his final preparations Leonard squatted on the rim of the mound and lit a cigarette.

"I'll be here in case you need assistance."

"Thanks."

"You'll begin as you always do by calling out some measurements?"

"Yes. You've got your notepad?"

"It's ready."

"I'm off!"

"Be careful!"

Mike carefully climbed down the pile of stones that ringed the hole. A few loose stones rolled down about him but he ignored them. When he stepped onto the little rock platform just below the rim he knelt on one of the steps and measured the distance to the opposite side of the aperture with a small sonic rangefinder.

"Three metres and ninety," he called to Leonard. Leonard jotted down the measurements in his little notebook.

"Yeah. Width of hole three metres and ninety. What shall I put down as the diameter of the mound?"

"Put thirty-five to forty metres. It could be more but we can't be more precise than that. The thing's not a perfect circle."

"OK."

"According to my tape measure the first steps are about one metre forty-six long, thirteen and a half centimetres wide at the narrow end and fifty-three centimetres wide at the wide end. The dimensions are almost exactly the same for each step. The steps are uh… about eighteen centimetres high, with a concavity that shows prolonged use."

"Yeah." Leonard read out the numbers individually: 1-4-6 long, 1-3 point 5 to 5-3 centimetres wide and 1-8 deep. Dimensions the same for all steps. Some concavity due to prolonged use."

That makes the shaft about ninety-eight centimetres in diameter," continued Mike.

"OK. Shaft diameter about 9-8." *Enough for a body to fall through!*

"The steps are volcanic rock. Very solid. Apparently not porous."

"Yeah. Volcanic rock. Not porous."

"That's it."

"OK."

Mike turned on his torch and cautiously pointed it down into the central shaft. The light did not reveal what lay at the bottom and all he could see were the winding steps that spiralled down into the blackness: *This hole could easily accommodate a falling body. But if it had been used to dispose of sacrificial victims, why the steps? Did they recover the bodies? And what was the purpose of the writing?* Mike recalled the human sacrifices of the Aztecs: *Perhaps the inscriptions are prayers to be carried to the gods by the victims.* Despite the heat the thought of bodies being thrown down the shaft almost made him shiver, and he tried not to think of what might lie at the bottom of the pit.

"I'm going down the steps now."

"OK," said Leonard from the top of the ridge.

Mike started his descent into the pit.

The inscriptions started four steps below the rock platform that marked the top of the winding stairs. The writing was in perfectly parallel columns about seventy centimetres wide and about ninety centimetres high, though the height of the columns varied considerably. The lowest of the inscriptions was about one metre above the steps, so that someone who could understand the writing would have been able to read it without stooping as he went down into the pit. The writing itself was quite small, no more than a few centimetres high. Mike's heart sank as he studied the symbols more carefully than he had previously. The cuneiform script, mixed as it was with little ideograms that were so reminiscent of Egyptian hieroglyphics, made no sense at all. He was not even sure whether the writing started or ended at the top of the pit. *Damn! It looks as though I will need Ohanian, after all!*

The necessity for caution as Mike descended into the pit soon put the mystery of the unknown script out of his mind, and his confidence rose as he slowly went down the steps. He took wide-angle photographs of the writing every five steps, making sure that his photographs overlapped at the edges. For every photograph he had to step back from the wider side of the steps to the narrow part, which was just over thirteen centimetres wide. Sometimes the rim of a step had broken off, leaving a jagged edge that emphasised the darkness beneath. Exciting though the descent was, it was monotonous and Mike had almost lapsed into a mechanical routine when, stepping back to take a photograph, he trod on a loose egg-sized stone and momentarily lost his balance. He almost toppled backwards into the shaft while the stone rolled away and fell behind him.

"Damn!" he cried, and then held his breath as he unwittingly waited for the stone he had dislodged to strike the bottom of the pit. It seemed an eternity before he heard a faint clatter.

"Are you all right?" Leonard's voice was muffled by multiple echoes.

"Yes. A moment's carelessness!" *There was no splash! The bottom of the pit is dry!*

"Be careful!"

"Of course!" *That was close!* Mike took a deep breath. *Face it chum, your reactions aren't as fast as they used to be!*

"Are you coming up?"

"No! But I'll be more careful!"

"Are you counting the steps?"

"Yes. I'm on the hundred and fortieth. The walls are almost black here with what – I think – had once been soot! But the writing is better defined down here than near the surface." *Better defined but still unreadable!*

He resumed his descent, taking pictures every five steps. Two hundred and ten steps down the writing stopped. Mike packed the flashgun and camera into his rucksack and held only the torch. The air was dry, but he thought he could detect a foetid smell that wafted up from the central shaft. *That's odd. I could swear there's an occasional updraft!*

"This place stinks!" he shouted merrily.

Leonard's reply was unintelligible because of the multiple echoes.

"I said this place stinks!" Mike shouted. "There must be a dead animal down there!"

Leonard shouted something back, but Mike could not make it out. *Hell! These steps are endless! It must have taken years to carve this.* The walls and steps were of solid rock and stained almost completely black. The writing had been quite discernible, however, as it was deeply engraved, but now that it had stopped Mike was able to concentrate more on the conditions around him.

It was cool in the pit, a welcome change from the dry heat outside. More than once Mike was sure there was a faint draft of air that sometimes wafted up the pit, carrying with it the noxious stench: *If it weren't for the damn smell, this venture could be quite pleasant!* Mike doggedly made his way down. The smell got worse, as did the darkness all around the small circle of brightness produced by the light from his torch.

4

At the 584th step Mike was still pointing the torch downwards when he saw that the last few steps sank into a sea of debris. *At last! So there are 590 steps in all.* He was on the point of taking a deep breath of satisfaction but refrained because of the stench. It was now almost unbearable. He waved the torch at the dense jumble of stones and dried mud that lay before him. He tried not to think of what might lie beneath.

The pit opened up into a hemispherical cavern whose floor was covered by rubble and the bones of animals. *Doesn't look too bad. All it needs is a good clean!* Standing on the last exposed step he shone his torch absent-mindedly across the cavern and his heart almost skipped a beat. Across from the stairs, above the rubble, was what looked like the top of an elliptical hole. The rubble extended into the hole.

A tunnel? I'll be damned! This would explain the air current!

The narrow aperture between the debris and the top of the tunnel gaped blackly and gave no discernible reflection to the glare of Mike's torch.

The walls of the cavern were too uneven for the sonic rangefinder to work, but from where he stood Mike estimated the dimensions of the cavern to be about six to seven metres, possibly larger. If the tunnel were circular and high enough to take the height of a small man then the rubble would be at least a metre and a half deep. *That would make the cavern four to five metres high at its highest! If the rubble covers eight or nine steps there would be about 593 steps in all!* Mike made a quick mental calculation: *The pit is over a hundred metres deep and I'm about eighty metres below the level of the plain! God, what a stench!*

Mike saw nothing that could account for the smell of putrefaction, which was almost overpowering. Scattered over the rubble were lots of jackal bones and the bones of what might once have been some kind of mountain goat, but they were dry and old. *Whatever is producing this smell must have died recently in the tunnel. It probably scampered over the rubble into the tunnel and could not climb out!* Mike looked at his watch. It was past six. *It will be time to go up soon, but first I must move some of this rubbish and take a better look at what's in the tunnel.* He stepped gingerly off the last exposed step and onto the layer of stones and dried mud, waving his torch so as to get an idea of what lay beneath him. The rubble under his feet shifted slightly but he did not lose his balance. As he slowly made his way to the opening he noticed that the debris was highest in front of the tunnel: *That's odd! It's as though someone has piled the stuff so as to make the aperture as small as possible!* For a moment all his attention was on the mystery of the unevenly piled rubble, but then he thought of a possible explanation: *Perhaps the pit flooded at some time and the water escaped into the tunnel, dragging the rubble with it.* It was not a very good explanation but it was all he could think of. *Oh well, this pit is old enough to have been flooded many times!* The crescent-shaped gap between the rubble and the top of the tunnel was about than twenty-five centimetres high.

He went down onto the rubble on all fours so as to peer into the aperture and grimaced. *I was right. The stench is coming from the tunnel!* But when he shone his torch into the narrow opening he could see very little, as the slope of the rubble prevented the powerful torch from illuminating anything but the farther walls and ceiling. There seemed to be dark shadows scattered along the end of the tunnel, but Mike refrained from looking too carefully because of the foul smell.

However, he did notice that the tunnel was roughly parabolic in cross-section, higher than it was wide, and extended no more than about six to ten metres before veering to the left. It was evidently higher than he had surmised, though he could not see the floor nearer to him because the angle was wrong. On his hands and knees, with his torch lying beside him, Mike moved back and started clearing the debris from the mouth of the tunnel. Despite his excitement he was fully aware of the possibility of something nasty lurking beneath the stones. He had to lift each stone carefully before throwing it behind him, as far from himself as possible. It was hard work and after less than an hour his hands and knees were sore. *We'll have to set up some kind of crane to clear this mess. Damn! It's almost seven!* Eventually Mike cleared enough space to be able to look down at the floor of the tunnel behind the rubble. The stench was now much worse but with an effort he brought up his torch and pointed it downwards, lighting up the space only a few metres from the opening. As the powerful beam shone onto the floor of the tunnel Mike gasped and his heart started beating wildly.

Lying at all angles, some lying on top of each other, some resting against the wall of the tunnel, were human skeletons. Mike tried to count the skeletons but because the torch could only illuminate a small area of the tunnel he gave up after the second try. *There must be at least ten of them, maybe more!* The skeletons extended as far as he could see along the length of the tunnel. The skulls had fallen off the neck bones of the bodies that were in a sitting position, but the skeletons seemed otherwise complete, with no sign of the scattering indicative of disturbance by animals. *So the bodies lay as they fell and decomposed undisturbed! The forensic boys and girls will have a field day here!* The bones appeared dry but were covered with stains of various shades of brown. Among the human remains lay badly corroded swords, spearheads and breastplates. *These people died defending the tunnel! What in heaven's name is at the end of the tunnel?*

But it was already past seven, and he had to return to the surface because it would soon be dark outside. Mike had enough self-discipline to suppress his curiosity and leave the work undone. He crawled back to the steps and started the long climb back in a mixture of high spirits at his discoveries and shock at what his discoveries had revealed. Half way up he had to use his torch, for it became too dark to see. In his frame of mind he did not think at all about the stench.

5

"Well?" Leonard sounded very relieved to see Mike's head pop up out of the pit. He was still squatting on the rim of the mound, smoking a cigarette.

"You've hardly moved since I went down there!" said Mike.

"Yeah! But I smoked almost a whole packet!"

"There's an oblong cavern down there, with a tunnel leading out."

"A tunnel?"

"As you Americans say: 'Yup'!"

"We must tell Kureishi!"

"He may expressly forbid me to go down there alone again. I'll try to find out what the tunnel leads to tomorrow morning. Then we'll tell him! Oh, and there's a godawful stench down there."

Leonard decided not to press the subject. "Did you find out what made the stench?"

"No."

"That's very strange."

"And," added Mike with a grin as they prepared to leave, "the tunnel is full of human remains!"

"What?" the American could not suppress his surprise.

"Human skeletons with bronze-age weapons lying all around them. I think their late owners died defending the tunnel."

"Why would they wish to defend a tunnel?"

"I've no idea. Perhaps it leads to something important. I hope to find out tomorrow."

"What about the photographs of the surface ruins?"

"To hell with them!"

"Mike, it's important that we photograph the surface ruins before they're all mucked up by the coming mob."

"I suppose you're right. But you can do that tomorrow while I'm having fun in the pit. Now let's get back to the Land Rover before it gets too dark."

"OK. But tell me more about the cavern and the skeletons."

"I don't want to talk about it now. Those old bones gave me the jitters."

Mike was very quiet as they made their way back. The Hittite records said nothing about fighting at the bottom of a pit. But then, they said nothing at all about the fighting with the temple priests! Leonard was also absorbed by his thoughts, but they were mostly about ElKureishi, and how he might react at not being told immediately about what Mike found at the bottom of the pit.

They were soon at the makeshift camp by the Land Rover. After a quick supper they sat under their little tent to drink their coffees. Mike lit his pipe. Leonard knew that this was the time when Mike was at his most expansive.

"Tell me more about the tunnel," said Leonard. "Any new ideas?"

"Well, I suspect that it's a natural tunnel, not carved by zealous fellows. Some gas, or possibly steam, must have been squeezed out somehow, back in primordial times when the rock was still soft. The hemispherical cavern would then have been a huge bubble whose compressed gases eventually broke through to the surface. That would also explain the shaft, which must have been the channel by which the gas pushed its way up to the surface of the hill. The zealous fellows would then have had to carve only the steps around the shaft. We'll have to check with the geologists."

"Have you any idea of what might be at the end of the tunnel?"

"Heaven knows! I almost regret not crawling through to see what it leads to. Its entrance is still almost choked with debris but I could have crawled through. I've made a sizeable gap now, but I didn't want to dislodge too many of the stones while lying on my belly."

"Yeah, you don't know what lives under the stones."

"Exactly. And it's totally dark down there, a hundred metres below the opening at the surface. My torch makes only a small circle of light, the rest is pitch black, but the gap is wide enough to show the length of the tunnel before it turns to the left. There was nothing interesting apart from the skeletons and the weapons. I didn't see any writing on the walls of the tunnel."

"How deep is the tunnel?"

"It's about eight to ten metres long before it turns. After that I don't know."

"You were actually back earlier than I expected." It was unlike Mike to come back on time from something so interesting.

"I ran up those steps in record time and only stopped once to have another look at the writing. I think the smell egged me on to get out. It almost drove me insane. I should have got used to it but I didn't."

"Exactly what kind of smell was it?" asked Leonard.

"Putrefaction I suppose, but very strong."

"A dead rat?"

"More like a thousand dead rats."

"In a four thousand year old hole full of dry stones?"

"And dry bones. Strange, isn't it? Anyhow, it was pretty awful. Most probably some larger creature died in the tunnel recently. There's quite a lot of wildlife around here. We don't see them because they see us first."

"Well, we shall get all the answers when the rest of us get here."

"Oh yes, but I'm going down again tomorrow morning. I'll write a preliminary report tonight after studying my photographs of the inscriptions."

"Do you have any new ideas about the inscriptions?"

"None. The writing is completely baffling! I've never seen anything like it!"

Leonard tried to persuade him not to go down the pit again before the rest of the expedition arrived, but Mike was much too excited to wait.

6

That night, Mike studied the photographs he had taken of the inscriptions. He sat cross-legged at the opening of the small tent, smoking his pipe and working on his laptop. Leonard lay at the back of the tent trying to sleep. None of the cryptographic programs on Mike's laptop were of any help. His frustration was such that he almost slammed the cover of the laptop shut.

"No luck, huh?" drawled Leonard.

"Why aren't you sleeping?"

"How can I sleep when you're huffing and puffing on your pipe like an old locomotive?"

"I'm sorry."

Leonard sat up. "Let's walk around a bit. It would give the tent a chance to get rid of all your smoke."

"Very well. I'll write the report tomorrow."

They walked almost to the foot of the ramp that led to the top of the hill. It was nearly ten o'clock and the stars shone brightly, casting a faint light on the clumps of boulders that were scattered before the ramp like huge molehills. There was no moon and Mike was very quiet.

"If there were any bandits around here they could easily jump us from behind these rocks," said Leonard.

"What would bandits be doing here?"

"I don't know. But this is a hell of an eerie place."

"I must admit these boulders give me the creeps," said Mike, "and I can't help feeling that someone is watching us."

"I get the same feeling."

"It must be all the little unaccountable noises," said Mike, "it's very quiet, so the slightest noise catches your attention before you realise it's just the wind."

"There you are being an engineer again. Must you explain everything?"

"I can't stand mysteries."

When they eventually returned to their small tent beside the Land Rover, Mike fell asleep almost immediately. Leonard tossed and turned for a while before he too fell asleep. During the night the wind rose and the cold air made Mike get up to close the flaps of the tent. They had somehow become loose, although Mike was certain that he had attached the straps securely before getting into his sleeping bag.

14

THE CAVERN-TEMPLE

1

"I FORGOT TO ask you," said Leonard over breakfast, "Did you take any photographs of the skeletons in the tunnel?" He popped a dried date into his mouth.

Mike had finished his breakfast and was drinking his coffee. "No," he replied, "I couldn't get a decent view from above the rubble. The opening was too small and the angle was wrong. I hope to do a proper job when I explore the tunnel this morning."

"Is there a lot of work left in clearing the rubble?"

"It's hard to say. A lot depends on the hardness of the dried mud. It gets harder as I dig deeper."

Leonard put away his coffee mug. His reservations about Mike venturing alone down the pit were still there, nagging away at the back of his mind. For want of anything better to say he asked: "D'you have an extra CF card for your camera?"

"I've got two spares," said Mike. He patted his pockets to make sure. "I won't be taking any more pictures of the writing but I shall use up a lot of camera memory on the skeletons. I'm also hoping..." He stopped, not wanting to tempt fate.

"Yeah, you're hoping that the tunnel will lead to something unbelievable. But if the tunnel were formed by hot gases or something like that, then it'll probably lead to more tunnels, or just cracks in the rock."

Mike shrugged. "I know. The poor fellows who died in the tunnel may have retreated down the pit to hide and may not have been defending anything. Still, you never know..."

"Don't build up your hopes, Mike."

"I'm not." Mike was all too aware of the possibility of disappointment. He changed the subject: "Oh, I've prepared the packed lunch. The usual stuff."

"It's not too bad in small doses. Uh…" Leonard squinted down at Mike: "Why are you tying an old shirt around your waist?"

"I scuffed my trousers yesterday and did worse to my knees and elbows."

"I still don't get it."

"I'll use this tatty old shirt to make kneepads and elbowpads!"

"Uh-huh. You'll look rather silly, you know!"

Mike smiled. "I suppose I will. Let's be on our way!"

Leonard finished his breakfast and they walked to the ruins as fast as they could, for even the normally phlegmatic Leonard was excited at the prospect of solving the mystery of the tunnel.

Not much later they stood on the rim of the mound. Mike tore the old shirt into long strips which he wrapped carefully around each of his knees, over his baggy trousers. When he was satisfied that the makeshift pads would not slide off, he did the same for his elbows. Leonard helped him tie the knots.

"I guess kneepads and elbowpads are a good idea if you expect to work on hands and knees," said Leonard, "But I must say you look ridiculous. We're lucky old Kureishi and the others aren't here to see you like this. You'll lose all respect!"

"The ghosts in the pit may laugh if they wish," said Mike. His thoughts were already at the bottom of the winding stairs.

"Have you got everything you need?" asked Leonard as Mike checked his equipment.

"I think so."

In addition to his camera and the usual tools, Mike had packed a short spade-cum-pickaxe and an omnidirectional lantern in addition to his torch. All but the lantern were stowed carefully in his rucksack.

"You will remember…" began Leonard.

"Yes I know. There are things that crawl and bite. That's why it's taking so long to clear the rubble."

"I guess that's it then!"

"I'm off."

Mike made his way nimbly down the conical slope to the opening of the pit and immediately started the descent. He had grown quite adept at negotiating the steep steps and was soon a long way down. His interest in the writing on the walls flickered for a brief moment when he paused to turn on the lantern, but his urge to get to the bottom of the pit quickly put all thoughts of the mysterious script out of his mind. The noxious smell was still there and got worse the deeper he descended.

When he reached the bottom of the pit he placed the lantern on the rubble at the centre of the cavern and immediately got down to work clearing the passage. Unlike the torch he had used the day before, the lantern illuminated the cavern walls evenly. Mike did not feel as isolated as on his previous trip, when he was surrounded by darkness except for the circular bright patch produced by the torch.

Mike prised away each stone carefully with the spade-cum-pickaxe, alert to the possibility that something that could bite or sting might be hiding underneath. Every so often he would get up and step back to photograph the exposed debris. He had expected to find stratified layers, but the jumble of rocks and stones held together by solidified mud was one inhomogeneous mass honeycombed by long, tube-like, empty spaces. Mike was at first baffled by these tubes, which were mostly about as wide as the small finger on his hand, and he wondered if they had been made by some kind of small burrowing animal, but he soon realised that they were only the casts left by pieces of wood that had rotted to dust after the mud had solidified. The casts were infested by beetles and many-legged things that looked like centipedes, and Mike had to be careful not to let any of the creatures get inside his clothes as they scuttled away when exposed to the light of the lantern.

Although Mike worked meticulously and methodically, he was anxious to get the clearing up done as quickly as possible and he did not stop to rest. The noxious smell was, if anything, worse than before and he was as curious to discover its source as he was to see what lay at the end of the tunnel. Yet he also wanted to find out what lay beneath the rubble, for the stones and dried mud had their own story to tell, and he painstakingly photographed each new layer that he uncovered. *The absence of any stratification implies that the structure above the pit suffered a single catastrophic collapse, with the rain gradually pushing down what had been caught by the steps! Was there a single collapse because the building was destroyed by fire?* The thought fanned his hope that the ruins on the surface were those of the community that supported the Amalishah temple, but if they were, then where was the temple itself? He had seen nothing on the surface that could be construed as the remains of an Assyrian temple, and the possibility that the inner sanctum of the temple of Amalishah could be deep underground did not occur to him.

2

After two hours of laboriously clearing the rubble his back and arms started to complain. He reluctantly stopped to rest and thought of lighting his pipe, but the all-pervading stench persuaded him that it would be a waste of good tobacco. The stones, animal bones and other debris he had carefully removed lay in two unsteady piles on either side of the tunnel entrance and the rubble, which continued a yard or two into the tunnel, was now less than two feet high. He could easily have stepped over it and ventured into the tunnel but he suppressed the urge to do so. His temperament was such that he could not leave any work undone: he had to see what lay beneath the rubble before he could give his full attention to the tunnel: *Just a little bit more work! I've got to know what was at the bottom of the pit when the surface structure caved in!* If the pit had been used to dispose of sacrificial victims the evidence might be there, albeit flattened by centuries of lying under the weight of the rubble.

He returned to his work of clearing the entrance. In the white light of the lantern the skeletons in the tunnel seemed to plead for attention but he ignored them; his mind wholly on what he might find under the stones and the compacted, solidified mud. After some twenty minutes of further work his arms and back started aching again, but just as he began to regret spending time shifting stones – when he could have been exploring the tunnel – his self-restraint paid off. Beneath a flat rectangular stone, and encased in a shapeless lump of dried mud, he saw the edge of something brown-and-white and smooth. He broke away the mud carefully, stopping only to take pictures of what he gradually exposed. It was an almost perfectly preserved but incomplete human pelvis. Mike knew enough anatomy to recognise it as that of a fully grown male. *Was this a sacrificial victim or did the fighting start in the cavern?* He got up and placed the pelvis carefully on the steps. One old bone meant very little, its late owner might have had no connection at all with the skeletons in the tunnel or the original function of the pit. The pelvis might have been that of an unwary traveller who had fallen down the shaft before the surface structure caved in and filled the cavern with rubble. *There might be many more bits of people hidden beneath this mess of stones and dried mud. Old bones are brittle; I'll have to be extraordinarily careful breaking up the mud!*

The presence of human remains suggested the possibility of finding artefacts. The pit must have collected rainwater periodically, but rain was a rare occurrence here, and if water had not seeped deep enough into the rubble to decompose bone it was possible that some metal might have survived too. *On the other hand, maybe not! I mustn't be too optimistic!* He decided to dig to the side of where he had found the pelvis. Although he used the pickaxe to gently break the hard solidified mud and lever away the larger stones, it was heavy work. He was dripping with perspiration when he found a corroded but still recognizable bronze sword encased, like the pelvis, in dried mud. *Ah! Rainwater didn't reach all the way to the bottom layers!* The bronze sword implied that any skeletons beneath the rubble were from the same group as the skeletons in the tunnel. *So there was fighting in the cavern! These fellows weren't trying to escape! They were defending the tunnel!* But he could not be absolutely sure, and for the hundredth time the thought came up: *What's at the end of the tunnel?*

He methodically photographed the debris every time he exposed another layer, and worked downwards systematically. Just as he reached bedrock, he found a crushed skull next to another sword. These he also carefully put on the steps. Then beneath the stones at the entrance of the tunnel he found a flattened human ribcage on top of which was a roughly rectangular sheet of heavily corroded bronze. *A breastplate! These were definitely not sacrificial victims!* There was no longer any doubt in his mind; the remains beneath the rubble belonged with the remains in the tunnel. He meticulously recorded the depth and positions of his finds and put the bones and breastplate on the steps as before, to be studied and analysed when the main party arrived. Eventually he had removed enough rubble to form a clear passage from the stairs to the tunnel. There was still a lot of work he could have done in the hemispherical cavern, but now that the tunnel entrance lay fully exposed Mike decided to forgo the excavation and see what the tunnel would reveal.

3

As Mike had suspected, the tunnel was a natural tube, formed when one or more primordial bubbles had rammed their way through the still unformed rock. The rugose walls were dark grey-brown and felt coldly damp to the touch, although there was nothing on the rough surface that could be interpreted as the final form of soot. The concave floor led slightly downwards where the tunnel veered to the left. Holding his lantern ahead of him, Mike advanced warily into the passageway, aware that the roof of the tunnel varied considerably in height. At some points it was no more than a few inches above Mike's head, at others it was higher than he could reach.

Mike put on thin plastic gloves before squatting to photograph and examine each of the skeletons in turn. As an archaeologist, he had come across human skeletons before, but they had always been ceremonially buried in soil and thus disturbed by the gradual shifting of the earth that enclosed them. Ceremonial burials and other *post mortem* disturbances somehow confer a degree of anonymity to human remains; bodies that have been formally buried lose all memory of their owners' final movements. This was the first time Mike could examine the remains of victims of an ancient conflict who lay exactly as they had fallen. Some of the skeletons lay in contorted positions which showed that they had died slowly and painfully, others showed that the body had collapsed suddenly, implying that the fatal thrust or cut had brought an almost instantaneous death. For someone with Mike's imagination, the skeletons were a gruesome but highly emotional sight for which no amount of experience could prepare him fully: *I wonder how Shakespeare would have described this tragedy! What last words would he have put in the mouths of the dying?* But then he thought of how the expedition analysts would react: *The forensic boys and girls will really enjoy this!*

The skeletons were all male. Some of their owners had died very young, when they were no older than boys, as testified by the incompletely fused sutures of their skulls. From the state of their teeth, Mike decided that the eldest would have been in their early forties. The rib cages of several of the skeletons showed inward scratch marks, indicating that something hard with sharp edges had been pushed between the bones with considerable force. *The forensic team should be able to determine whether whatever killed these poor fellows was straight or curved!* Hittite scythe-swords were curved, so if it could be proved that the weapons that had delivered the fatal thrusts were curved then it would be almost certain that the ruins were, indeed, those of the Amalishah temple! If Mike could find the remains of a Hittite sword then that would have furnished definitive proof, but Mike did not expect to find a Hittite weapon. Swords were hard-to-manufacture commodities and the Hittites would have made sure to take all their weapons with them when they withdrew: *Anyway, Hittite swords at the time of the Amalishah temple were probably made of iron. They would rusted away to nothing!* But whether this was the Amalishah temple or not the question that was uppermost in Mike's mind was: *Why did the defenders come down here? There must be something important at the end of the tunnel!* The question hung tantalisingly in Mike's mind as he systematically studied the skeletons and photographed each of them from several angles. When he had finished taking photographs of all the skeletons in the first part of the tunnel he left them undisturbed and almost ran, driven by a curiosity that almost matched his excitement. He held the lantern as high as the low passage allowed.

The tunnel veered to the left but then turned sharply to the right where, as far as he could tell, it appeared to run straight for about twenty metres. There were more human remains after the bend, though not as close to each other as before. All but one were scattered evenly along the first dozen metres of the corridor. Mike suppressed his impatience and photographed each skeleton methodically. The last skeleton he could see lay at some distance from the others. This one sat alone, resting, as it were, with its back against the wall. Balanced on its pelvis was a short and badly corroded bronze dagger. As with all the other skeletons that were not in a supine position, the skull had fallen from the neck. It lay on its side between the knee bones, and the mandible had become separated from the cranium. After taking more photographs, Mike picked up the skull, feeling a bit like Hamlet. It was the skull of an old man; what teeth remained were decayed, yellowed and well worn. After studying the skull, Mike replaced it exactly as he had found it. After taking yet more pictures he continued down the tunnel, which extended about ten metres beyond the skeleton of the old man. The tunnel became narrower and lower than before and ended with an oval aperture so black that it resisted the light of the lantern. Mike was almost overwhelmed by curiosity, but then he noticed that there was something lying on the tunnel floor just before the black oval: *Yet another skeleton? The last of the defenders?* Mike hurried to see what it was.

4

Lying almost at the end of the tunnel was indeed another skeleton.

It lay on its back, with the arms and legs lying parallel to its torso, palms against the floor, as though it had been placed there with great deference. Mike was so impatient to go through the opening that he was about to ignore the skeleton and rush past when he noticed that it was the skeleton of a woman.

A woman? A very tall woman, even by today's standards!

He stopped to study it, squatting beside the long leg bones and holding the lantern above his head. Then Mike looked for the skull, and he realised that the skull was missing.

Some archaeologists are lucky. In archaeology, perhaps more than in most other higher professions like Physics, Mathematics, or Medical research, luck plays a fundamental, all-important role. Howard Carter did not find Tutankhamun's tomb because he was noticeably more competent than the other archaeologists of his time. Schliemann did not find and identify the remains of Troy-Ilium because his faith in the core story of the *Iliad* was based on insightful archaeological knowledge. Most great archaeological discoveries were made because their discoverers had been *lucky*. But there was also something, other than luck, that those who achieved great archaeological discoveries had in common, though most other archaeologists who were not as fortunate often had it as well. That *something* was an obsession with the object of their quests. Mike was no exception. For more than fifteen years he had been haunted by the tale of the Amalishah temple, a tale that intruded into his thoughts whenever the duties and responsibilities of a university professor could be temporarily put aside. And central to his thoughts of the temple and its fate, whenever a lapse from professional concerns permitted him to indulge in speculation, was a deep, all-absorbing fascination with the shadowy figure of the woman who had been believed to be a goddess.

The few existing Hittite records that referred to the destruction of the Amalishah temple all stated, quite unequivocally, that the Hittites had brought back the head of the goddess of the temple, and that she had been a very tall woman.

The skull was missing. No less than Carter or Schliemann at their moments of triumph, when the objects of their dreams and fantasies had taken solid shape before them, Mike suddenly felt that he was among the lucky few of his profession when he contemplated, as though in a daze, at the mute female skeleton that lay, headless, before him.

Then his professional self clashed with the emotions of discovery, of triumph, and of sadness that had surged and mingled in his psyche. But the sense of elation was too strong and he could not prevent himself from suddenly getting up and saying quietly: "Is this all that remains of you, Amalishah?"

Then the professional self took control and Mike mechanically took several pictures before pulling himself away from the skeleton. Almost dizzy at the implications of what he might have discovered, he turned to the aperture of the tunnel and took the few remaining steps to where the oval blackness loomed before him. He held the lantern in front of him as he stooped to cross the threshold.

The light of the lantern dispelled most, but not all, of the darkness. Mike was unprepared for the sight that met his eyes. "This is the temple!" he cried aloud, **"I've found the temple!"**

5

A vast cavern opened up before him. The dome-like roof was at least twenty metres high, well beyond the capabilities of his sonic rangefinder, and almost at the outer reach of the powerful lantern's light. From the dark stone ceiling hung enormous stalactites, some almost two metres long. The cavern stretched out at least fifteen metres on either side of him, while ahead of him it extended almost eighty metres. Even the powerful lantern left the farther reaches of the cavern in semi-darkness. At least part of the cavern was natural, but much of it had evidently been hewn and sculpted out of the solid rock. Mike's lantern could only illuminate a small portion of his surroundings at a time and, as he moved forward, still in a daze, it took him several minutes to appreciate what the cavern contained. *Those poor fellows died defending **this**! Defending **her**!"*

On either side of him was a row of gigantic tapering pillars, considerably more than a metre in diameter at the base, which supported the dome of the roof. Between the rows of pillars was a wide aisle, more than twenty metres wide, which led straight from the tunnel to the far end of the cavern. The roughly cut and uneven walls were some three or four metres behind the row of pillars, while exactly between the rows of pillars, almost at the end of the aisle, was a huge, rectangular block of black stone that could only have been an altar. The length of the rectangular block was the length of a tall man, and at each of its four corners was a massive but heavily corroded bronze torch holder. The top of the block was flat and polished smooth.

An altar for human sacrifice!

The thought was sobering and he could not help but recall what the Hittites had written of the Amalishah temple:

> *...the home of the monster, the evil place...*

But they had said nothing about a cavern, or about a final battle at the bottom of a pit. Mike moved forward and the shadows moved eerily with him, as though they had minds of their own and feared the light.

The source of the stench lay in a heap on the flat surface of the altar. It was the putrefying body of a large mountain goat. Mike stayed well clear of the thing as he went on to examine what lay behind the altar.

At the end of the aisle, some three metres beyond the altar and extending to the back of the cavern, was a two-foot high, mud-brick dais whose stones had grown uneven with age. Upon the dais was a single massive stone seat with armrests and a high back. The seat had been cut from a black stone similar to that of the altar and its sides were covered with the same unknown writing that covered the wall of the pit.

The throne of the goddess!

The back of the cavern, some three or four metres behind the stone seat, had not been cut away, but was still in its natural state of convoluted stalactites and stalagmites that had melted into each other over the aeons, leaving only dark, narrow passageways between them that could, perhaps, lead to other caverns. Mike suspected that the whole of the cavern had been like that before the cavern was cleared and extended by cutting into the rock, leaving only the massive rock pillars to support the roof. There was nothing else in the cavern, just the altar with the bronze torch-holders, the dais and the seat on the dais, but the pillars and the sheer dimensions of the cavern gave the place an air of grandeur that held Mike spellbound.

The walls on either side of the cavern, behind the pillars, were dotted with almost circular holes in the rock, not more than about ten centimetres wide. A number of these holes were at shoulder level, the rest were scattered almost to the height of the cavern ceiling, which suggested that they were natural apertures made by whatever gas or liquid had formed the cavern and the tunnel.

Mike toyed with the idea of trying to squeeze between the stalagmites behind the stone seat to see what lay beyond, but he decided against it. The more Mike explored the cavern the more his initial joyful excitement gradually changed into something more akin to horror. The atmosphere was heavy, and the nauseating stench of the goat's carcase was all-pervasive, inescapable, despite the vastness of the cavern.

Hang on, Chum! A few years from now this place will be full of tourists in shorts and sandals, frenziedly clicking away with their cameras!

But the sense of horror did not abate, and like a foul growth it gripped his psyche in ice-cold tendrils that almost stifled the boyish joy that had accompanied his discoveries. *Oh come on, chum! You haven't been spooked by a few old bones and a sacrificial altar, have you?*

But many of the skeletons had lain in positions that spoke all too clearly of the agony in which their owners had died, and in Mike's over-excited imagination the altar was an all-too-clear reminder of the unspeakable acts to which it had once been accustomed. The words of the Hittite records kept flashing in his mind:

...the home of the monster, the evil place...

Mike brought out his torch the better to see the roof of the cavern, for at that height the light of the lantern was too diffuse to allow the examination of detail. Although the stench from the goat was almost unbearable, he methodically studied and photographed the contents of the cavern, writing detailed notes on the small notepad that he had brought with him. When he had finished taking photographs and making preliminary measurements, Mike climbed onto the dais and sat on the seat, his rucksack still on his back. With some shock he thought: *The last person to have sat here could have been Amalishah herself!*

The act of sitting on what could only have been the throne of the goddess felt sacrilegious, but he suppressed the feeling. *After all that work I deserve a rest and this is the only seat around!* The throne was cold and hard but well proportioned, so that Mike – who was not a small man – was able to sit comfortably despite the rucksack. But when he sat his body rested and the sense of horror receded, leaving his mind free to ask questions: *How did that goat get in here? And how in Heaven's name did it get to die on the altar?* Animals in a state of panic sometimes do silly things. *Perhaps it jumped onto the altar in a frantic bid to get out?* But the *presence* of the goat was harder to explain. Before he had cleared away the stones and the dried mud the space between the rubble and the top of the tunnel entrance might have been enough for a rabbit or even a fox to get through, but not for an animal as large as the goat. The goat would have had to crawl through – a distinct possibility for a rabbit or a fox but a physical impossibility for a large goat! *One or more of those holes in the walls or behind the stone seat must lead to the surface! That would explain the updraft.* The thought caused him to unconsciously shine his torch towards one of the larger holes behind the farthest pillars.

Immediately there was a scurrying sound as though his torch had disturbed something, or someone, who had been watching him from the darkness. Mike felt the hair at the back of his neck stand on end.

"Who's there?" he shouted in English before realising that anyone down there was unlikely to speak English. He got up and shouted again, first in Arabic and then in Turkish: "Who is there?"

There was no response.

It must be some damn animal!

Relieved by the plausibility of his explanation, the mischievous side of him reasserted itself and he shouted in Assyrian:

"I am a friend. I mean you no harm!"

There was an unmistakeable sigh, like the sigh of a young woman who exhales suddenly after holding her breath. Mike was no coward but the sense of horror that he had almost suppressed suddenly crystallised and he was gripped by a terror that he could not control. Overcome by an overwhelming need to get out of the cavern, he jumped off the dais and ran back towards the tunnel, skirting the altar and rushing between the rows of pillars. He ran mindlessly past the remains of the tall woman and paid no heed to the skeletons in the tunnel. He was still running when he reached the hemispherical cavern and saw, with dismay, that one of the piles of rubble had collapsed and now almost blocked the way to the steps. With unthinking haste he tried to jump over the stones. But he had forgotten the heavy rucksack on his back and did not quite make it. Falling short, he struck his foot against a protruding stone and fell headlong onto the pile of rubble near the stairs. His elbows hit the rubble with jarring force and he just managed to prevent his camera smashing against the stones.

Mike's mind went blank. There was a momentary pause, as though the world was waiting for him to move. Then Mike was violently brought back to his senses by a sharp searing pain in his left arm, between the elbow and the wrist, just outside the edge of the makeshift elbowpad.

"DAMN!"

Not knowing what had bitten him, Mike realised that there was no time to remove the rucksack or make a tourniquet. A dark red stain appeared on the strip of shirt that covered his elbow: *I've got to get to the surface!*

The pain spread rapidly to his shoulder. Clasping his arm tightly above the elbow, Mike hurried up the steps. He was halfway up when the pain became intolerable and he sensed that his strength was leaving him. His leg muscles felt soft and almost unable to carry his weight up the steep steps.

I must reach the surface!

By a supreme effort he managed to remove his rucksack and placed it and the camera gently on the steps. Then, slowly and racked by pain, he continued his climb up the stairs, holding only the lantern. The pain had now reached his chest and breathing had become acutely painful. His last thought before sinking into unconsciousness was: *Sunlight! I can see the sunlight!*

15

THE MILITARY ESCORT ARRIVES

1

IT WAS SHORTLY before noon when the pre-lunch activities of the expedition's base camp were disrupted by the roar of a huge military helicopter. All who were in the open stopped what they were doing and looked up. The craft, seemingly eager to entertain its captive audience, hovered uncertainly above the camp like a gigantic bumblebee trying to decide which side of a flower to alight on. When the helicopter finally started its descent, all the workers, including the cooks in the kitchens and the helpers in the laundry tents, had rushed out to the edge of the camp to watch. The helicopter settled down ponderously close to the small crowd of workers who had assembled not too far from the base camp's tents.

That must be the caving equipment! thought ElKureishi as he put on a tie before leaving his tent. *They promised to deliver it in three days and here it is! But why such a large machine?* The helicopter was indeed much larger than the one that brought the mail and the newspapers on alternate Tuesdays.

The pilot kept the twin rotors turning while the helicopter disgorged its load. The unloading was accomplished with military efficiency and with a deafening screech the helicopter rose into the air again less than twenty minutes later. When it was some three hundred metres above the camp it reoriented itself before flying in a straight line back towards its airfield. It left behind a dozen tightly folded tents, two heavy machine-guns, and a number of large wooden crates. Two of the crates were labelled 'Underwater Exploration Equipment' and two said 'Radio Apparatus'. The rest were simply labelled 'Army supplies'. Also left behind were an army major, two captains, and thirty fully armed soldiers carrying massive backpacks. When the aircraft lifted off the workers cheered loudly but the officers and their men waved goodbye to the pilot in silence.

When the helicopter was a mere speck in the sky and the sound of its engines could no longer be heard, one of the officers issued a sharp command and the men gathered together in three rows with the two captains on either side. At a second command the men and the captains followed the major towards the main body of the camp where the archaeologists and workers were waiting. The machine-guns, the tents and the crates were left near the place where the helicopter had landed.

Professor ElKureishi had not expected a military *escort* to arrive with the caving equipment. He had also not expected the escort to be so large: there would be almost as many soldiers as there were archaeologists! Worse, the presence of an army officer of significant rank meant that any *requests* he might wish to make to the military authorities would have to be through him. As ElKureishi saw it, these developments seriously weakened his position as sole leader of the expedition. But what the professor found most unpalatable was the fact that the soldiers had brought their own radio transmitter. Until now, the camp's only link with the outside world had been the transmitter that belonged to the university, and ElKureishi had complete control over who used it and why. The presence of a second transmitter, over which the professor would have no control, meant that the officer could appeal directly to higher authority whenever he disagreed with the way the expedition was run. The presence of Army officers also introduced a political element into the archaeological aims of the expedition.

The professor had enough acumen not to show his feelings and he welcomed the military escort courteously, but after the introductions were over he arranged to be alone with the senior officer: "I do not understand why you and your men have joined us, Major ElBalushi," said the Professor, "When I asked for caving equipment, it was my understanding that the armed forces would only assist us by bringing it here."

"The army may have a role to play now that you have found the temple you were looking for," the major replied pleasantly. He was in his early thirties, tall, suave and well groomed. He wore an army cap and dark glasses and his neat moustache was starting to go grey. His uniform was immaculate.

"The army has a role in everything," said ElKureishi gravely, and the officer was not sure whether the professor thought this was a good thing or a bad thing, "but I must stress that we are not convinced we have found the Amalishah temple. We may have found something else, something of little archaeological importance. Professor Townsend, the senior English member of our staff who found some ancient ruins on a flat hill, is very ill and has fits of delirium. Although his partner claims that the ruins he and Townsend have found were once the Amalishah temple, I must stress that this has not been confirmed!"

"I am aware of all that," said the major genially, "You were quite thorough in your report to Baghdad. But my superiors thought it best to give the Englishman the benefit of the doubt, and they assumed that he has found the unplundered temple you all hoped to find. So my men and I are here in case we are needed."

ElKureishi looked at him coldly: "This is an archaeological expedition, Major. I don't see why we would need the services of the armed forces."

"There are bandits in these parts, Professor. If you find anything of value, you will need to be protected."

"How would the bandits know if we find anything of value? We are in the middle of nowhere!"

"The bandits may be watching us now, as we speak. They will certainly have spies among your workforce. It is better to be safe."

2

ElKureishi had not thought about bandits. "I have people out in the field conducting surveys," he said, feigning concern about his *underlings*, "Are they in danger?"

"I wouldn't think so," replied the major, "The bandits would not risk pursuit for the sake of a few cameras or archaeological tools. Even the vehicles lent to you by the Army would be of no interest to them. But if you find ancient gold or valuable artefacts, that would be another matter. Certain kinds of artefact and ancient gold can be easily sold on the open market. You shall need military protection."

And you will take over! The Professor nodded, accepting the inevitable. "Very well," he said resignedly.

The major sensed the professor's concealed antagonism: "My men and I shall not interfere with your work, Professor Kureishi. We shall keep a low profile and stay out of your way as long as your personnel and any discoveries you make are not in danger."

The professor tried another tack to assert his authority: "Major, do you understand what we are doing here?"

"I am not an archaeologist," replied the officer. "But I hold a Ph.D in Physics from Imperial College in England and ancient history is one of my interests. I have read about the Amalishah temple and have been fully informed of your objectives. I think I understand a little of what you are doing."

The reference to Imperial College was to let ElKureishi know that the Major spoke English fluently. Because most of the Arab members of the expedition did not speak Turkish while most of the Turkish members did not speak Arabic, and because only a handful of the Western archaeologists spoke both Arabic and Turkish, the common language of the expedition was English. The major was telling ElKureishi that he could not be excluded from any serious discussions among the staff. The reference to the doctorate implied that the major could talk to anyone in the expedition on an equal basis. The Professor was discomfited, but he absorbed the information and saw the implications: *The authorities must have been waiting until we found something promising! They must have been preparing to take control. This man is not some hick soldier, he was carefully chosen! If he decides to interfere it will be difficult to outwit him. Let us hope that the main reason for his presence is to make sure the foreigners do not do anything untoward!*

"When do we join Professor Townsend?" asked the major, interrupting the Professor's thoughts.

"As soon as possible. He is being cared for at the hill where he found the ruins because we wished to move him as little as possible. He is suffering from a poisonous sting or bite. We sent our physician to take care of him the moment we heard and he is presently under sedation. After the base camp is moved to the hill he shall be given a private tent."

"The poisoning is not too serious, I hope."

"It could have been fatal but there is no danger now. Professor Townsend's partner, Doctor Ehrlich, gave the appropriate First Aid immediately. Our teams are well equipped for all eventualities."

"That is good. For your peace of mind let me tell you that my young Lieutenant Mursi is a fully-qualified army doctor."

"You brought a physician?"

"Naturally. If we come across bandits some of us may need urgent medical attention."

"But we have our own physician!"

"I know, but I was thinking of the worst scenario, Professor."

"The worst scenario, major?"

"I am sure your physician is excellent for treating toothaches, runny tummies and insect bites, but that is not like treating bullet wounds or performing amputations."

"So you think the bandits are a real threat?"

"Would I be here otherwise?"

"I see." ElKureishi was reluctant to accept the possibility of trouble from *bandits*. For him, such people existed only in newspaper articles and adventure stories.

"When will the people who are out on surveys return to your base camp?" asked the major.

"When they have completed their surveys the scout teams shall join us at the hill where Townsend found the ruins. I gave precise directions." ElKureishi's manner indicated that this was to be the end of the conversation, but the major appeared not to notice: "What kind of person is Michael Townsend?"

It begins! mused ElKureishi. "Professor Townsend is a very competent archaeologist of untarnished reputation. He has no interest in politics of any kind."

"I've read some of his professional work and look forward to meeting him."

ElKureishi was surprised: *A soldier who reads papers on archaeology?* "I am delighted that you share our interest in archaeology, major."

The major continued with his questions: "What about his companion, the American, Ehrlich?"

"Dr. Ehrlich is a historian with an international reputation. His areas of expertise include Assyrian, Babylonian and Hittite history. He also has no interest in politics."

"Why isn't Professor Townsend paired off with someone from a British university?"

"Dr. Ehrlich has been part of the London University staff for many years. He has worked as Townsend's partner on field trips almost as long."

"Is Professor Townsend married?"

"He is a widower. I believe his wife died tragically many years ago."

"Oh yes. I remember reading that in his *dossier*." At the word dossier ElKureishi could not suppress a scowl but the major smiled at him, indicating that he had all the information he wanted, at least for the moment.

"You said you're interested in ancient history," asked ElKureishi innocently, "Is archaeology your hobby?"

"Only the archaeology that concerns this tiny part of the world," replied the major, "I am familiar with some of its history and many of its myths."

This army man may become much more intrusive than he says! thought ElKureishi, but he said: "How interesting."

"And now, Professor," said the major, "perhaps you would tell me your immediate plans? My men are at your disposal to help with loading the lorries."

ElKureishi felt relieved: *At least we are off the subject of foreigners and their dossiers!* "I suggest we have lunch while I decide what to take and what to leave behind when some of the base camp is moved to the hill."

The major frowned: "Am I to understand that you are not ready to leave for the hill immediately?"

"Not completely ready," replied ElKureishi, "We cannot take everything from the base camp to the hill, and we shall only take the minimum necessary until we are sure that Townsend's discovery is important. As I said, there are still decisions to be made as to what we should take with us."

"These decisions should have been made when you were informed that your request for caving equipment had been accepted."

ElKureishi was unaccustomed to being hurried and was taken aback by the officer's bluntness. "This is an archaeological expedition, Major, not a military campaign. Decisions must be given the time they require."

"Just as well, then," said the major with a charming grin, "that I am here. I would prefer it if you got ready to move first, and we can have lunch on the way. While I wait, I would like to meet the younger members of the expedition."

The major and ElKureishi rejoined the others. The postgrads and postdocs had not been introduced and were keen to talk to the major. The officer was genuinely interested in what they thought about the pit and the ruins on the hill and he listened to each attentively. Eventually he turned to the only young person who had not spoken. "And you, Jehan," he asked the pretty postdoc, "Do you think that the ruins Professor Townsend found are of the Amalishah temple? You are the only person who has not given an opinion."

Jehan blushed visibly at being singled out. "I have not made up my mind yet," she answered quietly. "We have not examined the evidence firsthand."

The major smiled at her. "That is wise of you. Where are you from?"

"I am from Jordan," she replied, "but I am working with professor ElKureishi."

"I am sure we shall have many opportunities to talk again."

"I would like that."

The major exchanged a few more words with the postgrads and postdocs before he took leave of ElKureishi and rejoined his men.

3

To the major's annoyance they did have lunch at the camp after all, for it took the best part of four hours for ElKureishi to make his decisions and a further two hours to load the lorries. ElKureishi was not an effective people-manager and several decisions were made, then revoked, then made again. The Professor was not quite sure which responsibilities to delegate and which to keep for himself, but the major was careful not to interfere. The machine guns, the army crates, and most of the soldiers with their gear were assigned to two of the all-terrain trucks that the army had lent to ElKureishi's university. The remaining trucks carried archaeological equipment, tents, the junior officers and the archaeological personnel. After taking their first load to the ruins all trucks were to return to the base camp to pick up the workers and additional material. All inessential equipment was to be left behind in the care of some trusted workers.

When the trucks were finally on their way the major sat beside ElKureishi in the cab of the leading vehicle. "How long will it take to reach the ruins?" he asked.

"These trucks have to move slowly as they are heavily laden and some of our apparatus is very fragile. The terrain is treacherous, full of bumps and sharp rocks."

"So when shall I have the pleasure of meeting Professor Townsend and Doctor Ehrlich?"

"If we have no breakdowns we should reach the hill during the night. His vehicle broke down about a kilometre from the ruins and we shall set up a working camp near the tent he left behind. Tomorrow we shall move Professor Townsend so that he shall be with us."

"Why won't we camp at the ruins?"

"The ruins cover the top of what I was told is a low plateau with steep sides. The top can be reached by two ramps but they are apparently unsuitable for heavy vehicles. Townsend said that the ground is too soft. We shall camp near the hill and visit the ruins on foot."

"I suppose this will discourage my men from fumbling around the site."

"Oh there's no problem with that," replied ElKureishi, anxious to hide his apprehension. "Your men are most welcome to walk about as much as they wish. The ruins are apparently very old but quite robust."

"I'm very glad to hear that. If we do have trouble with bandits I'm sure the hill would make an excellent defensive position."

"What do you mean?" ElKureishi was worried at the thought of soldiers moving about freely during the excavations, setting up their machine-guns and other stuff.

"Don't worry, Professor. My men have strict orders not to interfere with your archaeological activities."

"I'm sure we shall all get on very well," said ElKureishi. He tried to sound relieved although he was not completely reassured. In that part of the world, soldiers tend to take upon themselves the role of policemen, and they often interfere in matters that do not concern them.

16

AN INTRODUCTION TO THE AMALISHAH TEMPLE
by Dr. Leonard Ehrlich

Prelude to an illustrated talk given to staff and students at the Kresge auditorium of the Massachusetts Institute of Technology in Cambridge, Massachusetts. As one of the co-discoverers of the Amalishah temple, Dr. Ehrlich was invited to give informal talks at a number of universities in the USA soon after the temple was discovered.

I WOULD LIKE, first of all, to thank you all for inviting me here. It is not often that an archaeologist is invited to talk about a recent archaeological discovery to an audience composed mostly of scientists and engineers. I must also apologise on behalf of my colleague, Professor Michael Townsend, for being unable to come himself. Professor Townsend, from University College, which is part of the University of London in England, deserves all the credit for finding the temple. Had it not been for his insight and brilliant interpretation of what little was known about the Amalishah temple it is quite probable that it would not have been found so soon. He cannot be here because he suffered some sort of venomous sting and has been in a coma for many days. However, he is expected to recover fully. I hope you don't mind getting introduced to the Amalishah temple by me. Before I show you the photographs I would like to say a few words about archaeology in general and the Amalishah temple in particular.

Archaeologists and historians sometimes say things with great confidence. Yet they are fully aware that they really know very little about what *actually* happened in the distant past. There are always gaps in our knowledge because we never have complete records. If we think of the panorama of past events as a jigsaw, then historians and archaeologists try to put this jigsaw together even though many pieces are missing. So when you read what historians or archaeologists write about events in the remote past you should remember that they have consciously or unconsciously selected from an incomplete jigsaw puzzle only those pieces that agree with their own personal inclinations and the fads and values of their times. All we usually have are a few pieces of the historical jigsaw that we try to bring together to make the best picture we can, even if the pieces don't always fit well with each other. Therefore, in a way that is very similar to what happens in the 'hard' sciences, ancient history needs to be constantly rewritten as new evidence comes to light. The most exciting part of an archaeologist's work is to discover new material and interpret what is found so as to add to the pool of historical knowledge. I should add something that Professor Townsend is fond of saying: 'There are three kinds of history: There is what really happened, which is often very complex and about which we know very little. There is what the historians and history books tell us, which changes as new discoveries are made. And finally there is Hollywood history, which is what we see in pseudo-historical films.' This last is often very different from what really happened or what the history books tell us, but unfortunately this is what many of the general public accept as truth.

The Amalishah temple flourished about four thousand years ago. Its main feature, of course, was the 'living goddess', Amalishah. The presence of someone who was claimed to be a real live goddess was very unusual even for temples in the remote past. We don't know of any other temples anywhere in the ancient world in which a god or goddess was a permanent resident, and it may be that the temple of Amalishah was one of a kind. The only thing we know about the goddess is that she was exceptionally tall and that she was supposed to have lived for several hundred years before she was killed. This compels us to surmise that she was not one person but a series of priestesses who assumed the role of 'goddess', so that a new Amalishah was somehow chosen after the previous one died. It's possible that they simply chose the tallest priestess in the temple. The important point is that, as long as the temple existed, there was always an 'Amalishah' living in the temple.

Be that as it may, the 'goddess Amalishah' was worshipped for many generations and there is some evidence that, in the early days of the temple, she wielded considerable influence, even over the Assyrian kings. However, her political influence waned with time, probably because her temple was almost inaccessible and very far from the centres of Assyrian power. It is also possible that her influence declined because, in the latter days of the temple, her worship entailed rather gory forms of human sacrifice. You must remember that the Assyrians were not averse to mass executions and horrific forms of torture, therefore if Amalishah's influence declined because the final forms of her worship became too horrific her rituals must have been unbelievably shocking! If we are to believe some of the few references to the goddess that we have, she fed on human blood.

The little that we know about the temple and its 'goddess' comes mainly from the writings of Assyria's neighbours, and they, perhaps not surprisingly, dwell on her more unsavoury aspects. Assyria's neighbours refer to her as a 'monster' and the Hittites repeatedly emphasised that she fed on the blood of young men. Is it possible that the senior priests and priestesses of the temple felt insulated enough to develop some sort of cannibalistic cult? It's possible. But what we do know for sure is that the Hittite king was so upset that he sent an army into Assyria to kill the goddess and utterly destroy her temple! Could the Hittites have attacked the temple for other reasons? The temple must have been very rich in its time. However, the Hittite records specifically claim that the Hittite army did *not* plunder the temple. It was as though they wanted nothing except to kill the 'goddess', and by all accounts they brought back only her head when they returned!

The economics of the temple must have been quite simple. We can be reasonably certain that in many ways the Amalishah Temple was not too different from the pilgrimage sites of our own day in that it depended heavily on pilgrims and wealthy visitors. For food they must have had goats and chickens, but not kine, since cows need grass and that would have been hard to find. Perhaps they also cultivated the land close to the temple, and it is probable that pilgrims to the temple also helped to replenish its food supplies

For defence the temple relied upon its impressive fortifications and its priests, who were armed. The temple complex was built on a flat-topped hill, between 54 and 60 feet high, and was surrounded by a thick wall. In theory, the temple was under the protection of the Assyrian kings, but defence must have been constantly on the minds of the priests because the temple was isolated and far from the Assyrian capital, Nineveh, so that any military support sent by an Assyrian king would have taken a long time to arrive.

For a long time we had no idea what the temple looked like, and most archaeologists, though not my friend Michael Townsend, believed that it lay on flat land. By careful scrutiny of the few references to the temple that survived, Michael came to the conclusion that it must have been built on a hill. He was right. We were all surprised to find that the temple complex was on a low flat-topped hill with steep sides. The temple itself was deep underground, but the surface complex was a sprawling collection of buildings enclosed by a protective wall. The complex had two entrances, one at the North-East and one at the South-West, and each entrance had a massive wooden gate and a tall guardian tower. You will see in the photographs that very little of these gates and their towers is left, except for piles of rubble. Access to the gates was via long ramps, which may have been constructed at the time when the temple was built. The temple complex occupied an area that was roughly oval in shape, more than 900 feet long and 630 feet wide. Since the temple had to be self-sufficient, its permanent occupants could not have numbered much more than about six hundred, and this rough number would include the priests, priestesses, their families, and the workpeople such as carpenters, those who farmed what land was available, and so on. We don't know the strength of the Hittite force that put an end to the temple.

The inner sanctum, the temple of the 'goddess' proper, was a vast underground cavern accessible only by a long winding staircase that led vertically down from the surface of the hill. The winding staircase was built around a deep pit whose entrance was at the centre of a large circular building. The geologists believe that the hill is all that is left of a prehistoric volcano that blew out its guts with such vehemence that its top was scattered into fragments, leaving only its base. Indeed, the area around the hill is covered with clumps of large boulders that shine dirty white in the sunshine. Between the boulders some hardy but stunted trees and shrub strive desperately to survive. On the side of the hill where the slope is least harsh, to the North-East of the Northern ramp, there was, and still is, a small grove of trees, indicating the presence of a stable supply of water. At night the hill and its surroundings become an eerie, almost depressing, place. There is no evidence of human habitation around the hill at the time when the temple was active, although some ten to fifteen kilometres to the North West there was once a village. This village was deserted before or at the time when the temple first became active. All that remains of the village are the husks of some of its huts, which were built of stone and mud bricks. And now I shall show you the photographs you have all been waiting to see.

17

A VISIT IN THE NIGHT

MIKE REGAINED CONSCIOUSNESS with a dull ache in his left arm and an alkaline taste in his mouth. As his awareness expanded he noted the complete absence of sounds and knew, somehow, that he was surrounded by darkness except for a weak source of light somewhere beyond where his feet should be. *It must be late at night! Where am I?* He resisted the temptation to open his eyes. *How did I get here?* His heartbeat accelerated as he remembered running desperately up the steps of the pit, goaded by the spreading pain in his arm and an uncontrollable terror. But the memory dissolved into a dizzy blackness and he could not recall reaching the top of the steps. *I passed out! Len must have dragged me up the steps and out of the pit.* The thought of Leonard awakened the analytic part of his mind and he reviewed the events in the cavern dispassionately: *The stink of the goat must have driven me round the bend! I was spooked by the wind blowing through the holes that are scattered along the sides of the cavern!* He took a deep breath and his heartbeat slowed to its normal pace. *I behaved like a complete ass!*

He opened his eyes and found that he was lying on a camp-bed in a large tent. *So Kureishi and the others are here! How long was I unconscious?* The source of the light was a gaslamp that someone had hung on a short, dead tree some ten paces from the opening of the tent. The yellow light of the gaslamp made random patterns of light and shade on the folds of a mosquito net that was suspended, like a curtain, across the open flaps of the tent.

Mike tried to sit up but was stopped short by a sharp pain in his arm. *Damn!* He fell back gently on the bed: *Watch it, chum! No sudden movements!* Lying on his back he stared at the ridge of the tent and wondered how long he had been unconscious. He had vague recollections of being carried on a stretcher; of having awakened under a strong light to babble like an idiot at anxious, unfamiliar faces; of hearing voices speak words he could not understand. But perhaps these were not memories at all; perhaps they were nothing more than the remnants of dreams. The images were in no particular order: just a jumble of disconnected scenes with only the pain in his arm common to all. *They must have drugged me to subdue the pain!* He looked at his watch. The luminous dial showed that it was almost half past three. *To hell with the pain! I can't sleep; I've got to get up.*

He got up in stages, moving slowly and deliberately until he was sitting on the bed with his feet on the floor. The pain was bearable as long as he was careful not to flex the muscles of his left arm. By the camp-bed was a foldable table with two small bottles, an empty plastic cup, and his glasses. On a chair was the box of English biscuits he had brought from England. His rucksack and battered old suitcase were on the floor in a corner. The suitcase had been left behind at the base camp but although he was sure he had shut it, it was now half open, showing that someone had opened it to take something and not bothered to close it properly. *Someone changed my clothes; I must have been unconscious for several days!* He continued to look around the tent. In another corner were his shoes and his laptop computer; his camera hung from one of the tent poles. At the foot of the bed were two neatly folded towels. Satisfied that nothing important was missing, he turned his attention to the mosquito net and tried to look out through the open flaps. From his sitting position he could see most of what lay within the light of the gaslamp, but the view was confused by the patterns of light and shade on the folds of the mosquito net and, anyhow, he was not wearing his glasses. He had expected to see other tents, but there was only the dead tree and, beyond that, vague dark shapes that could only be clumps of large boulders. *So I'm not on the hill!* It was all very quiet and peaceful, and he was half-thinking of lying back on the bed again when something in the shadows behind the gas lamp moved.

What's that? Mike strained his eyes to see beyond the range of the gaslamp. *Is that someone standing there? How odd!* After some effort he thought he could discern the faint silhouette of a person who stood, ghostlike, surrounded by darkness. Mike reached out and put on his glasses. The mosquito net prevented him from seeing anything clearly but his glasses helped and he was now sure there was someone there, someone tall who was standing without moving just beyond the range of the gaslamp. *Has Kureishi put guards around the camp?* The tall figure was hard to make out because it stood in almost complete darkness and the random patterns on the mosquito net prevented Mike's eyes from focusing. But as Mike stared at the figure it shifted slightly and something on the figure that had, until then, blended with the shadows, suddenly caught the light of the gaslamp and reflected it like a tiny mirror. The small glittering thing allowed Mike's eyes to focus and the figure assumed a recognisable shape.

Mike gasped: *In heaven's name!* Standing some way behind the tree, just beyond the range of the gaslamp, was what appeared to be a young woman. She was looking straight at him as though she could see through the mosquito net. The shock of seeing someone standing in the darkness and looking fixedly at him almost made Mike swoon: *The dizziness must be a side-effect of the medication!* Ignoring the pain in his arm, Mike got off the bed and gently moved the mosquito net aside without getting out of the tent. The woman retreated but continued to look straight at him with an intense gaze that he found impossible to interpret. Was she afraid of him? Was she just curious? There were hidden questions in that look but there was also wariness and great sadness.

What an attractive girl! No! She's not just attractive, she's very beautiful!

The woman was indeed extremely beautiful. Slim and unusually tall, with an oval face and a slightly aquiline nose; her jet-black hair formed a halo of gentle curls around her head that complemented her generous mouth. Around her neck hung the single red jewel that had caught Mike's attention; it sparkled like a small red star in the faint light of the gaslamp. But the most extraordinary feature of the woman was her eyes. They were huge, intense yet calm, with a watery beauty that spoke of a deep sadness tempered by an extraordinary energy.

Mike noticed that she stood barefoot and was wearing his tatty old raincoat. It was too short for her. *She must be very tall! Who is she? How did she get my coat?* The woman held Mike's coat tightly about her body with her hands on her chest and stood, unmoving, with her bare feet close together. Mike noticed that her feet were small for her size and well shaped. He smiled at her by way of greeting.

She did not smile back and, sensing that Mike was about to emerge from the tent, she receded further into the shadows. She moved with a graceful fluidity that reminded Mike of a jaguar he had encountered many years earlier in South America.

"Don't be afraid," he said in a low voice, "I won't harm you." He spoke in Arabic.

The woman shook her head to show that she did not understand; a simple movement accomplished with regal dignity. Mike was about to try another language when she spoke first. Her voice was soft and exquisitely feminine but very low-pitched, almost as low as the voice of a man: "I know you speak my language."

Mike was stunned. The woman was speaking Assyrian!

But it was Assyrian as he had never heard it spoken. Back at University College he had often bantered with his students in what he thought was ancient Assyrian, but perforce all who speak dead languages at UCL have an English accent and an English intonation. This was different. The young woman spoke with an alien inflection and guttural overtones that he was sure he could not reproduce.

"Who are you?" he asked from within the tent, in his own version of Assyrian.

There was a long pause, as though the woman was not sure whether she should answer the question, but then she made up her mind. "I am Amalishah," she replied in a voice barely above a whisper. "Amalishah of the children of Ashour."

Amalishah? In the stillness of the night Mike was certain he had heard the name correctly. He had no doubts at all about what she had said, but… *Amalishah?* After the initial shock he was tempted to laugh at the oddness of it all, but he did not wish to offend his unexpected visitor. *These ancient names are not used any more – why is she calling herself Amalishah? After the name of the temple?* But how could she know the name of the temple? He looked at her steadily, trying to gain time to sort things out. *She must be an orphan, the lost and wandering survivor of some feud between local villagers who remembered – somehow – the name of the temple. She might even be an Assyrian, one of the 'children of Ashour'.* There were still some Assyrians left, although Mike did not expect to find any in these parts. Was she alone? Women did not travel alone in the wastelands.

"Are you alone?" he asked.

"I am alone."

Almost certainly the survivor of some local tribal quarrel. She might have sought refuge in the wastelands and found the ruins of the temple. Blood feuds were not uncommon in this part of the world.

He remembered the box of English biscuits: "Would you like something to eat?"

She shook her head slowly, again with regal dignity.

In the long years since Mike's wife had passed away none of

the women he had met had seemed *interesting* enough to warrant a serious relationship, and he had come to think of himself as too emotionally hardened to feel drawn to any particular woman. Yet he felt compellingly, irresistibly, attracted towards the girl who now stood quietly some eight or ten yards away. *Don't be silly chum! She can't be much older than twenty, at most twenty-five. She's young enough to be your daughter!* But in the semi-darkness her poise and demeanour made her appear beautiful beyond anything he could have imagined possible. Mike was surprised to feel a sense of male protectiveness that he had always assumed had no place in the modern age.

Mike slowly came out of the tent. He had to stoop and this exacerbated the pain in his arm, but once out of the tent he managed to stand up straight. The girl stepped back so as to maintain the distance between them. "Please don't be afraid of me," he said softly. "I wish only to see you better."

She did not answer and Mike took the opportunity to look behind him. His tent was in the forefront of at least a dozen others, of varying sizes and shapes; all laid out with military precision. Small gaslamps were distributed sparingly about the camp. *This orderliness isn't like old Kureishi at all! Our expedition has acquired new members!*

When he looked forward again the young woman had disappeared.

Mike felt a pang of guilt and regret: *I frightened her and now she's gone!*

"Please don't be afraid of me," he said again in Assyrian, hoping that she had not run away. "I only wish to come closer so that we could talk." He spoke more loudly than before, but still low enough not to wake anyone in the camp.

"I would find talking to you agreeable," he heard her say, "but what is there that you and I could talk about?" In the brief moment that he had looked behind him she had moved farther away towards his right and was now standing motionless beside a clump of large rocks, outside the light of the gaslamp. But his eyes had adapted to the darkness and he could just see her outline. Behind her, at a distance, he could see the silhouette of the hill against the starlit sky.

"I would like to talk about *you*. Where you come from. Where you live. How it is that you are wearing my coat."

The woman beckoned to him. A dignified gesture, like a Victorian lady beckoning to a manservant, and Mike approached her warily. He was afraid that if he moved too fast she would flit away. When he was within talking distance she raised her hand and Mike stopped.

"It is kind of you to wish to talk about me," she said. "As for the coat I am wearing, it was lying on your *tent*. I borrowed it to hide my nakedness."

It took Mike a few seconds to interpret what he realised must be the Assyrian word for 'tent'. *My old coat was in the Land Rover. Someone must have tossed it on my tent.*

"You came here naked?"

"My clothes are... gone."

"If you wait I'll give you something better to wear."

She came slightly closer, watching his every move.

Ignoring the pain in his arm, Mike went swiftly to his tent and fumbled in his suitcase. He removed a clean shirt and trousers but was too much the Englishman to think of offering her underwear. He returned to the clump of rocks: "Here, try these on."

She approached him cautiously and took the proffered clothing with one hand. At close range he could see that she was taller than he, and he noticed that her unusually large eyes were framed by long black eyelashes that enhanced the whiteness of her skin.

"Please turn around so that I can put on the…clothes."

Mike turned around to allow her to dress. After a few minutes she said: "I am dressed," and Mike turned to face her. She handed him his coat and said: "I don't know what to do with these." She was referring to the shirt buttons and the trouser zip. Mike did the buttons and the zip for her, careful not to touch her, and indicated what she should do with the zip. *She is indeed a strange one. I wonder how she survived out here.* The trousers were too short for her but the shirt fitted her amply.

The small effort of buttoning the shirt had made the pain worse and Mike suddenly felt very weak: "Would you mind if we sat down?" he asked.

She nodded and sat on one of the rocks, facing him. She sat straight-backed with her knees close together and her arms by her sides. Mike sat two metres from her on the ground, the pain in his arm got much worse by the effort.

"Where are you from?" he asked, looking up at her.

"I live here."

I suppose these ruins could offer shelter to some lost waif. There might be enough puddles to provide water or perhaps even a spring, which we haven't found yet. But what about food? She does not look malnourished. In fact, she looks strong and healthy!

"Is your family near here?"

"I have no family."

Almost certainly an orphan from a blood feud! But the communities that spoke Assyrian lived far to the south. *I wonder how she got here. How did she find herself alone so far from everything? Maybe I shouldn't pry into personal matters.* "Do you know anything about this place?"

"This place?"

"I mean the hill, and the… old stones that cover it." Mike did not know the Assyrian word for 'ruins'.

"I know everything about the hill and the old stones that cover it."

Mike smiled, trying not to appear condescending: *Even if you've lived here for years, my dear, you wouldn't know everything about the hill and the ruins!* "Do you know that up there, on the hill, was once an ancient temple and that the name you gave me was that of the temple?"

"There were many small temples and shrines on the hill."

"Oh yes. But there was one main temple, to a goddess!"

She smiled wanly and the sadness did not leave her eyes: "The temple you speak of was underground. On the surface were minor temples, living quarters, craftsmen's workshops, storerooms and the defensive walls with the gates and their guard towers."

Mike was perplexed and slightly irritated. *How the devil does she know these things? She must have learned about the temple from someone!* He wanted to ask: 'Was your father or mother an archaeologist?' but he did not know how to put the question in Assyrian. *It's also possible that she doesn't know anything. It's possible that she made all that up!* So he asked: "How did you come to know about these things?"

The sadness in her eyes deepened, but she did not answer.

The loss of her family must have been traumatic and she does not wish to talk about it! She must have come here with someone who found the temple before me. Perhaps a freelance archaeologist or an amateur obsessed with the Amalishah temple. Then something terrible happened and she was left alone.

"What was your name before you called yourself Amalishah?"

"That was always my name."

In her loneliness she created a fantasy based on what she had been told or had overheard. In time she lost her mind, and gave herself the name of the temple!

She watched him patiently as he struggled to explain to himself what she had said. Finally he spoke, grateful that she had not interrupted his thoughts.

"When my friends awaken, they and I could help you."

"Help me? How?"

"Well," Mike was unable to think clearly, "We could take you to a city. Arrange for you to lead a normal life, like any other girl your age."

"Why would they wish to take me to a …city?"

Mike was not sure he understood the question. *Is it the word for 'city' she doesn't understand?* "A city is like a large village," he explained. "There you would meet other young people." *She might have lived in a village before she became part of an archaeological expedition!*

She smiled as though to herself and seemed to ponder over his words. "I think I understand. Why are you and your friends here?"

Mike was tempted to talk about the expedition and its objectives, but he realised that this was not the time for a lecture on archaeology. Anyhow, his Assyrian was not up to it. "We are here to study the temple," he said simply. "The temple whose name you use."

"Would *you* be willing to help me if I wished it?"

"Of course."

"Why?"

"Isn't that the human thing to do?" *I'm getting philosophical; damn those drugs!* She nodded slowly, as though trying to understand what he meant. "The human thing to do," she repeated, and her voice now reflected the sadness in her eyes. "Humans do a lot of things, not all good."

"We cannot leave you here."

"What is your name?" The question was abrupt, unexpected.

"Michael Townsend. My friends call me Mike."

"I am not your friend, Michael Townsend, though I would like to be. But if you wish to help me, I would ask of you one thing only: please do not speak of me to your friends."

"They cannot help you if they don't know about you."

"If the time comes for them to help me, I shall allow you to tell them about me."

He concluded that she was not ready to meet more people: *She must have lived alone for a long time and her isolation made her paranoid and homophobic!*

"Amalishah," he said, the name sounding strange when addressed to a living person, "my companions will awaken soon."

"I know."

"Perhaps you are right. It would be best if you do not meet them, not until you learn more of the world and its ways. You must have lived here for a long time and forgotten the world outside."

"I have lived here for a long time, yes." She smiled at him. It was a small smile, just a faint stretching of the mouth that did not fully erase the sadness in her eyes, but it was a warm smile, and it was the first time she had smiled at *him* rather than to herself. Mike felt his pulse quicken and there awakened within him an exhilaration that he had not felt since he was a very young man, the electric tingling that a boy from an all-male public school feels when he first meets a pretty girl. The fact that he was obviously so much older than her became irrelevant. He was entranced, captivated by her smile and the sadness in her eyes. He had never met a woman who could smile like that.

"If you wish," he said, and he almost stammered, "you and I can meet somewhere, at night when all are asleep, and I will tell you about the world away from the hill. The world is wonderful in ways that you cannot imagine, and I would very much like to tell you about it."

"I would be grateful if you would tell me about the world away from the hill. But remember, Michael Townsend, not to speak about me to your friends." It was not a request, not a suggestion, but an order spoken very evenly. She was not smiling.

"If that is what you wish, I shall not tell them about you."

"Then I shall meet you at night, Michael Townsend, halfway between sunset and sunrise. I shall be at the place where there are many trees close together, on the other side of the hill, near to where the hill slopes down."

That's the grove near the Northern ramp; not the ramp Len and I used. "Shall we meet tomorrow?" He felt like an adolescent who asks a girl out for the first time.

"Perhaps tomorrow night, perhaps not. I cannot say when I shall be there. But I will have hunted before I come, so that I would not be hungry when I meet you"

"I'll be there every night until I see you again." *Strange thing to say: 'Not hungry when I meet you'.* He thought of offering to bring her food, but people who have lived alone a long time sometimes developed strange habits and he decided against it. She got up and stood before him, waiting for him to leave first. Without further words Mike got up and walked the short distance back to his tent, leaving her standing behind him. He had completely forgotten the pain in his arm. When he reached his tent he looked back, but she had vanished into the darkness.

18

ON THE LORE OF VAMPIRES

1

MIKE WAS AWAKENED by a cool breeze across his face. Someone had opened the flaps of the tent and pulled back the mosquito net. There were subdued voices at some distance and he caught the tail end of someone's sentence. A man's voice was saying: "...I'm sure it'll work out great, honey!"

Ah! Americans.

A female voice answered: "I've organised the work teams. They know exactly what to do. All you have to do is supervise them!" *That sounds like Carol.*

"I'm sure I'll manage very well." *That's her husband, what's his name? Britten? No, Bradley.* The voices trailed off and Mike smiled. Things in the camp seemed to be proceeding normally. His watch showed a quarter past seven.

The open flaps gave a clear view of the hill and of the boulders interspersed with stunted trees that lay between the tent and the southern ramp. The gaslamp, now extinguished, hung from the branch of the dead tree just as he remembered it. The sight of the tree reminded Mike of his nocturnal visitor: *Amalishah!* – and he felt his heart pounding.

But in the bright sunlight the memory of the mysterious girl was too remote, too fantastic, to weave itself into the fabric of reality: *You must have been a dream, my beautiful Assyrian!* He reluctantly put the girl out of his mind and concentrated on the present. The pain in his left arm was still there but much less than he remembered. He got up, put on his sandals, and got out of the tent, still wearing his pyjamas. Carol and Bradley were gone, but there was a camp-shower just behind his tent and he needed a shower badly. *I must look a mess!* There was a considerable amount of stubble on his chin and his unkempt hair felt oily. He took a towel, his razor and a bar of soap and went to the camp-shower.

There were soldiers in the camp. Some carried automatic rifles and had pistols and commando knives attached to their belts. *Have the authorities revoked our leave to excavate?* The idea was chilling. *What would happen to the girl?* He pushed the thought away gently: *Don't be silly! She was only a dream!*

After a shave and a warm shower Mike returned to his tent and put on a clean set of clothes. He kept the sandals although they were wet from the shower. Not too far from his tent he found ElKureishi talking to an army officer. The professor had his usual *coterie* of postgraduates and postdocs hovering around him and hanging onto his every word.

"Ah, the sleeper has awakened!" said ElKureishi jovially. "It is good to have you back, Mike. Let me introduce you to Major Hussein ElBalushi; he's in charge of the military fellows." Almost as an afterthought he added: "Whom we are happy to have with us."

Mike shook hands with the major. "A pleasure to meet you, Major."

"The pleasure is mine," replied the major courteously. "I was looking forward to meeting you, Professor. You were sleeping rather fitfully for almost six days!"

"Six days?" Mike was very surprised.

"Yes, six days," said ElKureishi, "On and off. But when you were not sleeping you were not fully conscious and quite unintelligible. It was very difficult to feed you."

"How are you feeling, Professor?" asked one of ElKureishi's postgrads, a bright young lad from Basra.

"A bit groggy, but otherwise fine."

"That was quite a find, Mike," said ElKureishi, "There is no doubt at all that we have found the Amalishah temple."

"I take it you've all seen the skeletons?"

"And the writing on the wall of the pit," said ElKureishi. "Ohanian went practically insane with joy when he saw the writing! He says he never saw anything like it!"

The conversation was in danger of veering towards Ohanian's idiosyncrasies, which were among ElKureishi's favourite topics, but the major was not one for idle talk: "I am rather curious about the writing on the wall of the pit," he said, "Do you have any ideas about it, Professor Townsend?"

"Not really. Not yet, anyway," replied Mike, "It seems quite unique. But I am pleased that you find our stuff interesting, major."

The major grinned: "Oh, we are here in a purely protective capacity, Professor, but that doesn't mean that some of us aren't genuinely interested in your work."

"The major thinks we are likely to be attacked by bandits," said ElKureishi. He did not sound convinced.

The major's grin broadened: "*Only* if you find valuable artefacts. Especially if you find things made of gold or silver."

"That is not very likely now," said Mike, "As I'm sure you have seen, the cavern is not flooded. Any gold or silver must have been looted long ago."

"Oh, I'm still hoping we shall make some exciting finds!" said ElKureishi.

"Your forensic team has started working on the skeletons," said the major, "They are particularly interested in the remains of the tall female. You left her exactly as you found her?"

"I take it you are referring to the missing skull?" asked Mike, addressing the officer.

"Of course."

"I left her exactly as I found her."

The major nodded thoughtfully but remained silent.

"Did forensics come up with anything exciting?" Mike asked ElKureishi.

"According to the forensic team's initial conclusions," said ElKureishi, "She was old and infirm. She had all kinds of probably very painful problems with her hips and knee bones. That's all that can be said so far."

"Do you think it's the skeleton of the goddess of the temple, Professor Townsend?" asked the postgrad from Basra.

"I would think so," replied Mike. "The missing skull agrees with the Hittite records, as does the length of the bones. She was very tall."

"Who else could it be?" said ElKureishi.

"It could be the remains of one of the goddess's priestesses," said the major, "Or even of an unfortunate visitor who happened to be there during the Hittite onslaught."

"But then, why would the head be missing?" asked a Turkish postdoc. "The Hittites were not in the habit of decapitating their enemies. The decapitation of the goddess was unusual."

"They could have decapitated a priestess, or someone else who fitted the goddess's description, thinking it was the goddess," replied the major brusquely. "The Hittites were clever but not infallible."

"Are you saying that the goddess might have survived the Hittite holocaust?" said ElKureishi. "That is impossible, Hussein."

"Very improbable, perhaps, but not impossible," said the major. "We all make mistakes. The Hittites may have *thought* they killed the goddess!"

Mike was surprised by the major's reluctance to accept the female skeleton as that of the goddess. All historians and archaeologists who knew the story of the Amalishah temple accepted the Hittite claim; nobody doubted that the goddess had been killed.

"Are you *particularly* interested in the temple of Amalishah, Major?" asked Mike.

"Actually yes. I was brought up not too far from here. The local people have long memories and there are legends about the ruins on the hill."

"Really?" said Mike. "I would be very grateful if you told me some of them, when you find it convenient."

"I look forward to that, Professor."

"Let's all go to the refectory tent and have breakfast," said ElKureishi, "I'm quite hungry."

"Good idea!" said the major, and he stepped back to allow ElKureishi and Mike to go ahead of him.

2

The refectory occupied a central position in the camp and, not surprisingly, was in the largest tent. A generous breakfast was being served by three of ElBalushi's men who had been assigned to the kitchen.

"It is not often that we are waited upon by the army," said Mike.

"Soldiers must be kept busy," said the major. "Otherwise they may get up to all sorts of mischief." Mike laughed and the officer laughed back.

Most of the tables were occupied but ElKureishi's students collected enough empty chairs for the whole group to sit on both sides of a long table. Mike sat beside the major and across the table from ElKureishi. There was no conversation while the major and the senior archaeologists concentrated on the rich assortment of food that was on offer; it was intended to satisfy both Western and Middle Eastern palates.

When he had almost finished his breakfast, the major turned to Mike: "You had a lucky escape, Professor. You probably owe your life to that strip of cloth you had around your elbow."

Mike smiled: "And to my friend Leonard Ehrlich, who must have administered First Aid promptly and effectively."

"Oh yes, your attentive companion, Dr. Ehrlich," said the major. "Although the expedition's doctor is very competent, he would not have been able to do much had Dr. Ehrlich not pulled you out of the pit in time and done what was necessary. Our Army doctor, Lieutenant Mursi, has checked on your progress regularly."

"Dr. Ehrlich has helped me many times. Where is he, by the way?"

"He's on a tour of the United states!" replied ElKureishi with his mouth full.

"What kind of tour?" Mike was surprised.

"A lecture tour!" ElKureishi seemed to find the idea amusing. "The American universities who so generously sponsored us could not wait to be told about the discovery of the temple! He'll be back in a few days."

"They actually asked whether you, Professor Townsend, would have been willing to talk about your discovery," said the major, "But, given your condition, it was decided that Doctor Ehrlich should go instead."

"I'm sure he'll enjoy it. Len hasn't been back to the United States for several years."

"I personally think they should have waited until you were well enough to go," said ElKureishi, "But their urgency has to do with their sponsorship. An important discovery means that they are contractually obliged to move on to the second stage of funding us."

"When it comes to money, there are always wheels within wheels," said the major, "and the inner wheels have to be oiled regularly."

"That is all too true!" lamented ElKureishi.

Mike strongly disliked the system of grants and sponsorships that supported archaeological excursions but he was not quite ready to discuss it with people outside his profession. He turned to the major: "You said I was initially treated by the expedition doctor but that your Lieutenant Mursi checked on me regularly. Why was that?"

Professor ElKureishi, who was sitting across from the major, betrayed a certain gladness that someone – other than himself – had asked that question: "Come to think of it, Hussein, why did you insist on that?"

All eyes turned to the major. "I shall be frank with you," he answered, frowning. "I wanted to know what Professor Townsend was saying when he was delirious. Your physician would not have reported everything to me."

"And did your Lieutenant Mursi report *everything*?" asked ElKureishi darkly.

"I don't think so. Lieutenant Mursi was unable to understand most of what Professor Townsend said."

"That's because Mike was rambling in garbled Assyrian," said ElKureishi smugly.

"Why were you so interested in what I was saying?" asked Mike, addressing the major.

"As I said earlier, there are strange legends about this place. To put it simply, the ruins are supposed to be haunted and you might have seen something unusual. The villagers who lived not too far from here used to avoid this hill, especially after sunset."

ElKureishi laughed: "Haunted? Oh come now, Major!"

"You thought I might have seen a ghost?" asked Mike.

"Even ghosts don't haunt places for four thousand years!" said Jehan, the pretty post-doctoral student, who was sitting behind the major at the next table. She tried to smile at the major while munching her cornflakes but he seemed not to notice her. Several postgraduate students turned to listen to this unusual exchange.

The major took another mouthful and put down his spoon. "I don't know if it's a ghost that haunts the ruins," he said after he had swallowed his food. "My grandfather claimed to have seen the evil thing one very dark night. He insisted that it was flesh and blood, not a ghost. Something much worse."

"Why was your grandfather moseying around the ruins on a very dark night?" asked Carol, who was sitting beside her husband further down the long table. The conversation was gathering participants.

"Uh… moseying?" the major looked mystified.

"Sorry," said Carol. "That's one of those nice words from the U.S. of A. It means walking about casually, looking for something interesting without knowing what. A mosey is a mosquito, you see."

"Thank you," said the major. "But he didn't see the evil thing on the hill. He saw it prowling around his village when everyone but my grandfather was asleep. The village was not too far from here and the evil thing is said to wander, sometimes, far from the ruins on the hill. Like all the villages around here, that village is empty now. All the villagers have moved to the cities."

"Because of the evil thing?" asked Jehan.

"No," replied the major, "For economic and social reasons."

"What did you mean by 'something much worse' than a ghost?" asked ElKureishi before Jehan, who was young and idealistic, could turn the conversation towards the financial plight of the villagers.

The major shrugged. "The legends don't say what it is. But it is believed to be something evil, something from the very distant past."

ElKureishi was about to speak but refrained when Mike exclaimed: "Stuff and nonsense!"

The major turned to Mike with a polite smile, although his eyes were not smiling: "I am sure it would be stuff and nonsense in London, Professor," he said calmly, "but here, such things are believed to happen. Not frequently, of course, and certainly not regularly, but over the centuries many people have claimed to have seen the evil spirit of the ruins."

"As you said, Major, the people who lived around here had long memories," said ElKureishi placatingly, wishing that Mike had not lived up to his reputation for speaking his mind. He turned to his students: "It is not impossible that we have in these legends a legacy from the days of the temple itself. As I am sure you all know, the goddess was supposed to be immortal and she was very popular with the Assyrians of her time. Although the local people changed their religion several times over the last two millennia, it is possible that they clung to the myth of the goddess's immortality. It is a short step from that to the belief that something very much like her is still around, even if they do not actually know anything about the ancient goddess herself."

"A bit like the myth of King Arthur's return," said Carol, supporting ElKureishi in his attempt to soften the tone of the conversation.

"Perhaps that is so," said the major, not pleased by Carol's attempt at humour.

"And what is this evil spirit supposed to look like?" asked Jehan. She had a sudden dislike for people who did not take the major seriously.

"It's supposed to look like a very tall and stunningly beautiful young woman," replied the major, and Mike almost choked on his cereal.

3

At that moment they were joined by Ardashes Ohanian, the expedition's crypto-analyst. He had brought his personal folding chair with him but, before finding a place to put it down, he came over to Mike and shook his hand vigorously.

"I'm so glad to see that you are well now!" he exclaimed with enthusiasm, "We were all worried about you so much. How are you feeling?"

"I'm much better now, thanks," said Mike weakly.

"I hope you don't mind that your tent faces the hill," said Ohanian, setting his folding chair beside ElKureishi, who obligingly moved aside to make space. "That was my idea. I figured that you would sleep better if your tent did not face the hustle and bustle of the camp. We could turn it around if you wish."

"Oh no. I like it that way."

"I am anxious exceedingly to see your photographs of the writing on the wall of the pit." Although Ohanian's English vocabulary was impressive, he had frequent lapses of grammar.

"They're in my laptop and on a backup disk. We could work on them as soon as you're free."

"I'll have something to eat quickly and then we could see them. I'll meet you in the computer tent. Yes?"

Mike agreed, and Ohanian ploughed into his breakfast of bread, eggs and *halal* bacon, which was really beef that looked and tasted like bacon. The conversation turned to local history at the time of the Ottoman Empire. ElKureishi was an authority on the Ottomans and did not mind showing it. Mike finished his breakfast but was very quiet; he seemed to be fully absorbed by the patterns on his coffee mug.

4

It was late in the evening when Mike decided that he had had enough of trying to decipher the writing on the wall of the pit.

"You want to stop now?" said Ohanian incredulously. Apart from a single electric lamp, the only illumination in the computer tent was from the computer monitors.

"We're getting nowhere."

"Just a few more hours, Mike, and I'm sure the light we'll see!"

"I really can't, Ardash. I'm tired."

"Oh I'm sorry! I forgot that you are not recovered fully."

"No, I'm not fully recovered.

"May I have a printout of your photos? I'd like to work on the script tonight in my tent."

"Sure. You may borrow the backup disk and make as many prints as you like."

Mike left the disk with Ohanian and returned to his tent.

What did I see last night? Was it really a dream? He could not push away the memory of the girl with the huge eyes. *I could be going mad, but there must be a better explanation!* He got out his pipe and was about to light it when he remembered giving the girl a pair of trousers and a shirt. He turned to his suitcase and rummaged inside. Sure enough, a pair of trousers and a shirt were missing. *Oh Lord! It might not have been a dream!* His coat was lying on the chair next to his bed. He looked at his watch; it was 9:40 pm. The evil spirit of the ruins? Poppycock! That was just a young woman! Mike lit his pipe and stood at the entrance to his tent, puffing away vigorously. What's happening to me? First I'm spooked by the sigh of the wind and now by some local superstitions! But the questions about the girl remained: How did she get here? How did she know so much about the temple? Why did she call herself Amalishah? The questions were at the back of his mind as he berated himself for being so affected by what ElBalushi had said: Not a ghost but something much worse! What could be much worse than a ghost? What's much worse than a ghost, chum?

The answer came quietly of itself, like a little voice in his head: A vampire. A vampire is much worse than a ghost! *A female vampire, a lamia.* At which point Mike seriously doubted his sanity. *I can't really be considering the possibility that the girl is a vampire. That's impossible! It's ridiculous!* He shook his head and inadvertently scattered the ashes of his pipe all over his lap.

"Damn!" He quickly brushed off the ashes, noting with dismay that his trousers had a new set of tiny holes. He refilled his pipe and lit it. *There's no such thing as a vampire!* But ElBalushi was no idiot and he really seemed to believe in this 'evil spirit'. Moreover, a real orphaned girl, a real victim of some tragedy, would have jumped at the offer of help from Mike and his colleagues. *Or would she? If she's an amnesiac she could well have developed homophobic tendencies!* Like the writing on the wall of the pit, the girl was an enigma to which Mike had no answers. *There's only one way to find out. I've got to go to the little grove and confront her, if she comes.*

Although it was now well past ten o'clock, there were still people awake in the camp. They were talking quietly in their tents or moving from one tent to another. Mike felt grateful that his tent was at the edge of the camp. When there was no one about he extinguished his pipe and put it away. Then he put on a light jacket and took his torch before walking briskly towards the hill in the almost-darkness. The night was clear, with a gibbous moon, and the stars shone brightly.

It was quite a way from the camp to the grove. The camp was south-west of the hill, not too far from where the Land Rover had broken down, and Mike had to walk a considerable distance before reaching the grove, which was next to the ramp on the north-east of the hill. On the way Mike suddenly remembered the strange thing the girl had said shortly before they separated: *'I will have hunted before I come, so that I would not be hungry when I meet you'*. In the dark desolation around the hill, the memory gave him goose pimples. He reassured himself repeatedly that ghosts, werewolves and vampires did not exist – could not exist! But in the almost-darkness, with only the moon and the stars for company, and with the large boulders rising like enormous gravestones all around him, his self-reassurances felt weak and inadequate. Eventually, he found himself at the little grove on the other side of the hill, next to the northern ramp. There was nobody there. He waited for her until dawn, but she did not come. He returned to his tent: tired, confused and very sleepy.

5

"Mike?" It was Ohanian's voice. "Mike? Are you awake?"

"I'm awake now," Mike grunted.

"Let's have breakfast and then work on the inscriptions. It's almost seven!"

"Give me another hour or two, Ardash. I'm very sleepy!" *Damn monomaniac!*

"Oh yes, I forgot. You're still not well. I'll meet you in the computer tent later."

Mike grunted again and Ohanian left. *She didn't come! But then, she did not say she would come on the first night! Perhaps she'll come tonight? Or perhaps it was a dream after all? Whoever opened my suitcase could have given those trousers and shirt to the laundry boys!* Mike drifted back into sleep.

It was well past nine when Mike finished his breakfast and went to find Ohanian in the computer tent. Three postdocs were working on another computer. The cryptoanalyst was totally absorbed in his work.

"Hello, Ardash."

Ohanian looked up with a welcoming smile. "Hi Mike! You are better now?"

"I'm less sleepy."

"Good! Because I think it would take both of us to make progress!"

"You're finding it difficult?"

"Not difficult. **Impossible!**" Ohanian almost shouted the last word and raised both arms in a gesture of frustration.

"Well, tell me what you have tried so far."

Ohanian went into a long discourse on all the techniques he had tried, including quite a few that were unknown to Mike. When he had finished, Mike said: "Perhaps we should try something new."

"Yes. That is why I am glad so much you are here!"

But even Mike's innovative mind could not come up with something that gave hope of resolving the many puzzles. Despite all their efforts, the writing on the wall of the pit remained as mysterious as ever. They both forgot to have lunch, and worked solidly until Mike pushed away the keyboard. The postdocs on the other computer had left hours earlier and Mike was alone with Ohanian.

"Let's have coffee and think of something else for a while."

"Akh! I completely forgot!" exclaimed Ohanian, "I've got a large thermos with lots of good Colombian coffee!"

He poured out two cupfuls of moderately hot coffee and sat back in his chair.

"Nice coffee!" said Mike after a long sip.

"The trick is not to boil the water. That way, some of the dissolved oxygen doesn't fly away. I am sure the coffee with oxygen will sharpen our minds."

"Let's get our minds off the script, Ardash."

"What is there to think about besides the script?" asked Ohanian.

"Ardash, do you believe in vampires?"

"What kind of question is that when there is so much work to do?"

"Please indulge me."

"You have been talking to ElBalushi. The superstitious man."

"Yes and No. But do you believe in vampires, Ardash?"

"You are not joking?"

"No."

Ohanian had a sip of his coffee. "Akh! The coffee is almost cold."

"It's fine for me. Please tell me. Do you believe in vampires?"

6

Ohanian sat back in his chair. "My people have many tales of vampires," he said tentatively. He was obviously uncomfortable with the topic. "So do the Greeks, the Romanians who were once the Dashians, the Kurds who were once the Medes, the Iranians who were once the Persians. As far as I know, all the peoples who remember their folk tales have legends of vampires. Even the Turks, who are relative newcomers around here, have tales of evil things that can possess dead bodies. In 1813 there was supposed to have been a plague of vampires on the Greek island of Mykonos."

"When you say vampires, Ardash, do you mean evil beings that come out of their graves at night to suck the blood of the living?"

"From the little I know from my grandmother, who knew a lot of old folk tales, vampires are not necessarily evil."

"Not evil?"

"The notion of evil has changed in the last few centuries, Mike. For my people, something can only be evil if it causes people to turn away from God. In the West, anything that consciously chooses to prey on humans has come to be called evil. There is a significant difference."

"But what do your folk tales say of vampires? What are they like?"

"They are said to be like you and me, except that they are supposed to have gone through death and cannot bear the sunlight."

"What about the fangs and the bloodlust?"

"No fangs, Mike, no bloodlust, though some tales speak of the creation of a vampire through an urge unappeasable for revenge, which is a kind of bloodlust. You can also forget about silver bullets and the need for a stake through the heart. According to authentic folk tales – which does not mean they are true, of course – a vampire can be killed like any normal person, though decapitation is the surest way."

"Do your folk tales speak of how a vampire is made?"

"Mike, why don't you ask a physician? That is biology."

"Come on, Ardash! What is a vampire?"

"Twelve years ago, when I was working on my doctorate in mathematics, I read a lot about vampires. I was young and wanted to know what the old stories said about them. I don't mean stories like Bram Stoker's *Dracula*, but collections of legends authentic and folk tales. Did you know there is even a story of a vampire that appeared in England, at a place called Thetford?"

"No, but I've heard of the place. Please go on."

"So what is a vampire? Akh! It is hard to be brief! But I think it is someone who is supposed to have died but comes back to life, which is why the French call it *un revenant*."

"My French is patchy."

"Too bad. French is a very beautiful language. It means 'one who returns.'"

"Is it necessary for a vampire to have died, Ardash? I mean when it was a normal human being and had not yet become a vampire?"

"Anything that feels a thirst for blood can be called a vampire. There are vampire bats that like to drink the blood of animals and sometimes of humans. Fleas and mosquitoes may also be thought of as tiny vampires. But when bats and fleas are dead they stay dead."

"You know what I mean, Ardash. Does a *real* vampire have to go through death?"

"Apparently. In the early Christian church, it was believed that excommunication by a bishop would cause a person to become a vampire – but only after the person died. He would become a vampire because he could not find rest."

"What about in the modern church?"

"Maybe. I don't know. Why don't you ask a priest?"

"Because I never thought of this question before and there are no priests here."

"You have been listening too much to that fellow, ElBalushi."

"How do you think a vampire comes about, Ardash?"

"You want to hear the theory I came up with when I was still a student?"

"I do."

"You will find it boring."

"I assure you, I won't."

7

"OK." Ohanian was beginning to enjoy the conversation. His hands, which had been still thus far, suddenly started moving about meaningfully: "Imagine a very complicated machine whose function depends on very complex and interdependent mechanisms. If the machine is damaged so that one or more of its mechanisms no longer work, the machine would cease to perform the function for which it was designed, yes?"

"Yes."

"To use Physics terminology, such a machine would have only one eigenstate. Outside this primary eigenstate it would only be a pile of junk."

"Quite so."

"Now suppose that the machine is self-repairing. We cannot yet build such a machine with today's technology, but it is possible to build one, in principle. Biological systems do it all the time provided the damage is not fatal. Yes?"

"Provided the damage is not fatal."

"Now suppose this very complicated machine evolved through many stages, making use of its self-repairing mechanisms. All but the simplest self-repairing processes are necessarily goal-orientated, which means that they repair and replace while seeking for the optimal solutions that would maintain the working of the machine. A sophisticated self-repairing machine must therefore evolve as it exploits enforced changes and discovers better ways to satisfy its objectives. Yes?"

"Ummm... very well." Mike was not sure about the direction of Ohanian's exposition.

"Well, if the repair and replacement is according to some minimising principle..."

"You mean according to rules that try to minimise the expenditure of energy while repairing and replacing?"

"Or something more general, like we see when applying the calculus of variations..."

"Yes. I follow you now. Go on."

"So if the self-repairing machine follows some minimising principle then, during the machine's evolution, the machine could change by developing new components and bypassing but not discarding some of its old components. This would be the case if it costs the machine more energy to get rid of redundant components than to keep them and simply not use them. In its final optimal state, therefore, some of the old mechanisms would be redundant and unused, but not unusable. The machine could even have alternative mechanisms in store, so to speak, like the variety we find in the genes of bacteria that allows them to adapt to drugs. The machine works well, and performs its functions properly, even though it is using components quite different from those it started with. That is evolution in its true sense. No?"

"Ummm..."

"Yes. But now suppose that the machine is somehow disturbed in a way that does not damage any of its vital mechanisms. If the disturbance is slight the machine will recover and resume working in its normal state, the primary eigenstate. We know this from the theory of nonlinear systems with feedback. Yes?"

"I understand. I was once an engineer."

"Good. Very good. So I don't have to use baby language."

"Go on."

"But suppose the disturbance is not slight. Then the machine would be expected to cease to function altogether, yes?"

"Yes."

"However, because the machine is so complicated, and depends on so many complex mechanisms working together, it is also possible that some very specific disturbances would not incapacitate the machine, but instead push it into another, alternative but not necessarily inferior, state. In this state, where it may work in some ways worse and in some ways better than before, the machine would continue to function, with perhaps a few notable differences from its original state. We would say that the machine had a second, unsuspected, eigenstate due to its extreme complexity and the existence of the redundant mechanisms. Yes?"

"I follow what you're saying."

"Now imagine that this machine is not mechanical, but biological, for instance a human being. We all carry redundant parts, do we not?"

"Like little toes?"

"I had more sophisticated things in mind, things that are part of the human genetic makeup but which are not used in the way they were used by our remote ancestors."

"Go on."

"So, if a human organism is disturbed in a way that did not destroy the life functions but somehow activated some of the redundant mechanisms, would we not be able to say that the organism has been pushed into an alternative mode of living, biologically speaking?"

"Hm. An alternative mode of living. A different eigenstate of life.

Alive, but not in the usual sense. A vampire would be a human being in an alternative state of life."

"Yes, Mike. And remember that we do not know what life is."

"Would such alternative states be superior to the normal state?"

"I would say that in most cases they would not be superior. The Thetford vampire, by all accounts, was a pathetic creature."

"So there could be many different forms of vampire."

"I think so, if vampires exist at all. Have you ever heard of the Malay or Javanese devil-doll?"

"No."

"The Javanese call the devil-doll a *battara kara*. It was probably made from the body of a small child. It did not move or do anything, but if it were fed regularly on blood it would not decompose and its hair and nails would continue to grow."

"How awful! You say that this devil-doll was um... manufactured?"

"Yes. It would probably be the lowest form of vampire: practically immortal and feeding on blood but not active in any way."

"I see. But let us return to the more traditional form of vampire. What could push a human machine, if we can call it that, into an alternative state?"

"Who knows? A severe trauma perhaps? A certain very unusual form of injury? An enforced change in its chemistry?"

"What about excommunication? That brings in the supernatural."

"Not necessarily. In the old days excommunication would have been a very traumatic experience."

"What about the death experience? How would you explain that?"

"I am not a physician, but it seems likely that before it could enter an alternative mode of living a human body might need to go through a state of almost complete catalepsy. A state indistinguishable from death to anyone but an expert."

"You mean like a zombie?"

"Oh no! A zombie would almost certainly have suffered brain damage from the poison that is said to produce the almost-death. A vampire could have an intact brain, or even an improved brain!"

"What about the need for blood?"

"In the alternative mode of living, it could be that blood is the only food the body can digest. Remember the *battara kara*! The human machine in the second eigenstate would depend on different mechanisms to continue living. Some of these mechanisms might not work as efficiently as in the normal state."

"All that does not explain the horror with which vampires have been viewed."

"Mike, consider the psychological effects on a vampire made newly. When he looks at himself he is and is not his old self, and as a returner from the dead he inspires terror and is shunned and hated. Gradually he is isolated and develops anger and fear. He becomes, as you say, an anti-social outcast."

"You have deprived the vampire of its supernatural associations."

"Of course. There is no such thing as the supernatural, Mike. If something exists, it has to be natural. It has to follow the laws of Physics. That is true whether present-day Physics or Biology can explain it or not."

"Well, what you said is not convincing," said Mike, "But it is a theory, in a wishy-washy kind of way."

"Did I bore you?"

"Not at all. And thank you."

"So can we go back to the inscriptions now?"

"Yes, Ardash. By all means let us go back to the inscriptions."

Mike wanted to see the girl again more than ever. He worked late with Ohanian, but kept looking at his watch. At about eleven o'clock they decided to call it a day and Mike returned to his tent before, once again, setting off for the grove with his torch. But again, there was no one there. He waited until dawn. On the way back Mike seriously thought he was going insane.

19

TREASURE

1

MIKE'S TEMPERAMENT CHANGED after his second fruitless visit to the grove. He felt that something essential to his wellbeing had been found but then lost, leaving a cavernous emptiness within him that demanded to be filled. While working with Ohanian he frequently thought of quitting the expedition and returning to London. He needed to go back to the world of certainties and clear-cut realities. After all, he had made an important archaeological discovery and many of his views concerning the temple had been vindicated. It was perhaps time to move on and apply himself to archaeological matters other than the temple and its goddess.

Why didn't she come? The question seemed to be always there, calling softly for attention; often intruding unexpectedly. When Mike tried to push it away it resisted, lingering like a fog that refused to disperse in the sunlight. *Why didn't she come?* Mike struggled to embrace the only rational explanation possible: *She was just a dream! She didn't come because she does not exist!* The possibility that the girl was not real proved difficult to accept at first, but he persisted and, slowly, his conviction grew. Every objection to the idea that the girl had been a dream could be argued away: What of the similarity to ElBalushi's evil spirit of the ruins? ElBalushi was talking nonsense and the similarity was just coincidence! Why had she seemed so real and left such a strong memory? Because the medication made the dream so vivid! Why had she called herself Amalishah? Because the goddess encapsulated all that had filled the void in his life after his wife passed away. Why had he been so affected by the failure of his second attempt to see her? Because he had clung, oh so foolishly, to the notion that this girl could have filled his emotional emptiness.

The near-conviction that the girl was only a dream suppressed but did not eliminate his longing to see her. Every time he looked up at the night sky he yearned to be at the little grove again. He yearned for the *expectation* of seeing her, the *hope* of seeing her. He told himself a hundred times that it was impossible to be in her presence again because she did not exist. He argued with all the logic he could muster that to hear her voice once more was too much to ask of the heavens. But all the rational arguments in the world could not remove his secret wish that the girl was real. Because the wish was secret, even from himself, it engendered a persistent hope that gnawed tenaciously on his mind.

2

Mike and Ohanian did not make any significant progress with the script, and it was only because Mike's obstinacy was matched by Ohanian's obsession with deciphering the script that the two continued to work together despite a series of setbacks and disappointments. Mike became more morose and ill-tempered by the day. On the hill, meanwhile, the excavations and other activities proceeded furiously. The rubble at the bottom of the pit was carefully removed and – courtesy of Army engineers who visited the camp for a week – the spiral staircase was reinforced with concrete and steel. To prevent any stones from the surrounding mound falling down the shaft a stout wire mesh was put across the mouth of the pit; near the top where the spiral staircase began its long winding descent. But although ElKureishi and Carol tried to keep Mike abreast of all important developments, he remained aloof and politely refused their repeated invitations to visit the underground cavern again. Even the discovery of a concealed tunnel that led from behind the throne to what must have been the living quarters of the goddess and her priestesses could not persuade him to descend to the cavern-temple.

It was early afternoon, five days after Mike's second middle-of-the-night trip to the grove, when a somewhat portly and very excited Iraqi postgrad appeared at the entrance of the computer tent. He had evidently run all the way from the hill and was breathing in large gasps. Mike and Ohanian were sitting before one of the computers, bent forward and staring fixedly at the screen. The wooden table upon which they were working was strewn with paper covered by scribbled diagrams and calculations.

"They found it!" cried the postgrad after he had recovered.

Mike turned away from the screen and stared blankly at the young man. Ohanian frowned but continued to stare at the screen.

"They found it!" repeated the postgrad.

"What did they find?" Mike asked politely but without much enthusiasm.

"They found treasure!"

"Oh?" said Mike.

"Can't you see we are working?" said Ohanian.

"Carol sent me to tell you," said the postgrad patiently, his excitement undampened by the cool response, "that they uncovered artefacts of gold and silver and many statues!"

"Did they find any tablets?" asked Ohanian without looking at the postgrad. Tablets in the unknown script could provide important clues to its decipherment.

"Yes, they did find some tablets."

"Why didn't you say so?" Ohanian's interest was suddenly awakened.

"Where is all this stuff?" asked Mike.

"It's still where they found it. It's being brought out to be labelled, packed and catalogued. It's being prepared for transport from the hill to the camp, to be put in the storage tent!"

"Akh!" exclaimed Ohanian, "They'll put the tablets with the old bones! I can't bear the sight of those skeletons!"

"Don't worry Ardash," said Mike reassuringly, "You'll get to study the tablets without having to be anywhere near the skeletons!"

"I hope you're right!"

"When will the tablets be brought down from the hill?" Mike asked the postgrad.

"Shortly – I think. The treasure is being processed now, slowly and carefully."

"Where in the ruins was the treasure found?"

"In a kind of deep cellar beneath the remains of one of the larger buildings, not far from the pit. Beneath a lot of rubble there were steps leading down to a storage room. Probably a cellar, I think."

"Did they find anything with inscriptions other than the tablets?" asked Ohanian.

"I don't think they found anything else with inscriptions," replied the postgrad. He was evidently not too interested in inscriptions. "But they found many wonderful things! They found beautiful artefacts of gold and silver and the cellar was stuffed with food jars as well as statues, copper ingots and bronze artefacts. The priests must have hidden the treasure during or shortly before the Hittite attack."

"How do you know that?" asked Ohanian sharply. He disapproved of students speculating.

"Carol said so..."

"I see," interrupted Ohanian and resumed staring at the computer screen.

"It was Carol's team that found the treasure," continued the postgrad, speaking to Mike, "She said the stuff was uh... *stashed* hurriedly in no particular order." In trying to quote Carol the postgrad unwittingly mimicked her rather pronounced American accent and his face stretched sideways to one side as he said 'stashed'. Mike almost smiled but his inner turmoil reasserted itself and the smile died stillborn. "Were there any human remains?" he asked the postgrad.

"Not in the cellar. Some charred remains of men and two women were exposed when the remnants of the large building were removed. We still haven't found any skeletons of children."

No skeletons of children? In Mike's frame of mind a peripheral thought could assume engrossing proportions. *In a large community such as this there must have been many children!* He frowned and asked: "Are you sure that no remains of children were found anywhere?" He almost regretted his lack of interest in the ongoing excavations.

"Yes, Professor. I am sure."

Mike looked away. *They'll probably find all the children together, huddled in some secret room where the priests hoped the little ones would be safe!* Mike remembered pictures he had seen of air raid shelters in wartime Britain, and then his thoughts shifted to underground places where German children and their mothers had been cooked alive while their firebombed cities burned above them. "They *must* have found the remains of children!" he exclaimed..

The postgrad shook his head: "I don't think so, Professor."

Mike noticed that Ohanian was looking at him strangely. *My mind is running amok! I'm tired of working on this damn script while trying to control needs I can't manage!* He moved away from the computer. "Staring at the screen for hours has given me a headache," he said quietly, "Let's get out of this tent!"

Mike and Ohanian left the computer tent to see if anything had been brought down to the storage tent in the camp. Nothing had been brought down and there was nothing to see. They returned to their work. Ohanian was only slightly disappointed and had no trouble going back to his calculations, but he was surprised and a little concerned to find that Mike had lost interest. *Mike has changed,* he thought. *He is not as he used to be. Something is eating him up from inside.*

3

Later in the evening, after all excavations had stopped for the night, Major ElBalushi called a meeting of the senior staff. On behalf of his government he congratulated those who had organised the expedition, and he especially thanked and praised Mike for his insight and knowledge, which had served the expedition so well. He spoke English, to make sure that all present understood him perfectly. Many among the audience smiled ingratiatingly, but Mike suspected that after all the praise and the compliments the major was going to say something that would not be to everyone's liking. His suspicions were soon confirmed.

"You will all agree, I am sure, that the situation has changed dramatically," said the major after he had finished with the eulogies. "Until now, this was a purely scientific expedition, of interest only to specialists and experts like yourselves. Now you have found items that would be of incalculable value on the black market, and other markets besides. There are those who would give much, and take enormous risks, to lay their hands on what you have found here."

"If you are referring to bandits," interrupted ElKureishi. "As head of this expedition I can assure you that my staff and I shall cooperate fully with you and your men in the fulfilment of your duties."

"My men and I shall be most grateful for your cooperation, Professor," said the major with a politeness that did not quite tally with his deadly serious expression. "But I have not finished. The threat of bandits, or others who might take, shall we say, an illegal interest in your discoveries, is very real. So I am sure you will all agree with me that there is no alternative but to keep all that has been discovered near to where you have found it, on the hill. *There* my men can protect it; *here* in the camp on the plain its protection would be difficult if not impossible. The camp is on flat ground and completely exposed. It would be impossible to defend. I must therefore reluctantly insist that none of the precious finds be brought down to the camp. The storage tent shall be moved to the hill, somewhere of your choosing among the ruins, and it shall be guarded day and night by my men. No one shall henceforth have access to any of the new discoveries without my personal permission."

"Just a minute," said a female voice with an American accent. "The things we've found don't belong to you. You can't decide all by yourself what should be done with them!"

Good old Carol! thought Mike. The major would not be allowed to forget that it was Carol's team that had discovered the artefacts.

The major was unperturbed. "Madam," he said, "I am not deciding what shall be done with them. When the time comes to decide what goes where and who keeps what, I shall gladly step aside. But for the moment, when it is possible that further finds shall be made, it is my responsibility to ensure that all discoveries are well protected. This responsibility overrides all other considerations. My decisions in all matters of safety, including the safety of the personnel, are final."

"But," said an agitated voice, "What if we need to see some of the tablets that have been discovered? They could be of value tremendous in the decipherment of the script on the wall of the pit!"

The major smiled. "Dr. Ohanian, I shall see to it personally that you and Professor Townsend are provided with high-quality photographs of all artefacts that could help you in your work."

"Thank you."

"One more thing," continued the major. "It will be necessary to move all essentials, including foodstuffs, to the hill. It will also be necessary to move your tents close to the ruins and reactivate at least one of the wells on the hill by setting up the water-purification equipment. If the threat from bandits becomes imminent we may not have time to transport everything we might need to the hilltop, so it is better to move everything we need in advance. The vehicles will have to be left behind, of course. They may be left near the foot of the southern ramp."

There was some opposition to the idea of effectively moving the camp to the top of the hill, but the major was not to be swayed: "I appreciate that this may cause some problems to the ongoing excavations, but I repeat that my decisions in all matters of safety, including the safety of the personnel, are final."

The staff had no choice but to agree. The major was quite capable of having the *permits* to excavate revoked. When all discussions had died down, the major ended with: "I am sincerely sorry if some of you find my decisions difficult to accept. I am not unaware that moving all essentials, including your tents, to the hill shall break your routine and cause some of you many kinds of inconvenience. I can only assure you that it is for the best. Thank you."

"The meeting is now closed," said ElKureishi, but some of the people were already up and leaving, muttering quietly among themselves.

4

Mike was returning to his tent when ElKureishi caught up with him.

"What did you think of *that?*" said the Professor. "He is taking over, you know."

"I was flattered by his compliments," replied Mike.

"Mike, it is now *us* against *them*."

"I really don't understand what you mean."

"This talk about bandits is just a pretext for him to take control!"

"I don't think so. If the danger from bandits is real then he was being quite reasonable."

"Reasonable? How can you say that?"

"I can understand his point of view. I believe the major will make sure his men stay out of our way, just as we should stay out of theirs."

"But don't you see, putting all the tents, including the storage tent, on the hill will impede the excavations! Moving almost everything in the present camp to the top of the hill shall cause no end of inconvenience!"

"Only a little inconvenience, I am sure. The whole top of the hill is not being excavated at once, and when necessary the tents can be moved around, away from wherever excavations are taking place. The top of the hill covers quite a large area."

"I fear the soldier boys will impede the excavations more than a little, Mike. By pretending that it is purely for our protection they shall set up their... their weapons wherever they please, and they shall build things on the ruins that we would not be able to dislodge."

"My dear Nasser, if the threat from bandits is real it is better that we be on the hill, where ElBalushi and his boys can take care of us. The bandits in this part of the world have the reputation of being well organised, so if any bandits are going to make a grab for our stuff they are likely to be both armed and numerous. It might not be a bad idea to listen to the major."

"Mike, I'll be open with you. I think ElBalushi has his own personal reasons for being here."

"What kind of personal reasons could he possibly have other than our protection?"

"I don't know. But there is *something* on his mind. It might even have something to do with his idiotic ideas about a wandering ancient demon."

"What makes you say that?" *'Idiotic' is a strong word. Kureishi must be quite upset!*

"Did you know that he put armed guards on the ruins from the very first night we came here?"

"Before there was anything to guard?"

"Yes. And the guards were told to cry out and if necessary use their weapons the moment they saw anything out of the ordinary!"

"That's a bit odd, but I am sure everything shall be as you wish, Nasser. Give or take a few inconveniences."

"Have you seen what we have found, Mike?"

That's a sudden change of tack! "No. I'm not interested in things destined to gather dust in museums. At the moment, I only care about the tablets."

"Some of the things Carol and her team have found are extraordinarily beautiful. I *really* think you should see them."

Mike was about to decline, but there was an earnestness in the elderly professor's voice that would have been impossible to ignore without being rude.

"Very well. I'll see them tomorrow, with the major's permission."

"Why not now? For all you know the major will forbid anyone to see them tomorrow."

"It *is* rather late."

"I know. But I want you to be part of the whole expedition again, Mike, not just involved in the decipherment of the script. When you see the artefacts you'll appreciate what interesting work we are all doing and how much remains to be done."

Ah! He is mustering his forces. He would have made a fine politician. "Very well. Let's go and see the major."

5

Major ElBalushi was sitting in his tent, writing at his desk. He was wearing slippers and his shirt collar was open.

"May we come in?" said ElKureishi.

"Please do, and please accept my apologies for receiving you with such informality."

"It is for us to apologise for disturbing you," said ElKureishi.

"Oh no. I half expected a visit from at least one of you tonight and I am happy that you both came."

"Mike and I were thinking of seeing the artefacts. So naturally we came to ask whether it would be all right with you."

"You want to see the artefacts now? At night?" The major was surprised; this was not what he had expected.

"Professor Townsend has an inexplicable urge to see the artefacts," said ElKureishi good-naturedly, "he has not seen them yet."

"Oh well, all right. But the guards may find your late-night visit rather unusual, so I'll come with you." He put on his shoes and hung his pistol on his belt.

"Um… do you think you'll need that?" asked ElKureishi.

"For all we know, there are bandits even now around the hill, and we would make excellent hostages. In fact, I have a second pistol." He pulled open a drawer and took out a revolver with a long muzzle "Would you like to take it, Nasser? Just for tonight?" He offered the pistol to ElKureishi.

"No thank you. I wouldn't know what to do with it."

"What about you, Professor Townsend?"

"Why not?" said Mike, taking the weapon. "With two pistols, you and I could stave off a whole horde of bandits!"

The major laughed. "I'm not supposed to offer a weapon to a foreigner, but these are exceptional circumstances. Do you know how to use such a weapon?"

"Actually yes. I used to be a pretty good shot with a pistol. County champion, in fact."

"Just remember that I would like to have it back when we return."

"Of course."

6

They were almost at the top of the ramp when they were challenged by one of the fully armed soldiers who were on guard among the ruins: "Who goes there?"

The moon was covered by thin clouds and the hilltop was dotted with gaslamps, but the ramp was in complete darkness. Mike wondered how the guard could have seen them. He was unlikely to have heard them because their shoes made very little noise in the soft earth of the ramp. *Perhaps he heard our voices!*

"Major ElBalushi and two companions," the major shouted back as they cleared the ramp. "We're here to see the artefacts."

The guard came forward but did not lower his automatic rifle until he had saluted the major. He showed no surprise at the lateness of the visit. Mike noticed that the soldier was wearing night goggles: *So that's how he saw us. These fellows are well equipped!* The other guards were somewhere in the shadows, concealed by the darkness.

The artefacts were some distance away. They were not illuminated but lay exposed to the moonlight in neat rows. All the smaller objects had been carefully wrapped and were either in open cardboard cases or smaller cardboard boxes. Everything that was not in a case or a box was covered by thin plastic sheets. At the rear of the artefacts stood what was evidently a tall statue. It stood alone among the artefacts and was covered by its own plastic sheet.

"Are the tablets in boxes?" asked Mike.

"Don't be like Ohanian, Mike," said ElKureishi. "There is something much more interesting than tablets that I want you to see." He went over to the piles of containers and, bending down, turned on a switch. There was the whirring of an electric generator and the whole area covered by the artefacts was lit by powerful floodlamps.

"I'm impressed," said Mike.

"That's not it," said ElKureishi. He went over to the tall statue and gently removed the plastic sheet.

And there, brilliantly illuminated by the floodlamps, was the goddess of the temple.

Well over six feet tall and exquisitely carved of translucent white stone, she stood on a low pedestal with her left arm by her side and with her right hand slightly raised, holding a small owl in her palm. Around her hair was a golden diadem in the shape of small leaves that seemed to clasp her hair in place. The statue was uncoloured, but on her breast was carved a necklace that was inlaid with a large red jewel at its centre.

Mike felt the muscles at the back of his neck tighten: *Oh my God! It's her!* The likeness was indisputable, although the proud goddess was a far cry from the timid girl he had first seen wearing his old coat. Mike could not get his eyes off the statue.

"I present to you the lamia of the temple," said ElKureishi with a flourish, not quite sure what to make of Mike's shocked expression.

"What do you mean by a *lamia?*" the major asked ElKureishi, though his attention was fully on Mike.

"A lamia is a female vampire," replied ElKureishi, as though he was explaining something to one of his students. "I call her a lamia because a certain Apolothoros, a Greek traveller who lived around the fourth or fifth century BC, once mentioned 'the lamia of the temple' in his writings. For a while I thought it was a metaphor for the pit, but now I'm sure that it probably referred to *her*. I can well imagine human sacrifices made to someone as beautiful as that."

"If the sculptor created a fair likeness she must have been very beautiful," said the major, "What do you think, Professor Townsend?"

"She… must have been very beautiful," agreed Mike. He had almost said 'She is still beautiful.' He wished he had studied the ancient Greek's writings more attentively.

"Isn't the carving superb?" continued ElKureishi, "as good as a Praxiteles!" He did not noticed that the major was looking at Mike with an intensity that made Mike feel uncomfortable.

"I would say so, yes." Mike was stunned but in full control of his actions.

ElKureishi pointed to the crown of golden leaves: "Those leaves are covered in pure gold; we checked."

"Oh. Have you found the original crown?" asked Mike. He had not heard all that the professor had said.

"No, I was referring to the crown on the statue. The original crown, if it ever existed, was not among the artefacts. Neither did we find the original of the large red jewel, although we found a very large number of smaller precious and semi-precious stones. The jewel on the statue is of red glass, or something like that."

"Perhaps you will find the original in another dig," said the major.

"Probably not," said ElKureishi. "If she was wearing those things when she was killed, the Hittites would naturally have taken them.

That is probably why there was no jewellery next to her skeleton."

"It is such a pity that we cannot tell the colour of her hair," said the major in a conversational tone. "What colour would you say it was, Professor Townsend?"

"I would think it wasn't blonde," said Mike. *Strange question.*

"It was almost certainly black," said ElKureishi.

"Most probably," commented Mike. "The Assyrians were always depicted with black hair."

"One can find present-day Assyrian children with blonde hair and blue eyes," said the major.

"They are probably of mixed ancestry," explained ElKureishi.

"Her dress is also very interesting," commented the major, returning to the subject of the goddess. "The folds below the waist resemble the half-closed wings of a bird. I wonder what that means, if anything."

"Probably just the fashion of the time," said Mike.

"If we assume that it is *her* bones we have in the storage tent," said ElKureishi, "and we *have* to assume that, the statue must have been sculpted while the goddess was still very young. It is possible they made a statue for every new goddess."

Neither Mike nor the major answered.

"There are smaller statues too," said ElKureishi, eventually breaking the silence. "But nothing as breathtaking as this. Shall we unpack them?"

"No, thank you," said Mike, his eyes still held by the statue. "After *this*, anything else would be an anticlimax." He could not suppress an involuntary shudder.

"Are you cold?" asked the major. He was obviously watching Mike closely.

"A little. I forgot how windy it gets on the hill at night."

"It would be easy and quick to unpack one or two of the tablets," said ElKureishi.

"I really don't think I could do them justice at this time," said Mike. "Anyway, I would prefer to share the thrill of first seeing the tablets, or their photographs, with Ohanian."

ElKureishi seemed slightly disappointed, but he agreed. "Shall we go back then?"

"Yes, let's go back," said the major, "In case you are feeling a bit let down at not seeing the tablets, Professor Townsend, you will be happy to know that I have given instructions for all the tablets to be photographed first thing tomorrow morning. The photographs will be available tomorrow afternoon."

"Thank you."

ElKureishi carefully covered the statue with its plastic sheet and turned off the floodlamps. As though a spell had been broken Mike finally looked away, but he was left with a turbulent mind and an unrelenting thought that would not go away: *It's her! There is no doubt at all. It's **her!*** The orientation of the statue was such that the goddess's serene gaze had seemed to be directed straight at him.

20

THE MAJOR MAKES HIS CASE

1

THE NIGHT WAS dark and almost cold as they made their way back to the camp. The moon had not yet risen and there was a dust-laden haze that made it difficult to see. Each of the three men was totally absorbed in his thoughts until the major suddenly said to Mike: "I was told that you were interested in the goddess, Professor Townsend, long before you came on this expedition. Now that you've seen what she looked like, did she live up to your expectations?"

The question, out of the blue as it were, brought Mike back to reality with a jolt: *Watch it, old chum!* "I found her statue *mesmerising*," he replied cautiously.

"You were entranced by the goddess's beauty?"

"By the *statue's* beauty," said Mike, emphasising the distinction.

ElKureishi joined in: "The statue captures the very essence of woman!" he said enthusiastically, "She stands aloof and mysterious, yet is maddeningly feminine! I wonder how many young men fell in love with the goddess when they saw the statue, only to find she was a pain-racked old woman!"

"Oh, you must show more consideration for the goddess, Nasser," said the major.

"But that is precisely what she was!" said ElKureishi petulantly. "The evidence of her skeleton is quite clear!"

"*If* it is her skeleton," said the major, and he raised his eyebrows in mock exasperation as if to say 'We've been through this before!'

Mike withdrew again into his thoughts and the major was soon in a lively discussion with ElKureishi regarding the merits of a certain restaurant in Damascus. The major was in good spirits and when the three men finally stood in front of Mike's tent he was happy to concede that neither the food nor the belly-dancing at that restaurant were outstandingly good.

The camp was very dark and quiet, and the blackness of the night weaved its way between the tents everywhere except beneath the gaslamps, which formed little isolated islands of illumination. As always, someone had hung a lit gaslamp on the tree opposite the entrance to Mike's tent, away from the camp.

"I wonder why they put a lamp in front of your tent," said the major. "It's at the edge of the camp and would be more effective closer to the centre."

"That was Ohanian's idea," said ElKureishi.

"Maybe it's because my tent faces outwards," said Mike.

"So it does," said the major pleasantly, "You could leave the camp at any time during the night and no-one would notice!"

2

"Why would he wish to leave the camp at night?" asked ElKureishi.

"Oh, it's possible that Professor Townsend enjoys midnight strolls!"

"Well, it doesn't matter where they put the gaslamp!" said ElKureishi. "The camp will be moved to the top of the hill within the next few days." He allowed himself a frown to show his disapproval. The major pretended not to notice and said to Mike: "I trust you enjoyed your late-night trip to the hill, Professor Townsend?"

"I enjoyed it very much," replied Mike.

"If I may say so," continued the major, "You looked a bit shaken and much stirred when you saw the goddess."

Mike was surprised to hear the major bring up the subject of the goddess again: "I'm sure the statue has that effect on everyone who sees it for the first time."

"Especially at night," said the major. "In the daytime it will still be a thing of beauty, but then it would not be easy to forget that it is made of cold stone."

"It is certainly very lifelike," said Mike, trying to sound detached and clinical, but he had almost panicked: *Did I show recognition?*

Mike almost failed to hear ElKureishi say: "Your reaction was perfectly natural, Mike. Even I felt a strange fascination when I first saw the statue of the goddess."

"The face of evil is always fascinating," said the major, "That is why evil can be so seductive."

Mike turned to the major: "Do the local legends actually claim that the evil spirit who is supposed to haunt these parts was once the goddess of the temple?"

"The legends couldn't claim that," replied the major, "since it is doubtful whether the people who lived around here in the last two thousand years had ever heard of the goddess of the temple. But it is my personal belief that the evil thing of the legends can only be Amalishah. I believe she was never killed and continues to live!"

"How can you believe such a thing?" said ElKureishi dismissively.

But Mike wished to draw the major out: "So you believe your grandfather actually saw the woman of the statue, owl and all?"

The major gave a short laugh. "Not just my grandfather. A lot of people claimed to have seen the evil spirit, although no-one said anything about owls. In fact, my grandfather said she was completely naked!"

"Ghosts and demons are just superstitions," said ElKureishi, "With all due respect to your grandfather, Hussein, I think he was mistaken. The goddess lived approximately four thousand years ago. Your grandfather probably saw some poor beggar-woman looking for scraps of food. She was probably too poor to get clothes!"

"Tell us more about how your grandfather saw this evil thing," said Mike.

The major took a deep breath before answering: "My grandfather was still in his early teens when he saw the demon prowling outside his village very late one night. A dog was howling near one of the sheds and his father told him to go out of the house to investigate. Thinking that the dog was barking at a jackal he did not take any weapons, but instead of an animal he was shocked to see a very tall and beautiful woman without any clothes, exactly how the legends described the demon! It did not see him at first as it was too busy trying to quieten the dog, and he could have shot her then if he had a weapon. But he was unarmed, and for the rest of his life my grandfather deeply regretted not having killed the thing, for he knew that demons should have no place in this world."

"What happened then?" asked Mike.

"The demon saw him and escaped, running like the wind! My grandfather said that she would probably have attacked him if she did not have to run away because dawn was approaching."

"Oh? Is this evil spirit supposed to fear the daylight?" asked ElKureishi with a hint of sarcasm. "I thought demons can appear at any time they wish!"

"I don't know anything about other demons," replied the major, "But all the legends suggest that this particular demon is afraid of daylight."

"Granting that your grandfather saw a woman who happened to fit the legends," said Mike, "what makes you think it was Amalishah?"

"A few years after my grandfather saw the thing, most of the people of our village moved to the cities. My grandfather married and had children, and they in turn had children, and when I was born he grew quite attached to me, for I was his first grandchild. My grandfather never learned how to read or write, so after I went to school he made me write all the legends he knew about the evil thing in a scrapbook, and he made me mark all the places where the evil thing had been seen on a very old Ottoman map which had been in my family for generations."

"How could the legends have allowed you to mark the locations of the supposed sightings?" interrupted ElKureishi. "Legends are just vague stories!"

"Some of the legends were in fact just vague stories," said the major, "But the villagers never travelled far from their homes, and most of the legends mentioned the names of the villages where the sightings occurred. It was the locals' way of showing authenticity. The villages are now empty, but their names are shown on the Ottoman map." The major became suddenly quiet, as though he had remembered something that required all his attention.

"Please go on," said Mike, "You were telling us why you believe that the evil thing of the legends is the goddess of the temple."

The major continued: "Oh yes. Please forgive me, my mind wandered. Many years later, while I was stationed in Basra as part of the military team responsible for the safety of this expedition, I read the official report on the discovery of the underground cavern. The existence of the cavern proved that the ruins on the hill were the remains of the Amalishah temple and, of course, we were all very excited. When I returned home I brought out my grandfather's map and looked to see whether it showed the ruins on the hill. It did show the ruins, in an unimportant sort of way, but because my mind was now on the Amalishah temple I noticed that all the markings I had made were within a circle centred on the ruins! You can imagine how I felt when I estimated the radius of that circle and found it to be roughly equal to the distance a very fit person could travel on foot in half the night! In other words, the sightings are all within the greatest distance the evil thing could walk if it needed to return to the temple without getting caught by the daylight! This convinced me that the demon of the legends could only be Amalishah, the goddess who was believed to be immortal!"

"Hussein," said ElKureishi with a drawn-out yawn, "The woman who was Amalishah died four thousand years ago. We have her bones in a cardboard box."

"That is a presumption," said the major.

ElKureishi said something that sounded like 'Bah!'

"Your reasons for believing that the legends refer to Amalishah are not very solid," said Mike. "They use the improbable to prove the impossible."

"I understand that," said the major, "But this is an old country, Professor, and many civilisations have come and gone on this land. Each one left behind a little of itself, sometimes a memory of its culture, sometimes a memory of its beliefs, sometimes a bit of both. It is not impossible that one of the earlier civilizations left behind something that is more than just a memory, something evil and horrifying."

"But it *is* impossible!" said ElKureishi emphatically. "It is absolutely impossible! And we must not confuse legends with facts, especially if the legends speak of demons and evil spirits, which are impossible to the point of being laughable."

"We must not laugh at legends as though we are wise enough to know all that is possible and all that is impossible," said the major.

"But what you are asking from us is more than just respect for legends," said Mike, "You are asking us to believe that the woman who was once thought to be a goddess still lives after four thousand years!"

"Yes I am."

"I find it ridiculous to even consider such a possibility!" expostulated ElKureishi.

"You are forgetting," responded the major, "that her own contemporaries – and they covered many generations – wrote that she could not die of natural causes."

"Those who wrote such things were not her priests," said ElKureishi, "They did not know her personally. They wrote only what they had been told about her!"

"Our ancestors were ignorant of the higher truths that were revealed to us much later," said the major, "but they were neither foolish nor gullible. If they believed something that they could verify for themselves, it was probably true."

"Your ancestors were certainly not foolish or gullible" said Mike, "But ancient writings were often intended to be interpreted metaphorically or symbolically."

"Exactly!" exclaimed ElKureishi. "When the ancients wrote that the goddess was immortal they could only have meant that, over many human lifetimes, there was always someone at the temple who was said to be the goddess Amalishah!"

"We cannot say how the records are to be interpreted," said the major. "We know too little about the minds of the ancients." He seemed to be losing interest in the argument.

3

Mike was too keen on the subject of the goddess to let the discussion slip away. He said half-jokingly to the major: "Don't you think it would be interesting to meet whoever or whatever it is who is supposed to walk in the night? If it is the goddess, as you claim, it would give us the opportunity to learn, as you say, about the minds of the ancients!" Mike was aware that he was treading dangerous ground, but he wanted to push the major as far as he could.

The major gave Mike a long, hard look, and when he spoke again he spoke directly to Mike: "It would indeed be a great opportunity to learn about the minds of the ancients," he said, choosing his words carefully, "but it would be *very dangerous* to speak to the demon, Professor. They can be very beguiling, these things, if they want something from you."

"What could the goddess possibly want from me?" asked Mike innocently.

"Your blood, perhaps?"

Mike found the major's reply disturbing. "I don't believe in vampires," he said quietly, "and you have given us no reason to believe that this supposed evil thing has ever harmed anyone!"

"We only have the stories of those who survived meeting the demon," said the major, "we do not know what happened to the others!"

"There may not have been any others," said Mike, "the demon, as you call it, may be quite harmless – assuming it exists."

"Oh it certainly exists!" said the major.

"I am not convinced," said Mike. "I think we are fortunate to have found a very beautiful statue of the goddess. Let us leave it at that."

He brought out the long-muzzled pistol from his belt and handed it to the major. "Well, we didn't need this after all!"

"We can't be sure of that," said the major. "It is possible that nothing sprang at us out of the darkness only because two of us were armed." He put away the pistol.

"First you talk about demons, now you bring up the idea of bandits again," said ElKureishi, "I think you are trying to frighten us and I don't understand why!"

"I am not trying to frighten you," said the major calmly, "But I am responsible for the safety of everyone on this expedition. It is my duty to make you aware of any dangers you might meet."

"I think it is time for us to retire," said Mike, "We shall have ample opportunity to discuss demons and bandits another time"

"Please remember my warning," said the major, "I say to you again, Professor: they can be very beguiling, these things, if they want something from you."

"I'll remember," said Mike, "If I ever come across the goddess."

They bade each other good night and Mike entered his tent. ElKureishi and the major left, talking quietly in Arabic.

21

A TRYST WITH THE LAMIA

1

THE CRUNCH OF the major's heavy footsteps faded away into the silence of the night. ElKureishi's shaky voice lingered for a little while longer but then it, also, faded away. The only sound left was a rasping squeak from the gaslamp outside Mike's tent as it swung from side to side in the night breeze.

Well, they're gone! Mike sat on his camp bed but did not turn on his table lamp. The table lamp was much too bright and he felt, somehow, that it would be easier to confront the events of the evening in the dim light of the gaslamp that hung outside his tent: *I've got to think things through!* The luminous dial on his watch showed 10:03.

It had not been long since Mike had succeeded in persuading himself that the girl was nothing more than a drug-enhanced dream. But the idea that the girl did not exist was merely a flimsy refuge created to preserve his peace of mind, and when ElKureishi pulled the sheet off the statue all thoughts about the girl being a dream vanished in an eruption of renewed hope that the girl was real. Even as Mike beheld the statue he knew that the resemblance of the girl to the goddess could not be explained on rational grounds. Like a catastrophic tidal wave that carries twisted and convoluted debris on its hump, the explosive surge of hope carried questions that Mike could not answer without stretching the boundaries of what he, a professional archaeologist, would consider *rationally acceptable*.

ElBalushi's insinuations during the walk back to the camp had only added to Mike's emotional turmoil. The major evidently suspected that Mike had experienced some form of contact with *something* when he was down in the cavern, and his innuendos in the course of the conversation showed that he believed that Mike was concealing the real cause of his panic. But although Mike could easily dismiss the major's suspicions as the product of a superstitious mind, he could not so easily dismiss the major's beliefs regarding the woman who walked around the hill at night because they propped up his hope that the girl was real. *What would ElBalushi have said if he had known about my dream?* The major would have jumped on the idea that Mike had been visited by a vampire.

Mike had always regarded himself as a totally rational man, an engineer turned archaeologist. He *needed* not to believe in vampires. But as he sat alone in his tent, conscious of the intermittent squeaking of the gaslamp and the darkness that surrounded the camp, he felt exposed and vulnerable to invisible and unexplainable forces. *The major was right about one thing, this ancient land remembers its past!* He unconsciously perceived the handing back of the long-muzzled pistol as a symbolic gesture that shunted away all the physical and psychological protection the modern world had to offer: *I could have been wrong about the resemblance of the girl to the goddess. When I see the statue in daylight I shall probably find that there is hardly any resemblance at all!* Yet as he sat on the camp bed his rationalisations seemed volatile, elusive, difficult to reconcile with his feelings. The more he tried to think rationally the more his thinking became confused and distorted. He was beset by seething, clamouring emotions that he could not suppress. The girl he had seen, or had dreamt of seeing, was *indubitably* identical to the woman whose statue had been carved in milk-white stone some four thousand years earlier. The similarity extended to the large red jewel of her necklace.

The resemblance of the statue to the girl can only be a coincidence! But the harder he tried to accept the resemblance as coincidence, the deeper his thinking degenerated into chaos. Disconnected thought fragments started to intrude without warning:

Vampires don't exist!
The girl was only a drug-enhanced dream!
Does ElBalushi have a personal agenda?
*Vampires **can't** exist!*
Vampires are not necessarily evil!
*There **are** no vampires!*

Although Mike's thinking was turbulent and without direction, each individual thought fragment was remarkably clear. It was like trying to think while having to listen to the drumming of a mad drummer whose sole purpose was to disrupt Mike's attempts to organise his thinking. Whenever he tried to focus his mind the chaos reasserted itself as an unrhythmic hammering that eliminated the likelihood of any control over his thoughts: *Vampires can't exist! ElBalushi is wrong! Ohanian was talking nonsense!* However, the thought fragments continued to roar past in his mind, oblivious of his attempts to restore order. One solitary phrase returned again and again as though to defend his sanity: *Vampires don't exist!* But, like the chorus of a Greek tragedy, the recurrent theme only served to distil and concentrate his emotional turmoil.

At the back of his mind Mike knew that he could not bring his thoughts under control because his rational arguments were little better than sophistry: *The resemblance of the girl to the statue **must** be a coincidence! But ...coincidence? Coincidence has limits!* The circumstances had blatantly exceeded the limits of coincidence. *And what of Balushi's observation that the sightings of the 'evil thing' were inside a circle centred on the Amalishah temple?* The major was unlikely to have erred in something so crucial to his belief that the 'evil thing' was Amalishah herself.

Only one consciously generated thought eventually managed to affect the turbulence in Mike's mind: *I must see her!* The chaos subsided slightly. *I **have** to try and see her again!* The intruding thought fragments seemed to hesitate, as though waiting for Mike to make a decision. *If she exists she's just a lost girl! She can't be a vampire! There **are** no vampires!* But the alternative forced its way into his thoughts and he could only shake his head in futile resistance: *And if she **is** a vampire and intends to kill me... does it really matter? I **must** see her!* The possibility of seeing the girl seemed to open a gate in his mind, a gate through which the intruding thought fragments could escape and leave him free to think. *If she kills me, who would grieve for me? Only Len would grieve for me!* The latent decision to see her again – the revived hope of seeing her again – slowly but inexorably subdued the chaos: *My wife is dead. I have no children and no siblings or living parents! Only Len shall grieve for me... so what does it matter if she kills me? I **must** see her!* For the time of a heartbeat his thinking stopped in the mental pause that precedes a decision: *I shall go to the grove tonight!*

The chaos of intruding thought fragments vanished.

Having made up his mind, Mike waited in his tent, suppressing all doubts and fears, until he was sure everyone was asleep. Then he hurriedly left for the grove. He took his torch and a small hunting knife. He wished he had ElBalushi's long-muzzled pistol but he had returned it to the major as agreed.

2

When Mike rounded the hill the moon had climbed only a little way among the stars and had a strangely yellow hue. The Northern ramp was only a few hundred metres away and in the light of the yellow moon the boulders at its foot seemed like huge unhealthy teeth that rose vertically from the ground. *What in heaven's name am I doing in this dark and lugubrious place, beneath a sickly yellow moon, driven by the hope of meeting a vampire?* The thought reminded Mike of a poem he wrote during his schooldays:

> *The dazzle of your smile*
> *Has enchanted me*
> *And like a moth to a flame*
> *I hasten to my doom*

No, I must not think of her that way: **Vampires don't exist!** *I am going to the grove in the hope of meeting an extraordinarily beautiful lost girl!* The ground was rough and uneven, full of hidden cavities that could cause him to stumble or, worse, sprain an ankle, but although the sallow light of the moon barely illuminated the way he did not turn on his torch, for despite his fixation on seeing the girl he did not forget the guards who paced unseen at the top of the hill.

The grove loomed ahead of him like an enormous black shadow that rose menacingly from behind the ramp. As he climbed the side of the ramp to get to the grove, Mike became aware of a weakness in his knees and a coldness along his spine: *This is fear, old chum! ElBalushi has infected you with his superstitions and you are afraid of what you might meet!* But the fear was controllable, not at all like the terror that had seized him in the cavern, and Mike entered the grove boldly. *The yellow moon and this dark grove make a perfect setting for meeting a vampire!* He quashed the thought but impulsively touched the small hunting knife in his belt. Its hilt pressed reassuringly against his side.

His watch showed 11:37 but he could not see anyone in the grove. *She's not here! Was she a dream after all?* His disappointment was like a black cloud that settled slowly and heavily, darkening his hope and leaving him angry, frustrated, and struggling against a feeling of futility. Yet his hope was not wholly extinguished and he resisted the temptation to get back to the camp: *Not just yet! She might still come. It's not yet midway between sunset and sunrise.* He looked dazedly around him for something on which he could sit and found the fallen trunk of a dead tree. It had been a small tree, not quite thick enough for its trunk to be used as a bench, but it had to do. He sat wearily on the fallen tree, facing the ramp, unsure of what he should do. The minutes passed with agonising slowness and his despondency grew until, having finally given up all hope, he held his head between his hands and thought ruefully: *Old chum, you've made another silly trip in the hope of meeting someone who doesn't exist!*

But the thought had barely congealed when a soft voice came from behind him: "I am pleased that you came."

He sprang up and whirled around. She stood before him, less than three metres away, still wearing the trousers and shirt he had given her. The trousers were too short for her – he had noticed that before – and the red jewel hung from her necklace just as he remembered. Just like the jewel on the statue of the goddess. In the filtered moonlight of the grove the girl looked even more beautiful than in his memories, infinitely more beautiful than the statue. But it was, nonetheless, as though the statue had come to life.

"I am sorry I did not come sooner," he stammered. His pounding heart prevented him from breathing normally.

"I know you came twice already."

He managed to say "Why didn't you speak to me?" He wanted to say so much more.

"Do you find it easy to speak to *me*, Michael Townsend?"

"Why should I not?" This was not what he meant to say.

"Because we are very different, you and I."

He had not expected her to say that. "Yes, we are very different," he admitted, "I do not find it easy to talk to you."

"It is much harder for me, Michael Townsend. I have not spoken to anyone for a very long time."

"Amalishah…" he began, but could not continue. That name could only be brought up casually to Leonard, or to ElKureishi, or even to Major ElBalushi. Here, in her presence, in the shadow-haunted grove, it evoked malignant ghosts and primordial fears. He looked away, feeling an inexplicable pang of guilt at his negative emotions.

She read his guilt but misinterpreted its cause: "You have spoken of seeing me to your friends?" she asked. He expected this particular question to come in the tone of a rebuke, or of an accusation, but it was spoken only with great sadness.

"No Amalishah, I have not spoken about seeing you to my friends. But one of the people in the camp spoke about someone who could only be you, someone who walks near the ruins at night, and he said things about you that I find hard to believe."

"And so you came with a small knife, just in case his words were true." The sadness was now much deeper, almost tangible.

He was about to say 'the knife is not because of you', but he was unable to lie to her.

"I was afraid," he said simply.

She sighed and her shoulders slumped, a relaxation of the back muscles that sometimes happens when one is reminded of something one deeply regrets. But she quickly straightened again and her large black eyes opened wider: "You fear me, Michael Townsend? Now that you have seen me again and spoken to me? You fear me?"

There was pathos in her voice and an earnestness which Mike found compelling. He managed to say: "I don't think I fear you. Though I find it difficult to believe who you are and I do not understand what you are. What are you?"

"I was hoping that you would find that out from me, in time, when we know each other better."

"What *are* you?" he repeated.

"What am I?" She smiled sadly, a faint stretching of the mouth that accentuated the sadness in her eyes. "I do not really know what I am. I am a *hur-iah*, an accident of fate. That is what they used to call children who were born… different, perhaps deformed, not like normal children. But I was not born… like this."

"When I first saw you," he said, his voice firm, "I thought you were just a beautiful girl who was lost in the wastelands and found shelter in the ruins of the temple. When I woke up the next day, I thought you were a dream. Then some of the people I work with mentioned an evil demon who haunts these parts at night and said that it appears as a beautiful woman. Yet I was almost sure you were a dream until I saw a statue they dug up. It looks exactly like you."

"A statue of white stone?" Her voice was trembling.

"Yes."

She looked away for a moment, as though overcome by emotions she did not wish to divulge, and then said: "It has been such a very long time since I've seen that statue. Your mention of it awakens memories."

Am I really talking to someone who is four thousand years old? The thought was staggering, rationally unacceptable. *I can't believe that! She's just a lost girl who has developed delusions from living alone among these damn ruins!* Yet he had to admit to himself: *I'm still afraid, though I don't know of what!*

He remained silent but his expression must have told her something of his thoughts, for she asked quietly: "What do *you* think I am, Michael Townsend?"

He chose his words with care: "I think you are a person who has lived alone for a long time." His answer was intentionally ambiguous. He was clinging to the idea that she was just a lost girl, but he did not wish to openly oppose any beliefs she might have about herself.

"I did live alone, yes, and for a very long time. I don't know how many planting seasons came and went since my temple was destroyed, but they were many. More than one can count. Does that frighten you?"

"Why should it frighten me?"

"Because you don't understand how that could be. Most people fear those whom they do not understand. They invent tales of sorcery and demons, and call those whom they do not understand *evil*. Thus they justify their fear. And is fear not the brother of hatred, Michael Townsend? Or has that changed?"

Mike did not answer at once. "No, that has not changed," he said slowly, and he paused as he searched for the appropriate words: "But I cannot hate you, Amalishah."

"It is easy to hate, Michael Townsend, and sometimes one hates without knowing it. For a long time I hated the Hittites because they killed all who were dear to me and destroyed the temple that was my home. I even hated them for not killing me when they had the chance because I so much wanted to die when death had danced so wantonly around me. But then, in time, I grew up and stopped hating. I am thankful to my long loneliness for helping me grow up. When one is with others, one unwittingly follows their way of thinking, but when one is alone for a long time, one eventually finds the right way to think. Why do you say you cannot hate me?"

"Because I do not believe you are evil, Amalishah. I don't think I can hate someone who is not evil." The words came easily.

"What if I told you that I was the cause of many deaths, some with my own hand?" She turned away and walked slowly towards the middle of the grove, as though she was trying to walk away from what she had just said. Mike followed her, conscious of the knife-hilt pressing against his side. He almost hated the knife.

"I would try to believe you but still not hate you," he said.

She did not answer and they were soon in the middle of the grove. Here the trees were densest and the moonlight percolated through the branches to form insane patterns of light and shade on the trunks of the trees and on the soft, uneven ground. She entered a bright patch of moonlight and stopped walking away, although she did not turn to face him. The moonlight was no longer yellow and it covered her in glowing silver as she stood, unmoving, with her back to him. As Mike watched her, spellbound by the magical effect of the moonlight, she raised her arms to the moon in supplication, and with her palms up she murmured: "Wise Suen, brother in the sky, *help me!*"

Although she had her back to him and there was no overt threat in her actions, Mike felt a surge of unease at her invocation of the Moon God. For a brief moment he was transported back to ancient times when people prayed to the Moon and offered the Moon God the lives of those who had been brought to his altar.

"Why do you call upon the Moon God?" he asked lamely.

"Because even I, it seems, can succumb to foolishness that I know can only bring me pain," she replied, still with her back to him.

Without thinking, he blurted out: "Do you intend to kill me, Amalishah?"

"Why would I wish to kill you?" Her voice expressed astonishment, but he could not see her face as she had still not turned to face him.

"I don't know. To drink my blood perhaps?"

She spun around to face him, a lightning movement faster than his eyes could follow, and for the first time he saw anger in her eyes. But he also saw that her eyes were brimming with tears: "Yes Michael Townsend, I have fed on human blood! Many men and many boys fought desperately and uselessly as I held their trembling bodies and drained them of their life!"

He stared at her mutely, taken aback by the vehemence of her outburst. But somehow he did not feel fear, and her anger vanished as suddenly as it had appeared, to be replaced by an ineffable sadness. As he continued to stare at her, she said very quietly: "Would it help our understanding of each other if I said that I have not drunk human blood since my temple was destroyed? Would it help you wish to know me better if I said that I never, *never* wanted to drink the blood of men, but only did it when I had no choice?"

He was unable to think clearly, and could only say: "I want to be your friend, Amalishah."

"You offer me friendship?"

"Yes."

"I could easily kill you, Michael Townsend. That little knife you carry would be of no use against me. Do you still offer me friendship?"

"Yes!"

"True friendship is built upon loyalty and trust. How can you trust me when your friends would say I am evil and you know that I could kill you?"

"I make up my own mind in such matters. When the time is right I shall try to persuade those friends who say you are evil that they are wrong."

"Then you shall lose some of your friends, Michael Townsend. So let me tell you something else before you offer me friendship again. I would find it very difficult to become someone's friend. I have seen too many friends grow old and die, and every time a close friend died something in me died also. I have become wary of friendship. It lasts for too short a time and the price is too high."

"Are you rejecting my offer?"

She came closer to him and looked deeply into his eyes, and as she held his gaze the ground beneath his feet seemed to grow soft and he almost lost his balance.

"No, Michael Townsend," she replied, "I am not rejecting your offer of friendship. You are knowledgeable and wise, and since my temple was destroyed you are only the second person I have spoken to who accepted me for what I am. My heart yearns for your friendship. But it was lonely to be a queen, and lonelier still to be a goddess, and loneliest of all to be a furtive creature of the night, feared and hated by everyone who knew or guessed what I am. My loneliness changed me, and now I am hard like a Hittite sword. I am wary of accepting friendship."

"Why are you telling me this?"

"Because I want you to know what friendship between us could cost you, and what it would cost me."

His heart was pounding but after a few moments he managed to say: "Then let us not talk about friendship. Let us allow loyalty and trust to grow naturally between us. We have a lot to learn from each other. You come from a world that is of great interest to me but about which I know very little. You can teach me about your world. That is what you can give me. That is what I ask of you."

Although the rational part of his mind still hoped that she was *a lost girl whose loneliness drove her insane* the other part, the irrational emotional part, had fully accepted that the beautiful woman before him had lived as a goddess at the time when the temple on the hill was young and vibrant with life. The conflict between the rational and the irrational parts of his mind had not yet risen to trouble his consciousness.

She did not answer at once. After a long pause she said: "And what would you give me in return? What can I learn from you?"

"You must know that when my friends and I leave, many others will come."

"You will *leave?*" The question was direct, poignant.

"Yes. We shall leave when our work here is finished. In time there will be new people living here. They shall live off visitors who will come to see the ruins and the cavern temple. The visitors shall come from all over the world, curious and expecting to be entertained. You shall not be able to continue here as you have before, Amalishah. To survive these changes, you shall need someone to help you adjust."

She looked down, thinking about what he had said. As she thought, she unconsciously pushed her hands into the pockets of her trousers and Mike could not resist a smile: *Pockets are so convenient when the hands have nothing to do!* Eventually she said: "Yes, I would need someone to help me adjust. You could help me adjust to your world and I would tell you what I remember of mine. That would be a fair exchange."

She is coming to realise that she cannot continue as before. She knows that her life is in my hands! But he remembered the major's warning: *'They can be very beguiling, these things, if they want something from you'.* He pushed the thought away: *No! She may be deluded or insane, but she is not deceitful!*

3

"Were you in the cavern when I removed the rubble that blocked the entrance to the tunnel?" he asked.

"Yes."

"So it was you who sighed."

"You spoke my language and said you were my friend. I knew your words were empty because you did not know I was there, but I had been alone for so long that I forgot the need for silence."

So there was contact, of sorts, down in the cavern. He wondered what might have happened if he had not panicked but stood his ground, or if he had tried to determine whether the sigh he had heard was caused by the wind or something else. *Such questions lead nowhere!* "Why was there a dead goat on the altar?" he asked.

She laughed. It was the first time he had seen her laugh. It was the laugh of a woman who has cause to remember that she had once been a child. "That was the idea of someone who came to my temple long before you!"

"And you spoke to him?"

"Yes. There were many, many visitors to the cavern before you, Michael Townsend. Most of them hoped to find precious things. At first, it was easy to elude them or frighten them away, but as time passed they became more persistent. And then came a strange man with two companions and they entered my cavern temple. His companions looked like the men I had known but he looked different. He had yellow hair and a short yellow beard and his eyes were blue, like yours, and he was taller than most of the men I had known. He had neither shield nor spear and, unlike the others who came with him, he carried a straight sword. I was very curious about him. When he and his companions entered my temple they did not rush around looking for gold. They stood in awe, holding their torches above their heads, and the one with the yellow hair and blue eyes stood quietly and for the time of a few breaths he wept."

"He *wept?*"

"Yes. Tears flowed down his cheeks. That was when I realised he was not like the others who had come to my temple before him. So I came out of the shadows and spoke to the yellow-haired man. He did not understand me but one of his companions did and he translated my words, and so the yellow-haired man and I talked. I asked him why he had wept and he said that it was because of what had been lost!"

"He wept because of what had been lost?" Mike did not understand.

"It was as though he could see what my temple had once been. He understood that much that was once beautiful had been destroyed forever. When he told me that he wept because of what had been lost that simple phrase went straight to my heart. It established a bond between us. With the help of the companion who spoke my language we discussed many things, and I learned that the Children of Ashour were no longer important and the Hittites were gone."

"Did he ask who you were?"

"Yes, and I told him."

"Was he surprised?"

"Very surprised, but not frightened. I think he had seen many strange things in his life and this was just one more."

"When he left, did he ask you to go with him?"

"Yes, but I declined. He said that I could be a goddess again, but I did not wish to have to pretend any more. He understood."

"So he left you, alone among the ruins."

"I was not yet ready for change. I had almost got used to my loneliness and I explained that to him. It was his idea to put a dead animal in the cavern when men came. He said that a bad smell would help keep away the greedy and the curious. Since then I always put a dead animal on the altar when people came. It helped, until you came."

"When did the yellow-haired man come?"

"A long time ago. He was not a Hittite and he was not of the Children of Ashour. He said he was an *Ionas*."

"A Greek! You spoke to an ancient Greek!"

"You know about them?"

"Yes! Do you remember his name?"

"He had a lovely name which meant 'a gift of the god Apollonos'. I had not heard of that god."

And we all thought the writings of Apollothoros were just hearsay! The Greek must have had his reasons for not giving the location of the temple. Was it to protect Amalishah? "What happened to the Ionas?"

"I don't know. He stayed for a short while and then he and his companions left. I was very sorry to see him go and I never saw him again. He was the first person who accepted what I am without fear."

Did the ancient Greeks know about vampires? What did the word 'lamia' mean to an ancient Greek? The thought of vampires reminded Mike of Ohanian.

"Amalishah," he said, "Do you know anything about the writing on the wall of the pit that leads down to the temple?" He could not bring himself to say 'your temple'; the notion that she was just a normal girl who had developed delusions was still strong.

"I was there when the inscriptions were carved."

"Why is the writing different from other Assyrian writing?"

"Because that is the writing only I and my High Priest used when we wrote to the high priests of other temples. It was different from normal writing because it was not meant to be read by all who could read."

That would explain why the script appears nowhere outside the temple! "Would you tell me what the inscriptions say?"

"If you wish me to."

"I would be grateful. Shall we sit down?"

She nodded and sat cross-legged on the ground. Her movements were fluid and graceful, exquisitely feminine, with a dignity that Mike had not seen in modern women. *She moves like a beautiful cat taking its place on the sofa!* Mike could not help staring, fascinated. After a moment he also sat cross-legged on the ground, facing her, waiting for her to speak.

4

Her back straightened and she closed her eyes. Her expression changed. Mike was no longer in the presence of a *lost girl*; the woman before him was once again a proud and reserved Assyrian queen. With her eyes closed, she spoke in a haughty monotone as though reciting something she had almost forgotten:

> "The Queen of the land is a great Queen. She is Queen over the land of the Children of Ashour and Queen over all the lesser Kings and Queens who are vassals of the Queen of the Children of Ashour. The lords of our land and the people of our land adore our Queen for she is good, like a mother to us, like the Earth Mother. She makes sacrifice to herself and to all the gods of the sky and of the land, the gods of the rivers and of the lakes, the gods of the wind and of the rain and of the thunder, and the gods are pleased with her sacrifice. The fields yield their crops abundantly and the animals thrive and there is no hunger, for there is food aplenty. The people are content and there is no conflict among us, for she rules with justice and compassion. Her armies keep our enemies at bay and there is no trouble at the borders, for she is wise beyond Wisdom and good beyond Goodness. Our enemies fear her for she is strong beyond Strength... "

"Stop!" exclaimed Mike, and she opened her eyes. He felt the fear of the *unexplainable* rise within him and his mind was in an uproar again. *She cannot be inventing this! Her tone is just right, her words are just right!* As the conflict between the facts before him and the beliefs he had held all his life rose at last to assault his consciousness he was once again bewildered and beset by confusion. The rational part of his mind struggled to explain what was happening in familiar terms but it failed and it knew that it had failed: *My God! She actually is what she says she is!* Mike *felt* the limits of what he found *acceptable* expand to encompass beliefs he could not have accepted earlier.

"So how does the story end?" he husked.

She took his question literally: "The last writing on the wall of the pit says:

'After she died from an illness that no-one in her kingdom could cure she was brought back by Wise Ones from the lands far beyond the land of the Children of Ashour. She was brought back by Wise Ones from the land in which the sun rises. She was brought back, unchanged but different, so that she would not die again and would continue to be a mother to her people.'

That is how the writing ends."

Mike sat back. He was still shocked and confused, but things were beginning to fall into place: *Unchanged but different! A lamia!* "You were brought back after you died? How did it happen that you died and were brought back?"

She shrugged her shoulders like an adolescent girl and said: "I was brought up to be queen and became queen when I was still very young, barely a woman. Then after a number of planting seasons I fell gravely ill and everybody knew that I was going to die. But I had no husband and no children and there was no one of royal blood to be my heir. Without a strong king or queen my land would have fallen into strife and become prey to our enemies. My people sought everywhere in my lands for someone to cure me but there was no one who knew how, and so they brought Wise Ones from a very distant place to make me well. But I died just before they arrived, and all they could do was call me back. They called me back and I returned as I am. I returned to be the queen of my people but I was different."

She came back a lamia! She was like the girl she had been when she died, yet different! "How were you different?" he asked, and his voice sounded hoarse from the strain.

"I felt different. My illness was gone and I was never ill again. But I could no longer bear the sunlight. It burned my eyes and my skin.

And I could only feed on fresh blood, not solid food. I was also able to sleep whenever I wished. There were other differences, but they are not important."

"You fed on the blood of people?"

"Only during the reign of the last king I knew. Before that I fed on the blood of animals."

I am in the presence of a vampire! This is incredible! Yet, having finally accepted the incontrovertible, Mike felt no fear, only tremendous excitement at having come across something so unbelievably alien to normal human experience.

5

"And then, what happened to you?"

"For a time, nothing. I lived as Queen in the way I had lived before. But because I could not bear the sunlight I eventually moved to the hill and the underground cavern. It was far from my home but it suited me well, for it allowed me to hide my weaknesses."

"Your weaknesses... you mean your inability to tolerate the sunlight?"

"Yes, and my inability to eat food like everyone else. The cavern inside the hill was extended and the top of the hill was built upon with stone and wood. The wood had to be brought with great labour from beyond the wastelands. The inscriptions were written on the wall of the pit after the buildings were completed. I was then only a queen, not a goddess, and the cavern and the buildings above were only my palace, not a temple. There were many soldiers but few priests, and the priests served the customary gods. For several human lifetimes I ruled as best I could by delegating my authority. I tried to rule wisely but it was not enough. A king was eventually chosen to rule far from here in my name."

"Were you on good terms with the king?"

"There were many kings who ruled in my name. One after the other, each king was crowned, lived and died while I remained young. At first our relationship was good, but my land grew more difficult to govern and I was far from where important events occurred. There were often quick decisions to be made and I was not there to make them. Because it took a long time for messages to travel between me and the king, I gradually withdrew from affairs of state and, when it was realised that I would not grow old and die, I began to be thought of as a goddess. The soldiers around me were replaced by armed priests, and the cavern that had started off as a palace became a temple."

"How did you adapt to the role of goddess?"

"When they called me a goddess I had to pretend to be one, and in time I almost believed it. Being a goddess is very attractive to one who is still young in mind."

"And then the Hittites came."

"They came like a storm in the night. They came and brought destruction and death, but that was many, many plantings seasons later."

"Why did the Hittites come? Were your people at war with the Hittites?"

"No. But they had good reason to attack my temple. The last king I knew called himself the Great King and troubled the lands of our neighbours. He loved collecting precious and beautiful things and was inclined to mount campaigns against our weaker neighbours to obtain what he wanted. Because I was by then considered to be a goddess, I was unable to interfere. Being a goddess makes one dependent upon one's worshippers."

"But why did the Hittites attack the temple?"

"The Great King made sure the Hittites would destroy my temple."

"Why?"

She looked away and a dark shadow seemed to pass over her face. "When one thinks of oneself as The Great King, there is no room for a goddess with whom to share power."

"I understand. How did the Great King entice the Hittites to destroy your temple?"

"He insisted that I only drink the blood of prisoners. They included young men and boys abducted from Hittite villages. The Great King knew this would anger the king in Hattusas."

"You could not refuse to drink the blood of prisoners?"

"I could not refuse. The man who called himself The Great King did terrible things to whoever dared disobey him. If I refused to follow his wishes he would have blamed the priests and priestesses who were closest to me, and he would have had them killed in the cruellest of ways."

"Why did he um… persuade the Hittites to destroy the temple? Surely he could have done that himself very easily."

"Not easily. He was greatly feared, but even he could not order the destruction of an Assyrian temple without reason. And this was the only temple with a living goddess who was still loved by many."

"So he had the Hittites destroy the temple and try to kill you."

"Yes. The Hittites avenged their dead boys, and the boys from other lands, by putting an end to the world I knew. They set fire to all the buildings on the hill and killed everybody, the good and the bad, the young and the old, the men and the women, but they killed without cruelty. Only the children and some of their mothers survived because I had sent them away before the Hittites came."

So that is why we did not find the remains of children! "The Hittites believed they had killed you."

"They were wrong. Their prince killed someone else, an old and infirm priestess who was very dear to me. He had the chance to kill me but did not; I do not really know why. The Hittite prince was wounded and perhaps he was tired of killing."

So ElBalushi's guess was correct! The Hittites killed someone else thinking it was the goddess! "How did you survive all the years after the temple was destroyed?"

"At first with great anguish and anger. When I walked night after night among the ruins the betrayal of the Great King was like a raging fire in my breast. I lived in anger, but also in fear because I knew that if I were found alive by soldiers sent by the Great King I would certainly have been killed. But as the planting seasons passed the Great King became less important in my thoughts. I gradually forgot the cries of my priests who had died trying to protect me. When the smell of burning wood was long gone I found that I tended to remember only the times of the earlier kings, when the buildings with their fluttering banners towered above me and there was much talking and laughter. I remembered the evenings when I played with the children of my priests or watched the normal activities of the temple. And as I remembered I would sit among the ruins and weep."

"Like the *Ionas*."

"His tears echoed mine. That is why I had to speak to him."

"But there must have been long times when nothing happened. How did you prevent yourself from going mad?"

"Much of the time I slept, except when some animal disturbed me, and then I fed before sleeping again."

"You slept?"

"Yes, I can sleep for long times. I sleep like the dead, without dreams. None that I can recall, anyway. That is the story of Amalishah."

She put her hands in her lap, palm against palm, and looked down. Mike realised that she did not wish to continue with the story of her life and he remained silent.

6

"But now I have a question to ask you, Michael Townsend."

"Please ask it."

"Do you know of others like me?"

He thought for a moment before answering, recalling what Ohanian had said about vampires.

"I don't know," he said slowly. "There are stories. Superstitions. I never believed them. Those like you are always depicted as evil, but you are anything but evil, Amalishah."

"I have lived on human blood, Michael Townsend, and I can do so again if I have to. Is that not evil?"

"Evil is a disease of the soul, Amalishah."

"Do I have a soul, Michael Townsend? If I have a soul, why don't I die and release it?"

"We don't understand why people grow old and die. You said that you were not born as you are, so when you... you became what you are, your body was changed so that it would not grow old. People have always wanted to find out how not to grow old. They still do. It is not evil to stay young, Amalishah."

She reflected upon what he had said; then spoke quietly: "You are indeed wise, Michael Townsend, and I now believe that you do not fear me. That makes it easier for me, for I can trust you more. May I call you Mike? You said your friends call you that."

"Are we friends now?"

"Not yet. But we are on the right path."

"Then please call me Mike."

She nodded.

7

The pre-dawn light was chasing the stars away.

"Amalishah, it will be difficult for us to meet here regularly. Someone is bound to notice my absence. Also, I need to sleep at night for I have a lot to do during the day."

"I understand."

"I think I shall be able to meet you here, not tomorrow night but three nights after that. In the meantime I shall try to make arrangements to go to Mosul, and if these arrangements are successful I would like you to come with me to Mosul, if you wish."

"What is Mosul?"

"Mosul is a place that is not too far from here. It has many, many people and is very much like the rest of the world. In Mosul it shall be easy for me to help you learn about the world around us."

"Why do you need to make arrangements?"

"Because I cannot just leave my friends and go to Mosul. I have to tell them that it is necessary for me to leave and I have to find a way for you and me to get there. And I have to find a place in Mosul where we can stay. I shall tell you what arrangements I have made when I see you. When I um... *find* a suitable house we can go to Mosul and I can at least teach you the Arabic language." Mike did not know the Assyrian words for *to rent*.

"Arabic? That is a language I have never heard of. Is Arabic your language?"

"No. But Arabic will be the most useful to you. In Mosul we can live together until you are ready to come out and live in the world."

The haughtiness returned: "How shall we live together, Michael Townsend? Shall I be your slave? Your concubine? One of your wives?"

"You shall be my companion, Amalishah. You shall teach me about your world and I shall teach you about mine. I ask for nothing more."

"Won't your wives object?"

"Where I come from we have only one wife. I used to have a wife, but she died and I did not marry again. We had no children."

"You live without a wife? How strange. Do you have many slaves?"

"We don't have slaves any more."

"How is it possible for a man to live alone and without slaves?"

"It is possible. My world is very different from yours."

She digested the information. Very quietly she said: "I have a lot to learn. I must agree to go with you to Mosul as your companion." She seemed resigned but not displeased.

"And there is another thing," he said, "I have to get you some proper clothes. The clothes you are wearing look rather crumpled."

"That is because I wash them every two days."

"You wash them?" *There must be some places around here that we haven't found yet!*

"Of course. There is no one to wash them for me. I can also sew my own clothes if you would get me cloth and whatever else I shall need."

"I shall get you some clothes like the clothes women wear and whatever else you will need to change them to your taste."

"Thank you, Mike. I shall wait for you here every night starting the night after tomorrow, in case you return early from Mosul."

"Please don't! Every night you wait for me you risk being seen."

"No, Mike. With those heavy shoes that you and your friends wear I can hear your footsteps long before I can be seen. And I can tell the sound of your footsteps from those of other men."

8

They parted without ceremony. On the way back, Mike felt completely, unreservedly dedicated to the welfare of this alien *being*. It was with some surprise that he admitted: *I think I am in love with her. I think I've been in love with her since I first saw her!*

Back in his tent he lay on his camp bed with his head on his palms. He felt happy, a sensation he had almost forgotten. How breathtaking for an archaeologist to make a tryst with a lamia who was almost as old as civilization! But despite his elation – had she not said 'I shall wait for you here every night... in case you return early from Mosul'? – Mike knew that there was no time for amazement and wonder. To prepare Amalishah for life in the modern world would be a delicate operation fraught with possible disasters. *I've got to plan things with care!* He yawned and his eyes closed. *But this is not the time to make plans; I'm too tired to think clearly!* Yet his mind was too agitated to suppress all the options that his imagination conjured up, and he could not help thinking that the train of events might lead him to make a little speech to his colleagues: 'Ladies and gentlemen, I would like to introduce you to Amalishah. She is a vampire and was once the goddess of this temple!' He chuckled to himself as he imagined the expression on Leonard's face. But then he saw again the serious side of things: *No, I have to take her to Mosul. Away from ElBalushi.* With the certainty of those who are about to drift off into sleep, he felt he had at last understood the major's personal mission: *He intends to kill her!*

22

THE CLERIC AND THE SOLDIER

1

FOR MANY YEARS Professor Nasser ElKureishi had taught a course called *The Evolution of Ethics,* and for every one of those years he had introduced the course with the rhetorical question: "Can we know where we are going if we don't know where we come from?" The patent aim of the course was to inspire his students with an awareness of the role of history in modern society, a role that, in his opinion, was generally undervalued. The professor's zeal in advocating the cause of history and, by extension, of archaeology had been strengthened by his appointment as leader of the international expedition, and he saw the raising of public awareness regarding the expedition's purpose and activities as an important part of his job. What better way to kindle the media's interest in the expedition than to arrange a visit by a socially prominent figure?

At ElKureishi's personal invitation, a well-known senior cleric and judge, *Qadi* Haidar Mohsin Abdel-Rahman ElTurujman, arrived at the expedition's base camp to witness for himself the kinds of things archaeologists do. The *qadi* was accompanied by two photographers, one tall and the other short, from two competing newspapers. Both photographers carried enormous but obsolete cameras. The twin-rotor helicopter that the army had put at the *qadi's* disposal landed near the foot of the Northern ramp, just outside the boulders that were scattered randomly in a broad ring round the hill, and the cleric had barely set foot on solid ground when he was enthusiastically greeted by ElKureishi himself. A few steps behind the professor, and showing somewhat less enthusiasm about the *qadi's* visit, was the reception committee that the professor had personally selected and organised. This unwieldy group included Major ElBalushi, all the senior archaeologists of the expedition and a small number of postdocs. Its core was meant to provide the judge with a *guarde d'honneur* that would accompany him during his tour of the camp.

After ElKureishi and the cleric had gone through the customary greetings, they made their way slowly up the ramp. As they climbed the long loose-soiled incline the professor formally introduced each member of the reception committee in order of rank. As a result, the climb appeared interminable to the *qadi*, all the more so because his soft-heeled slippers kept coming off as he laboured up on the soft soil. The *qadi*, who was well past middle age, was breathless and wet with perspiration by the time he reached the top of the ramp. The two photographers took photographs as they hovered discreetly just outside the circle of archaeologists and postdocs who surrounded the cleric.

When the statutory introductions were duly completed, the *qadi* was taken to the refectory for coffee and sweets. Here he met the postgrads and postdocs from ElKureishi's university team who had not been chosen to be part of the welcoming committee. Being young, or perhaps out of post-adolescent pique for not having been selected to be part of the reception committee, they immediately engaged the Qadi in heated discussions regarding his views on ancient history. The *qadi* was by nature a quiet man who liked solitude and meditation, and he did not particularly enjoy the persistent attention of those who, in the hope of impressing ElKureishi and their own professors, wanted to know his opinions on a wide range of subjects regarding Assyria and its neighbours. The *qadi*, beset by questions from all directions, tried to answer as best he could, but he soon realised that a defensive attitude was not the best policy and he decided to take the offensive: "And in your studies of history," the *qadi* finally asked one of the more vociferous postgrads, "did you find the time to become acquainted with the less ancient history of your country?" The *qadi* was hoping to divert the questions from the time of ancient Assyria to the time of the Caliphate, when Baghdad had played a pivotal role in the social evolution of the Middle East. The *qadi* was well versed in the history of the Caliphs.

"Do you mean in the last hundred years?" asked the postgrad to whom the *qadi* had addressed the question.

"Do you mean during the Ottoman Empire?" asked a postgrad from Izmir.

"You are referring, no doubt, to the unfortunate events in Palestine," said a doctoral student from Jordan.

331

Anxious to avoid a digression into politics, ElKureishi hastily intervened: "Our students come from all over the Middle East," he said affably, "and they are naturally most familiar with the more recent histories of their own countries. But we don't want to tire you with more questions. Would you like to talk to some of the overseas members of the expedition?"

"Yes, of course. Thank you." The *qadi's* moan of relief was heartfelt and audible to all around him.

ElKureishi beckoned to Carol and Bradley, who were standing behind the postgrads. Everyone's attention turned to the Americans.

2

Apart from the formal and very brief introduction earlier, Carol and her husband had never met a senior Iraqi cleric before and, partly out of genuine interest, partly out of curiosity, they had managed to nudge themselves as close to the *qadi* as the circle of postgrads permitted. The conversation between the *qadi* and the students had been conducted in the local dialect of Arabic and much of it had escaped Carol and Bradley, who were familiar only with *Nahawi*, the classical form of the language. Now that ElKureishi had invited them to talk to the cleric, Carol felt slightly ill at ease.

But the *qadi* smiled warmly and said in perfect English: "It gives me great pleasure to meet people from as far away as America who are interested in the ancient history of my country. I am so happy to meet you. Professor ElKureishi has spoken about you on the 'phone when he invited me here."

Carol and Bradley had expected an Islamic judge as socially prominent as *Qadi* Haidar to be reserved and aloof towards foreigners, so they were surprised and charmed by his words. Bradley muttered something about how glad he was to meet an Islamic judge and Carol, who was tall by Middle Eastern standards, tried to shrink to the size of the diminutive *qadi*. She gave the cleric a brilliant smile: "Professor ElKureishi has been our friend for a long time. My husband and I are very proud to be working with him."

ElKureishi smiled approvingly. "It was Carol's team that discovered the treasure," he said, deftly introducing a fertile topic of conversation.

"That must have been very exciting for you," said the *qadi* to Carol.

"It was," agreed Carol. "Bradley and I had known about the

Amalishah temple for many years and our university in the U.S. of A was among the first to sponsor this expedition. But I must admit that we didn't really fancy our chances of finding the temple, let alone discovering wonderful artefacts."

The *qadi* nodded. "I am surprised that you had heard of the Amalishah temple when you live so far away."

"Oh, the Amalishah temple is known all over the world, at least among archaeologists."

"And why do you think that is so?" asked the *qadi*.

Carol looked thoughtful: "I think the tragic end of the temple and its resident goddess have a lot to do with its fame. The tragedy provides human interest and the goddess adds several interesting questions. Moreover, the fact that the temple's name was erased from the Assyrian records provides mystery. Human interest, unanswered questions and mystery, what archaeologist can resist such a combination?"

"When you put it like that," said the *qadi*, his eyes twinkling, "I would say that the Amalishah temple would be like a magnet to any self-respecting archaeologist. But did you know that for a long time and until recently these ruins had a somewhat sinister reputation among the locals?"

Major ElBalushi was suddenly very interested in what the *qadi* was saying. "You are familiar with the local legends, *qadi*?" he asked in English before Carol could answer. This was the first time he had spoken to the cleric apart from the ritual exchange of greetings during the introductions. Until this moment he had secretly believed that the time he would have to spend with the *qadi* was going to be totally wasted.

"I am not *familiar* with the legends," replied the Qadi, addressing no-one in particular, "Just aware of their existence. I believe the ruins are supposed to be guarded by some kind of *djinn*."

"Major ElBalushi thinks that the guardian *djinn* is none other than the goddess of the temple herself!" said ElKureishi.

"How could the local legends have claimed that the guardian spirit was Amalishah herself when nobody knew that the hilltop ruins were those of the Amalishah temple?" said Carol, speaking to the major. She was aware of ElBalushi's beliefs but wanted to make sure that the *qadi* did not think that these beliefs were shared by the archaeologists.

"I never said that the local legends identified the evil spirit of the ruins as Amalishah," said the major with a broad smile, "That is my own personal belief. But the locals knew that there were ruins on the hill, and they believed for a very long time that on dark nights *something* prowled around these ruins and the surrounding countryside, even though they knew neither the history of the ruins nor the identity of the prowler."

"Perhaps the major is alluding to the fact that archaeologists sometimes have a lot to learn from local lore," said the *qadi*, "It is often said that archaeologists approach their excavations with a spade in one hand and lots of foreign books in the other. But their books only contain eclectic versions of what was written in other, older, foreign books. So it is said that the archaeologists sometimes miss out on relevant facts because they do not condescend to ask the locals what they know."

"That's unfair," said Carol, "I cannot think of a single instance where the archaeologists could have learned something archaeologically useful from the locals and didn't bother to ask!"

"I can think of at least one instance," said Mike unexpectedly. He was standing behind Carol and, although he had been formally introduced to the cleric, he had not taken part in any of his discussions.

"Ah, Professor Townsend," said the *qadi*, nodding towards Mike, "And what instance is that?"

"Oh, I apologise for intruding. I was just thinking aloud."

"Please tell us," insisted the *qadi*, "A specific instance would be useful to know."

"Well," said Mike, "Archaeologists have been looking for the tomb of Alexander in all sorts of unlikely places in Egypt. Yet local tradition places the tomb beneath the Nabi Daniel mosque in Alexandria. This local tradition is admittedly comparatively recent, but it nevertheless seems to have bypassed the Egyptologists!"

"Are you saying you know the location of Alexander's tomb?" asked ElKureishi. He could not hide his astonishment.

"Not at all," replied Mike. "I am merely saying that until the first half of the twentieth century there was a tradition, among Alexandrines, about the tomb's location. Whether that tradition is correct or not I cannot say. The point here is that the Egyptologists appear to be totally unaware of what the locals believe, or at least used to believe. They only look at the places that agree with their own theories."

"And how did you come upon this information about Alexander's tomb?" asked Carol.

"From an Alexandrine friend, who now lives in Oxford."

The *qadi* rubbed his grey beard thoughtfully. "Are you perhaps saying, Professor, that the Amalishah temple might have been discovered sooner had archaeologists paid more attention to local knowledge?"

"I think so," replied Mike thoughtfully, "Though in all fairness I should say that it is difficult for archaeologists to talk to the locals before mounting an expedition and, once an expedition has been mounted, it is usually too late. Expeditions are most often guided by the rigidly set beliefs of their sponsors."

Things were getting too philosophical for ElKureishi. "There is a lot to see and I think it's time our honoured guest was given a tour of the ruins," he said hurriedly to Mike. Mike nodded understandingly and ElKureishi turned to the *qadi*: "I am sure you shall find the underground cavern very interesting. It is the heart of the temple."

"And you must see the things we dug up," said Carol, "After you've toured the ruins and been down to the underground cavern."

"I'm afraid I shall have to give the cavern a miss," said the *qadi*, speaking to both ElKureishi and Carol. "But I would be very grateful if I were shown the treasure immediately after my tour of the ruins. I have to return to Najaf soon after lunch."

"You mean you're not going to visit the cavern?" asked Carol. She could not hide her disappointment.

"I am no longer a young man," said the *qadi*, touching his chest just above his heart, "and going down those many, many steps and then up again may not be good for me!"

"Oh, I'm so sorry!" exclaimed Carol.

The major stepped forward to get closer to the judge. "The army helicopter shall be taking you to Najaf, *qadi*?" he asked.

"Um… yes."

"Would it inconvenience you in any way if I came along? I have some things to do at the army base in Najaf and it would be a great help to me if I could come with you."

"It would give me immense pleasure to have your company on the helicopter, major. But how would you get back to the hill?"

"That won't be a problem. I'll take an air force plane to Mosul and then borrow a car from the army base."

"Then I shall look forward to enjoying your company on my return trip!"

3

The *qadi* and the photographers, accompanied by ElKureishi and some of his staff, were shown around the hilltop. The students who had been strategically scattered among the ruins had been instructed to look busy and, if possible, to *do interesting-looking things using the latest equipment*. At the end of his tour the *qadi* looked tired but pleased.

"I never knew archaeology involved so much work!" he said, "Or involved so many hi-tech tools!"

"It is no longer a simple matter of digging and looking for things," said ElKureishi gravely, "Archaeology is now a science. Every find has to be scrupulously noted and recorded. Even the most trivial discovery! The best part is trying to understand what has been discovered while sitting at the end of the day, in the comfortable shelter of our tents."

"You were very fortunate to have discovered valuable and interesting artefacts," said the *qadi*, "I am very anxious to see them."

ElKureishi led the group to the storage tent with the *qadi*, who was slightly shorter than he, walking briskly beside him. As they walked the professor gave a running commentary on the ruins.

"This temple must have been quite magnificent," said the *Qadi* as he paused to catch his breath.

"And opulent despite its isolation!" replied the professor, stopping abruptly in front of the entrance to the storage tent. The cleric turned and gave a long look at the ruins around him. His look showed a genuine interest, which was not lost on ElKureishi.

"We are fortunate that the temple was destroyed and then forgotten," said the professor, "had the Amalishah temple fallen into disuse gradually, like the majority of the other temples, most of its treasures would have been lost. The treasures of the Amalishah temple were expressly hidden by the priests just before or during the Hittite attack, and thus saved for posterity."

"God works in ways that are sometimes difficult to understand at the time, but which only become clear much later," said the qadi. He indicated to ElKureishi that he was ready to be shown the contents of the storage tent.

"Now that you have seen the ruins and the excavation work, I am sure you will find the artefacts particularly interesting," said ElKureishi.

"Yes, I am sure I will."

The major had decided that, apart from himself, only ElKureishi, Mike and Carol with her husband Bradley were to accompany the *qadi* into the storage tent. The photographers were on the point of following the *qadi* inside when the major stopped them: "This is not a good time to photograph the discoveries," he said matter-of-factly. The photographers protested but the major cut them short: "It is not yet time for pictures of the artefacts to be shown to the public!" The photographers withdrew, none too happy.

ElKureishi had hoped that pictures of the *qadi* standing beside some of the expedition's discoveries would have figured prominently in newspapers and popular journals as well as the televised media. He was surprised and not a little annoyed when the major dashed his hopes, but the major's tone permitted no argument. The professor wondered if the major was displeased at the fact that he had not bothered to ask his permission about letting the artefacts be photographed. In fact, the major was merely reluctant to advertise the amount of gold, silver and sellable artefacts that had been discovered.

4

The more flamboyant artefacts had been taken out of their boxes and put on display on long tables borrowed from the refectory. The statue of Amalishah was given pride of place. It stood between two tables on which were displayed a number of crowns and tiaras of pure gold or silver as well as exquisite statuettes carved of different kinds of stone. The storage tent was well lit and the jewels in the crowns and tiaras glittered brightly. The *qadi*, however, was much more interested in the statue of Amalishah.

"What a beautiful statue," he said, impressed by the life-size effigy.

"The goddess Amalishah," said ElKureishi grandly, "Whom the major believes still walks among the ruins at night."

"Do you really believe that, Major?" asked the *qadi*.

The major felt slightly embarrassed, but he was not a man to shirk what he saw as the truth.

"I do. I believe she was never killed and still lives."

"But how could she have lived so long? The temple is, what, four thousand years old?"

"The ancients believed she was immortal."

"But have we all not outgrown such beliefs?"

"My family's roots were not too far from here, qadi, when there were still villagers who knew the old customs and traditions. The legend of a woman who does not die and walks about the hill at night was never challenged by the local people."

"Don't get too involved in this discussion, qadi," said ElKureishi pleasantly, "The major is quite convinced in the truth of his beliefs."

Carol felt disappointed in ElKureishi. It was unfair, she thought, to bring up the major's personal quirk as a means of scoring status points just because the major had forbidden photographs of the artefacts. Mike simply looked away, pretending to be engrossed in one of the golden crowns. He knew how much ElKureishi had been hoping that the newspapers would carry photographs of the discoveries, but he was not so much concerned about ElKureishi's way of getting even with the major as he was reluctant to listen to a discussion of Amalishah. He found the mention of her name, in what he considered a trivial context, distasteful.

The qadi showed great interest in the exhibits, and listened carefully to the lengthy explanations of individual artefacts provided by ElKureishi and Carol. Mike remained silent, and he was greatly relieved when the qadi suggested that it was time for lunch.

"Of course!" said ElKureishi, "you must be very tired from all this talk on ancient artefacts and a wandering goddess."

"Not at all," said the qadi, "But it is getting late and I must be going back to Najaf."

They returned to the refectory, which was now almost empty except for some soldiers, and had an uneventful lunch. The major sat with his men, claiming to have urgent army matters to discuss. When the qadi had finished his meal he went over to the major's table.

"Do you still wish to leave with me?" he asked the major.

"Oh yes. Thank you. It will save me a long drive!" The major got up. "I have finished my lunch and am ready to leave."

"Then please allow me a few minutes to thank everyone for their hospitality and then we can go."

The major nodded and took leave of his men.

The qadi thanked everyone profusely, especially ElKureishi. The goodbyes took longer than Mike would have liked but the etiquette of Middle Eastern good manners had to be observed.

5

As the helicopter rose into the air the roar of its rotors drowned all possibility of conversation. However, once the craft was airborne and had reached its cruising altitude the noise became tolerable. The *qadi* leaned over to the major.

"Unlike some foreign archaeologists," he said conversationally, "I am very interested in local lore."

"You are referring to the thing that is said to haunt the ruins?"

"I am. I noticed that you appear to have a personal interest in this legend."

"It is one of many local legends and stories."

"But you believe that the goddess of the temple still lives, although thousands of years have passed since her temple was destroyed. That is an unusual thing to believe."

"I do believe that. The people who used to live not too far from the ruins had many stories about her."

"But you must have personal reasons for such an unusual belief, major. Have you seen her?"

"No. But my grandfather believed he saw her and Professor Townsend might have seen her when he discovered the cavern. He was bitten by something when leaving the cavern and was delirious for a short time, during which he said some strange and surprising things."

"You think he was bitten by the *djinn* who prowls about at night?"

"Oh no! He was bitten by something unpleasant but ordinary, most probably some kind of insect or venomous reptile. The wound caused him to lapse into delirium. But I suspect he saw or heard something while he was in the cavern before he suffered the bite, something that frightened him enough to make him careless. Mike Townsend is not the kind of man who is easily frightened."

"I suppose not. Despite his reputation as a scholar and his boyish looks he must be quite tough. Such people usually are. What strange and surprising things did he say?"

"Most of what he said while he was delirious was unintelligible, but what was not unintelligible was very strange."

"I see. But if he was delirious he would be expected to say strange things, would he not?"

"He spoke of hearing a woman's voice in the cavern, *qadi*. That is very strange even for someone who is delirious."

"And what did the woman's voice say?"

"That was not clear. When he mentioned the woman's voice he lapsed into a strange language, probably Assyrian."

"Forgive me for saying this, major, but the ramblings of a delirious man and a few legends passed down by uneducated villagers do not make a strong argument for the survival of an ancient goddess."

"I know that, *qadi*, but my grandfather had actually seen the… thing. And I have studied the reports of her sightings. My studies strongly suggest that the legend, though incredible, is true."

"What was there to study?"

The major told the *Qadi* about how he had mapped the sightings and how their distribution had agreed with the distance from the temple that someone who must travel only at night could walk.

The *qadi* was very thoughtful. "And what did your grandfather say about her?" he asked, "Did he talk to her?"

"No. He saw her only fleetingly. She ran away as only a demon could run when she realised that she had been seen. The story was told to me by my grandfather, who had fought in several tribal wars and was known to be a brave man. Nevertheless, he had found the sight of her, a totally naked and very tall woman just as the legends described, quite terrifying."

"Was she frightening to look at? According to her statue she was quite beautiful."

"Certainly beautiful. But my grandfather believed she was an affront to God. He was not frightened by her looks, but because she was something evil!"

"Do the legends say that she is an affront to God? Or that she is evil?"

"Not specifically. But what else could she be if she continues to live past her allotted time?"

"No-one can live past his allotted time, major. If God saw fit to allot her a very long lifetime, what business is that of anyone?"

"Is it not the business of every true believer to recognise evil? How else could one be a sword of one's religion? One must destroy evil when one comes across it!"

"Destroy it?"

"Naturally. I am a soldier, *qadi*, and my grandfather had said many times that he would have killed her if she had not run away with the speed of a gazelle!"

The *qadi* did not answer at once, but when he spoke his words were uttered with absolute conviction: "Beware of pride, major. Anyone can believe himself to be a sword of his religion, but the thinking man has to weigh his thoughts and actions, lest he strike blindly in the mistaken belief that he has Divine approval."

"Is a thinking man, then, to wallow in sophistries and leave alone what he perceives to be evil?"

"If she had tormented those who lived beside her home, or if, because of her long life, she had tried to usurp the powers that belong only to God, then you would be right in calling her an affront to God," said the *qadi* solemnly, "For to bring physical harm without reason, or to try and mislead people away from the true path, must be construed as wrong according to the tenets of our religion. But you believe that she was never killed and so continues to live, therefore her only sin, in your eyes, is that she has lived for a very long time. I see nothing wrong in that!"

"But only a demon would give a person an unnaturally long life!"

"Is not a long and healthy life the avowed aim of every normal person? Is it not one of the aims of medical science to give a long and healthy life to everyone? Why accuse her of great sin for achieving, in a way that we do not understand, only what so many of us desire to have?"

"We desire a long but *natural* life, *qadi*!"

"That is true. But what is a natural lifespan for some may be very long for others. The allotment of lifespan is God's prerogative, and His alone."

This was not what the major expected a *qadi* to say. "I am not a *qadi* or a *mufti*," he said, speaking very slowly, "But I believe I can tell what is evil and what is not."

The cleric understood that the major had made a decision to impose a death sentence. He did not find this particularly shocking, for it was the *right*, indeed the *duty*, of a true believer to kill someone whose actions were intentionally contrary to Divine Law. Someone who flouted Divine Law could indeed be described as an affront to God. But the decision to impose death was not to be taken lightly and, if taken on insufficient grounds, was itself a sin against Divine law. Irrespective of whether the survival of the goddess of the temple was nonsense: it was the *decision* that mattered in the case of the major, the *intention* to kill without sufficient warrant. So although the *qadi* could see that the major believed strongly in the reality of the survival

341

of the goddess, and although this belief was evidently irrational and strongly open to question, it was clear to him that the major had made a decision that was against the deeper teachings of the religious code that he, as a *qadi*, an Islamic Judge, had a duty to uphold.

"Before you take it upon yourself to make so important a judgement, major, remember that even a *qadi* or a *mufti* cannot always tell what is good in the eyes of God or what is bad, or even what is right and what is wrong. As you know, to be a judge in our tradition one must first know that the truth in an unfamiliar situation can only be achieved, with God's help, through *ijtihad*. We must struggle within our hearts to find God's will. As simple humans, this is sometimes only possible if we are shown the way by Divine intervention."

"Are you saying that I shall be shown how to act if I see her?"

"In such an important matter, when you alone have to decide whether to take a human life or not, you shall have to wait until you are given a sign that you can understand."

The major did not answer and the *qadi*, having made his point, changed the topic of the conversation to more mundane matters.

23

THE SPY

1

SELIM WAS A tall, wiry man in his early forties; an electrician by trade. He was very good at his job and had authentic testimonials from satisfied customers to prove it. However, he lacked formal qualifications because he had learned his skills by apprenticeship, and as more and more of his younger competitors carried official certificates from technical schools he found it increasingly difficult to get work. His income dwindled and both his wives (only one of whom was legal) nagged him incessantly about his inability to provide for them and his nine children. His deteriorating circumstances made him fare little better with his acquaintances, who never returned his 'phone calls and, on the few occasions when they met him accidentally in the street, would either nod hurriedly and walk past or pretend not to see him. Selim endured the nagging from his wives and his slide down the social ladder with stoicism if not with grace, but then a friend of a friend introduced him to Jawad and a world of opportunities opened before him.

Selim joined the loosely connected gangs of burglars who were part of Jawad's multi-tentacled organisation. He specialised in the disconnection of electrical security systems and his reputation as an expert electrician quickly spread throughout the underworld. Such was his fame that he was regularly invited to the large cosmopolitan cities to apply his skills against the security systems of banks, warehouses and, in particular, the homes of the *very*-well-to-do. His income soared and his wives no longer complained about there not being enough food on the table. And yet, Selim's star was none too firmly attached high in the firmament, for runaway success exposed a particularly unsavoury trait in his character, and it was not long before his fellows in Jawad's burglary network thought of him as a liability rather than an asset.

What alarmed Selim's fellows was the extreme brutality with which he treated the rich men and women whose homes he opened up to be ransacked. To be sure, most of those who worked for Jawad were no strangers to brutality, but Selim's colleagues feared that his excesses would prod the normally phlegmatic police into a no-holds-barred, doggedly tenacious pursuit. The burglary branch of Jawad's organisation was vulnerable to persistent police investigations because it depended heavily on free agents, such as informants and fences, who owed no loyalty to Jawad and could not be easily controlled. If a sizeable reward were offered, or if the police threatened to get the information they wanted through 'whatever means proved necessary' from someone they captured, the free agents would readily snitch on their fellows and bring Jawad's burglary business crashing down like a house of cards. It was therefore vital for the police never to be too keen to apprehend the burglars, and to this end unmarked envelopes full of neatly stacked banknotes regularly found their way to certain police officers. As an added precaution the proceeds from the burglaries were kept below the threshold that would alert the newspapers. However, it was understood by all concerned that neither generous bribes nor restraints on the appropriations would prevent a ruthless and systematic police crackdown if someone with influence were seriously injured or killed.

2

Jawad heard of the growing apprehension regarding Selim during a *majliss*, the monthly meeting where profits and losses were discussed, new ventures assessed and problems aired. These meetings were open only to the inner circle of Jawad's organisation. Apart from the lawyer who attended in case legal advice were needed, the active participants were Jawad and the dozen or so well-heeled criminals who ran the separate branches of his organisation. Coffee and sweets were served by some of Jawad's lackeys and order was maintained, when necessary, by Jawad's armed bodyguards, two of whom were posted at both entrances of the sumptuous room in Jawad's house where the meetings were held. One particular *majliss*, like all the others, started with a lackey reading out the agenda. Half-way down the list was: *"Selim the electrician, whose behaviour while on the job could cause problems."*

Jawad was annoyed to hear that Selim was proving troublesome because he had recruited him personally and, being the kind of man he was, saw any criticism of his appointee as a slur against himself. When the lackey finished reading Jawad ignored all other items and said harshly: "What is the complaint against Selim the electrician?"

"I was told that it is not a serious complaint," hurriedly replied the lackey, "but that it could become serious if not dealt with."

"Who wishes to speak about this? I want to know everything!"

Everyone expected the man in charge of the burglaries to speak, but it was the lawyer who answered: "It was I who asked that this matter be put on the agenda, Jawad *effendi*. The matter was brought to my attention and I believe it deserves to be discussed."

Jawad was surprised: "It is unusual for a lawyer to speak about such things. You must think it is very important."

The lawyer nodded politely. "Yes, Jawad *effendi*, I do think it is important."

"So speak!"

The lawyer was a bald, corpulent middle-aged man with a thin moustache. Despite his high position in the hierarchy of the *majliss* he had enough experience of Jawad unpredictable temper to appreciate the need for caution. He stood up and cleared his throat loudly before speaking: "As *everyone* here knows," he began ponderously, bending forward slightly every time he emphasised a phrase, "our burglars have always taken what they wanted with a *light hand*. They would get into a rich man's home, or a warehouse, or a bank, or a large department store, and help themselves only to what was *easily available*. They were not greedy and they avoided having anything to do with the homeowners and their servants or with the guards at the banks, warehouses and large stores. That way nobody was hurt and the police investigations *did not last long.*"

"Get to the point," muttered Jawad.

The lawyer cleared his throat again: "Yes, *effendi*. From what I have been told by several sources, this Selim is not satisfied with what can be acquired easily. He wants to lay his hands on *everything* and becomes very nasty if thwarted. He is particularly nasty when the target is a rich man's home. On at least three occasions he made the lads use *a door* to crush the fingers of the homeowner, one finger at a time, until the man gave them the combination of his safe. On two occasions he beat the lady of the house savagely and would not stop until she told him where she had hidden her jewellery." The lawyer paused for effect before continuing: "Rich men can afford a burglary or two since their property is always insured, but they cannot afford to *lose fingers* and they cannot allow their wives to be *beaten up!*"

"How did you come to know these things about Selim?" asked Jawad coldly.

"Selim's ways are common knowledge among the active burglar groups, *effendi.*"

"That may be, but how did *you* get to know about this?"

"I know some of the lads who took part in the burglaries with Selim, *effendi*, because my duties bring me close to those who get into trouble with the authorities. The lads who recently worked with him complained to me only last week, and their stories were confirmed by the lads who have worked with him in the past. All who have worked with the man – from the boys who climb the walls to the fences who dispose of the goods – fear that Selim's viciousness will arouse the police and bring a rain of troubles down upon our heads!"

"Did anyone try to talk to Selim about this?"

"Many tried, Jawad *effendi*, but Selim is not a man who listens to advice."

"That is all too true," said the man who ran the burglary operations.

Jawad clicked his fingers contemptuously: "I was talking to my lawyer!"

"A thousand pardons, *effendi.*"

Jawad turned back to the lawyer: "Is Selim not the best electrician we have in our pockets?"

"Yes, *effendi*. Nobody doubts that."

"So what does it matter if he breaks the fingers of some rich men or beats up a few women? Does he not always get results?"

The lawyer nodded with unctuous politeness: "Yes, Jawad *effendi*, he always gets results. But rich men sometimes have *powerful friends*, and it is only a matter of time before Selim breaks the fingers of a rich man with *very powerful friends*. If such a man gets his fingers broken or his wife beaten he will not sit quietly and weep. He will not mourn the money he has lost and curse the pain in his hand. When our lads are gone he will roar with rage and not rest until his powerful friends *compel* the police to hunt down the man who did these things! The police will pursue Selim until they catch him, and they *will* catch him, *effendi*, because he is like a dead rat among sacks of grain; he produces a *stench* wherever he goes, a stench that will lead them to him!"

"A stench?" said Jawad. "What do you mean?"

The lawyer changed metaphor: "I am saying that Selim's ways are like a signature that cries: 'Look! It's me again!' His methods make him stand out from other burglars. The fury he ignites in the hearts of rich homeowners cannot be forgotten! And when, as is sure to happen one day, a homeowner has very powerful friends, then the powerful friends will order the police to hunt Selim until they catch him, and when the police catch him they will beat him until he tells them who he works for. They will beat him until he points his finger at *us!*"

Jawad smiled icily: "Thank you. I will think carefully about what you said and I shall deal with Selim in my own way. Now let us turn to other matters."

The lawyer sat down, unsure as to whether he had made his case convincingly.

3

Selim's excesses were not discussed further at the *majliss*. Jawad was sure that all this fuss about the electrician was a waste of time, and he had made up his mind to let Selim continue as he pleased before the lawyer had finished speaking. Jawad was confident that any police investigation could easily be made to lead nowhere. That night, as he lay in bed with Aisha, his lover and *confidante*, Jawad went over all that had been discussed at the *majliss*. Jawad always told Aisha what had been discussed at meetings because, although he would not admit it, he needed her approval of his decisions. Jawad was tired and spoke in a languid monotone as he lay naked on his back while Aisha snuggled beside him, wearing only a silken shirt that showed off her long legs. The only illumination in the hot and humid bedroom was from two candles in a crystal holder, and the girl struggled to stay awake as Jawad droned on about what had been said at the *majliss* and what needed to be done. She was still struggling to stay awake when Jawad brought up the matter of Selim, which he had left to last because he considered it to be the least important. When Aisha heard what the lawyer had said she was suddenly wide awake.

Aisha hated cruelty and did not underestimate the possible repercussions of Selim's treatment of the people whose homes he helped burgle. When Jawad stopped speaking she said quietly: "You were clever, my love, not to show how important the problem of Selim is to you. When you resolve this problem nobody must think that you acted because of what was said about Selim at the *majliss*. They must believe you were aware of his excesses and had already made plans to deal with him."

"What do you mean?" Jawad growled. He had no intention of doing anything about the electrician and did not fully understand what Aisha was saying.

"I am sure you know how to deal with this dangerous man, my dearest. The lawyer is not stupid and what he said cannot be ignored. You cannot allow the police to poke their long noses into your burglary business and if Selim continues in his ways it is only a matter of time before his doings enrage someone with a lot of influence."

"Many of those who have influence also have secrets they do not wish to be known," said Jawad with a sly grin, appearing wolf-like in the candlelight. "A little blackmail in the right places will silence the complaints and any police investigation will fizzle out!"

Aisha caressed him in the way he liked best. "You are too wise to depend on blackmail, my love. What if the people involved are not susceptible to blackmail?"

"There are ways other than blackmail, woman!"

"Of course, light of my eyes. A man such as you has unlimited resources. But why risk putting your resources to the test? Isn't the safest way just to push this Selim aside?"

"He is too useful to be pushed aside!"

"No man can be that useful to someone like you, Jawad. From what you said, Selim could easily kill a rich homeowner who provoked him, and if the homeowner happened to be an influential person the police would hunt Selim relentlessly. You have many electricians, my dearest. Why not get rid of this Selim?"

Jawad tried to argue, emphasising Selim's extraordinary skill at disarming security systems and extolling the revenue he had brought in, but when it came to persuasion he was not in the same league as Aisha, whose subtle softness could change the mind of any man without him realising that his mind had been changed. When Aisha's persuasive skills had run their course he could only protest: "I cannot throw Selim out! He knows too much about us! And I cannot have him killed because the lads will think I made a mistake in recruiting him!"

Aisha smiled at him with a look of profound admiration: "Everyone knows you don't make mistakes, my love. The fault lies with those who brought Selim to you. They failed to tell you that he hated the wealthy and that this hatred would make him act without restraint. But you don't need to have him killed; just make sure he doesn't get any work. The opportunity to rid yourself of him will come."

Jawad frowned wordlessly at the ceiling, like a little boy who has been refused a treat without understanding why, but Aisha knew that she had won, and to consolidate her victory and ensure that he would not change his mind she rewarded him with pleasures that only very clever women can devise.

4

The opportunity to get rid of Selim came in the form of some personnel agencies that were recruiting workers on behalf of a foreign-sponsored archaeological expedition. After a long private talk with Selim, Jawad ordered him to apply.

Selim produced numerous testimonials and had no trouble demonstrating his electrical skills to the personnel agency and the archaeological expedition's agents. The panel who interviewed him were impressed by his intelligence and charmed by his pleasant demeanour. He was appointed Chief Electrical Technician and in less than a month everyone in the expedition knew how competent and efficient he was. When Selim casually mentioned to ElKureishi that he had a lot of free time on his hands the professor listened sympathetically, and when Selim volunteered to take on additional responsibilities his offer was gratefully accepted. Selim was invited to choose whatever extra duties he wished, and one of the jobs for which he volunteered was to help look after the two powerful radio transmitter-receivers in the expedition's camp.

5

The Army had set up an office in Basra to monitor the archaeological expedition, and because this office was under the command of one Colonel Haleel, for want of a better name its officers and NCOs were collectively known to all but the expedition's manual workers as 'Haleel's boys'. Major ElBalushi had entrusted the job of *liaison officer* to young Sergeant Ali, who was also responsible for the safety of the Army's radio. Sergeant Ali had to make sure that the radio was manned at all times, and he took this responsibility so seriously that he slept in the radio tent. But Sergeant Ali's most important duty was to change the Army radio's carrier frequency just after 7 a.m. every morning. The daily change of carrier frequency was to make it impossible for anyone to listen in on the communications between the Army office in Basra and the expedition's military escort. The frequency was re-set every day according to a secret timetable known only to Major ElBalushi and some of 'Haleel's boys', and the major would come into the radio tent promptly at 7 a.m. to give Sergeant Ali the necessary instructions. After the major had left, Selim would usually join Sergeant Ali in the radio tent for a morning chat. The Chief Electrical Technician could be quite genial when he wanted to and Sergeant Ali, who was innocent in many ways, liked him.

Selim's *other* duties were to keep Jawad informed of all important developments in the archaeologists' camp. This he did with his own compact transmitter-receiver that he kept well hidden, but because his radio had to be small in size its range was not greater than about fifteen kilometres. Selim's messages therefore had to be sent first to another of Jawad's men, Aslan, who was camped not too far from the hill. The information was then relayed to Jawad via Aslan's portable but powerful radio.

Aslan had been given the task of relaying the information from Selim because he was one of Jawad's most trusted lieutenants. For the same reason he was also to keep an eye on Selim lest the electrician decided to sell his services to Arroussi, or to anyone else. Aslan knew that if Selim decided to throw his lot with Arroussi the old bandit would appoint his own intermediary to forward the information from Selim, which meant that he would have no use for Aslan and would probably send someone to kill him. So Aslan had to remain within range of Selim's radio without the electrician knowing, or being able to guess, Aslan's exact location.

When the expedition moved to the foot of the hill Aslan had followed at a respectable distance on his carefully muffled scooter. A scooter is the ideal mode of transport for someone who never washes and who almost never changes his clothes and who only has to carry fuel, water and rations, a few blankets, and a portable transmitter-receiver. Aslan camped some twelve kilometres from the hill in a well-camouflaged lean-to that could not be seen from the camp or by anyone who approached the hill from the cities. The camouflage also concealed the lean-to from the Army helicopters that brought the weekly mail and other necessities to the expedition's camp. Aslan's water and rations were replenished every fortnight by a courier whom Jawad trusted. Apart from Aslan, only Jawad and the courier knew where the camouflaged lean-to was stationed.

Selim contacted Aslan only when he had something to report. He had contacted him after Mike had informed ElKureishi about the ruins on the hill, and then again when ElBalushi and his soldiers arrived at the expedition's base camp. Thus, Jawad knew the numerical strength of the military escort and what weapons they had brought with them. Jawad also knew the coordinates of the temple, for Selim had lost no time in obtaining them from Sergeant Ali when the expedition moved to the foot of the hill.

Selim was not the only spy among the expedition's workforce. Among the manual workers were three low-grade criminals who worked for Jawad but who only had a vague idea about what the archaeologists were doing and no idea at all about Jawad's plans. Their orders were to keep Selim informed of everything out of the ordinary that they saw or heard. The information they brought Selim was copious but mostly irrelevant, and he had to sift through much random verbiage before deciding what would be of interest to Jawad. Unlike the spies among the manual workers, Selim had a good grasp of what the archaeologists were doing and what Jawad needed to know.

6

When Carol and her team discovered the artefacts Selim reported immediately to Aslan: "They found treasure!" he said excitedly. He was speaking from his private tent, which was among those of the manual workers. The camp had not yet been moved to the top of the hill and Selim's tent was close to the foot of the southern ramp. It was four o'clock in the afternoon and the tents of the manual workers were deserted.

"How much gold?" asked Aslan laconically. If Aslan were excited at the news he did not show it.

"I don't know exactly, but the treasure is much more than a man can carry."

"What's in it?"

"Lots of small jewellery, some gold plates, many heavy gold ingots, a great number of bronze things and several crowns of gold and silver."

Like everyone in the camp, Selim had been allowed to see the artefacts soon after they were discovered.

"What kind of crowns?"

"The kind important priestesses used to wear. They go round the head and are inlaid with jewels and have long pendants on which hang more jewels. There are also silver artefacts and statues that should sell for a lot of money. One of the statues is life-size and very heavy, but it is a real beauty and should fetch a good price."

"What are they going to do with the treasure?"

"It'll probably be kept in a large tent that they've modified for the purpose, together with the bronze things, the pottery they found and some boxes full of old bones."

"The bronze things and pottery are useless; the museums are full of them. Are the bones of any value?"

"They're just old bones!"

"Are Kureishi and his foreign cronies looking for more treasure?"

"I think they're hoping to find more treasure. They're still digging everywhere and don't seem too anxious to send the treasure away."

"Good! I'll tell Jawad at once."

7

On the following day, Selim's report was to be less pleasing to Aslan: "ElBalushi wants the foreigners' camp moved to the top of the hill!"

"Where shall the treasure be kept?"

"On the hill of course! And it shall be guarded day and night by ElBalushi's men."

Aslan hated soldiers as much as he hated policemen, and he could not resist making his feelings known: "May ElBalushi's house burn down and his children perish! I've seen that hill, it will be difficult to kill the soldiers without risk to the treasure. We won't be able to use grenades freely!"

"Many are sure to die," agreed Selim. "Let's hope it's mostly Arroussi's jackals."

"It's more likely to be our lads who'll get the drubbing," said Aslan. "You know Jawad, he will want his lads to be at the forefront of things!"

"Well, you and I will be safe."

"Just make sure you're always close to the two transmitters!"

"Don't worry! They'll both be useless just before anyone realises that Jawad is coming. I can get into the radio tent any time I want because that idiot Ali trusts me!"

"Who is Ali?" asked Aslan suspiciously.

"He's the sergeant in charge of the army transmitter."

"Oh yes. You mentioned him before. He must be a very gullible idiot to trust you!"

"When you tell me that Jawad is on his way to the hill, I shall press the sharp edge of my knife against Ali's throat and he will trust me even more!"

"How do you know that Ali will be alone?" Aslan wanted to be certain that there were no flaws in Selim's plan.

"He is always alone with the army radio after Balushi has left."

"That is good, but don't cut Ali's throat until you're sure you have the day's radio frequency!"

"Don't worry! I'll only kill him when I'm sure he has told me what I want to know!"

"Are you sure the frequency is not shown on the Army radio?"

"I've already told you that the frequency display has been removed!"

"So how does the idiot Ali set the radio?"

"He's got some gadget to help him. He won't let me see it so I don't know how it works."

"Remember that I *must* have the radio frequency! Without it I won't be able to fool the dogs in Basra if they call while our lads are killing the soldiers!"

"I know that."

"Does the Army still call at least once a day?"

"Just once and it's always a routine call. They talk to Ali and ask if everything is normal."

"They don't ask for Balushi or anyone else?"

"They only asked for Balushi once and they never asked for anyone else. They don't care who they talk to and it's very unlikely they'll ask for Balushi while our lads are storming the camp."

"What about the other radio? Is it still idle most of the time?"

"I have already explained to you that the university radio is only used to call *out* from the camp. It is used by the old fool Kureishi when he wants something."

"All right. Just remember to get me the new frequency and destroy both radios when I tell you that Jawad is on his way!"

"I'll remember. You remember to remind Jawad that the attack on the foreigners must not be on a Tuesday. That's when the helicopter brings in the mail and other things."

"Jawad knows that. Oh, I almost forgot. Jawad wants to have a list of what's in the treasure."

"How am I supposed to get you a list? The treasure is guarded day and night!"

"There must be an inventory somewhere. Steal a copy and read it to me."

"I'll try. But it may take some time."

"Treat it as urgent, like all Jawad's commands."

"Very well."

"And remember to get yourself and all the workers off the hill as soon as you can after the shooting starts. If you take too long you could get killed."

"Will you stop worrying like an old woman? I and the lads will start a panic among the workers when the attack starts. We'll all rush down the hill together!"

"Remember to run down the ramp on the *southern* side!"

"You've already told me that many times! I know that I'm supposed to escape that way!"

"And I'll tell you again so that you don't forget."

"I won't forget but suit yourself."

"And don't forget the inventory!"

"I won't."

"That's enough then."

Aslan turned off his radio. He knew that Jawad and Arroussi had agreed to kill all the workers as they ran down the southern ramp, but he had been instructed by Jawad not to tell Selim "in case he has friends among the workers." Unlike the northern ramp which was next to the grove, the southern ramp offered no cover and was shorter and much steeper. There would be nowhere for anyone running down the incline to hide and the slaughter would be easy. It was no concern of Aslan's if Selim and the other spies happened to get killed with the workers. After all, the smaller the number of Jawad's lads who survived the attack, the greater would be Aslan's share of the treasure.

24

MIKE PREPARES FOR A SHORT TRIP TO MOSUL

1

THE EARLY-MORNING SUN was shining brightly when Mike entered the computer tent. Ohanian was bent over a pile of A4-sized photographs, holding a magnifying glass. Beside the photographs was a plastic cup half full of coffee.

"Good morning, Ardash!"

"Hello, Mike." Ohanian did not look up.

"Are these the pictures of the newly discovered tablets?"

"Yes."

"Anything interesting?"

Ohanian pulled himself away from the photographs and looked up at Mike despondently. "*Aman!*" he exclaimed with an expression of utter misery, "The writing on most of the tablets is usual Assyrian cuneiform! The writing on the rest is in other languages ancient but well-known! There is nothing like the script on the wall of the pit!"

"Don't worry, Ardash, we'll crack it yet."

"It looks without hope! We can learn nothing from these tablets!"

"I wouldn't say that. The tablets could prove that the temple of Amalishah had links with other temples as well as institutions outside Assyria. They could give us a good idea of what these links were."

"I guess so. But I have found nothing exciting yet."

"What do the tablets contain?"

"All kinds of messages, including grocery lists!" Ohanian looked up at the ceiling of the tent and shook both his fists: "There is nothing that could help with the script!"

Mike sat down on a chair away from the computer. "May I have some of that marvellous Colombian coffee of yours?"

"*Of course!*" Ohanian sprinted across the computer tent and brought his thermos and a paper cup to Mike. "It'll be much hotter than the last time!" he said enthusiastically. He poured the coffee and handed the steaming cup to Mike.

Mike had a sip and looked thoughtful. Ohanian said: "You want to talk about the script, Mike?"

"No, not about the script, Ardash. I'm thinking of going to Mosul for a while. I miss the 'phone and the internet. In Mosul I'll also be able to order books and papers that might help us decipher the script!"

"You are going to Mosul because of the papers and books? You can order them through the university on Kureishi's radio and have them delivered here!"

"I'll probably die of old age by the time the red tape is sorted out! And speaking of old age, I'm also no longer too keen on camp life. I'm getting to dislike lukewarm showers!"

Ohanian laughed. "Me too. I really hate lukewarm showers! In Mosul we can stay at my cousin's house. He is a jeweller and his family are very nice people. They have a large house with two modern bathrooms."

"Um, I would rather go to Mosul on my own and rent a small house or flat."

The cryptoanalyst looked stunned: "Don't you want to work with me any more?"

"That's not it at all, Ardash. It's just that there is someone I want to be alone with for a while."

"Ahh! So you are not as old as you say and the lukewarm showers are not cold enough!"

Mike smiled but made no comment.

"How shall we communicate when you are in Mosul?" asked Ohanian.

"I'm sure we can arrange something. Kureishi is quite generous with his transmitter when it comes to university matters."

"Yes, I know. Umm...is the lady from Mosul?"

"No, and she doesn't speak a word of Arabic. I'll have to teach her."

"Where is she from?"

"I'm sure you'll meet her some day."

"When will you be moving to Mosul?"

"I don't know yet. That will depend on how long it takes to find a place to stay."

"Do you want my cousin to find you a house or flat?"

"Thanks, but I'll manage."

"If you stay near my cousin's house you and your friend shall be able to enjoy his wife's cooking. It's fantastic cooking! And she can cook English food too, or French if you prefer."

"I'm sure her cooking is excellent, but I don't want to inconvenience anyone. I intend to leave for Mosul today to make arrangements. I should be able to leave immediately after I tell ElKureishi about my plans."

"Have you talked to Leonard about moving to Mosul?"

"I have, though I'm not so sure he heard all I said. He was much too anxious to tell me about his lecture tour in the 'States."

"Oh? How long was he gone?"

"He was gone for a couple of weeks and only returned two days ago."

"I envy him. I would like to visit the United States of America so much."

"Well, your turn will come, I'm sure." Mike downed his coffee and got up to leave.

"You are going to see Kureishi? To tell him you are going to Mosul for a few days to make arrangements for a much longer stay?"

"Yes."

"Then I may not see you before you leave. Good luck with the house!"

"Thanks." Mike dropped his empty coffee cup in the bin and left the computer tent.

2

"I don't understand your sudden desire to go to Mosul," said ElKureishi, "Don't you want to work on the script any more?" He was not very pleased with Mike's decision to move to Mosul.

"Of course I do. At the moment that seems to be the only field in which I can make a contribution to this expedition."

"Don't be so modest, Mike. You have already made enormous contributions. Even if you do nothing more you will continue to be an inspiration to the students. But why move to Mosul?"

"Well, in Mosul I can exchange data by 'phone or internet with colleagues who could help me with the script. With a proper address, I shall also be able to bring over books and technical papers that contain the most recent advances in cryptographic analysis. I think that I can be more productive there than here."

"Hmm. Your reasons are excellent and I see that I must reluctantly let you go. Would you like some coffee?"

"No thanks. I've just had some with Ohanian."

Kureishi smiled knowingly. "Your trip wouldn't have anything to do with last night, would it?"

"Well yes. In a sense. The statue reminded me of someone I would very much like to see again." *If you've got to lie, Chum, it's always better to stick close to the truth!*

"Oh, you had a letter in the weekly mailbag?"

"She never writes to me, but I believe she'll be in Mosul soon."

"That's wonderful, Mike. A man needs a woman for the health of his body and his mind. But uh… I'm afraid I have to impose two conditions on your trip to Mosul."

"What are these conditions?"

"Well, the first has to do with money. As you know this expedition has been very, very expensive."

"I know."

"Then you will understand my first condition. It is this: your trip to Mosul will have to be at your own expense. Is that OK with you?"

"Of course. What is the second condition?"

"You take Ohanian with you. I am sure he shall be a great help both with the script and as a guide in Mosul, where I believe he has a cousin."

Damn! "Oh?"

"Mike, I want him to benefit from your communications with your colleagues abroad! Ohanian is one of the best in his field but he is a bit of a loner and has few overseas contacts. Moreover, his obsession with the script has isolated him from everyone in the camp except you. Is it OK if he comes with you?"

The request is reasonable. Ohanian is part of Kureishi's staff and if the script is deciphered the old boy wants some of the credit to go to Ohanian. "As long as he doesn't have to stay with me."

"But of course. I did not mean that he has to live with you. I am just hoping that you would help him expand his horizons a little. They have contracted too much since he saw that script!"

"I'll see what I can do." *Ohanian's horizons will certainly expand if he meets Amalishah!*

"Have you arranged transport?"

"I was hoping to borrow one of the Land Rovers."

"Take the best one for as long as you wish. We are hardly using them at the moment. When do you intend to move?"

"I don't know yet. I am intending to go to Mosul right away to look for a place and to make other arrangements. I'll need to apply for a 'phone line, for instance. Getting a 'phone line in Mosul takes a long time, I believe."

"It takes a very long time. Sometimes several weeks, even months, depending on which part of Mosul you will be staying in. Ah! Just a minute!"

ElKureishi reached into the drawer under his desk and produced a small notepad. He quickly wrote down a few lines and tore out the top sheet.

"This is the name and 'phone number of a very close friend of mine who now lives in Mosul. He used to be a professor at the University of Baghdad and he has quite a few influential friends in Mosul. If you have any trouble 'phone him or visit him. He will offer you all the help he can."

"Thank you."

"You are still very much part of this expedition, Mike."

"Thanks again."

"Are you going right away?"

"If you have no objection."

"God speed!"

Mike was about to leave Kureishi's tent when the professor said: "You know, Mike, it's very strange. Last night, after you saw the statue of Amalishah, the major said that you were probably going to do something unexpected. And here you are, moving to Mosul!"

3

"Oh! Hello again, Mike!"

"Hello, Ardash." Mike took the seat next to Ohanian.

"You've spoken to Kureishi?"

"Yes I have. He said I should take with you me."

Ohanian grinned broadly and spread out his arms as though to hug an extremely fat person. "I think that is a *very* good idea. I'll stay with my cousin and you shall rent a little house where you shall stay with your friend. When you find time free you'll work with me on the script and... **Akh!**" Ohanian looked as though he had been struck by lightning.

"What is it?"

"What if they find more tablets while we're away? What if these tablets contain writing in the script of the pit?"

"I'm sure someone will let us know. Anyway, we'll be in frequent touch with the camp. They'll be happy to send us photos of any new tablets they find with the Tuesday helicopter. If something is found that could be of help with the script we'll be told."

"Are you still thinking of going to Mosul right away?"

"My bags are packed. The sooner I find a house the sooner we'll be able to move to Mosul."

"How will you get there? Will you take one of the Land Rovers?"

"Kureishi has given me free use of one of them for as long as I wish."

"Would you mind calling my cousin when you reach Mosul? He will need to know when to expect me."

"Sure, give me your cousin's number and I'll give him a ring the moment I find somewhere to call from."

Ohanian searched through his diary until he found his cousin's 'phone number. He wrote the particulars on a scrap of paper and handed it to Mike. "And you'll be back soon?"

"I should be back in three days, maybe four. But things might take a wee bit longer 'cos I'm hoping to arrange for a 'phone line after I find a suitable house to rent."

"I hope you don't expect to get a 'phone line the moment you rent a house! This isn't England, Mike."

"I know, but I'll see what I can do." Mike got up to leave.

"Goodbye, Mike."

"'Bye, Ardash."

25

DECLARATIONS

1

IN SOME PARTS of the world things take longer to do than one expects, and instead of a few days Mike spent the best part of a week in Mosul. After the silent solitude of the wastelands the city had felt loud and bewildering. The cacophony of vendors' calls, raucous shouts, beeps and hoots, not to speak of plentiful sonorous blasts from lorries and trucks, continued throughout the day and only dropped to tolerable levels at night. All but the broadest roads were chronically jammed with vehicles of all shapes and sizes, and everywhere densely packed people either loitered on the pavements or else dashed about hurriedly in singe-minded pursuit of their business. Mike tried to imagine how the crowds and the noise would affect Amalishah: *A few months away and I can barely tolerate the noise and the milling multitudes! Could she ever grow accustomed to such chaos?* But Amalishah could not bear the sunlight and would only go out at night: *It'll be easier for her at night... the noise is less loud at night... the crowds are less mad at night... and I'll always be there, holding her hand!* He tried to see Mosul through her eyes, and was surprised at how many things he would have to explain to her, and sometimes justify.

Although Mike left Mosul early in the morning it was after ten in the evening when he reached the hill. He parked the Land Rover among the other vehicles in the expedition's 'car park', which was a roughly semicircular area some hundred metres from the foot of the southern ramp, just outside the ring of rocks that surrounded the hill. It had been chosen, by tacit consent, because it was the nearest place to the ramp where the ground was flat and almost devoid of rocks. The archaeologists' camp had been moved to the top of the hill for some time, soon after Carol's team had made their discoveries, and it was largely due to the major's tact and organisational skill that the move was accomplished smoothly and without undue inconvenience.

When Mike stepped out of the car the moon had not yet climbed above the black bulk of the hill, and in the starlight the tall rocks that stood between him and the hill appeared ominous and unfamiliar: *What if Balushi's right? There could be dozens of cutthroats lurking among the rocks!* But the thought was easily dismissed and he reached the foot of the ramp without mishap. All thoughts of bandits evaporated as he trudged wearily up the incline. He had to carry his suitcase instead of rolling it along, for its tiny wheels were useless on the soft earth.

Although the southern ramp was steep it was short compared to the northern ramp, which was more than two hundred metres long, and it was not long before Mike entered the camp. The workers' tents were dark but the lights in some of the archaeologists' tents were still lit, so that the silhouettes of their occupants as they prepared to sleep reminded Mike of the *wayang*, the shadow theatres he had seen during his trips to the Indonesian archipelago. Mike paused in front of the computer tent; the flaps were loosely closed but, at the far end of the tent, a solitary lamp struggled with the darkness. *Ohanian is still working!* Mike felt sorry for the obsessive cryptoanalyst, and momentarily regretted not having told him that the writing in the pit was no longer a mystery, but he suppressed the impulse to enter the computer tent and tell Ohanian to have a rest. *He'll meet Amalishah soon enough and she'll tell him everything he wants to know!* He smiled to himself: *I just hope he survives the shock of seeing her!*

2

He reached his tent without encountering anyone and, once inside, carefully closed and fastened the flaps behind him. He did not turn on his gaslamp in case the light attracted visitors, and anyway, he found the darkness welcoming. In the dark he could savour the thought of Amalishah waiting for him in the grove. His watch showed 10:37 and she would probably be there around midnight. Hopefully, everyone but the guards would be asleep before it was time to leave. He sat on the edge of his camp bed and lit his pipe. The influx of nicotine cleared his mind and he went over all that he had done in Mosul. Had he forgotten to do anything important? *No, I believe I did everything I had planned to do!* The house he had rented was comfortable though sparsely furnished, and with the help of ElKureishi's friend he had managed to ensure that there would be a working telephone within two weeks. He had 'phoned Ohanian's cousin, as promised, and Armen had turned out to be a jolly fellow who was overjoyed to hear that Ohanian would be staying with him soon. Between chores, Mike had found time to do some shopping for Amalishah.

3

Almost everyone in the camp was asleep by 11:30. The two guards who patrolled around the storage tent were careful not to make any noise but the faint crunch of their army boots occasionally betrayed their whereabouts. The storage tent was near the centre of the camp, close to the pit, while Mike's tent was at the periphery and closest to the northern ramp. When Mike's watch showed fifteen minutes to midnight he listened carefully for the sounds of the guards, and when he was certain that they were both on the farther side of the storage tent he set out cautiously for the grove. Apart from the starlight and the faint light of the rising moon, the sole illumination was from the lamps that were always left on near the latrines. Apart from his flashlight, Mike carried a large plastic carrier bag of the kind used by expensive shops.

She was waiting for him deep within the grove, standing straight and totally immobile with her arms by her side and her bare feet close together. The almost leafless branches of the grove's twisted trees formed a lattice that dappled the moonlight, and where the silver beams touched her skin her complexion appeared to be completely white, like Pendelic marble. She was wearing the clothes Mike had given her when they first met, and her expression was so much like that of the statue that it seemed as though the effigy of the ancient goddess had been dressed in trousers and a wrinkled shirt. Her complete lack of movement made Mike wonder if vampires could sleep on their feet with their eyes open, but as he approached her she turned her head to face him and her mouth broke into a warm smile. Before he could smile back she was running towards him, her face beaming. She stopped two paces away.

"Have you made your arrangements?" she asked. Her expression was that of a happy child and he had a sudden urge to drop the carrier bag and hug her, but he thought better of it and just stood before her awkwardly, holding the carrier bag.

"I found a nice house with a large garden just outside the city. You will like it!"

"There is nobody living in the house?"

"Those who were living there have left."

"I hope you didn't *make* them leave!"

"No, they left of their own accord." Mike did not wish to explain *renting* in Assyrian.

"But there is furniture?"

"Yes, there is some furniture."

"Is there a well?"

"It has everything we need. We can move in any time we like. I should finish what I have to do here in a few days, and then we can go, if you are ready."

"I shall be ready when you want me to be. How long will it take us to walk to Mosul?"

"We won't walk. We'll go in a..." There was no Assyrian word for 'cross-country vehicle'.

She grinned with delight. "In one of the chariots with four wheels and no horses?"

"Yes."

"Will it be a big one or a little one?"

"A little one. They are faster."

"What do you call the little ones in your language?"

"It is called a *car*."

"And what do you call the big ones?"

"A big one is called a *truck*."

"Ah Mike! I wanted to travel in a *car* or a *truck* from the moment I saw them! They are very noisy and sound angry. Are they dangerous?"

"Only if you get in their way!" Mike laughed. "Oh, I brought you these." He gave her the bag he was carrying. She took the bag and tried to open it but found it difficult because it had a concealed zipper. He gently took it back and showed her how to open it.

"It's just like the *zip* on your trousers," he explained.

"The sliding thing is called a *zip* in your language?"

"Yes."

"It's a funny word, '*zip*'! Such a short word for something that must take a long time to make. Your language has some funny words: *zip... car... truck...*your words are so short!" She examined the contents of the plastic bag as she spoke.

4

The bag contained two knee-length skirts and three blouses, all neatly folded, in addition to assorted ladies' underwear. It also contained a pair of black soft-leather shoes with low heels. Mike had removed all the tags.

"Ahh! Thank you, Mike!"

"I didn't know where to find sewing things."

"No matter! These clothes are beautiful! Which of these clothes would you like me to wear when we next meet?"

"Would you mind wearing the light blue skirt and the white blouse? They would look very pretty on you."

"I shall wear the light blue skirt and the white blouse. May I put on the shoes now?"

"Please do. I hope they fit you. I remembered that you have small feet for your size."

She put on the shoes and took a few steps to try them out. The shoes fitted perfectly.

"It has been such a long time since I wore shoes!" Her face was radiant. "I am very pleased, Mike. Thank you!"

"I am happy too," he said, but then he suddenly looked serious: "Amalishah, there is something you must know about our trip to Mosul."

She looked at him inquiringly, alarmed by his sudden change.

"I have to bring a friend along, although he shall not live with us in Mosul. I have not told him about you but I shall have to tell him before we go."

5

She frowned as she thought about what he had said and he waited for her response. Eventually she said: "If you think it will be all right to tell him, I cannot object."

"He is a good man, Amalishah, and he knows a lot about… your kind."

"Is he your friend?"

"Not in the way you mean, but he could be. I trust him."

"Is it the friend who pulled you out from the pit?"

"No. It is someone else."

"A stranger? I am afraid, Mike!"

He moved forward and took her hand in his, squeezed it reassuringly. She squeezed his hand back and the strength of her grip made him wince in pain.

She was immediately concerned: "I'm sorry I hurt you!" she exclaimed.

"I'm all right." He smiled weakly as he nursed his hand. "I did not realise you were so strong!"

"We have a lot to learn about each other."

"I know."

"Mike, I fear what might happen if you tell someone about me."

"You have nothing to fear, all I ask is that you trust me."

She looked away and spoke very quietly: "I have no choice but to trust you." He did not know what to say and remained silent. A soft wind rustled through the branches above them and the latticework of shadows and light that covered her body trembled. She turned to face him and her expression spoke of awakened fears and doubts. He understood her feelings but still he said nothing, unsure of what to say, and after a deep breath she continued: "Amalishah is in your hands. If you betray her no one shall blame you; she least of all."

He did not answer at once because he found it difficult to express what he wanted to tell her, but eventually he said: "I *cannot* betray you, Amalishah."

"Cannot?" Her face was a beautiful but emotionless mask; the lack of any expression somehow emphasised the question.

"Yes. I cannot."

"Why do you say you cannot betray me? We are from different lands, different times. You owe me no loyalty, Mike."

"Perhaps not, but I am in love with you."

"In love with me? What does that mean?"

"It means that my soul feels empty and incomplete without you," he replied, avoiding her eyes, "and my heart only knows happiness when you are with me."

6

Even as he spoke he realised that he was making a declaration of love to a woman who had once been a queen and a goddess, a woman who had been worshipped by countless people and who for centuries had the power of life and death over her subjects. He did not know how she would react, and he suddenly feared that he had overstepped the mark. He tried to suppress the thought that she could be deadly if offended.

But she responded with surprising calmness, her face still a beautiful but emotionless mask: "Do you know what you are saying, Michael Townsend? Do you understand *what* it is you are saying it to?"

"I know what I am saying, and I am saying it to the woman I love."

Her total lack of expression remained but her eyes suddenly filled with tears in which the reflected moonlight sparkled like tiny diamonds. "I used to be a woman, Mike, a very long time ago, but now I am something else." She spoke with a calm dignity tempered by immeasurable sadness.

"You are still a woman, Amalishah. A very beautiful woman."

"No, Mike. I only have the appearance of a woman. I am a *monster* who feeds on blood and does not grow old." She could not conceal her bitterness, her deep aversion to what she had just said.

Without thinking he took her in his arms and held her tightly. She was taller than he, but that did not matter as he breathed her female perfume, felt the shapely curve of her narrow waist. "Don't ever say that again!" he husked.

She broke away: "Love between us is foolishness, Michael Townsend! Can't you see that such… such emotions can bring us both much pain?"

"If this be foolishness, then I am the greatest of all fools, Amalishah."

"You are not a fool, Michael Townsend, but even the wise can succumb to foolishness."

"Only if the gods who rule our lives wish it so," he replied, "and if the goddesses one sometimes meets permit it." He managed a smile.

She smiled back through her tears and the dappled moonlight danced in silver ripples on her wet cheeks. Then, as though her worries suddenly ceased to matter, she said gravely: "Such feelings are new to me, and I have prayed that they would pass me by, but Amalishah must let you know that she is a fool too, Michael Townsend."

His heart missed a beat and he could only say: "Why would you wish these feelings to pass you by?"

For a moment her eyes closed in an expression of despair, but then she took a deep breath and said firmly: "Because, Michael Townsend, no matter how many years we spend together, the day will come when you shall leave this world, and when that happens my heart shall shrivel and grow old beyond measure. Only my body will remain the same."

He could not bear the anguish in her voice, he had to say something that would reassure her, somehow: "But your body will still be young, Amalishah, and in time a young body can heal the heart and make it young again."

"No Michael Townsend, for I speak of the old age that comes when all hope of finding happiness again is lost."

"In your new life you shall live in a world you cannot yet imagine. You will meet many people! Perhaps you feel that way now because you have not met many other men."

She laughed softly, without mirth, and the bitter sadness returned: "I have met a hundred times more men than you have, Michael Townsend! It is *because* I have met so many other men that I know how different you are, and that is why I know that *you* are what was missing in my life. You cannot be replaced."

To his surprise she moved forward and took him in her arms. She lifted him up and held him the way a strong man would lift and hug a child, and Mike was once again shocked by her strength. But the shock melted away as she held him tightly, and he felt lost in her, absorbed by her, totally immersed in her. As she held him he lost all control and kissed her. He kissed her on the mouth with a passion he had never felt before. He had expected her lips to be cold, like an English winter, but her lips were warm and sweet, like the sunshine of ancient Assyria.

7

She put him down abruptly and with a frown she said: "What did you do to me?"

"I... *kissed* you." He did not know the Assyrian word for 'kissed' and used the English word.

"Why?"

"That is what a man and a woman do when they are in love. It is an *expression* of love!"

"I liked it. But I have never done that before."

"Not ever?"

"When I was a goddess no man was allowed to touch me, and any man who tried would have been put to death!"

"I am sorry."

"Oh no! You are different. I have never felt for a man like I do for you."

"Are you still afraid of us going to Mosul with a stranger?" he asked. He was not used to compliments and felt ill at ease. *This damn English upbringing!*

"Yes, Mike, but only a little. As long as you are with me I will not be afraid of strangers. The only fear that is left now is at the thought of leaving the place I know as home. I know very little of what lies far from the hill."

He took her hand in both of his just as a night bird chirped once.

"I promise that you shall have a new home, Amalishah. You shall come with me not only to Mosul, but also to my home that is far away. I want you to be my wife and be part of my world. I cannot live without you."

She backed away from him and turned her head, as though to see the bird that had chirped. "But are you sure you can live *with* me, Michael Townsend? I can learn your language and your customs, I can grow close to those who are part of your life, but I am not like you or your friends. I cannot bear the sunlight. I cannot eat food like other people. *I don't grow old!* What will the people around you think? What will they do to you?"

"They don't need to know anything that we don't want them to know."

"Then your life will change completely. You must know that before you make any promises."

"I do know that."

She approached him and looked deeply into his eyes. Very deliberately she said: "Then I shall make you a promise too, Michael Townsend. When you grow old and leave this world, I shall follow you."

"Don't promise that!"

She smiled at him, a teasing smile, the smile of an adolescent girl who asks to be kissed for the very first time: "*Kiss* me, Michael Townsend. Just *kiss* me."

8

They agreed to meet at midnight three nights later. Amalishah suggested they meet at what was left of the ancient village whose ruins were about two or three kilometres from the hill. The village had lain empty since the time when the temple was built, and all that remained were a few crumbling walls and the remains of a well. The archaeologists had decided that the ruins were not worth excavating and the place was deserted at night. Mike was to come with Ohanian and pick her up in a Land Rover, *a chariot with four wheels and no horses.* Picking her up would require only a small detour from the shortest way to Mosul.

26

THE MAJOR CONFIDES IN MIKE

1

MIKE HAD FINISHED breakfast and was on his way to the computer tent when he met Major ElBalushi.

"How was your trip to Mosul?" asked the major. Mike noticed that the major was unusually pale and had dark bags under his eyes.

"Quite successful," answered Mike, "I was back last night."

"I understand you shall be leaving us in a few days, with Ohanian."

"The change will do us both good."

"Mosul is a lovely place," said the major, "But I don't think it will lessen Ohanian's obsession with the script! I hope he doesn't try to take too much of your time when you are with your lady friend."

"Oh, you know about her?"

"Kureishi told me about her. We are very happy for you, Professor. I hope you don't mind my mentioning her?"

"Not at all."

"Will she be waiting for you in Mosul?"

"I expect her to arrive in Mosul at about the same time as Ohanian and I."

"I suppose you got in touch with her while you were in Mosul?"

"It is very difficult to get in touch with anyone while I am in the camp. The mail is reliable but very slow." *The major doesn't usually pry into private matters. There's something on his mind but he doesn't know how to bring it up!*

"Yes, it is collected only on Tuesdays." The major seemed to lose interest in Mike's 'lady friend' and stared vacantly into the distance.

"Is everything all right with you, Major?"

"Oh I'm so sorry Professor! My thoughts wandered. Please forgive me…"

"You do not seem to be your usual self, Major."

"It's just that I haven't been sleeping very well these last few nights."

"Is something wrong?"

The major's eyes narrowed and he looked at Mike as though to say: 'Can I trust you?' Then he abruptly made up his mind and said: "Actually yes, Professor. Something has happened and it's worrying me."

"Does it have to do with the safety of the expedition?"

"Why don't you come with me to my tent? As the senior member of the um... overseas contingent there are certain things you should know."

2

Mike followed the major to his tent. ElBalushi offered Mike a chair and said: "Shall we have some coffee, Professor? What I shall tell you is strictly between us, and coffee is a good way to seal an agreement."

"I understand. I would certainly like some coffee. Thank you."

The major poured the coffee and offered Mike a plastic-wrapped sheet of apricot paste: "Would you like some *amareldeen*, Professor?"

"No thank you. It sticks to my teeth."

"It sticks to mine too, but I still like it!"

The major solemnly cut a square of apricot paste for himself, folded it carefully and put it in his mouth. Then he sat in his chair, chewing thoughtfully. Mike waited for him to speak first.

"Ah, you English," said the major. "I am in no doubt that you are very curious about what I have to tell you, and yet you show no curiosity at all."

Mike tilted his head slightly, as though to say 'Well, that is how we English are!'

The major understood but did not respond. He sat back in his chair and lit a cigarette. After taking a long, noisy sip of his coffee he said: "As you know, Professor, in these troubled times there is extensive cooperation between the police forces of different countries. A few days ago I was informed that our police have picked up certain rumours that are circulating among the members of the um... *underworld* in my country. Similar rumours have apparently been picked up by the police of some of our neighbouring countries. The rumours were confirmed by police reports. It would seem that something big is happening, or is about to happen."

"And you think this big event may have something to do with us?"

"I hope it doesn't but I fear that it might, Professor. Um… may I call you Mike? It would make talking candidly so much easier."

"Of course."

"And please call me Hussein."

"Thank you."

"According to the rumours and the police reports," continued the major, "At least two large criminal organisations are pulling in their members. In several places the level of criminal activity has declined significantly. Also, the police have lost track of many known criminals. That would imply that members of at least two criminal gangs have been moved away from their usual uh… hunting grounds, presumably to join together for some big operation."

"Approximately how many people are we talking about?"

"Dozens, at least. Perhaps hundreds if they join up".

"I really cannot see what this could mean. I really don't know how criminal gangs operate, Hussein, here or in my own country."

"Then let me explain. Large gangs always have a hierarchical structure. At the top of the organisation is the gang leader, who has the power of life and death over the gang members. He or she makes the final decisions, sometimes alone and sometimes in consultation. Immediately below the gang leaders there are lawyers, accountants and the *entrepreneurs* of the criminal world. These people are criminals only by association, so to speak; they never get their hands dirty and are often linked to legitimate businesses. They run the accounting systems of the larger gangs and negotiate deals with, for example, foreign arms manufacturers when it is necessary to procure certain kinds of weapon. Then there are uncategorised rungs in the criminal ladder, part-timers, informers, and so on. At the bottom of the hierarchy there are the more-or-less specialised groups. They actually do the dirty work and can act independently. Sometimes, such a group may be affiliated with more than one criminal organisation."

Mike nodded to indicate that he had absorbed the information.

"The hierarchical structure ensures that when the police catch someone he is practically always from the bottom of the hierarchy, so that it is very difficult to prove that anyone from the higher levels was involved. This is the first reason for the hierarchical structure. The second is to allow the leaders to bring together two or more groups when the task at hand requires more men, or a wider range of skills, than a single specialised group can provide."

"So you're saying that organised crime here is a bit like the Army, where the generals can combine different units to bring together the skills and ordnance required by the military objectives."

"Precisely. Away from the cities the gang leaders are, in fact, mini-warlords. The gangs can be thought of as illegal armies composed of criminals."

"Perhaps there is going to be a gang war," said Mike, "And the gangs are redeploying their members."

"That is what the police appear to think. But gang wars are usually preceded by things like little skirmishes and tit-for-tat assassinations. To my knowledge there have been no reports of such activities. I fear that something else is being prepared, and that it involves us."

"So far, we have only worried about bandits, Hussein. Now you are telling me that we might be the target of organised crime?"

"In the cities, they are called 'organised crime' or 'criminal gangs'. In the countryside and the mountains they are called 'bandits'. They are often the same people, or at least they work for the same gang leaders. The days when small bunches of mountain bandits worked autonomously are over."

3

Mike digested the information. "So you are saying that at least two criminal organisations are pooling their resources to attack us? Why would they target us? Most of our equipment is useless to anyone but archaeologists, and all we have found are some old statues and a few gold and silver trinkets."

The major smiled politely. "Do you have any idea of the monetary value of what this expedition has dug up?"

"No. I am not concerned with such things."

"We radioed a detailed inventory to Baghdad and they provided us with an estimate of the value of the archaeological finds. It is a little above eighty million dollars!"

Mike was astounded. "I see. Such an amount could well be an inducement, I suppose, for one or more gangs to rally their forces."

The major smiled: "And eighty million dollars is a conservative estimate! On the black market, with wealthy collectors and a few rich but unscrupulous museums competing for bits and pieces, the net value would be much higher. Perhaps triple that amount."

"But how would the bandits know the monetary value of our finds? Surely 'Haleel's boys' can be trusted?"

"May I add that a copy of the inventory that we radioed to Baghdad has disappeared? There were two copies in my safe but now there is only one."

"You are saying that there are spies in our camp?"

"Probably among the workforce, perhaps even among the students. Some students may not be able to resist blackmail or threats to their families, not to speak of the promise of a rich reward."

"But you have, what, twenty-odd armed and trained soldiers, and two heavy machine guns!"

"Over thirty soldiers, Mike, not including me. But the spies will have told whoever has designs on those eighty million dollars how many soldiers we have and what weapons we have brought with us. These criminal gangs are flexible; they will pull in as many men as they need, and they can acquire weapons that will make our machine guns look like water pistols!"

Mike understood why ElBalushi went through the trouble of explaining the structure of the criminal organisations. This was not something the Western mind could grasp easily; criminal organisations in the West were often highly sophisticated, but they did not have the ability to put together as many men and weapons as they needed. He also understood why ElBalushi was worried. "So it's not your usual common bandits you are worried about, but a force tailored to deal with whatever we have here!"

The major took another noisy sip of his coffee. "Quite so," he said laconically.

"And in what form would this attack take place, major, if it ever happens?"

"I can't say," replied the major, "but since the gang leaders don't have much respect for the lives of their underlings they will probably make a frontal attack, using an armed mob as so much cannon fodder."

"They're not likely to have something like a tank, are they? Only a tank could climb up the ramps."

"No, Mike. The illegal purchase of a tank, or anything like that, would send loud alarm signals through the police networks. The bandits can't risk that. Their method would probably rely on stealth and surprise. They would probably hit us as hard as they can when they hope we don't expect anything to happen."

"Which is why you're taking the rumours and the loss of the

inventory so seriously."

"Yes. We must rely on even the most flimsy indication that they are aware of what the archaeologists discovered and the most indirect suggestion that they are gathering their troops."

"Have you spoken to ElKureishi about this?"

"I mentioned the threat from bandits many times. But I did not tell him my recent suspicions about the likelihood of criminal organisations pooling their resources. It would frighten him but I would not expect him to do anything useful."

"Why are you telling *me* all this?"

"I am hoping that you might try to persuade ElKureishi and Carol that the threat of an attack on the camp is serious. As I said, you are the senior member of the overseas personnel. ElKureishi thinks I'm using the threat of bandits as an excuse to take control. Carol has taken charge of the foreigners now that you're tied up with Ohanian and she won't deviate from what she believes are her archaeological duties."

4

Mike realised how much he had lost touch with what went on in the camp. "But are ElKureishi and Carol doing anything at all about the threat from bandits?"

"They don't accept that the threat exists!" replied the major with some exasperation, "Kureishi is still moaning about having had to move camp to the hill and Carol has persuaded her husband to pester me regularly with complaints about the inconveniences she is suffering."

Mike laughed softly, but his mind was not wholly on ElKureishi or Carol. *What would happen to Amalishah if we are attacked? She might try to help me and get in the way. She could get killed! She knows nothing about modern weapons!*

The major sensed that Mike's thoughts were being distracted. He said: "ElKureishi should not be too difficult to persuade. It's Carol who might prove obstinate."

"Why is that?"

"Because she will not concede that organised crime in these parts is different from that in Europe or America, where criminal organisations tend to keep a low profile. Your criminals may sell drugs or steal from building sites, they might also organise protection rackets, but they tend not to attack travellers or hijack lorries. On rare occasions they may rob a train or an armoured car, but that is so unusual that it becomes big news. So in Europe and America organised crime is mainly the concern of the police. Your general public has little direct contact with them. Here, organised crime is much more visible and the organised gangs often prey on the public directly. It's not too bad in the cities, but they can be very aggressive in places where the police do not have a strong presence."

"Like out here."

The major nodded: "Yes, away from civilisation." The major lit another cigarette. Mike said: "But even if I persuade ElKureishi and Carol of the possibility of an attack by bandits, there is very little they can do."

"Well, I have taken all the precautions I can," said the major. "The men are in place and the machine guns are in place. What Kureishi and Carol can do is to put an end to irresponsible behaviour. I don't want the archaeologists to become paranoid, but many of them have taken to wandering off away from the hill and having picnics in the wastelands, others are taking leisurely drives to the ruins of the ancient village that is not too far from the hill. That is very dangerous! Archaeologists, and especially foreign archaeologists, would make excellent hostages."

"I'll have a word with my colleagues."

"Thank you. And, by the way, Mike, it would be a good idea if you, also, refrained from your midnight walks."

5

Mike was stunned but did not show it: "Was I followed?"

"My men cannot leave their posts. They only report what they observe."

"I promise, Hussein," he said smoothly, "No more midnight walks." *But if he knew that I went out to meet someone he would have said so!*

The major continued: "I don't want to scare anyone, but you and your colleagues can only be protected by my men if everyone stays on the hill!"

"Do your superiors know that you expect bandits to make a grab for our discoveries?"

"Yes. They said that it is natural for me to worry about such things in my position."

"They did not take you seriously?"

"They always take me seriously. But they are unwilling to send reinforcements unless I have something more concrete than suspicions based on distant rumours and a missing inventory."

The major's words made Mike adjust his perspective of the situation: *But that is actually all he has! Rumours and the disappearance of an inventory! But what further evidence might one expect at this stage? Short of catching a bandit trying to climb up the hill we cannot expect any stronger evidence And if some criminal organisations found out that we are sitting on eighty million dollars in the middle of nowhere, it is very likely indeed that they would try to do something about it!*

"If we are attacked," Mike said, "How long would it take for help to arrive?"

"Not less than two hours and probably much longer," replied the major. Then he added: "Assuming we can radio for help."

"Why shouldn't we be able to radio for help?"

"If their spies can nick an inventory, they can disable the radios!"

"But your headquarters, 'Haleel's boys' as we call them, call your radio every day. If they don't get a proper response they will know immediately that something is wrong!"

The major carefully stubbed out his cigarette and lit another. "Not immediately," he said quietly. "If they don't get a response on the Army radio they will apply for permission to try the university radio. That may take as much as an hour given that they are not allowed to use private communication channels. If the university radio also doesn't work *then* they'll suspect that something is wrong. After that, the question of whether we are under attack will probably be debated with Colonel Haleel and then between Haleel and his immediate superiors. So far, the discussion will be at a military level. Whether something needs to be done may *then* be discussed at a still higher level, the political level. Finally, *if* it is decided that something needs to be done, there shall be further discussions about what specific action should be taken."

"That's a bureaucratic nightmare!" exclaimed Mike, "Surely your presence implies that the threat of bandits is taken seriously!"

"The threat yes, but not the imminence of an attack. Don't be too harsh on 'Haleel's boys', Mike. The bureaucratic hurdles are understandable. We are not at war, yet my superiors may have to decide whether to deploy our soldiers against civilians, some of whom may be foreign nationals!"

"What about the police?"

"They are not equipped for this sort of thing."

"From what you've said, it would be a miracle if any help gets here within twenty-four hours! If these bandits are any good, we may not survive until help arrives!"

The major took a deep breath: "There is some hope. I gave you the worst scenario. It's possible that they will not be able to disable the radios, or perhaps Colonel Haleel may have had thoughts similar to mine, and when he is told that both radios don't work he'll cut through the red tape and say 'What the hell! Let's send in some combat helicopters just in case!'"

"Hussein, that kind of thing happens only in stories and films!"

"But it's not impossible."

"What sort of chap is this Colonel Haleel?"

"I've never met him and have only spoken to him on the 'phone, but being responsible for a foreign archaeological expedition could be seen as a comfortably easy job. So he's probably a political appointee."

"So he's probably a moron!" Mike had a low opinion of political appointees.

"Not necessarily, and being a political appointee could mean that he knows the right people. If he does, and if he's not a moron, his chances of cutting through the red tape would be quite good!"

6

The idea of bandits mounting an attack on the archaeologists' camp was too alien for Mike to accept fully. His mind was naturally averse to any form of violence. But there would certainly be a market for the expedition's discoveries, and more than eighty million dollars would perhaps be irresistible to a gang leader, a 'mini-warlord', if such people existed. He wished he had his pipe with him; for he believed he could think more clearly when he smoked his pipe.

"Do your men know about the possibility of an attack?" Mike asked.

"They know, I keep them informed of all relevant information, including rumours I hear about from Haleel's boys. But they have orders not to show that they are in a state of alert."

"Major…" began Mike.

"Please call me Hussein, we are talking like brothers now."

"Oh yes, I forgot. Er… Hussein, wouldn't a simple solution to our problem be to transport the finds to Baghdad as soon as possible? If the bandits get to know about that they may not attack the camp."

The major shook his head. "I suggested that to ElKureishi, but he and Carol are vehemently against it. Neither of them seriously believes we could be attacked by a large force of bandits, and they don't want the finds out of their sight until they are absolutely certain that nothing more will be found. Their usual excuse is that a lot of work remains to be done on the artefacts before they are ready to be shipped away."

"That is probably true. I suppose the international nature of this expedition has something to do with their disinclination to divide the finds between here and Baghdad. Our actions are guided by undercurrents of competition and jealousy between our sponsors."

"Very eloquently put," said the major, "Carol and ElKureishi seem to think that if some of the archaeological finds were in Baghdad, and some here, it would be harder to allocate the spoils equitably."

Mike downed his coffee. "I see no alternative but to ask Kureishi and Carol to speed up the search for more artefacts. Unessential measurements, recording and map-making can be postponed while they concentrate on using the metal-detectors. It shouldn't take long to be reasonably sure that no metal artefacts remain to be found."

"That would be another thing for you to do, Mike. I've tried to urge ElKureishi and Carol to concentrate on looking for metallic objects, but they told me in no uncertain terms to mind my own business where archaeological matters are concerned!"

"I apologise for that. It is obvious that safety and archaeology are closely intertwined in this situation, though they are at cross-purposes."

"I would be grateful if you reminded your colleagues of that."

7

Mike got up and put his coffee cup away. There were still questions he would have liked to ask, but he did not wish to take more of ElBalushi's time; the major could do with some sleep. *But wait, there's one very important question!*

"How would the spies communicate information to their masters? You said that a copy of the inventory of the discoveries has disappeared. The information would have to be sent by radio. If there is a third radio in the camp we can find it. Even a portable transmitter is a bulky item!"

"I've thought about that, and my men secretly searched everyone's personal belongings. They did not find any portable transmitters."

Mike was shocked and he sat down again: "You had everybody's personal belongings searched?"

"Naturally. And all outgoing mail is checked personally by me. This is not England, Mike, and the stakes are very high!"

Mike accepted the explanation. *The stakes are indeed very high! If ElBalushi is right about the bandits we could all get killed! He must do everything he can to protect us!*

"But if you haven't found any transmitters, wouldn't that simply mean that there are no spies among us, and that we are not likely to be attacked by bandits?"

"With at least eighty million dollars stored in a tent it is more than likely that there *are* spies among us, but that they have devised some other way of keeping their bosses informed. Or perhaps they hid their transmitter very well, if they're using a transmitter."

"We are in the middle of nowhere, Hussein. What else could they use?"

"It's possible that the spies convey messages to a courier who comes at regular intervals. That is why my men keep a 24-hour watch to see who leaves the camp, and at what times. They have orders not to interfere because we don't want the bandits to know we're on to them. But I always get to know who leaves the camp, and when."

"Has anybody been leaving the camp at night?"

"Only you, Mike."

"Surely you don't think I'm a spy?"

"The thought crossed my mind but, after doing some fairly extensive checking, I'm certain you're not a spy for the bandits."

"That's a relief," said Mike. He could not conceal the sarcasm and the major was annoyed: "That still leaves the *reason* for your midnight walks unexplained, Professor!"

He didn't want to say that! He's very tired and has a lot on his mind!

"And what reason do you think I could possibly have?" Mike asked quietly. *Let's put all our cards on the table!*

The major shrugged. He regretted having said what he did but it was too late to back down. "Meeting someone in secret, perhaps? A very dangerous secret friend?" The major refused to look Mike in the eye.

"Are you talking about ghosts again?"

"Worse than ghosts, Mike. I warned you about her!"

"What makes you think she is my friend?"

"She would be only pretending to be your friend, Mike. Just pretending."

"Be that as it may," said Mike, "How long have you thought I've been in touch with... this person?" He almost said 'Amalishah', but that would have been an admission.

"Ever since you mumbled something about a female voice in the cavern. Dr. Mursi did not understand everything you said while you were delirious, but he understood enough. And she is not a person, Mike. She is a *thing*! A very clever *thing* who managed to survive for a long, long time!"

"What would you do if she were real and you met her?"

"I have no doubt that she is real," said the major flatly. "And if I meet her, I'll kill her!"

"Why?"

"Because she is an abomination in the eyes of God and I am a sword of my religion!"

Mike nodded grimly: *For this man protecting the camp is just a job, killing Amalishah is a sacred duty! Nothing can change his mind. If he had the choice between saving the camp and killing Amalishah he would ignore the bandits and kill Amalishah!*

The major was looking at Mike intensely, expecting a remark along the lines of what the *Qadi* had said, but Mike's only response was: "And you think that this... this abomination, as you call her, has somehow singled me out?"

"I do."

"Why would she choose me?"

"I don't know why she would choose you. Maybe it's because you're the first one she met. After all, you found her cave."

"So you think she lives in the underground cavern?"

"Not necessarily the one you found. That cavern leads to many others and she probably knows them all. But we shall flush her out, sooner or later. If she tries to escape she would need to walk for a long time and is sure to get caught by the sun! Sunlight will kill her, as I'm sure you know. Perhaps she hopes you will provide her with fast transport!"

The major's words tore through Mike's emotional defences. He felt as though a heavy weight had suddenly materialised in his chest. *Yes I know that sunlight will kill her, and here I am helping her escape in a Land Rover at night! Is that why she singled me out? Because I'm gullible and can provide fast transport?* The memory of Amalishah as he had last seen her in the moonlight – so beautiful and so innocent – was sullied by misgivings. Her actions and her words, which he remembered so clearly, took on sinister overtones. Mike took a deep breath. "This supernatural stuff is too much for me," he said bitterly, "You have given me enough to worry about with your talk of bandits!"

"The bandits are indeed the more pressing problem. Hopefully, you and Ohanian shall leave for Mosul before the bandits attack."

"You mean *if* they attack."

The major chuckled mirthlessly. "They *will* attack, Mike, sooner or later."

Mike got up to leave. "I shall have a word with ElKureishi and Carol about the need to intensify and complete the search for metal artefacts."

"And don't forget to remind them of the need for caution. No unnecessary trips off the hill!"

"I won't forget," said Mike as he left the tent. The major remained slumped in his chair and did not look up.

27

THE BANDITS: AISHA

AISHA'S PARENTS WERE *Circassians. The Circassians were never numerous, but their young men were once famous for their wildness and, throughout the Ottoman Empire, their young women were reputed to be the most beautiful in the world.*

Aisha's mother was only sixteen when she was ready to give birth to her first child. In accordance with tradition, she was to have the child in her own home. An experienced midwife was called in and she carefully examined the young mother-to-be. To the family's dismay she predicted medical complications and refused to take responsibility for the delivery. Mehmet, the father of the unborn child, called the hospital at once, and he was so distraught with anxiety that his mother had to calm him down. He smoked one cigarette after another and paced back and forth impatiently as he waited for the ambulance. But Mehmet was not concerned about his young wife; he was a wealthy man who knew that a wife could be easily replaced. What concerned him was the possibility that he might lose a son, for he was confident that the baby would be the first of a long string of boys.

The young wife entered labour while still in the ambulance and was taken immediately to the emergency ward of the hospital. The physicians, after a lengthy operation, succeeded in saving the lives of both the mother and her baby. But the mother's life was bought at a heavy price: she would never be able to give any brothers or sisters to the little girl she had brought into the world.

When the obstetrician informed Mehmet that his baby was a little girl he was greatly disappointed, but when she added that his wife would not give him any more children he felt as though the Earth beneath his feet had opened up to swallow him. In a society where men pride themselves on the number of boys they beget, a man such as Mehmet could only interpret such news as a betrayal on the part of the woman he had married.

"What sin did this woman commit," Mehmet asked his mother, "For the heavens to curse me so?"

"The woman is blameless!" the mother answered, "And be not angry at the heavens whose ways are not for us to understand. The baby is healthy and beautiful and you should be proud of your little girl. Give your daughter my name, so that I may live on in her!"

And so the baby was called Aisha, after her paternal grandmother.

For many years Mehmet nursed a sullen anger mixed with shame. When he and his wife were alone together he never failed to remind her of her betrayal. She, young and isolated from her own kin by her husband's relatives, was vulnerable to his accusations and lived a life tormented by guilt. She tried to please her husband in every way she could and, by the time Aisha had become a beautiful little girl of ten, it would have seemed that she had succeeded in making Mehmet's resentment towards her a thing of the past. However, subsequent events proved that his anger and his shame had never, in any real sense, been lost.

Aisha's childhood was not unhappy. Certainly she did not lack any of the material things that can be made to appear very important to young children. Mehmet was a wealthy landowner and, as Aisha grew to be an intelligent and lively teenager, he never refused her anything that she needed or asked for. Yet Aisha was never close to either of her parents, and when her grandmother passed away she felt completely alone for the first time in her life. She was only fifteen, a difficult age for any young girl.

Aisha sought for purpose in her life through her schoolwork, and was so successful at school that there was talk among her many uncles and aunts that she would go to university one day, perhaps to study some esoteric field such as chemistry or biology or engineering. Mehmet proclaimed proudly to all his friends that his daughter was not only beautiful but destined to become a scientist or an engineer.

And Aisha was indeed beautiful. As one of her more poetically minded admirers had written to her:

'Ivory can never match the colour of your skin;
Emeralds can never match the colour of your eyes;
The purest copper can never match the colour of your hair.
Diamonds can never match the brilliance of your smile.
Oh why won't you deign to look at me, Aisha?
Why do you condemn me to hide among my friends
And caress your beautiful body only with my eyes?'

Had Aisha's life continued normally, she would have gone to university. With her brilliant mind and warm personality she would most probably have had a successful career and a happy family life.

That was not to be. Barely a week after her sixteenth birthday, Aisha had completed a short errand for her father and was walking home in the early evening when a long limousine full of happy and drink-intoxicated young men pulled up beside her. Two well-muscled youths jumped out of the car and tried to push her into the back seat. Aisha resisted and one of them slapped her hard across the face several times. Then two more youths came out of the limousine and all four managed to push her into the car. Though she was very frightened she continued to fight and they beat her mercilessly to stop her resistance. They continued to beat her even when she was so dazed and exhausted that she did not notice that the limousine had stopped in a deserted part of the town. They only stopped beating her when they were satisfied that she could offer no further resistance. The happy young men then proceeded to rape her one at a time, repeatedly violating her while she moaned from the pain and teetered on the edge of consciousness. When they finished enjoying her body they drove back and left her within sight of her own front door. She was left naked, bleeding and unconscious.

Mehmet was standing in front of his house, seething with anger because his daughter had taken so long to return from her errand. When he saw passers-by stopping and gathering less than half a block away he strolled over casually to investigate. Mehmet's feelings were very complex when he realised that the body that lay naked on the pavement was that of his daughter. He stayed away but called the police, and when they eventually arrived they covered Aisha's body with an old coat before taking her to the nearest emergency ward. Mehmet paid all the bills but he did not visit his daughter while she slowly recovered in hospital. Nor did he allow anyone else to visit her, not even her mother. When the police, knowing he was a wealthy man, came up with one pretext after another as to why they could not prosecute those who had gang-raped his daughter he neglected to provide the customary financial inducements, and when Aisha was finally released from hospital he refused to let her back into his house. It can only be surmised that the man had finally found a way to avenge himself on the wife who, in his eyes, had so unjustly betrayed him.

Aisha was given shelter by a distant aunt on her mother's side. The aunt was poor and unmarried, and she treated Aisha as a servant and a burden. The young girl who had shown so much promise lost all hope of a happy life and, late one night, when her aunt was asleep, she quietly left the house and wandered aimlessly along the empty streets. After hours of wandering she found herself standing on a bridge that straddled a polluted and foul-smelling river. As she stood staring at the dark water that flowed silently beneath her, she was approached by a middle-aged, rough-looking man.

"Girl, what are you doing here?" the man asked, not unkindly.

She did not answer. The middle-aged man repeated the question: "Girl, what are you doing here?"

"I am thinking of jumping into the river!" she answered, as though talking to herself.

"All lives must end some day. Why the hurry?"

"An empty life must be cut short."

"Come with me and you may find hope."

"There is no hope for me."

"Perhaps there is no hope among the people you know. But I can show you new people and another world, a secret world that exists in parallel with the one you know. In my world we make use of opportunities as they come and take whatever pleasures we find. We enjoy a freedom of sorts, and if you come with me your happiness will be in your own hands."

And that is how Aisha met the bandit leader, Attila. Although he was middle aged and she was only sixteen he became her lover and mentor. He treated her with kindness and generosity, and he taught her to be independent and ruthless. Her despair had gouged out painful hollows in her psyche that readily admitted independence and ruthlessness, and these hollows also admitted the kind of wild hopes that only those outside society's conventions can enjoy. Most importantly of all, he taught her that the pleasures of the flesh are best enjoyed when unencumbered by emotional attachments. This also fitted well within the painful hollows of her psyche.

She lived with Attila for over two years, content though never happy. But at the end Attila's health deteriorated and he was judged unfit to lead his gang of bandits and thieves. He was unceremoniously deposed as leader and all his possessions, including the girl whose life he had changed, were taken from him by his successor, Jawad. Not long after he lost Aisha, Attila was found dead by his own hand on the bridge where he had first met her.

28

THE BANDITS GATHER

1

ASLAN WAS A stocky, heavily-built thug in his late thirties. As one of Jawad's oldest companions, he was completely trusted by Jawad and the higher echelons of Jawad's organisation. However, he was not popular with Jawad's rank and file because he was prone to unpredictable violence, and at the slightest provocation (and sometimes without any provocation at all) he was all too ready to use his knife on friend and foe alike. Normally sporting no more than a stubble, he now had an unkempt beard because he had been watching the archaeologists' camp for several months, from the early days of the expedition, when ElKureishi had sent out the Land Rovers to survey the surrounding wastelands, to the final move from the plain to the top of the hill.

Jawad had surmised that money-laden organisations would not sponsor the expedition unless there was a real possibility of rich rewards, and he had made sure that he would be kept informed of all developments. Aslan was fully aware of the importance of his task, which was to relay messages from Selim, Jawad's principal spy in the foreigners' camp, to Jawad himself. Aslan would set up his lean-to in places where there was no chance of being seen by anyone, just within the range of Selim's small transmitter. To avoid being accidentally seen by visitors to the archaeologists' camp, including the weekly helicopter that carried the mail, Aslan's lean-to and scooter were heavily camouflaged by a light mesh of string and cloth whose colours matched those of the surrounding wastelands. Provisions were supplied by a courier, who was the only person, apart from Jawad, to know the exact location of Aslan at all times. Now that Jawad had teamed up with Arroussi to storm the archaeologists' camp and take the treasure that had been found in the ruins, Aslan's job had become absolutely crucial. He was to intercept any calls from the Army office in Basra so as to conceal the fact that the archaeologists' camp was under attack. The attack was no imminent.

2

On this very important day, Aslan was worried because it was past four-thirty in the afternoon and Jawad had not arrived. The day was dark and depressing, with dull grey clouds scattered thickly across the sky like great bloated birds of indeterminate shape. Although the sun occasionally managed to shine through the gaps, the intermittent shafts of light were too few to mellow the harshness of the wastelands. To someone less anxious than Aslan, the changing patterns of light and shade might have been construed as beautiful, but they did nothing to raise Aslan's spirits, and he smoked continuously as he sat on a foldable stool beside the wing of his lean-to, barely finishing one cigarette before lighting another.

Jawad and Arroussi had agreed that they and their men would convene and make camp at Aslan's lean-to on the eve of the assault on the expedition. The assault was to start early in the morning of the day after the bandits convened. Aslan's lean-to was close enough to the hill for the travel time from the camp to the hill to be short, yet sufficiently far for the bandits' camp not to be visible from even the highest point on the hill. Two days earlier, Jawad had told Aslan that he would be at the lean-to at four, at the latest, because Arroussi was to arrive at five. Jawad had stated emphatically that he wanted to reach Aslan at least an hour before Arroussi. Jawad and the lads would be travelling in a huge truck that Jawad had bought a week earlier, a monstrous vehicle that had previously belonged to a mining company. Aslan did not know how many trucks Arroussi would have, but he was certain that there would be more than one.

Aslan could not understand how Jawad could be late on such an occasion and risk arriving after Arroussi. Something must have happened. Every few minutes Aslan raised his binoculars to scan the horizon, but every time he saw only the bleak and empty landscape of the wastelands. When Aslan was not scanning the horizon with the binoculars he stared vacantly at his filthy blankets that were scattered under the lean-to, or else stared, equally vacantly, at his battered metal coffeepot, half-full of strong coffee, that was perched on his small camping stove. The coffee had been brewed an hour earlier and was no longer hot. On the ground before him, beside the transmitter-receiver that was always by his side, was an empty wide-mouthed jar that had previously contained sugar. When the taste of stale nicotine became too strong, Aslan would remove the cigarette from his mouth and spit richly into the empty jar. It was a little game he played in an attempt to get his mind off Jawad's lateness, but it did little to alleviate his anxiety, and it did nothing to lessen his worries that something had happened to Jawad.

3

Could the attack on the hill have been postponed? Such things are not postponed at the last minute and Jawad would surely have called to let him know in good time! What if Arroussi arrived before Jawad? Aslan had not been told what to do if Arroussi arrived before Jawad. Aslan would not know what to say to Arroussi.

At ten minutes past five Aslan's nerves almost gave way and he tried to calm himself by drinking coffee straight from the spout of the coffeepot. The coffee was cold and tasted vile and he wished he had not finished the sugar, but the bitter taste somehow reminded him to check the radio's battery. Had Jawad called and not managed to get through? No. The battery was working perfectly. Jawad had not called.

Could Jawad have lost his way? That was impossible. Jawad had the precise coordinates of the lean-to and his truck had a satellite navigation system that could be used in the wastelands. Could the navigation system have failed? Things often malfunctioned in the wastelands, but Jawad also had a directional receiver that was tuned to a homing beacon on Aslan's transmitter. The homing beacon on the radio receiver was dependable and had been routinely used by the courier who brought Aslan his provisions. To avoid giving Arroussi Aslan's coordinates, Jawad had provided the old bandit with a similarly tuned directional receiver to show him the way to Aslan's lean-to. What if Jawad's navigational system as well as his directional receiver had failed? Then *Shaitan* himself must be out to stop Jawad! Aslan muttered a garbled prayer that his father had taught him. What if Jawad's truck had broken down? God help the man who had sold Jawad the truck! But if the truck had broken down, or Jawad had somehow got lost, surely he would have called to tell Aslan what to do when Arroussi arrived? Yet Jawad had not called. Had Arroussi decided to kill Jawad somewhere in the wastelands? This was what Jawad would have done if he thought he did not need Arroussi's help. If Arroussi had waylaid Jawad in the wastelands the lads would have put up a fight and that would explain why both Jawad and Arroussi were late.

The possibility that Arroussi might have killed Jawad was not in itself disagreeable to Aslan. Jawad was a difficult man to work for and his ventures were not always successful. Aslan felt no loyalty to Jawad other than that which enabled him to survive; he would be quite happy to work for Arroussi. But Arroussi had a reputation for thoroughness and if he killed Jawad he would make sure that none of Jawad's close henchmen survived, which meant that he would also try to kill Aslan! But would Arroussi kill Aslan? Arroussi knew that the office in Basra called the Army radio in the foreigners' camp every day, sometimes more than once. They were sure to call during the attack and only Aslan, who knew how to intercept the call provided he were given the day's code by Selim, would know how to fool the Army office in Basra into believing that everything was as normal! But what if Selim had betrayed Jawad and was now working for Arroussi? If Selim had betrayed Jawad then one of Arroussi's men could easily do Aslan's job, and Aslan would then be as useful to Arroussi as a cockroach in his shoe! If Selim were working for Arroussi then Aslan'a life was in serious danger!

4

By six pm Aslan's anxiety had turned into a stomach-twisting fear of getting killed. Every large rock he could see became a potential hiding-place for an assassin sent by Arroussi, and several times he thought of calling Jawad, But every time he decided against it. If Jawad were dead there would be no point in calling, and if something else had gone wrong then Jawad could be in one of his moods and would be furious if Aslan called him without good reason. Better to wait and call Jawad only if he saw Arroussi's trucks! If Arroussi's trucks were in sight he would have a *good reason* to call and Jawad would not think he was being impertinent. Fortunately, Aslan would be able to see any approaching vehicles long before the camouflaged lean-to became discernible in the subdued light. What if he saw Arroussi's trucks but Jawad did not respond to his call? Aslan would be sure that Jawad was dead. His only hope would be to turn off the homing beacon, get on his scooter and get away as fast as he could! Aslan scanned the horizon with mounting desperation.

Ayyah! Is that a faint column of dust on the horizon? It was some time after six and the light, such as it was, was beginning to fail. Aslan's hands trembled as he held the binoculars and strained his eyes to see how many trucks were coming. If there was more than one truck it would be Arroussi and Aslan would try to call Jawad. He mentally prepared himself to flee if Jawad did not respond. If there was only one truck it would be Jawad's and Aslan could forget his worries.

Not much later, Aslan was quite sure that only one truck was coming, and before long the huge vehicle was clearly visible as it zigzagged ponderously over the treacherous terrain in the general direction of the lean-to. So Jawad was alive and in no great hurry! Aslan radioed Selim.

The electrician answered immediately: "Talk!" He must have been waiting with his radio stuck to his ear.

"I can see Jawad's truck! He'll be here soon."

"Wasn't he supposed to be there at four?"

"Never you mind. Jawad can be here any time he pleases!"

"I've been waiting more than two hours for your call! This is not the time to make me take risks!"

"That's what you're paid for! Tomorrow morning get the day's radio frequency immediately after Balushi leaves the radio tent and disable the two radios in the foreigners' camp. Then wait for my call. I'll need the day's radio frequency as soon as possible!"

"I know the plan."

"Just make sure you do your job properly!" Aslan broke off the call and put down the receiver. *Too much depends on this Selim. If he fails to get the day's frequency we're all finished!* Aslan tried to relax. Jawad was coming and Aslan would not have to make any decisions! Aslan breathed a sigh of relief but his smoking caught up with him and he started coughing uncontrollably.

5

Aslan had stopped coughing when the huge truck was close enough for its occupants to see him. He climbed on a flat rock and waved one of his blankets. The vehicle stopped zigzagging and made straight for the lean-to. The roar of its engine became louder until it stopped, within a stone's throw of Aslan, with a screech of aging brakes. The driver turned off the engine and Jawad emerged from the cab: "Have you heard anything from Arroussi?" he shouted hoarsely to Aslan. His face was grim.

"Greetings, Jawad!" replied Aslan pleasantly. "No, I haven't heard anything from Arroussi." Hoping to elicit a more cordial response he added: "Arroussi is late!"

Jawad scowled but did not answer. He signalled to the men to get off the truck and they wasted no time climbing down and scattering around the lean-to to stretch their legs and relieve themselves in plain view. Despite the enormous size of the truck they had been squeezed uncomfortably between piles of blankets, rucksacks, wooden trunks, cardboard boxes and crates of ammunition, and they all felt stiff from the long journey. When all the men were out, Aisha and the driver got out of the cab. Aisha wore camouflage fatigues, as did Jawad and some of the men. The truck was left with the wooden trunks and some cardboard boxes full of mineral water in plastic bottles. The trunks were empty except for padding and Aslan guessed that they were to contain the gang's share of the gold and silver on the return trip.

The men were unusually sullen as they bunched together in small groups and talked gloomily among themselves. They started to eat some of the food they had brought with them: bread, dried meat, cheese, hummus and olives. Some had also brought home-cooked food like *dolmas* and *imambayelde*. Before the men had settled down, Jawad shouted that they had better smoke their cigarettes quickly because they would not be allowed to smoke when there was no daylight left. Fawzi, one of the new recruits, dared ask 'Why won't we be allowed to smoke when it gets dark?' He was immediately hushed and his fellows furtively explained that it was because the flames of their lighters would be visible from a great distance. "But we can't be seen from the hill!" Fawzi had protested. He was answered by: "Some of the foreigners might be digging for treasure away from the hill, you idiot!"

Although Aslan was technically second in command he was rudely rebuffed when he attempted to engage Jawad in casual conversation. Even Aisha, who always tried to smoothen things over when Jawad was in one of his moods, avoided talking to Aslan and did not speak more than a few brief words of greeting. Clearly, something had happened on the way that had made Jawad very angry, but Aslan dared not ask

Jawad any questions. When Jawad was in one of his moods he was dangerously volatile and could find any question offensive. On the other hand, if Jawad were still in a bad mood when Arroussi arrived there was no telling what he might do, so Aslan had to find a way of getting back into Jawad's confidence, if only to prevent him from saying or doing something that would get them all into trouble with Arroussi.

But Aslan could do nothing if he did no know what had happened on the way. He wandered among the men exchanging banal pleasantries and hoping that someone would volunteer information, but the men were reluctant to talk to him. Aslan had almost given up when he noticed that Fawzi, the new recruit, was standing alone away from the others. Fawzi was known to be rather dim, but he was in awe of Aslan and might be induced to talk.

6

"Fawzi, why are you standing so far from the lads?"

"Greetings, Aslan," replied the young man sulkily, "I just want to be alone."

"By the end of tomorrow, you shall be a rich man, my brother. That is a reason to be happy!"

"Don't you know what happened?"

"Of course I know what happened! But you are a clever man and I would like to hear again what happened from someone as perceptive as you!" Aslan spoke in a low voice although they were unlikely to be heard.

"I've had enough of Jawad and his moods!" said Fawzi irritably. He spoke louder than he should have.

Aslan found the comment potentially useful. "Fawzi my brother, if you tell me what upset you I could do something to make you feel better! You know that even Jawad listens to what I say!"

"We all think very highly of you, Aslan. You are like an older brother to all the lads."

"Thank you. That is why I feel sad when I see a promising young man like you standing alone and unhappy. Now tell me what happened. I want to hear your version of why Jawad is so angry."

"You won't tell anyone if I speak openly?"

"Of course not. What you say will be our secret forever!"

"Then I'll tell you everything! I'm sure there are some things that even you don't know. The driver of the truck is my friend and he told me exactly what happened."

"I knew you were an intelligent man from the moment I saw you!" Aslan was now sure that Fawzi was a fool.

"As you know," said Fawzi, "Arroussi called Jawad to say that he would be three hours late. The call was put on the truck's loudspeaker so that Aisha could hear what was said, and according to the driver, who heard everything, Arroussi used very polite words and Jawad was flattered. But you know how it is with Jawad, after the call he thought about what Arroussi had said and the more he thought about it the angrier he got! He worked himself up until his temper flared, like a fire that smoulders for a short time and then suddenly bursts out in hungry flames. The driver said that he'd never seen Jawad so angry!"

"What did Jawad say when he was angry?" asked Aslan, hiding his impatience.

"The driver told me that Jawad kept saying things like: 'How dare he make me wait!' and 'I'm not that old dog's servant!'"

"Just as I've been told," said Aslan, "Jawad was furious because Arroussi said he was going to make him wait three hours!"

"Ayy! The more Jawad thought about it the more he became convinced that Arroussi was late only to insult him. And the more his woman, Aisha, tried to calm him down the more he shouted at her!"

"So what happened? You must tell me everything if you want me to help you!"

"I'm telling you exactly what happened. As I told you, the driver is my friend and he saw and heard everything because he was in the cab with Jawad and Aisha. Jawad was furious because he thought Arroussi had belittled him and was treating him like a servant. When the woman tried to calm Jawad down she must have said the wrong thing because he became even angrier!"

"And then?"

"Jawad ordered the driver to stop the truck and said that he wanted to be late too! The driver thought that he needed a pee but he didn't. He just wanted to sit in the truck and do nothing! So they all waited until the woman finally said something about there being no point in waiting in the middle of nowhere. This made Jawad completely crazy. He opened the door, jumped out of the truck, and pulled the woman out. Then after shouting at her some more he hit her and pushed her down and…"

"And what?"

"He pulled down her pants and fucked her in front of everyone!"

Aslan pretended to be shocked: "Just as I've been told! What an insult to the lads! You are right to be upset, my brother."

"Ayy! He has no respect for us at all!"

"You're right! No respect at all! And then what happened?"

"Not much. The woman started to weep and would not return to the truck and Jawad called her a whore and shouted that if she did not return to the truck *at once* he would leave her to die in the wastelands!"

"What did she do?"

"What could she do? She returned to the truck like a beaten dog!"

"Yes, that is what I had been told," said Aslan. "You have every right to be upset, my brother. How can Jawad expect the lads to respect him after he fucked his woman in front of them all?"

Fawzi spoke loudly: "Ayy! When he's angry he doesn't care what we think! The thought of all the gold on the hill has gone to his head!"

Aslan looked behind him in case someone had crept up and was listening: "How much of that gold do you think Jawad wants to keep?" he asked in a low voice.

"I think he wants to keep it all! He wants the lads to get killed!"

"Do the rest of the lads know that?"

"No. But I'll make sure they do!"

"You're a brave man, Fawzi. Think of how much more gold you will get if something happened to Jawad!" Aslan smiled at Fawzi as he spoke, but there was a cunning malice in the smile that Fawzi did not notice.

"You're right, Aslan. If Jawad is killed we shall all get a greater share of the gold!"

Aslan did not answer. He now had a way of getting back into Jawad's confidence, a necessary step to take before Arroussi arrived. He patted Fawzi on the back and promised to make sure that Fawzy would get more gold than the other lads when the plunder was divided among the men.

7

Jawad and Aslan had finished their meal and were sitting at some distance from the rest of the men. They sat cross-legged on the ground facing each other, smoking continuously and saying very little. Aisha, her copper-red hair in a long thick ponytail that fell down her back almost to her waist, stood behind Jawad but did not take part in the conversation, such as it was. She had learned how to survive, and her latest humiliation had been pushed aside and stored in a secret compartment of her heart with all the other affronts and indignities she had suffered. She watched wordlessly, engrossed by the silent tension between the two men, fascinated by their abrupt movements when they raised their cigarettes to their mouths, sucked in the smoke, and then exhaled. Aslan avoided looking at Jawad directly and made sure that his exhaled smoke never touched Jawad, but Jawad exhaled as he pleased, and did not care if his smoke went straight into Aslan's face.

Why do men smoke so much? Aisha suspected that most of the men she knew smoked cigarettes because they thought it made them more attractive to women, but as a woman who followed her own convictions, Aisha had not yet decided what would make a man attractive to her: *Perhaps all men are pigs, and it is my fate to be at the beck and call of this particularly uncouth pig!*

Although he had eaten and smoked, Jawad's mood had not improved much. Aslan, who had been with Jawad since the time when the bandits were led by Attila, knew that he would continue to mull over any real or imagined affront until his temper got the better of him, and Jawad's temper could flare up unexpectedly more than once. He kept his eyes on Jawad all the time, studying his mood: *Jawad should have felt better after fucking Aisha, but perhaps that didn't work because it made him worry about having offended the lads! Worrying always makes his anger worse, and if his mood doesn't improve he might say something to Arroussi that could get us all killed!* Aslan had to get Jawad's thoughts away from Arroussi's late arrival, but it had to be done carefully and in as roundabout a way as possible. *I will make Aisha deal with him! She will know what to say.*

"Arroussi should have known that his lateness would be offensive to a man like you," Aslan said politely, sounding sincere and indignant. Aisha, who was standing behind Jawad, was startled and glared at Aslan, but said nothing.

As expected, Jawad exploded: "That accursed spawn of a filthy dog!" he shouted, "We agreed to meet at five and at the last minute he tells me that he shall be three hours late! Who does he think he is?"

Aisha expected Aslan to speak, but when he remained silent she said: "Have some more to eat, my love, you may still be hungry and food always makes you feel better." Jawad nodded absent-mindedly and fumbled in his rucksack for more bread. When he found a loaf he bit into it angrily and Aisha noticed that his hand was shaking: *I should have seen this while we were in the truck! This is more than just anger at Arroussi's lateness! He is very worried. He is unsure about how the arrival of Arroussi and his men will turn out!* Aisha knew that despite his arrogance and bravado Jawad was secretly afraid of Arroussi. "My love, that old man's lateness won't make any difference to your plans," she said soothingly, "You shall take the hill tomorrow, as you planned."

"But who does he think he is? Making me wait for him like a servant?" Jawad sounded unappeasable but Aslan knew that Aisha was on the right track.

"He is just being cautious, my love. He must be frightened because he doesn't know how well you have prepared everything."

"That doesn't excuse his lateness!"

"Of course it doesn't! Nothing can excuse rudeness to someone like you. But he is worried and afraid."

"What is he afraid of?" Jawad sneered. He intended to be sarcastic but there was a plea for reassurance in his voice.

Aisha put her hand on Jawad's shoulder. "The spies among the workers on the hill are *your* men and not his, my love, and it is *your* man who has the only radio contact with the spies. You are in a position of strength."

"But he has more men than I have!"

"That is not so important, my love. If you so wished you could make sure that when Arroussi arrived he would be greeted by army helicopters with machine guns and rockets. With Arroussi out of the way and your men in place, *you* could attack the hill any time it pleased you"

"I don't have enough men!"

"But you are clever and resourceful, and if you decided to take the hill on your own you could make sure that Arroussi and his men got nothing but bullets."

For a moment Jawad was visibly tempted and Aisha held her breath, terrified that he might decide to take the hill on his own, but then he said: "To get rid of Arroussi too soon would not be in my interest!"

"*You* are wise enough to know that, my love, but *he* cannot be sure.

He has good reason to be afraid!""

Jawad nodded as he chewed. Aisha continued: "Even Arroussi must feel vulnerable when dealing with someone like you. As you always say, powerful men must always beware of those who would betray them if they could. Arroussi is also powerful in his way, but he must be terribly afraid of you at this moment!"

"Afraid of me?"

"Of course, my love."

Jawad turned and patted her thigh.

8

Aslan decided that this was the time to make use of what he knew: "Aisha is right about the need to be wary of traitors, Jawad," he said conspiratorially. "I think you should know that there may be trouble with one of the lads."

"What kind of trouble?" Jawad growled.

"You know the new recruit, Fawzi? He is thinking that his share of the gold would be too small as long as you are leader."

"Fawzi is an idiot!"

"Yes Jawad. But the thought of all the gold that belongs in your pocket is making him ambitious, and his ambition could spread among the lads."

Jawad had not expected that of Fawzi. He looked at the men who were standing or sitting not too far from him, and his eyes narrowed as he searched for Fawzi. When he found him he got up and walked over. Something in Jawad's gait made all the men turn to watch. Fawzi was standing alone, holding a piece of bread in one hand and a piece of cheese in the other. He smiled weakly as Jawad approached, but his face turned pale.

"What have you done?" Aisha hissed at Aslan.

Aslan did not answer. He watched calmly as Jawad took hold of Fawzi by the hand and led him further away from the others. When they were alone there was a brief altercation and Fawzi could be heard earnestly protesting his loyalty. Then Jawad made a sudden lunge and Fawzi crumpled to the ground with Jawad's knife in his stomach. As Fawsi lay on the ground with his legs kicking feebly, Jawad pulled out his knife and wiped it casually on Fawzi's shirt before walking slowly back to Aslan and Aisha, smiling with satisfaction.

"He'll be much calmer now," muttered Aslan while Jawad was still out of earshot.

Jawad returned to his place and sat across from Aslan. Aisha stood behind him, as before. Fawzi's body was dragged away out of sight, alive but unconscious. He would die soon, and be left unburied because nobody had thought of bringing a spade.

9

Jawad was in a noticeably more pleasant mood after killing Fawzi, though it was evident that his rage was still there, smouldering beneath the surface.

"Now we all feel safer," said Aslan to Jawad. The bandit leader nodded and Aisha nodded too, though for different reasons. Her already low opinion of Aslan had dropped much lower.

"Go and find out when Arroussi will be here," Jawad said curtly to Aslan

"Yes, Jawad. We must not let him forget that you are waiting." Aslan got up and went to his radio.

Jawad said nothing while Aslan was away, and Aisha continued to stand passively behind him, absorbed in her thoughts. A few minutes later Aslan returned. Before he could speak, Jawad shouted: "Is the old dog still expecting to be three hours late?"

Something in Jawad's tone made Aisha think: *He's still dreading the encounter with Arroussi!*

Aslan replied with extreme deference: "I did not speak to Arroussi himself, Jawad, but whoever spoke to me said Arroussi will be here before eight."

"By then it will be dark!" snorted Jawad. "They cannot use their headlights and one of their trucks will fall into a ditch or hit a rock!"

"The man I spoke to said they would be here before it is completely dark. As you so wisely pointed out, Jawad, they have to be. They cannot use the headlights and they cannot drive in total darkness."

"What if they get lost?"

Aslan nodded as though agreeing with Jawad but said: "They cannot get lost, Jawad. They don't know where we are, but they are guided by the beacon on my transmitter, same as you were."

Jawad found another way of expressing his anger. "Are you sure you understand what you and Selim are supposed to do tomorrow?"

"Yes, Jawad. As soon as you and Arroussi leave for the hill I shall give Selim the go-ahead. He will get the day's radio frequency from Sergeant Ali and send it to me immediately. He will then disable the radios. If the Army dogs in Basra call I shall pretend to be a radio operator in the foreigners' camp and reassure them that all is well. I shall do that until you have the gold and are on your way home. Only then will I leave on my scooter."

"Good. I suppose Selim knows what to he has to do. Does he know I am here?"

"Yes, Jawad, he knows you are here and knows what to do. As you instructed me, I told him the attack was planned for tomorrow morning at about 8:00."

"That was the original plan. Now I'm thinking of mounting the attack before 7:30. How early can Selim get the day's radio frequency?"

Aisha decided to intervene: "Jawad, the army radio operator gets the day's frequency from ElBalushi at about 7.00. We cannot be sure that ElBalushi will have left the radio operator's tent before 7:15. Selim said that he always stays in the radio tent for about fifteen minutes. If we tell Selim to get the day's Army frequency before that he won't be able to enter the tent because ElBalushi will still be there. If we leave for the hill too early we might arrive before Selim disables the radios."

"It should take Selim no more than a few minutes to get the day's radio frequency from Ali and pass it to Aslan!"

"Perhaps, my love, and perhaps not. Ali is unlikely to give Selim the secret frequency without some resistance. We should give Selim at least twenty minutes to get the frequency and disable both radios!"

"So what if he hasn't disabled the radios before we get there?"

Aisha tried very hard to conceal her irritation at Jawad's inability to grasp the need to follow a schedule. "Don't you see, my love?" she said sweetly, "Selim has to get the day's frequency and then disable the two radios *before* we arrive. If we arrive too soon ElBalushi's guards shall see us before the radios are disabled and the soldiers may kill Selim and manage to send a call for help. It is essential that Selim gets the frequency and disables the radios *before* we arrive."

"You are making it all too complicated!"

"I am sorry, my love. Let me put it in a simpler way. If we arrive too soon the soldiers will be alerted and Selim may get caught before he has completed his task!"

Aslan nodded, effectively siding with Aisha. "I think it will take at least thirty minutes for the trucks to reach the hill from here. The ground gets more rocky near the hill and the trucks will have to be driven slowly."

Jawad looked at him angrily before turning to Aisha: "Stop standing behind me!"

"Yes, Jawad." She padded her way around him and sat on the ground beside Aslan. Jawad spoke angrily to Aisha: "Did I not say to you yesterday that Selim should get the radio frequency tonight from Balushi? It was your idea, woman, that he gets it from that fool, Ali, tomorrow morning. Now we have to wait at least until 7:15 in the morning before we can leave!"

"Selim might have to kill whoever he gets the frequency from," said Aslan, pretending that the murder of Sergeant Ali had not already been decided, "And to kill Balushi tonight may not be as easy as killing Sergeant Ali. Unlike Ali, the major is rarely alone and, from what Selim has told me, he is clever and usually armed. What if Selim fails and Balushi kills *him?* Then Balushi would guess we were coming and radio for help at once. We would have no choice but to run for home as fast as we can in the dark, hoping that the army helicopters would not catch us while we're running!"

"Selim could get to Balushi tonight while he is sleeping alone! He cannot be sleeping with his weapon under his pillow! We could attack the hill tonight!"

"My love, we discussed this before. It would not be wise to attack in the dark, and we might as well reach the hill at about 8.00 tomorrow morning as planned."

"I like working in the dark and I hate waiting!"

"I know, my love. But if we attack in the dark we would risk damaging the treasure and we could also end up shooting one another. Worst of all, Selim has informed Aslan that some of the soldiers are equipped with night goggles. If we attack at night we would be groping about in the dark while they picked us off, one at a time, like wooden chickens in a fairground."

1 0

Jawad scowled and Aisha decided that there was a better way to get his mind off Arroussi. She managed a seductive smile and arched her body coyly: "I think we should prepare to go to bed soon after Arroussi arrives."

"You think I'm in the mood for sleeping?" Jawad barked.

"I can promise you pleasures, my love, that will make the *houris* in heaven blush!"

Jawad's anger subsided at the thought of exotic delights. She pressed her advantage: "You haven't made love to me properly for a long time," she cooed, and her body language said: *The time of Arroussi's arrival is not important. Think about our stay here during the night. I can make it very exciting for you!*

Jawad grinned lewdly, a malevolent grin: "Wasn't the last time *proper* enough for you?"

"I did not have time to enjoy the last time you made love to me, my dearest, but tomorrow you shall be richer than you are already, and to celebrate your coming triumph I want to give you a special performance tonight."

"What if I'm not in the mood?" he teased.

"You are always in the mood, my love, like all great men. And I would like to make sure that you are completely satiated before tomorrow so that you are not tempted too strongly by the foreign women!" Aisha smiled as she spoke.

Jawad grunted: "Huh! So you don't want me to enjoy the foreign women?"

"You are free to do as you wish, my love, but you know that I am more than a match for any foreign woman."

"Some of the foreign women may be prettier than you!"

"Prettier, perhaps, but none will have a fire for you that can match mine."

Jawad changed the subject: "Did you bring my blankets?"

"They're still in the truck, my love. I'll prepare our bed out of sight of everyone."

Aisha got up to go to the truck and Jawad's eyes followed her hungrily. She walked with the grace of a panther and the voluptuousness of her figure was not lessened by her loose-fitting fatigues. When she was out of sight behind the truck, Jawad spoke roughly to Aslan: "Make sure you get tomorrow's Army frequency correctly!"

Aslan nodded respectfully: "I shall listen carefully and set my radio at once."

"And you know what to say if the Army calls?"

"Yes, Jawad. I shall say that Major ElBalushi and Sergeant Ali are at a meeting with the foreigners."

"Don't say Ali is at a meeting, you sheep-brained dolt! Sergeants don't go to meetings! You must say Sergeant Ali is on guard duty!"

"You are right, Jawad, as always."

"Go back to your radio. The son-of-a-dog may be trying to call us."

Aslan returned once again to his radio. When Aisha returned she sat across from Jawad; she looked thoughtful as though preoccupied by uncertainties, but Jawad did not notice.

11

The evening dragged on and the drop in temperature caused a light mist to form, its dampness making it seem colder than it really was. Aslan stayed under his lean-to beside his transmitter. Some of the men covered themselves in their blankets and tried to sleep. Aisha had made a comfortable little nest behind some boulders, out of sight of the others, and she lay with Jawad under the blankets. Despite Jawad's sexual arousal they could not make love because Arroussi could arrive at any moment. It was getting dark and the brighter stars were already shining through the light mist.

Shortly before eight they heard the rumbling and creaking of trucks in the distance. Jawad threw off the blankets and jumped up. "I hear Arroussi's trucks!"

"Yes, Jawad." Aisha got up and folded the blankets neatly. "But they are still some distance away. Sound travels far in this emptiness."

Jawad went to where the others were standing and listening attentively. The men had also heard the sound of the trucks and some were moving about, collecting their things and checking their weapons. Aisha followed Jawad, aware of his sexual frustration and knowing that his temper could flare again at the slightest provocation.

"Arroussi is coming," Jawad shouted to his men. "When they're here stand in a line on either side of me – not too close – facing them! Don't fall asleep on your feet and make sure your weapons are ready! Arroussi may have decided he doesn't need us!"

The men nodded and prepared their weapons, their attention was fully on the noise of the trucks. The rumbling and creaking grew louder as they waited nervously but they could not see the trucks because of the mist.

12

Not much later the black silhouettes of five trucks loomed out of the misty semi-darkness. They had their lights off and moved slowly over the rough ground, tilting this way and that, making the extendable ladders that hung by their sides swing loosely. As they approached they slowed down further before separating and coming to a stop on either side of Jawad's vehicle. Aisha stood beside Jawad, holding her Kalashnikov at her waist. Jawad's men spread out in a thin line on either side of Jawad, facing Arroussi's trucks.

Arroussi's men poured briskly out of the trucks and stood in a half-circle, facing Jawad and his men with their weapons at the ready. They were heavily armed and two carried launchers for rocket-propelled grenades. Each of Arroussi's trucks had carried at least thirty men, and Jawad noticed with some envy that Arroussi's trucks were practically new, with large and powerful engines. But they were smaller than Jawad's and he was glad that he had bought the old but enormous vehicle.

When all the men had come out, Arroussi's son stepped down from the cabin of one of the trucks. Jawad glared at him but said nothing. Then Arroussi and his bodyguards alighted from the cabin of the truck that was farthest from Jawad. Jawad stepped forward impatiently but before he could say anything the old bandit said in a booming voice: "What is a woman doing here?"

Jawad was caught wrong-footed. "This is Aisha," he replied, trying to sound firm and confident: "She is my woman and is always with me."

"I thought we agreed not to bring anyone who cannot fight!"

"I can hold my own with any man," said Aisha coldly.

Arroussi ignored her and spoke again to Jawad: "I have half a mind to turn back and make you pay for all my expense and trouble!"

This was too much for Jawad and he was on the point of making an insulting remark when Arroussi's son, Mukhtar, intervened: "Father," he said, "If this woman can fight like a man and will not jeopardise the business at hand, why make an issue?"

To Aisha's surprise Arroussi appeared undecided. Mukhtar continued: "The gold is almost within reach, father. If we turn back now, we might never get another chance. The woman is not important!"

"All right, then. As long as everyone knows she'll get no special treatment!"

Aisha cast a quick glance at Mukhtar: *Arroussi listens to his son?* Her attention was still on Mukhtar when, to her further surprise, the young man turned to her and said gently: "Is that all right with you, Aisha? You shall have no special treatment, but you shall be given the respect owed to any man."

She gave him a half-smile.

Jawad was very annoyed that Mukhtar dared speak to *his woman*. "Aisha does not expect special treatment!" he said brusquely. "She doesn't need it!"

"Before we waste any more time talking about the woman," said Arroussi gruffly, "I think it might be a good idea if our men get to know each other. It might prevent accidents later."

It was not a good idea for the two gangs to stand facing each other, weapons at the ready, for too long.

"Of course," said Jawad, and waved his hand to indicate that his men could move forward and mingle. Arroussi nodded to his men and they lowered their weapons. One at a time they stepped forward and began to talk quietly with Jawad's men. Both Jawad and Arroussi knew that this was a critical moment. They waited to see how the men would interact. Personal vendettas between members of different gangs were not infrequent and there was a good chance that there were some old scores to be settled. When it was clear that there was not going to be any trouble Arroussi said: "I would like to talk to you, Jawad. It would be best if we were not too close to our men."

"Yes, we have to discuss tactics. Aisha would have to be present too."

"She is your business, not mine," retorted Arroussi.

13

The talk between Arroussi and Jawad lasted less than half an hour. Most details, including the manner in which the treasure was to be divided, had already been settled during previous negotiations. The talk was mostly about how the men were to be deployed and how the weapons were to be used. Aisha thought that Jawad was too anxious to complete the talk quickly and made too many concessions, but she had to admit that she had only herself to blame. As she expected, the moment the meeting was over Jawad practically dragged her to the little nest she had prepared.

An hour later it was completely dark except for the starlight that seeped out from between the clouds; the moon had not yet risen and the mist was still there, although it was less dense than before. Jawad and Aisha lay uncovered and completely naked despite the cold. They were both breathing deeply and were covered in perspiration. Aisha's red hair, which now fell loosely to her shoulders in thick straight strands, looked blue-grey, like everything else in the starlight, but the Circassian's white body seemed to glow in the dark like a pale ghost.

Aisha sat up and said quietly: "Arroussi has made sure he always has some of his men around him, my love." Jawad was lying on his back, and she bent forward to rub his chest sensuously. He always liked that after they had made love.

"I know!" he answered sleepily.

"Don't you think you should also have some of your men around you during the attack?"

"I can take care of myself. Anyway, I don't have men to spare!"

"It would be a wise precaution, my love."

"I don't need bodyguards! Arroussi is an old coward!"

"Do you still intend to kill him?"

"Of course I intend to kill him! And I shall kill his son with my knife, so that I can enjoy watching his eyes grow dim as his miserable life drains away. I don't like the way he kept looking at you." Jawad's intellect was never too sharp after he had made love, although his mood usually improved.

"This is not the time for jealousy, my love. We are heavily outnumbered and the killing of someone like Arroussi could prove difficult and ill-advised." She was careful not to say 'Arroussi and his son'.

"I'll kill him when the hill is almost taken and there are only pockets of fighting left. I'll make it look like an accident."

"It may not be easy to kill him while we are still fighting the soldiers."

"It would be the best time to kill him."

"Shouldn't we consider alternatives to killing that old man?"

"Don't annoy me, woman!"

Aisha sighed audibly, the sound of a woman whose anxieties are not taken seriously. She shook her head in frustration, making her long hair swing one way and then the other. In sunlight, such a gesture would have inflamed the passions of any healthy man, forcing him to take her wishes seriously. Here, with only the stars and the sexually satiated Jawad to witness it, the gesture was wasted.

Jawad closed his eyes and was about to drift off into sleep, but Aisha wanted to know more about how Jawad planned to accomplish the deed, if he had any plans at all. The killing of a man such as Arroussi was not a trivial matter and she was strongly against it.

"Jawad, I really don't think it is a good idea to kill Arroussi while we are fighting the soldiers. We don't know what his men might do if Arroussi is killed. They might turn against us!"

"His men hate him as much as I do. They'll be happy to work for me after he and his son are dead."

"Jawad, I don't like this. He has more than three times as many men as we have."

"I don't understand your reluctance to let me kill Arroussi when I please!"

"He is a powerful man, my love. Even if you succeed in killing him there may be repercussions long after we are back home."

"What repercussion can there be if there are no witnesses?"

"Some of the workers or the foreigners might see you kill him, and maybe later mention the killing of Arroussi to others. In time, Arroussi's friends are sure to learn how he died."

"When it's all over there won't be anyone left except my men and possibly some of Arroussi's, and I can persuade them to keep their mouths shut."

"You are planning to kill all the workers? And all the archaeologists?"

"This is too important to leave witnesses, beautiful one."

"Jawad, the workers are poor people with families!"

"Are you becoming sentimental?"

"Of course not, but killing indiscriminately could start all kinds of vendettas against us. At the least it would make us social pariahs, and killing the archaeologists would bring foreign pressure on the police to catch us."

"The police have tried to catch me before. I dealt with them very effectively!"

"This would be different, Jawad. There are powerful people behind this expedition!"

Jawad grinned: "That is why killing them all is the only way to ensure that after tomorrow we shall live in luxury without worries. When the treasure is converted into money I shall live like a king, and you shall be the envy of all women!"

"Am I not that already?" There was a resentment in her voice that she could barely conceal.

"Only because you have *me*," he taunted.

She climbed over him and knelt astride his stomach. *Kings have harems. Is he planning a little accident for me too?* "Why don't we discuss how you intend to do this thing?"

"I don't need to discuss it with *you!*"

"Don't you trust me?"

"Of course I trust you. But I won't listen to you trying to change my mind!"

"Jawad, my love, even the smaller share of the gold is more than enough for us!"

"It's not enough for *me!* I told you I intend to live like a king!"

"Jawad, you can live like a king without making new enemies. Killing Arroussi and his son is bad enough, but killing the workers and the archaeologists could bring us problems we cannot foresee."

"Get off me, woman! I've got everything planned in my head!"

Instead of getting off him she moved forward onto his chest and clamped his head tightly between her thighs. "You are only a man," she murmured, "and your head can be crushed so easily!"

His ears were covered and he could not hear her, but his lust was aroused once more and he moaned with pleasure. When she loosened her thighs he pressed his head forward and buried his tongue deep within her, but she was too absorbed in her misgivings to enjoy it.

29

THE MURDER OF A SOLDIER

1

"SELIM!" HISSED THE short, bandy-legged man.

It was late morning and the sun was shining. But the air was damp and despite the sunshine there was the promise of rain, perhaps in the evening, perhaps at night. The sky was speckled with small grey clouds that slowly coalesced, forming larger, darker, clouds. Selim was alone in the tent reserved for electrical repairs, working on a metal detector whose insides were scattered over his workbench. He looked up and stared coldly at the bandy-legged man who had parted the flaps of the tent: "What do you want?"

The man was very excited: "They've found more treasure!" he exclaimed.

"Are you sure no one can hear you?" Selim asked sternly.

"Yes, yes!"

"Is there much gold?"

"I don't know."

"Is there *any* gold?"

"I don't know."

Selim sighed: *Why are fools so good at wasting people's time?* "How did you find out about this supposed treasure?"

"I was at the north-south trench... when someone said that the Turks had found beautiful things... beneath a pile of stones... large stones!" The bandy-legged man was so overwhelmed by what he was saying that he ran out of breath several times as he spoke.

Selim put down the screwdriver he was holding: "Did you go to look?"

"Naturally!" The bandy-legged man nodded vigorously. "I left what I was doing and went to look at once! There was a hole like a low tunnel that went deep beneath the stones... and there was a lot of scaffolding and..."

"Don't waste my time!"

"Yes, yes! The treasure was wrapped in soft paper padding and was being brought out in large bundles by some foreign students."

"Not the workers?"

"No. The bundles were heavy but the workers weren't allowed to carry them!"

"I see." *So whatever they found was fragile!* "Were there lots of bundles?"

"Ayyah! Lots! About six! Maybe ten!"

"Did you see what was inside any of the bundles?"

"I couldn't!"

"They might have found nothing but pottery, you idiot! Find out what was inside the bundles and don't bother me again unless you're sure they found gold or silver!" Selim picked up his screwdriver, pushed a screw into a small hole in the metal detector and screwed it in tightly. He expected the bandy-legged man to leave but he did not: "Will you tell Jawad that it was I who told you about the new treasure?"

"If any treasure was found. Now go!"

The bandy-legged man was about to leave when Selim called him: "Wait!"

"Yes, Selim?"

"Do you know today's date?"

"Yes. It is the 14th."

"Does that date mean anything to you?"

"No..." the bandy-legged man looked perplexed: "Should it mean something? Is something important happening today?"

"No. Nothing is happening today. Now go!"

The bandy-legged man left, mystified and very confused. Selim returned to his work on the metal detector: *The date meant nothing to him! So the lads in the camp haven't heard anything!* The workers' grapevine was very efficient, any hint that something was happening or about to happen would be embellished and disseminated through the workforce in no time at all. Selim found it hard to concentrate on repairing the metal detector: *Tomorrow I shall be a rich man!*

2

A week earlier Aslan had called to say that on the 14th of the month Jawad and Arroussi, with as many men as they could muster, were to convene at Aslan's lean-to. This was the precursor to the attack on the foreigners' camp that Selim had been waiting for since the discovery of treasure. The attack would start on the morning of the 15th. Until the visit of the bandy-legged man Selim had not allowed himself to be unduly keyed up by Aslan's message. There was an old saying that the heavens tended to mock those who wished too strongly for something to happen, and Selim did not want to jeopardise his chances by building up his hopes. But surely the discovery of more artefacts on the day before the attack was a good omen! Even if no gold or silver were found, a new discovery on this important day could not be just coincidence! *The heavens sent me the bandy-legged idiot so that I would know that my dreams will come true! The heavens are smiling upon me, telling me that Jawad will succeed and I will become rich!* For the first time during his stay on the hill Selim felt he could indulge freely in his daydreams without fear of tempting fate. Being an obsessively vindictive man, his first thoughts were on how he would use his wealth to bring pain and humiliation to those who had offended him in the past, but his thoughts soon turned to a very attractive Jordanian girl he had often seen in the camp. She had long legs, the eyes of a doe and a skin as smooth as pale jade. She had figured prominently in Selim's night-time fantasies for some time, but he had never dared hope that the fantasies would come true and – until now – he had tried not to think of her during the day. But Selim now believed that the heavens were smiling upon him, and he was sure that Jawad would let him have the girl when all the soldiers were dead and it was time for rewards! *Surely Jawad will remember how he depended on me to disable the radios and get the day's frequency from Ali! Surely he shall not refuse me the Jordanian girl!* Of course, Selim would have to kill the girl after he had finished with her, but this only made thinking of what he would do with her more exciting. On many a night Selim had imagined her on her knees pleading for mercy, weeping and begging to be allowed to do *anything* that would please him, *anything* that would prolong her life. Selim had an active imagination in such things, and his sadistically erotic thoughts mingled deliciously with his expectation of sudden wealth. Selim forced himself to return to his work. He picked up his tools and resumed the repair of the metal detector.

3

Jawad had told Aslan that he would arrive at Aslan's lean-to at four in the afternoon. Aslan was to call Selim immediately after sighting Jawad's truck, to let him know that the preparations for next day's attack were under way and to answer any queries that Selim might have. This was to be Aslan's last radio talk with Selim. In anticipation of Aslan's call shortly after 4pm on the 14th of the month, Selim had retrieved his transmitter-receiver from its usual hiding-place during the night of the 13th and hidden it beneath the false bottom of his iron toolbox, which he kept in his tent. Keeping the transmitter in his tent was dangerous, as it was possible that the soldiers would carry out another search of the workers' quarters, but it was much safer than retrieving it from its hiding-place during the day.

Shortly before four in the afternoon Selim took his metal toolbox and made his way casually to the southern ramp. The bandy-legged man had not returned and Selim assumed that the Turkish team had only found pottery. This was disappointing but could not be helped. Selim did not go directly to the southern ramp but made a slight detour so as to walk past a group of soldiers who were standing idly by the refectory.

"Hey Selim," shouted one of the soldiers pleasantly, "where are you going with that heavy toolbox?"

"I'm going to the car park," Selim replied, equally pleasantly, "There is a problem with the electrics of one of the 'Rovers and I've been told to fix it.".

"It looks like you've got all your tools in that box! Are you thinking of taking the whole car apart? "

"I don't know what's wrong with the electrics so I'm taking all the tools I might need. It's better to carry everything once rather than find I'm missing something and have to come back to get it!" The walk from Selim's tent to where the expedition's vehicles were parked normally took more than ten minutes, and walking down the southern ramp, which was covered by loose earth full of small stones, was particularly irksome.

"That metal box looks very heavy," joked another of the soldiers,

"Would you like one of us to help you carry it?"

"I would like that very much!" said Selim, "But whoever helps me carry my toolbox will end up quite a bit shorter by the time he reaches the car park!"

"Well, none of us can afford to get shorter. So you'll have to carry it on your own!"

"I was afraid you would say that," laughed Selim, "but thank you anyway!"

He waved at the soldiers and continued towards the ramp that led to the car park. *What fools! They will all die tomorrow because they didn't bother to check my toolbox!* The soldiers' missed opportunity to find his radio reinforced Selim's belief that Jawad's success, and his own god fortune, were pre-ordained.

Having made sure that no one would wonder why he left the camp, Selim continued to the car park. The soldiers were suspicious of everyone who left the camp ever since he had taken the inventory from ElBalushi's safe, and they were sure to check his story about a problem with one of the Land Rovers. But the story was true and would be corroborated. Selim had known about the faulty electrics for over a week but had done nothing about it because he needed an excuse to leave the camp during the afternoon of the 14th, so that he could wait for Aslan's call away from the camp. Now that the archaeologists had stopped going on picnics, the car park was usually deserted and Selim could take as long as he wished to repair the fault while he waited for Aslan to tell him of Jawad's arrival

4

The fault in the Land Rover turned out to be trickier than Selim had expected but, even so, the repairs had been completed for more than an hour when Aslan called. Selim had waited with growing impatience inside the vehicle, and even thinking of what he would do with the Jordanian girl had not made the time pass faster. It was past six o'clock when Aslan called and Selim was hungry and annoyed. He tried not to show his annoyance and said nothing about the new discoveries because, after all, Jawad would not be interested in the finding of more pottery. Anyway, he was too anxious to return to the camp to have supper. Fortunately Aslan was not in a talkative mood and Selim was soon back on the hill. After leaving his toolbox in his tent and covering it with dirty laundry he made straight for the refectory. The meal turned out to be unusually good and Selim was in a happy mood when he finished his supper and returned to his quarters, but his mood changed when the bandy-legged man came to his tent and peered in sheepishly.

"Selim?"

"If you have something to say keep your voice low," growled Selim, "There are people all around us!"

The bandy-legged man entered the tent and closed the flaps behind him. He was, if anything, more excited than he had been in his previous visit: "I have very good news!"

"Talk!"

"Yes Selim. The Turks *did* find treasure. Lots of it! They found clay jars full of pretty little trinkets. Some were made of gold, others were made of silver and some were made of bronze! The trinkets were all mixed up!"

"Are you sure?"

"I was told that one of the jars broke as it was being carried and lots of little things made of gold and silver and bronze fell out and scattered all over the ground! That is why everything had been wrapped so carefully. The jars broke easily because they were heavy with gold and silver things!"

"Why didn't you tell me earlier?" *If only this idiot had told met before I talked to Aslan! Now I have to call Aslan tonight!*

"I came earlier but you weren't here!"

"Very well," said Selim coldly, "Thank you for coming again!"

"Does that mean a lot more money for all of us?"

Selim ignored the question: "Where is the new treasure now?"

"In the storage tent. With the other things they found."

"Are you sure?"

"Yes, yes! They let me carry one of the jars to the storage tent after they had added more padding and wrapped it very carefully. You will tell Jawad that it was I who told you about the new treasure?"

"I'll try. Now go!"

The man left.

Selim found it difficult to feel pleased at the news. He had a bad feeling about having to call Aslan one final time. It would have to be in the middle of the night, just a few hours before the attack on the hill. He had to call because if he did not tell Aslan about the newly discovered gold and silver Jawad could accuse him of withholding information. He would probably get very angry and might not give him the Jordanian girl to do with as he pleased!

5

The night was misty and cold, and the heavy clouds were laden with rain: *It hasn't rained for weeks and it will probably rain while Jawad is coming for the treasure! It might even rain now!* Selim pushed his long knife under his belt and put on a knee-length loose black leather coat. With his small radio tucked under the coat he made his way cautiously to the western edge of the hill. It was the safest place from which to call Aslan at night, as it was rarely patrolled by the guards because the precipitous drop made it unlikely that anyone would climb to the hilltop from there. The western edge of the hill was also where Selim normally hid his radio, behind a loose stone that overhung the precipice. The hiding-place was not too far from his tent, which was at the northern edge of the camp. Selim's intention was to quickly tell Aslan about the new discoveries and then return the radio to its hiding place. With a bit of luck and common sense the guards could be avoided. Even so, Selim moved with extreme caution, for although the night was dark and the hiding place was not too far there were two armed soldiers guarding the storage tent and at least three other soldiers patrolling around the camp.

Selim reached the remains of the western defensive wall and looked carefully around him to see if anyone was in sight. It was very dark except for the lanterns that were distributed around the camp, mostly around the latrines. He could neither see nor hear any of the guards and Selim squatted on the slightly elevated rubble, taking what concealment he could from the bushes that grew profusely on the stony ground. The thin mist diffused the light from the lanterns, the closest of which was about a hundred metres away.

With his eyes peering into the semi-darkness in case anyone approached from the camp, Selim turned on his transmitter. It made a barely audible hum but no light came on, for Selim had removed all LEDs from the device. He pressed the button which activated the bleeper on Aslan's radio.

"Aslan!" he whispered.

There was no answer.

The son-of-a-whore is sleeping! He waited a few seconds and then pressed the button again. "Aslan!" This was as loud as he dared.

There was no answer. Selim was about to press the button for the third time when a voice behind him said sleepily: "Who are you talking to?"

There was barely enough time to hide the transmitter under the leather coat. No time at all to fold the aerial. Selim had expected any guards to come from the direction of the camp and be silhouetted in the dim light of the lamps above the latrines, but whoever had crept up on Selim had come along the edge of the precipice, probably along the rubble of the defensive wall, and in that direction there was only darkness. Selim's first reaction was acute fear and he felt the muscles at the back of his neck tighten, but the fear quickly changed to fury: *It's not right that I get caught tonight! In a few hours Jawad will be here and the girl would have been mine!* With icy deliberation he turned to look, expecting to see one or more guards. The image of the girl, which had dominated his thoughts since the first visit of the bandy-legged man, dissolved in a cloud of anger.

But there was only a single soldier behind him, a young man, no more than a boy. His hair was in a dreadful mess and despite the cold he was barefoot and wore only a jacket and a pyjama top over his military trousers. Selim noted that the boy was not carrying a weapon. "Who are you talking to?" the boy asked again.

Selim did not answer at once. The soldier was no more than three metres away and Selim got up to face him with deliberate slowness. It would not do to alarm the boy. The transmitter under Selim's coat pressed against his chest and he could feel his heart pounding against the flat metal.

"I'm talking to my younger brother," Selim said softly. He knew it was a stupid thing to say but it was all he could think of. "It is a dark and lonely night and I miss him terribly." *The dog has to be kept quiet at all costs!*

"Your brother's name is Aslan?" The soldier looked confused; he found Selim's reply vaguely suspicious but he was too sleepy to think clearly.

"It *was* Aslan," said Selim in a sad voice. "He is dead now, but I always call his name when I am alone and look up at the stars."

"But there are no stars tonight. They are covered by clouds!"

"Oh the stars are there," said Selim. "Even if we can't see them. Tomorrow it may rain and I won't be able to come alone to this quiet place and think of my brother."

417

"I understand," said the boy. "I lost my father recently, and although I am a grown man I sometimes cry at night when I am alone. I say: 'Father! Where are you?' and wonder if he can hear me."

"I also wonder if my dead brother can hear me," said Selim as he moved closer to the boy. "But I try not to shed the tears which come to my eyes when I think of him. I don't want him to see my tears. We loved each other dearly and that would make him sad."

"How did your brother die?" The young soldier was no longer suspicious; he found it natural to go to a lonely spot to mourn a dead brother.

"He died of an illness... a terrible illness," replied Selim, and again he moved closer to the young soldier. The boy did not move back and Selim moved closer still.

"My father also died of a terrible illness," said the soldier, "it was very difficult for all of us, especially my mother, but there was nothing we could do to save him except pray."

Selim took the initiative: "But what are *you* doing here?" His right hand crept stealthily towards his knife. The boy was now less than a metre away.

"I... I came out for a walk because I couldn't sleep," stammered the boy. He was visibly embarrassed. "I had a nightmare. I dreamt that my father was calling me to join him!"

"And that frightened you?" asked Selim caringly. He placed his left hand on the boy's shoulder. "I would not be frightened if I dreamt that my brother was calling me!"

"Yes. Dreaming of my father frightened me! I don't know why. I fear..." The boy stopped abruptly and was suddenly fully awake. He raised his hand and pointed accusingly at the thin metal shaft that protruded from Selim's coat. Selim had not managed to fully retract the aerial of his radio.

Before the boy could cry out, Selim pulled him forward by the shoulder and swung his knife viciously under the boy's throat, tip uppermost. There was a ripping sound and a gush of blood spurted over Selim's coat and shoes. The boy made no more than a faint gurgle as he fell to his knees and then collapsed face down onto the stony ground, his hands clawing at the earth. Selim knew that the boy would not make any further sound and, satisfied that he had made his kill as quietly as possible, dragged the still-moving body to push it over the edge of the precipice, head first. But when the head and arms hung over the precipice the boy's belt caught on something in the rubble and would not move further. Selim's temper flared and he kicked the boy repeatedly, hoping to dislodge the snag, but the body would not come loose and Selim's added effort, made in anger and without due care, caused a few large stones to fall from the remains of the defensive wall. In the silence of the night the stones clattered loudly as they hit the stony ground below.

One of the guards in the camp gave a cry of alarm and there was a flurry of voices from the direction of the storage tent. The north-west of the hilltop was suddenly illuminated by a blaze of floodlamps.

Selim cursed under his breath: *May the souls of this dog and his father burn forever in hell!* In a desperate panic he tried to lift the boy so as to heave him over the edge but stopped when he realised that the now alerted guards would probably hear the thud of the body hitting the ground. *Better leave him as he is and hope that the guards won't find him!* Crouching low, he pulled out some dry bushes and covered the body as best he could. There was no time to hide the transmitter behind the stone that overhung the precipice. After a quick look to see if anyone was coming he loped awkwardly back to his tent. He just managed to enter his tent and throw his blood-stained shoes under the bed when he heard the sound of several pairs of boots coming his way. Selim fell on the bed and covered himself with a blanket so as to hide his blood-spattered coat in case the guards came into his tent. He prayed fervently that none of the soldiers had seen him.

He could only wait to see if anyone would come in pursuit. The minutes passed with agonising slowness but there was no further sound of approaching guards. So the soldiers had not seen him! Selim continued to wait, unsure of what he would do if the soldiers entered his tent. Eventually, he heard one of the guards say: "It must have been some stones falling off the side of the hill. This happens sometimes without cause." A few minutes later the sound of boots moved away and then the floodlamps went out. Selim took a deep breath and got off the bed to wipe the blood off his shoes. His bloodstained coat he stuffed into his laundry bag. *If they find the body in the morning it will make no difference, Jawad will be on his way and they'll have no time to worry about one dead soldier when Jawad arrives!* He hid the transmitter in the secret compartment of his toolbox and fell again on his bed, feeling suddenly exhausted. He would explain everything to Jawad the next day and Jawad would forgive him for not letting him know about the new treasure because he had killed a soldier. Jawad would be very pleased about that. All in all, things had worked out well. He calmed himself down by thinking of the Jordanian girl and his erotic thoughts soon mingled with the fog of sleep, bringing sweetness to his dreams.

The boy died silently as he lay partly on the hilltop and partly over the edge. His blood drained copiously from the gaping wound and fell soundlessly onto the ground below.

30

THE LAMIA IS CAPTURED

1

IT WAS A vibration in the rock that would have been totally inaudible to human ears, but the lamia awakened instantly. She had been sleeping in her favourite *place-for-rest*, a small lightless cavern deep beneath the ground between the hill and the deserted village. Although she knew that it was still light outside, she sat up sleepily and blinked as she focused on the noise that had intruded into her sleep. The rumble was muffled and distorted by distance as well as by the layers of earth and rock that lay above her, but she recognised the faint vibrations as the sound of a *truck*. When Mike's friends had arrived at the hill their *trucks* and *cars* had shaken the ground with the rumble of a hundred chariots.

She was not fully awake: *Could that be Mike and his friend coming to pick me up at the deserted village? No. That is for tomorrow night, half-way between sunset and sunrise!* The thought of her appointment with Mike brought on a passionate longing to see him and her imagination soared: *Tomorrow Mike shall take me to a city!* When she was a child her father had taken her to many cities, and she remembered how each had been different, how the people of each city had different customs and sometimes even spoke the language slightly differently. When she became queen she had had to travel across her lands to meet her people, and she remembered the cluttered houses, the towers of the palaces, the endless enclosing walls whose ramparts had been decorated in her honour with bright-coloured banners: *That was a long, long time ago. Things were simpler then!* She sighed as the flashbacks cascaded through her mind. She redirected her thoughts and imagined walking through narrow, earth-paved streets with Mike, stopping only to look at the wares of the peddlers or the colourful fruit of the fruit-sellers... *But wait, wait! Mosul may not be like the cities I remember... in Mosul I might be like a child in a dark place, frightened and bewildered! She smiled: Mike shall be my oil lamp! He shall shine beside me!* The thought of Mike brought joy, hope and a sense of security, but these feelings crumbled as she realised that she was indulging in dreams: *Have you not dreamt enough during the countless nights of your solitude? You must contain your hopes! The gods often mock those who hope too strongly!*

She became pensive as her hopes dissolved and became doubts. Her life in Mosul might not be as idyllic as she hoped. She knew very little about the people in Mike's world. If they were like the Assyrians she had known their perception would be limited and it was possible that they would see her either as a goddess or as a monster. She would not let them see her as a goddess, but if they saw her as a monster would they not try to kill her? If Mike tried to protect her could they not also try to kill him? She would never allow that, she would destroy herself rather than let her presence bring danger to Mike. She would gladly die if that were the only way to save the man to whom she had given her body and her soul... *If I have a soul*, she reminded herself, and the thought brought her back firmly to the present.

There was only one truck. It was still far but was moving closer. She wondered if these could be the people Mike had said would come to live around the remains of the temple. By pressing her ear against different parts of the cavern wall she could tell the direction from which the sound came. She guessed that the truck was heading towards the temple, but when the rumbling sound stopped she was puzzled because the truck was evidently still far from the hill. The truck had stopped in the direction of the deserted village; perhaps close to the village ruins.

What if they are not friends of Mike? Despite her long life, the lamia still held a tribal view of humanity. She knew that people of different countries were usually on amicable terms but competed in everything and often fought their neighbours to increase their wealth or replenish their resources. As a queen and a goddess she had learned that such relationships also existed between individuals, and she had classified people as *friends, enemies,* and those who were too far to be relevant. Her ways of classifying people had remained essentially unchanged during the long years of her loneliness, although now her social criterion was Mike, and people would be *Mike's friends, Mike's enemies,* and the rest who were too far to be relevant.

She was curious and slightly apprehensive about the newcomers, but she wanted to wait for the sunlight to be completely gone before she ventured above ground, for even the remnants of sunlight would be painful. The area around the hill was honeycombed with underground tunnels and over the millennia she had discovered that many of these tunnels led from her underground caverns to openings from which she could get to the surface. Some of these exits she had not used for a long time and it was possible that they were no longer usable; others she had used recently. One of the latter was the dry well in the deserted village. It lay in the open space at the centre of the ruins and was flanked by a few parched trees. The dry well was just a round hole in the rocky ground, a pace wide and many paces deep, and was concealed by a large flat stone that the wind always covered with earth. Many times small groups of *Mike's friends* had left the hill in a horseless chariot and come to the deserted village. When the distinctive noise of their *car* had awakened the lamia she had hurried to the well, driven by a childlike curiosity to find out more about *Mike's friends*. They would sit on rugs and talk in a strange language, unaware that she was quietly listening from beneath the flat earth-covered stone, enjoying the proximity of people from Mike's world. Sometimes, when they were at some distance from the well and the sun was covered by thick clouds, she would be more curious than cautious and lift the flat stone just enough to brave the sunlight and peep for a few seconds. She would watch for as long as she could while they ate strange food and drank from long, odd-shaped jars. She was always surprised at how much they laughed while they spoke, and she had often wondered whether Mike also laughed a lot when he was with people he knew.

The lamia realised that she was daydreaming again, an understandable habit for someone who had not felt a sense of urgency for centuries: *These newcomers might not be Mike's friends. Perhaps they pose a danger to Mike!* Her apprehension returned and she became impatient, but to emerge now would be painful as there could still be some sunlight left. The sunlight would be gone in a little while and she would emerge from the well to reconnoitre. If the truck had stopped not too far from the ruins it was possible that, by the time it was dark enough for her to venture out, the newcomers would have wandered into the deserted village. That could be dangerous and she would have to be very attentive, sensitive to any noise the newcomers might make: *I should be able to know where they are unless they are intentionally quiet and waiting for me!* The thought brought distant memories of fear and persecution. Not all strangers who had come to the temple had been lured by the hope of finding treasure; some had come to kill the *thing* that was said to haunt the ruins. *But that was long ago, when I had not yet learned to be careful. Now nobody remembers me. These newcomers are not here to hunt Amalishah; they are here for something else!*

2

When her instincts told her that the sunlight was gone she put on some of the clothes that Mike had brought her from Mosul. She first put on what Mike had called *underwear*. It was strange clothing whose only purpose, she surmised, was to keep her outer garments from touching her private parts. Then she put on a light blue skirt. She was at first suspicious of the *zip* on the skirt, but after a few fumbling attempts she found that it offered no problems. Zips were fun! She pulled the zip up and down several times, marvelling at how it kept the cloth together. The blouse was a different matter as her fingers were not used to dealing with buttons, but that was also dealt with, after some effort. Should she wear the shoes? *No, better leave them behind, they make too much noise on hard ground!* What about the jewel that hung from her neck? *Better leave that behind too, it would glitter in the moonlight!*

It was time to get to the well. She made her way swiftly through the totally dark tunnel that linked the cavern to the deserted village. As she ran she thought of how easily she could become accustomed to wearing these new clothes. They were very comfortable and the cloth was smoother than anything she had worn before. When Mike had first shown her the dresses and blouses she had been surprised at how even the colours were, at how they *blended* so perfectly into the cloth. Apart from the *tiny flat round things* that held the blouse closed, these clothes were much better than anything she had ever worn. Even Assyrian queens did not have cloth as smooth as this! *But I must not think of those times. I shall start a new life soon! With Mike!*

Even she could not see in the complete darkness of the labyrinthine tunnels, but she knew from long experience all the passageways beneath and around the hill. She could tell where she was in the tunnel by the texture of the rock and the shapes of the bumps and cracks. She could run very fast and it did not take her long to reach the bottom of the well. Many, many planting seasons earlier the shaft of the well had been much deeper and had extended deep into a hole that stretched far below the level of the tunnel from which she came, but she had filled in the hole so that she could stand beneath the shaft that led up to the opening on the surface. The tunnel continued beyond the shaft but she had only explored it once many planting seasons earlier and had found that soon after the well it narrowed and became impassable.

Standing at the bottom of the shaft she explored the cavity above her with her fingertips, seeking the familiar handholds. The opening at the surface, covered by the large flat stone, was almost three times her height above her. When she was ready to clamber up the shaft, she paused for a few seconds to listen carefully for any sounds from the village. She could hear the sound of muffled voices but these were at a considerable distance away. From close by there was only the faint sighing of the wind through the remains of the mud-brick walls in the deserted village.

When she was satisfied that there was nobody in the vicinity of the well she sprang upwards into the shaft and climbed rapidly by bracing herself against the sides with her arms and legs. She had almost reached the flat stone at the mouth of the well when she heard the rumblings and creaks of more trucks in the distance. She stopped immediately and her body became rigid while she held herself motionless just below the top of the shaft. She could tell that there were many trucks this time. They were still far from the village but they were getting closer, and they appeared to be going to the same place as the earlier truck. She waited patiently until the sounds stopped. There was some brief talking in loud voices and then only a confused hubbub, suggesting that the newcomers had settled down and were all talking at once. Still she waited, poised beneath the flat stone, until she was sure that no one would come towards the village. Then she quietly lifted the stone and looked cautiously out to see if there was anybody among the ruins. The stars were covered by clouds and the moon had not yet risen, but there was ample light for her to see. Only a faint mist impeded her vision. The ruins were deserted. She silently shifted the flat stone aside and lifted herself out of the well.

3

She crouched beside the opening of the well like a cat ready to pounce while her ears probed the stillness around her. When she had confirmed that there was nobody in the vicinity of the ruins she quietly pushed the flat stone back over the mouth of the well and covered it carefully with earth.

There were rain clouds in the sky, travelling swiftly like long black shadows that hid the stars as they passed. The moon would be up soon, and she had to make sure that she was completely alone before any moonlight managed to slip through the dense clouds. She sniffed the damp air: *It will rain! Perhaps later in the night, perhaps tomorrow.*

From the well she could not see the trucks or any of the newcomers because some low crumbling walls were in the way, but she could hear the newcomers' voices clearly. The trucks had stopped farther from the deserted village than she had estimated, more than two hundred paces from the ruins in the direction away from the hill. She wondered if the newcomers *intended* the deserted village to lie between them and the hill: *Probably not. Anyone coming to the temple from the direction of the land of the Hittites would pass that way!* The village lay on a natural road, and she remembered that when the Assyrians had been on good terms with the Hittites many richly laden caravans, bringing pilgrims and gifts, had come this way. *The newcomers came on the best way for their trucks, but they stopped far enough for Mike's friends not to be able to see them even if they left the hill!*

To see farther the lamia moved away from the well and took the risk of standing up. She could now see six trucks in all, one noticeably larger than the others, just visible through the mist. The newcomers' camp was too far to see any details and, surprisingly, the camp was completely dark, for despite the rapidly falling temperature the newcomers had not lit any fires. *They don't want anyone to know they're here!* The lamia was now convinced that the newcomers were not *Mike's friends.*

Cautiously, she made her way towards the trucks by flitting from one clump of boulders to another, sometimes crouching, sometimes on all fours. It took her longer than she would have liked, and she was only half way to the newcomers' camp when a brief gap in the clouds bathed the landscape in silver and black.

Moon god! Brother in the sky! Do not betray me!

The newly risen moon obliged by hiding behind a cloud. The clouds, herded by a strong wind, were gathering into a thick canopy with gaps that gradually grew smaller and less frequent.

4

The intermittent moonlight permitted her to get to within less than a hundred paces of the camp, close enough for her to see the faces of the newcomers. There were more of them than she had suspected. *There are at least two hundred of them!*

The trucks had stopped close to where the ragged man had lived ever since Mike's friends had come to the hill. The ragged man had lived alone and had built himself an *incomplete tent* that offered some protection from the wind and the sun. The lamia had heard his arrival soon after Mike's friends had arrived. He had used something that made a lot of noise, like a little horse with wheels. She had not understood why he had not joined the others in Mike's camp, or why he was so preoccupied with the odd box-like toy that never left his side. Now that many others had joined him she realised that the ragged man belonged with the newcomers, not Mike's friends. There was much that she did not understand.

These new people did not laugh and she did not like the way they behaved. They spoke furtively and she sensed a tension in their voices: *These men have violence on their minds! They are like a raiding party before a raid!* Her suspicions deepened when she was close enough to notice that many of the men wore clothing that would blend with their surroundings in daytime. *They would only dress like that if they don't want to be seen easily!* The only weapons that she could identify were knives, which were in short sheaths tied to their belts. They carried no shields and they had no spears or swords or bows, but she was in no doubt that the stubby metallic things that some held at their waists, or the long metal-and-wood things that some carried over their shoulders, were weapons.

She knew that Mike's friends had found the statue of white stone, so they must have found the other things that her panic-stricken priests had hidden in the deepest of the food-cellars. Over the centuries many people had come to search for the hidden riches of the temple, but they had not found the food cellar because it was buried beneath the rubble of the living quarters of the senior priests. Were these people after the gold? Why else would they come but not go to Mike's friends and greet them? Why else would they carry weapons? *These men intend to attack the hill!* The thought that Mike might be in danger gave her an uncontrollable sense of apprehension.

She decided to watch what they would do. Some of the men gathered around the ragged man with the box-toy and he talked to them at length, as though explaining the function of this thing that seemed so significant to him. Although the lamia did not understand anything that the ragged man said, she concluded that the box-toy was somehow important. If these people were Mike's enemies then perhaps the removal of the box-toy would weaken them. What if they were not Mike's enemies? The box-toy would have to be returned, somehow.

Meanwhile there were other people to observe. There was only one woman. She had red hair (red hair!) and was obviously the mate of one of the leaders, a man with yellow hair. The man with yellow hair spoke harshly to all but a very tall man with a grey beard, who was also apparently one of the leaders. When most of the men were either sleeping or trying to sleep, the two leaders had a talk away from the others with only the red-haired woman and a tall young man sitting with them. The tall young man had a strange thing on top of his nose. Mike also wore such a strange thing, and he had explained to her that it made him see better.

The four only talked for a short time, and they talked as though they were merely confirming things that had been decided before. The red-haired woman did not speak, but the men spoke in tones that showed that there was little trust between them, although they pretended otherwise. When the yellow-haired man had finished talking with the two tall men he took hold of the woman's wrist and pulled her roughly to a place that was hidden from view. At first there was silence, but then the yellow-haired man made all sorts of sighs and grunts and the lamia guessed that he was making love to the red-haired woman: *These people are very different from us! They can behave like animals. Could he not have waited until everyone was asleep?* Although she was astonished at this *uncivilised* behaviour, the lamia was not interested in their lovemaking and decided that the only thing of importance was the box-toy. If it were a weapon then she would take it and make sure that Mike got it.

5

The sighs and grunts of the yellow-haired man eventually stopped and for a short time he talked sleepily with the woman. The lamia waited patiently until she was certain that everyone was asleep. She waited a bit longer to be sure and then crept cautiously towards the place where the ragged man slept beside the box-toy. The sky was covered in clouds and it was almost completely dark, as the newcomers had still not lit any fires. The lamia noticed that, unlike the raiding parties of her day, the newcomers had not posted any guards, which implied that the newcomers believed themselves to be the only dangerous men in the vicinity.

The ragged man's *incomplete tent* was next to the *trucks*, and there were men sleeping all around it with their bodies pointing in all directions. Padding softly in her bare feet, the lamia circled the camp and approached the ragged man's *incomplete tent* from the side that had the least sleeping men. The ragged man was snoring loudly as he slept beside the box-toy. The lamia noticed that he had something tied around his wrist but, not knowing what a cable was, she did not realise that whatever was tied around the sleeping man's wrist was connected to the box-toy she intended to carry away. The clouds moved away from the moon just as she lifted the radio, and the faint tug on the cable awakened Aslan.

"Yah!" he shouted, immediately awake. **"Leave that thing alone!"**

Shocked at her own carelessness, the lamia put the box-toy down. The ragged man's shout awakened everyone in the camp and the lean-to was surrounded by coarse-looking men. Some of them held knives while others held the stubby metal things that the lamia felt certain were weapons.

The lamia's first reaction was an almost irresistible urge to run but she did not know the power of the stubby metal weapons. If she tried to run it was possible that even her extraordinary speed would not save her. She stood with her arms at her sides, unmoving in the faint moonlight, her face expressionless.

Arroussi bellowed: "Don't turn on any lights! And no shooting!"

Someone lit a cigarette lighter but turned it off immediately. To Arroussi's annoyance, Jawad lit a small candle.

"Who is this woman?" Jawad barked, "Is she one of yours, Arroussi?"

"Don't be an idiot!" Arroussi barked back, "She must be one of the foreigners! And put out that candle!"

"Let's kill her then," said Jawad calmly as he blew out the candle. He approached the lamia with his knife pointing forwards. The blade glittered in the moonlight.

"No, wait!" exclaimed Mukhtar. "She might be useful as a hostage. We cannot do anything sensible in the darkness. Before we set out tomorrow we can ask her what she was doing here. We can also ask about the camp's defences. She might know something useful!"

Jawad was going to ignore Mukhtar but Arroussi stepped forward: "My son is right," he rasped, "You can have the pleasure of killing her tomorrow, Jawad, *after* we question her! She was obviously after the radio!"

"Yes, that is curious, don't you think?" said Mukhtar, "Perhaps she knew how much our plans depend on Aslan's radio."

"How would she know that?" asked Aisha.

"Perhaps they know more about us than we suspect!" said Mukhtar.

"Are you saying that one of my men is a traitor?" growled Jawad, and there was dreadful menace in his voice.

"I'm only saying that we should question her before we do anything hasty," replied Mukhtar evenly. Although his assault rifle was pointing at the ground, his finger was on the trigger and the rifle could quickly be raised to point at Jawad. Mukhtar had been warned about how unpredictable Jawad could be.

"What I would like to know is how she got here," said Arroussi, "It would take someone hours to walk here from the hill, and she is barefoot."

"If she had come by jeep after we arrived we would have heard it," said Aisha, "and if she was here before we arrived we would have seen her jeep before it got dark."

"So a jeep must have brought her here and left before you arrived," said Mukhtar.

"If she were hiding in the ruins we would have caught her!" said Jawad angrily, "Some of my men explored the ruins when it was still light and there is no place she could hide!" He was anxious to break this exchange between Mukhtar and *his woman*.

"She might have been hiding behind a boulder outside the ruins," said Mukhtar, "That could mean that the army knows about Aslan!"

"That is not possible!" exclaimed Aslan. He was alarmed at the possibility that the people on the hill knew of his presence.

"She is obviously a spy!" someone said.

"Perhaps not," said Mukhtar, "Perhaps she just wanted to spend the night in those old ruins. If she's an archaeologist, she might have wanted to know what the old stones have to say."

"Alone?" said Aslan. No woman he knew would want to spend

the night alone in the wilderness. Least of all among ruins that were probably haunted.

"Why not?" replied Mukhtar, "These foreign women are different from ours; they are much more independent and sometimes get strange ideas."

"It is certainly possible that she only wanted to study the ruins and spend the night there," said Aisha, "As an archaeologist she might have been brought here, expecting to be picked up tomorrow. Aslan's shelter is far enough not to have been seen when she was dropped off."

"Then it is possible that she has one or more companions," said Mukhtar, "What could she do alone among the ruins?"

"I would rather believe she is an Army spy!" snarled Jawad, "That would explain her interest in Aslan's radio!"

"The army would not send a woman to do a man's job!" Arroussi said evenly. "Even a woman as tall as this one. And they would certainly not send a foreigner!"

"Then she is most probably an archaeologist who wanted to explore the ruins of the village," said Mukhtar, agreeing with Aisha, "And when she saw us she naturally hoped to get hold of the radio to warn her people on the hill."

"You are probably right," said Aisha, addressing Mukhtar but keeping her eyes on Arroussi.

"Let's not be stupid!" said Jawad with a sneer, "The foreign woman must be a spy! Tomorrow morning I shall pry the truth out of her before I kill her!" He stared at Aisha, daring her to contradict him.

The fierce jealousy that came over Jawad whenever Mukhtar spoke to Aisha annoyed Arroussi, but this was not the time to do something about it. Jawad had to be distracted and placated before he did something silly that would jeopardise the success of the attack on the hill. He addressed Jawad directly: "Let's tie her up and get up early to interrogate her. I have no doubt that if she knows anything useful you will be able to bring it out of her."

"I look forward to asking her lots of questions first thing in the morning!" said Jawad, putting away his knife, "and I can promise you that she will not enjoy it!"

"Meanwhile," said Arroussi, "I'll send some of my lads to look around the old ruins, in case there is someone else there."

"Send your son with them," said Jawad, "He is the one who thinks there may be other spies."

Arroussi nodded to Mukhtar.

"I'll go at once," said Mukhtar, "If that is what you wish, father."

Arroussi saw that his son understood the need to appease Jawad. "Yes. Go now and take five men with you. Remember that if more foreigners are hiding out there in the dark they may be armed."

When Mukhtar had left, Arroussi said: "We must tie the woman securely."

"Why not tie her to a truck?" suggested Aisha, "The trees around here wouldn't hold a goat." The trucks were just beyond the place where the men had been sleeping.

"That is a good idea," replied Arroussi. He was about to order his men to tie the woman when Jawad said: "*My* men will tie her up. To *my* truck!"

"Very well."

Jawad ordered some of his men to take the lamia away. "Tie her up tightly," he added, "She is very tall and could be strong."

They could not find any rope but Jawad's truck had a hauling winch at the front, so they tied the lamia's hands behind her back with the spare wire cable of the winch. The cable was of plaited steel and was stiff, so that they had to use a pair of large pliers from the truck's toolkit. She offered no resistance as they wound the cable tightly round her wrists and then her ankles, and she let her body go limp when they pushed her to the ground and attached her feet to the fender of Jawad's truck.

CONFIDENTIAL MEMO

From: Major-General Murad Sharkaoui
To: Colonel Badr ElHaleel

IN CONFIDENCE

Further to the information recently conveyed to you regarding the possible amalgamation of two or more criminal organisations it has been brought to my attention that an illegal but well known supplier of black-market weapons has sold and delivered to a buyer or buyers unknown

1.   A large number of <u>assault rifles and ammunition</u>.
2.   Two <u>rocket-propelled grenade (RPG) launchers</u> with an unknown number of grenades.

The delivery of the above took place between five and eight days prior to the date of this communication.

As you know, terrorists and those with political grievances have a special interest in RPGs but our sources are adamant that the ammunition and the weapons were NOT purchased for political ends. The said sources cannot be named but are deemed reliable.

Please consider the above information as pertinent to any decisions you may need to make regarding the international archaeological expedition for whose safety you are responsible. Given the possible urgency of said decisions you shall not need clearance from me but consider yourself as acting with the authority of the Ministry, which will need to be informed as soon as possible though not necessarily prior to the implementation of your decisions. I remind you that a serious misadventure to the archaeologists and/or the accompanying students is certain to have long term repercussions at both national and international level.

Please do NOT convey the content of this communication to the officer in charge of the military escort.

[Signature]

Major-General Murad Sharkaoui

[Stamp with date]

433

32

THE LAMIA ESCAPES

THE LAMIA LAY unmoving on the cold, damp ground with her hands tied behind her back and her feet attached to the fender of Jawad's truck. The bright moonlight came and went, subservient to the whim of the passing clouds and diffused by the light mist. Although the thick wire cable around the lamia's wrists and ankles had been twisted viciously so that the coils dug into her flesh, she was not particularly uncomfortable. The pain was dull and easy to forget. Nor was she unduly worried; she was sure she could break the bonds whenever she wanted.

As she waited for the men around her to return to their sleep, she tried to fathom the strange emotions that came to her unbidden, like the leaves that fall, one at a time, from a dying tree. She found these novel emotions interesting, for they revealed facets of her character that had never before been stimulated into existence: *It's the newness of being captured! Of being so close to my enemies! The newness of being touched by strangers!* Before Mike she had only been touched by her parents and her personal female servants who had helped her dress and undress. Her heart beat faster than usual and she felt aimlessly agitated. Were these emotions fear? No, she could remember how fear felt. This was different: *I have never been captured before and my emotions are wild and difficult to control!* But whatever these emotions were they offered no help at all, and with an effort of will she suppressed them and calmed herself down.

The truck was at the edge of the bandits' camp and the sleeping men were all to her left. To her right was empty desolation interrupted only by boulders and the occasional stunted tree. None of the men had lain down to sleep less than seven paces from her. Were they afraid of her? Although she had not understood their language she had not sensed any fear of her in their voices or in their body language. Quite the opposite, their body language showed that they considered her physical abilities contemptible. So they could not have known what she was. Had they known they would surely have killed her. So why did they lie down to sleep so far from her? *They do not trust each other! Their leaders must have ordered them to keep their distance from me!* This said something about the intentions of the leaders. *They intend to use me somehow!*

She listened to the breathing of the men closest to her, focusing on the breathing of each man in turn. Yes, they were all asleep. It was time to get rid of her bonds and escape. She took a deep breath and tensed her arms to try and loosen her bonds, once, twice. The thick wire loops hurt her wrists but did not give way.

What kind of rope is this?

She tried again, exerting as much strength as she safely could, but again the winch cable proved too strong. She would break her bones before she would sever the thick metal strands. For the first time in her long life she felt defeated and helpless.

She felt a coldness creep up her spine and her heart thumped louder, faster. Her chest ached from the pounding. *This is fear!*

She did not want to die, not this way, not trussed up like a sacrificial animal. She tensed her muscles once again, as hard as she dared, but again the metal cable did not yield. *Mike, is this how my brief dream of happiness shall end?* It was not the uncouth men she feared, but the sun. Dawn was yet far but it was sure to come, and even if the sky were covered by clouds enough of the sunlight would seep through to burn her to death, slowly and very painfully.

To forget her fear she thought of Mike. She imagined what it would have been like to live with such a knowledgeable man, among people he knew, among friends. She imagined the joys of travelling with Mike to places she had never heard of, of meeting the people of distant and wonderful lands. But these imaginings all carried the reminder that they were never to come true, and her thoughts inevitably led back to the hopelessness of her predicament. No matter how hard she tried she failed to subdue her fear and the thoughts of what-might-have-been only inflamed her sense of helplessness. She was going to die here, and Mike might never know why she had not waited for him to take her to Mosul. Who would tell him of the burnt corpse these uncivilised people would find in the morning? The thought of Mike never knowing what had happened to her was too painful and she closed her eyes tightly: *Don't think of Mike or of what might have been! Think of how you can escape dying from the sunlight!* But the more she thought of escape the more she realised that there was no way out, and so intense was her concentration that, for a brief moment, she lost control of her mind and she saw, like an echo of distant memories, a kindly face looking down at her. The eyes were huge and the grey-black beard was beautifully trimmed: *Father! You have not visited my thoughts for such a long time!* The face was frozen in a loving smile and she felt a sudden joy interwoven with an almost overwhelming nostalgia. *Father, are you so alive in my heart because I shall be joining you soon? Will you remember me after all those years?*

Very briefly the clouds melted away from the Moon, and the moonlight washed away the vision. The lamia felt desperately, hopelessly alone. She looked up at the silver orb: *Moon God! Brother in the sky! Help me!* But the moon could only peep intermittently through the clouds and offered no help.

Her mind teetered between fear and sadness, and she almost failed to hear the sound of furtive movements from behind the boulders where the red-haired woman lay with her yellow-haired mate. But there was no doubt now that someone was coming towards her very stealthily. The lamia half hoped that it would be the yellow-haired man with his knife: *Better the knife than the sun!* The lamia pretended to be asleep until whoever was stealthily approaching her was two paces away, then she opened her eyes and turned her head to face him.

It was the red-haired woman. She was barefoot and wore only her trousers and a loose shirt. When she saw that the lamia was aware of her presence she put her finger to her lips to indicate the need for silence. The lamia understood but could not guess the woman's intentions. The red-haired woman squatted beside her and the lamia offered no resistance as she was gently turned over onto her side. Holding the same heavy tool that the men had used to tie her up, the red-haired woman silently undid the bonds on her wrists. The cable was stiff and it was not an easy task, but the lamia was almost overcome by hope.

When the lamia's hands were freed the red-haired woman undid the bonds on her ankles. The lamia got up with a bound and the woman stood up too, facing the lamia who was a full head taller than her. The lamia smiled and nodded gracefully by way of thanks. The red-haired woman did not smile back, but took her silently by the hand and led her a short distance away from the camp.

Ten paces from Jawad's truck the red haired woman whispered very quietly in broken English: "You free now!"

The lamia did not understand the words but guessed their meaning: "Why are you doing this?" she whispered in Assyrian. She did not expect to be understood.

The red haired woman seemed surprised at the guttural tones, but she said in English: "Something very bad will happen. If you want to be alive go away far. Run!"

The lamia nodded as though she understood. She took the red haired woman's hand and squeezed it gently before turning away and running towards the deserted village. The speed with which she ran made Aisha gasp.

Later, Aisha wondered why the tall foreign woman had run towards the ruined village and not the hill.

33

THE BANDITS SET OFF FOR THE HILL

1

IT WAS SOON after dawn when Aslan rushed to tell Jawad that the prisoner had escaped. Jawad was sleeping soundly with his head nestled in Aisha's bosom and did not hear Aslan approach, but Aisha was a light sleeper and half-opened her eyes to see who was coming. When she saw that it was Aslan she moved her hand away from the assault rifle that was by her side under the blanket. Aslan ignored Aisha and gently shook Jawad's shoulder: "Jawad! The woman's escaped!"

Aslan's voice percolated into Jawad's sleep but did not awaken him completely: *Who is this idiot?* He groaned in protest.

"Jawad wake up! The foreign woman's escaped!"

It sounds like Aslan... But then the message sank in: **"What?"**

"The woman has escaped, Jawad!"

Jawad pushed Aisha away and threw off his blanket with a loud curse. Springing to his feet he grabbed Aslan by the shirt collar: "What do you mean she's escaped?"

Aslan cringed and barely managed to whimper: "She's gone!"

Jawad hastily put on his clothes: "How could she be gone, you son-of-a-dog!" His voice was an octave higher than usual. Aslan cringed all the more.

At the sight of Jawad's uncontrollable fury Aisha felt that she had awakened into a nightmare. She did not regret what she had done but it was only now that she fully confronted the possible consequences: *If someone saw me with the foreign woman Jawad will kill me very slowly!* She waited under the blankets without moving while Jawad got dressed: *Best not to attract attention – but I must not appear indifferent in case he feels slighted and directs his fury at me!* She remained silent and totally motionless, staring wide-eyed at the cloud-laden sky, ready to let Jawad know how shocked she was at the news. But it was soon apparent that Jawad was too furious to notice what she was doing. When he left without further words she got up and collected the blankets. She folded them neatly and placed them on the ground.

With Aslan in tow Jawad hurried to where the lamia had been tied to the fender of his truck. Arroussi and Mukhtar were already there, surrounded by some of their men. Jawad's men were also there but they stood in the background, unsure of what to do because they knew that Jawad would be in a murderous mood and did not want to get in his way. The rest of the men shuffled about aimlessly like wasps around a threatened nest; none of them spoke, and the only sound was the deep voice of Arroussi, who was talking to a stocky middle-aged man: "And you're sure the bindings were secure?"

"Yes, I checked them last night before going to sleep, as you told me."

"The woman could not have undone them herself?"

"No. The winch cable had been twisted very tightly and whoever released her would have had to use pliers or some other tool. He probably used the same pliers Jawad's men used to bind her. They had been left on the ground."

"Could the woman have broken the cable somehow?"

The middle-aged man shook his head. "Tewfiq, an elephant could not break that winch cable!"

Jawad just managed to catch the end of the conversation. "What's all this about the woman escaping?" he shouted at Arroussi. The old bandit said something quietly to the middle-aged man and the man hastily withdrew. Aslan, fearing that Jawad would be offended at not being answered immediately, said in a timid voice: "The woman must somehow have broken her bindings!"

Arroussi heard what Aslan said but spoke to Jawad: "I have just been told that the prisoner could not have broken her bindings. Someone *released* her, probably using your pliers!" Arroussi was not used to being shouted at, but this was not the time to waste anger on Jawad. He was mainly concerned with the escape of the prisoner and was prepared to be tolerant of Jawad's rudeness.

"How do you know it was done with *my* pliers?" Jawad shouted, "Haven't *you* got any pliers in your trucks?"

"Jawad, it doesn't really matter whose pliers were used to release her! The point is that someone used pliers to untie the captive! She escaped with someone's help!"

"Why did you say it was done with *my* pliers?"

"Your pliers were lying on the ground next to your truck!"

"My lads must have dropped them after they tied her up!"

Arroussi's patience was being tried to the limit. "Please let's not talk about pliers! What is important is that someone *untied* the foreign woman! She did not escape on her own!"

"Are you saying that one of *my* men untied the foreign woman because he used my pliers?"

"No Jawad. Anyone could have released the foreign woman using your pliers. The question we must answer now is: What do we do about it?"

Jawad was not prepared to make any constructive suggestions and just glared at Arroussi blankly, as though his fury had deprived him of the power of speech. Mukhtar said: "There are really two questions, Father: How do we identify the man who released the tall woman? And did she have time to warn the Army escort? The second question is the more important!"

2

Jawad had not thought beyond the fact that the woman had escaped, and he had not considered the possibility that she could have warned the Army unit on the hill. He seized the opportunity to disagree with Mukhtar: "No! The first question is the more important! We cannot take the hill until we catch the man who did this. There must be a police spy among your men!"

"Or yours!" retorted Arroussi.

"There cannot be a spy or a traitor among my men," said Jawad with a scowl. "No spy would dare join my men and none of my men would dare to turn traitor!"

Mukhtar could see that his father was beginning to lose his temper. "No spy would dare join my father's men either," he said placatingly. He did not want the antagonism between his father and Jawad to escalate. "So it is most likely that there is no spy, although there might be a traitor."

"And why would one of the men turn traitor?" sneered Jawad. "The woman could not have had enough money to bribe anyone! One of the men must be a police spy who did not want me to torture her while I asked her questions!"

Aslan added: "The police spy must have helped her escape because he knew that Jawad would torture her!"

Mukhtar thought for a moment. "My father took every precaution to make sure there were no spies among his men, and I am sure, Jawad, that no man would dare be a spy among yours. But it is possible that the foreign woman did manage to bribe someone. She was quite attractive and some of the men are young. She might have offered herself to one of the men on condition he released her."

"You may be right," said Arroussi broodingly. "Jawad and I made sure that there were no police spies among our men, but nobody can guard against a lovesick fool!"

"Well!" said Jawad venomously, "If your son is right, I want to lay my hands on that lovesick fool. I would physically rip out his private parts and let him bleed to death screaming in agony!"

"I feel the same way, Jawad," said Arroussi. He turned to his son: "Mukhtar, you were among the first to find that the woman was gone. Did you look at the footprints around the spot where she was tied?"

"I did," said Mukhtar, "But there were many footprints. All I can say is that whoever released the captive was barefoot, but then so were Jawad's men when they tied her up and most of us are barefoot even now. Also, many of the men went behind the boulders to relieve themselves during the night. There are footprints everywhere. I could only distinguish the prisoner's footprints at some distance from us, where she ran away."

"Your son can read footprints?" asked Jawad. He was impressed but did not want to show it.

"It's something he learned at summer camps in America," replied Arroussi matter-of-factly, "As you know, he studied at a university in America."

Jawad anger took a turn for the worse at the mention that Mukhtar had studied in America. Without thinking he said: "Your son's stay in America could have made him soft on foreign women!"

Arroussi gave his son a quick look. *To save the tall woman from torture is the kind of thing my son might do!* Yet he felt no anger towards his son, only a sudden fear for his life: *If my son released the foreign woman then even I might not be able to save him from this bloodthirsty maniac!* Arroussi turned and looked steadily at Jawad: "Mukhtar was with me all night!"

"Are you sure?"

"Very sure!" Arroussi replied icily, daring Jawad to contradict him. *If Jawad persists in this I might have to kill him!*

But Jawad realised that he had gone too far. There was only Aslan to help him while Arroussi was surrounded by his men. Arroussi could easily kill him, and Jawad was also suddenly horrified at the possibility of losing face: it *could* have been one of his men who had released the woman! *One of the lads who tied her up! The touch of her warm body could have inflamed some idiot's passion!* With a shrug he said: "Perhaps we should look for the lovesick fool after we have the gold."

"That is an excellent idea," said Arroussi. "We'll find the traitor after we get the gold. We shall have more time then."

3

Mukhtar said: "It would help us if we knew *when* the prisoner escaped!"

"How would that help us?" asked Jawad.

"The hill is many kilometres away," replied Mukhtar. "Even if she ran for much of the time it's likely that she hasn't reached the hill yet. Why don't we find out whether the Army escort has been warned before we decide anything?"

"Selim will be expecting my call after about 7:15," said Jawad. "If I call Selim now his radio will be off."

"Then there is nothing we can do until 7:15," rasped Arroussi. He looked at his watch. "It's only six-forty. Let's eat quickly and get ready to leave."

"I still want to get my hands on whoever released the woman!" Jawad snarled, "Whether she managed to warn the foreigners or not!"

"I don't think we can do much now," said Arroussi, "So we might as well eat. Please call your man Selim at 7:15 and let me know what he says."

The men prepared for a quick breakfast. Whether they attacked the hill or whether they ran for home it was going to be a long day, and it was possible that they would not have time to eat later. Someone asked: "Can we light a fire to make coffee?"

"Yes," said Arroussi, "Light small fires without smoke!" The only stove in the camp was Aslan's and that was not enough to make coffee for all.

Jawad's provisions were in his rucksack, which had been left behind with Aisha. As he walked back to the place where he had spent the night he noticed that Aslan was following closely behind him. "What are you coming with me for?" he shouted, "Go and make me some coffee!"

"Yes, Jawad."

"Bring it to me and then get back to your radio!"

"Yes, Jawad."

Aslan brought his stove from the lean-to and joined Arroussi's men who were making coffee. The rest of the men were busy eating or collecting their gear, which they tossed into the trucks.

Aisha was waiting for Jawad, standing fully dressed in her fatigues and with the blankets neatly folded on the ground beside her. She had washed her face with wet tissues and her hair was in a neat ponytail. "So the woman has escaped, my love," she said quietly, "Do we know how?"

Jawad responded by kicking the pile of folded blankets.

"If she has warned the Army escort we might have to change plan," continued Aisha, picking up the blankets and folding them again.

"I don't think she had time to reach the foreigners. We'll catch her and kill her on our way to the hill!"

"How did she escape, my love? Were her bonds improperly tied?"

"Someone released the cable and set her free. I'll find out whether she warned the foreigners when Aslan calls Selim."

"Do we know who let her escape?"

"Not yet. It was probably some lovesick idiot brought by Arroussi. He let her go in exchange for sexual favours!"

"It's not yet seven, my love. Let's have something to eat and then decide what to do."

"I just want coffee!"

"You must eat something. The coffee Aslan is getting you will not be enough." *And eating may improve your mood!*

"What's the point of eating now? If that accursed whore warned the foreigners we'll eat in the truck as we rush for home hoping to escape the army helicopters!"

"So it's possible that we don't attack the hill?" Aisha tried not to sound hopeful. She had been unable to put the intended massacre of the workers and the foreigners out of her mind: *The killing of Arroussi is not important any more, but the killing of the archaeologists and the workers would be a dreadful tragedy. So would the killing of Mukhtar.*

443

The last thought surprised her.

"No!" shouted Jawad, "Of course the attack is not off! The foreign woman did not have time to reach the hill. When we catch up with her I'll hack her head off with my knife the moment I see her! Slowly, one hack at a time!"

"Of course my love."

Aisha remembered how fast the foreigner had run. She had untied the foreigner's bonds sometime in the middle of the night, but did not know the time. At the speed the woman could run she might have reached the camp and the combat helicopters could already be on their way. Aisha's hopes and fears see-sawed in her mind: *But surely the woman could not run at that speed over any distance, and the hill is almost fifteen kilometres away!* Could the woman's escape be used to persuade Jawad to call off the attack? It was worth a try, provided she was careful not to arouse his suspicions. In a humble voice she said: "My love, we must find out if the woman warned the camp."

"Don't tell me what to do!" Jawad snapped as he left. Aisha picked up the blankets and followed him meekly. Her face was expressionless but she was praying fervently: *Please God, let the tall woman be safe among her friends! Make Jawad call of the attack! Please spare us the carnage!*

4

Aslan was sitting impassively next to his radio.

"It's almost seven," said Jawad, "Call Selim and ask him if the camp has been warned!" Jawad had eaten a large breakfast and his anger at the escape of the woman was still there but under control.

"I should call him just after 7:15 at the earliest, Jawad. ElBalushi might still be with Ali and Selim might not have done anything yet!"

"Call him now!"

"Yes, Jawad."

Aslan called Selim with Jawad bending over his shoulder to listen in. Selim answered almost immediately.

"Why are you calling me now? It's not yet seven. You're lucky I'm alone in my tent!" Selim's nerves were evidently on edge.

Jawad heard what Selim said and grunted: "Huh! She didn't warn the foreigners!" He backed away from Aslan, whose body odour was very unpleasant.

"Is anything unusual happening at the camp?" Aslan mumbled into the microphone.

"What?" said Selim. "Talk clearly!"

Aslan repeated the question, more clearly this time.

Selim must have answered in the negative because Aslan turned to Jawad and shook his head: "Nothing's happened!" he said quietly.

"Is he sure?" asked Aisha.

Aslan spoke again to Selim and then turned to Jawad: "He is sure everything is normal. He wants to know why we think something might have happened."

"Tell him everything shall be explained later." Jawad was smiling. "Tell him to get today's frequency as soon as he can and not to wait for your call. Tell him to call you immediately after he gets today's radio frequency!"

Aslan conveyed the message and switched off the communication without waiting for a reply. Aisha was on the point of saying something but decided to remain quiet. Jawad returned to Arroussi to tell him that the woman had not warned the foreigners.

Arroussi was very pleased with the news. He bellowed at the men: "The foreign woman didn't reach the hill yet and the radios in the camp shall be disabled soon!"

All the men cheered, including Jawad's. The possibility that the foreign woman might have warned the military escort, and that combat helicopters could already be on their way, had been preying on their minds. Only Aisha and Mukhtar did not seem very enthused by the news. Mukhtar took his father aside and said: "We must not feel safe until the radios are disabled, father. Perhaps we should not leave for the hill until we are sure that the military escort will not call for help. Until we are sure of that we won't know whether to drive towards the hill or away from it!"

Arroussi nodded and put his hand on his son's shoulder. "I see that you have kept your head, Mukhtar. I'm glad. Leaders must never rejoice prematurely. But it was necessary to give the men hope, as doubt or despair would cloud their thinking. If necessary, we shall take their hope away later."

"So what shall we do now, father?"

"Now I have to make sure that our friend Jawad does not leave for the hill while there is still a chance that the escort is warned before the radios are disabled."

Jawad was not at all pleased when Arroussi told him that they

445

would have to wait for Selim's call. "That is not what we planned!" he said, showing his annoyance.

"I know," said Arroussi gravely. "But what good would it do if we set out to attack the hill only to realise, too late, that Selim failed to get the secret frequency because the woman warned the military escort?"

"What if Selim forgets to call Aslan?"

"This not something he can forget," said Arroussi, "if Selim doesn't call then we'll wait for a short time and then know that something is wrong!"

"I hate waiting!"

"I know, Jawad. But if your Selim is any good we won't have to wait long."

"Even if the woman reaches the hill it's possible that ElBalushi won't try to call for help until it's too late!"

"It's possible," said Arroussi, "but we can't depend on that happening. Balushi is more likely to call for help the moment he hears about us."

Jawad put his hands in his pockets and shrugged. He always did that when he felt compelled to bow to circumstances: "As you said, it will be a short wait!"

"I hope so," said Arroussi amiably

"How long should we wait for Selim's call?" asked Mukhtar, "If Selim is caught he will never call us. We have to decide now on how long we are prepared to wait."

Before Jawad could reply, Arroussi said: "Perhaps we should wait until 7:45? Does that sound reasonable to you, Jawad?"

"Make it eight o'clock," said Jawad, making sure that he had the last word.

5

Selim radioed Aslan soon after 7:30. Aslan ran to tell Jawad, who was standing with Aisha, Arroussi and Mukhtar.

"The radios in the foreigners' camp are destroyed and I've got today's frequency!"

Jawad could not control his joy. He slapped Arroussi on the back and shouted: "Let's go! The gold is waiting for us!"

Arroussi looked down at Jawad and smiled broadly, he was too pleased to be offended by the sudden familiarity. Aisha looked away and tried to hide the tightness in her chest. Mukhtar noticed Aisha's pained expression and frowned, but he remained silent. The men did not cheer when told that the attack was on. They climbed into the trucks sullenly because, now that the attack had been decided, they were suddenly aware that many of them would not live to enjoy the spoils.

With Jawad's truck in the lead the bandit force sped towards the hill as fast as the terrain allowed. Only Aslan was left behind. His scooter lay on the ground next to his lean-to and he sat beside his radio, under the lean-to, wearing his headphones. He was to stay by his radio until 7 in the morning of the next day. Although Jawad expected the attack to be over before nightfall, he wanted Aslan to be able to reassure the Army in Basra for as long as possible. The Army office could call at any time, and they could call more than once.

34

ASLAN IS REMOVED

1

THE SIX TRUCKS were mere specks in the far distance, barely visible beneath the canopy of iron-grey clouds that covered the morning sky, when Aslan suddenly sensed that something was horribly wrong. Dangerously wrong. He felt like a bird in a cage with an invisible cat clawing at the bars. The acute sense of unease had struck without warning while he was lying under his lean-to, thinking of nothing in particular, enjoying the silence after Jawad and Arroussi had left. But now Aslan was tense and alert: *Someone is watching me!* Aslan always paid heed to instinctive warnings and he sat up to scrutinise the part of the landscape that was visible from beneath the lean-to. There was no-one he could see. Somewhat reassured, he took a deep breath: *It must be the dismal weather. It hasn't rained for weeks and it will rain by the bucketful soon!* He looked up at the sky: *There must be a lot of electricity in the air... they say that electricity in the air makes people nervous!* But Aslan had experienced sultry weather before and it had never given him such disquiet. He got up and scrutinised the landscape again, this time in all directions, but again he could not see anyone. Did not Jawad say that one or more companions of the tall foreign woman might be hiding in the ruins of the deserted village? *Arroussi's son was to clean up the place but perhaps he didn't search well enough! Several stupid foreigners might be hiding in the ruins and watching me!* The village ruins were too far for someone there to pose a threat, but just to make sure Aslan brought out his binoculars and scanned the ruins. There was no-one to be seen: *If some foreigners are watching me the idiots are too frightened to show themselves!* Aslan muttered a string of choice insults directed at all foreigners. The insults made any foreigners hiding in the ruins seem less threatening and Aslan's unease almost withdrew. *Well! They can watch until they die of thirst!* Aslan made himself comfortable under the lean-to with his radio beside him.

But the unease was back in full force ten minutes later. *Maybe it's not some stupid foreigner watching me, maybe something else is wrong!* Could the radio be faulty? A problem with the radio would be a catastrophe! Aslan checked the wiring and methodically tested the radio. There was nothing wrong with it. He checked to see if it had been set at the correct frequency. As far as he could remember what Selim had told him the radio frequency had been set correctly: *So what is making me feel like this?* Aslan was bordering on panic and his imagination sought refuge in his memories. Many years earlier, when Aslan was not yet twenty, he had spent some months in Egypt, and in the Eastern Desert he had met an old Bedouin who had told him something very strange: The old man had said that, before a battle in which many will die, the Angel of Death strolls casually among the men and marks those he will take and those he will leave behind. Nobody can see the Angel of Death, of course, but each man feels his presence, and such is the mark of the Angel of Death that those who are doomed to die feel confident and unafraid while those who will survive feel uneasy and apprehensive. That is why, the old man had explained, those who are chosen to die enter the fray joyfully while those who shall live feel anxious and melancholic. Aslan had not paid much attention to the old Bedouin's words, but now, completely alone and with the oppressive weather weighing upon him, what the old man had said seemed likely to be true. But then, the unease implied that he was safe! *Maybe I feel this way because many of the lads shall die while I sit here safely!* He chuckled to himself: *May the soldiers kill off the lads like flies! Every lad who gets killed makes my share of the gold bigger!* The treasure in the foreigners' camp was never far from his thoughts and the possibility that Jawad might fail to take the hill never occurred to him.

Aslan was pleasantly preoccupied thinking of his share of the gold when a drop of rain fell on the radio with a sharp *plink*. Although he had expected it to rain he cursed loudly. The plastic of the lean-to had too many holes to be effective against a downpour and he was lazily thinking of getting up and covering it with the larger of his two louse-infested blankets when the radio bleeped. *Ayyah! The dogs are calling already!* With a twinge of excitement he realised that the attack on the hill could have started already. This made it easier for him to play his little charade! It would be amusing to talk to the fools in

Basra knowing that their fellows on the hill were being slaughtered! He put on the headset and spoke into the microphone: "This is Private Musa!" He was sure he sounded just right.

It was Selim: "Are they gone?"

"Of course they're gone! They left soon after your last call and may be at the hill already! Why are you calling on the Army frequency?"

"To check that you got it right!"

"Have you nothing better to do?"

"No. I am alone and everything is quiet here."

"Jawad may be there right now!"

"If he is, nobody noticed. There is no alarm in the camp. Everybody is going about their business as usual."

"Are you sure?"

"Of course I'm sure."

"Nobody knows what happened to Ali?"

"They're too busy with their stupid digging to look in the radio tent. But let me give you some advice: Talk more slowly when you answer the call from Basra. Musa is known to be a slow talker."

"I'll remember. Are you sure none of the dogs in Basra know Musa personally? I can't mimic his voice!"

"Don't be stupid! The dogs in Basra are *officers* and Musa is a private! None of them would know him personally and if they talked to him before they wouldn't remember his voice. But they might remember that Musa speaks slowly, like an idiot. So talk like an idiot, it shouldn't be difficult for you!"

Aslan ignored the jibe: "Are you sure that both radios are dead?"

"They're as dead as Sergeant Ali. They are permanently dead."

"Where are you calling from?"

"The tent where I usually work. Ah! That reminds me of something I was meant to tell you: the Turkish team found more treasure yesterday morning!"

Aslan reacted angrily: "Why didn't you tell me when I called yesterday afternoon?"

"It wasn't sure then."

"You should have called me at night so that I'd tell Jawad this morning! Now he'll think you want to make him look like a fool in front of Arroussi!"

"I tried to call you at night but a soldier caught me bleeping you. I killed him but I couldn't call again!"

"*You* killed a soldier? I thought you only played with screwdrivers

450

and soldering irons!"

"The more the fool you!"

"Did the Turks find much gold?"

"I don't think they found much. But enough to make a difference to our share."

"I'll tell Jawad about the new finds if I get the chance. You must remember to escape down the *southern* ramp when you run down with the workers."

"I'll remember."

"Now get off the radio!" With a croaking laugh Aslan broke off the communication. His unease had evaporated when he heard that more gold had been discovered, but there was no point in trying to tell Jawad now. Whatever Jawad was doing he would have turned off the radio in his truck.

2

The day got steadily darker and Aslan covered the lean-to with the larger of his two blankets. The tip about talking slowly was useful and he felt much better after talking to Selim: *More gold? That was good news!* Jawad had left him a plentiful supply of cigarettes, coffee and sugar as well as some food. He lit his small stove and prepared to make some sweet black coffee. While the coffee was brewing he wrapped himself in the remaining blanket and lit a cigarette. The nicotine gave a boost to his mood: *That's much better!* When the coffee was ready he had a long sip and felt confident enough to face anything the soldiers in Basra might say when they called.

Aslan's thoughts returned wistfully to the gold that was waiting in the foreigners' camp. According to Jawad the treasure that the Americans had found was worth a hundred million dollars! And now the Turks had found more gold! That would make it *more* than a hundred million dollars! Aslan would be rich soon! More than a hundred million dollars to be shared among a few survivors! *Jawad is sure to push our lads into the worst of the fighting!* Aslan smiled at the thought that his share would increase with every lad who got killed! Aslan imagined the lads storming the hill with Jawad egging them on regardless of casualties. He smiled with satisfaction. With his share of the gold Aslan would lead a life of luxury. He would get rid of his scooter and buy himself a luxury car! Maybe two cars, one red and one blue! He would buy several flats and live off the rent. He would have every woman he wanted!

But Aslan was a worrier: *For the gold to reach my pocket I must first convince the dogs in Basra that all is well!* But Aslan had no idea what the callers from Basra might ask. *What if they ask something like: 'How is your wife, Musa?'* Aslan's heart started beating wildly. Selim had spoken to Aslan about Private Musa several times but had not said anything about a wife. *No! An officer won't ask Musa about his wife!* But what if the devil made the caller ask something equally personal? *What if Musa had an operation on his leg and the caller says 'Remind me, Musa, was it the left leg or the right leg?* Aslan realised that this line of thought was becoming silly and he put a stop to it: *I must remain calm! If I am calm I'll be able to answer anything they ask!* Aslan had a fairly good idea of what Private Musa was like. Musa was not yet nineteen and knew a little about electrical things. He had often helped Selim with simple repairs, which is why Musa manned the radio when Sergeant Ali had other duties. *I think I know enough about electrical things to answer any technical questions they ask!* He sighed and glanced at his watch. It showed 8:50. *Musa may be dead already!* Aslan found the idea of impersonating a dead man amusing. He smiled wryly as he gulped down the rest of his coffee and lit a cigarette, letting his thoughts settle comfortably on wealth and women. He was on his third cigarette when his reverie was cut short by the bleep of the radio. *I must keep calm!* He picked up the headphones and put them on. "This is Private Musa." He remembered to talk slowly but his heart was beating wildly again.

An educated voice asked: "Is Sergeant Ali there?"

Aslan froze. This was an officer and Aslan had never spoken to an officer before. With an effort he said: "Sergeant Ali is on special guard duty this morning!"

"When will he be back on the radio?"

"I don't know. The guard shifts today are… longer than usual." Aslan had never been in the Army and did not know how long guard duty could be.

"Why is Sergeant Ali on special guard duty? Is something wrong?"

"Everything is normal. But the camp is being reorganised because the Turks have found more treasure."

"We've heard about the new finds. Could you call Major ElBalushi please?"

"Major ElBalushi is in an important meeting with the

archaeologists."

"I see. We need to talk to him."

"Is it urgent?" asked Aslan, suddenly worried. The officer might *order* 'Private Musa' to call the major.

There was a pause, then the caller said: "It's not urgent. Please ask Major ElBalushi to call us when he can."

Aslan breathed a sigh of relief. Encouraged by his good luck he said: "Perhaps I can convey a message to him?"

"That would be helpful. Please ask him to send us an inventory of the new finds. Colonel Haleel wants an inventory as soon as possible."

"I'll remember to ask the major to send an inventory to Colonel Haleel."

"Thank you, but please also ask him to call us as soon as it is convenient."

"Very well, I'll ask him to call you as soon as he can. Would it be all right if he gets in touch with you tomorrow? He's very busy today."

There was another, longer, pause. Then: "I shall call again later. Are you sure everything is all right at the camp?"

"Yes, everything is normal. We are very busy because the camp is being reorganised." His heart was pounding and he had to make an effort to talk slowly.

"I see. Please tell Major ElBalushi about the inventory and ask him to call us."

"I will."

The caller signed off and Aslan removed the headphones. He found that he was perspiring profusely. *But I think I did well! I could fob them off again if they call and ask for Ali or Balushi. They won't suspect anything as long as somebody answers!*

3

Aslan returned to his fantasies but it was not long before he noticed, from the corner of his eye, that someone was standing behind him and to his left some ten metres from the lean-to and next to the boulder on which he had stood to wave at Jawad's truck. Whoever it was must have crept up stealthily, hidden by the wing of the lean-to, and only now stepped into view. Aslan's sense of unease, which had diminished but not gone, took on the palpable nature of terror: *Arroussi has sent someone to kill me! He was waiting for me to talk to the dogs in Basra before showing himself!*

Aslan removed the blanket he had wrapped around himself and dropped it beside him, careful not to show that he was aware of the intruder. He had good reason to be afraid if this were one of Arroussi's men. All the firearms had been taken by the men for the attack on the hill and Aslan's only weapon was his knife. If the intruder had a firearm he could use it from where he stood, but Aslan hoped that he would come closer, perhaps to taunt him before finishing him off. If the intruder came close enough Aslan would throw his knife. But the intruder kept his distance.

Aslan had the habit of putting on an idiot grin when faced with an assailant. As one of Jawad's more experienced assassins he had found that this ploy sometimes baffled his opponent and gave Aslan time to assess the situation. With the idiot grin in place Aslan got up unhurriedly and then suddenly turned to confront whoever was standing beside the boulder. When he realised who it was he grinned all the more. It was not one of Arroussi's men; it was the very tall foreign woman who had tried to steal his radio the night before!

She was barefoot and appeared to be wearing the same clothes she wore the previous night, but her head and shoulders were covered by what seemed to be a short skirt, which had been opened up into a sort of hood. *She's afraid of getting wet! But why is she here?* Perhaps she had come back to try to steal his radio again. *She must be an extremely stupid woman!* Aslan noticed that the woman's face and arms were very red, as though she had been severely sunburned. *But there's no sun! Maybe she's ill!* Since all the foreigners were to be killed, Aslan could do with her as he pleased, and if she were ill that would only make her more pliable and add to his fun! *It must have been she who was watching me earlier!* The woman carried no weapon and therefore seemed harmless, but somehow Aslan could not help thinking of the Angel of Death strolling casually among those who were about to die.

Aware that Aslan had seen her, the tall woman approached to within a few metres and pointed at the radio, indicating with a nod that he was to give it to her. *The stupid whore wants the radio again!* Aslan shook his head emphatically. "No!" he said in guttural English. The tall woman seemed undecided. She swayed slightly as she stepped closer to the lean-to and leaned against the frame, as though she were dizzy. *She's not just stupid, she's ill! That's why she didn't go back to the foreigners' camp!* Aslan thought of letting Jawad know that the camp had not been warned but it was too late for that: *No matter. But when I see him I'll let him know that I killed her slowly, the way he would have done it!* Aslan savoured the thought of telling Jawad how skilfully he had killed the foreign woman, how he had prolonged her agony.

Because of the hood over her head, Aslan had not been able to see the foreigner's features in any detail when she stood beside the boulder, and it had been much too dark to see any details on the previous night, .but now that she was closer to him he studied her leisurely. Although she was unusually tall she was very attractive. Her face was a perfect oval and despite the sunburn – or was it some kind of fever? – her skin was without blemish and her jet-black eyes were uncommonly large, larger than those of any woman he had seen, infinitely more beautiful than the eyes of the heavily made-up women he normally frequented. But Aslan did not spend much time on her face. Her light knee-length skirt pulled his attention downwards to her legs and then to her pubic region, where it lingered as though stuck by some animal magnetism. Her hips were too narrow for Aslan's earthy tastes, but what he could see of her legs – which also appeared sunburned – were long and straight and her ankles were beautifully shaped. Aslan liked his women to have long legs with well-shaped ankles. It had been some time since he had slept with a woman and his lust was quickly kindled. The fact that she was a foreigner made the prospect of enjoying her body doubly exciting.

He stared at her, his lust beginning to show as a hardness in his loins, while she looked back at him through half-closed eyelids, as though she was not fully aware of his presence. *She's definitely not well! Good! She won't be able to put up much of a fight!* Again the woman pointed at the radio and nodded, but now she was frowning. *Is she threatening me?* Aslan thought of the sharpness of his knife and laughed as he shook his head and again said "No!" emphatically, more loudly this time. *It would be such a waste to kill her without having some pleasure first!* But the woman did not seem to understand and remained motionless, as though waiting for Aslan to give her the radio. *She doesn't know what to do!* Aslan decided to take control of the situation. "Come you to me, darling!" he said in broken English. The idiot grin was back on his face. "Come near! Not be afraid!"

4

The woman did not answer; she seemed to be in a daze. Aslan was sure she understood him: Didn't all foreigners speak English? Perhaps her illness made her confused. "You not understand, eh?" Whether she was ill or not, the tall foreigner was sure to run if he made any threatening movements, and Aslan was in no mood to chase her. But if he could conceal his intentions he could get close enough to grab her and hold her securely! In his mind he could already feel her hot body pressed against his, struggling vainly against his superior strength. Aslan was not tall but he was stoutly built and uncommonly strong, and he had no doubt that taking this skinny woman against her will would be as easy as it would be enjoyable.

"Aslan will be good to you, darling!"

He moved closer to her, his arms hanging by his sides, and the idiot grin changed into a grin of anticipation. The tall woman did not move back and continued to watch him without expression. He thought she was unaware of his intentions: *She is really very stupid!* Aslan was pleased because he believed he had a way with stupid women.

Under normal circumstances her apparent lack of fear would have made Aslan more cautious, but his passion was so inflamed that he could think of nothing but the satisfaction of his lust. He approached her to within arms reach and still she did not move away. He raised his left arm slightly, as though to calm her down. Very soothingly, he said: "You very beautiful, darling…" and in mid-sentence he lunged at her head with one hand while he tried to pull out his knife with the other. He intended to pull her down to her knees by the hair and point his knife at her face.

He never reached her. His left arm was less than half stretched when she slapped him with such force that his jaw cracked and his neck bones came apart. Aslan's eyes widened in disbelief and then froze, wide open, as he collapsed to the ground and lay completely still. But the lamia almost collapsed too. Dizzy with pain, she dropped the skirt that was covering her head and shoulders and seized the large blanket that lay on top of the lean-to. She was about to cover her head and body to protect herself from the sunlight when she noticed the lice and, with a grimace of disgust, held the blanket at arm's length. Sensing the scent of the lamia the lice dropped off, first in a steady stream and then a few at a time, like wine from the tap of a barrel that has almost run dry. When she was sure that the last louse had fallen the lamia covered herself with the blanket. Then she picked up Aslan's radio, with the headphones and wires attached, and ran as she had never run before towards the remains of the ancient village.

456

The lamia had found that a salve made of lard and clay would allow her to brave the daylight for short times, and before venturing out to get the box-toy for Mike she had smeared her whole body with all the salve she had left. The salve had offered some protection, but she had never been away from the dark for so long and although the day was heavily overcast there was enough sunlight to burn her. When she reached the ruins of the village she made straight for the well and frantically pulled away the large flat stone that concealed the aperture. Holding the radio with the headphones trailing, she almost fell down the shaft of the well in her desperate bid to reach the darkness. The radio struck the wall of the shaft several times but she did not notice. Every part of her that had been exposed to daylight was on fire, burning like red-hot metal on her skin. Sometime during the run back to her lair she lost the headphones.

35

RENEWED SUSPICIONS

1

IT WAS ALMOST 7:10 but Major ElBalushi was still in the radio tent chatting with Sergeant Ali. The major would normally have left by then, but the sergeant was due to take his first leave and was in a particularly talkative mood. While he adjusted the Army's radio to the day's frequency he gave the major a rambling description of the men's latest efforts to entertain themselves. The major was aware that his men often found their stay on the hilltop excruciatingly tedious and he was genuinely interested in the sometimes bizarre activities they devised to escape their boredom. The latest fad was chess, and the men had organised a competition amongst themselves with the winner getting to play, over the radio, against the winner of a similar competition among the lower echelons of 'Haleel's boys' in Basra. The major had his doubts about the practicality of his men playing chess over the radio, especially since their recent attempt to play backgammon over the radio had ended in disaster. He reminded Sergeant Ali of the disagreements and arguments that had arisen concerning the throws of the dice.

"Oh no! It's not like that at all in chess!" the sergeant exclaimed, "There are no dice and Haleel's boys won't be able to cheat!"

"And the cheating was all on the side of Haleel's Boys, of course?"

The sergeant swore by all that he held holy that neither he nor any of his friends had ever cheated in backgammon.

"Well," said the major, "Many people play chess over the radio. It's quite feasible if everybody follows the rules."

"We always follow the rules, Major!"

"That is good to hear. How will you play when you're on leave for five days?"

"The competition started three days ago and I won my first game yesterday. I shall play my second game after I return from seeing my family. "

"I wish you a happy stay with your family and a good trip home and back."

"Thank you, Major!"

"And when the Basra office calls remember to tell them about the Turkish team's discoveries yesterday morning."

"Oh, I told them about the newly discovered artefacts yesterday. They called in the evening. They were very pleased at the new finds but a little disappointed because there was not much gold."

The major laughed: "We can't expect to find a large amount of gold every time!"

Sergeant Ali nodded in agreement: "Yes, Major." The major left the radio tent and Sergeant Ali made some final adjustments to the radio.

Sergeant Ali's imminent departure reminded the major that Mike and Ohanian would be leaving for Mosul. He felt strangely forlorn: *Who will I talk to when Mike is gone?* Unlike everyone else, the major could not leave the hill. The ministry had ruled that the commander of the military escort should stay at his post until the archaeologists had completed their work and all discoveries had been removed from the hill. The major knew that one of the reasons he had been chosen was because he was a bachelor and did not have the legal right to take days off. *Oh well, being in charge has its compensations...*

The major had not seen the new finds and decided that this would be a good time to check on their progress. As he walked towards the storage tent, which had been extended to accommodate the new discoveries by the Turkish team, his mind turned to the weather: *What a dismal day! I've never seen such a dark morning!* The dark clouds were racing across the sky as though pursued by something dark and malevolent that was hidden from view. *And it's getting darker! It's going to rain in torrents and the archaeologists will have to stop their excavations!* The major was convinced that it was only a matter of time before the camp was attacked by bandits, and he deplored anything that interrupted the work and lengthened the stay of the archaeologists on the hill. The darkening sky certainly did not bode well for archaeological digging, and for a brief moment the major considered whether he should return and ask Sergeant Ali to get a weather report. He paused in his stride and almost turned to go back to the radio tent but then changed his mind: *We don't need to know how long the rain will last! The archaeologists will get back to their work the moment the ground is dry enough!* Had he turned to go back he would have seen Selim skulking behind the radio tent, glaring at him balefully.

2

The Turkish team had found a substantial store of pottery with gold, silver and bronze trinkets not far from the southern ramp. Although this second find was not as spectacular as the first, its discovery had taken everyone by surprise because no one had realistically expected to find any more artefacts. The Turkish team had celebrated by cooking some mouth-watering Turkish dishes, which they had added to the previous evening's menu.

When the major reached the storage tent he found Carol and ElKureishi standing outside the entrance, within sight of the pit. They were discussing restoration work.

"What news of the latest finds?" asked the major after the usual greetings. He knew that Carol and Bradley had been up early to help Professor Efremoghlou, the leader of the Turkish team, with the classification of the artefacts.

"We're making good progress," said Carol. "Professor Efremoghlou and his team have finished sorting out the trinkets and the pottery is being reassembled."

"He and his team must be very happy. Are the artefacts in good shape?"

"The pottery was very fragile and most of it is in pieces, but it shouldn't be too difficult to harden the clay and put the pieces together. The gold and silver trinkets are practically in perfect condition because they're small and compact. However, the bronze trinkets are oxidised and need a lot of restoration work before they can be properly catalogued and packed."

"Is the restoration work to take place in the storage tent?" asked the major.

"Yes," replied Carol, "That is why we needed to extend the storage tent. But we haven't started the restoration work yet".

"Don't you think the restoration work should be done at the university in Baghdad, where there are better facilities?" asked the major.

"I was just discussing this with Carol," said ElKureishi, "We agreed

460

that preliminary restoration work can be done here quite satisfactorily. That would greatly please Efremoghlou and his students."

"But it will take much longer," said the major.

"Yes it will take longer, of course, since they shall only be able to work on a few artefacts at a time and with less sophisticated equipment," said ElKureishi, "But our Turkish colleagues should have the privilege of working on the artefacts first."

"I understand," said the major. He had come to accept the rivalry between the teams. "Do you think I could have a look at the new finds?"

"Of course," exclaimed Carol enthusiastically, "Professor Efremoghlou is working very hard in the storage tent but he would be delighted to show you the new discoveries! Some of the artefacts will be very beautiful when restored."

"I'm afraid I won't be able to come with you," said ElKureishi, "I've got a meeting with some of my students."

"We shall miss your expert comments," said the major.

"There is actually very little to comment on," said ElKureishi. "There is no doubt that the items of the first hoard we found were hidden deliberately, perhaps when the temple became aware that it was under attack by the Hittites. The new finds were apparently deemed unworthy of concealment and were probably left where they were normally stored."

"Yup," said Carol, "What the Turkish group found must have seemed of secondary importance to the priests. I find this surprising given the high level of artistic skill shown by some of the artefacts."

"I am not at all surprised at their sophistication," said ElKureishi pompously, "We know that, at least in its early days, the temple was in touch not only with several other temples but also with the Assyrian king – with a line of consecutive kings, in fact! This suggests that the temple wielded considerable influence. Any gifts to the temple during this period would have been of the highest quality!"

"Are you saying that the goddess dealt with affairs of state?" asked the major. He was pleased that the conversation had taken an interesting turn.

"It would seem that way, at least until she fell from favour," said ElKureishi.

"I wish we knew *why* she fell from favour," said Carol thoughtfully. Like almost all archaeologists, Carol believed that the title of 'goddess' had, in fact, been held by a sequence of priestesses, but she always

461

referred to the goddess of the temple in the singular. Her admiration for whoever played the role was not lessened by the loathsome activities the goddess was reputed to have indulged in. Any woman who could influence an Assyrian king in affairs of state, and from a distance too, must have been a formidable person.

"The answer to why she fell from favour might lie in tablets we haven't discovered yet," said ElKureishi.

"Or perhaps in the writing on the wall of the pit," said the major.

"Well, Mike and Ohanian will continue working on that in Mosul," said Carol, "Mike told me he's going to have all kinds of books and journals sent there. Also some new cryptanalysis programs. I'm sure the writing on the pit wall shall be deciphered before too long."

3

The conversation was interrupted by a soldier who ran up to the major and saluted smartly. The major turned to the soldier: "Yes?"

"Major, there are at least two large vehicles coming our way from the northwest! They could be trucks or lorries, but we cannot tell yet what they are!"

"Please excuse me," said the major. He turned to address the soldier who had brought him the news. "How far are they?"

"They would not yet be visible from ground level, but as seen from the northern machine gun nest, they've just crossed the horizon. I would say at least nine kilometres, possibly more."

"That's about six miles!" said Carol. She could not think in metric units.

The major spoke to ElKureishi: "Nasser, are your teams expecting any large deliveries?"

"No," said the Professor, "And even if we were, they would not arrive so early in the morning. It's not yet eight o'clock."

"Yeah," said Carol, "Arriving now would mean they travelled at night, which would be crazy!"

"Why would it be crazy?" asked the major absent-mindedly. His thoughts were being drawn to other things: *Is it finally happening? God help us!*

"Because archaeological equipment, especially if it consists of large items, tends to be very fragile," said Carol. She did not enjoy having to explain the obvious. "If the archaeological equipment travelled at night over this dreadful terrain there would be a good chance that it would be seriously damaged!"

"Yes, of course," said the major.

"Anyway, we're not expecting anything that would require a truck or a lorry, let alone more than one!" said ElKureishi, anxious to have the last word.

The major noticed that his heartbeat had accelerated wildly. "We might be having uninvited company," he said calmly as he suppressed a sudden need to frown. Carol was about to say something but the major interrupted her: "I'm sorry, but I have to go and see what is happening." *And if things go badly I'll never see the new discoveries!*

The major and the soldier went as fast as they could to the northeastern part of the hill and climbed the mound of rubble that had once been the temple's northern guard tower. The mound provided the highest vantage point on the hill and was a logical emplacement for the machine gun that guarded the northern ramp. To prevent subsidence under the weight of the machine gun nest the rubble was enclosed at its base by a low brick wall as well as wire mesh and steel supports. The nest itself consisted of several layers of sandbags piled around a thick concrete ring slightly more than half a metre high that was open on the side away from the ramp. A corporal and two privates were standing within the nest. The corporal was looking into the distance with powerful binoculars. When the major climbed the mound the corporal saluted and passed the binoculars wordlessly to the major. The major took a long look at the tiny cloud of dust just below the horizon before speaking to the corporal: "I think there are more than two trucks. What do you think?"

"I think so too, although it's hard to see because of the dust raised by the first two trucks."

"And the poor light," added one of the two privates; the weather was getting darker.

The major nodded but did not answer. He took another long look through the binoculars. "They're coming rather fast over the rough ground, don't you think?"

"Yes, major," replied the corporal. "They must be doing between fifteen and twenty kilometres per hour, maybe more. That's very fast for this rough ground"

4

"So it's definitely not archaeological equipment," said ElBalushi as he passed the binoculars back to the corporal. "Your eyes are better than mine, can you make out how many trucks there are and what they're carrying?"

The corporal looked through the binoculars. "No major. They're too far and it's impossible to see through the dust. But from the length of the dust cloud I would say there are more than five trucks."

The major took a deep breath. "Corporal," he said briskly, "Go quickly to the camp and check the radio tent. Make sure Sergeant Ali is armed and tell him to be alert and to stay by his radio at all costs. Then get six armed men and have two of them guard the radio tent to make sure no-one enters. With the other four men collect all the workers and tell them to get to their tents and stay there until told otherwise. Don't mention the trucks to the workers but make sure they understand that they must not leave their tents! When you've done that, let the word be passed around discreetly that all our men are to pick up their weapons and expect further orders. Be as quick as you can!"

"Yes, major."

"Go!"

The corporal hurriedly gave the binoculars to the major and clambered down the mound. ElBalushi was very thoughtful for a few seconds and then looked again through the binoculars. The cloud of dust was now well below the horizon.

"Major," said one of the privates, "I think the trucks are full of men."

"Can you see through the dust?"

"No major, but at that speed they must be having a very rough ride. Any archaeological stuff would be shaken to pieces. It's got to be men."

"I agree with you. They may be here in less than twenty minutes. Both of you go and collect all the men you need to tell the archaeologists and the students to convene in the storage tent at once. Say that I have something important to tell them and will join them as soon as I can. Go!"

The two soldiers climbed out of the nest and clambered down the mound. The major remained alone in the machine gun nest, looking through the binoculars at the tiny cloud of dust that grew steadily larger. He was still looking through the binoculars when the corporal returned, accompanied by a young soldier with unruly hair.

"Major!" shouted the corporal breathlessly as he approached the mound.

"Speak!"

The corporal looked around him to make sure that no one was listening. "Major, Sergeant Ali's been murdered and both radios have been seriously damaged!" The corporal's face was pale and he was struggling to breathe.

"Are you sure *both* radios don't work?" The major tried to suppress a sudden throbbing pain in his temples.

"Private Musa checked them both," he indicated the young soldier who was standing stiffly at attention beside him. "What do we do with the body of Sergeant Ali? His throat has been cut and there is a lot of blood."

"Leave Sergeant Ali where he is and don't tell anyone about him. We are under attack. Is the machine-gun at the southern ramp manned?"

"Yes major. Captain Allawi is there with a full crew. Shall I leave the two guards at the radio tent?"

"Tell them to join the other men on the perimeter. Pass the word that all the men are to take up their battle positions at once. When you have done that make sure that all spare ammunition for the machine guns is in the nests. Oh, and please pick up the two walkie talkies from my tent. Take one to Captain Allawi and bring the other to me."

"Yes, Major."

"And make sure that the archaeologists and students are not told about Sergeant Ali and the radios under any circumstances!"

"Yes, Major."

"Go!"

5

The corporal ran off and ElBalushi addressed Private Musa, who was still standing at attention. "Have the workers been told to return to their tents and stay there?"

"Yes, major. They are all in their tents!" Private Musa spoke very slowly, as though he had trouble choosing his words.

"Don't stand at attention, boy. And speak faster if you can. We are short of time!"

"Yes, major."

"What about the archaeologists and the students? Are they all in the storage tent?"

"Not all of them, but all have been told to go there immediately and our men are talking to those who are refusing to leave their work." The boy made an effort to speak faster. "Some archaeologists and students are reluctant to leave their work because they know they will have to stop if it rains."

"I want the archaeologists and students to get to the storage tent NOW!" roared the major, "Get what help you need and make the archaeologists leave whatever they're doing at gunpoint if necessary!"

"Yes, major."

"Go!"

Private Musa scampered away.

There was a lot of shouting and running about in the camp as the soldiers took up their battle positions, but the major's attention was focused on the approaching cloud of dust. The six trucks were quite discernible now. The binoculars showed them to be large open trucks and they appeared, as far as he could judge, to be full of standing or crouching men. When the major eventually looked away he saw that a few archaeologists were entering the storage tent. He could see that some of them were not very pleased. 'Let them grumble,' he thought, 'playtime is over.'

When the major entered the storage tent the archaeologists, the postdocs and the students were all there. They had been talking heatedly but they fell into a sullen silence when the major entered and stood before them.

"I believe we are under attack by bandits," said the major without preliminaries. A few people started talking at once but the major raised his hand for silence.

"We are under attack," repeated the major. He spoke gravely. "You are to stay in the storage tent because the bandits are after your finds and they are unlikely to throw grenades at the place where the discoveries are kept. They would not risk damaging the artefacts. Whatever happens please don't leave this tent without very good reason. Any questions?"

"Has the office in Basra been informed?" asked ElKureishi. His face was grey.

"All possible precautions have been taken," replied the major.

"How would the er... bandits know which is the storage tent?" asked Professor Efremoghlou.

"The bandits are probably well informed about us. We must assume they know where the artefacts are kept."

"I find it hard to believe that there are still bandits in this day and age," said Carol, "where are they from?"

"From information I have received," replied the major, "They would be of several nationalities. They got together because you found treasure and because we are in the middle of nowhere."

There was a tense silence as the implications of the major's last words sank in. "Where will the workers be?" asked Jehan, the pretty postgrad. She looked concerned and her eyes had not left the major from the moment he entered the storage tent.

"In their tents, out of harm's way and out of our way. Any more questions?"

"Can we help?" asked a Turkish postgrad. "Some of us have had military training."

"Perhaps later, but thank you for your offer. At the moment I cannot risk any of you getting hurt."

"Can we arm the workers?" asked another postgrad, "Even if they can't tell a butt from a muzzle they're sure to be of some help to the soldiers."

"We cannot rely on untrained men," answered the major curtly: *And there may be at least one traitor among the workers!* "Any more questions?"

Everyone was too stunned to ask more questions.

"I want you to know that everything is in place. My men know how to deal with the situation. Thank you for coming."

The archaeologists and students immediately started talking loudly among themselves. The major turned to Mike: "Professor Townsend, will you step out of the tent with me for a moment?" Mike nodded and followed the major out of the tent.

6

When they were far enough not to be overheard ElBalushi said: "The radios have been made useless and my radio operator has been murdered. I don't know when, or *if*, anyone will come to help us.

467

Certainly it seems unlikely that anyone shall come in time to stop the attack."

"Could some bandits have gotten into our camp unseen?"

"I don't think so."

"So there must be at least one traitor among us," said Mike.

"We suspected that, but we cannot do anything about it now. He or they must be among the workers as my men have all been screened and all your fellows have been checked. I ordered all the workers to remain in their tents to prevent the traitor or traitors from doing more damage."

"Let's hope that works."

"The archaeologists and students must stay in the storage tent unless they have good reason to go somewhere. But if they leave they must get back as quickly as possible. I would be grateful if they were not told about Sergeant Ali or the radios."

"Of course."

"It's possible that the bandits will spare the university teams if they don't get in their way. If the bandits reach the storage tent then, no matter what they do, nobody is to try and stop them. The bandits can be very murderous."

"I understand."

"Can I rely on you to make sure nobody panics or does anything foolish?"

"I'll do my best."

"If the attack succeeds this may be goodbye."

"I know."

They shook hands and the major was about to return to his men when he hesitated.

"Yes Hussein?"

"Mike, one more thing in case I don't make it. Don't forget what I told you about *her*. I may not be around to remind you."

"I know. You said: 'They can be very beguiling those things if they want something from you.' I haven't forgotten."

At that moment a burly sergeant ran up to the major and saluted absent-mindedly, as though preoccupied by something terribly urgent.

"What is it, Radwan?" asked the major wearily.

The sergeant looked at Mike and then at the major as though to say 'Perhaps the Professor should not hear this.'

The major shook his head with impatience: "Speak freely!"

468

"Private Rashidi has been murdered!"

For a moment the major appeared to have been struck dumb. Then he said: "Where was the body found?"

"At the western perimeter. The sides of the hill are very steep there."

"Any idea who did this? Or why?"

"No, major."

"Did you see the body?"

"No major. I was with Captain Allawi and his men when the body was found. When the captain was informed he ordered me to run over and tell you. Captain Allawi sent someone else to call doctor Mursi."

"How was Rashidi killed?"

"I don't know, major."

"I think I'd better see this. Mike, have you got a strong stomach?"

"You don't expect me to accompany you!"

"It will make you take the bandits more seriously and you might notice something that we miss. Come, we may have no more than ten minutes before the bandits reach us!"

7

Private Rashidi lay on his back beside the remains of the western defensive wall. His feet were close together and his arms were by his sides, palms down. Dr. Mursi was kneeling beside him and two fully armed soldiers were standing by.

"What can you tell me, Dr. Mursi?" asked the major before he and Mike had reached the corpse.

"There is little to say," replied the physician, "His throat was slit by a violent lateral thrust that cut across the Adam's apple. The cut was administered by something very sharp; the sharp end of a well-honed knife perhaps. There is almost no laceration."

"Why is he so pale?" asked Mike. Rashidi's face had the colour and texture of white wax.

"He has lost a lot of blood," the physician replied casually. He turned to speak to Major ElBalushi about other matters relating to the murder.

But there was no blood that Mike could see anywhere around the corpse. As he stared at the dead soldier he felt as though something very cold had touched him at the back of the neck, something cold that sprouted freezing tendrils. He heard his own voice whisper:

"What happened to the soldier's blood?"

Dr. Mursi was too busy speaking to the major to hear the question, but as he listened to the physician the major noticed that Mike was almost as pale as Rashidi. He assumed that Mike was shocked by the sight of the corpse. When Dr. Mursi finished speaking he said: "Mike, you had better return to your friends in the storage tent!"

"I'll be all right," said Mike, "Who could have done this?"

"I don't know," replied the major, "Perhaps whoever killed Sergeant Ali, perhaps someone else." He looked at Mike pointedly and added: "Perhaps *something* else!"

"I thought of that too," said Mike quietly and he stepped back, away from the major and the dead man, and stumbled towards the storage tent. The major was too busy examining the body to notice Mike leave.

"*Rigor mortis* has not quite set in," said the major, "When would you say the murder took place?"

"It's hard to say," replied the doctor, "It was a cold night. Between three and six hours ago. I could give you a better estimate later, if you wish."

"Why is Rashidi drained of blood?"

"We found the body half-hanging over the edge," replied Dr. Mursi. "Much of his blood had poured out of the wound to the ground below."

"So there is a simple explanation," said the major, "Did you hear that, Mike?"

But Mike was gone.

8

As though to escape from what he had seen Mike broke into a run, but he could not escape from the memory of Rashidi's bloodless corpse: Why couldn't you wait? *Why did you have to feed on a man just because I was not going to take you to Mosul?*

As he ran to the storage tent Mike passed several groups of ElBalushi's soldiers. They stared at him oddly; the sight of one of the senior archaeologists running while seemingly in a daze was not a common occurrence. Some nodded to him as he passed but he ignored them. *Why did this have to happen on the day I was meant to take you away from here? I don't know how you found out about the bandits, but after all we said to each other, all that we planned together, would you have killed me like you killed that poor boy?*

Before he reached the storage tent Mike stopped to look at the mound of the pit. His outer calm concealed the frenzied turmoil of his thoughts. *You would have waited for me tonight and I would have taken you away from here. I don't really care if you made a dupe of me. I can't blame you for wanting to get away. This place was a prison that held you without hope for most of your long life. I just wish you had not deceived me so easily. I wish you hadn't killed that boy!*

And I wish I didn't miss you so much!

The storage tent was adjacent to the mound and Mike hesitated before entering the tent and turned to gaze upon the mound. As he stood the morning silence was shattered by a violent concatenation of single shots from automatic rifles and a continuous rat-tat-tat from both machine-guns. The noise seemed to come from all directions at once. The clamour of the weapons provided a fitting accompaniment to the frenzied thoughts that seethed in Mike's mind.

36

THE BANDITS AT THE HILL

1

IT WAS ABOUT eight in the morning when the bandits approached the hill from the north-west. Jawad's huge truck was in the lead, and he sat in the cabin with his arm dangling outside the window. In a few places the ground was still damp from the heavy mist that had covered the land during the night, but mostly it was dry enough for the trucks to raise clouds of dust as they travelled as fast as the terrain allowed. The mist of the night had vanished, dispersed by the same wind that herded the thick grey clouds across the sky. Very rarely, small gaps would appear in the billowing greyness and slim rays of sunlight would struggle to reach the ground, like the groping hands of luminous angels. Aisha almost smiled at their ephemeral beauty as she sat between Jawad and the driver, engrossed by her thoughts.

Jawad had forgotten his anger at the escape of the foreign woman and exchanged crude pleasantries with the driver regarding the sexual charms of foreign women in general and of those on the hill in particular. Aisha pretended not to hear what was said on the few occasions when Jawad's voice intruded into her thoughts, and eventually Jawad realised that Aisha was not paying attention.

"Why aren't you talking?" he asked.

"Foreign women are of no interest to me," she replied coldly.

Jawad laughed. "You'd better not get into the habit of ignoring me," he said, "Or I won't let you enjoy my gold!"

"I don't need your gold, Jawad," she replied almost inaudibly, and after the briefest of pauses she added, more loudly: "You are enough for me."

Jawad laughed again. "You don't fool me!" he exclaimed, "All of us are thinking of the gold that is waiting for me on the hill!"

Aisha did not answer, and Jawad asked the driver how he intended to spend his share of the gold.

"I have no plans," the driver replied laconically.

"What?" Jawad was astounded. "Soon you shall have more money than you have ever had in your life and you have no idea how you are going to spend it?"

"I have always been poor," the man replied, "And from a very young age I learned not to dream of what I would do if I became rich. Such dreams would only have made my poverty seem harsher."

Jawad found the driver's reply annoying. "You are a fool!" he said, and turned his attention to the hill, which in the shadow of the clouds appeared as a dark grey mass.

As the trucks approached the hill its silhouette began to show detail. When struck by one of the rare, intermittent rays of sunshine its colours showed a kaleidoscope of grey-brown and orange-brown tones. The closer they got to the hill the more it mesmerised Jawad, and his face pointed resolutely towards it, like some unerring compass, despite the detours that the driver was compelled to make because of rocks, small trees, and treacherous hollows.

Jawad was actually thinking furiously. In his mind the attack on the hill was as good as over, and yet he had a growing apprehension that a direct assault without any preparatory ceremony would not do justice to the rapturous climax that, in his mind, was already within his grasp. He felt that the assault on the hill and the riches that awaited him, like the favours of a beautiful woman, had to be courted and were not to be hurried. To reach out and just grab what he wanted might offend whoever or whatever controlled the dispensation of *luck* in the wastelands. This was as close as Jawad got to being superstitious, and he did not want to tempt Fate by accepting her gifts too quickly lest he showed a lack of respectful appreciation.

Somewhere at the back of Jawad's mind was the dim memory of something he had once heard about the ancients. He had a vague memory of being told that the ancients used to make blood sacrifices to their gods before embarking on a venture. The idea of blood sacrifice was attractive to Jawad and he struggled to remember more about this *ritualised killing*. However, because he considered his acquisition of the foreigners' gold as practically a *fait accompli*, and because his knowledge of ancient history was severely limited, he could not understand that the purpose of sacrifice had been to appease the gods and avert setbacks. He surmised that the purpose of sacrifice was to display gratitude – in advance – for gifts that the gods were about to bestow, and so felt that he should approach the riches that awaited him with an appropriately flamboyant preliminary ritual. What better ritual than a multiple sacrifice? Moreover, even if whatever god dispensed luck in the wastelands was indifferent to sacrifice, a *ritualised killing* would enhance Jawad's pleasure in receiving the god's gifts! The true glutton does not rush to consume a delicious meal, but consciously delays the golden moment, and thus shows his appreciation, by first savouring a string of appetizers.

For Jawad, the climax of the day, the end product of careful planning and endless fantasising, was much more than just the stretching of his arms to lay his hands on the gold: it included the contrived demise of Arroussi and his son. The killing of Mukhtar, in particular, was something to be savoured, a special gift from whatever god, demon or angel ruled over the hill and the surrounding desolation. *And I, like the noble ancients, shall make a sacrifice! A sacrifice worthy of the great gifts that are waiting for me!*

2

When the trucks were about three kilometres from the northern ramp, Jawad turned abruptly to the driver: "Don't go straight towards the hill," he ordered, "Turn left and drive in a wide circle around it."

"Now?"

"When we reach those large boulders." Jawad pointed at a prominent distant clump.

"Yes, Jawad."

The boulders in question were less than two kilometres from the hill. They were surrounded by lesser rocks and the truck had to slow down considerably as it approached them. Its suspension creaked and groaned as usual.

"Turn now!" barked Jawad when they were almost at the boulders. The truck veered to the left and swung eastwards. Jawad stuck his head out of the window to see whether Arroussi's trucks were following. He was gratified to see that they were as close behind as the dust cloud raised by his truck allowed.

The trucks had driven fast over the rough ground and Aisha had found the trip not only depressing but also uncomfortable. However, she was not so much affected by the physical discomfort as by her misgivings about the attack. She could not get the tall foreign woman out of her mind and her thoughts teetered between horror and hope: *The foreigner could not possibly have covered the whole distance to the hill at the speed with which she had run when she escaped; she must have slowed down somewhere! She must have stopped to catch her breath! What if the trucks catch up with her as she making her way back to the hill?* The closer they came to the hill the greater the chances that they would overtake her, or find her hiding behind a rock. *I would not be able to stop Jawad from killing her! He will kill her bit by bit, agony upon agony, to give the men a spectacle of how cruel he can be!* Her thoughts turned to the men at the back of the truck: *And some of them would relish the spectacle!*

Aisha felt an overwhelming sense of bitter impotence, and as her thoughts roamed far from the hill and the wastelands she felt hot tears flowing down her cheeks.

"Why are you crying?" Jawad asked suddenly

"I am not crying!" She had not realised that Jawad was staring at her.

Jawad lost interest before she had completed her words and Aisha took a deep breath. She accepted that Jawad was completely absorbed by the prospect of sudden riches; perhaps he was also thinking of how he would kill Arroussi and his son. She had failed to dissuade him from that, but could she change his mind about killing the archaeologists and the workers? Unconsciously she turned to look at him and he, noticing that her attention was on him, glared at her suspiciously and said: "Why are you looking at me like that?"

She felt a sudden sickening terror. *The idea that the gold is within his reach has made him more reckless than usual. He feels invincible! If the whim takes him he could easily kill me in this barren place!* She pushed away her fears and asked quietly: "Why do you want the trucks to drive around the hill?" *Are we circling the hill because he hopes to find the tall foreign woman?*

Jawad ignored her and the feminine part of her rebelled. She *had* to make him listen to her. "My love," she said in her normal voice, "Do you want Arroussi to think you are up to something?"

"I don't care what he thinks!" he replied angrily. He found the question annoying but of no importance.

"My love," she repeated, "Now more than ever we don't want to make Arroussi suspicious!"

"Eh?" He had not thought of that. Arroussi must not become suspicious! If his suspicions were aroused they would be difficult to quell and killing a suspicious Arroussi could pose problems.

"I said we should not awaken his suspicions," persisted Aisha, "Not now when we depend on him to achieve what we want. You know he doesn't trust us!" She almost said 'You know he doesn't trust you!'

Jawad seemed confused for a moment, but then he said: "I want those accursed soldiers to see us!" He was not in the habit of explaining his actions, no matter how thoughtless, but he knew that Aisha was better than he at understanding people and now he needed her to help him test an explanation that would prevent Arroussi from becoming suspicious. "I want the soldiers to see how many we are," he continued. "I want them to feel terror!" Explaining his decision to Aisha was a tentative rehearsal of what he might have to say to Arroussi.

She would not grant her support too easily: "What if this ElBalushi and his men are not the kind to feel terror? What if he uses the time we waste going around in a circle to prepare for our assault?"

Jawad did not have the patience for such talk. "What can Balushi do?" he asked brusquely, "He can't call for help! He has only two machine guns and thirty men!"

"Yes, my love, but we mustn't annoy Arroussi or make him suspicious."

Without acknowledging the validity of her comments, Jawad looked back at the following trucks and waved his arm up and down outside the window. Arroussi's truck flashed its lights in response.

"Stop the truck!" ordered Jawad.

The vehicle came to a stop in a cloud of dust. The following trucks slowed down and stopped. Arroussi's truck came to a halt alongside Jawad's enormous vehicle.

Arroussi shouted hoarsely from his window: "What antics are you up to now, Jawad?"

Jawad had to bend forward to look at Arroussi because Aisha and the driver were in the way. He was reassured to see that Arroussi was more curious than angry.

"I think it might be a good idea if we drove around the hill before attacking!" Jawad shouted back. "It will give our men a feel for the place and the soldiers will be frightened when they see how many we are!"

"Do you expect them to surrender?" asked Arroussi mockingly.

"I don't think they'll surrender!" replied Jawad, and he laughed loudly as though Arroussi had make a hilarious joke, "But frightened men fight badly!"

Arroussi was surprised; he did not expect Jawad to show any kind of insight. "Perhaps it is not a bad idea to show our strength," he said, "We have time to spare. Very well, you lead and we'll be right behind you."

Jawad's truck lumbered forward and Arroussi's trucks followed.

Aisha unconsciously shook her head. She had expected Arroussi to oppose this new idea of Jawad's. The movement, though small, was noticed by Jawad and he was struck by the thought that she had opposed his ideas ever since they had camped beside Aslan's lean-to. This was not strictly true, but as his jealousy and rage swelled up the suspicion that *his woman* was not wholly on his side became a certainty. His conviction was all the more intense because it was linked to the *other* certainty that this had something to do with Mukhtar, the *educated* butter-hearted son of the old fool. Perhaps it would not be enough to kill Arroussi and Mukhtar. After taking the gold he could have any woman he wanted and Aisha would be irritatingly superfluous.

3

The trucks had almost completed their circuit around the hill when Arroussi's trucks turned away towards the southern ramp. Jawad was absorbed by thoughts of Aisha flirting with Mukhtar and did not notice immediately, but when he saw Arroussi's trucks making their way towards the hill he vented his fury on the driver: "You imbecile!" he cried out, "You brought us too close to the hill and now Arroussi will start the attack before me! May you and your father and your mother burn forever in the flames of Hell!"

"What do you want me to do?" asked the driver timidly. He was afraid; Jawad was very dangerous at times like this.

"Follow them! I want you to drop me off at the southern ramp."

"Drop you off?"

"Yes, you idiot! Must I say everything twice?"

The driver was about to say something but Aisha said: "You and Arroussi had agreed that we and our men would attack the northern ramp and deal with the soldiers there. You agreed that we would be with our men!"

"I've changed my mind! My truck and the lads will go there but

I want to be at the southern ramp with Arroussi! That is where the workers will run down!" He did not care if Aisha guessed why he wanted to go to the southern ramp. He had a brilliant thought about how he would make his magnificent sacrifice.

Arroussi's trucks stopped just before the boulders that were scattered, like huge molehills, around the southern ramp. Arroussi and his men were getting off not too far from where the expedition's vehicles were parked.

When his truck was within ten metres of Arroussi's vehicles, Jawad shouted: "Stop!" The truck stopped. "I and my woman are getting off," he said to the driver, "are you sure you know what to do?"

The man nodded contritely. "We go past the west side of the hill and drive around to the northern ramp. When we hear shooting we go up the ramp as fast as we can. We smash into the tents so that our men can get behind the soldiers who are guarding the northern perimeter."

"Good! Just don't drive into the large tent! That tent contains the treasure. And don't let the truck fall into a hole!" He flung open the door of the truck and, holding his assault rifle, jumped out. Aisha was not sure what to do and hesitated, but Jawad reached over and pulled her out roughly by the arm. "Come on! You're coming with me!"

"You're hurting my arm!" protested Aisha as he dragged her along the seat.

"What's the matter with you?" he shouted, "First you cry and now you sleep! COME OUT!"

Her face expressionless, Aisha alighted deftly from the truck, holding her assault rifle and a box of ammunition.

Jawad was in too much of a hurry to be patient. He cursed loudly as he slammed shut the door of the truck. "Go!" he shouted to the driver. With a loud roar the huge truck reversed and then turned away, its suspension creaking loudly. Jawad turned to Aisha and pushed her ahead of him. "Come on! I want you to run in front of me!"

"Why are we at the southern ramp?" she asked.

"Without me that stupid son of Arroussi is sure to let some of the workers escape!" Aisha almost swooned: *I don't want to watch the massacre of the workers!*

The last of Arroussi's men were jumping out of their trucks and most were already spreading out cautiously along the southern side of the hill. They used the boulders for cover although they were beyond the effective range of the machine gun that guarded the southern ramp. Jawad and Aisha found Arroussi and his son squatting behind some rocks, surrounded by their bodyguards. They were about twenty metres from the foot of the ramp.

"Why are you here, Jawad?" Arroussi growled. Mukhtar pretended to be unaware of Jawad's presence.

"My men know what to do!" replied Jawad, not quite answering Arroussi's question, "I want to be where the killing will start!" He placed his hand on Aisha's shoulder and pushed her forcefully down to her knees before squatting beside Arroussi.

"Suit yourself," growled Arroussi, "My men will attack the perimeter in about fifteen minutes. They're taking up their positions."

"Can't they run faster? My men are anxious to get among the soldiers but my truck won't go up the ramp unless the shooting starts!" Jawad stood up and stared at the top of the southern ramp.

"Get down!" said Mukhtar coolly, "You are almost within range of the machine gun on the hill and there may be sharpshooters with long-range rifles!"

Jawad quickly squatted behind the rocks. He had not considered the possibility of sharpshooters with long-range rifles among ElBalushi's men.

"Are you sure the workers will run down the southern ramp?" asked Arroussi, he was not happy with the idea that Jawad could change his plans without consulting him.

"My men will make sure the workers come pouring down the ramp after the shooting begins," said Jawad.

"What about the soldiers?" asked Mukhtar, "Won't they try to stop them?"

Jawad snorted: "The soldiers are already too busy worrying about how to stay alive!"

"So why are you here?" asked Arroussi for the second time.

"I'm here to make sure none of the workers escape!"

Arroussi shook his head and looked at his watch. Aisha half hoped that Mukhtar would intervene on behalf of the workers, but the young man remained silent. She was on the verge of saying 'Do we really have to slaughter the workers?' but the look on Jawad's face made her change her mind. He would kill her without warning if she tried to speak against his wishes in front of Arroussi and his son. They all waited in silence.

4

Arroussi looked at his watch and said: "My men will attack the perimeter... now!"

Almost immediately the silence was shattered by repeated volleys of gunfire from all around the hill. They were answered by scattered shots from the hilltop and the rattle of the heavy machine gun that guarded the southern ramp. A few seconds later there was the rattle of the second machine gun in the distance.

"Ah! My truck is climbing the other ramp on its way to the tents!" exclaimed Jawad, "that was the machine gun guarding the northern ramp!"

"The soldiers around the hilltop don't seem to have been affected by our display of strength," said Mukhtar calmly, "Their shooting is deliberate and without panic."

Jawad looked at Mukhtar disdainfully but said nothing. The sound of concerted gunfire from around the hill rose and fell, then became sporadic. The machine gun at the northern ramp continued to fire in short bursts.

"The battle is almost over!" said Jawad triumphantly, "My men are on the hill!"

"We'll see," growled Arroussi, "Where are the workers your spy was supposed to send down the ramp?"

"They'll be coming down the ramp soon, don't you worry! Remember, no witnesses!"

Arroussi looked very grim. Mukhtar was looking at the ground, as though he was ashamed of what was going to happen. The machine gun guarding the northern ramp continued firing for a time but then stopped, as if it were waiting for something.

For intuitive reasons she could not explain, Aisha felt that the silence was a natural prelude to the horror she expected to unfold. *Please*, she prayed, *Please Oh God! Let the workers stay on the hill!* But then, as though to give substance to her fears, some sixty tiny figures appeared at the top of the ramp. They at first seemed unsure of what to do, but then, as though urged to action by some unseen force, they raised their arms and ran down the steep incline shouting and gesticulating. They ran with their arms held high to show that they carried no weapons.

"Please don't kill us!" some shouted.

"God is greater!" shouted others.

The remainder just shouted incoherently as they ran down the ramp, stumbling frequently in their haste. When the foremost workers had almost reached the bottom of the ramp Jawad grabbed Aisha's assault rifle and surged forward. With an assault rifle under each arm he ran past Arroussi and swiftly covered the distance to the bottom of the ramp as though to greet the shouting, frightened men. He was laughing wildly as though possessed: *This is my sacrifice! I'm going to make my sacrifice!*

5

The workers saw him coming and slowed down. Some smiled nervously at Jawad. All held their arms rigidly above their heads. Jawad stopped laughing and smiled back as he ran towards them. The workers eyed his weapons fearfully but were deceived by his smile; had they not been reassured by Selim that the bandits would not harm them? But when Jawad was among the first of the workers he whirled around and opened fire with both weapons. The workers closest to him fell to the ground while most of the others, blind with terror because they suddenly became aware of what was waiting for them, staggered about waving their arms because they could not decide whether to run back up the ramp or fall to their knees and beg for mercy. Arroussi joined Jawad and, weaving between the terrified men so as not to present an exposed target to the machine gun on the hill, opened fire on the workers. All the workers were at the bottom of the ramp and there was no escape. Some died quietly, a few died screaming in fear and pain, and some died pathetically calling for help. The massacre was completed by Arroussi's bodyguard, who advanced beyond Arroussi up the ramp. When only a few workers were left standing, Jawad and Arroussi withdrew to the protection of the rocks just as the heavy machine gun on the hill spat flame. Two of Arroussi's bodyguards spun like dervishes and fell among the dead and the dying, but the remaining bodyguards managed to escape. Despite the breeze and a light drizzle there was a stench of blood and burnt gunpowder.

Aisha had covered her eyes and was weeping softly. Mukhtar, who had not joined in the killing, not for the first time in his life wondered what he was doing among people who found killing so enjoyable.

37

FIRST STAGES OF BATTLE

1

THE STORAGE TENT sprawled roughly to the west of the camp, less than ten metres away from the edge of the circular mound that enclosed the pit. Mike had not been down to the cavern since that fateful morning when something venomous had bitten or stung him. Now, convinced that he would die before the day was over, and with his mind aflame with the conviction that he had been betrayed – and deceived! – by her whom he had loved so blindly, he longed to see the cavern again. The feverish gunfire that came from everywhere around the perimeter of the hilltop implied that the bandits were attacking from all sides. *But they're being kept at bay, at least for the moment! Would it matter if I took a few minutes to see the cavern again? Just once more?* There was a small torch in his pocket.

But what if he confronted her down in the darkness? What would he tell her? How would she react if he told her that the trip to Mosul would have to be postponed indefinitely? No doubt she knew that already. No doubt she was furious at having lost her chance to leave the hill and extend her domain. *She killed the boy to show me how angry she is!* Her reaction to seeing him in her cavern, now that he would no longer be useful, could be singularly violent and probably lethal: *But is it not better to be killed by someone you love rather than by those damn bandits? Yes! I need to be with her again!* But then the wax-doll face of the blood-drained Rashidi floated across his mind and a wave of mixed emotions choked his yearning to see her.

Mike stood undecidedly outside the closed flaps of the storage tent, unable to make up his mind whether to enter or not. He turned his back to the pit. He was engrossed by his thoughts when the machine gun that covered the northern ramp fell silent. *Why would they stop shooting?* The soldiers at the machine gun nest exchanged a few hurried shouts with those on the perimeter but Mike was unable to understand what was being said. *I hope the major is all right!*

The tents impeded his view of the machine-gun nest but from the silence he guessed that all activity at the north-east of the hill had stopped. The second machine gun, at the south-west, also fell silent. The exchange of automatic fire from around the perimeter almost stopped. *Is it over? It's probably just a lull!*

Mike thought of going to the machine gun nest to check on the Major but decided against it. He was not ready to face unpleasant possibilities. He pulled open the flaps and entered the storage tent. There was a flurry of short bursts of automatic fire somewhere to the south but Mike was too surprised at what he saw to pay much attention.

In heaven's name!

He stared in disbelief at what had been done with the cardboard boxes that contained the ancient bones and the artefacts. When he had accompanied the major out of the storage tent the boxes had been lying in neat rows on low pallets. During the short time that he had been outside, the boxes had been stacked like bricks, on top of each other, along all but one of the four sides of the storage tent. They formed three sides of a rectangular enclosure within which the archaeologists and students sat in small huddled groups. The entrance to the tent, on the fourth side of the rectangle, was free of boxes.

Mike unconsciously looked for the statue of Amalishah. It stood alone, to the right of the tent's entrance, away from the stacks of boxes, and had been covered with several layers of plastic sheet. *For added protection, I suppose. But protection from what? The plastic would be no protection at all against bullets or worse...* Mike felt grateful that he could not see the face of the statue, but the feet and the low pedestal were exposed and he noticed that the statue had a small scratch on the right ankle. The minor detail held his eye and, for some unaccountable reason, saddened him. *Get her out of your mind! Only a few hours ago she killed a man to feed on his blood!* It was a non-verbal thought, composed of fleeting fears and suppressed emotions, but the bitterness that assailed him was easy to verbalise: *It seems that I won't be providing you with a Land Rover, after all, and you won't be able to get out of here... none of us will get out of here!*

His thoughts were interrupted by Carol's cheery voice: "Hey, Mike! Come on over and sit with us!" She was sitting with her husband and ElKureishi. Someone had brought in chairs from the refectory and

483

there were plenty of empty places. *How can she be cheerful when people are getting killed not too far from here? Doesn't she hear the shooting?* He managed to get his thoughts under control: *She doesn't know how little hope there is! And she hasn't been betrayed by someone she loves!* The last thought brought a pang of pain and he examined his feelings. His anger at Amalishah was compounded by the frustration of his hopes and his own undeniable fear. There was no doubt that he was afraid to die, but his fear of death was not wholesome; it was not the fear of a happy man who faces death bravely. It was distorted and pathological; the death-fear of a man who feels he has been deceived and betrayed, the fear of a man left holding onto an empty life that mocks him.

2

"Oh come on, Mike! Don't be so gloomy!" Carol was beckoning wildly. He waved back. He was in no mood for chitchat with a compulsively cheerful woman and he looked around for someone else he might join. But there was nobody else. Leonard was talking earnestly with some students, apparently oblivious of the danger that, for Mike, was creeping ever closer as the minutes dragged by. No, he couldn't face young men and women who would probably be dead in a few hours. His eyes fell on Ohanian, who sat on his own. The cryptoanalyst was sitting alone staring at the floor, his face darkened by a deep frown.

Mike decided to compromise and went over to Carol and the others. "Do you mind if I ask Ohanian to join us?"

"Not at all," said Carol, "Yeah, bring him over!"

Mike approached Ohanian. "Come on, Ardash. Come and sit with Carol and ElKureishi. I'm going to join them."

Ohanian looked up. "Mike!" he exclaimed wretchedly. "What things terrible are happening? Akh! The computers are sure to get damaged in this stupidity and our work will be lost!"

"I'm sure the disks will be safe."

"I hope so, Mike. When will all this stop?"

"I don't know"

"This is very bad! These Akh…bandits are after the artefacts and we cannot do anything! They'll probably smash everything they don't want to take, like the tablets and the computers with all our work!"

Mike managed a half smile: "It's a pretty awful situation, yes, but I'm sure the army fellows can handle the bandits." Mike was not used to lying but he assured himself that this particular little lie was justified.

Ohanian was inconsolable: "We were meant to go to Mosul tonight and now look what happens!"

"The trip to Mosul may have to wait a little. Come, old friend, let's sit with Carol and ElKureishi."

Ohanian spoke in a conspiratorial whisper: "Carol will make me go crazy!"

"Perhaps, but you seem to be more down in the dumps than I. Carol will cheer us up, or else drive us both crazy."

Ohanian got up despondently. "Mike, I think I'm too sad to talk."

"Carol will cheer you up."

Mike and Ohanian joined the others.

"This is very exciting!" said Carol as Mike and Ohanian sat between her and ElKureishi. "Imagine, real-life bandits and those brave soldiers protecting us! Definitely something to tell our grandchildren when we're old!"

"*If* we see our grandchildren again," muttered ElKureishi, who had many grandchildren.

"I suppose it is very exciting," said Mike coldly. Carol's apparent inability to understand the danger seriously annoyed him. "Was it your idea, Carol, to use the boxes with the artefacts for protection?"

"It was actually Bradley's," replied Carol. "ElBalushi said that the bandits wouldn't want to damage the artefacts, so why not use them for protection?"

"You should have had them stacked *outside* the storage tent," said Mike, "That way the bandits would see them and not shoot in our direction."

Carol did not catch the sarcasm but ElKureishi did: "Mike, this is not the time to be flippant!"

"Why d'you say he's being flippant?" asked Carol suspiciously. She was not used to sarcasm and she had missed Mike's completely.

"I don't think Mike approves of putting the artefacts in the way of stray bullets," said Bradley.

"It was *your* idea!" snapped Carol.

"Oh, I suppose it doesn't matter," said Mike. *So Carol is as worried as we are, but she's doing a good job at hiding it! She's a brave woman!* His annoyance lessened but did not go away. It now focused on ElKureishi's passivity: "I'm surprised you allowed the boxes to be used as a shield, Nasser."

"You think I'm still in charge here?" said the elderly professor wearily.

"Of course you are!" *Damn! Why am I trying to cheer him up?*

"The army is in charge now!"

"Only in military matters. You are still the senior member of this expedition, and within those boxes is a large part of the expedition's purpose!"

ElKureishi looked away and did not answer.

"Perhaps Bradley's idea wasn't that good after all," said Carol. She was concerned about ElKureishi and thought that Mike's comments would upset him. She spoke hurriedly to the elderly professor, who was slumped in his chair and looked older than usual: "If you wish, Professor, the students can put the boxes back on the pallets."

"I don't think it will make any difference," said ElKureishi. He knew what bandits were capable of. They would destroy everything they didn't want to take.

Although the storage tent, with its recent extension, was the largest on the hill, there was not much room for the archaeologists and the students.

"If we put the boxes back on the floor we shall keep tripping over them," said Mike, "So we might as well leave them as they are."

"OK," said Carol.

"Let's just hope they're not hit by any bullets!" said Ohanian. He was thinking of the tablets in the boxes. A stray bullet could smash one or more clay tablets to pieces.

"Yeah! Let's hope so!" said Bradley.

"It's almost quiet outside," said Ohanian. The continuous shooting had stopped and there was only intermittent gunfire.

"Oh my God!" exclaimed Carol. "Do you think the bandits are gone?"

"Is that possible?" asked Ohanian hopefully.

"I doubt it," said Mike. "There's an awful lot of them and they wouldn't give up so easily."

Carol was about to answer when there was a tremendous explosion followed by several smaller explosions. It was like the sound of a large bomb followed by the quick cracks of multiple fireworks. Carol screamed and her husband immediately put his arm around her.

"It's all right, honey," he murmured. "We're safe here."

Carol put her head on her husband's shoulder and sobbed quietly:

"Brad, I'm afraid! I can't keep trying to be cheerful!"

"You don't have to be cheerful, honey. Don't worry, we'll be all right." She snuggled closer to him, still sobbing.

"I'd better go and see what that was!" Mike hurried out of the tent. Ohanian stared after him, feeling deserted and alone.

3

The major was half way up the machine-gun emplacement, crouching outside the ring of sandbags that encircled the machine gun nest. It was raining softly and the sky was at its darkest, but there was little sound of gunfire and both machine-guns were silent. Half way up the northern ramp were the remains of an enormous truck. It was burning furiously and giving out a column of black smoke. Several bodies were lying around the twisted, burning metal and a few were scattered down the ramp, away from the hill.

"Keep your head down!" hissed the major.

Mike quickly did as he was told.

"Mike, you shouldn't be here!"

"I know. What happened, Hussein?"

The major smiled sardonically. "Oh, we were attacked from all sides. The trucks carried six full truckloads of armed men!"

"I mean, how did that huge truck get there?"

The major shrugged: "There must have been some choice idiots in that truck. First, they drove around the hill as though unsure of where to attack, and when the shooting started this big truck rushed up the ramp as though chased by devils. It got bogged down by the soft mud and my men peppered it with heavy-calibre bullets."

"And then?"

"Well, the truck should have reversed but it didn't. It kept trying to come up the ramp until it stopped completely. It was full of men and when it was clear that the truck wouldn't go any further most of them jumped out, shouting and shooting. They didn't hit anyone but the machine gun took all those you see lying there. Those that survived ran down the ramp and we got a few more as they ran."

"What about the explosion?"

"The machine gun must have caused a petrol leak. The truck burst into flames and exploded some minutes after it stopped, as did several of the grenades carried by the bandits who were still in the truck."

"What's happening now?"

"I think the whole lot have pulled back to lick their wounds. But they'll be back, and they'll be less foolhardy this time."

"What's happening at the other ramp?"

"Mike, you don't want to know."

"Tell me."

"According to what Allawi told me on the walkie-talkie, the workers decided they didn't want to stay in their tents. For some reason they went to the southern ramp and ran down like frightened sheep. They ran down the ramp right into the arms of the bandits!" The major shook his head in disbelief.

"And then?"

"Then? They were massacred! They were mowed down like... like... I don't know like what!"

"How many survived?"

"The southern ramp is steeper than this one, Mike. They could not run back fast enough to escape."

"*All* of the workers were killed?"

"*Ay wallah!* All of them. Not one escaped! There's some insane maniac among the bandits, a fellow with yellow hair. Allawi said that he jumped out from behind the rocks and opened fire on the workers at close quarters, using two automatics. Then some other bandits joined him to complete the job."

"Why didn't your fellows shoot the maniac?"

"He's a clever maniac. He stood among the workers while he killed them. And he kept darting around, like a demon!"

Mike bowed his head at the horror of this news. *What made the workers leave their tents and run down the ramp? They didn't stand a chance!* Some of them had been Mike's friends. Many of them were young. Almost all had families.

"The workers were expressly told to stay in their tents!" husked Mike, he found it difficult to speak.

"They were told, but they didn't listen."

"Why did the bandits have to kill the workers? They were harmless."

"You must understand what kind of people these criminals are," said the major, "One of their rules is never to leave witnesses."

"So they intend to massacre us too?"

"If we let them."

Mike felt sick. Guessing Mike's feelings, the major said: "How are things in the big tent?"

"We have idiots among us too," replied Mike. "Somebody had the bright idea of using the boxes with the artefacts as a protection against bullets."

"We should send someone down to let the bandits know that if they shoot at the big tent they might damage what they came to steal." The major smiled weakly.

Mike could not smile back. "Do you have any idea what their plans are?"

"I don't know what their plans are now. I think they originally planned to overwhelm us in one bold attack from all sides. As the big truck came up the ramp the bandits from the other trucks tried to swarm up the sides of the hill. But the driver of the truck misjudged the softness of the ramp and the others underestimated the training of my men. None managed to reach the edge of the hill, let alone the top."

"How did they expect to climb the sides of the hill?"

"They brought extendable ladders. But their informant or informants failed to tell them how high the hill is."

"I see. Did any try to run up the southern ramp?"

"That ramp is steep and well covered by the second machine gun. It would be foolish to run up that incline."

"What about casualties?"

"They lost at least a dozen men when the truck was stopped and perhaps twice as many were killed trying to climb the sides of the hill. My men are very good."

"What of our casualties?"

"You mean apart from the workers? No casualties among my men, except for Sergeant Ali and Private Rashidi."

"I would have expected more organisation from these bandits."

"They're just an armed mob, Mike."

"What do you think they'll do now?"

"I have no idea. But they now know that only the two ramps are vulnerable. If they silence the machine guns they will try to creep up the ramps and wear us down. They have the advantage of numbers and the ramps are very uneven, so crawling men can find cover."

"How many are they?"

"They must have been between two hundred and three hundred. They're not that many now, but they'll be more cautious."

"But if they can't storm the sides of the hill and they can't climb the ramps they're stuck!"

"They still have the initiative. And if they know our radios don't work they may wait for darkness. They may also have weapons they haven't used yet."

Mike raised his head above the machine gun nest to have a look at the bandits. The whole length of the ramp was visible from the gun emplacement, but he could only see the burnt truck and the bodies of the dead; the remaining bandits were concealed behind the rocks at the foot of the ramp.

"Hussein, can I get a rifle? I'm a good shot."

"With a pistol, you said."

"Yes. But with these assault rifles one doesn't have to aim too well. One just sprays bullets."

"You are welcome to join us, Mike. But it's safer for you to return to the others."

"The storage tent's too crowded."

"Is there enough food and water?"

"There's no food or water in the storage tent, but at least the latrines are close by."

ElBalushi half smiled. "That's good. The frightened ones won't make a mess!"

The rain grew heavier.

4

There was a long whistling sound followed by a small explosion at the centre of the hill. Mike raised his head again and saw that one of the tents was burning.

"That was a rocket propelled grenade," said the major. For a moment his calm expression vanished and was replaced by one of apprehension. But he quickly regained his composure and said flatly: "I was hoping they wouldn't have anything like that!"

"Why didn't they use the RPGs before?"

"The angle is wrong. They must get close before they can knock out the machine guns. That was a wild shot. Let's hope that they're getting impatient and foolish!"

"They must know that time is not on their side," said Mike hopefully. "Haleel's boys would have radioed and found that there was no answer."

"We don't know when the office will radio us. They sometimes call in the evening."

Mike felt a compulsion to do something useful: "Where can I get a gun?"

The major said "Ah, yes!" and spoke to the crew of the machine gun nest. After a few words he turned back to Mike and handed him an assault rifle and some ammunition.

"Can you use this?"

"I haven't used one before but I only need to know how to load it."

The major showed him the safety mechanism and how to load the weapon.

"You realise it's not easy to kill a man?"

"I'm frightened enough to do anything!" replied Mike.

"That describes all of us perfectly."

The sound of automatic weapons resumed. This time it was concentrated at the southern ramp though there was intermittent shooting from all around the perimeter of the hill.

"They're back!" said the major. "Come with me to the other nest. It sounds as though we'll be more useful there!"

"I wish it weren't raining!"

"It's worse for them. They'll find it hard to get a handhold if they manage to reach the sides of the hill and the ramps are slippery."

The major gave some instructions to the crew of the machine gun before he and Mike clambered down the mound.

They passed quickly behind the soldiers who were positioned around the edge of the hill. The men were lying on their stomachs, deployed in pairs along the low ridge that had once been the ancient protective wall. The ground was muddy and small rivulets were pouring down the side of the hill at several points. Although the bandits fired almost continuously, the soldiers seemed to fire only when a bandit was exposed.

"Are we short of ammunition?" asked Mike breathlessly.

"No. But my men are trained not to shoot unless they have a clear target. They are also very careful. That is why we've only had two casualties."

Mike almost said 'One of our casualties was not because of the bandits!' but he decided that it would be better to say nothing.

With their heads low and the bandits' bullets flying above them, they made for the second machine gun nest.

5

The machine gun that guarded the southern ramp had been installed at the top of the pile of rubble that had once been the southern guard tower. It was not as high as the nest that faced the northern ramp, but was otherwise similar, with an open concrete ring surrounded by sandbags. The bandits who were firing at the defenders were less than two hundred metres away, concealed by the clumps of boulders that lay just beyond the foot of the ramp. Scattered all over the lower end of the ramp lay the bodies of the slain workers.

"Oh my God!" exclaimed Mike when he saw the corpses.

The major remained silent.

They climbed the pile of rubble as fast as they could and were soon crouching beside the sandbags that surrounded the concrete ring. "How are things here?" asked the major after he had caught his breath.

"A few of the bandits tried to run up the ramp but we stopped them," answered Captain Allawi from within the nest. "They managed to lob some grenades which fell short."

"Did you inflict any casualties?"

"We got a couple after the murder of the workers and we hit some of those who tried to run up the ramp. They are lying there, just above the workers."

"I suggest you take it in turns to rest," said the major, "It is enough if two of you are watching the ramp."

"Yes, major. But I suggest that you have a rest too," said the captain, "I think the main attack shall come after nightfall."

"You are probably right, but I cannot afford to rest until I'm sure that all the men are equipped and ready."

"We are worried about the RPGs!" said a soldier from within the nest.

"They can't use them effectively as long as we stop them getting up the ramp," replied the major.

"At the rate they're firing," said Allawi, "It is only a matter of time before some of us are hit. They know that they can wear us down, and the fewer we get, the easier it will be for them to get up one of the ramps."

The shooting from behind the rocks reached a new peak. The major and Mike lay on the ground as the machine gun answered back, spattering the mud around the rocks at the bottom of the ramp.

"Did you get any?" asked the major.

"I don't know. It's hard to tell because they keep darting between the rocks."

"Pray that the Basra office tries to call early today," said the major. "And that God gives Haleel and his boys wisdom and decisiveness!"

"May God hear us!" said Captain Allawi, and he was echoed by the two other men behind the sandbags.

Mike and the major withdrew from the nest on all fours.

"Allawi is right," said the major as they crawled towards the perimeter of the hill, "They are trying to wear us down. I must see to the men around the perimeter. They might need ammunition."

"I'll come with you."

"You don't have to."

"It's better than being cooped up in the storage tent," said Mike, "And I'm one more gun."

"At a time like this, I would welcome help even from your friend," said the major.

Mike raised his head momentarily to stare at him, and a bullet whistled past his ear.

"Keep DOWN!"

"Yes dammit! I forgot!"

They moved cautiously, bent forward, along the hill's perimeter, stopping only to talk to the men who lay in pairs along the sides of the hill. There was no shortage of ammunition and the men seemed to be in good spirits.

38

THE BANDITS LICK THEIR WOUNDS

1

JAWAD WAS INSANELY pleased as he handed Aisha's weapon back to her. She accepted the weapon without looking at him and held it by the butt, letting the barrel hang down. Perhaps she feared that the barrel would be too hot to touch; or perhaps she was too aware of what the weapon had been used for.

Arroussi was panting for air: "Are you satisfied?" he asked Jawad as he slid a new magazine into his assault rifle.

"*Ayyah!* That was a job well done!" Jawad grinned broadly and burst out laughing.

"What's so funny?"

"Don't you see? If those sheep-brained dolts weren't so afraid to kill a worker or two they could have got both of us!"

"You enjoy killing, don't you?"

"Don't *you?*"

"I only kill when it's necessary. I don't enjoy it."

Jawad guffawed loudly and Aisha looked away. Mukhtar withdrew behind a rock and retched uncontrollably.

"Your son is vomiting!" said Jawad with a self-satisfied grin.

"Yes, he is."

"He's not really up to this sort of thing."

"He'll learn," replied Arroussi grimly.

The bodies of the workers were scattered near the bottom of the southern ramp like grotesquely crumpled dolls. Their blood oozed into the soft grey-brown earth, mingling with the dampness of the soil. Here and there an arm or a leg moved spasmodically but there was no sound other than the patter of the rain, the whining of the wind and the clicks of weapons being reloaded. The stench of blood and spent cartridges was carried away by the wind and the workers stopped moving.

"You're as pale as a corpse," said Jawad to Aisha as he leaned against a rock, "You know I despise squeamish women and have no time for them!"

"I know that," replied Aisha, and she was about to say more when she was interrupted by a tremendous explosion. A ball of black smoke rose high into the air from the other side of the hill. Several smaller explosions followed in quick succession.

"That was your truck!" said Arroussi to Jawad. He looked worried.

"That was the machine gun nest!" shouted Jawad, "My men were to lob grenades the moment they were within throwing range!"

Arroussi and Mukhtar looked at each other but said nothing. They both knew the sound of grenades. The loud explosion and the ball of black smoke that rose high above the hill were almost certainly the result of a large fuel tank blowing up.

"Listen, there is no more shooting from the other side!" exclaimed Jawad, "My lads have wiped out the resistance!"

"Perhaps the soldiers surrendered," said Mukhtar dryly.

"We'll soon know how things are at the northern ramp and around the perimeter," said Arroussi quickly. He wished his son would not bait Jawad, but Jawad was too engrossed with the idea of a quick victory to pay attention to Mukhtar. He toyed with the strap of his assault rifle while looking lustfully at Aisha's body. The killing had awakened his libido and he was in the mood to celebrate in the way he liked best, but she pretended not to notice.

2

It was not long before one of Arroussi's men came up and gave a brief summary of events on the other side of the hill. The man spoke directly to Arroussi and avoided looking at Jawad. The news was bad. Jawad's giant truck had not made it to the top of the ramp because it got bogged down in the soft mud and was riddled by heavy-calibre bullets from the machine-gun. Then it exploded. There were many casualties among Jawad's men. Arroussi listened patiently without interrupting while Jawad gaped as though he could not believe what he heard.

When the man finished speaking Arroussi stood quietly, looking down at his feet: "How many casualties at the northern ramp?" he asked quietly.

"We could not count the dead," replied the man, "But many of the men in the truck did not escape."

"What about our casualties from around the hill?" asked Arroussi.

"A few were killed trying to climb the sides. Some were killed before they even reached the hill. The ladders were useless!"

"Thank you for the information," said Arroussi quietly. He turned to Jawad and said: "I am sorry about your men. And your truck."

Jawad was furious: "The soldiers must have weapons we did not know about!" he shouted. "It's Selim's fault! He failed to warn me!"

"You heard my man's account," said Arroussi, "The truck got stuck in the mud before it reached the top of the ramp! That was just bad luck! Bullets from the machine gun must have punctured a fuel pipe and then caused a spark that blew up the truck!"

Jawad spoke to Arroussi's man: "Before the truck blew up… didn't my lads try to take the machine gun?"

The man shook his head. "They tried but could not. There is no cover between the truck and the machine gun. And there were also soldiers shooting at them from both sides of the ramp! Your men did all they could!"

"Those cowards!" exclaimed Jawad. "I'll kill them when this is over!"

Arroussi dismissed his man, who joined the others behind the boulders. Then he turned to Jawad, who was muttering to himself incoherently. Much as he hated doing it, Arroussi felt it necessary to mollify Jawad. If Jawad turned against any of his own men the cohesiveness of the attackers would melt away. "Jawad," he said, and he tried to make his voice sound as reasonable as he could, "It was just bad luck that your truck didn't make it!"

"My men should have run *up* the ramp instead of *down!*"

"They would have all been killed. That is a heavy machine gun up there, and Balushi's men are obviously well trained!"

Jawad felt he was living in a nightmare. His dreams had dissolved like honey in hot water and his impotence against the unexpected turn of events suddenly overcame him. "So what do we do now?" he asked Arroussi weakly. He was surprised to find that his anger had evaporated.

"If we had an armoured tank," answered Mukhtar, "We could send it up the northern ramp." He could not stop staring at the corpses of the workers.

"Shut up!" barked Arroussi.

But Jawad did not have the energy to respond. All he could say was: "We have to think of something else. A different plan."

3

Arroussi realised that Jawad had switched from a state of optimistic exuberance to its opposite, which was worse. To be useful he had to be reeled in, cajoled into a constructive awareness of reality.

"As you heard," said Arroussi, "My lads weren't too successful either. None of them reached the top of the hill. Not one of my men even managed to climb the sides of the hill! The attack was too spread out and the defenders fought well."

"I heard," said Jawad. He sat down with his back against one of the rocks. "So what shall we do now?" He sounded like a little boy who had joyfully put his toy boat in the river only to see it whisked away by the current. Aisha tried not to look at him. She knew that, as long as he lived, whenever Jawad remembered this moment of weakness he would get furious and vent his anger on her because she had been there.

Although he had already made up a plan, Arroussi did not answer at once. If Jawad lapsed into silliness, and people like Jawad could burst out in tears just as easily as they burst out laughing, he would kill him. All Jawad's men were on the northern side of the hill and Aisha would understand. She would understand if Arroussi killed Jawad because he had jeopardised the discipline of the men. If she did not understand, he would ask Mukhtar to *make* her understand. Mukhtar was educated and could speak persuasively to someone with Aisha's intelligence. Aisha's bitter repugnance at Jawad's glee when he was killing the unarmed workers had not escaped Arroussi.

But Jawad managed to pull himself together. "So what shall we do now?" he asked yet again, but this time much more robustly.

Arroussi noticed the change. "Without your truck to make a hole in the defences and put some of your men behind the soldiers we have no chance of scaling the sides of the hill. We must concentrate our attack on one of the two ramps. Hit it with all our men at once."

"Eh? And what about the heavy machine gun?" sneered Jawad.

"We'll take it out with the RPGs."

"**Yes!**" Jawad's hopes and secret plans came alive again. "We will remove the machine guns with the RPGs! We should have used them before the attack!"

"We cannot use the RPGs from behind the rocks," said Arroussi, "It's too far to aim properly and the grenades would either fall short or fly over the machine gun."

"So let's send someone up the ramp!"

Arroussi shook his head. "Anyone who gets close enough to do something useful will be torn to pieces by the machine gun. We'll attack the ramp when it's dark."

"That's too long to wait!"

"If your man destroyed the radios we have time. We will wait for darkness. But we'll tell our men to take pot shots at the hill all the time. It will keep our men busy and prevent those up there from having a rest."

"Why not send an RPG in one of the foreigners' jeeps?"

"Because it will need to get around the truck that's blocking the ramp! And if it gets stuck too we shall lose more men!" Arroussi was running out of patience with Jawad.

4

Jawad was in no position to argue. He had only Aisha to back him up while Arroussi was surrounded by his men. "Very well," he said, "We'll attack when it's dark."

Arroussi nodded but, almost in a whisper, Aisha said: "The soldiers almost certainly have night goggles."

Arroussi turned to her: "Are you sure?"

"Selim, our chief spy in the foreigner's camp, said he saw some boxes labelled 'night vision equipment', or something like that."

"A lot would depend on how many night goggles they have," said Mukhtar.

"Selim did not say how many boxes he saw," said Aisha.

"It makes no difference how many they have!" exploded Jawad. He was enraged that Mukhtar had entered the discussion and that Aisha had talked to him again. His voice rose as he said: "They have night goggles! That's all there is to it! So we lose a few more men. It doesn't matter how many men we lose as long as we take the hill!"

"Is there any way of getting through to your man Selim?" asked Arroussi calmly.

"He should still be up there," said Aisha, speaking to Jawad and trying not to look at Mukhtar. She moved closer to Jawad, letting him feel the warmth of her body and hoping to get his mind off Mukhtar. She did not know that Aslan had been instructed to tell Selim to come down the ramp with the workers.

"Selim is dead!" said Jawad angrily. "He and my other spies died with the workers. I did not think they would be of any further use."

Aisha closed her eyes and turned away.

"Too bad," grunted Arroussi. "They might have been of great help to us now." He was disgusted by Jawad's disregard for the lives of his men: *Jawad controls his men only through fear. Given the choice, they would probably kill him!*

"What's done is done!" said Jawad.

Arroussi nodded. "It's agreed then. We'll wait for darkness. That would give us a better chance of knocking out one of the machine guns with an RPG."

"You're forgetting the night goggles!" said Jawad.

"They can't have too many night goggles," said Mukhtar, "And when it's dark it is most likely that they would spread them out among the men on the perimeter. They will fear that some of our men will climb the side of the hill and throw grenades."

Before Jawad could answer, Arroussi said: "My son is right. The men at the machine guns would not need night goggles. In the dark they could send a stream of bullets at anything they thought was moving."

"I don't like waiting!" Jawad almost shouted the words.

"Neither do I," said Arroussi. He thought for a moment, then spoke again: "When it's dark we can pretend to be attacking the ramp with a lot of shooting and shouting, but actually keep most of our men under cover. In the confusion two men with the RPGs can crawl unseen along the sides of the ramp. In the darkness one or both should be able to get close enough to knock out the machine gun."

"Have we decided which ramp to attack?" asked Mukhtar.

"The northern ramp," replied Arroussi.

"It's longer than the other," said Mukhtar.

"Yes, but it's much less steep," replied Arroussi, "The men will move faster as they climb in the mud. And then there's the grove. In the darkness it could offer some concealment, as would the burnt-out truck."

Mukhtar nodded.

"My only argument against waiting for nightfall is that it would give time to the authorities to guess that something is wrong," said Aisha, addressing Jawad. She still entertained the hope, no matter how weak, that the attack would be called off. But she knew that Jawad would be impossible to live with if they returned empty-handed.

"Aslan will deal with that," said Jawad confidently, "Until tomorrow morning he should make them believe that everything is normal." Jawad had felt excluded from the discussion between Arroussi and his son and needed to make himself heard.

"What if they insist on talking to someone they know?" asked Mukhtar.

"We'll have to risk that," said Arroussi, "We can't give up now. Not after what we did to the workers. We can't leave witnesses. Especially not the foreigners."

"Would foreign witnesses make that much difference?" asked Aisha: *Could I persuade them to spare the archaeologists? What happened to the foreign woman?* Aisha could not forget her look of deep intelligence mingled with childlike innocence. For the first time since she had left home Aisha had felt a sense of sisterhood: *That foreigner could have been my friend!*

Arroussi shrugged. "Woman," he said, "If any foreigners survived they would blab to their newspapers and the authorities would never give up their investigations."

"Wouldn't it be more difficult for them to give up their investigations if we kill the archaeologists?" persisted Aisha.

"Yes, they won't give up for a long time," replied Arroussi, and Jawad found the older man's patience with Aisha astonishing, "But without witnesses they'll spend weeks trying to puzzle out what happened, especially if this Aslan convinces the Army in Basra that everything was normal until tomorrow. Even if they manage to trace the attack on the archaeologists to us, by then we would have had time to prepare our alibis."

"What are alibis?" asked Jawad without thinking, and he suddenly hated himself for showing his ignorance.

"Oh, alibis are made-up stories about what we were doing instead of being here," said Mukhtar glibly.

I will truly enjoy killing this man! thought Jawad. He smiled warmly at Mukhtar: but only with his mouth, his eyes were freezing cold.

Mukhtar was going to say something polite but Jawad had turned away to stare hungrily at Aisha's voluptuous body.

5

The weather was still deteriorating. The thick black clouds continued to amass above the besiegers and the besieged, and it was certain that there would be a cloudburst, perhaps before the sun had set.

"I think I should join my men at the northern ramp," said Jawad, "I want to make examples of those cowards!"

"Shouldn't you let your man Aslan know what happened?" asked Arroussi. "He might be expecting the attack to be over soon, and could decide to leave if it rains."

Arroussi was reluctant to let Jawad join what was left of his men, who were probably at the foot of the northern ramp. Jawad was still very angry at the failure of his truck to breach the defences and he was quite likely to say or do something to his men that would infuriate them. If Jawad's men rebelled they would kill him, and Arroussi would find it difficult to control what was left of Jawad's men during the night attack on the hill.

"I told Aslan not to go home until tomorrow morning," said Jawad irritably, "Anyway, my radio was in my truck! I cannot get in touch with Aslan."

"You can use my radio."

"Aslan doesn't need to know anything!" Jawad had no wish to tell Aslan that the first attack had failed.

"As you wish," said Arroussi, "But do you think we should talk about the night attack? We have made no plans about that."

"There is nothing more to say. We wait until it's completely dark and then pretend to attack the northern ramp so that your men with the RPGs can creep up along the sides and knock out the machine gun!"

"Would you agree, Jawad, that some men should be posted around the foreigners' vehicles in case someone decides to steal a jeep?" Arroussi was willing to speak in the humblest of tones in order to get Jawad into a more cooperative mood.

"Two men should be enough."

"I agree with you, Jawad. I'll send off two men at once."

Jawad had not expected Arroussi to agree to anything he said so quickly: *The old fool lost as many men as I did. Maybe more. He knows he is not better than me!* His ego replenished, Jawad grabbed Aisha's hand and pulled her away from the others: "Now you come with me to the northern ramp! I want to see the mess those idiots made!"

"I have a better idea, my love," said Aisha with a sensuous smile. Like Arroussi, she did not want Jawad to get to his men while in such a mood. "Since we have some time, why don't we stop for a while behind some rocks on the way?"

"No. I want to confront those cowards now!"

"There is no hurry, my love. And why confront your men before the attack? You can confront them later, after you've taken the gold!"

Jawad seemed undecided, but Aisha squeezed his hand tenderly and rubbed her body sensuously against his. He gave in and they made their way to some tall rocks holding hands. Arroussi breathed a sigh of relief.

39

THE LONG WAIT

1

IT WAS MORE than three hours since the bandits had withdrawn to the shelter of the rocks. They continued to fire their weapons sporadically at the soldiers on the hill, but the shooting was haphazard and came in waves, as though someone would fire his weapon on a whim and others would join in for the joy of it.

For the greater part of the morning Mike and the major patrolled the perimeter of the hill and chatted with the soldiers. The men lay, in pairs, on their stomachs along the remains of the protective wall with their rifles at the ready and their eyes never straying from the boulders that surrounded the hill. Although their discipline had not wavered during the assault, and although they were keen to show that their morale was high, the major knew that his men were fully aware of how precarious their situation was. He, like his men, knew how lucky they had been when the soft earth – or was it Providence? – had stopped the huge truck from reaching the top of the ramp and spewing out its murderous load.

Mike and the major climbed wearily onto the mound of the pit and sat on the rim. The top of the mound was not high enough to be in the line of fire of anyone at ground level close to the hill, and the bandits were unlikely to have long-range rifles.

"I'm tired of keeping my men in a state of alertness," said the major, "And they're tired of waiting and doing nothing."

"Yes," said Mike thoughtfully. He brought out his pipe, filled it carefully and lit it, "Yet what can you do other than exhort your men to keep their eyes open?"

"I just hope I didn't overdo my exhortations," said the major, "A state of constant alert is tiring, and tired men can become complacent. A moment's lapse could allow a stealthy bandit to climb the side of the hill and throw a grenade."

"Or use one of the damned RPGs."

"Oh I think they'll save the RPGs for the main attack," said the major, "They can't have too many rocket-propelled grenades."

"I suppose they're expensive," said Mike.

"Quite expensive, and unlike terrorists these bandits don't have unlimited funds. They wasted one rocket grenade but they won't waste any more. They'll probably try to use them on one of the machine gun nests!"

"Are you saying that the next assault will start with one or two cretins with RPGs creeping up one of the ramps to try and knock out its machine gun?"

"That's their most likely move."

"And if they succeed there'll be nothing to stop the rest from pouring in like angry wasps!"

"Yes. Almost nothing except my men on either side of the ramps, which may not be enough." The major regretted saying that, for his words would only increase Mike's despair. He lit a cigarette and said, as calmly as he could: "My men are aware of the danger of a bandit creeping along the side of one of the ramps and using an RPG. That is why it has not happened yet."

"But will they be able to stop them when it's dark?"

"They're good soldiers and two will have night goggles. There's a good chance they'll stop them."

Mike did not answer.

"We mustn't give up, Mike. There's still hope, you know."

"Hope?" said Mike. *Hope?* His thoughts turned to Amalishah, to her large black eyes and raven-black hair, to her dazzling smile. His yearning to see her felt like an open wound in his chest: *I mustn't think of her! She killed a man only because she realised I wasn't taking her away from here!*

The major said emphatically: "Yes, there's hope. Haleel might do something."

"Oh yes, Haleel."

"Sooner or later he'll be told that both radios don't work." The major's voice was steady despite his weariness.

Mike looked away. "I suppose you're right…" *Eventually it shall be reported to him, and then he'll come up against a bureaucratic wall! What will happen to Amalishah when I'm dead?*

The major took a long drag from his cigarette and stared at the desolate landscape. Mike's sparse words had done little to alleviate the sense of impending doom they both felt, but like any good officer he had to keep up everyone's morale as best he could.

2

To a casual onlooker who did not notice Mike's pipe or the major's uniform, the two might have looked like naughty schoolboys taking a brief respite from mischief. The major was absorbed in his thoughts and smoked one cigarette after another. After a while Mike looked at his watch and said: "It's been considerably more than three hours since they've done anything."

"There has been some shooting," the major reminded him.

"That was to remind us that they're still here. What do you think they're doing now?"

"I don't know. They seem to be waiting for something."

"Reinforcements?"

"I don't think so. There must have been considerably more than two hundred of them. That is probably all they've got. But although they lost a lot of men there are still enough to take us, if luck is on their side."

"Luck? I thought you had a doctorate in physics."

"Luck, Providence, God, call it what you will. I'm old enough to have noticed that things sometimes work consistently one way and then, at other times, just as consistently in the opposite way."

"You might as well believe in astrology! With the stars supposedly favouring one thing and then another."

"No, Mike. A belief in astrology would be against my religion."

"And you think that luck is presently on our side?"

"That truck was stopped, wasn't it?"

"And you think that luck may continue to favour us? Do you really think that Haleel might do something in good time? Before we're all dead?"

"Luck will continue to favour us, *insha'allah*, if it is God's will."

Mike felt uncomfortable; the conversation was at risk of degenerating into triviality. Worse, it could end up wallowing in theology. He took a deep breath: "Is there anything we can do to improve our position?"

"Not really. We've done all we can."

"I wish it would rain seriously! It would make them uncomfortable!"

"It *has* rained, though not seriously."

"I meant *real* rain."

The major laughed mirthlessly. "*Real* rain would make my men uncomfortable too. Why not see how the people in the storage tent are doing?"

"I almost forgot about them. Well, all right, let's visit my colleagues."

"Hm. Let's wait until I finish my cigarette!"

"Let's wait until I finish my pipe!"

They both smiled, but Mike's smile was brittle and soon vanished. "I am reluctant to be with people who entertain hope when I have none," he said.

"I feel the same way," replied the major, "But there is always room for hope, and perhaps it would be good for you to be with your friends at a time like this. I think you should remain with them when I go back to my men."

"We can't keep these cretins at bay for too long, can we?"

"My men and I will fight to the last bullet. That is what we were trained to do. Your job would be to keep your friends from losing what hope they have."

Mike shook his head: "Hussein, I saw the workers lying like so many mangled lumps of meat. I don't think I can put on a cheery face in front of my colleagues. Not while I know there is very little hope for any of us."

"It won't be easy, but you are the only one who can keep your colleagues' hope of rescue alive."

"Why should I?"

The question was out of character for Mike. The major was surprised until he realised that Mike was struggling with feelings other than a fear of dying. He tried to see the implications of the question and suddenly got a fleeting glimpse of Mike's convoluted emotions. It was a sudden and instinctive empathy, such as happens only between similar men at a time when they both expect to die: *He is thinking of _her_! I did not realise how emotionally involved he is. He must have spoken to her and she has bewitched him!*

But Mike's question, for all that it revealed, deserved an answer. "Why should you help your companions not to lose hope?" asked the major, "Because although you are not an officer, Mike, you are a gentleman and that is the right thing to do."

"You've lived too long in England, Hussein. And even in England

506

such things are becoming out of fashion."

"Perhaps I have. But we both have duties, even at a time like this. Duty is the same everywhere and at all times."

"I don't give a damn about duty right now!"

"You're thinking of *her*, aren't you?"

"Her? Who do you mean?" The major's words were veering towards a subject Mike wished to stay away from.

"Your secret friend."

"You said yourself that she cannot be my friend!"

"I used the term loosely. Tell me Mike: Can one talk to her? What is she like?"

"Do you still want to kill her? If she exists?"

"I know she exists, and I have no choice but to try and kill her."

"Let's not talk about her, please Hussein."

The major remained silent: *According to what everyone says, Mike was obsessed with the goddess of the temple for years. The goddess was a fascinating myth, an alluring idea around which he could wrap his thoughts, his dreams, his work. And then he must have met her in the cavern, and seeing her alive would have been something that he would not even have dreamt of! Her evil beauty bewitched him and he fell in love with her. Now he believes she killed Rashidi and feels betrayed. He is wrong about that but I must never tell him even though his heart is broken. It is for his own good, although a broken heart is a poor companion when death is beckoning from around the corner!* Since Mike's pipe was still going strong the major lit another cigarette.

3

It was more than an hour after they had sat on the rim of the mound when Mike and the major entered the storage tent. Mike felt slightly self-conscious carrying an assault rifle but nobody commented, although he got some strange looks, particularly from Ohanian. Everyone waited for the major to speak.

"You may have noticed that there hasn't been any serious shooting for some time," began the Major pleasantly, "The bandits tried to storm the hill but my men held them off."

"Are the bandits gone?" asked ElKureishi.

"No, they are not gone," replied the major, "But I think they will change tactics. They lost one of their trucks at the northern ramp and quite a lot of men, but I don't think they lost enough men to lose interest in the gold you have dug up."

"What will they do now?" asked one of the Turkish postgrads. He had been in the Army and liked clear-cut answers.

The major looked at the young man, trying to assess how best to answer. The young Turk was a handsome lad, intelligent and clearly level-headed. "I don't know what they will try next," said the major, "But the truck is blocking the northern ramp so I don't think they shall try to send a vehicle that way again."

"What about the southern ramp?" asked Carol.

"Even the Land Rovers would find it difficult to climb the southern ramp. It is too steep and the ground is soft and wet. It would be completely impossible for a vehicle to climb now because of the rain."

A young postdoc at the back cleared his throat. The major looked in his direction and the young man stood up to speak: "What if we offered to give them some of the treasure? Would that make them go away?" The postdoc stared at ElBalushi defiantly.

There were murmurs of protest from some of the archaeologists but the young man did not back down.

"How dare you think that we could make such an offer?" said ElKureishi sternly.

The postdoc stood his ground: "Given the alternatives," he said, "My suggestion is reasonable."

The major nodded understandingly. "Your idea is not devoid of merit," he said, "And under different circumstances I would support it because it could save your lives and the lives of my men. But I don't think we can negotiate with those people. They would break any agreements they make."

Mike remembered the slaughtered workers: *He's right. They've gone too far. After killing the workers they must eliminate all witnesses. They cannot be reasoned with. They wouldn't stick to any agreement they make.*

The young man sat down. The archaeologists and the students were about to start arguing among themselves but the major cut them short: "We have to put this lull in the fighting to good use," he said. The hubbub subsided. "I have arranged a rota for my men to get something to eat. I suggest you get something to eat too. Some of the students can go – very carefully – to the food stores and bring back food and water for everyone, but don't bring back more than you need."

"How long shall we all be cooped up together in here?" asked a female student timorously. She was a young Iraqi girl who had had a somewhat sheltered upbringing and felt uncomfortable being with men in circumstances that imposed a certain degree of intimacy.

"You can expect to be in this tent until tomorrow," replied the major, "And if any of those who shall go to get food and drink know where candles and electric torches can be found, let them bring them here."

"Are we to stay here until tomorrow then?" asked Leonard. He did not like what he had heard and wanted to confirm the unpleasant part.

"That is very possible, doctor."

"Uh… we noticed that Mike is carrying a gun," said Bradley, "Are we all to be armed?"

"I don't think that will be necessary. Professor Townsend has some experience with weapons and volunteered to help. He has been very useful, but he shall now stay with you and will not need a weapon. None of you shall need weapons. If the bandits manage to get into this tent you would perhaps be safer if they find you unarmed."

"Major, when can we expect the next assault?" asked Professor Efremoghlou.

"I can't say. Perhaps after dark."

"When did you radio for help?" asked ElKureishi.

That was the question the major was hoping would not be asked. "We have done all we can."

But the professor insisted: "That is not an answer to my question!"

The major took a deep breath. "The answer to your question is 'We have not radioed for help.'"

There was a gasp of dismay. "Why not?" asked ElKureishi, suddenly pale. "Why in Heaven's name did you not radio for help?"

The major spoke through clenched tenth: "Both radios are not working!"

"How is that possible?" asked Carol.

"The weather must have caused a sudden and unpredictable surge of current from the generators," interjected Mike, "such a sudden surge would have burnt out the radios." *Let's hope nobody realises I'm talking nonsense! But they must not know about Ali!* Ohanian looked at Mike quizzically but said nothing.

"Can't Selim repair at least one of the radios?" asked Professor Efremoghlou.

The major spoke before anyone could comment: "That is not

necessary. As you know, the authorities in Basra call us regularly. When they find that our radios do not respond they will know that we are in some kind of... trouble."

"Exactly how much trouble are we in?" asked Carol.

The major was about to say 'That remains to be seen,' but he stopped himself and said: "So far we have held our own very well."

"Why shall we need candles?" asked ElKureishi, "We have electric lights."

"All the power has been transferred to the floodlamps. The floodlamps have been moved to cover the ramps in case the next attack occurs after dark."

"What about the perimeter?" said Professor Efremoghlou, "It cannot be left in darkness."

"The light from the ramps shall illuminate the perimeter too, to some extent. Some of my men on the perimeter have been issued with night vision goggles. Nobody will get past them."

The archaeologists and students fidgeted and murmured among themselves, but before anyone could ask any more questions the major raised his hand and said: "I have to go now. Please use the time you have wisely."

The major left, taking Mike's weapon with him. Mike found a chair and sat down. He did not wish to talk to anyone and nobody spoke to him. Everyone was deeply preoccupied with his own thoughts.

40

AISHA AND JAWAD BREAK UP

1

ONCE ALONE BEHIND the tall rocks with Aisha, Jawad let his rage take over. Arroussi was not there to make stupid comments, and he could freely show how he felt! His rage had festered within him from the moment he had heard the bad news about his truck, and it had fed itself at every opportunity until it had become a burning poison in his chest. His breath came in short hissing gasps while he tightened and released his fists with every breath: *Were it not for those cowardly dogs I would now have been on my way home, laden with gold!* But his men had failed him! The gold was still on the hill and he had to play second fiddle to Arroussi! *I'll kill the cowards when I finish enjoying the woman... I have no use for cowards!* But the worst thing was that the snivelling cur, Mukhtar, dared talk to his woman whenever he pleased! *And she, the filthy whore, talks back even though she knows it displeases me! Perhaps she makes eyes at him behind my back! Perhaps she and the cur are plotting to kill me!*

Although the targets of Jawad's anger were beyond his reach, Aisha stood before him, wearing only her shirt. She stood with her long legs slightly apart and her hips pushed seductively to one side. Despite what she felt about the massacre of the workers she desperately wanted Jawad to forgo confronting his men. Aisha could think of no reason for Jawad's anger other than the supposed cowardice of his men and the loss of his truck, and she hoped to turn his mind away from murder by using her body to stimulate and then gratify his desires. She felt certain that a strong dose of pleasure would calm him down. It had worked before, and it could work now... she smiled at him invitingly: *Come to me, my love. Forget your anger in the pleasure that awaits you...* She gave him a warm, reassuring smile but he only glared at her malevolently. Her smile and her open invitation only served to focus his rage upon her. With an inhuman growl he grabbed her savagely by the throat and pushed her down to her knees before lashing out frenziedly with his fists. He had vented his anger on her many times before, but it was never like this, never with such vehemence. Aisha was terrified and alarmed but, throttled by his hold on her neck, she could only raise her arms to ward off the blows. Her distress only inflamed his sadism and he struck her repeatedly until she went limp. He released her and she crumpled to the ground, but it was only when she lay trembling, curled into a whimpering ball, that Jawad's lust became stronger than his need to hurt her. He kicked her viciously to make her open her legs and then fell upon her to indulge his sexual urge. It was with a brutality he had never shown before. When he finished he got up, adjusted his clothes, and stalked away to join the others. He had intended to murder her and had not spoken a word during the whole encounter, but by the time he finished his anger was mixed with other feelings and he somehow forgot to kill her, or perhaps felt that what happened to her was unimportant.

Aisha regained consciousness while Jawad was adjusting his clothes. When he left her terror of him lessened and the pain hit her suddenly in all parts of her body, but it was her feeling of worthlessness that hurt most, and she burst into uncontrollable tears. She remained naked on the ground behind the tall rocks; bruised, bleeding and weeping silently.

2

It was cold and wet, but not yet completely dark, when Jawad rejoined Arroussi and his men near the base of the southern ramp. "What a gloomy lot you all are!" Jawad exclaimed with unusual joviality, "Have you forgotten that you'll be rich in a few hours?"

Arroussi was sitting alone, preoccupied with concerns about his son, staring dourly at the ground. He was pulled abruptly away from his thoughts and looked at Jawad with annoyance: "We'll only get rich if there are no more setbacks!"

Jawad waved his hand dismissively: "There won't be any more setbacks!"

"I hope you're right!" Arroussi rasped.

"I know I'm right. Are we still thinking of attacking the northern ramp when it's completely dark?"

"There is no reason to change what we agreed. Where is your woman?"

"She will be joining us soon. She's behind the rocks, weeping like a little girl!"

Arroussi guessed the reason for Jawad's unusual pleasantness. "Your woman must be weeping because you were such a good lover!" he said sarcastically.

"Yes I was!" said Jawad, missing the sarcasm. "I enjoyed myself immensely! Her body was so warm and soft that I..."

"Please don't talk like that in front of the men," interrupted Arroussi, "Some are young and must not be made to listen to such things!"

"Oh yes," said Jawad with a laugh, "We must not corrupt the young!" He walked over to a flat bench-like rock and sat down; yawned and stretched his legs. He had completely lost the need to confront the men who had fled down the ramp when the truck got bogged down. Arroussi looked away and resumed staring at the ground. He could not forget that his son had been sick after the massacre of the workers: *I can understand why my son did not take part in the killing, but why did he have to throw up after the killing was finished? Why did he have to show such weakness?* Arroussi had no illusions about the kind of men he led: *My men expected my son to cut a bold and dashing figure! A little reckless perhaps, a little wild and irresponsible maybe, but always hard as iron!* The old bandit was convinced that by being sick Mukhtar had lost the respect of the men. Unless something was done the story would spread and the men would invent crude jokes that would make his son a laughing stock: *Why did he have to vomit like a frightened child?* But Arroussi was unable to think of anything he could do that would help Mukhtar, and the more he struggled with the problem the more resentment he felt towards his son.

"Father?" Arroussi had not noticed that his son had returned.

"What do you want?" he snapped angrily.

Mukhtar knew the reason for his father's anger. *He thinks I'm weak, not fit to be his son! He thinks I vomited at the sight of the blood! But it was the needlessness of the butchery that disgusted me, and that madman merrily prancing about and spinning like a dancer as he killed the workers!* Mukhtar had never understood why his father had been so ready to go along with Jawad and agree to massacre everyone in the foreign expedition. He had made his feelings known soon after Arroussi's first meeting with Jawad at the Turkish baths:

"Father, I am appalled that you agreed to a butchery!"

His father had replied: "When we've taken the ancient gold and are back in our homes the authorities will mount an investigation and seek witnesses. Anyone on the hill left alive would be able to point the finger at me and Jawad! We must ensure that the authorities cannot find anyone to testify against us!'

Mukhtar had found the argument hollow: 'The prosecutors will not need witnesses from among the foreigners and their helpers, father! Many of our men are habitual criminals who will pass into the hands of the police sooner or later. At the first interrogation they will blab all they know about who was responsible for the attack! Our own men are our greatest liability! There is no need to kill all the foreigners and those who work for them!'

'Are we then to do nothing to protect ourselves from prosecution?'

'We can draw on the usual methods of bribery, coercion and clever lawyers!'

To this Arroussi had remained silent, and it was only now, as he remembered the bitter altercation he had had with his father, that Mukhtar understood why his father had agreed with Jawad to murder everyone in the foreigners' camp: *My father was afraid that Jawad would think he was weak!* For the first time in his life Mukhtar perceived his father's limitations. He was brought back to the present by his father's gruff voice: "I said, 'what do you want?'" said Arroussi irritably.

Mukhtar manged to keep his voice firm: "I've just come back from the place where the foreigners park their jeeps and trucks. I think we should put more guards there. In the falling darkness a group of soldiers can overcome our two men and escape."

Before Arroussi could answer, Jawad drawled: "The dogs on the hill are too frightened to do anything other than wet their pants!"

Arroussi ignored Jawad. "And how will the soldiers overcome our guards?" he asked his son mockingly, "They can't rush down the southern ramp. They know that some of our men are watching it!"

"In this poor light some of ElBalushi's soldiers can climb down the sides of the hill and then meet where the vehicles are parked. We cannot watch the whole perimeter and some soldiers may get through!"

"Ha!" Jawad smirked, "Those idiots won't even dream of climbing down the sides of the hill! And you are an idiot to think they'll try!"

Arroussi ignored Jawad again: "Why should they want to drive off in one of the vehicles? The soldiers are too few as it is and they cannot afford to get fewer. And even if any manage to escape they won't be able to reach anywhere in time to bring help!" Arroussi did not try to hide his anger at his son.

"There may be a radio hidden in one of the vehicles, father, or they may hope to meet someone who is on the way here. Anyone coming to the hill through the wastelands is sure to have a radio!"

Arroussi realised that his son was right. He frowned and nodded, but before he could speak, Jawad said: "Are the men who are guarding the machines too few to make you feel safe?"

Mukhtar turned to Jawad: "None of us should feel safe as long as some of the soldiers can escape and call for help!" He spoke as politely as he could.

"If it will make your son feel safer," said Jawad to Arroussi, "Why not burn the foreigners' machines?"

"Because we might need them!" Arroussi was tempted to add: 'And because we don't have enough vehicles now that your truck is a burnt-out hulk!' but he decided not to say anything that might irritate Jawad. He addressed his son: "How many men do you want to take, Mukhtar?"

"I think five or six should be enough. I'll tell them to scatter and hide among the rocks that surround the vehicles. We'll join you and the others at the northern ramp when the main attack starts."

Jawad laughed. "You want to take as many as *six* men? If you're so frightened why don't you just *vomit* all over the trucks so that nobody will want to touch them?"

3

Arroussi was shocked at the direct affront to his son but managed to control his anger. The men around him were all suddenly silent, staring at him and Mukhtar, and he felt the tension rise. Yet if he intervened that would only confirm that his son was a weakling. He nodded with a frown to Mukhtar, effectively saying: 'Deal with this yourself!'

Mukhtar got the cue and said evenly: "Perhaps you should be more careful what you say, Jawad." His voice was calm, but he looked at Jawad directly as he spoke. This was a warning and Jawad, not unexpectedly, took it as a personal insult. He sprang to his feet and moved menacingly towards Mukhtar. "You feel safe because your father is here, boy? But your father cannot help you – this is between you and a real man!"

As he moved towards Mukhtar, Jawad expected the boy to crumble and apologise, but Mukhtar only removed his glasses and put them in his shirt pocket. Jawad found the measured response provocative and this further aroused his anger. He said nothing but when he was close enough to Mukhtar he swung his fist viciously at the young man's head and braced his other hand to punch him in the stomach. To everyone's surprise Mukhtar smoothly evaded the blow and Jawad almost lost his balance.

Mukhtar said hurriedly: "Jawad, this is not the way..." He hoped that Jawad would desist, but Jawad was too furious to desist. He took another vicious swing at Mukhtar's head and, once again, the young man evaded the blow. But when Jawad lost his balance for the second time he tripped him with his foot. Jawad fell forward and ended up sprawled ignominiously on the ground. Mukhtar stepped back.

With an obscene expletive Jawad was up in an instant and, consumed by rage, pulled out his knife. With the speed of a striking snake he sprang forward, holding his knife before him. Arroussi could only watch and hold his breath as Jawad closed in to kill his son. The men watched mutely, wondering what Arroussi would do if Jawad killed Mukhtar. But in the split second that Jawad thrust his knife forward his wrist was caught in an iron grip and he felt the sharp tip of Mukhtar's own knife beneath his jaw: "This has gone far enough, Jawad!"

Shaking with fury Jawad tried to twist his wrist out of Mukhtar's grip but he was unable to free it. "This has gone far enough!" repeated Mukhtar.

Jawad again tried to free his knife hand but again he failed and the tip of Mukhtar's knife pushed upwards beneath his jaw just enough to draw blood. **"Drop the knife, Jawad!"**

Jawad had not felt fear for a long time and the sharp pain beneath his jaw suddenly became his only reality. His knife hand was powerless and from the speed at which Mukhtar had reacted he knew, without any doubt at all, that before he could kick or lash out with his other hand the knife beneath his jaw would push upwards all the way. He could almost feel the metal tear through his mouth, crack his palate open and dig into his brain. Burning with fury yet terrified at the possibility that his life could end suddenly, Jawad hesitated but then let his knife drop to the ground. Mukhtar released Jawad's wrist and took several steps back before putting his own knife away. "We must not fight amongst ourselves, Jawad."

Without a word Jawad picked up his knife and returned to sit on the bench-like slab of rock, staring sullenly at the hill. The men resumed talking among themselves, pretending that nothing had happened. The blackness of Jawad's thoughts was unfathomable.

"I think you should take six men and go!" said Arroussi to his son. He was breathing heavily.

"Yes, father." Mukhtar took his assault rifle and ordered six men to follow him to where the foreigners' vehicles were parked. Arroussi noticed the alacrity with which the men responded: *So my boy is only soft when it comes to unnecessary killing! He has never killed a man but in every other way he is as hard as I am.* He nodded to himself with satisfaction: *This little unpleasantness has served a useful purpose. There will be no jokes about Mukhtar's vomiting!*

4

Just then Aisha emerged from behind the rocks. She came back unobtrusively and kept her head down as she squatted not far from Jawad. Jawad ignored her and continued to stare sullenly at the hill. Arroussi noticed that that she was limping slightly and that although her face was dry her eyes were red and swollen: *I'm truly sorry for that woman. Jawad would not survive without her and yet he treats her abominably. Still, she is fortunate not to have seen my son get the best of that maniac. He would kill her at the first opportunity if he thought she had witnessed his humiliation!*

Some time after Mukhtar was gone Jawad said pleasantly: "Before the attack starts I shall tell my men to burn the foreigners' jeeps and trucks!" He had pacified himself with the thought that Arroussi and his son would soon be dead, so why remain angry?

"As I said before, we might need them," replied Arroussi, "If we have to leave in a hurry the more vehicles we have the easier it will be to disperse and the harder it will be for anyone to catch us."

"Why should we leave in a hurry?"

"The attack on the hill is not over, and it is not certain that the army believes that nothing is wrong."

"I have already explained to you that my man Aslan will keep the authorities happy at least until tomorrow! We shall be on our way home with the gold long before that!"

"We must consider all possibilities," replied Arroussi.

"Ah yes, we must consider all possibilities!" said Jawad, pretending to mock Arroussi but feeling that he had been put in his place once more. Arroussi wandered off to join a small group of his men who were standing some distance away and Jawad felt slighted at being left alone: *Just wait, you filthy dog! You will die soon! And you will die horribly, I promise you! And your son shall also die horribly!*

As he sat on the flat rock Jawad consoled himself by imagining various scenarios in which he killed Arroussi and Mukhtar in unpleasant ways. His spirits rose, for he slowly came to realise that mounting the second attack on the hill after dark had its compensations. The darkness would provide better opportunities to dispose of Arroussi and his son! All he would have to do is stay close to them, and in the heat and confusion of battle, with bullets flying in all directions, who would notice that the two dogs were knifed or shot from behind? *Once Arroussi is dead his men shall rally around me! They will accept my leadership gratefully!* Jawad began to feel increasingly optimistic about his prospects of getting the lion's share of the gold. It was not long before other advantages of waiting until darkness presented themselves. He beckoned to Aisha: "Come here, woman!"

Aisha was sitting despondently a small distance away from him, her face an expressionless mask, compulsively cleaning her assault rifle. She placed the weapon gently on the ground and came over to where Jawad sat upon the bench-like slab of stone. He did not move to offer her a place beside him and he smiled when he saw her limping.

"Yes, Jawad?" She stood before him, her face still a blank.

"We have some free time and nothing to do."

"Shouldn't we see how your men at the northern ramp are doing?"

"My men can take care of themselves."

"Jawad, the men should be told of the change in plan. They should not be made to wait until nightfall without knowing what you and Arroussi have decided."

"I'll tell them after I spend some time with you again." He looked pointedly at the clump of rocks behind which he had ravished her earlier.

Aisha felt as though a black cloud had suddenly enveloped her: *Does the pig never have enough?* "I am sorry, Jawad, but I'm not in the mood to be alone with anyone."

She had never refused his advances in the past and he thought: *She must have seen me fail to kill Mukhtar!* He glared at her fixedly. "Not in the mood?" he said venomously, "What does 'not in the mood' mean?"

"My love, you were so good the last time that I am exhausted."

"I don't care if you're exhausted. *I'm* in the mood again, and you'll do as I want!"

"Please, Jawad. This is a difficult time for me."

"You'll feel better after you give me pleasure!" He described what he wanted her to do in the crudest words he could think of, wishing to humiliate her in front of Arroussi and his men.

"I am not a slave girl, my love, to give you pleasure in whatever way you want, whenever you want!"

She could see his anger growing but did not care.

"You are my whore," he said in a loud voice, "You shall come with me now and do everything as I want it!"

"I am not a whore, Jawad." She looked him straight in the eye, but without anger.

"You dare reject me?" he asked in a sibilant whisper.

"Jawad, I don't know how this day shall end. There are many things on my mind."

Jawad grew livid. *She is thinking of Arroussi's son! It is he who is on her mind!* "Things on your mind?" he hissed, "What things do you have on your mind?"

"It has been a long day, Jawad, and the worst may be yet to come."

"The only thing on your mind must be to think of ways to give me pleasure!" He pointed at his genitals to emphasise his .meaning. She found the gesture deeply offensive and, for the first time, allowed herself to be angry: "I don't want to give you pleasure now, Jawad. Your clothes are spattered with blood and you stink of sweat!" She knew that he was quite capable of killing her but was well past caring:

Jawad's face froze, then his eyes narrowed and he smiled at her coldly. Very slowly he raised the muzzle of his rifle until it pointed at her head. She looked down at him without expression, imagining what it would be like to feel the bullets digging into her face. But Jawad did not pull the trigger. Still smiling coldly, and without lowering the weapon, he got up and stood before her: "I *will* have my way with you, you know, whether you're in the mood or not!" He pushed the snout of his rifle hard against her breast: "You'll be a dead whore soon, but

519

not until you give me pleasure exactly as I want it!"

The pressure of the rifle's snout was painful but she said nothing and did not back away: *I've been dead for a long time. I just wasn't sure until today!*

When Jawad saw that she was not going to say anything, he lowered his weapon, still smiling coldly, and casually passed it to his left hand. Then his smile changed into a feral snarl and he slapped her across the face with all his strength. He hit her twice, once with the palm and then, as she reeled from the blow, with the back of his hand. The violence of the blows loosened her ponytail and strands of her red hair fell to her shoulders, but she made no sound and did not move away.

"You can wait here and keep Mukhtar company when he returns," he said malevolently, "He will smell of jasmine and wild flowers!" He did not know what Arroussi or his men might do now that he had mentioned Mukhtar.

Jawad strode off. As he passed Arroussi he said: "I shall expect you and your men at the northern ramp when it's fully dark. Don't forget the grenade launchers."

Arroussi did not respond but stared at Jawad with an expression that was almost sad. Aisha lowered her head and turned to face the empty landscape. She wished Jawad had pulled the trigger and put an end to her miserable existence, but the tears that would have brought some relief refused to flow. She walked away and only stopped when she was at some distance from everyone.

5

When Jawad was gone Arroussi ambled over and stood close to Aisha. "I am sorry about what happened," he said.

She turned to face him. The kindness with which he had spoken threatened to release her tears but somehow she managed to hold them back. "I'll be all right," she stammered, almost in a whisper. She looked at Arroussi steadily just as a gentle breeze blew her hair over her eyes. The breeze cooled her face and made it easier to hold back the tears. She brought out a small elastic band from her pocket, pulled her hair back and briskly re-arranged her ponytail.

"Let's talk," said Arroussi, "I'm old enough to be your father. You can talk to me and open your heart. The men cannot hear us."

She smiled bitterly but remained silent.

"When all this is over, will you go back to Jawad if he'll have you?"

"Never!"

"Then don't worry about his threats, you are under my protection now if you want it, for as long as you wish."

"Thank you. Why are you being kind to me?"

"Perhaps because I still have some humanity left. Do you find that surprising?"

"Yes."

He smiled. "But if you are under my protection, you must never lie to me, do you understand?"

"I understand."

"Then tell me," and he paused for a moment, "Was it you who let the tall foreign woman escape?"

"Yes!" She expected Arroussi to pull out his knife and slit her throat, but instead he threw back his head and guffawed. When he finished laughing he said: "You are a very brave woman, Circassian. Under different circumstances, and if you had a fat dowry, I would have thought you the perfect mate for my son. He obviously likes you."

"Why do you say he likes me?"

"Oh, I am sure he knew it was you who released the captive. He did not mention that there were two pairs of tracks leaving our camp. He would have been able to tell that both pairs of tracks were made by women."

"And you think he did not say anything because he likes me?"

"Why else? Jawad would have killed you if Mukhtar had not said that the tracks were all mixed up."

"I am grateful to him for that."

"Keep your gratitude to yourself. You shall not see him again after all this is over."

Aisha did not expect such a blunt statement. "Don't you want your son to be like you?"

Arroussi nodded to himself: *That is perceptive! She is a clever woman!* "Mukhtar would not wish to be like me, and will therefore not need a woman like you by his side. I own a number of legitimate and very lucrative businesses that are more suited to his temperament. Anyway, the days of bandits are almost over. The world is getting too small for us."

"How is the world getting too small?"

"The police are getting smarter."

"But the opportunities are increasing. People have more wealth."

"That is true, but it is better protected."

"I see."

"Also, as we bandits see the wealth around us, we become more greedy. That is our main weakness. Jawad is planning to kill me, is he not?"

Aisha took a deep breath. "Jawad is always planning to kill someone, but he doesn't always do it."

"That is a non-committal way of saying 'yes.'"

She did not answer, and Arroussi changed the subject.

"By breaking up with Jawad you shall lose your share of the gold."

"Do you think I care?"

"At the moment, perhaps not. But circumstances change."

"When I get back, if I get back, I shall try to find some kind of employment. I won't need Jawad's money, or anything else from him."

"And what can you do?"

"I don't know."

"Perhaps I can help you, though it may not be easy. Can you read?"

"I have had some education."

"That always helps. Do you have a family?"

"I am dead to them."

"I see. Well, the future is full of surprises. I suggest you get some rest now, but be careful. Jawad is vindictive."

"I shall be careful. And thank you again." She bowed her head.

Arroussi withdrew and Aisha stood alone, engulfed in her thoughts.

41

The Archaeologists meet the Lamia

1

After the failed morning attack the bandits were left without instructions. They spread out aimlessly, like rats in an empty granary, and loitered behind the boulders that surrounded the hill. They then hardly moved at all, for whenever a bandit left the protection of the rocks a flurry of rifle fire would send him scurrying for shelter. The bodies of Jawad's men by the burned truck, like those of Arroussi's men who died trying to scale the sides of the hill, remained undisturbed, as did the corpses of the slain workers. None of the bandits thought that attending to the bodies of erstwhile friends, or rifling the pockets of the dead workers, was worth the risk of getting shot.

The dark morning turned into a darker afternoon but the bandits paid little attention to the weather. They ignored the intermittent drizzle and whiled away the time playing backgammon or talking loudly about how they would spend their share of the gold. When they lost at backgammon, or when their thirst for gold became more than they could bear, they vented their frustration by firing their automatic rifles exultantly in the general direction of the soldiers on the hill. Occasionally, a bandit would feel happy and raise his voice to sing a few lines from songs that were currently in fashion. The singing was always out of tune.

To the archaeologists and students in the storage tent the singing and the exultant gunfire were an affirmation of the confidence with which the bandits viewed their eventual triumph. The mood of hopelessness, which had started when the major had disclosed that no plea for help had been sent, grew steadily worse, fed by the relentless howling of the wind. By late afternoon the archaeologists and students were certain that some particularly potent form of assault was being prepared and, by dusk, they were like the occupants of a besieged medieval castle who waited in crestfallen silence, cowed by the knowledge that the enemy was tunnelling beneath the walls to plant barrels of gunpowder that would blow away their defences.

Not long after the cloud-hidden sun passed below the horizon the storage tent fell into complete blackness. Yet such was the mood of despondency that no-one called for light. It was only when an eerie high-pitched wail rose above the howling of the wind that the silence was broken by Professor Efremoghlou: "What a ghastly noise!" he said sombrely, "I've never heard anything like it!"

"It makes my blood freeze!" said Jehan, the Jordanian postgrad.

"It's just the wind!" said Efremoghlou hastily, anxious not to add to the students' fears, "It's only frightening because of the darkness."

"The wind never wailed like that!" whimpered a female student at the back of the tent.

"I'm sure it has something to do with the direction from which the wind is blowing," explained Efremoghlou reassuringly, "Each direction of the wind makes a different note! Haven't you heard of the colossi of Memnon in Egypt? In ancient times they were believed to sing when the morning wind blew!" *A little archaeology might nudge their thoughts away from our predicament!*

"This is not singing!" said Jehan, "It's like the crying of a lost soul!"

"A soul lost in Hell!" said the female student at the back of the tent.

"I'm certain this horrible noise is just the wind," insisted Efremoghlou, "What else could it be?"

"Back in Oklahoma," said Leonard gloomily, "Some folks would say it was the wail of a banshee!"

"What's a banshee?" someone asked in the darkness.

Leonard did not answer and there was silence. He regretted having spoken, for down in Oklahoma there were folks who believed that a banshee was a harbinger of death.

The silence was broken by Carol: "Don't say things like that, Leonard! It's just the wind blowing through the tents and outbuildings!" And for good measure she added emphatically: "Banshees don't exist!"

"Yes, of course," agreed Efremoghlou. He did not know what a banshee was and could only surmise that it was something malevolent that wails in the dark: *I wish Leonard had kept quiet! We're all worried enough as it is!* But those who knew what a banshee was, even if they did not believe in banshees, were dismayed by Leonard's comment and the atmosphere of gloom deepened.

2

The eerie wailing died away as mysteriously as it had begun, leaving everyone with the sensation of having been touched by the inexplicable, a feeling that added to their apprehension and sense of foreboding. The weather continued to worsen and the drizzle changed to a steady rain that struck the thick PVC of the tent with a muffled drone. Not much later, erratic flashes of lightning, followed by long peals of thunder, began to roll across the desolation. At first the lightning lacked robustness, for it was far and obscured by intervening clouds, but when the main part of the storm eventually reached the hill the flashes grew brighter and the peals of thunder became almost deafening. Nobody in the storage tent managed to sleep.

Mike sat on an armless chair holding his empty pipe. He had run out of tobacco but, overcome by the lethargy of hopelessness, had not bothered to put away his pipe. When he eventually poured the cold ashes on the floor he felt a twinge of guilt which he quickly suppressed: *Who cares if there's ash on the floor? We'll all be dead by morning!* He put the pipe in his pocket and turned to look around him, but although he strained his eyes he could not see anyone in the darkness. Without the solace of his pipe he felt frustrated and the silence of his colleagues annoyed him. He wished they had not lost heart so readily: *They didn't even ask who might have put the radios out of action! We're like sheep waiting to be slaughtered!* But at least there had been no emotional displays and Mike was grateful for that; he would have found emotional displays embarrassing: *What had Leonard said about us Englishmen? He'd said we were emotionally constipated!* He smiled acerbically in the darkness: *We don't show our emotions! We bottle them in!* His thoughts wandered and then, because they were beyond his conscious control, they homed in on the lamia's radiant face when she welcomed him on his return from Mosul. He could almost hear her say: 'I shall wear the light blue skirt and the white blouse. May I put on the shoes now?' The darkness sharpened the memory and his heart ached as he remembered that he was meant to pick her up at midnight: *Yes, we bottle our emotions and sometimes they choke us!*

He took a deep breath and exhaled slowly: *Chum, you'll be dead by morning! You won't see her again. Get her out of your thoughts!* Like everyone in the storage tent, Mike believed that the bandits would swarm over the camp sometime in the hours of darkness, well before daybreak. Hussein and the soldiers would put up a gallant fight, but the bandits' victory was inevitable. There were too many of them and they had rocket-propelled grenades. Despite his own troubles Mike could not help feeling sorry for the major: *Hussein did his best to warn us of the danger of bandits, but no one believed him! Not us, not Haleel's boys in Basra!* And again his thoughts returned to the lamia, for the thought of ElBalushi's warnings about bandits inevitably brought the major's *other* warnings to mind: *And I, also, paid no heed to Hussein's warning!* With the jolt that often accompanies the recollection of a nightmare, Mike remembered the pallid face of the young soldier who had been left drained of blood by the precipice: *I was warned about you but didn't listen! You pretended to care because you wanted me to take you away from here, and I believed you cared because I wanted so much to believe you!* He tried to push the thought of her away but the effort only produced a fleeting memory of her enormous eyes, alive with intelligence but tinged with sadness: *Oh God how I miss you! I wish I could be sure you were safe!* Mike admonished himself for letting her intrude so easily into his thoughts: *Damn it chum! We're all going to die soon! If only there was something we could do!* Suddenly restless, he peered around him; but there was only darkness.

3

The postdocs and students had chosen to sit or lie at the rear of the storage tent, away from the entrance. Some talked amongst themselves in inaudible whispers while others dozed fretfully in their chairs or on the floor. The senior archaeologists sat silently together at the front, opposite the entrance but with a sizeable empty space between them and the opening. Their chairs faced this way and that as though conversation could be tolerated but not encouraged. Even Carol was quiet as she sat leaning against her husband with her head on his shoulder and her eyes staring vacantly into the blackness. The flaps of the tent were closed but not secured.

The thunder and lightning eventually abated but the rain became a downpour. The wind-driven raindrops struck forcefully against the PVC of the storage tent with a booming patter. Several people fidgeted in their chairs and Mike realised he was holding his pipe again, more tightly than before: *It's only the rain, chum! It's only the rain!* But for a moment he had imagined the rapid dum-dum-dum of the raindrops to be the ghosts of the slaughtered workers asking to be let in: *I'm losing my mind!* And he would have continued to contend unsuccessfully with his thoughts had Ohanian not suddenly cried out: **"We shall all go crazy if we go on like this!"**

Ohanian's cry of exasperation caught everyone's attention. Mike turned towards Ohanian with a bemused smile but said nothing; he could not see his friend in the blackness. He returned his pipe to his jacket pocket. Some of the sleeping students and postdocs opened their eyes but closed them again when they realised there was nothing to see. ElKureishi jerked upright for a moment but, intimidated by the utter blackness around him, slumped down again in his chair. Only Carol reacted positively: "You're right!" she answered in a voice almost as loud as Ohanian's: "Don't you think we ought to have some light? Nobody said we shouldn't have some light!"

"I'm darn sure we'd all feel better if we could see each other!" drawled Leonard.

"I don't think it would make any difference at all," said ElKureishi dejectedly.

"Do we have any lanterns or electric torches?" said Mike: *Ah action! Something to wrench me away from my thoughts!*

"We didn't find any lanterns or torches when we went to get food and water," replied a student, "We were in such a hurry to get back that we only brought a box of candles. They were in the refectory!"

"So where are the candles?" said Mike.

"I think they're right here," said Leonard. The battered cardboard box that contained the candles had been left close to his chair. The candles were of different lengths and girths; all had previously been used by the workers.

A large, thick candle was lit and secured with molten wax to the wooden seat of an empty chair between ElKureishi and Leonard. The senior archaeologists were illuminated by a flickering yellow-orange light.

"That's much better!" said Carol. She was no longer leaning against her husband.

"Shouldn't we light more candles?" drawled Leonard, "The tent is draughty and the candle may go out."

"Yeah!" said Carol, "And the light doesn't reach those at the back!"

"Why light a second candle?" said ElKureishi, "Do we really want

527

to see how miserable we are?" The strained faces he could see only made his depression worse.

Carol was about to argue when Mike noticed a shoebox-sized object on the floor of the storage tent, half a metre from the opening.

"What's that?" he asked in surprise, pointing at the object.

Carol leaned forward: "It wasn't there before!"

"How'd it get there?" asked Leonard, speaking without his usual drawl.

Mike got up wearily and went over to pick up the object. It was heavy for its size and there were some cables attached. Several students and postdocs got off their chairs and came over to have a closer look. Those who had been lying on the floor sat up, rubbing their eyes.

"What is it?" asked Carol.

"It's a radio transmitter!" Mike replied. He could not suppress his excitement.

"How'd it get there?" asked Leonard again.

"A soldier must have found it and brought it here!" Mike answered: *This must be the radio that belonged to the spy! The radio Balushi's men had looked for! It's quite large; strange that they couldn't find it! But why did they bring it here?*

"Where would the soldiers have found a radio transmitter?" asked a student.

"In the tent of one of the workers, I suppose," said Mike: *In the tent of the traitor, the man who cut the throat of the radio operator!* He held the radio gingerly, as though it were tainted with blood.

"Why would one of the workers have a transmitter?" asked Carol.

"Who cares!" drawled Leonard.

Mike held up the radio in the candlelight: "Does anyone know how to use this thing?"

One of the Turkish postgrads said: "I've used a transmitter-receiver like that when I was in the army." He came to stand next to Mike, his eyes glued to the radio.

Mike handed it to him: "Can you work it?"

"I think so."

Everyone's attention was on Mike and the Turkish postgrad. The young man examined the radio but when he turned it over to look at its underside there was a grating sound followed by several small thumps. The postgrad shook his head and said, almost in a whisper: "I don't think this radio will work."

4

There was a murmur of disappointment and Mike asked: "Why not?"

"Because its insides are in little pieces!" answered the postgrad irritably, his intense disappointment expressed itself as irritation.

Mike nodded absent-mindedly: *The bastard who disabled the radios would naturally not leave his own radio in working order! Ah! But if he didn't expect his radio to be found it's possible that he didn't disable it properly!* He took the radio back from the postgrad and shook it gently. Although the rattle was not encouraging he asked the postgrad: "Do you think you can fix it?"

"I am not an electrician," replied the young man, "I wouldn't know how to fix it. Anyway, it needs a battery and a headset!" He held up the cables that hung from the side of the radio and singled one out. "Do you see this wire? That's for the battery!"

Mike would not give up easily: "Perhaps I can fix it. What voltage does it use?"

"Twelve volts. See? It says so right there. Twelve volts DC!"

Mike nodded: "I believe there are transformers and rectifiers in the tent that belonged to that electrician fellow, what was his name?"

"Selim," someone said.

"Oh yes, Selim," said Mike, "If we can find the right tools in his tent we should be able to connect the radio to the generator and rig up some kind of DC power supply. We can use the headset from one of the two main radios!" *But I'll have to get the headset myself because the body of Sergeant Ali might still be in the radio tent!*

"The insides are all in pieces!" protested the postgrad. His disappointment continued to sound like anger.

"Perhaps they're just loose!" said Mike, "If they're not broken we might be able to put them back in place and make the thing work. Does anyone have a screwdriver?"

One of the students had a Swiss Army knife. He opened the screwdriver attachment and handed the knife to Mike. Mike pulled up an empty chair and put the radio carefully on the seat: "Let's see what we can do with this!"

The Turkish postgrad placed the chair with the candle beside the chair with the radio.

"Mike, do you think you can make the radio work?" asked Leonard.

"It's worth a try!" said Mike hopefully, "But I would need another candle or two!"

"Shouldn't we call Selim or one of the military?" asked Efremoghlou, "This looks like a job for someone with specialist training."

"The major gave explicit orders that all the workers are to stay in their tents," said Mike carefully. This was not the time to tell anyone that the workers – and probably Selim – were dead. *But if Selim were the traitor he would be alive. He was certainly intelligent enough to be the spy!*

Efremoghlou frowned and said: "I really think this should be done by someone with specialist training!" He was sure that archaeology and electronics did not mix well.

"If the soldiers could fix it they wouldn't have brought it here!" said Carol sharply.

"I was once an engineer," Mike said, as though engineers could fix anything. He hoped that he had not forgotten the electronics he once knew.

Someone stuck two more thick candles on the chair seat and lit them as Mike squatted in front of the radio and tried to apply the screwdriver. "Damn!"

"What's wrong?" said half a dozen anxious voices.

Mike explained that the screwdriver on the Swiss Army knife did not fit the little screws that held the cover of the radio to the base.

"Keep trying!" said Carol encouragingly, her eyes aglow with hope. The rain had slackened and they could hear each other clearly. Mike nodded and continued with his efforts to remove the cover while everyone watched expectantly. After a lot of effort he eventually succeeded in turning the screws with the point of the knife, but when the screws were removed and the cover was taken off it was clear that the radio was beyond repair.

"Well, that's that!" said Mike curtly, trying hard to hide his disappointment, "The thing must have had quite a battering. It will never work again!"

Everyone looked away and ElKureishi covered his face with his hands. At the back of the tent two female students started to weep. To make matters worse, a sudden gust of wind blew out the candles so that the tent was again in total darkness. Several students cried out in dismay but Mike said firmly: "Who's got a light?"

"I'll light the candles!" said Ohanian and he brought out his cigarette lighter. But no sooner had he lit the candles than he looked up and gasped: *"Akh Asdvadz!"* and crossed himself.

5

The lamia was standing just within the opening of the storage tent, less than three metres from the men and women who stared at her mutely, shocked into immobility. She stood straight backed with her arms by her sides, her feet close together and her head bent slightly forwards. She wore a white blouse with a medium-length blue skirt and on her feet were soft-leather shoes. Her black hair was held in place by a delicate diadem of golden leaves that glistened in the candlelight, and around her slender neck was a necklace with a single large red gem. Apart from her clothes and shoes, it was as though the statue of Amalishah had come to life.

Taller than everyone except Leonard and Bradley, the lamia gazed down serenely at the faces that stared at her uncomprehendingly. She stood completely still, her mouth touched by the faintest of smiles. Mike could only stare at her, unable to speak. In the golden glow of the candles she looked beautiful beyond description. There was the scraping of chairs being moved as the senior archaeologists backed away. Only Mike and Ohanian remained in place.

With an effort of will Mike found his voice: "Why are you here?" he blurted out in Assyrian. Like the head of a sea monster that rises ominously above the waves ElBalushi's warnings had surfaced in his mind, awakening doubt and suspicion, yet his words felt inadequate and unnecessarily harsh, and he wished he had spoken more softly or said something else.

In response to Mike's abrupt question the lamia closed her eyes and slowly turned her head. When she opened her eyes again she was looking straight at him: "You would not have met me tonight," she said simply. "I thought that giving you this thing might help you all."

Although her voice was almost as deep as a man's it was maddeningly feminine and Mike was entranced: *Where in Hell did she get the radio?* He managed to stammer: "We are under attack by... by bad people!" He wanted to say more but his Assyrian failed him:

"I know," she said quietly

"You don't understand," he said, suddenly angry at her and at himself, "You and I are not going anywhere!"

The lamia's ghost of a smile remained as though frozen, but for the briefest of moments her eyes betrayed surprise and pain. Then her expression became cold and haughty and she spoke with exquisite dignity: "Have your friends changed the way you think of me, Michael Townsend?"

This was not the warm and childlike Amalishah Mike had known, and he realised that his angry words had caused her to change back into someone he had never met. He was now facing an Amalishah who remembered that she had once been an Assyrian queen, a goddess with the power of life and death over everyone around her, the goddess of the temple whose ruins were all around him. She was also, he reminded himself, an extremely dangerous woman who had killed many times and could easily kill him if she wished. For a moment he felt remorse at having caused the change in her, but the thought that she had reverted to her previous *persona* against her will was quickly extinguished by the memory of ElBalushi's words: *'They can be very beguiling, these things, if they want something from you.'* He wanted to cry out: 'Why did you have to kill that boy?' But he remained silent, his emotions in turmoil.

6

Although the lamia had spoken in Assyrian and with a guttural intonation that was unfamiliar to all but Mike, several of the people in the tent had understood what she said, and before Mike could decide how to respond everyone started talking at once:

"Who is this woman?" asked ElKureishi hoarsely.

"What is she saying?" asked the Turkish postdoc. He did not understand Assyrian.

"Is she one of the bandits?" asked Carol.

"She's talking Assyrian!" said Bradley, "Very fluent Assyrian! She can't be one of the bandits!"

Ohanian had realised who she was the moment he saw her, but he was so numbed by the shock that he was not quite sure he was awake. The existence of the lamia was totally fascinating, astounding, even miraculous, and yet strangely acceptable. He finally understood why Mike had asked about vampires while they were working on the script, and the bandits were suddenly of no importance.

"Where did she get the gemstone and the crown?" asked Efremoghlou, "We looked for them everywhere!"

The question brought Mike back to reality: *Chum, you are going to die tonight. Pull yourself together and deal with this!* Yet all he could do was speak the truth even though he knew that it was unlikely to be believed: "This is Amalishah," he said matter-of-factly in English, "She has lived in the ruins of the temple for a very long time. The diadem and the necklace are hers."

There was silence. Then Carol laughed sardonically: "Mike, are you saying that this is the woman who lived here as a goddess? The one who killed people?"

"Mike, can't you see that what you're saying is just plain mad?" exclaimed Leonard.

ElKureishi had already formed his own explanation. He glared at Mike accusingly: "Ah, this is the friend you were supposed to meet in Mosul!" he said, "I suppose you brought her with you when you returned!"

Mike looked at him vacantly, too shaken by events to say anything. The lamia gave ElKureishi a brief supercilious glance as though she would not condescend to give him her full attention. ElKureishi ignored the lamia and, encouraged by the lack of response from Mike, spoke to him the way one would speak to a miscreant: "Oh yes! You brought her to the camp without letting anyone know! I want you to tell me how you managed to smuggle her into the camp and hide her from all of us!"

"There's no rule that says we can't bring guests for a short time!" protested Leonard. Carol joined Leonard in the defence of Mike: "He was probably too busy preparing for his move to Mosul to tell us about her!" *This is a hell of a time for Kureishi to get prudish!*

ElKureishi guessed what Carol was thinking and found it necessary to voice his thoughts explicitly: "Didn't you hear what *Professor* Townsend said?" His attention was on Carol but his voice became shrill as he pointed a finger at Mike: "*Professor* Townsend said that the crown and the gemstone *are hers!* He evidently found them somewhere but kept them hidden so that he could give them to this woman! That's why he brought her here and didn't tell anyone about her!"

Carol's mouth opened as though she were going to speak but she held back and closed her mouth. Despite her loyalty to Mike she felt that the old professor had expressed the only explanation possible. While ElKureishi was speaking, Leonard had frowned and looked down at the floor. He had understood all that the lamia had said and things did not make sense: *Hell! A girlfriend wouldn't say what this woman said!* The Mike he knew would never steal ancient artefacts, but what if Mike had gone insane because he couldn't decode the script? He was under pressure to decode the script and had never failed before. An extraordinarily beautiful girl who looked so much like Amalishah could have made an unstable Mike believe she was the goddess: *She certainly looks like the statue of Amalishah! Mike was obsessed with the goddess for years and could have fallen very hard for this lookalike!* A completely besotted Mike might well have hidden the jewels to give them to her! *But why would she speak in Assyrian? She can't think we're all going to believe she's the goddess!* Leonard looked up at Mike and said: "Mike, I personally don't give a shit about the crown and the jewel, but I feel you should explain why this woman is here!" *Hell! I hate doing this to Mike but I must admit that old Kureishi is probably right!*

Carol joined in: "If this woman is pretending to be Amalishah she's trying to trick you, Mike! The real Amalishah has been dead for four thousand years! Her bones are in a box in this tent. This woman might even be in league with the bandits!"

With a shock Mike became aware of how serious the accusations were. He was being accused of stealing or of being insane, or both. It was also clear that his friends were ready to accept ElKureishi's accusations. But he was not used to being disbelieved and could only affirm what he knew to be the truth: "I've already explained who this woman is," he said quietly, "She's not in league with the bandits, and I can only say again that the diadem and necklace are hers. They always were. I didn't give them to her."

Leonard shook his head and looked down: *Mike's gone nuts! He's forgotten giving this woman the baubles because he's convinced she's Amalishah!*

"Oh my God!" cried Carol, "Mike, you mustn't believe she's the ancient goddess!"

"Mike, listen to me," pleaded Leonard, "We found the headless bones of the goddess! She was killed by the Hittites!"

"The goddess was not killed," said Mike evenly, "The bones were of someone else."

"That's ElBalushi's crazy idea!" exclaimed Carol, "You mustn't believe that!"

Leonard persisted in trying to bring Mike to his senses: "If the goddess escaped there must have been a way out of the cavern. If so, why didn't her priests use it?"

"Akh!" interjected Ohanian impatiently, "The priests were not trying to escape! They were protecting their goddess from an enemy who had followed them down the pit!"

ElKureishi stood up as though he was going to say something important, but all he said was: "This woman came out of hiding because she knows we are all going to die! She couldn't leave the jewels behind and didn't bother to take them off!"

"It may be that Professor Townsend has gone crazy," said Efremoghlou, "But he is not a thief!"

"How can Mike believe the ancient goddess still lives?" expostulated Carol.

Ohanian, not quite sure how to respond, rose to Mike's defence: "She spoke in ancient Assyrian!" he said, emulating Leonard's appeal to reason, "Did any of us ever hear the tongue ancient spoken like that before?"

"So what?" retorted ElKureishi.

So she is who Mike says she is! thought Ohanian, *And she can answer all our questions about the script, and the temple!* He was so engrossed by what the goddess could reveal that he forgot to speak and only nodded to himself several times.

ElKureishi interpreted Ohanian's repeated nods as a sign of acquiescence. "So she speaks Assyrian!" he continued, still standing and now speaking forcefully to all who would listen. "I say again: So what! And she speaks in a strange way. So what! Anyone who speaks Assyrian can put on a strange accent! Many tall pretty women can be made to look like the statue of Amalishah! I would like to know what this man hopes to gain from such a charade. Does he really think we'll believe that this woman is the goddess of the temple? If we survive this situation I shall see to it that *Professor* Townsend is convicted of stealing ancient artefacts and ruined professionally!" And before anyone could think of something to say, ElKureishi suddenly turned to the lamia and shouted in Arabic: "Who are you? How dare you stand before us wearing those things? Take them off at once!"

The lamia did not understand his words but no one had *ever* spoken to her in that tone of voice. Her body tensed and the ghost of a smile vanished as she glared down in rage at ElKureishi, who glared back, a defiant but comparatively diminutive figure. Mike was suddenly afraid for the old professor's life. He looked pleadingly at the lamia: "Please leave this place," he begged. But she ignored him and continued to glare at the old professor with eyes wide open with fury.

"Oh yes!" shouted ElKureishi again in Arabic, unaware of the danger, "Leave us! **Get out!** And when you leave don't take the stolen things with you!"

Ohanian stepped forward. *I've got to get Mike out of this mess! He's too honest to see a way out – and if Kureishi isn't careful he might get killed!* He casually placed himself between ElKureishi and the lamia. "If you are referring to the diadem and the red jewel this woman is wearing, Professor," said Ohanian soothingly, speaking directly to ElKureishi and trying not to think of the lamia standing directly behind him, "You shouldn't worry about them. They're not ancient! When Mike realised how much his girlfriend looked like the statue of Amalishah he sent my cousin in Mosul some photographs of the diadem and the necklace on the statue and asked him to make copies. My cousin is a jeweller well-known and excellent!"

The lamia's deadly glare moved from ElKureishi to Ohanian and Mike's throat tightened, so that he could barely husk: "Ardash, don't stand so close to her! She doesn't know you're trying to help me. She can kill you!"

But Ohanian only smiled at Mike as though to say: *I know!*

ElKureishi was too busy trying to absorb what Ohanian had said about his cousin the jeweller to hear Mike's warning or see Ohanian's response. He looked at the senior archaeologists for support but, finding none, turned to stare at Ohanian in shocked disbelief. Most of the archaeologists were glad the unpleasantness was lessening and things were being resolved in a plausible way.

"Professor ElKureishi," said Efremoghlou with a smile, "It is evident that Mike is not his usual self. He's gone temporarily insane and believes this woman is the goddess of the temple! His madness made him forget asking Ohanian's cousin to make copies of the jewels on the statue. I'm sure he will return to his senses when all this is over and there will be no need for recriminations."

Only Leonard could not accept Ohanian's explanation: *There wasn't enough time for Ohanian's cousin to make anything!*

Carol felt relieved, but only slightly. "Your *cousin* made the jewels?" she asked Ohanian. There was doubt and confusion in her voice. The situation was turning and twisting and nothing could be pinned down.

"My cousin is a jeweller well-known and excellent," Ohanian repeated pleasantly to Carol. The lamia stood directly behind him and he could almost feel the warmth of her body; he had never been so frightened in his life. "The crown is gold plated and the jewel is paste.

If you come to Mosul, Carol, my cousin can make you any kind of jewellery you like. Even copies of the things this woman beautiful is wearing!"

In a trembling voice Carol managed to say: "Thank you. But under the circumstances that may not be a good idea."

7

Mike was too absorbed in the lamia to fully come to terms with what was happening. The voices around him receded into a blurred hubbub and he spoke to her earnestly: "When the bad people get to us they will kill us! I am sorry that I will not be able to take you away from here. I really wanted to. But please save yourself!"

The lamia heard the sincerity in his voice and her attention shifted from Ohanian to him. The tension in her body slowly dissipated and the faint smile returned. She spoke to Mike with less coldness: "Save myself, Michael Townsend?"

"Yes. Go and hide somewhere! You'll be safe. The bad men don't know about you! They will kill us all because they're after the gold, but they won't look for you!"

In carefully measure tones the lamia said: "If you wish to die with your friends, Michael Townsend, then I wish to die with you."

Mike did not expect her to say that. "I don't understand," he said softly.

"You heard me," she said without emotion. In her language, 'to hear' and 'to understand' overlap in meaning.

"But why would you wish to die with me? You don't have to die. Someone else, one day, will get you away from here!" Mike's thoughts were in turmoil again and ElBalushi's warnings were demanding attention.

"Because," and the lamia paused for a long moment before speaking very slowly once again, "Because I once lost everyone whom I knew and loved, Michael Townsend. I do not wish that to happen again."

The implications of what she said slowly sank in. Mike felt dizzy, as though a great worm that had been eating away at his brain had been removed and left an empty space that made him feel weak and disorientated. But his mind felt free: *Balushi is a prejudiced idiot and I am an even greater idiot! So she killed a man because she had to feed! Who can tell how hungry she was! Don't we all have to feed?* The doubts that had been torturing him were replaced by a sudden and overpowering concern: *She mustn't die! She must leave us and escape!* "I don't want to die," he said, "But when those bad people get here they shall kill everyone they find. You can escape because they think that only my friends and I are here!"

"You won't die if you come with me," she said quietly.

"What?"

"You won't die if you come with me," she repeated. "I came to take you away, if you wish to come."

His doubts returned. They were weaker but tinged with suspicion at her motives: "I can't leave my friends!"

"So bring your friends with you."

"Mike," said Ohanian, absent-mindedly speaking Assyrian, "Go with her! The bad men will not notice that one of us is missing and you at least will be safe!"

The lamia appeared surprised. She turned to Ohanian with a warm smile, the smile of a child: "You look like a Hittite but you are Mike's friend. I want you to come too."

Ohanian felt privileged. He bowed stiffly by way of thanks, the way his grandfather used to do at formal occasions. The lamia nodded at him regally and Leonard thought: *Lord Almighty! The woman also thinks she's Amalishah! And Ohanian has gone loony too! He thinks this woman knows a way out!*

The others just stared.

"Ardash," said Mike in English, "Things may not be as they seem. She might be intending to kill both of us!"

"If we stay here we'll die anyway," replied Ohanian, also in English. "At least with her there's some hope! She might also know something about the script!"

"She just wants me to get her away from here, Ardash. She can only get away from here by car!"

"Does she understand the writing on the wall of the pit?"

"Of course!"

"Then it's worth the risk!"

"Why are you talking like this?" said the lamia, "There may not be much time."

Mike was finally able to think clearly: *If she knows a way to get around the bandits she won't kill us immediately. Above all she wants me to get her away from here! We'll take our chances when we get to*

Mosul – if we get to Mosul! "So who's coming with us?" he asked loudly in English.

"I'd rather put my trust in ElBalushi and his men," said Carol. Her husband nodded mutely.

"I don't understand any of this," said Leonard, "Count me out too!"

"I'm coming with you and... your girlfriend," said Ohanian.

Mike looked inquiringly at the others but they all shook their heads.

At that moment there was a burst of automatic fire accompanied by the rat-tat-tat of a machine gun. Everyone looked in the direction of the northern ramp and the students all started talking at once. They were silenced by the sound of a horrendous explosion. The lamia covered her ears with her hands: "Mike?..."

"It's all right," he said reassuringly, "It's just a loud noise!"

The lamia nodded, accepting his reassurance.

"It's the beginning of the end!" intoned ElKureishi.

"Come, Ardash," said Mike hurriedly, "We can do nothing here. If we escape we might be able to summon help."

"I'll get some candles."

"If you're leaving, *Professor* Townsend," said ElKureishi with a sneer, "Why don't you steal more artefacts? Take all you wish! You know which boxes to open."

Mike was about to answer but Leonard drawled: "Don't listen to him, buddy. Just get yourself and Ohanian out of here. I'm not sure who this woman is, but she might just possibly know a way past the bandits."

"Thanks, Len. I'll explain all this to you some day!"

Leonard smiled sadly but did not reply; the others looked away. Ohanian collected his things and took some stout candles from the cardboard box.

Mike said: "Let's go!" just as an unusually bright flash of lightning lit the tent.

The lamia turned in one swift motion and disappeared through the opening of the storage tent. Without looking back, Mike and Ohanian followed a few moments later.

42

Hubris and Nemesis

1

It was dark, wet and windy when Arroussi and his son made their way to the northern ramp. They were followed by some one hundred and seventy men, the greater part of Arroussi's force. A dozen had been despatched around the hill in case any of the defenders tried to clamber down the sides. Three of the six men Mukhtar had taken to guard the expedition's vehicles had decided to join the main force, leaving only three with the lorries and Land Rovers.

According to the agreement between Arroussi and Jawad, Jawad and his men were to wait for Arroussi's arrival at the rocks near the foot of the northern ramp, but Arroussi could not forget that Jawad had left the southern ramp in a foul mood. It was possible that when he joined his men he had behaved in his usual ill-tempered way and gotten himself killed. The loss of Jawad would not change Arroussi's plans for the attack on the hill, but killing their leader might have changed Jawad's men into blood-crazed thugs who would resist any attempt by Arroussi to impose discipline. This could pose problems as discipline was essential if the attack were to be in carefully thought-out stages. If Jawad were dead and his men refused to toe the line Arroussi decided to have as many of Jawad's men killed as necessary. On the other hand, when Jawad had left the southern ramp his fury was directed mostly at Aisha, so it was possible that he had not crossed the line and was still alive. In that case the agreement to join forces in the assault against the soldiers would take place as planned. As he approached the foot of the northern ramp Arroussi prepared himself for any eventuality.

There was no obvious path from the southern to the northern ramp, and the puddles, rocks and slippery mud that littered the way might have caused a few mishaps had Arroussi and most of his men not carried small electric torches. The lights of the torches fanned out and lit the falling raindrops to produce glowing yellow-white cones which showed, from some angles, fringes of pale rainbow colours. To Mukhtar the moving column of men with torches seemed like a procession of Christmas decorations: *Ah Christmas in America! A different world where people can follow their conscience! Here I must be loyal to my father and participate in the murder of people who could have been my friends...*

Arroussi's fears of fatalities at the northern ramp were unfounded. Jawad and his men were waiting for Arroussi in the darkness. All were calm as they crouched behind the rocks that were scattered about the foot of the northern ramp. Jawad had given orders that no fires were to be lit for he did not want the soldiers to estimate how many men were stationed near the foot of the ramp. When he saw Arroussi and his men carrying lit electric torches his anger flared up and he shouted above the howling of the wind: "You're late! It's long after sunset!"

"I was hoping the rain would stop," replied Arroussi as softly as the howling of the wind allowed. Arroussi was almost glad to see Jawad as things would be much simpler that way. In the presence of his men Jawad had evidently regained his customary arrogance but Arroussi thought it best not to antagonise him.

"And why are you all carrying lit torches?" continued Jawad, "Do you want the soldiers to count your men?" He pretended not to see Aisha, who stood a few paces behind Arroussi.

"As you said earlier," replied Arroussi, "It is a good idea to make the soldiers afraid. If they see how many we are they might panic and forget to follow orders!"

Jawad scowled but he turned to his men and shouted: "Turn on whatever lights you have!"

Only two of Jawad's men had brought any kind of light and Jawad was further irritated at the thought that the soldiers on the hill would take note of Arroussi's men and not his. "Why didn't you bring electric torches?" he shouted at his men, "Now you'll have to lurch around in the mud like blind dogs!"

In the presence of Arroussi the men were not willing to accept Jawad's insults, and because they felt safe in the darkness one shouted back: "Don't call us dogs!"

The others joined in: "You didn't tell us to bring electric torches!"

And one mustered the courage to shout: "Ayyah! It's your fault we don't have torches! You told us we would have the gold before sunset!"

This was too much for Jawad and he almost screamed: "We wouldn't be here in the dark if you dogs and sons-of-dogs had not left my truck to run down the hill like cowards!" Evidently his anger at his men had been suppressed but not extinguished. The men did not answer, but they closed in on Jawad, glaring at him menacingly.

Jawad was too furious at the unprecedented insubordination to realise that after waiting for most of the day in the cold and rain, without news and with very little food, his men were at the end of their tether, but Arroussi did not miss the signs of a possible rebellion. "Are these all of your lads?" he asked mildly: *If Jawad insults them again they might kill him and I might not be able to control them!* Jawad's attention was forced away from his men. "All the cowards who are still alive are here!" he replied.

Arroussi shook his head in exasperation: *Jawad had convinced his men that victory was going to be quick. They feel betrayed and need encouragement, not scolding!* "I was told, Jawad, that many of your lads showed great courage when the truck was stopped on the ramp!"

"These idiots don't have any courage!" Jawad sneered.

"I'm sure they will run up the ramp bravely when the time comes!"

"That's only because they want to get to the foreigners' gold!"

"That is true of all of us," replied Arroussi coolly, "Why else would we face that machine gun in this dreadful weather?"

Jawad gave a cackling laugh: "You're right! That's why we're all here! To get the foreigners' gold!"

"Don't you have any wounded?" asked Mukhtar unexpectedly.

Jawad momentarily lost his composure but then answered hastily: "There are no wounded among my lads!"

Arroussi was shocked but did not show it: *He's left his wounded to die!* He gave a sign to his son 'Don't say anything more!' and Mukhtar nodded. Arroussi had not brought a physician, but he had brought some medicines and his wounded had been treated as well as the circumstances allowed. They were lying in moderate comfort in one of his trucks.

2

Jawad became aware that his men were standing very close to him, within range of a quick stab with a knife, and he moved closer to Arroussi. "It's dark enough and the gold is waiting," he said without enthusiasm, "Let's start the assault!"

"There's no hurry," said Arroussi, "Before we start, perhaps we should go over what we agreed."

"More talk? What is there to talk about?" Jawad wanted his men to move away from him. Now that Arroussi was there to take command if necessary the possibility of getting stabbed was very real.

"It's always a good idea to make sure everyone understands the plan of action," replied Arroussi calmly, "It's possible that some of your men don't know what you and I decided earlier."

"Oh very well!" Jawad turned to his men and spoke loudly with what he thought was an ingratiating smile: "When it's as dark as the mouth of hell, and the soldiers are soiling their pants because they can see how many we are, I and Arroussi shall give the order for all the men to shout loudly and shoot at the hill! This will make the soldiers even more frightened and they will keep their heads down. While they are trembling with fear, two of Arroussi's men with grenade launchers shall creep along the sides of the ramp and blow the machine gun away. Then we'll rush up the ramp to kill the soldiers and get the gold!" He turned back to Arroussi: "There! Now my lads understand everything!" To Jawad's relief, his men moved back and were no longer glaring at him malevolently.

"Good!" said Arroussi, "My men already know the plan." He was about to turn away when Jawad said: "And what have we agreed to do with the foreigners?"

Arroussi gave Jawad a hard look: *He is paying me back for Mukhtar's question about his wounded!* "Is it necessary to speak about that again?" he asked.

Jawad tried to mimic Arroussi's gruff voice: "It's always a good idea to make sure everyone understands the plan of action." He expected his men to laugh but they did not. Arroussi nodded resignedly: "We have agreed… that none of the soldiers or the foreigners are to be left alive." He wished that Mukhtar had not been there.

"Make sure that *all* your men know that," taunted Jawad, "We don't want anyone to escape the way the tall woman escaped last night!"

Aisha tensed and became very pale. It would be easy for Arroussi to put an end to Jawad's bluster by disclosing that it was she who had released the tall foreign woman. But Arroussi simply shrugged: "Just make sure your men do what they have to do," he said, and Aisha relaxed.

"Oh, my men will do what they have to do," Jawad persisted,

"though some of us may want to have some fun with the foreign women before we kill them."

"Enjoying the foreign women may cost us time we cannot afford to waste," said Arroussi brusquely, "better to finish the job quickly, load the trucks and leave immediately!" *If the men are allowed to make pigs of themselves they won't stop until they've all had their share of pleasure. This could take all night!*

"I'm sure your lads will want to do the same," said Jawad with an arrogant grin.

Arroussi shook his head. "There will be ample time for pleasure when we have the gold and are safely back. We need to get away from here as soon as we can!" *I don't share this maniac's faith in his radio man!* He turned towards his men, who were listening in silence. But Jawad had not finished: "If you're hoping to use some of the foreign women for your own pleasure," he said, making sure that the men around them could hear, "then you had better tell your men not to kill the pretty ones too soon!"

Jawad felt he could goad Arroussi as much as he pleased. He knew that the old bandit would not harm him when the assault on the hill was imminent. Arroussi frowned darkly but ignored the taunt. Jawad raised his voice: "Tell your men to leave the best foreign women for you. Tell them how many you want!"

Arroussi froze with anger and was going to say something, but he calmed himself down: *He is trying to show my son that I am no different from him! I must not let this disgusting man irritate me!* "I don't need a woman," he said bluntly without turning to face Jawad, and in the wavering light of the torches, from the corner of his eye, he saw that Mukhtar was pleased by what he had heard. Mukhtar was very close to his mother.

Jawad grinned: "Of course, I forgot that you're too old to enjoy a woman."

This was too much for Mukhtar: "When you speak to my father," he said coldly, "please remember that there are certain things that must not be talked about."

"We must not talk about your father's age?" Jawad replied mockingly, again making sure that everyone around them could hear him. He grinned as he spoke but, as though by accident, he raised the muzzle of his assault rifle until it pointed at Mukhtar. Arroussi indicated to his son to let the jibe pass. He turned to Jawad and said evenly: "Will you lead your men up the ramp when the machine gun is silenced?"

"Will *you* lead yours?"

"I'll be with them, but I'm leaving my son behind. If something happens to me I want my son to survive. I hope you don't mind." *If Jawad tries to kill me it will be during the run up the ramp, when everyone will be looking ahead. He must not get the chance to kill my son!*

"Do as you please," said Jawad. "I'll be with my men. They'll need to be told what to do when they reach the top of the ramp." Although he spoke casually, Jawad was thinking furiously about how his plans would need to be changed. If Mukhtar were left behind it would be harder to kill him.

3

The rain became a downpour and the raindrops made a loud pattering as they struck the rocks. Arroussi decided to start the attack when the rain was heaviest, as this would make it hardest for the soldiers on the hill to see the two men with the RPGs crawling along the sides of the ramp. He wandered among his men making pleasantries and giving encouragement, but when he reached Atef and Salah, the two men with the RPGs, he quietly told them to turn off their torches and leave.

"Are you sure the soldiers won't see us?" asked Atef. Now that his moment had come the man was not so sure it was a good idea to leave the protection of the rocks.

"We are all in God's hands," replied Arroussi, speaking to both Atef and Salah, "and when you are close to the hill you will be out of the line of fire of the machine gun while you crawl along the side of the ramp. Don't forget to keep covering your faces and hands with mud so that you will be invisible in the dark!" This was to lessen the likelihood of the two men being seen by soldiers with night goggles, but Atef was not convinced that this was going to make him invisible and he muttered a quick prayer. Salah asked: "Why are we to take only one rocket grenade each?"

"You will only need one. Don't fire your RPG unless you are sure to hit the machine gun!"

"But we have four grenades in all!"

"I know, but I want you to leave two behind. They are heavy and will make it harder for you to crawl along the side of the ramp. Now go, and may good fortune go with you!"

Atef and Salah left and Arroussi noted the time. Jawad did not notice their departure as he was staring at the hilltop and trying to figure out how he would kill Mukhtar.

Exactly ten minutes later Arroussi ordered all men with lit torches to turn them off. Mukhtar said: "Should we start shouting and shooting to distract the soldiers, father?"

"Not yet," said Arroussi. The rain and the wind were now lighter and it was no longer necessary to shout to be heard.

"In this rain we'll keep slipping like donkeys as we climb the ramp!" said one of Arroussi's men.

"That cannot be helped!" answered Arroussi. He looked at his watch and shouted: "Take up your positions as close to the ramp as you can and get ready to open fire on the machine gun when I give the order!"

"If we leave the rocks the machine gun will slaughter us!" someone shouted.

"There are enough rocks close to the ramp to give you cover," said Arroussi.

"Are the lads with the RPGs ready to go?" another man asked, he was behind Arroussi and did not need to shout.

"Atef and Salah are already gone," Arroussi replied.

Jawad was close enough to Arroussi to hear him: "What!" he shouted, "You didn't tell me that the men with the RPGs are gone!"

"I thought you saw me talking to Atef and Salah," Arroussi replied, "I am sorry you didn't know that the first part of the attack has begun!" He suspected that Jawad was preoccupied with something but did not know what.

"You should have told me before you sent them off!"

"Yes, Jawad. I should have told you before I sent them off. I apologise!"

"Is it time to distract the soldiers, father?" said Mukhtar: *Jawad must not start an argument now!* He tried not to look at Jawad.

"There's no point in shouting and shooting too soon," said Arroussi, "I'll give the order when Atef and Salah are at least half way." He had estimated that if Atef and Salah moved cautiously and stopped often to keep covering their exposed parts with mud it would be at least fifteen minutes before they were ready to climb to the top of the ramp and fire their RPGs.

Mukhtar nodded, although it was too dark for his father to see now that the torches had been extinguished. He felt the tension growing in the men and wished, with mixed feelings that the attack would start soon. The rain and the wind had made the strain of anticipation in the men almost unbearable, but some of soldiers had night goggles and he knew that his father was anxious about whether the men with the RPGs could manage to crawl along the sides of the ramp without being noticed.

Suddenly there was a single shot from the hill and a cry: "Aah! Help me!"

"That was Atef!" someone shouted, "I know his voice!" ElBalushi had anticipated that the bandits would try to crawl along the sides of the ramp.

"How can they see in this black night?" a man husked, "Do they know magic?"

"Of course not!" said Arroussi hastily, "They don't know any magic. Atef was unlucky or careless!" Many of the bandits were superstitious and Arroussi wondered whether he should tell his men that some of the soldiers had night goggles: *No, that would sap their courage!* The idea that some of the soldiers could see in the dark would horrify them. Atef was probably dead, but it was now sixteen minutes since Atef and Salah had left and Salah should be in position by now. He shouted hoarsely: "Start shouting and shooting at the machine gun!" *The soldiers' attention must be kept away from Salah!*

With a loud shout everybody started shooting in the direction of the machine gun, not bothering to aim. The shouting and the sound of gunfire was deafening and the flashes of the automatic weapons illuminated the bandits as well as the rocks behind which they crouched. A few seconds later a single floodlamp from somewhere near the machine gun nest came to life and illuminated the ramp. The light was so bright that it was impossible to look at it directly despite the rain.

"Put that lamp out!" shouted Jawad.

The order was unnecessary, as the men were already aiming at the light although the floodlamp was beyond the effective range of their weapons. They were shooting continuously when a solitary silhouette, distorted by the rain and hardly visible in the glare of the floodlamp, rose up ungainly more than half way up the ramp. The attention of the defenders must have been on the bottom of the ramp because the machine gun remained silent. The figure, casting a long shadow that penetrated deep into the curtain of rain, reeled as though drunk.

"It's Atef with his RPG!"

"He's wounded!"

Most of the bandits stopped shooting in case they hit Atef. Others shouted exhortations: "Come on, Atef!"

"Fire your weapon!"

The soldiers at the machine gun became aware of the danger and opened fire. The silhouette twisted and fell, but before the man hit the ground he inadvertently fired the RPG in the direction of the attackers.

"Watch out!"

"The grenade!"

All the shooting stopped and everyone scattered in terror as the rocket-propelled grenade rushed towards them in a blaze of red light. The bandits dispersed in all directions, many of them leaving the protection of the rocks, and the machine gunners, momentarily able to see the horde at the bottom of the ramp, opened fire a second time. Some men were hit while the missile flew over the bandits in a long arc and exploded with a loud thump somewhere far beyond the rocks.

"Get that lamp you idiots!" shouted Jawad.

The shooting started again with more success. The lamp went out with a loud metallic *clang* and the machine gun fell silent, but most of the bandits continued shouting and shooting.

"That machine gun has a long range!" someone close to Arroussi said.

"Was anyone hit?" shouted Arroussi.

"Some of us are dead because of Atef!"

"That idiot Atef!"

"Mukhtar is down!"

4

"Mukhtar!" shouted Arroussi desperately, his voice hoarser than usual because of his anguish, "Mukhtar, are you all right?" He ran blindly, not thinking of the machine gun, in his desperation to find Mukhtar. The shouting of the men and the din of the automatic weapons drowned his words. The men kept shooting in the general direction of the machine gun nest but Arroussi could do nothing but look frantically for his son. The only light was from the almost continuous flashes of the automatic weapons.

"I think he's over there!" someone said, and Arroussi rushed to find his son.

Mukhtar was lying on the ground beside a large boulder. He was curled up with his hands on his abdomen. When his father saw him he hurried to kneel beside his son and took hold of his hand.

"I think I'm all right, father," said Mukhtar weakly, "The bullet was spent. It must have bounced off something before it hit me."

Arroussi examined the wound by the light of his cigarette lighter. "It's not deep," he whispered, "but the bullet fragmented and you need to be treated before the wound gets infected. Some of our men have medicines and can help you!"

"No please, father. The men are needed on the ramp!"

The noise of the shooting rose and fell as Arroussi gripped his son's hand tightly.

Suddenly there was a loud explosion and for a brief moment the machine gun nest was bathed in incandescent smoke. The men stopped firing and emerged from the shelter of the rocks to look.

"Atef reloaded and fired his RPG!" someone shouted.

"Atef is dead. It was Salah!"

The machine gun nest burned fiercely. Despite the rain the cloth of the sandbags was on fire. Arroussi gave a booming bellow: "Take the hill! Don't wait for me!"

With a roar of triumph the bandits rushed towards the ramp. They were met by repeated volleys of shots from the hill and although some fell the rest stormed onwards. The frenzied mob was almost a third of the way up the ramp when three floodlamps came on and illuminated the ramp. The attackers stopped, half expecting the machine gun to come back to life, and some retreated in panic. But the weapon, surrounded by a crown of fire, remained silent, and despite the powerful light of the floodlamps the mob pushed on again. Shouting obscenities at the defenders they tried to reach the burnt-out truck, but the wet, slippery ground slowed them down and many had to fire their weapons crouching on their knees in the mud. The rain became a light drizzle and the bandits cheered.

5

Arroussi appeared to have been left completely alone, kneeling beside his son and holding his hand. His attention was wholly on Mukhtar, who lay motionless on the wet ground, and he did not see the crouching figure that glided stealthily towards him from the shadows of the rocks. He only realised that something was dreadfully, painfully wrong when he felt the knife cut downwards through the muscles of his shoulder and dig into his lungs, scraping against his shoulder bones. Paralysed by the pain and unable to breathe his eyes rolled upwards. He felt that he was spinning dizzily, falling through a sea of agony, and during the split second before his eyes rolled up the last thing he saw by the light of the floodlamps was the shocked face of his son. Then Arroussi's spirit left him and his mind evaporated into nothingness. But he remained on his knees and did not fall because the knife that was wedged tightly between muscle and bone was held by a strong hand. Only when Jawad finally twisted his knife and wrenched it out did Arroussi slowly collapse. He turned as he fell until he lay on his back beside his son, staring sightlessly at the black sky and the falling rain.

"Aha!" said Jawad pleasantly, "Two maggots lying side by side in the mud! Whose eyes shall I gouge out first? Eyeballs make a lovely *pop* when they're gouged out!"

"You cowardly pig!" muttered Mukhtar.

"Not you," said Jawad conversationally. "Not yet. I want you to watch what I do to your father!" He stepped on Arroussi's chest and bent forward, waving his knife above Arroussi's face, making sure that Mukhtar could savour the glint of the blade in the light of the floodlamps. He was gratified to see that Mukhtar could not help staring, wide-eyed with horror, at the shining blade of the knife.

"Jawad, please don't!" pleaded Mukhtar. He was too weak, too shocked, to move.

Jawad laughed and spoke calmly as he continued to wave the knife: "You are still wearing your idiotic glasses, you piece of excrement. Good! You will be able to watch me pry out your father's eyes!" He laughed again, with almost hysterical glee: "If you listen carefully, you will hear the *pop* as I dig out each eyeball!"

But before Jawad could carry out the mutilation there was a burst of automatic fire from behind him and to his right. His side exploded in blood and gore and he jerked upright as he turned to face his assailant with a look of surprise. Recognition came slowly and perhaps he tried to smile, or perhaps he wished to say something, but all he could do was curl his lips in a feral snarl and cough up a thin trickle of blood. Jawad knew that he was going to die, but even so he did not concede defeat. Propped up by his hate he slowly turned his knife away from Arroussi and pointed it at Mukhtar's chest as he stumbled sideways, intending to fall on the young man with his knife pointing down. Aisha fired again and Jawad's whole body shook as the bullets ripped into his head and torso. The knife fell from his hand and he collapsed limply beside Mukhtar and lay still, but Aisha did not release the trigger until the magazine was empty.

"Aisha!" Mukhtar exclaimed as he turned with difficulty to face her. The noise of the shooting had abated, for the bandits were no longer shooting wildly as they struggled against the slippery mud. Some sought shelter from the soldiers' fire behind the bodies of their fallen comrades, others tried to reach the burnt-out truck but found it impossible due to the fire of the soldiers on either side of the ramp. Aisha squatted beside Mukhtar on the side away from Jawad's body. "Come. This is our chance to get away from all this."

"I cannot leave my father!"

"Your father is dead. He is waiting for you to close his eyes."

Biting his lip to suppress the pain, Mukhtar sat up slowly and turned towards his father, who was lying on his back beside him with his eyes wide open. In the light of the floodlamps Arroussi looked completely white, even his grey beard appeared white. Gritting his teeth Mukhtar leaned forward and closed his father's eyes.

"Say your goodbyes and let us go," said Aisha hurriedly, "When they take the hill the men will be back, wondering what happened to your father and to..." She could not say Jawad's name.

"I cannot leave my father! You go. There are only three men guarding the foreigners' vehicles. Deal with them and take one of the vehicles!"

"When the men come back they'll be crazy with gold. If they see you wounded they'll kill you!"

"I know, but I cannot leave my father."

"Your father would want you to survive. Let us go!"

"I can't get up and walk!"

"Yes you can! Your father said it is not a deep wound. I'll help you."

Mukhtar squeezed his father's hand and slowly pulled himself away. He managed to get up with Aisha's help.

Mukhtar was tall but slightly built, and Aisha had no trouble half-carrying him as they half walked, half limped towards the place where the expedition's vehicles were parked. They were on the other side of the hill, not too far from the foot of the southern ramp, but the distance seemed infinite to Mukhtar.

43

THE MAJOR SEES THE LAMIA

1

IT STARTED AS a tiny faint glow far beyond the northwest edge of the hill. Were it not for the utter darkness it would have been too dim to be visible, but the four men in the northern machine gun nest noticed it immediately. The major looked at it through his binoculars.

After a while, the sergeant asked: "Can you make out what it is?"

The major could not hide his frustration. He lowered his binoculars brusquely and said: "I can't even tell how far it is! The rain blurs all detail!"

"The rain is sure to stop soon!" said Private Hassan soothingly. He was the youngest of the machine-gun crew and had a cheery disposition.

Very slowly, the serpentine glow stretched eastwards until it became a hazy phosphorescent line that twinkled as it made its way around the hill.

"Could it be the headlights of a convoy of cars or lorries?" the sergeant asked.

"Even allowing for the rain," answered the major, "the lights are too dim to be headlights!" The men were too cold and wet to comment further, but when the rain momentarily stopped the major hurriedly passed the binoculars to Private Hassan: "Your eyes are the sharpest here! What do you make of it?"

The young soldier looked steadily through the binoculars for a short while, but then the rain started again and he passed them back to the major: "I think it's a long column of men carrying lights!"

The other private said: "Whatever it is, it's getting closer. It's moving towards us!"

"It can only be the enemy from the other side of the hill," said the major, "They are coming to join their friends who are behind the rocks beyond the foot of the ramp!"

"There are shorter ways to get to their friends near the bottom of our ramp," said the sergeant, "why would they follow such a wide arc around the hill?"

"Perhaps because they found out this morning that some of our men on the perimeter are very good with long-range rifles," replied the major, "and they know that carrying lights makes them stand out in the darkness!"

"So why do they carry lights?" asked Hassan.

"Because they can't see in the dark!" said the sergeant impatiently.

The other private said: "They're stupid! They should have left before it got dark!"

"Yes, but one mistake doesn't make them stupid," said the major, "We must not underestimate them! Bringing flashlights shows forethought. At least one bandit leader realised that a daytime attack might fail!"

"You're right," commented the sergeant, "it could be fatal to underestimate them."

The snakelike glow converged into a luminous pool behind the rocks at the foot of the ramp. The major looked again through his binoculars and said: "From the glow of their lights, there must be at least a hundred and fifty of them behind the rocks!"

"They must have realised that the sides of the hill are impossible to climb," said the sergeant, "and decided to focus their attack along the ramps!"

"Attacking both ramps would expose them to two machine guns," said the major. "Unless they attack again from all sides they will probably attack only the northern ramp!"

"Why the northern ramp?" said the sergeant, "The other is much shorter!"

"The southern ramp is shorter but steeper. It would be much harder to climb in the rain." The major lowered his binoculars and added grimly: "And they probably know that Allawi's machine gun covers the whole of the southern ramp whereas near the hill our machine-gun does not cover the flanks of the ramp!"

"Why is that important?" asked Private Hassan, "They can't run along the flanks!" Before the major could answer a voice called out from near the base of the machine gun mound: "Major! Major!!"

The two privates climbed briskly upon the concrete ring to look down over the sandbags, but it was too dark to see anything. The sergeant barked: "Who goes there?"

"It's Private Kurdy," said the disembodied voice. "Is the major there?"

The sergeant fumbled around the floor of the nest until he found an electric torch. He shone it on the soldier and shouted: "Come closer! I want to see your face!"

Kurdy approached the mound with his body bent forward. He felt exposed and vulnerable in the light of the torch and kept turning this way and that as though trying to push himself into his helmet. The major stood up: "What is it, Kurdy?"

"Major, the enemy has amassed behind the rocks near the bottom of the northern ramp!"

"We know that, we saw their lights, but thank you. Where are you stationed?"

"Immediately to the left of the ramp. We can see between the rocks and with field glasses we saw the enemy arrive, then spread out and take cover!"

ElBalushi's men were deployed in pairs around the perimeter of the hill. About one in four pairs had been issued binoculars and, in case any bandits tried to sneak along the sides of the ramp, one man on either side of the northern ramp had been equipped with night goggles. There were three pairs of night goggles in all, and the remaining pair was at the machine gun nest that covered the southern ramp.

"If you could see them, why didn't you shoot?" The soldiers had orders to shoot at any bandit who presented a target.

"They're too far to see without field glasses, major. We could only see their lights, and in the darkness and the rain we would not have been able to shoot accurately!"

"Just as well you didn't shoot, then," said the major, "Let them think we don't know they're there! Do you know how many they are?"

"Only approximately major. We could not tell for sure because they arrived in a long line and then scattered. We estimated about one hundred and seventy men with lights, maybe slightly less, maybe slightly more."

"Could they be as few as one hundred?"

"No, major. Definitely closer to two hundred."

"Are you sure, Kurdy? This is important!"

"We counted as carefully as we could, major. At least one hundred and seventy!"

555

The major nodded to himself: *They've brought together all the men they can spare! There can be no doubt that there will be a concentrated attack at the northern ramp!* "Thanks for the information, Kurdy. Have you and the others on the northern perimeter got enough food and water?"

"Yes, major. When shall the floodlights be lit? Without them it's impossible to keep an eye on the whole length of the ramp."

"That is why your partner and another man on the other side of the ramp have night goggles! But a floodlamp will be turned on when the time is right."

"Very well, major."

"Return to your post, Kurdy. And remind your partner with the night goggles to pay special attention to the flank of the ramp! Especially near the hill. Also remind your comrade with night goggles on the other side of the ramp!"

"Yes, major." Kurdy saluted and left. The major picked up the walkie-talkie to talk to Captain Allawi at the other machine gun.

2

There was one walkie-talkie at each machine gun nest and one with the man who controlled the floodlamps. The three walkie-talkies were connected so that each operator could hear what the other two were saying.

"Allawi, did your man with the night goggles report any activity?"

"No Major. Nothing is happening here. But it's very dark and I wish we had more night vision equipment."

"We'll have to make do with what we have!" The major took a deep breath: "Allawi, about a hundred and seventy of the enemy from the southern ramp have joined up with their friends behind the rocks at the foot of the northern ramp!"

"One hundred and seventy! That could be all who were previously stationed here, at the rocks near the bottom of the southern ramp. Could that be all the men they have left?"

"Probably not, for that was only the men who carried lights, and more men must have been waiting for them to arrive. Others must be deployed around the hill. Given how many there were and the casualties they sustained, I expect just under two hundred to attack here. That is enough for a massed assault up the northern ramp if they use all their firepower as they climb!"

"So it seems that you shall have all the fun!"

"Maybe not. Enough of them may have been left behind for a covert attack at your end. As many as twenty men might try to sneak up your ramp!"

"We can deal with that. Our man with the night goggles can see the whole of *our* ramp as well as its flanks. But if we are attacked we would need at least one floodlamp to make proper use of the machine-gun. Who is manning the switches?"

"Corporal Murad. He's in the tent with the generators and he's got the third walkie-talkie. He can hear everything we say."

"That makes things simpler; we won't have to repeat ourselves. Has the grove been infiltrated? It's ideal for snipers!"

"It's too dark for snipers unless they have night goggles. It is very unlikely that the enemy have night goggles, and they must know that our heavy-calibre machine gun can spray the grove and dislodge any snipers. I don't think they'll bother with snipers!"

Corporal Murad cut in: "Should I turn on any of the floodlamps without being told if I think it necessary?"

"It might be better if you don't," replied the major, "Timing is important and the decision is best left to those in the machine gun nests. But use your discretion."

"Yes, major."

The major addressed the captain: "Allawi, how is morale at the southern edge of the hill? The men have been on alert all day."

"Morale was good when I last inspected the men on the perimeter. They are calm but vigilant and we have rotated watch duty, as you ordered, so all of us have had some rest. We have also been well fed."

"If all this ends favourably remind me to thank the men who distribute the rations!"

Allawi chuckled drily: "We are all very grateful to them. Do you think the enemy has weapons they haven't used yet?"

"Well, they cannot have artillery, and if they had mortars they would have used them this morning, but we know that they have at least one RPG launcher. We don't know how many grenades. The machine gun nests are vulnerable to RPGs if they are fired from near the top of a ramp!"

"They won't be able to get near the top of our ramp!" said Allawi confidently, "Our man with night goggles is watchful and I shall bring on the floodlamps if necessary. But bandits with RPGs could crawl along the flanks of your ramp and then climb up to get into position for his RPG!"

"That's my main worry, which is why there are men with night goggles on both sides of our ramp. Are you in touch with the men on the periphery near your nest?"

"We keep an eye on them and they on us. But if the main attack is at your end you may need reinforcements. If nothing continues to happen on our side of the hill I could send you some men from the southern perimeter as well as two from our nest. One gunner with night goggles and I are enough to operate the machine-gun effectively."

"Keep your men for the moment, captain. We don't really know what will happen and can only hope that we have guessed the enemy's intentions correctly."

"Very well. I'll send some men only if I think they're needed. May God help us!"

"May our prayers be heard!" echoed the major, "And be grateful for the rain, Captain. It makes the ramps slippery and will hamper the enemy more than us!" The major signed off.

3

"We can't see anything in this darkness, major," said Private Hassan, "when will you order one of the floodlamps to be lit?"

"When it shall come as the worse possible surprise to the enemy! For now we must depend on the night goggles of the men on either side of the ramp!"

"The goggles have a narrow field of vision," said the sergeant, "Let's hope they…"

"They've turned off their lights!" interrupted Private Hassan. The rocks at the bottom of the ramp were again in complete darkness. The major stared at the blackness of the ramp: *Is this how the attack will start? Will they try to crawl silently up the ramp in the dark?* He was about to ask Murad to turn on one of the floodlamps when there was a single shot followed by a cry of pain. The cry appeared to be quite close. The major stiffened: "Did any of you see anything?"

"It's too dark," said the sergeant.

"And the rain is too thick," added Private Hassan, "but I think the shot was fired from the left of the ramp. Probably by the man with night goggles!"

The major was too stunned to answer at once: *The enemy managed to crawl quite far along the sides of the ramp!* He started to say "I think so too..." when he was interrupted by the sound of shooting and loud shouting from behind the rocks at the bottom of the ramp. Bullets began whistling over the head of the men in the machine-gun nest, and they lowered their heads as much as they dared, hoping to avoid flying bullets while trying to see what was happening at the bottom of the ramp. "They must be attacking!" said the sergeant, his voice was strained.

The major spoke calmly into the walkie-talkie: "Corporal Murad, please turn on one of the floodlamps that cover the northern ramp!"

A floodlamp to the left of the machine gun mound came on immediately. It bathed the ramp with an intense white light that was scattered and diffused by the rain, but the sides of the ramp were too steep to be fully illuminated and remained in relative darkness. The shooting from the foot of the ramp waned briefly but then intensified again. The gunfire was now aimed primarily at the floodlamp, even though it was beyond the effective range of the bandits' automatic rifles.

"There doesn't seem to be anyone at the bottom of the ramp!" said the sergeant, "If they're not attacking, why are they shooting and making so much noise?"

"They're trying to distract our attention from the sides of the ramp!" said the major, "I should join Kurdy and the man with the night goggles. Keep your eyes open and remember that the enemy may have RPGs!"

"Our lives depend on not forgetting that, major!"

The major climbed over the concrete ring and the sandbags and made his way warily down the mound on the side away from the ramp. He crouched as low as he could to avoid stray bullets and ran to the two men who were lying on their stomachs to the left of the ramp. He lay down in the mud beside them.

"Why did you shoot? We heard a shot and a cry."

The soldier with the night goggles answered without turning: "A man was crawling along the side of the ramp. I think I got him but I'm not sure."

"Can you see the man you shot?" the major asked. His body heat would show on the night goggles.

"No major, he's either dead and getting cold or hiding behind something. The sides of the ramp are full of deep ridges and there are

559

bushes and small trees."

"The enemy is trying to crawl along the sides of the ramp with RPGs!" the major shouted to all who could hear, "We don't know how many RPGs they've got!"

The bandits continued shouting and shooting. A storm of bullets whined above the men on the northern perimeter and thudded around the floodlamp or into the side of the mound with the machine gun. Occasionally a bullet *pinged* and ricocheted when it hit something solid. *They're concentrating on the floodlamp!* The major saw that despite the light of the floodlamp the rocks at the foot of the ramp were illuminated as though by fireworks. *God the Merciful, there may be too many of them!*

The two men with the night goggles watched the sides of the ramp but all the others concentrated on the rocks at its far end. After all, that was where an attack along the northern ramp would start.

4

The major was startled when the machine gun fired a short spurt and then stopped. He looked down at the ramp and in the rain-scattered light of the floodlamp he was just in time to see a figure half way to the top stagger and fall slowly to the ground. *God help us! One of them almost made it!* Before the man hit the ground there was a loud crack followed by the shriek of a rocket-propelled grenade. The major held his breath but the shriek grew fainter, not louder.

"The rocket is going in the wrong direction!" exclaimed Kurdy. The shooting from behind the rocks stopped and the major could not help raising his head again to look. For a brief moment the RPG flew upwards and the bright red light of its rocket showed the bandits running between the rocks in all directions. Suddenly able to see the bandits, the machine gunners opened fire. There were distant screams and shouts of panic from around the rocks.

The red glare vanished abruptly while the grenade was still rising high in the air. Suddenly bereft of the thrust of its rocket it plummeted down and fell somewhere behind the boulders with a dull thump. In the lull that followed ElBalushi mentally urged the machine gun crew to keep firing: *Don't stop! Some of them may still be in the open!* But the weapon on the mound remained silent while the shooting from behind the rocks resumed. The soldier with the night goggles said:

"That must have been the man I shot!"

"You only wounded him," said the major, "and he climbed half way to the top of the ramp!"

A bullet hit the floodlamp and it went out with a loud metallic *clang*. The ramp went completely dark. The bandits shouted louder and their shooting intensified.

"They're still trying to distract us!" shouted the major, "There must be at least one more man with an RPG!" He was about to instruct Murad to turn on another floodlamp when there was a short shriek from a rocket followed by a blinding flash and a deafening explosion. A fountain of white fire rose from the machine gun nest and sprouted luminous streamers that shot upwards, shattering the darkness. A fraction of a second later a shower of concrete chunks mixed with sand fell around the pile that supported the machine-gun nest or splashed into the small puddles that were everywhere. Small bits of concrete fell as far as the men on either side of the ramp. The major could only think: *God help the crew!* Despite the cool weather he felt drops of perspiration running down his forehead. But he felt no fear at all for the situation was too calamitous, too tragic, to allow debilitating emotions.

5

The major shouted above the din of the gunfire: "Has anyone been hurt?"

"We're both unhurt but the machine gun nest is burning!" shouted one of the soldiers on the other side of the ramp. Despite the rain, the sandbags around the machine gun nest burned fiercely. The din of the shooting had abated and the major was just able to hear a quick burst of gunfire from the other side of the ramp. The man with the night goggles said drily: "I think I shot the man who fired the RPG!" Salah had been unable to repress his joy at destroying the machine gun and, believing he was invisible in the darkness, had got up and danced on the top of the ramp.

"They'll be rushing up very soon!" said the major. He was surprised at how calmly he spoke: *The sandbags are wet and should not burn. The bastards used an incendiary grenade!*

"Major," said Kurdy, "If the fire reaches the ammunition belts there will be heavy-calibre bullets flying in all directions. Some may hit the tent with the foreigners!"

The major said: "I know, but we cannot leave our posts to warn them!"

One of the bandits behind the rocks at the foot of the ramp gave a loud bellow and with a roar of triumph the bandits streamed out from between the rocks and rushed up the ramp. But the ground was wet and slippery; some slipped and fell while others made slow progress as they clambered, sometimes on all fours, along the slippery mud. The attackers could only be seen by the flashes of their weapons and both men beside the major fired only when they could guess the location of their targets. There was similar intermittent shooting from the other side of the ramp and from almost the whole of the northern perimeter. The major spoke into the walkie-talkie: "Corporal Murad, please turn on another floodlamp!" Three floodlamps came to life almost immediately and the movement up the ramp faltered, but only for a moment. In the rain-scattered light of the floodlamps the bandits were small black blobs that moved slowly up the ramp in little patches that sometimes separated and sometimes grouped together. The mass of the bandits was not close enough to the top of the ramp for the remains of the truck to provide protection, but it was only a matter of time before one or more would reach the burnt-out hulk. Despite the concentrated fire from both sides of the ramp, the horde of stumbling, crouching men moved up the ramp inexorably, shooting and shouting profanities as they climbed.

"With the machine gun gone," said Kurdy, "they'll move into the grove`!"

The major was too concerned about the floodlamps to answer. With the enemy getting closer it was only a matter of time before all three floodlamps were hit, and there were no more floodlamps in reserve on the northern perimeter. The major spoke into the walkie-talkie: "Murad, please turn off two of the floodlamps!"

Nothing happened.

The major repeated the order: "Murad, turn off two of the floodlamps!"

But again there was no response. The major's stomach muscles tightened involuntarily: *Murad has been hit!* "I must go to the switches!" he said breathlessly. He rose and made quickly for the generator tent, bending low to avoid the bullets that were flying all around him. He held the walkie-talkie in one hand and his long-muzzled pistol in the other. His other pistol was in its holster on his belt.

6

When he was sufficiently far from the edge of the hill the major straightened up and ran as fast as he could: *The nest is still on fire but the ammunition has not exploded: the fire may be outside the concrete ring! If the grenade exploded against the concrete the machine gun could still be usable!* Only the machine gun could stop the mob that was pushing its way up the ramp, oblivious of casualties. *If the ammunition does not explode I must get to the nest and try to reactivate the weapon. But first I must turn off two of the floodlamps!* The tent that housed the generator was not far from the storage tent, on the side away from the machine gun, and the major reached it safely. There were fewer flying bullets here because the bandits' fire was divided between the floodlamps and the men on the perimeter, but there were still enough random bullets to pose a serious hazard. The rain reflected enough light for the major not to trip over the body of Corporal Murad, who had left the generator tent to see what was happening and been hit in the head. He lay sprawled just outside the tent, holding the walkie-talkie tightly in his right hand. After hesitating only long enough to make sure that he could not do anything to help Murad, the major pushed the flaps aside and entered the semi-darkness of the tent. Then he stopped abruptly because, in his frantic state of mind, he could not remember the location of the switches: *Please God, please help me!* For several agonisingly long seconds he groped around the tent until, eventually, he found them: *Ah! God be praised!* He turned off two of the floodlamps and the light outside dimmed noticeably. *What if the single floodlamp is hit? Should I stay here to turn on another?* He was trying to decide whether to stay at the switches when the flaps of the tent opened and he could just see a dark figure standing at the entrance. The major raised his pistol: "Who are you? Answer or die!"

"Captain Allawi sent me to work the floodlamps when Murad did not respond!"

"Thank God!" The major relaxed: "Did Allawi send any others?"

"Four more. I've taken Murad's walkie-talkie. Have you still got yours, major?"

"Yes. But don't wait for orders. When the floodlamp goes off turn on another. Don't turn on the last one unless it's necessary!"

"Yes sir."

The major left hurriedly, still holding his walkie-talkie in one hand and the pistol in the other: *I must get to the machine gun! The ammunition has not exploded and I may be able to stop that mob before it reaches the top of the ramp!* Although the floodlamp was aimed primarily at the surface of the ramp its blindingly bright light was scattered by the rain and illuminated almost the entire northern perimeter. *Thank God for the rain! The mud is slowing them down and nobody can climb the sides of the hill!* The major ran towards the mound of the machine gun. *The bastards are taking huge casualties but even if a fraction of them reaches the top they'll get behind my men and we'll be finished! My men are spread thinly and cannot look behind them as well as at the ramp!* As the major ran towards the machine gun nest he noticed that the rain had almost extinguished the flames: *Thank God for the rain!* But then an unusually close flash of lightning lit up the sky and he halted, blinded by the light. When his eyes recovered he happened to be looking at the storage tent, which was now between him and the machine gun nest. He was on the verge of starting the last sprint towards the machine gun when he saw a tall slim figure emerge gracefully from the storage tent and move swiftly towards the mound of the pit.

7

It's HER!

The rain that buffeted his face suddenly felt icy cold. Without thinking he raised his pistol and fired. The figure stopped and turned to look at him. Despite the distance and the rain he was sure that their eyes met and he knew that he could not conceal his hatred: *She knows I am hunting her!*

The major was going to fire his pistol again when he saw that she was not alone. Two hunched figures had emerged from the storage tent and were running towards her. He could not be sure but he thought he recognised Mike and Ohanian.

"Get out of the way!" the major shouted at the top of his voice. His hand was shaking and he did not want to risk hitting his friends.

Mike was too preoccupied to hear him above the din of the shooting and when the major looked again the tall figure had disappeared. The major hesitated – should he go to the machine gun or should he pursue the *thing* he had vowed to kill? If he went to the weapon he might be able to save some of his men, but *she* was an abomination in the sight of the Almighty! Never had he felt so torn between conflicting needs.

From the sound of the conflict he guessed that the rush of the bandits had been slowed. But the bandits were now almost three quarters of the way up the ramp, and they were shooting at his men on the perimeter as well as the floodlamp. The firing from his men was now intermittent, suggesting that the bandits were taking cover behind the burnt-out truck and among the trees of the grove. *My men are managing to hold them back, but for how long?* The major made up his mind: he might never get another chance to kill the abomination. He ran towards the mound that encircled the pit. As he ran the rain lightened and suddenly stopped. There was a half-hearted cheer from the bandits. *So they didn't like the rain either!* The major almost smiled bitterly as he reached the mound that surrounded the pit.

The mound was not easy to climb. The heavy rain had softened the clay and made the climb treacherous. He put the walkie-talkie in one of the pockets of his jacket and pushed the long-muzzled pistol under his belt before starting to climb desperately on all fours, his eyes smarting from his own perspiration. He was driven by something that was more than hatred, much greater than a sense of duty. He felt that this was the moment he had been prepared for, and although the sounds of the struggle reminded him of how desperate the situation was, his resolve to do what he *must* drove him on relentlessly: *In God's name I have to kill her! But I must do it quickly for there is very little time!* The rain started again, in torrential proportions.

He clambered up the muddy slope to the top of the mound and looked down into the pit. A faint orange-yellow flickering glow seemed to shine out from the shaft. *So Mike and Ohanian brought candles. They are not too far below and she is ahead of them! I must hurry or she will escape!* And then he heard the sweet rattle of the machine gun. *God be praised! Allawi's men reached the weapon and managed to work it!* With renewed vigour he started down the incline towards the gaping hole that was noisily swallowing the rainwater. The wire mesh that lay across the aperture to prevent stones from falling down the shaft looked flimsy and delicate beneath the water. *That won't stop me from falling through! I must be careful not to slip!* But he was in too much of a hurry and not careful enough. Before he could start his descent down the slope the wet clay unexpectedly moved beneath his feet and he lost his balance. His body turned as it fell and he found himself staring at the black sky and then at the mud and then again at the sky as he slid down. The hole of the pit seemed to expand, like a yawning mouth, to greet him. He was almost submerged in slimy, muddy water when he slammed against the wire mesh. For a moment he hoped it would hold him, but with a grunt of rending metal the mesh pulled away from its supports and the major fell down the shaft into the blackness, his arms waving helplessly as he tried to get a hold of anything that would slow his fall.

44

Decisions at Headquarters

1

COLONEL HALEEL CALLED the Army office in Basra at 17:03. The 'phone was picked up immediately: "Lieutenant Sayyaf speaking."

"This is Colonel Haleel. Sayyaf, has Major ElBalushi been informed that I want an inventory of the new finds?"

"I did not personally tell him, Colonel. I called the expedition this morning but Major ElBalushi was at a meeting with the archaeologists. I spoke to a Private Musa and told him that you had asked for an inventory. He promised to tell the major and ask him to call us as soon as possible."

"Why didn't you speak to Sergeant Ali?"

"Sergeant Ali was on guard duty."

"I see. Did this Musa say when Major ElBalushi was likely to call?"

"He said that it would probably be tomorrow."

"*Tomorrow?* How long does a meeting last?"

"Private Musa said that they were very busy today. He said they were reorganising the camp because of the new discoveries."

"Major ElBalushi is not there to help reorganise the camp!" The colonel paused, struck by a worrying thought: "Sayyaf, have you talked to this Private Musa before?"

"No, Colonel. I usually talk to Sergeant Ali. But I checked the personnel list and there *is* a Private Musa at the foreigners' camp."

"Did this Musa ever answer the Army radio before?"

"Not to my knowledge, Colonel. I never spoke to him before today."

"Lieutenant, I wish to speak to Major Khidr."

"Yes Colonel. A moment please."

"Major Khidr speaking."

"Khidr, please call the foreigners' expedition and ask to speak to

Major ElBalushi. Remind him to send me the inventory of the latest discoveries and add that I also want a translation in Turkish!"

"In *Turkish*, Colonel?"

"Ankara University called me this afternoon. They heard that the Turkish team made important discoveries and they asked if we could provide them with an inventory in Turkish as soon as possible."

"Would it not be better if we made the translation ourselves after we received the inventory?"

"Their translation will be better than ours. They've got at least one senior Turkish archaeologist and, anyway, it would be faster if they made their own translation. We wouldn't need to have the translation validated officially. And Khidr..."

"Yes, Colonel."

"Have you spoken to Major ElBalushi often enough to know if you were speaking to him and not someone else?"

"Yes, Colonel. I have spoken to him many times."

"When you have spoken to ElBalushi please call me back to confirm that umm… the inventory and the translation will be on their way to me soon. I want you to *insist* on speaking to the Major!"

"Do you think that something is wrong, Colonel?"

"There may be nothing wrong but I don't like the sudden unavailability of both Balushi and Ali. And I don't understand why Major ElBalushi cannot call your office before tomorrow!"

"Yes, Colonel. I'll get in touch with the expedition at once."

2

Major Khidr called back at 17: 37: "Colonel Haleel, please."

"Speaking."

"This is Major Khidr. We called the expedition but the army radio does not respond and neither does the university radio."

"Are you sure you called both radios on the correct frequencies?"

"Yes, Colonel. We were very careful. And we called each radio several times!"

"And *both* radios did not respond?"

"Yes, Colonel."

"Has this ever happened before?"

"No, Colonel. "

"I see." The colonel hesitated for a moment, then made up his mind: "Major, I want you to 'phone the Air Force base in Mosul and ask to speak to the commanding officer. Tell him, on my authority from the Ministry, to put three armed attack helicopters on standby without delay. They must have enough fuel for prolonged action at the camp of the foreign archaeologists and must carry enough troops to retake the camp if it has been invaded. Give him the coordinates of the camp."

"Give the coordinates of the archaeologists' camp on the 'phone, Colonel?"

"If the helicopters are needed, getting them there quickly is more important than keeping the location of the camp secret!"

"I understand. The commanding officer will want to know who will authorise the dispatch of the helicopters once they're fuelled and ready."

"Tell him that I shall call the base to authorise the dispatch myself after I inform the minister of the situation."

"Yes Sir."

"And keep trying to get through to either of the two radios in the archaeologists' camp. If you speak to ElBalushi, and are sure that it is ElBalushi, call me at once!"

"What if I call you after the helicopters have left?"

"I shall have them recalled."

"I understand, Colonel. Is there anything else I can do?"

"You and your staff are to remain in the office until further notice!"

"Of course, Sir."

"I will call the minister now." The colonel hung up.

Major Khidr muttered to himself: 'Haleel has sat on a wasp!' He spoke to the lieutenant: "Sayyaf, please get me the Air Force base in Mosul; I need to speak to the commanding officer urgently!" Then he turned to the NCO who was sitting, ashen faced and stock-still, in front of the office transmitter: "Keep trying to raise the foreigners' expedition. You *must* get through if at all possible!"

45

DOWN INTO THE PIT ONCE MORE

1

WHEN OHANIAN FOLLOWED Mike out of the storage tent he thought he heard the distinctive bang of a pistol. Until then his thoughts were completely on the lamia and he had paid little heed to the sound of gunfire from the northern ramp. But the pistol shot was from somewhere close by, much nearer than the ramp, and it intruded forcibly into his awareness: *Are the criminals already among us?* He stopped and looked around anxiously, half expecting to be confronted by an armed ruffian: *I wish I had a weapon!* But Ohanian had never used a weapon and knew that he would not be able to kill a man, not even in self-defence: *I wouldn't know how to use a weapon! I am not a fighting man!* Fortunately, no ruffian loomed out of the shadows and his fear of the bandits subsided. Because he had not dared look beyond his immediate vicinity he did not see the major, who was less than fifty metres away.

Mike was a short distance ahead, hidden by a cloud of raindrops that sparkled as they fell in the light of the distant floodlamp. Behind the sparkling raindrops there was blackness, and Ohanian could not help thinking that the blackness concealed the ruins of the temple where the goddess had once killed people and fed on their blood. The bandits withdrew from Ohanian's thoughts and his terror of the lamia reasserted itself: *If this woman is the ancient goddess she is in her home... why would she have changed?* His mind conjured images of the goddess's victims in the last moments of their lives: *Did she kill them before she sucked out their blood?* Did they die slowly as their blood was sucked out? The way ahead seemed filled with evil portent and the urge to run back to the storage tent almost overwhelmed him.

With considerable effort he managed to suppress his fear: *I cannot leave Mike alone with her!* He spurted forward and caught up with his friend.

"Why did you stop, Ardash?"

"I… I thought I heard a shot!" Ohanian stammered.

"So did I. It has nothing to do with us. We must hurry!"

Mike ran towards the mound of the pit and Ohanian followed, but not as speedily.

"Don't dally!" shouted Mike, "There are bullets all around us!"

"Akh yes!" Ohanian could not get his mind off the lamia and had forgotten about the bullets: *But if she's really the goddess she could answer every question of every archaeologist who has heard of the Amalishah Temple!* "Can you see her, Mike? I can't see very well in this rain!"

"She's gone down into the pit!"

"What? I can't hear you!" The shooting from the ramp was very loud.

Mike raised his voice above the noise: "I said she's gone down into the pit!"

"In the dark?"

"She knows the way."

"Of course she does!" Ohanian muttered to himself

They reached the mound. Its wet sides glistened like dark-grey granite in the rain-diffused light of the floodlamp.

2

With stray bullets splashing into the mud around them, they climbed the slippery slope frantically on all fours, using hands and feet. When they reached the rim of the mound they rested on their knees, panting, trying to catch their breath and hoping that no bullet would hit them.

"The rain is getting worse!" complained Ohanian.

"We've got to get down this thing!" said Mike as he stared down the funnel of the mound. The prospect of climbing down the slippery, rain-flooded surface to the dark hole of the pit was daunting. The rain-diffused light of the floodlamp only illuminated the rim; the hollow was in shadow and the rain cascaded furiously down the sides, gurgling loudly as it poured down the shaft.

"Be very careful!" warned Mike, "The mud can slide away from under you!"

"If one of us slipped… that wire mesh wouldn't take our weight, would it?"

"Probably not. Be thankful there is some light from the floodlamp!"

"Not in the pit!" Ohanian lamented, "Akh! Why aren't there any lights in the pit?"

"The power's been diverted to the floodlamps. But at least there won't be any bullets once we're off the rim. Let's go!"

Mike turned and began to crawl backwards down the funnel on all fours.

Ohanian was not particularly well coordinated and he was not sure he could cope with making his way down backwards. He found breathing difficult under the heavy rain, but he could not stay on the rim, not with bullets flying around him. Gingerly he turned around and began the descent on his stomach. His predicament reminded him of a time when he was a very young boy and had poured a small bucket of water on a lizard. The poor creature had almost drowned as it struggled to get away in the mud: *God is punishing me for that!* The water that seeped through his shirt felt icy and he was certain that his head was heavier because his curly hair was soaked with water. *What am I doing here? Why didn't I stay home with my parents?* The mud was slimy, like earth mixed with thick oil, and he had trouble pushing against the stones and rubble beneath: *I'm sure I'll be all right!* But he suddenly found that he had nothing to grasp and he started to slip with increasing speed towards the hole.

"Mike!"

Mike reached out and grabbed him by the wrist: "Hold on, Ardash!"

"Let go of my wrist or I'll pull you down with me!"

"I'm holding on to something!"

Ohanian managed to dig his feet into the rubble beneath the mud: "I'm OK now!"

"Are you sure?"

"Yes. I'm sorry dreadfully. I'll be more careful!"

They managed to reach the little platform at the top of the spiral stairwell. Although it had seemed like an eternity to Ohanian, the climb up the mound and the descent into the pit had lasted little more than a few minutes.

3

The spiral stairwell was covered in muddy water but felt reassuringly firm. Ohanian took a deep breath and mumbled something incomprehensible.

"Are you all right?" Mike asked.

"Yes, thank you. But I have never been in my life so frightened!"

"Let's go down the steps!"

"They're very slippery!"

"I know, but at least the floor won't slide away. Hold my hand. Careful now!"

They made their way down the spiral steps cautiously. When they were one tier down they were sheltered from the rain but it was almost completely dark.

"I think I'll light a candle," said Ohanian. He brought out his lighter and tried to light two of the candles he had brought. The candles had been in his pocket and the wicks were almost dry but the pit was draughty. He eventually managed to light one of the candles and then the other. He handed a candle to Mike: "Here!"

"Thanks. Let's go!" They proceeded down the steps.

The mud and water poured down the shaft in a gnarled brown column that writhed and wriggled as it reflected the flickering light of the candles. Sometimes it struck the winding staircase and spattered muddy drops all over Mike and Ohanian, threatening to extinguish the little flames. Ohanian followed Mike down the steps until he reached the inscriptions. "Mike," he said, reluctant to continue, "This place is very spooky but the writing… it's beautiful!" He stared in awe at the inscriptions on the wall and Mike remembered that this was the first time Ohanian had been down the pit. Ohanian had never seen the original script and the work he had done was based on Mike's photographs.

"These steps were much worse the first time I went down," said Mike reassuringly. "I didn't know whether they could take my weight and there was a god-awful stink! Now the steps have been reinforced and there isn't that vile smell any more!"

"I can smell foetid mould and centuries of decay!" said Ohanian seriously.

"That's your imagination, Ardash. Come on!"

Ohanian was on the point of following Mike down the steps when he hesitated.

"Now what's the matter, Ardash?"

"Mike, I'm afraid very much!"

"So am I. The water makes these steps very slippery."

"I'm afraid of *her*, Mike!"

"Keep going!" Mike could not say more, and from the way he spoke Ohanian realised, for the first time, that Mike was struggling with his own fears.

Very cautiously they went down the steps, holding their candles away from the water that was pouring and spattering down the shaft. Ohanian was frowning with obvious distress; the writing on the walls had done little to turn his mind away from his fears. He remembered being told of the skeletons of the priests that had lined the tunnel at the bottom of the pit and shuddered: *The poor priests died to protect her! Now they're just old bones in cardboard boxes and **she** is waiting for us!* The horror twisted his insides: *Calm yourself! She's not supernatural, she is just different from us!* But the thought was not enough to alleviate his fears. *Think of all the wonderful things she knows!* Even that did not stop his heart pounding and he unconsciously clutched the little cross that hung around his neck.

4

The lamia was waiting for them at the fourth tier of the staircase. She was standing impassively against the wall of the pit, her hands behind her back. Ohanian crossed himself and hoped that she would not understand what that implied. Mike was about to say something but she raised her finger to her lips. She seemed to be listening.

"We are not alone," she husked, her voice low, "someone has followed you!"

She bent forward and looked up, trying to see through the water that was funnelled down the shaft. Mike and Ohanian could hear very little above the sound of falling water. Even the distant gunfire could not be heard distinctly.

"No one would follow us here!" said Mike in Assyrian.

"It's the soldier who gives orders," said the lamia quietly. She had watched the soldiers many times, secretly, hidden by shadows.

Oh my God! thought Mike, *Balushi has seen her and has left everything to follow us and kill her!* Mike was surprised to find that he still felt an overpowering protectiveness towards the lamia. The analytic part of his mind had decided to put his feelings on hold because there were too many questions that needed answering, but ElBalushi's single-minded hatred of the lamia could not be ignored; he would kill her at the first opportunity. "We must go down quickly!" he exclaimed, and he almost touched the lamia to emphasise the urgency of the situation. He pulled his hand back just in time and only said: "That man wants to kill you!"

"I know," replied the lamia, and she half-smiled at Mike, a resigned smile: "I saw that in his eyes." She showed no inclination to escape.

"Please," Mike said, "Let's get away from him!"

"I will not run like a frightened animal, Michael Townsend. I shall wait for him."

Dammit! She's playing queen again! "That man can kill you, Amalishah. He…"

A heavy thud on the wire mesh forced them all to look up. In the flickering light of the candles and through the falling water they saw the wire mesh bulge inwards as it momentarily supported what looked like a writhing black mass. Then some of the screws that held the mesh gave way and the major plummeted down the shaft enclosed in a cocoon of muddy water. Mike and Ohanian froze with shock but the lamia reacted instantly.

With lightning speed she pushed Mike and Ohanian against the wall of the pit and turned towards the falling body that was plunging down towards them. The major's arms were flailing in all directions as he tried desperately to catch something, anything, that would arrest his fall but his hands only scraped ineffectively against the sides of the shaft. The lamia braced herself and, with her arms stretched out, caught the major around the waist. Before Mike and Ohanian had realised what had happened she was putting him down gently on the steps.

5

ElBalushi stood dizzily for a few moments, trembling with shock. Then with a look of utter horror he backed away from the lamia and pulled his pistol from its holster.

"No!" shouted Mike. The major ignored him and quickly climbed a few steps until he stood behind Mike, out of the lamia's reach. His eyes narrowed into black slits as he pointed his pistol at her chest.

"Don't do it, Hussein!"

The pistol did not waver and Mike thought he could see the muscles of ElBalushi's trigger finger tighten. "Hussein, NO!"

Although the major was still in shock he knew that here, in this wet and dismal place, he at last had the chance to end the long life of *her* whom he had vowed to destroy. But he could not just pull the trigger and do what his grandfather or his great-grandfather would have done. His life had not been as simple as theirs. And as he tried to consciously *decide* what action to take he almost heard, like an echo from the past, the *Qadi*'s warning: *'Beware of pride, major. Anyone can believe himself to be a sword of his religion, but the thinking man has to weigh his thoughts and actions, lest he strike blindly in the mistaken belief that he has Divine approval!'* The major's past convictions clashed with an upsurge of doubts he never knew he had and he was paralysed by an agonising uncertainty. The strain of his inner conflict crept slowly, muscle by muscle, to his face and the muzzle of the pistol started to shake as the opposing tendons of his hand pulled in opposite directions. Slowly, very slowly, the major lowered the pistol.

"You saved my life," he said quietly in Arabic, breathing in short gasps. "I must accept that as a sign from God that I am not to kill you." He returned his pistol to its holster. To himself he added: "We cannot always understand the ways of the Almighty!"

The lamia could not comprehend the words but she could read his emotions. From the way the major had pulled out his pistol she had realised it was a weapon, perhaps it was the thing that had made she loud noise when he first saw her, but after she had set him down she had shown no emotion and had watched him calmly, like a spectator who attentively follows the unfolding of a play.

"I need to return to my men," said the major curtly, ignoring the lamia.

"Hussein," said Mike, "We cannot go back with you. Not with her."

"I understand. Why are you here?" Still under stress, he spoke in clipped tones.

"She is taking us away. To help us escape whatever shall happen on the hilltop."

"Does she know a way out?"

"She said she knows a way out."

"Then go with her. Perhaps it's safer than up there. I must return to my men. There is little time and although there is some hope the battle

576

is not going well for us!"

The major was about to run up the steps when the lamia looked up and said: "There is a new sound! Something is coming. It is still far away and I do not know what it is." The torrential rain had almost stopped and the water that fell down the shaft was no more than a loose collection of gurgling trickles. The sound of gunfire could be heard clearly, punctuated by short bursts from the machine gun.

The major looked at Mike: "What is she saying?"

"She says there is a new sound. She says something is coming but it is still far away."

"I can only hear my men defending the hill," said the major, his face tense.

"I don't hear anything but the sound of guns!" said Ohanian.

"Her hearing is better than ours," said Mike.

"What could be coming?" said Ohanian, "It is probably another truck full of bandits!"

All four stood and listened, waiting anxiously. The major's frown was like a dark shadow on his face but Mike and Ohanian showed no emotion as they waited stoically to see how things would work out. The lamia stood impassively, her eyes half closed. Eventually, interspersed with the gunfire and at the threshold of human hearing, they could just make out the *thwack thwack thwack* of helicopters. The sound of shooting lessened and finally came the continuous *BRRRR…* of a rapid-fire machine gun.

"It's the US cavalry!" shouted Ohanian.

"God be praised," the major said quietly. Mike nodded and found himself saying: "Amen." Ohanian muttered something in his own language that nobody understood.

6

The major's mood changed completely; he was a happy man. The pressure to return to the surface and be with his men had been relieved. "Do the others know about her?" he asked Mike almost pleasantly.

"They think she is my girlfriend," Mike answered.

"And Kureishi was happy to let her take the crown and that big jewel with her?"

"Kureishi thinks I stole them," said Mike, "She was wearing them

577

when she appeared to everyone in the storage tent. I could not ask her to leave them behind!"

"Of course not. But ElKureishi could cause you trouble, Mike, when all this is over."

"I tried to explain that they are copies," said Ohanian, "That they were made by my cousin the jeweller for Mike's girlfriend. I'm not sure I convinced anyone."

"I see," the major said with a boyish grin. "When I get back I'll let everyone know that you were both well and, though I hate lying, I shall also say that I was impressed by how well Ohanian's cousin made the uh… copies."

"Thank you, Hussein."

"And Mike, another time perhaps you shall tell me how …uh your girlfriend got hold of shoes, a skirt and a blouse?"

"I will tell you, Hussein, another time."

"What will you do once you're out?"

Mike's plans had not gone beyond getting away from the hill. "I don't know yet," he admitted, "I think I'll try to hot-wire one of the expeditions' trucks."

"That's not as easy as some people make out," said the major. He got a small bunch of keys from his pocket and removed one of the keys, offered it to Mike: "This is the key to my Land Rover," he said, "You can return it to any army base at your leisure. There's a compass in the glove compartment and bottles of water in the boot."

"Thank you." Mike took the key.

"I have to go now!" The major turned to Ohanian: "Doctor Ohanian, may we meet again under better circumstances."

"Akh yes," replied Ohanian awkwardly, "May we meet somewhere bright and dry!"

The major suddenly became very grave: "Mike, please tell the lady that I am grateful to her for saving my life."

Mike translated the major's words and the lamia showed her acknowledgement by nodding briefly to the major. ElBalushi was about to run up the steps when he stopped and removed the long-muzzled pistol from his belt.

"Take this, Mike," he said, handing the pistol over, "You never know… um, there may be bandits in your way."

Mike took the weapon. It felt heavier than he remembered: "Thank you. Is it loaded?"

"I loaded it. It's got six bullets."

"Goodbye, Hussein. And thank you."

"Goodbye, Mike." The major turned and climbed up the steps two at a time.

Mike pushed the pistol down into his belt, wondering if he would ever need to use it.

7

"What is that noise?" asked the lamia. The sound of the helicopters' rotors could be heard clearly over the sound of gunfire.

"What noise?" asked Ohanian, before realising who he was speaking to. He had not spoken directly to the lamia before.

The lamia smiled. "The noise that made you all so happy."

"That was the sound of…" Mike did not now the word for 'rescue' in Assyrian.

"That was the sound of unexpected help!" said Ohanian.

"Your friends are safe now?" said the lamia.

"I hope so," said Mike.

"And you still want to come with me?" She spoke to Mike, but although she spoke without expression it was evident that she was trying to hide a mixture of emotions.

Mike looked directly at the lamia and spoke slowly: "There is a little house in Mosul where I promised to teach you the ways of my world. That house is waiting for us. I cannot speak for my friend."

The lamia's face lit up and she turned to Ohanian: "Do you still want to come with us?" She smiled as she spoke, the smile of a contented child.

Ohanian looked confused for a moment. His heart was beating wildly again. He frowned and said after a long pause: "Yes. I'll come with you and Mike."

"What is your name?" asked the lamia.

"Ardashes," said Ohanian, his voice shaky.

"Then let us go now." The lamia's smile broadened: "And do not be so frightened of me, Ardashes. I mean you and Mike no harm."

Ohanian stared at her for a moment, then smiled back.

46

THE ELECTRICIAN, AGAIN

1

SELIM SAT CROSS-LEGGED on the floor of his tent with tears streaming down his face. Only minutes earlier a lull in the shooting had exploded with hysterical cries of "Don't kill us!" and "God is greater!" followed by the clatter of assault rifles. Selim did not need to see the killing to know that all who had run down the ramp had been slaughtered: *They were massacred and I was to have died with them!* Selim felt no pity for the workers or his fellow spies; it was the narrowness of his escape that tormented him, the fact that Death had passed him by only because of a fluke of fate. He covered his face with his hands and wept uncontrollably, his whole body shaking.

Selim had foreseen that the soldiers could not leave their posts during the attack and would not stop the workers from moving to the head of the southern ramp. He and the other spies had gone with the workers, like sheep-dogs herding sheep to their pen, but when the last man had started down the ramp Selim had changed his mind and returned to his tent, hoping that nobody would notice: *If I join Jawad and the lads they will make me take part in the attack on the hill! I could get killed!* And there had also been the hope that if he stayed on the hill he could, with some luck, knife a soldier or two in the back: *Then Jawad might increase my share of the gold! At the very least he would not refuse to give me the Jordanian girl!* Selim sighed as he remembered the girl who had figured so prominently in his daydreams. But these hopes were dashed now. Jawad had expected Selim to die but Selim was alive. Jawad hated surprises: there would be no gold, no Jordanian girl.

As the only non-archaeologist with professional skills, Selim had acquired the status of unofficial leader among the workers. They had gathered outside his tent at the first sounds of conflict and had wanted him to explain what all the shooting was about. Selim and the other spies had previously agreed on what to say in order to persuade the workers to leave the hilltop: "Do you know *who* is out there?" Selim had asked the frightened workers as ominously as he could, "That's Jawad and Arroussi with their lads! ElBalushi and his soldiers don't stand a chance against them!"

A few of the workers had heard of Arroussi but none had heard of Jawad:

"Who is this Jawad?"

"Is he Arroussi's son? I've heard that Arroussi has a son."

Selim had smiled knowingly, hinting that he knew more about Jawad and Arroussi than he was willing to divulge: "Jawad is not Arroussi's son, but he is sure to be Arroussi's heir!"

"Sure to be Arroussi's heir!" had intoned a heavily-built man with a deep voice. He was the most imposing but least intelligent of the spies and Selim had instructed him to agree with everything he said.

"Let me tell you," Selim had intoned, "Arroussi is like a little lamb compared to Jawad!"

"Like a little lamb!" the heavily-built man had echoed.

"But what do Jawad and Arroussi want?" a worker had asked.

"They want the gold, of course!" Selim had answered, "and to kill the foreigners!"

"But how do *you* know who is out there and what they want?" another worker had asked.

"I know a lot about these things," Selim had asserted confidently, "And I know that if we don't get off the hill soon we shall die!"

The workers were simple folk, and Selim had known that they would believe anything he said if it were spoken with conviction. A worker had protested: "But Major ElBalushi said that we should stay in our tents!"

"What does ElBalushi know?" Selim had retorted, as though the question betrayed unlimited stupidity. "The soldiers are here to protect the foreigners, not us! If we stay here we shall never see our families again!"

After that it had been easy to persuade the workers to collect their meagre belongings and congregate at the head of the southern ramp. The electrician had convinced them that they had nothing to fear if they rushed down the ramp together. When Selim was sure that they were all at the head of the ramp he had shouted at them to run down as fast as they could. They had barely taken a few steps when he sneaked off and made his way to his tent.

2

Now Selim was alone in his tent, trying to come to terms with the notion that he had almost been killed: *Aslan knew about this! I'll kill the pig if I see him again!* But then he realised the futility of the thought: *Why kill Aslan? This is Jawad's doing! He must have told Aslan that my death would increase his share of the gold!* Selim toyed with his knife as he thought of Jawad, but then he shook his head: *I cannot kill Jawad; I am no match for him!* The more he thought about his predicament, the worse it seemed: *I will never get the chance to kill Jawad! He never trusts anyone who disobeyed him and if he finds out that I am alive he will have me killed! And he will have my wives and children killed!* The memory of his wives and children made Selim weep bitterly.

Eventually, Selim noticed that the shooting had stopped: *Jawad's attack on the hill failed!* This was a welcome development; it gave him time to think and plan: *But there will be a second attack and this one won't fail!* What would happen after the lads swarmed over the camp? When the raping and the killing were over the men would search everywhere for valuables. They would find Selim and tell Jawad that he was alive and Jawad would have him killed: *I must escape before Jawad and the lads take the hill!* He would take one of the expedition's vehicles and drive to some town far from Jawad! What if he got lost in the wastelands? *Insha'Allah I will not get lost!* But how would he escape? *I could join the soldiers and wait for a chance to climb down the side of the hill!* But there could be ruffians all around the hill – what if he were caught? He would be handed over to Jawad, who would kill him. And what if he never got the chance to climb down the hill? He would get killed with the soldiers when Jawad took the hill. And what if the bandits failed to take the hill? It was improbable but not impossible that ElBalushi and his dogs would prevail: *If some of Jawad's men are taken captive they would point the finger at me and say: "He was the chief spy! He killed Sergeant Ali!"* The soldiers would tear him apart.

His only chance was to lie low and hope that the second attack would be at night. In the mayhem and the darkness he would try to escape and make it to the jeeps. What if Jawad or Arroussi had left guards around the vehicles? If the guards were from Jawad's lads he could persuade them to let him take a Land Rover – but any guards would probably be from Arroussi's jackals! They would not know him and would probably kill him out of hand. Selim felt boxed: every way out carried heavy risks and staying in the camp meant certain death. It was a very long time since Selim had prayed: *Help me! You are said to be merciful! Please let the second attack be at night! Please help me escape!*

After much self-pity mixed with fervent prayers, Selim convinced himself that the second attack had to be after dark: *They don't need to attack again soon because Aslan will convince the idiots in Basra that nothing happened! The second attack will be after dark and I will escape while the camp is in chaos!*

Having made a decision Selim felt hungry. The foreigners were in the storage tent and the soldiers were stuck at their posts, looking outwards towards the enemy. There was no movement in the camp. Selim picked up his rucksack and, very cautiously, went to the refectory. It was empty, as expected, and he ate as much as he could before filling his rucksack with cans of food and bottles of water. He remembered to take a can opener. Then he hid in the tent of one of the workers to wait until it was time to escape. The tent was clean and the mattress, though stained, had been aired regularly and did not smell. He lay on the bed and wept, mumbling to himself. Only his self-preservation mattered now, the gold that lay in the storage tent was no longer important and even his family meant nothing to him. He would gladly have exchanged the lives of his wives and children for a sense of safety. After all, women were plentiful and he would have no trouble finding other wives and breeding more children.

3

Between the battle of the morning and the night-time attack at the northern ramp Selim remained in the worker's tent. It was pitch dark when the shooting started again but he was too frightened and stupefied by the blackness to attempt his escape. When the tarpaulin of the tent suddenly glowed with a faint yellow-grey light, Selim knew that a floodlamp had been turned on. This complicated things but still Selim did nothing, paralysed by his terror of getting caught by the soldiers or the bandits. It was only after what seemed like a very long time that Selim heard the sound of helicopters, and his first thought was: 'That idiot Aslan! He failed to fool the army!'

The certainty that the soldiers were going to win made it imperative that he get away from the hilltop. Any prisoners the soldiers captured were sure to identify him: 'He's the man who killed Sergeant Ali and the young soldier!' He could not tarry any longer. He got up and warily stuck his head out of the tent, squinting in the rain. He could see the searchlights of two helicopters hovering above the northern ramp with their machine guns blazing. A third helicopter hovered a short distance away. *Jawad and Arroussi must be having a hard time; insha'allah they shall both get killed!* But the sight of the helicopters spitting death at the bandits terrified him. *There will soon be soldiers everywhere! I must get to the jeeps before the helicopters land.*

ElBalushi's men had left their posts and were standing in little groups, watching the helicopters strafe whoever was still trying to climb the northern ramp. Even the foreigners had left the storage tent to watch. Selim loped to the south-western side of the southern ramp, bending forward like a penitent ape. The rain had lessened but the floodlamp at the southern ramp had been turned on and Selim saw that the machine gun nest was empty. With many a glance behind him, he managed to half-lope, half-slide down the side of the southern ramp, expecting to be shot in the back at any moment. But the soldiers were too busy watching the helicopters, and Selim left the hill with little more than a contemptuous glance at the corpses that were sprawled, forgotten by all, at the lower end of the ramp.

4

Selim knew where Arroussi's trucks had been left, and he felt a senseless anger when he noticed that the trucks were gone: *So some of the pigs escaped! May they perish in the wastelands!* The expedition's vehicles were not too far and Selim walked quickly towards the rocks that formed a ragged ring around the trucks and Land Rovers. Sometimes he stopped and crouched and listened, suppressing his urge to run lest someone noticed the movement. There was little cover, but although the rain had stopped the moon had not yet risen and Selim made as much use of the darkness as he could. The sound of the helicopters stopped just as Selim reached one of the large rocks that encircled the hill, indicating that all three craft had landed on the hilltop, and Selim felt that this was a good omen. But although the first stage of his escape had been achieved without mishap, he knew that the final run to the vehicles could be the most dangerous part of his escape: *If there are guards they would be soldiers!* Moving very cautiously from rock to rock, Selim approached the expedition's vehicles.

The moon had risen but was intermittently covered by wind-driven clouds. Selim could just make out the expedition's trucks and Land Rovers, parked in neat rows and surrounded by rocks and boulders of all shapes and sizes. Were there any guards? Selim could not see anyone. He moved stealthily, loping in his ape-like gait, and swiftly covered the distance to a large rock that was only a few metres from the closest truck.

Selim dared not look around the rock but, with his back pressed against it, he listened intently. There were no sounds. Were the vehicles unguarded? There would be at least two soldiers to look after the vehicles, and they would talk to each other as they patrolled between the vehicles. But there was no sound of talking and there was no crunch of footsteps. The moon peeped out from between the clouds while Selim listened and waited, and he had almost decided to run past the lorries to the nearest Land Rover when the silence was broken by angry whispering. The voices came from the far end of the parked vehicles: *They are behind the trucks – near the jeeps!* It sounded as though several men were having an argument while trying to make as little noise as possible. *These can't be soldiers! Soldiers would have no reason to whisper!* Selim moved cautiously away from the concealing rock to look. His attention was on the vehicles and he almost tripped over something soft but heavy.

It was the bodies of two soldiers, one lying across the other: *Ayyah! The guards! They were careless and had their throats slit!* Selim could just make out four armed ragged men standing close together near the Land Rovers: *They've killed the guards but the fools are standing around wasting time!* The four men were arguing in muted tones, waving their arms and pointing repeatedly at something a short distance away. The object of their argument seemed to be a long-haired woman who was kneeling beside the prostrate body of a tall slim man. Although the woman had her back to Selim, he recognised her as Aisha, Jawad's woman.

This was worrying to Selim: *If Aisha is here Jawad can't be too far away! Where is he? He must not see me!* Selim could not see Jawad anywhere, and the long fellow who lay on the ground was definitely not Jawad. *Could it be that the arrival of the helicopters separated*

Jawad from his woman? Selim shook his head: *Jawad would not leave his woman behind! Not if she were alive! She might tell everything about him to the soldiers!*

Selim waited to see what would happen but Jawad did not appear and the argument appeared to be getting worse. Selim recognised one of the men as Nabil, a taciturn burglar whom Selim had worked with in the days when he disarmed burglar alarms. The other three were unknown to Selim; they were either from Arroussi's lot or from among the dispensable ruffians that Jawad had recruited for the attack on the hill. Hoping that Jawad would not appear unexpectedly, he decided to approach the men.

5

Selim strode out from behind the rocks feigning an air of confidence. He hoped that they would have enough sense not to shoot, for the sound of an automatic weapon would be heard by the soldiers on the hill.

"Hello lads!" he said in a stage whisper.

"Who is this?" exclaimed Nabil. The bandits raised their weapons and turned to glare at Selim. Aisha cast a quick look at Selim but did not get up. She seemed in great distress.

"Don't you recognise me, Nabil? It's Selim!"

"Oh it's you. We thought you were killed with the workers!"

You son-of-pig! Is this all the welcome I get? Selim smiled: "So you don't know all Jawad's plans! Where is he?"

"Jawad is dead. Somebody shot him full of holes!" Nabil seemed confused, tired and outpaced by events. "We have his woman here."

"And who is the corpse?"

"The man lying there is Arroussi's son," Nabil replied, "He is not dead yet."

"Where is Arroussi?"

"He's dead too. Someone knifed him."

Selim could not help smiling. *Both Jawad and Arroussi dead? Things are much better than I hoped!* "So why don't you finish off Arroussi's son and get away from here?"

"We can't make up our minds about that," said Nabil. "Arroussi's son could be useful. His family is very rich and would pay handsomely if we delivered him alive."

So that's what the argument is about! The men got nothing for their pains and Arroussi's son could be worth a lot of money. "You're right. It is a good idea to keep Arroussi's son alive. Where are the rest of you?"

"The helicopters and the soldiers got all Jawad's lads except us. They also got most of Arroussi's jackals. Those who weren't killed managed to escape in their trucks."

"So you are all that is left of our lads?"

"We think so. Arroussi's jackals wouldn't let any of us escape with them. Those of us who tried to climb into Arroussi's trucks were shot!"

"So why didn't you take one of the foreigners' trucks? Or one of their jeeps?"

"We tried but we couldn't start either the trucks or the jeeps," replied Nabil sheepishly, "we haven't got any keys!"

Selim was about to laugh but he remembered how vulnerable he was and suppressed the urge. "So you're lucky I came along!" he said with a broad smile. "I can start any of the trucks I want!"

"That is good. What shall we do with the woman?" asked Nabil.

Ah! They expect me to settle their argument! Selim wondered if he should keep the woman for himself. To hell with his wives! Aisha was far prettier and smarter! And she knew most of Jawad's business connections. With Jawad and Arroussi gone and this woman by his side he could start his own organisation! But perhaps not. If he took Aisha he would be seen as a usurper, and it would only be a matter of time before he was blamed for the deaths of both bandit leaders – and Arroussi had many friends and relatives! Selim could become the target of a well-financed vendetta.

"She is useless," he replied after a moment's thought, "Nabil, kill her!"

But instead of pulling out his knife Nabil looked at Aisha hungrily. She was still kneeling beside Mukhtar with her back to the men, oblivious of what they were saying. "I would like to have some fun with her first," said Nabil, "I've always fancied her!"

Selim pondered for a moment; there was no time for this sort of thing but it was best not o antagonise Nabil. Nabil carried an assault rifle but he only had his knife. "Very well. Have your fun and then kill her. But don't take too long."

"Ayyah!" exclaimed Nabil gleefully.

But another bandit sad: "I want her too! We must not kill her before I'm finished!"

587

"I'll have her first!" said Nabil. "I found her!"

"But I found Arroussi's son, and he is more important!"

"So have Arroussi's son!" retorted Nabil.

Everyone laughed except Aisha, who was too involved in nursing Mukhtar to pay attention. She knew that the men valued Mukhtar's life because his family was wealthy and might pay a generous reward, but now that Jawad and Arroussi were gone she had no part to play and had not given any thought to the worth of her own life.

6

"Nabil shall have her first," said Selim firmly, "Get on with it!"

With a broad grin, Nabil laid down his assault rifle and went over to Aisha: "Get up!"

She looked up at him in surprise. "Shouldn't we be going soon?" she said quietly, "Mukhtar will die if he is not taken to a doctor."

"That can wait!" barked Nabil, leering at her.

"Wait for what?"

By way of answer Nabil took hold of Aisha's upper arm and pulled her roughly away from Mukhtar. "Come on woman, this is your lucky day!"

"What are you doing, Nabil?"

"I want you away from him!" He yanked her up so that she stood before him, held by his grip on her arm. At that moment the clouds moved away from the moon and everything was bathed in silver.

Aisha looked at Nabil's face with horror.

"Selim!" she cried. But Selim was looking away and seemed to be sharing a private joke with the other men. Aisha struggled violently and tried to escape but Nabil was too strong for her. At first he found her struggles amusing, but he soon lost patience and cuffed her playfully on the side of the head: "Come on woman! It'll be some time before that half-man can give you any pleasure. I can give you what you want right now!"

Aisha tried to slap him but he parried her blow easily: "Stop fighting, woman!"

But she fought like a tigress and in the scuffle managed to scratch his face. Nabil howled in pain and then, with a loud curse, hit her so hard with his fist that she stumbled backwards and fell to the ground. She lay trembling from shock, staring at the blackness of the sky with her eyelids fluttering.

"You'd better not give me any more trouble!" Nabil growled, glaring at her as she lay barely conscious on the ground. "Take your trousers off!"

Aisha did not respond and Nabil moved forward and stood between her legs. "I said take your trousers off!" He started to unbuckle his belt.

'It is finished' she thought, 'If only I could die now!' But although her despair made her almost lose consciousness it was not enough to end her life.

Naked from the waist down, Nabil squatted between her legs and tried to force them apart, but she resisted him and he could not pull off her trousers. Cursing furiously, Nabil moved forward and climbed over her: "Stop struggling you stupid whore!" But she struggled all the more and scratched his face again, more deeply this time so that his blood flowed down his cheeks. This was too much for Nabil. His lust vanished and was replaced by a murderous fury. He took hold of her neck with one hand and held her down, throttling her. With the other hand he took hold of a heavy stone and raised it high above his shoulders, intending to smash it down on her head. Aisha closed her eyes and waited for her life to end, but the blow never fell. A single shot rang out and the fury on Nabil's face melted away. He released her neck and with his arm still held high he dropped the stone before collapsing like a deflating balloon. Aisha tried to push the lifeless body away but she seemed to have lost all her strength. Mukhtar turned weakly onto his side to see who had fired the shot that had saved Aisha. Selim and the three other men stared wide-eyed at the hill, hardly daring to move, terrified that the gunshot might have attracted the attention of the soldiers.

47

BEHIND THE CAVERN-TEMPLE

1

OVER THE MILLENNIA the tunnel that led to the cavern-temple had been kept dry by the rubble that had blocked its entrance, but when the pit was cleared and the rubble removed there was nothing to stop rainwater spreading to the tunnel from the hemispherical chamber at the bottom of the steps. A large area of water would have raised the humidity of the cavern-temple and accelerated the corrosion of any metal artefacts that remained to be discovered, and so the archaeologists had built a low dam across the entrance of the tunnel to confine rainwater to the hemispherical chamber. The dam had proved adequate against the night's heavy rain, but it had transformed the chamber into a circular pool that looked black and forbidding in the candlelight.

"Akh!" cried Ohanian, "We can't get across this!" He stood precariously on the lowest step above the level of the pool.

"The water can't be deeper than the height of the dam," said Mike.

"If the floor of the chamber is like a bowl," argued Ohanian, "the water at its centre could be *much* deeper than the height of the dam!"

"Why have you stopped?" the lamia asked from across the pool. She was waiting at the tunnel entrance.

"We're not sure how to cross this water," Mike answered.

The lamia looked at Mike with an expression of suppressed amusement. Goaded into exasperation, Mike said to Ohanian: "She just crossed this pool and her skirt isn't even wet! I'm sure you'll be all right!"

"My legs are not as long as hers and I cannot roll my trousers high enough!"

"It might help if you take your shoes and socks off," suggested Mike.

"This is where you were bitten or stung, is it not?" said Ohanian, "What bit you or stung you could be waiting for us in the water!"

"Very well, so don't take off your shoes and socks, but we can't stop here!" Mike rolled up his trousers and stepped into the black water with his shoes on. He reached the tunnel entrance without mishap and said: "Come on, Ardash!"

Ohanian looked agitated but showed no inclination to follow. The lamia resolved the impasse by taking off her shoes and, holding her skirt above her knees, stepping over the dam and wading across the flooded chamber to where Ohanian was standing. To his consternation she lifted him up and, holding him with one arm the way a man would carry a large pillow, carried him bodily across the pool to the tunnel entrance. She lowered him gently onto dry ground and said impishly: "Now your shoes will not get wet!"

"Thank you!" stammered Ohanian, still holding his lit candle and visibly shocked at having been carried so easily. Mike could not suppress a smile as they hurried down the tunnel, with the lamia in the lead.

2

The air in the tunnel was considerably colder than in the pit and Mike noticed that Ohanian was shivering: "Are you cold, Ardash?"

"A little, but I'm more scared than cold! Did you see how easily she lifted me? What chance would we have against someone like that?"

"You're quite right. She's very strong."

"Akh! She has disappeared again!"

"She's down the tunnel ahead of us. She doesn't need the light of our candles!"

The tunnel was longer than Mike remembered, and in the shifting candlelight the shadows on the rugose walls intertwined and disentangled continually, like the fingers of skeletal hands that would not stay still. Mike could not help thinking of the priests whose bones had lain for centuries along the tunnel floor: *If ghosts exist this place should be haunted! The poor fellows cannot be at peace while their remains are stored in cardboard boxes!* The tunnel and its shadows likewise induced Ohanian to think of the priests: "This is what the tunnel must have looked like to the priests and priestesses with their oil lamps!" he whispered.

"I suppose so, although they probably used torches instead of oil lamps."

"And it must have looked like this to the prisoners who were dragged and pushed to where the goddess was waiting!"

"Ardash... this place is bad enough as it is!"

"I'm sorry!"

Ohanian kept quiet after that, but Mike's imagination was ignited and he could not avoid thinking of the captives: *Were they taken to their deaths one at a time? Did they struggle? Did they scream for help? They must have known they were fodder for the goddess!* The lamia had told Mike that she had fed on human blood only during the reign of a single Assyrian king, that she had fed on prisoners with extreme repugnance, that the king had given her no choice because he wanted the Hittites to attack the temple... *Yet she could not wait to kill when she thought I wouldn't be able to take her to Mosul!* The wax-like face of the young soldier who had been murdered in the night flashed in Mike's mind: *She must have craved human blood all the time! She concealed her craving and pretended to care for me only because she hoped I'd take her away from the hill!* Mike felt furious at having been duped and having his emotions exploited. With a sudden spine-chilling horror he saw his present situation in a new light: *Perhaps she also lied about there being a way out of this damn hill! Perhaps she is taking us to a place where she can kill us and hide our bodies so that they'll never be found!* The sense of horror brought an all-enveloping fear and he sought refuge in the thought of ElBalushi's long-muzzled pistol. However, try as he might he could not imagine himself directing the weapon at her and pulling the trigger. As though the memory was permanently at the back of his mind, the *ecstasy* he had felt when he kissed her for the first time blocked any notion of intentionally harming her. He could fear her but not hate her, and as he remembered their first shared moments together his fury at her betrayal changed into something altogether more complex, weaker and ambiguous: *If I touch her again, if I savour the perfume of her body again, I would not be able to pull the trigger! I could never kill her just to save my life!* And so, despite severe misgivings, his attitude softened and he found himself giving her the benefit of the doubt: *Perhaps there is a way out, after all. Perhaps she killed the boy to appease her craving for blood so that she wouldn't be tempted to kill us on the way to Mosul!* Yet he felt weak and frustrated at how easily he had been vanquished by feelings he could not control.

3

As Mike and Ohanian approached the end of the tunnel they saw that the lamia was waiting for them. Framed by darkness, she stood facing them impassively just within the cavern-temple. In the flickering candlelight she looked very pale.

They emerged from the tunnel and Ohanian husked: "So this is the grotto that was the goddess's temple!" The candlelight could not reach the farthest parts of the cavern and Ohanian brought out another candle from his pocket and lit it. It made little difference at first, but when his eyes adapted to the low illumination behind the lamia he became aware of the cavern's vastness: "Aah!" he exclaimed, staring at the huge stalactites and the massive columns that helped support the roof, "This is amazing truly!" The lamia did not understand his words but she understood and appreciated his awe: "This place was only a hollow cavity before my people came," she said engagingly, "With a lot of work they extended the cavity and carved the pillars. It took many planting seasons to make it like this."

The lamia's tone charmed Ohanian and he was about to respond but Mike snapped in Assyrian: "We don't have time for this!" Ohanian was taken aback by Mike's shortness but, aware of his friend's conflicting emotions, chose not to speak because he expected the lamia to show anger. However, the lamia's reaction was only one of disappointment, she lost all expression for a moment and then looked down, as though beset by painful thoughts. Ohanian was about to say something conciliatory but the lamia turned away abruptly and walked swiftly towards the dais, striding in long steps past the sacrificial altar as though she wished it not to be noticed. Mike followed wordlessly a few steps behind her, his face a grim mask. When Ohanian reached the altar he could not help whispering in English: "Mike, is it on this thing that she drank the blood of the prisoners?"

"Probably."

Ohanian said something but it sounded so much like a whimper that Mike ignored it.

The lamia got onto the dais with an effortless jump. Mike was a few metres behind her, not yet on the dais, watching her closely. If she were to revert to what she had once been it was most likely to be here, next to the sacrificial altar, next to her massive throne. He felt ready for all eventualities, even to the possibility of pulling out the pistol and warning her of its lethal capabilities. But the lamia did not revert back, and only hesitated for a moment before moving diffidently towards the black throne. She reached out and passed her hand lightly, almost lovingly, over the smooth backrest, and as she caressed the cold surface her eyes closed and she appeared to be listening to something beautiful but distant, something only she could hear.

Satisfied that no perilous transformation had taken place, Mike climbed onto the dais. The lamia instantly withdrew her hand and looked away, but not before he noticed that her eyes were wet with tears. He could not suppress a rush of empathy and heard himself say, with a kindness that surprised him: "I promise we'll come back one day, Amalishah. This is not the last time you see your cavern."

The kindness in his voice surprised her too: "I am afraid of your world, Mike," she said softly, "and my heart is reluctant to leave what is left of mine."

"You shall become part of my world," Mike answered quietly, "And, if you wish it, I shall always be with you; holding your hand as long as I live."

When he said 'as long as I live' the lamia shuddered visibly, as though struck by a sudden gust of freezing air. Mike saw her tremble and frowned, not sure how to interpret her reaction, but then Ohanian climbed onto the dais. The lamia left the black throne without a backward glance and disappeared into the cavern wall behind it. The shadows made it difficult to see the opening through which she had vanished.

"A private entrance to the cavern-temple?" Ohanian whispered in English.

"I think so," replied Mike, "Carol mentioned an almost invisible cleft in the rock. She said it leads to more tunnels but they haven't been explored yet."

"I am more frightened now," said Ohanian.

"We have to go on."

Mike followed the lamia through the opening, his hand on the butt of the pistol under his belt. Ohanian hurried behind him, afraid to move forward but terrified of being left behind. They were now in a dark passageway, narrower than the tunnel that linked the hemispherical chamber to the cavern-temple. Unlike the wrinkled walls of the tunnel, the walls of the passageway were smooth and in parts shiny and worn, showing that they had been touched by countless passing hands.

4

The air in the passageway was humid, musty and cold, and a short distance ahead Mike could just make out black gaping doorways on either side. "Where are we?" he asked the lamia.

"This is where my white priestesses and I lived," she answered, "It was known as the Sacred Quarters, and no males were allowed here."

"What are white priestesses?" asked Ohanian incongruously.

"They were the priestesses closest to me," replied the lamia. "Most of the priestesses lived above ground, but the white priestesses were my friends and they lived here with me. A few lived normally long lives, but almost all died young. I do not know why."

"The air here is not very healthy," said Ohanian.

"I did no know."

"Can we see inside the rooms?" Mike asked.

"Of course."

The doorways led to small, roughly rectangular enclosures which varied in size and shape, as did the heights of their ceilings. They were completely empty, damp and cold, with frayed cobwebs on the walls and rock floors that were uneven and covered in dust. At the before-last opening the lamia stopped and said: "My white priestesses and I used to sit and talk in this room."

The opening led to a large room with rough sloping walls and a large oblong hole at the far end. From the hole came the faint gurgling of running water.

"An underground stream?" Mike asked.

"Yes, but not much water," replied the lamia. "There is a spring inside the hill. This room is also where my white priestesses used to wash, when we did not sit and talk."

"Weren't they cold?" interjected Ohanian.

"My priestesses often lit a fire below the hole that leads to the running water," replied the lamia, "It kept them warm and the smoke left through the hole. I was never cold."

"Which was your room?" asked Mike.

"The next one. It is the last."

"Why was your room farthest from the cavern?" asked Ohanian.

"So that my priestesses would not disturb me as they went back and forth while I slept."

The lamia paused in front of the last doorway: "I have not been in this room for a very long time," she said, "not since my priests entered the Sacred Quarters. That was on the night when the Hittites attacked the temple."

Little was known about the last hours of the Amalishah temple and Mike asked: "Why did the priests break the rule and enter the Sacred Quarters?"

"My priests did not break the rule willingly," explained the lamia, "They were almost mad with fear because the Hittites had destroyed the northern gate and were threatening to come down to the cavern-temple itself." She spoke without emotion, as though recounting a distant dream. "Driven by terror the priests entered the Sacred Quarters because they wanted to take anything that would burn. They removed all the wooden doors and emptied the rooms of everything that was wood or cloth. They had already stripped the cavern-temple of all but a few torches. They wanted to light a great fire at the bottom of the steps in the hope that the heat and the smoke would deter the Hittites from coming down."

"But the Hittites came down anyway," said Mike gravely.

The lamia spoke almost inaudibly: "The Hittite prince was not easily deterred."

Mike finally understood why the walls of the pit had been covered in soot. "May we enter your chamber?"

"If you wish. I shall go in after you and your friend."

5

Mike was reluctant to lead the way, but there was no door, nothing that could trap them inside. He suppressed the urge to remove the pistol from his belt and entered what had once been the lamia's private bedchamber. Ohanian followed him hastily, afraid to be left alone in the passageway with the lamia. The room was L-shaped, larger and higher than the bedchambers of the priestesses but smaller than the room in which the lamia and her priestesses had sat and talked. Through the thin layer of dust Mike saw that the floor was perfectly flat and had once been polished. Along one of the walls the rock had been carved into shelves. From the far end there was again the gurgling of running water, but the opening from which the sound came was not visible from the doorway. The lamia entered the room as Mike reached the corner of the L.

"Did any of your priestesses live in this room with you?" Mike asked as he studied a thin crack that ran up the wall and halfway across the ceiling.

The lamia did not answer at once: "I lived alone," she said eventually. From the way she spoke Mike felt that something was wrong and he turned to look at her. She was just inside the door, and he saw that she had covered her face with her hands and was weeping silently.

"I am sorry," he said, "This room must bring back many memories."

"Memories only live in the heart," she answered, "They are not real." She wiped away her tears with the back of her hand.

"Why is she crying?" asked Ohanian in English.

"She is unloading her life," replied Mike.

Hidden from the entrance by the corner of the L was a rectangular opening in the rock wall, like a small window. Mike thrust his candle into the opening and saw a small stream that fell down a miniature waterfall, frothing and bubbling as it fell. Without thinking, Mike dipped his hand in the water and was startled to hear the lamia say: "Do you find the water cold?"

She was standing close behind him but he had not heard her come up: *I must remember that she can move without making any sound!*

"The water is very cold," he answered, moving away from her. "Where does the stream go?"

"I do not know. When there is no rain for a long time the stream becomes very shallow, but it is never dry."

"So you always had water."

"A goddess must be clean at all times."

Mike did not answer. He wandered around the room, trying to imagine how it might have looked when it was the goddess's bedchamber. Ohanian stayed close to him.

"The rooms and corridors are now dark and empty," said the lamia, "but they were once bright with the light of many torches. You would have liked my bedchamber: Along the wall were two wooden stands for torches, and to the right was a table with chairs, all intricately carved. There was a large wooden bed, also intricately carved, and on the shelves were gifts brought by pilgrims. Some were beautiful and precious, brought from distant lands."

"Were the furnishings all made of wood?" asked Ohanian.

"There were water jars and other things made of clay or stone, and the walls were covered with ornately-patterned cloths woven by the most skilful of my priestesses."

"Everything that would burn was taken away?"

"Everything. Taken away and burned. I stood outside the door and watched my room being emptied. Before that, when we first realised that the temple was under attack, the precious gifts were taken away by the white priestesses to be hidden."

"Where was your bed?" Mike asked.

The lamia pointed at the large square opening: "My bed was near there, just under the opening. The sound of running water helped me sleep."

6

They continued down the tunnel. Occasionally they would reach a fork and the lamia would wait for Mike and Ohanian to catch up. When the tunnel separated into four branches the lamia stopped just inside the third.

"Where do the other passages lead?" Mike asked

"One leads to a cavern like the underground temple, only smaller. That was for rituals that the male priests were not allowed to see. Another passage leads to a place where we kept things that were not needed. The last leads to the well of the deserted village. We shall not go there because it is far from the horseless chariots."

"Are we still under the hill?" asked Ohanian. After many turns the tunnel had begun to slope gently upwards.

"No," replied the lamia. "We are now at some distance from the hill. The tunnel leads away from the hill and then returns. That is why it is so long." Mike wondered why the tunnel was so intentionally long; carving into the rock could not have been easy with bronze-age tools.

Some time later the passageway veered to the left. The roof was covered with short limestone stalactites and the texture of the walls changed, although it was difficult to tell their colour in the candlelight.

"Where are we now?"

"We are back under the hill."

Mike was wondering how far these tunnels extended when the lamia stopped and raised her hand to indicate that they were not to pass her. He raised his candle to see what lay beyond. Ohanian raised both his candles.

A short distance ahead the passageway widened and then showed a high arch, a tall inverted U made of closely packed stones. On each side of the arch was a statue, taller than Mike but shorter than the lamia, carved of dark stone similar to the stone of the sacrificial altar. The statues showed stout, muscular men with full beards and close-fitting but unadorned helmets. Their straight hair fell from beneath their helmets and reached down to their shoulders, and their long beards were combed in waves that seemed to vibrate in the shaking light of the candles. They wore no armour other than thick breastplates, and beneath the breastplates were short-sleeved robes that were held around the waist by wide belts. The robes extended almost down to the feet, which were shod in thick-soled sandals. Each statue held a small circular shield with its left hand and had its right hand on the pommel of a broad sword that hung from its belt. The statues glared forbiddingly, threatening to pull out their swords, challenging anyone to pass.

"Who are they?" asked Mike. The ferocious gaze of the sentinels was hypnotic.

"They are guardian priests," answered the lamia.

"So that's what the warrior-priests looked like!" whispered Ohanian excitedly in English.

Mike nodded to Ohanian and asked the lamia: "What are they guarding?"

"They guard the dead," replied the lamia quietly, "We are close to the place where the bodies of the priests and priestesses were put to rest after they died."

Mike's attention returned to the statues and he wished he had his camera. It had been left in his tent, now part of another universe.

The lamia seemed to be waiting, as though unsure whether to proceed, or perhaps she was trying to recall something. Then she bowed to each statue in turn and recited in a lilting voice:

> "Oshim and Ashim, permit us to pass.
> We venerate the dead but bring no gifts.
> The dead are beyond all worldly pleasures."

For a moment it seemed to Mike that the expression of the guardians softened, but then the lamia passed swiftly between them. Mike and Ohanian hurried after her and the statues were soon absorbed by the darkness behind them.

7

The passageway became higher and sloped upwards. When it levelled again it turned sharply to the right and Mike saw that there were closely spaced rectangular alcoves on both sides, like small squat windows. They reminded him of the catacombs he had seen in Italy. Along the passageway, every fifteen metres or so, were larger apertures that might have been entrances to other tunnels. The alcoves were in two rows, with the upper row at about the height of Mike's shoulder and the lower row at the height of his knees. There was no writing around the apertures but some had been decorated with intricate flower motifs. The carving was crude, suggesting that the artisans had wished to complete their work hurriedly: *The sculptors were probably anxious to get away from here!* Mike put his candle into one of the alcoves to see inside. He pulled it away quickly.

"That had once been Mirish," said the lamia without stopping, "She was pretty and very kind but died young." The lamia continued down the tunnel.

"How many people are buried here?" asked Mike.

"I have not counted them," replied the lamia, "But I remember many of their names."

"Are all the priests and priestesses buried here?"

"Yes, but not just priests and priestesses. Their families are also buried here, as are others who lived in the temple."

"Just in this one tunnel?"

"The resting place of the dead has many branches. The tunnels were extended about every hundred planting seasons."

"Why is the burial place so far from the temple?"

"It is not too far," said the lamia, "if one could travel through the rock. It would have been disrespectful to the dead to have made their resting place easy to reach."

"I understand," said Mike: *The long winding tunnel would also keep the smell of the decomposing bodies away from the living quarters!*

"What happened to the bodies of those who were sacrificed to the goddess?" asked Ohanian unexpectedly.

"Ardash!" hissed Mike.

The lamia stopped and turned to face Ohanian, but he did not look away.

"The sacrificial victims were not buried here," she said softly,

"Their bodies were taken from the cavern temple by the priestesses and handed over to the priests. The priests buried the bodies in a special place beyond the rocks that lie around the hill."

"Without ceremony?" persisted Ohanian.

"They were buried with a special ceremony of gratitude because they gave their lives to the goddess of the temple." The lamia's voice was down to a whisper. "The young men who were sacrificed were considered holy after they died. The priests believed that their bodies were imbued with some of the sanctity of the goddess."

Mike had not failed to notice that the lamia had said 'the goddess' as though referring to someone other than herself. *Perhaps that phase of her life is truly over! Time will tell.* "Shall we go on?" he said.

"Yes," replied the lamia, "But I am glad Ardashes asked me these questions. He needs to know that the woman who walks with you now is no longer the goddess of the temple. Perhaps you need to know that too, Mike."

Mike did not reply and a wave of sadness passed across the face of the lamia. But the expression passed fleetingly, leaving no trace.

8

They continued down the passageway. Mike tried counting the graves but soon lost count. At a point where the roof of the tunnel boasted an unusually ornate cluster of stalactites the lamia halted: "We shall get out here." She pointed at one of the rectangular apertures in the upper row.

"Through a grave?" asked Mike, surprised.

The lamia shook her head. "This opening was never a grave. Come!"

"I cannot climb into this. There is nothing to hold on to!" Mike was unwilling to use the lower grave as a foothold.

With a smile the lamia took him by the waist and lifted him up easily, like a large adult placing a child on a high-chair. He had been reminded of her tremendous strength when she had caught the major as he fell down the shaft, and again when she carried Ohanian, but being lifted so effortlessly sent a shiver down his spine and he felt an echo of the fear that was troubling Ohanian: *The time to be afraid of her hasn't come yet; she still needs me to provide transport!* His cynicism brought surprise and a spasm of guilt: *You're all mixed up, chum.*

Lovesick boy and cynical old man! He suppressed his emotions and focused on the present. The air in the hole seemed fresher, different from the air in the passageways.

"Crawl through," said the lamia behind him, "There is nothing to fear."

Mike crawled on his stomach. He was on his third candle, which he held ahead of him while he pushed himself along with his elbows. He had barely crawled two body lengths when a faint scraping behind him made him aware that Ohanian had also been lifted and pushed into the hole. "Do not be afraid, Ardashes," he heard the lamia say, "I shall be right behind you."

Mike smiled: *That won't lessen his worries!*

They were in a long, roughly horizontal, oval tube that sometimes turned gently to the right or left. Mike could not tell whether the tube had been carved out of the rock or whether it was natural, but it felt cold and damp. Its sides were rough to the touch and full of cracks that must have formed due to the gradual settling of the huge mass of the hill above them. Most of the cracks were no wider than the blade of a knife, but some were large enough to give refuge to a mouse or a snake, not to mention scorpions: *I must not think of creatures that sting or bite!* Several times he saw small things scuttle away just beyond the light of his candle and disappear into the cracks, but they moved very fast and he could not tell whether they were mice or large insects. The air became fresher as he crawled, and the level of the tube rose more often than it fell. The crawl seemed interminable, but he surmised that he had been pushing his way for less than twenty minutes when a rush of cold air raised his hopes that he was approaching the end of the tube. He cupped the flame of his candle and tried to look ahead: *Is that a blue light ahead of me?*

It was not a blue light but the radiance of the moon, which at first appeared blue because Mike's eyes had become accustomed to the orange-yellow glow of his candle. Mike blew out the candle and crawled faster to reach the opening. He wanted desperately to look outside.

9

Mike emerged from the tube onto a small ledge on the side of the hill. The air felt fresh and there was a smell of wet earth and damp stone. The ground was only a few metres below, and everything was pure silver in the moonlight except for long black shadows cast by the ever-present boulders and a few forlorn trees. The rain had ceased and all that remained of the earlier downpour were small puddles that glistened like polished mirrors. In the foreground, within reach of the ledge, was an enormous flat-topped rock like the cap of a huge silver mushroom.

Mike had no difficulty getting onto the flat-topped boulder from the ledge and clambering down to the ground. He tried to see whether Ohanian had come out from the tube but although he could see several ledges on the hillside he could not see the ledge with the hole: *How convenient, the stone provides a way down while concealing the hole from anyone at ground level!*

"Mike! Where are you? I can't see you!"

"I'm here! Get onto the big rock and climb down!"

"The view is beautiful!"

"I know. We have to hurry. Come on!" Mike's watch showed that it was past eleven-thirty.

After many grunts and muttered complaints Ohanian stood beside Mike. The hill loomed above them, looking strangely unfamiliar. The helicopters had either landed or left and the moon-bathed landscape was eerily silent except for the faint whistling of the night breeze through the rocks.

The lamia climbed down the boulder with the smooth movements of a cat. She moved so fast that Mike wondered whether her crown of golden leaves would fall off her head but it held fast. Mike thanked her for getting him and Ohanian off the hill.

"*The obligation is on me,*" she replied in formal Assyrian.

"I think we should get away from here quickly," said Ohanian in English, "The rocks around us make hiding-places ideal for bandits escaping from helicopters!"

Mike nodded. "You're right." He turned to the lamia and said: "Where are we?"

"We are at the foot of the hill near the side where the rising sun first appears," she answered, "The chariots-without-horses are not too far."

Mike looked around him for any sign of the bandits. Misinterpreting the action, the lamia said: "Mike, you do not have to take me with you if you do not wish to."

"Amalishah," said Mike, and he saw Ohanian flinch as he

mentioned her name, "You got us away when we were in danger. It is now for us to get you away from here."

"You are under no obligation."

Mike took her hand and squeezed it gently: "There *is* an obligation," he said, "although it is unimportant compared to dreams and hopes."

"I thought you had forgotten the dreams and the hopes."

"Not forgotten," said Mike, "Just put aside. There are some things I wish to understand better."

The lamia frowned and looked down, but did not pull her hand away. "I shall wait until you understand what your heart should be telling you, Michael Townsend."

Mike did not know how to answer, and was unsure whether an answer was expected.

1 O

They skirted the hill and made their way towards the place where the vehicles were parked. The southern ramp was only a little way ahead when the lamia said: "There are people among the chariots!"

"How do you know?"

"I can hear them. There are at least three, probably more."

"Then we have to be very careful."

"Perhaps I should go ahead," suggested the lamia, "I am used to hiding from people."

"Your days of hiding are over," said Mike, "We shall stick together. We don't know who these people are and it is best if Ardash and I deal with them if we have to. If they're bad men they can be very dangerous, even for you."

"Would they not be dangerous for you, Mike?"

"Not if we are careful. Besides, I'm armed!" Mike took out the long-muzzled pistol that the major had given him, held it with the muzzle pointing away from her.

"I thought that the strange weapon was to be used against *me*," said the lamia. She was smiling, but it was clear that she was trying to hide some resentment.

"The soldier who gave it to me thought I might need it for protection against bad men," said Mike, avoiding her eyes.

"How could the little thing you are holding from the wrong end be used for protection?" she asked, referring to the pistol, "It only makes a loud noise!"

She thinks the pistol is some kind of club! No wonder she felt no fear of Balushi! "It should be enough if we come across some bad men," he said. "Now let us get to the uh... horseless chariots. I'll lead the way."

The lamia seemed unsure and Mike said: "Come. We must get to the horseless chariots before we can start for Mosul."

The lamia shrugged, a happy-child shrug, the shrug of a little girl whose father, after many postponements, finally decides to take her to a place of wonders.

48

THE ELECTRICIAN EXPOSED

1

THE BANDITS WERE too stunned to speak. They looked mutely at the rocks around them, numb with shock and surprise. The bullet had struck Nabil at the back of the head and so must have come from somewhere behind the boulders in the direction of the hill. But it was impossible to see anything clearly. The moon coated everything in stark silver that allowed no colours, and the intensely black shadows confused all outlines.

Selim was bewildered. "No shooting!" he muttered between his teeth, "Please no shooting!" *It can't be the soldiers, they would have killed us all! But if these idiots start shooting the soldiers will come to investigate and we shall all get killed! With Allah's help the soldiers might ignore that one gunshot!*

"Put your weapons down on the ground!" ordered a firm voice in Arabic. The echoes made it difficult to locate its source.

"It's a foreigner!" whispered one of the bandits.

"He's either a very good shot or very lucky!" whispered another.

"Be quiet!" hissed Selim, "We must find out how many they are!"

"He sounds as though he's alone!" whispered the bandit who had first spoken. Selim and the three remaining bandits were agitated and baffled, but they were not frightened enough to put down their weapons. They strained their necks as they scrutinised the surrounding rocks in the hope that whoever had shot Nabil would betray his location. Selim, who had only his knife, stood motionless, facing the direction from which he believed the shot had come. He had already made up his mind that his best policy would be to persuade the foreigner that he was not one of the bandits. But it had to be done subtly, without making the ruffians suspicious: *I can speak the foreigner's language and I am sure these idiots cannot. But I have to be careful; they will kill me if they realise I am betraying them!*

"I said put your weapons on the ground!" ordered the voice again, and this time Selim recognised the speaker: *Ah! It's that stupid Englishman, Townsend!*

"How do we know you won't kill us if we put our weapons down?" asked one of the bandits.

There was no answer.

Selim weighed the possibilities: *If there are soldiers with the Englishman they would have killed us all by now. They would not take prisoners, not after they saw what the bandits did to the workers. So there are no soldiers with the Englishman!* Selim recalled the English he had learned at school and which he had practised at the camp: "What are you doing here alone, Professor Townsend?" he asked good-naturedly in English but with a heavy Arab accent. He tried to sound stressed, as though he were a prisoner.

"Hello Selim," said Mike, speaking Arabic. "Please tell your friends to drop their weapons or I shall shoot you all, starting with you."

Selim could not suppress a smile. *He would only come to the vehicles if he is trying to escape! Why would he try to escape now that the helicopters have come? He must have stolen some of the gold!* The ramifications of this possibility were not lost on Selim, who was alert to opportunities. "Professor Townsend!" he said, "These are not my friends. These murderers had taken me and the woman prisoner! You came just in time to save her. Thank you!" He sounded genuinely grateful.

"Please tell the three men to put down their weapons!"

"If I do that, they will kill me, Professor!" protested Selim in English.

"You're probably right. Are there any other prisoners?" Mike asked in Arabic.

"Only I and the woman were taken prisoner," replied Selim. "The wounded man on the ground is one of the murderers. All my worker friends were killed." The last phrase was added for good measure.

2

Selim and the bandits now had a good idea of Mike's position. They turned their assault rifles in his direction but with the muzzles pointing downwards, waiting for a signal from Selim.

"I'm glad you weren't killed with the other workers," said Mike, "But if the weapons are not put down at once I shall have to shoot you all, one at a time."

Selim looked around him but there was nothing he could use for cover. There were no suitably large rocks and the vehicles were too far. The Englishman might shoot him if he made a dash, perhaps the excellent shot at Nabil was not just luck. He spread his arms wide and assumed an expression of abject shame: "I'm not a brave man, Professor, and I get upset when someone points a gun at me!" As he spoke, he strolled casually to his left, passing between Mike and one of the bandits. "Look at me, Professor!" Selim waved his arms to show that he was not holding anything: "I am completely unarmed!"

The bandit behind Selim, realising that for a split second Mike would not be able to see him, raised his assault rifle so as to spray the rocks the moment Selim got out of the way. But although Mike was not sure whether Selim had concealed the man intentionally, he expected the bandit to seize the opportunity to use his weapon. So when Selim moved away Mike was ready, and the bandit's rifle had time to fire only once before Mike's pistol barked back. The bandit collapsed, shot in the forehead, and the other two hastily dropped their weapons and stood very still. Selim quickly raised his hands above his head, alarmed that the Englishman could shoot so well.

"I now want you to drop the ammunition you are carrying," said Mike in Arabic, "and any other weapons you have."

The two bandits complied at once. Selim did not touch his knife.

"The woman is to get up and stand with you," ordered Mike.

Aisha got up groggily and stood a few metres to the right of Selim. She looked bewildered and distraught but she raised her hands above her head.

"Thank you. Now, all of you, stand back from the weapons and the ammunition!"

Selim, Aisha and the two remaining bandits moved back a few paces.

Mike stepped out from behind some boulders. He was holding the long-muzzled pistol with both hands, pointing it at Selim: *The traitor who murdered Ali and disabled the radios could well be the electrician; that would explain why he escaped the fate of the workers!*

"You are alone Professor?" asked Selim. He sounded concerned, but he could not stop himself from grinning.

Mike ignored him. Without taking his eyes off Selim or the

bandits, he spoke to Aisha: "Lady, are you all right?"

"I'm all right. I owe you thanks." Her face was bruised and one of her eyes was swollen. She kept her hands high above her head.

"Who is the man lying on the ground?" asked Mike, his pistol always pointing at the electrician.

"As I have already told you, he is one of the murderers," replied Selim hastily before Aisha could speak. "He is the son of one of their leaders!"

Aisha, fearing that Mike would execute Mukhtar on the spot, exclaimed: "But he is a good man! Please don't kill him! He is badly wounded and will die if he is not taken to a hospital quickly!"

Mike cast a quick glance at Mukhtar just as Selim said: "Professor Townsend cannot be concerned with the life of a murderer!"

Mike noticed that there was a dark stain around the waist of the wounded bandit, and that the man had not moved at all after he had turned on his side. The woman appeared to have spoken the truth: the wound probably needed urgent medical attention. On the other hand, if he was one of the bandits, allegedly the son of one of the bandit leaders, Mike would not owe him anything. Mike's pressing concern was to find a way out of this predicament: He could not shoot the two bandits in cold blood and Amalishah's presence meant that he could not take them prisoner and hand them over to the army. Moreover, Selim's role was unclear, and he was intelligent enough to be the most dangerous of the four.

"Professor Townsend cannot be concerned with the health of a murderer," repeated Selim, "He has more important things to think about." Selim wanted to make sure that Aisha would not switch loyalties. Mike disregarded the remark and said: "I want you all to step back further, away from the weapons."

The two bandits did as they were told but Selim expostulated in English: "You cannot think I'm one of these murderers, Professor!"

"Just do as I say," said Mike calmly.

Selim stepped back, scowling.

When they were all about five metres from the discarded weapons Mike called out in Assyrian: "Ardash, come out and pick up the weapons!"

Ohanian stepped out into the open and quickly collected the four assault rifles and the ammunition. There were also three grenades, which he handled with great care.

"Akh! What do I do with all these things?" he asked in Assyrian.

He held the weapons as though they were so much useless metal

"Hang on to them," replied Mike in English. "Would you know how to use them?"

"Of course not!"

"Just hang on to them, then. Here, give me one of the rifles."

Ohanian handed one of the rifles to Mike, who checked the magazine and made sure the safety catch was not on before pointing the weapon at Selim and the two bandits. He then pushed the long-muzzled pistol into his belt. Selim guessed that Mike had not decided what to do with him or the bandits, and was thinking how Mike's indecision could be used against him.

3

"Are you going to kill us now?" asked one of the two bandits.

"Englishmen don't kill people without reason," said Selim. He hoped that Mike would find the statement disarmingly flattering: *I am sure this Englishman never killed anyone before today! He is probably disturbed at having killed Nabil and the idiot who couldn't shoot properly. If one of us has a go at him the Englishman would hesitate!* Selim hoped that the Englishman would not notice the knife at his side, wedged under his belt and hidden by his coat.

"Ardash," said Mike quietly in Assyrian, "Give Amalishah the grenades and two of the automatic rifles. Keep one of the automatic rifles for yourself." The lamia came out from behind the rocks and, without looking at the bandits, walked swiftly over to Ohanian. He wordlessly handed her the three grenades and all but one the assault rifles. Without taking his eyes off Selim or the bandits Mike said in English: "Ardash, remember that given half the chance these fellows would happily slit your throat. You may have to use the rifle you are holding."

"Mike, that would be what you English call 'taking the law into your own hands'!" Ohanian was evidently shocked and outraged by what he had seen. Mike had killed two men!

"There is no law out here, Ardash." Mike leaned over to release the safety catch on Ohanian's rifle and said: "All you have to do is point the thing and pull the trigger!"

"I'll use it if I have to, Mike."

Mike was going to say more when he noticed that the bandit

woman was looking at the lamia strangely. To his surprise she suddenly exclaimed: "I am very glad to see that you are alive, foreigner!"

"You know this woman?" Mike asked the lamia in Assyrian.

"I owe her my life," replied the lamia. She smiled warmly at Aisha, who smiled back.

"Then, lady, you had better stand with us!" said Mike in Arabic, speaking to Aisha but with his eyes on the bandits: *There seems to be an interesting story here but it'll have to wait!*

"You wish me to stand with you?" asked Aisha incredulously. This stranger's willingness to trust her was something outside her experience. Even Attila had never trusted her completely.

"Yes. It seems the tall lady owes you a favour. And I promise you that we shall take your wounded friend to a hospital as soon as we can."

Aisha muttered "Thank you," and lowered her hands. She came forward but stopped a few metres away from Amalishah: "I would embrace you," she said, "but your friends might think I want to take one of the weapons you are holding!" The lamia did not understand the words but she could read people's emotions.

4

Selim had taken note of the lamia's crown and the large red jewel that hung around her neck the moment she had emerged from behind the rocks. He had never looked at the statue of Amalishah closely, as his attention had been wholly on the gold and silver artefacts, but he knew enough to guess that the crown and the jewel were ancient. He thought he understood why the Englishman and Ohanian had chosen not to remain on the hill and greet the rescue party from the helicopters. Speaking English he said: "We must kill the murderers and go away from here, Professor."

"I am not an executioner," Mike replied coldly in Arabic, "I suppose your bag contains food and water. Let them take some and start walking across the wasteland!" *If Selim is one of them they would expose him now!* Walking across the wastelands with limited food and water could be tantamount to a death sentence, but Mike was more concerned with getting rid of the bandits. Instead of opening his rucksack Selim said in English: "We will need food and water more than they, Professor!"

"We need only take water," said Mike in Arabic. "Now open your bag and give them enough food and water for two or three days. By that time they might find a village or a well if they're lucky." Selim reluctantly opened his rucksack and pulled out four cans and three bottles of water.

"Would Selim be travelling with us to the hospital?" Aisha asked.

"I cannot let him go with the other two," said Mike, "They will kill him for the food and water."

Despite her joy at seeing that *the tall foreign woman* had survived, Aisha had not fully committed her loyalty to the foreigners. She had never befriended any foreigner before, and she did not know whether to trust them even if they appeared to trust her. But she felt that she had no alternative under the circumstances, not if this Englishman had promised to take Mukhtar to a hospital. Perhaps Englishmen kept their promises. She decided to side with the foreigners because she knew that if Selim travelled with them Mukhtar would never get to a hospital.

"There is something you should know," she said quietly in Arabic. "Selim is one of *them*. He killed the soldier who was with the radios!"

"I see," said Mike thoughtfully, "I suspected as much. Then he will go with the other two. If they kill him, or if he kills them, it will be none of my doing."

"Don't believe this woman, Professor Townsend!" shouted Selim. "She is just a whore! She was the whore of one of the leaders of the murderers!" Selim was too concerned about his safety to care if his voice was heard by anyone on the hill.

"Take one more can and one more bottle of water." ordered Mike. "Then be on your way! But keep in mind that I shall report you to the authorities and know that they will have no trouble finding you."

"If the police come after me I shall tell them about the gold and the jewel you stole!"

"Just leave the water and be off!" said Mike, offended but not surprised.

Selim reluctantly took out a can and a bottle of water from his rucksack, but his rage was such that he could not leave without venting his anger: "I shall not forget this, Aisha," he snarled, "I shall find you and kill you!"

Ohanian felt compelled to say in Arabic: "I would not take his threat seriously, lady."

Mike reacted more effectively, he pointed the muzzle of his assault rifle at Selim's face and visibly tightened his finger on the trigger.

Selim noticed and raised his arms higher: "I am going, Professor! I am going!"

Selim walked away hurriedly, leaving his rucksack behind. The two bandits followed him, stumbling with weariness. Aisha immediately rushed to Mukhtar's side and put her hand on his forehead. "I think he has a fever," she said, her voice scarcely above a whisper, "If we try to take him to Mosul in his present state he might die."

"I know," said Mike grimly, "but we must take him to Mosul, lady. Only a hospital can save him!"

49

THE LAMIA LEAVES THE HILL

1

HIS TEMPERATURE WAS very high but the gentle touch of Aisha's hand on his forehead made Mukhtar regain consciousness. He opened his eyes and murmured: "Who are these people?" His words were indistinct, as though his tongue were swollen.

"They are friends," Aisha answered as she took his hand in both of hers. He was wet with perspiration and, miraculously, still wore his glasses.

"Friends? What friends?"

Aisha squeezed his hand. "They're foreigners who promised to help you."

"Foreigners? Do they know who we are?"

"Yes."

Mukhtar raised his head to look behind her: "Where are Selim and the others?"

"They're gone," she said soothingly, "You shall be taken to a hospital in Mosul."

He closed his eyes and said: "I'm very cold, Aisha."

"We'll be on our way soon and you'll be warm in the car."

She cradled his head in her lap. Mukhtar tried to keep his eyes open but the struggle to remain awake took a lot of effort and he lost consciousness.

Aisha was deeply worried about Mukhtar's fever but felt completely powerless to help him. She got up wearily and looked down at him as he lay at her feet, her anxiety and frustration showing in the tight knots of her fists. Then she turned to see what the foreigners were doing.

Ohanian was examining his assault rifle as though it were an alien artefact; he found the weapon repulsive but also, somehow, deeply fascinating. Mike was staring at the wastelands in the direction in which Selim and the two bandits had left. The lamia stood alone, totally unmoving and with her eyes half closed, deep in her thoughts. Aisha was on the point of speaking to the lamia when Ohanian saw her looking in his direction and said: "How is your friend?"

"He is alive," replied Aisha, unsure of what tone to take with the foreigner, "But he is very hot with fever and may not be able to travel."

"We have to be sure the trip does not make the wound worse," said Ohanian.

"How can we be sure of anything?" she replied, unable to conceal her despair. "He has lost a lot of blood and his forehead is like fire. I do not know what I can do but I have seen men die when they become like this!"

"Has the wound been dressed?"

"Only superficially. I do not have any bandages or medicines. To make matters worse, the bullet shattered. It is not a clean wound!"

"Akh! The bullet must have bounced off something before it hit him."

"Yes."

Ohanian looked at Mukhtar: *He doesn't look like a bandit. He wears glasses and looks like a decent young man. I wish I could do something. Ahh!*

"Lady," he exclaimed excitedly, "The expedition's trucks are probably unlocked and might contain some First Aid stuff!" Without waiting for Aisha to comment he hurried over to the trucks. They were parked just beyond the Land Rovers, close to the hill.

The trucks were not locked and Ohanian went from one to another, bringing out whatever he thought might be useful. When he returned he was carrying two First Aid kits, some blankets and a donkey jacket. The donkey jacket was in poor condition but the blankets had never been used and were still in their plastic bags.

"That's all I could find," he said breathlessly as he brought the things to Aisha, "The First Aid kits should help you deal with the wound."

"Thank you! Thank you so much!"

Aisha immediately opened one of the First Aid packets and set about treating Mukhtar. She carefully pulled back his bloodstained shirt and began cleansing the wound with sterile swabs. Ohanian knelt beside her, hoping that he might be able to help while trying to suppress his revulsion at the sight of the blood and torn flesh. Aisha noticed his discomfiture and said: "You don't have to be here. I have dealt with wounds before!"

Ohanian nodded and got up so violently that he bumped into the lamia, who had been standing silently behind him, wanting to see how the red-haired woman treated the wound. The unexpected physical contact with the lamia brought a sudden pang of terror and Ohanian grew pale: *Akh! What if the sight of blood opens her appetite?* For a moment he imagined her holding him in her powerful arms and thrusting long fangs into his neck. "I'm sorry!" he stammered.

The lamia smiled at him, a tired smile: "Ardashes, you must not fear me," she said quietly.

"I'm sorry," he repeated, "I did not expect you to be so close behind me!" *She doesn't have fangs, you silly man! Her teeth are beautiful!*

"Why is she putting white powder on the wound?" asked the lamia.

"To help it get better," replied Ohanian, trying to calm himself, "To prevent the wound from..." He did not know any Assyrian words for 'getting infected'. *She probably doesn't know what an infection is!*

"I understand," said the lamia, "She is putting on the white powder to stop badness from getting into the wound."

"Uh something like that. What would you have done?"

"I don't know. I have never had to help a wounded man. Such things were done by those who knew about wounds and sickness."

Ohanian nodded. He felt guilty and embarrassed at having shown his fear. But he appreciated the deftness with which she had managed to calm him down: *She is like a wise and very intelligent child. It would be wonderful to get to know her better!*

He turned to Aisha, who was applying bandages. "The wound is not as bad as it might have been," he said, "It did not appear deep."

"It was better than I feared, though there is not much I can do about any bullet fragments that might be scattered inside him. The danger is infection, which may have set in already."

"But you have done what you needed to do against that."

"Yes. There is hope thanks to you. I am grateful."

Ohanian helped Aisha cover Mukhtar with the blankets.

"He shall feel less cold now," she said.

"We shall get him to a hospital soon, lady. He shall be all right."

2

Ohanian went to Mike, who was still watching the bandits recede from view. They were three small specks that moved slowly in the moonlight, barely distinguishable from the shadows of the stunted trees and boulders that were scattered across the landscape.

"The young man's wound is being dealt with," said Ohanian, "Why are you still looking at these vile people? They're very far from us!"

"Not far enough," said Mike, "I'm waiting for Selim and his friends to put a hefty distance between us in case they decide to double back"

"What mischief can they do if they come back?"

"I don't know, but Selim is a resourceful fellow when it comes to mischief."

"Mike, I'm worried about that poor wounded man. The wound has been cleaned, covered in antiseptic powder and bandaged, but the bullet fragmented and bits may be still inside him. If we don't get him to a hospital soon he may not survive."

"I know." Mike paused. "Very well, let's get him into ElBalushi's Land Rover."

Mike and Ohanian went over to Aisha, who was kneeling beside Mukhtar.

"We must carry your friend to the car," said Mike, "It must be done very carefully so that there is no stress on the wound."

"I shall help as much as I can," replied Aisha.

"By the way, what is his name?"

"His name is Mukhtar Arroussi," she replied as she stood up. "My name is Aisha. I don't use a surname any more." She offered her hand gracefully, astonished that she could still remember *proper behaviour* after all her wretched years with thieves and murderers.

Mike took her hand: *Rather strange behaviour for a bandit's woman, but perhaps she has seen better days.* "Professor Michael Townsend," he said formally. "My friend is Dr. Ardashes Ohanian. He and I shall carry Mukhtar to the car. We shall leave as soon as we can."

With Aisha's help, Mike and Ohanian carried Mukhtar to ElBalushi's Land Rover. The vehicle was easily recognisable because of the Army insignia. It was a long-wheelbase model and with one of the rear seats folded it easily accommodated Mukhtar with his knees drawn. He remained unconscious while they carried him.

Once Mukhtar was safely inside the vehicle Mike turned and gave a long look at the lamia. She was standing alone, deep in her thoughts, and Mike's expression softened for a moment before hardening again. Ohanian guessed the direction of Mike's thoughts, and he said softly in English, "Mike, my friend…"

"Yes?" said Mike abruptly. His thoughts had been interrupted.

"My friend, it is not every man who is lucky enough to find the woman of his dreams, and if that woman also cares for him, then that is a gift beyond measure."

"And how would he know that she would not discard him, perhaps even kill him, once she got what she wanted?"

"*Look* at her Mike," said Ohanian pleadingly, "Forget her beauty, for that is only a distraction, just *look* at the way she behaves in your presence. *Listen* to the way she talks to you!"

"She is very clever, Ardash. She would know exactly how to beguile me. She knows that I am predisposed to believe her."

"And what would she gain by deceiving you?"

"She would gain access to the world outside! She would no longer be restricted to feeding on animals that come within her reach! Once outside she would be able to prey on people again! She has already done so once!"

"You cannot be sure she killed the young soldier!" said Ohanian. Mike had told him his suspicions regarding the death of the boy who had been murdered on the night before the attack on the hill.

"Who else would kill the boy and drain his blood?" said Mike.

"I don't know. But he might have been killed by one of the traitors in the camp. Do you really believe that she would go to all that elaborate pretence of caring for you just to get away from here and feed on people?"

"Why not? She cannot travel to a city on her own, and she knows she cannot continue to live in her caverns. I told her that in a short time the hill will be overrun by archaeologists and tourists who will look into all the nooks and crannies!"

"You told her that?"

"I have. It's the truth."

"All right, so she knows that she cannot continue to live here. But that does not mean she intends to feed on people. She has not done that for a time very long, Mike."

"Perhaps not that long," said Mike coldly.

Ohanian remained silent for a few moments. Then he said: "You are not sure that she did that. As I said, the young soldier might have been killed by Selim or one of his friends."

"And would they have drained the boy of blood?"

Ohanian thought for a moment. "If you are sure it was her then we should go back."

Mike replied very curtly: "If I need your advice I'll ask for it!"

Ohanian looked away, biting his lip.

"I'm sorry, Ardash. I didn't mean to be rude."

"It's all right. My people have a need compulsive to give advice. We often get on people's nerves."

3

The lamia had guessed why Mike had been staring at Selim and the two bandits. She approached Mike and said: "The bad men are far from us now. Even I cannot see them. They were walking fast and I don't think they shall come back."

"They were walking fast to make the best of the coolness of the night," said Mike, "the sun and heat make travel on foot difficult during the daytime."

"Where shall you take the wounded man?" asked the lamia.

"To Mosul, where we hope to find a place that can heal his wound."

"Is Mosul far?"

"It is near what you might have known as Nineveh," replied Mike. He looked at Mukhtar as he lay unconscious in the vehicle. Mukhtar occupied a fair portion of the space available.

Aisha noticed that Mike was looking at Mukhtar. "He is asleep," she said apologetically. She seemed to be worried about something and Mike looked at her inquiringly. "Is there something you want to say?"

"Professor," she said quietly, as though she found it difficult to speak, "There is something I should know before we leave. When we reach a hospital in Mosul, what will you tell the doctors about Mukhtar?"

Mike thought carefully before answering. "It is a little late to ask about that."

"I know. But I am tired and a bit confused. It is better that I ask you now, before we're on our way."

"I shall try not to say anything that will get either of you into trouble."

"Thank you," said Aisha, "Mukhtar is truly a good man. He is an educated man who had no wish to get mixed up with the bandits but had no choice. One of the bandit leaders was his father."

"And you?" asked Mike, "Did you also have no choice?"

Aisha looked away, turned to gaze at the hill so that he would not see the tears in her eyes. "People like me always have a choice," she said slowly, "But sometimes we make the wrong decisions. If you wish you can tell the authorities that Mukhtar was there because of me, and that only I was there willingly."

"That will get *you* into trouble," said Mike.

"I am not important," said Aisha, "and my life is probably over whatever happens."

Mike was surprised. "Let's wait and see," he said, "And I want you to know that you needn't worry about hospital fees. I'll cover all expenses."

Aisha had not expected that. These foreigners were not at all like the men she had known! "You are a man of honour, Professor," she said solemnly, "But you needn't worry about hospital fees. Mukhtar's mother is very wealthy and she will make sure Mukhtar is not a burden on anyone."

"Very well."

4

While Mike and Ohanian put the bandits' weapons in the car, Aisha turned to the lamia, who was standing a short distance away, her face a blank.

"I owe you thanks," she said, "When I cut you loose I did not expect any reward." The lamia was a head taller than Aisha and she looked down at her benignly, trying to guess the meaning of her words. Aisha recalled that the *tall foreigner* could not understand her. She put her hand on the lamia's arm and smiled, trying to express her feelings without words, but then suddenly she fell forward and embraced the lamia tightly, bursting into tears. To Mike's surprise the lamia embraced her back and said: "All will be well." Aisha did not understand but the lamia's voice was comforting, and her evident compassion went beyond language.

Not knowing what to make of this display of sisterhood, Mike entered the Land Rover and turned the ignition key. The engine started immediately.

"Get in!" said Mike.

Ohanian opened the side door for the lamia but she would not get in.

"Mike," she said, "How long would it take the horseless chariot to get to Mosul?"

"Because of all the delays we shall be there after daybreak," said Mike.

"Then I cannot come with you."

"What!? Why not?"

"The daylight will burn me. You must leave me behind, Mike."

5

Mike was thunderstruck. He had stupidly, unforgivably, forgotten about the danger that sunlight posed to the lamia. "I cannot leave without you," he said, trying not to sound emotional. "If you stay, I'll stay."

"No. You must go quickly. The wounded man needs help. If you still want to see me after you have gone, you may come back for me at some later time."

"Amalishah, I cannot leave without you."

"You must," she replied, "That wounded man needs help urgently. Please don't stay here any longer."

Mike did not know what to say. He had promised the red-haired woman that he would help Mukhtar, and there was no doubt that Mukhtar was in desperate need of medical help, but he could not leave Amalishah behind. ElBalushi might find out that the lamia had not left the hill and could easily revert to his obsession with killing her.

"Mike," said Ohanian in English, "Why can't she come?"

"Because the morning sunlight will burn her!" he replied impatiently, this was not the time for explanations. *Why are we speaking in English?*

"Akh! So that part of the vampire myth is true!" muttered Ohanian. He frowned and then exclaimed: "Um...would you be willing to take a chance, Mike?"

"She will *burn* in the sunlight, Ardash! What kind of chance can I take?" Mike sounded desperate: *Are we never going to get away from this damn place? She must get away!*

"Perhaps we can protect her from the sunlight," said Ohanian, "Please consider what I'm thinking."

"What are you thinking?" Mike sounded tired, worn out.

"It is not the light that would burn her, Mike. She has no trouble with light. She can take the moonlight and the light of our electric torches. It is *sunlight* that is dangerous to her!"

"That's true. Go on!"

"Well, it seems to me that we could arrange for her to come with us safely. There is a risk, but if I'm right the risk is small."

"Please explain!"

"What is the difference between the light from candles or electric lamps and sunlight?"

"Don't give me riddles, Ardash!" Mike was almost exhausted. It had been a long day and his wits were not at their best.

"The ultraviolet! It is the ultraviolet that burns her, as it does us. Ultraviolet burns us too, Mike, but to a degree much lower. The windows of this Land Rover are made of thick normal glass! Normal glass is not very transparent to ultraviolet and the window glass in Elbalushi's car is tinted as well! So very little of the ultraviolet spectrum will get through. If we cover her so that no direct or reflected sunlight gets to her, she ought to be all right!"

Of course! Amalishah has had little experience with glass and would naturally think that all sunlight would harm her! But the windows of the military Land Rover are of reinforced glass and would cut off most, if not all, of the ultraviolet! With some care she should be safe in the Land Rover!

"Well, what do you think?" said Ohanian.

Mike considered what Ohanian had said: *Ardash is speaking English because the decision to take her must be mine. Given the choice, she would refuse unless I asked her myself!* "Ardash, you may be right. There is a risk but it is not as great as the risk to her life if she remains behind!"

"I think so. Sooner or later, ElBalushi will know that she is still at the temple. He will see it as a sign divine that he is to kill her!"

Mike turned to the lamia, who was waiting passively to see where this unintelligible discussion would lead. "Amalishah," he said in Assyrian, "It may be safe for you to come with us. If you stay in the... *car*, and if we cover you so that no direct sunlight gets to you, you should be safe."

"I am afraid of the day's light," she replied, "But if you think I

622

would be safe then I shall come with you."

"I think you would be safe as long as you stay in the *car*."

With some trepidation, the lamia entered the rear of the vehicle and took the seat behind Mike. Ohanian closed the door behind her and sat next to Mike at the front of the car. Aisha sat cross-legged beside Mukhtar, between the lamia and the tailgate. The assault rifles and the grenades were on the floor in front of Ohanian, lying in a pile next to the worn-out donkey jacket. Mike put the engine into gear and the vehicle set out. Ohanian's seat had been pushed forward so that he had very little leg room, but he was pleased that they had finally left the hill.

50

ON THE WAY TO MOSUL

1

THE ONLY REMINDERS of the earlier cloudburst were shallow pools of water in the hollows of rocks. The orange-red moon had completed its journey towards the horizon and the night sky, almost empty of clouds, revealed stars that twinkled like tiny diamonds strewn over black velvet. Major ElBalushi's Land Rover sped towards Mosul as fast as the terrain allowed.

Ohanian slept fitfully in the front seat with his head on the rolled-up donkey jacket and his knees pressing against the assault rifles, grenades and ammunition that had belonged to the bandits. Occasionally he would mutter in his sleep and his body would twitch. Aisha could not sleep and her attention was divided between the sleeping Mukhtar and Mike. The lamia sat straight-backed and silent behind Mike, with eyes half closed and fixed on the blackness ahead. Her thoughts were veiled by an expression of benign haughtiness such as one sometimes sees on statues of ancient royalty.

Daybreak was less than an hour away and Mike was concerned about the lamia. He was by no means convinced that it was the ultraviolet in the sun's rays that would burn her. It could be another part of the spectrum, a part that would not be shielded by the glass of the Land Rover. He wished he could pick up speed so as to lessen the time she would be exposed to daylight, but greater speed meant more bucking and rolling, and this would endanger the life of the wounded man.

As the stars started to fade Mike found it increasingly hard to resist the need for sleep. More than once he lost consciousness and awakened just in time to avoid hitting a rock or falling into a depression. At every abrupt awakening he kicked down on the brakes in near panic, causing the Land Rover to lurch forward and swerve violently. Ohanian was too tired to take in the danger of an accident, but Aisha, fearing that something might happen that would delay Mukhtar's arrival at a hospital, grew increasingly agitated. Eventually she suppressed her natural reticence and asked Mike: "Where is this tall woman from, Professor? Her language is strange and she seems to understand little of what we say."

Aisha's question must have coincided with whatever was troubling Ohanian's sleep, for he awoke with an overwhelming fear that Mike might say more than he should about the lamia. *If this wild woman realises that Amalishah is not a normal person she might become hysterical! We could end up travelling with a female Balushi!* "She comes from somewhere far away and very different from here!" he said hurriedly.

"But where is she from?" persisted Aisha, trying to bring Mike into the conversation.

Ohanian understood what Aisha was trying to do and gave Mike a hard nudge with his elbow. "Um… Mike?"

"What is it?" responded Mike irritably. Aisha's questions had passed him by completely.

Ohanian answered in English: "I think Aisha is trying to make sure you stay awake by asking questions about Amalishah!"

2

The fog in Mike's mind cleared slightly: "What questions?"

Ohanian reverted to Arabic: "Aisha wants to know why Amalishah is with us although she doesn't speak our language."

Mike thought for a moment before saying: "Oh, she is my *fiancée*. We've known each other for a long time." He spoke Arabic but deliberately used a French word because he thought Aisha would not understand. He hoped that the ensuing explanations would divert the conversation away from the lamia, but to his surprise Aisha said: "Your *fiancée*! How wonderful! When are you getting married?" She pronounced the French word perfectly.

Mike failed to notice the unexpectedness of Aisha's response. "We don't know yet," he said flatly, "Probably when we settle in Mosul." *Provided she doesn't burn alive when the sun comes up!*

But Ohanian was intrigued. "You speak French?"

"I used to," replied Aisha. "It is a romantic language and I used to love French literature, but now I have forgotten how to speak French."

"You loved French literature?" exclaimed Ohanian. "I love French literature too! But if you loved French literature how could you forget the language?"

"It is easy to forget a language if one does not practise it."

"Where did you learn French?" asked Mike, suddenly curious.

"At school. All of us were taught French and some of us had the chance to study French literature," said Aisha.

"I did not know they taught French literature in government schools," said Mike.

"I went to a private school," said Aisha quietly.

"Selim said that you were uh... the woman of one of the bandit leaders," said Mike. He did not mean to be callous, but his concern for Amalishah made him tactless.

"Selim spoke the truth when he said that."

"What made you leave your private school?" asked Ohanian. He wanted to know how someone who loved French literature could end up with homicidal criminals.

"One's life sometimes takes unexpected turns," said Aisha bitterly. She remembered the exuberant young men in the limousine, her father's refusal to let her return home, the hardships she had endured with her aunt, the fateful meeting with Attila: *All that could so easily never have happened!* Overcome by a sense of shame she looked away.

"And what of the young man?" asked Mike, unaware of Aisha's rampant emotions, "Did he drop out of school too?"

"Oh no!" said Aisha, "Mukhtar graduated from a university in America!" She was relieved that the subject had moved away from her.

"What did he study at university?" asked Ohanian.

"I don't know."

Neither Mike nor Ohanian said anything and the conversation died. Mike's thoughts returned to the danger that sunlight might pose to Amalishah, a very real danger that was looming ever closer. Aisha pondered on how little she really knew about Mukhtar; how tenuous their bond was. She didn't even know if there was a bond at all.

3

The lamia remained motionless and quiet, as though asleep with her eyes half-open. Mike could not see her directly because she was sitting behind him, but he did not want her to think that he had forgotten her danger. "Are you afraid?" he asked softly in Assyrian. *Stupid question! But she mustn't bottle up her fear! Better to talk about it!*

"Yes."

"As long as you stay within the *car*, you should be safe from the sunlight." *God Almighty, I do hope I'm right!*

"It's not just the coming sunlight, Mike. I have never travelled so fast before."

Mike suddenly realised how terrifying the ride in the Land Rover must be to her. He remembered his grandmother, who would hide her fear of speed by talking incessantly whenever she travelled in a car at more than twenty miles per hour. For four thousand years Amalishah had not travelled faster than her legs could run.

"You shall get used to it," he said softly. "How did you travel when you were young?" His doubts about her had been shelved away and all but forgotten; it was very pleasant to talk to her normally.

"By chariot or palanquin," she answered, "Although I saw others travel by camel or in carts pulled by bullocks or..." She said something that Mike did not understand, but which he guessed must have meant some animal. Perhaps she meant 'donkey' or 'mule'. He knew the Assyrian word for 'donkey', but she had used another word. The Assyrians used to hunt wild donkeys for sport. What were wild donkeys called? *Onagers!* Mike felt the small gratification of remembering a word he hardly ever used, his thoughts wandered but he reined them in: *We take mechanical contraptions so much for granted! Our speed must be terrifying for Amalishah!*

"Did you travel a lot when you were young?" asked Ohanian.

"As a child, yes. As a queen, only a little. As a goddess, never."

"Where did you travel as a child?" asked Mike.

"I travelled with my father. He was always going to cities and towns where he would meet people. My father would ask a lot of questions before he gave orders."

"Your father must have been very wise," said Ohanian.

"A ruler without wisdom leads his people astray," the lamia replied.

Ohanian pushed the crumpled donkey jacket aside and sat back in his seat: *Her father was an Assyrian king, of course! When we reach Mosul I shall ask her a million questions!*

4

The land about them gradually changed. There were more trees and they appeared to be much healthier than the trees of the wilderness. They had also come upon a road, of sorts, which allowed them to pick up speed. Several times they passed deserted villages in various stages of decay. The lamia asked: "Why are the villages empty?"

"The young people moved to the cities," replied Mike, "And the older ones either joined them or remained behind until they died."

"How could the king allow this? It is a waste of good soil."

"There haven't been any kings here recently," replied Mike. "The rulers are usually from among the common people."

"That must be why the villages are empty," said the lamia, "The common people care only for their homes and families. For a king, the whole land is his home and the nation is his family."

Mike was glad that Amalishah seemed to be getting her mind off the coming daylight and the speed of the Land Rover, but he was too busy driving to enter a debate about the relative virtues of a monarchy. Ohanian, however, saw the chance to talk about history, his favourite subject after mathematics and cryptoanalysis. "It is much more complicated than that," he said.

"Was there war?" asked the lamia.

"There were many wars in this land," said Ohanian, "Some big, some small."

"But the Hittites are gone!"

Ohanian became thoughtful: "A long time ago different invaders came from distant lands. They settled in the lands of the Hittites and then fought against each other." *There were Babylonians... then the Romans came and they eventually became the Byzantines... and the Persians fought the Byzantines until the Arabs exploded onto this land and smothered the ancient cultures... and then the Crusaders weakened the Byzantines and opened the gates for the Seljuks and the Ottomans!* Each of the invaders had brought appalling misery to Ohanian's ancestors. The lamia noticed that history weighed heavily on him and decided that it would be better if his thoughts were brought back to the present.

5

"Ardashes, teach me about these weapons!"

"Eh? What weapons?"

"The ones on the floor in front of you!"

"Akh! What do you want to know?" *Mike might not like this!*

"These weapons kill with a loud noise. How do they do that?"

Ohanian was at a loss: "Uh... Mike?"

"Go ahead, Ardash! Tell her about some of the wonders of the modern world!"

"I am not one to instruct in the use of guns and grenades!"

"You know enough!"

Ohanian shrugged. *How does one teach someone from the Bronze Age about assault rifles and grenades? Better to take a heuristic approach: One must start with the basics!*

"This is a *bullet*," he began, pointing at a bullet in an ammunition box. "It is the bullet that does the harm. The key is to propel it towards your enemy with sufficient force."

"Like an arrow!" said the lamia, her eyes widening.

"Yes, but much faster. You can see an arrow fly, but not a bullet!"

"*Where* is it propelled in the weapon?"

Ohanian showed her the tube of an assault rifle. The lamia said "Ahh!" and then asked: "*How* is it propelled?"

Ohanian envisaged some difficulty in explaining the idea of an *explosion* but to his amazement the lamia grasped the concept after very little explanation. After that the function of the cartridges was easy to explain. Ohanian decided that this lesson could turn out to be quite enjoyable despite his distaste for the subject. He would much rather have talked about the indecipherable script, but this was definitely not the time for that. The lamia seemed very excited, which meant that she was not actively worrying about the sunlight or the speed with which the Land Rover was gobbling up the distance. Aisha fell asleep, assured that Ohanian would continue talking and keep Mike alert.

The assault rifles were too long to be moved easily in the confined space and remained mostly on the floor, but the grenades were small enough to be handled. The lamia was surprised that an *explosion* could cause so much damage and had to be reassured that the grenades were harmless until the pin was pulled and the handle released.

"But if they quickly break up with a loud noise and kill those around them, of what use are these *fruit-like things?* They would kill whoever pulls the pin and releases the handle!"

Ohanian explained that the grenades exploded a short time after the pin was pulled, so that they could be thrown among those they were intended to kill.

"These *fruit-like things* are strange weapons," said the lamia, "They are thrown like stones!"

"Not like stones," said Ohanian. "Stones have to be thrown hard!"

"And with great accuracy," added the lamia. "I know because that is how I hunted the animals on which I fed when I lived alone."

"You hunted by throwing stones?" Ohanian was astonished.

"Yes. The bows and arrows in the temple rotted away and I could not find the right wood to replace them. So I used stones! At first it was difficult, but gradually I became very good at throwing stones accurately and fast!"

"Well, you don't need to throw these weapons hard. They explode on their own a short time after you pull the pin."

"So shouldn't we prevent them from rolling about on the floor of the *car?*"

"There is nowhere else to put them," said Ohanian.

"Give me the garment you were sleeping on!"

Ohanian handed her the donkey jacket and she carefully put the three grenades in the pockets, two in one of the side pockets and one in the other. The pockets had buttons and the lamia wanted Mike to see how deftly she dealt with them.

"Why did you do that?" asked Ohanian. He wanted to know why she put the grenades in the pockets.

"So they don't roll about and kill us accidentally."

"I told you they're harmless until the pin is pulled!"

"Why take chances?"

6

The stars had dissolved in the slowly brightening sky when Ohanian finished giving the lamia a crash course on modern weapons. The lamia had found the idea of a *trigger* very interesting and had asked whether there were other weapons Ohanian had not told her about. Ohanian told her about aircraft and artillery, with Mike interrupting several times to fill in as much detail as his Assyrian allowed. When Ohanian finally fell silent the lamia seemed saddened by what she had learned.

"And is this what the new world is about?" she asked, "*Cars* and things that carry people through the air and weapons much more deadly than bows and arrows?"

"There are many other things," replied Ohanian, "Some good, some bad. But the most important things in the world are *ideas*, for it is on the quality of its ideas that a civilization must be judged."

"Aren't we getting a wee bit philosophical?" said Mike in English.

"She is deep enough, Mike. And what do you expect at this hour of the night? Or is it morning?"

"True. Sleeplessness is as good as five pints of beer when it comes to maudlin thoughts!"

Ohanian smiled: "Just don't drive into a rock or a tree!"

Mike smiled back: "I'm trying!"

They drove on while the sky became brighter.

"Are all the windows up?" asked Mike in English.

"Yes," said Ohanian, "Soon we shall need the air-conditioning."

"There is no air-conditioning."

"Akh!"

"Remember to make sure she is completely covered by the donkey jacket until we're certain that the glass will protect her."

"Of course. And she should cover her legs in the remaining blanket." Ohanian could not conceal the fact that he was very worried about the lamia. The sky was grey-pink and the sun would rise soon. The rocks on the ground became fewer as they were now on a dirt road. The Land Rover travelled at a good speed.

"The sun shall look down upon us soon," said the lamia.

Mike and Ohanian exchanged glances. The upper part of the lamia's body was covered by the donkey jacket and the lower part was protected by the blanket. The hood of the donkey jacket was pulled over her head.

In due course the sun peeped over the horizon in a glory of blazing light and the lamia shuddered as though she was suddenly very cold. Mike and Ohanian waited for her to say something but she remained silent. Her body remained stiff as the vehicle slowly filled with light.

"Does it hurt?" asked Mike and Ohanian together.

"The light feels hot but... no, it doesn't burn!"

"God be praised!" exclaimed Ohanian in English.

"Let's not be too confident," said Mike, "She hasn't got the full dose yet!"

The light awakened Aisha, who looked about her sleepily before turning to Mukhtar, who was fast asleep.

"He looks better," said Ohanian, "The sleep must be doing him good."

"I think so," said Aisha, "Do we have far to go?"

"We should be reaching some villages soon," replied Mike, "We shall be able to get water and food."

"We still have some water," said Aisha, "Would you mind if we just drive on?"

"Ardash?" asked Mike.

"Yes. Let's drive on Mike. The sooner we get to a hospital..."

He was interrupted by the thud-thud-thud of bullets digging into the spare tyre attached to the back of the vehicle. The tyre deflated with a hiss but the rear glass was undamaged.

7

Because Mike's attention had been on the road he had not looked in the rear-view mirror and had failed to see the truck that was approaching rapidly from behind. The truck was less than a hundred metres away.

"Damn!" cried Mike with considerable vehemence, "Those goddamn bastards again!" He pressed his foot down on the accelerator and the vehicle surged forwards.

"It's one of the murderers' trucks!" cried Aisha.

"I know. Everyone get down!" shouted Mike.

They all crouched low as the gap between the Land Rover and the pursuing truck widened, but the Land Rover was now heaving violently and virtually flying over the rocky ground. Mukhtar screamed in pain.

"You must slow down, Mike, or you will kill him," said Ohanian, "He is full of bullet fragments!" Aisha looked very worried but said nothing.

"I can't slow down! The bastards will kill us all!"

"Slow down, Mike," said the lamia quietly, "Stop at some distance from them. Talk to them. Find out what they want. Offer my crown and jewel if you think it will help."

"We can outrun them!" said Mike defiantly in Assyrian.

"You will kill the wounded man," said the lamia.

632

The truck had speeded up recklessly and was gaining on them despite Mike's efforts. Something landed some ten metres to their left and there was a deafening explosion. Dirt and small stones struck the side of the Land Rover.

"They've got some kind of cannon!" said Ohanian.

"They've got some of the *fruit-like things* that make *explosions!*" said the lamia.

"They've got a grenade launcher," said Mike in English. "I'd better stop."

Mike slowed down and the vehicle came to a halt. The bandits' truck stopped about fifteen metres behind the Land Rover.

"How did they find us?" said Ohanian.

"They must have guessed we're heading for Mosul, and this is the shortest way!"

"What shall we do?" asked Aisha.

"That depends on them. That near miss with the grenade was a warning shot. It meant 'Stop!' It also meant 'we have more grenades and are prepared to use them!'" He spoke to Aisha: "Perhaps you should check that all our assault rifles are loaded and working."

"Yes, Professor."

The door of the truck opened and Selim stepped out. He was holding a white rag.

"It's Selim!" said Ohanian in Arabic, "He wants to talk!"

"Don't trust him, Professor!" muttered Aisha.

"I don't," said Mike.

"Selim was humiliated at the parking lot," said Aisha, "And he is a vindictive man who will not forget a humiliation. Yet he refrained from killing us all with the RPG. That means that he wants to get something from us before he takes his revenge."

Mike did not reply.

The lamia remained serene, unmoving and silent. If she was concerned about how things would work out she did not show it.

5 1

AND THE SCALES FELL FROM HIS EYES

1

SINCE LEAVING THE hill, Mike had believed that the saga with the bandits was well and truly over. The re-emergence of Selim therefore came as something of a shock: *Will we never get rid of these vermin?* Now Selim stood in the sunlight, about ten metres behind the Land Rover; ahead of the truck and to its left. He looked supremely pleased with himself as he waved the white rag above his head. Mike continued to sit in the Land Rover, staring at Selim in the wing mirror. He had no option other than to deal with the fact that the bandits were back – with a grenade launcher! In a resigned voice he said in Arabic: "I think I had better go and talk to him." He spoke to no one in particular.

Ohanian nodded in reluctant agreement, but he was frowning gloomily: *This is like a forced move in a chess game. Mike has to go and talk to that evil man!* Aisha recognised in Mike the I-don't-care-anymore manner of a man struggling against loss of hope: *The Professor is more tired than any of us and feels defeated! He will be no match for Selim if he feels like this!*

"Please don't go yet," she pleaded, "Let us first make some kind of plan."

"What kind of plan can we make?" said Mike angrily, "They can fire their grenade launcher at us any time they want!"

Aisha shook her head: "I don't think they will use the RPG as long as the tall lady's crown and jewel are in the car."

Ohanian's gloomy frown lightened: "And if you look carefully at that evil man," he added in English, "You will see that he is confident extremely. That could make him do something foolish!"

"Your friend is right," said Aisha, not quite sure of what Ohanian had said but guessing that it was meant to boost Mike's confidence.

Mike shrugged and gave a lopsided smile: "Thanks for the encouragement. Perhaps we can outwit these people after all. Now I've got to go!" He felt better.

"Please not yet, Professor," said Aisha, "You will take one of the automatic rifles?"

"No, Selim might see that as a provocation. I'll take the pistol."

"That is only a toy gun!" said Aisha, referring to the long-muzzled weapon.

"It's a very accurate pistol and easy to conceal." He checked the firing mechanism and made sure the safety was off. "I'm hoping that Selim will think I'm unarmed." He tucked the pistol in his belt, at the back and out of sight, and made sure it was covered by his desert jacket.

"Selim is not easy to fool, Professor," said Aisha, "and he will remember your pistol from the time you shot Nabil. Take an assault rifle but then pretend to change your mind and drop it after you leave the car. If you do that he may think you don't have another weapon."

"Very well."

"And beware of his knife! Selim can throw it without warning and he is as fast as a striking snake!"

"I'll remember that."

Aisha was reluctant to let him go: "How many cartridges are in the pistol?"

"There are four left."

"That should be enough. And while you are talking to Selim I shall get out and stand behind the car so that I can use my automatic rifle more effectively if you need help."

"Don't get out too soon! Selim's friends may take a shot at you if you get out of the car unexpectedly. Stay inside until I give you a signal to get out."

"What signal?"

Mike thought for a moment. "I'll raise my hands to my head, as though I'm frightened or very worried – like this!" Mike put his right hand to his temple. "When I do that, ask them something and get out of the car slowly with your weapon pointing down. They probably won't shoot you if you're talking to them."

"I'll make sure they don't shoot me. Oh, and please, if you can, let us know how many men are in the truck."

"When I know for certain I'll put my hands behind my back and show you with my fingers!"

"I'll keep my eyes on you, Professor." She reached over and took hold of three assault rifles, made sure they were loaded, and handed one to Mike and one to Ohanian, who took it hesitantly.

Mike noticed the hesitation and said: "Remember you might have to use that, Ardash!"

"Don't worry," replied Ohanian resolutely, "If I need to protect you I'll use it. Should I get out and stand behind the car too?"

"You'll be safer in the car. If you need to shoot, lower the window and fire the assault rifle through the open window so they don't see the muzzle. Don't try to aim and above all, don't expose yourself!"

At that moment Selim bawled in a loud voice: **"I am waiting to talk to you, Englishman!"**

Mike turned to the lamia. "When I leave," he said in Assyrian, "please lie down! *Bullets* cannot pass through the back of the *car.*"

"I understand, Mike."

Mike turned off the engine and was about to open the car door when the lamia almost whispered: "May the gods be with you, Michael Townsend."

"And what of the goddesses?" said Mike, trying to dampen the gravity of the situation.

"One goddess will always be with you," she replied quietly with a faint smile.

Mike smiled back, a goodbye smile, and got out of the Land Rover carrying one of the assault rifles. He was surprised at how calm he felt. Selim was waiting with the white rag in one hand and the other hand on his hip, a confrontational pose accentuated by an arrogant grin.

2

When he saw Mike leave the car armed with a rifle Selim lost his grin and let the white rag fall to the ground. Mike knew that this was a critical moment. Pretending to be utterly bewildered, he looked around him vacantly and then, as though suddenly making a difficult decision, raised the rifle and tossed it away. Selim's grin returned as Mike walked diffidently towards him with his arms by his sides and his palms facing forwards: *Look humble, chum! None of your customary cockiness!* The sun was shining through the clouds and there was no wind at all; the only sound was that of the engine of the bandit's truck.

It had not been turned off and emitted a deep growl punctuated by intermittent rattling.

Selim's only weapon seemed to be a heavy knife held prominently at his waist by a broad sash, which sagged under the weight of the knife. Mike's thoughts raced furiously: *Could there be a pistol at the back of the sash? Probably not. Selim and his two friends didn't have a pistol and the new lot are unlikely to have brought one!* Mike studied the occupants of the truck.

There were only three men in the vehicle: one in the cab and two at the back of the open truck. Mike had not seen any of them before and all were staring at him suspiciously: *They're not happy with Selim's idea of bringing me here; I must convince them I'm harmless!* The man in the cab sat scowling with his shoulders hunched and both hands on the steering wheel. *He's ready to give chase in case we make a run for it!* Could the driver have a firearm beside him in the cab? It was to Selim's advantage for the bandits to display all the firepower they had: *If the driver has a firearm he wouldn't conceal it. So he probably doesn't have a firearm – but he could use the truck as a weapon!*

At the back of the truck one of the two bandits was leaning against the cab holding a double-barrelled shotgun. His finger was on the trigger and the muzzle remained trained on Mike as he moved towards Selim. The man was big and muscular, with a drooping black moustache, and he glared at Mike with a dark expression. Mike avoided looking at the man: *Not the thinking type! He doesn't trust me at all and is likely to pull the trigger if he thinks I'm staring at him!* The other bandit, a small wiry man, sat precariously on the tailgate with a loaded grenade launcher resting on his shoulder. His attention kept darting from Selim to Mike and back again. *He's waiting for a signal from Selim to blow up the Land Rover!* Could Aisha get a clean shot at the bandits at the back of the truck? The man with the shotgun was protected by the cab and the bandit with the grenade-launcher couldn't even be seen from the Land Rover as long as he was sitting. *Ah! But he can't fire the grenade without getting up! That's a split second lost!* The more immediate danger was from the shotgun. His preliminary assessment over, Mike considered the other question: *Where are Selim's two erstwhile companions?* He scanned the terrain behind the truck as well as behind the Land Rover but there was nobody there. *Where **are** the two cretins? I can't plan anything without knowing where they are!*

3

Mike stopped about four metres from the electrician: "Hello Selim. I am surprised to see you again!" He spoke Arabic.

Selim's grin broadened: "I am sure you are surprised, Englishman! Was I not lucky to have found some friends in the wastelands? And was I not lucky that my friends had a shotgun and an RPG with two grenades?"

So there are no other weapons! And that's the only grenade they have left! "What happened to the other trucks?"

"They are in heaven, Englishman. As you know, the very big truck was trashed at the hill. The other trucks were chased by the helicopters and broken into little pieces. My friends in them were also broken into little pieces!" Selim shook his head in mock sadness.

"But this one got away," said Mike, "And you had the good fortune that it managed to find you and your two friends!"

"My two friends are no longer in this world," said Selim, and again he shook his head in mock sadness. "But my new friends are much better, especially the one with the RPG!"

So he got killed his two companions for their food and water! Mike put his hands behind his back and held out three fingers to show Aisha and Ohanian that there were three men in all. "There are always accidents in the wastelands," he said solemnly, "but you were very lucky to have been picked up by your new friends!"

"I am protected by an angel, Englishman! Did you know that this was the third time my angel protected me?"

A plan of sorts was forming in Mike's mind, but it relied on split-second timing and he was not sure it was feasible. If Selim's need for revenge was aroused he would give the go-ahead to the fellow with the grenade-launcher without provocation. A lot depended on how much Selim wanted Amalishah's crown and jewel. For the plan to work Selim had to be flattered, humoured, made to feel in control. His irritating verbosity had to be encouraged. In deferential tones Mike asked: "How did your angel protect you three times, Selim?"

Selim did not answer at once: *Is the Englishman mocking me? Do Englishmen believe in angels? Probably not, he's just a heathen!* Abruptly he shouted: **"Why did you take so long to get out of your car?"**

Mike remained calm. Very humbly he said: "My companions are very frightened of you, Selim. They did not want me to come out of the car and talk to you!"

Mike's answer was flattering to Selim: *I am the lion and the dogs are frightened of me! I must frighten this English dog more!* His grin grew cold and, very leisurely, he pulled out his knife and toyed with the pommel as though trying to decide whether to answer or throw the weapon. Mike pretended to stare at the knife in abject fear and was pleased to see Selim's cold grin turn into a smile of satisfaction. Still toying with the pommel of his knife Selim said: "Your friends are wise to be afraid of me, Englishman!"

"Please tell me how your angel is protecting you, Selim. It is not often that someone is guarded by an angel."

Selim took his time in answering. He did not want to exchange pointless words with the foreigner but feared that if he did not give due credit to the angel his help would be withdrawn. Eventually he said: "It is a story of wonders, Englishman! I might have gone down the ramp with the stupid workers and got killed but my angel held me back. And when I slid down the hill after the helicopters came I might have been shot by the soldiers, but my angel made them blind and they did not see me. And then this truck managed to escape from the helicopters but it got lost!"

"It got *lost?*" Mike sounded incredulous. "How could it get lost?" *The more he talks the less likely he is to blow up the Land Rover!*

"It is a miracle, isn't it? My friends wanted to drive straight but they drove in a circle! It was dark but they couldn't turn on any lights because of the helicopters. They thought they were driving straight but my angel made them drive in a circle and find me!"

"Don't they have a compass?"

Selim sneered as he said: "I don't think any of them knows how to use a compass. Anyway, they haven't got a compass. So they went round in a circle until they found me. Am I not very lucky, Englishman?"

"An angel is surely protecting you, Selim!"

"I think so!" Selim's grin vanished and his face hardened: "You must not forget that my angel is still protecting me now, while we speak! Do you understand that, Englishman?"

"I can only agree with you, Selim. An angel must be protecting you!" Mike's voice expressed hopelessness mixed with fear. "But what do you want from us?"

Selim's grin returned. He shrugged and raised his hands as though to say: 'I'm not asking for much!' but he said menacingly: "I want you to give us all the money you have as well as the things you stole, the

639

golden crown and the jewel! I also want Mukhtar, if he's still alive."

"I see," said Mike, pretending to be surprised at Selim's demands. "Yes, Mukhtar is still alive."

"Then you will give him to me!"

"Don't you want Aisha?"

Selim smiled insolently, the way a cat might smile at a bird caught in its claws: "No, I don't want Aisha; she can stay with your friend and the tall woman in the car. I just want your money and Mukhtar and the ancient things you stole, the things the tall woman was wearing. Do you have a lot of money with you?"

"Well yes, of course. All the money my friends and I had. But we hoped to use part of it to pay for Mukhtar's hospital fees!" *If he thinks there's a lot of money in the car he'll be less willing to blow it up too soon!*

"Forget Mukhtar. He will come with us. How much money is in the car?"

"I don't know exactly. A few thousand dollars?" *I must arouse his greed but he mustn't think I'm exaggerating!*

"Is that all? I expected rich foreigners to have more!"

"I don't know how much money my friend and the tall woman brought. You are right, perhaps there is more than just a few thousand dollars in the car."

"Pray there is enough to make me feel generous, Englishman!"

Mike was in no doubt that when the electrician got what he wanted he would give the go-ahead to the fellow with the grenade launcher, but he had to play the role of the naïve foreigner to the full: "If we give you what you want," he said innocently, "What will happen to us?"

Selim returned the knife to the sash at his waist and spread his arms in a gesture of benevolent generosity. "I shall, of course, let you go on your way in peace!"

The man with the shotgun guffawed and Selim gave him an angry look. Mike noticed that the bandit on the tailgate was grinning: *Good! They're starting to enjoy this little game of Selim's. They must be made to believe that the game is as good as won!*

"You can have Mukhtar and all our money," said Mike, "But surely you can't ask for both the crown and the jewel. Apart from the money, that's all we've got!"

"I know that's all you've got, Englishman, but in return you'll be allowed to stay alive and drive away!" He made a squiggly gesture with his fingers as he said 'drive away'.

"The crown and the jewel belong to the tall woman," said Mike, feigning indecision, "We didn't steal them."

Selim laughed mirthlessly: "That is not important. You will tell the tall woman or Aisha to bring them and all the money in your car to me!"

"I shall have to go back to the car and ask the tall woman if she is willing to give up her crown and jewel."

"You will *not* go back to the car, Englishman. You will shout for someone to bring me the crown and the jewel and all the money in the car!"

"What about Mukhtar?"

"My driver will bring Mukhtar to my truck once I get the money, the gold and the jewel."

"Mukhtar cannot walk!"

"Then my driver will drag him to me."

"What if I refuse to give you the crown as well as the jewel and the money?"

"If you refuse…" Selim shrugged and his eyes grew cold, although the grin remained.

4

Mike pretended to be confused. "I know you're not a killer, Selim," he said in seeming desperation. "You're the best electrician I've ever met! A true professional! I didn't believe Aisha when she said you killed the soldier in the radio tent. I am sure we can reach some sort of agreement." *I've got to convince him that he's almost won, but the victory must not appear too easy or he'll suspect a trick!*

Selim could not hide his pride at having killed more than once: "Oh, I also killed one of Balushi's men near the edge of the hill late at night!"

Mike was dumbfounded. "*You* killed the young soldier?" *My God, it wasn't Amalishah!*

"Of course it was me, and I shall have you all killed if you don't do exactly as I say!"

"But," and Mike almost stammered because he was dazed by the enormity of what he had just learned, "The body of the soldier was drained of blood! How did you do that?"

Selim found the question comical: "The idiot died with half his body lying over the edge of the hill! His blood gushed from his throat

641

like water from a faucet and fell down to the rocks!"

Mike felt relief, anger at himself, guilt: *She didn't kill the boy and I treated her abysmally! But this isn't the time for remorse!* Mike's heart was pounding and the adrenaline surge sharpened his senses: *I've got to find a way to get us out of this mess, if only to make it up to her!* "Please, Selim," he pleaded, "Would you accept only the money, Mukhtar and the crown? There is a lot of money in the car and the red jewel isn't worth much!"

"Don't waste my time, Englishman."

Mike appeared defeated, distressed, the way only a thief who is forced to give up all his loot can be distressed. He shook his head as though confused and wandered aimlessly forward, like a man too stunned by defeat to remain in one place. The seemingly random displacement brought him closer to the man with the grenade launcher and so close to Selim that Mike feared that the electrician would make a quick stab with his knife, but Selim was too pleased by Mike's apparent distress to use his knife and the men in the truck were greatly amused by Mike's apparent misery. In a show of wretched hopelessness Mike raised both hands to his temples.

Immediately Aisha shouted: "Do you have any water to spare?"

"What?" exclaimed the man with the shotgun. He was so astonished by the absurdity of the question that his attention turned from Mike to Aisha, who was getting slowly out of the Land Rover. The man with the grenade launcher did not move but his attention was no longer on Mike or Selim.

Selim laughed. "Isn't it funny?" he said loudly to the men in the truck, "How women ask stupid questions when they are afraid to die?" The bandits at the back of the truck grinned and exchanged glances. The muzzle of the shotgun drooped and the man with the grenade launcher relaxed visibly. Nobody was looking at Mike.

This was the moment Mike was hoping for: *Lord! Let their fingers be loose on the triggers!* And with that thought he moved faster than he had ever moved before. He reached behind him for the pistol, pulled it from his belt, pointed it and fired, depending more on instinct and training than on deliberate aim. There was a loud bang and the man with the shotgun died suddenly and collapsed. The shotgun fell to the floor of the truck with a clunk. The man with the grenade launcher sprang up just as Mike fired three more times, hitting him thrice in the chest. He lurched sideways and tumbled backwards off the back of the truck. The grenade launcher fell to the ground behind the truck

642

beside him. Before Selim could react Mike scooped up the grenade launcher and, pointing it away from the Land Rover, fired the missile. At that moment Aisha opened fire and shattered the windscreen of the truck. The driver cursed loudly and ducked just in time. With a scream of gears the truck lunged forward and the engine stalled.

But for all his speed Mike was not fast enough to get away from Selim. The grenade was still in the air, screaming as it flew towards the empty landscape, when Mike felt Selim's strong arm around his neck and the sharp point of Selim's knife pressing against his side.

"Drop the pistol Englishman!"

Mike dropped the empty pistol just as the grenade exploded somewhere in the distance.

Livid at having been tricked, Selim snarled: "Now you will order the tall woman to bring me..." he stopped, for the tall woman appeared before him as though by magic. Selim was astounded at the speed at which she had covered the distance.

"You will give me the knife," she said in Assyrian.

"What is she saying?" said Selim, "And what is happening to her?" For although she was wearing the donkey jacket and the hood was over her head the lamia was burning in the sunlight. The skin of her face was slowly turning a fiery red.

"Go back to the *car!*" Mike husked, "Let Aisha deal with this!"

"I'm not leaving you alone with this man," said the lamia evenly. She took off her crown and ripped the jewel from around her neck, offered them to Selim. But even as she spoke the skin on her face and hand slowly dried and curled back, revealing pink flesh. As Selim watched in horror the tissue became covered in dark brown splotches.

"She will give you the gold and the jewel if you give her your knife," said Mike, trying to conceal his anguish at what was happening to the lamia.

Selim did not have a free hand. He tried to grab the crown and the jewel from the lamia's hands while still holding the knife but she was too quick for him. "Give them to me!" he hissed. But the lamia just looked at him calmly, holding her crown and jewel just out of his reach. Selim stared at her in horror as the flesh of her face pulled back, exposing her teeth and gums.

"She will give you the gold and the jewel if you give her your knife," repeated Mike.

"She will take my knife and give me nothing!" shouted Selim, trying not to stare at the lamia, but he realised that he had little choice.

Too many things had gone wrong and he was confused. If he killed the Englishman Aisha would shoot him, her weapon was aimed at him and he knew how good she was at using it. With a dreadful scowl he made up his mind and abruptly proffered his knife to the lamia, pommel first, trying not to look at her face. In a lightning movement the knife was snatched from his hand and the crown and jewel came within his reach. Selim pushed Mike away and grabbed them roughly before dashing to the truck and climbing into the back. "Drive off!" he shouted to the driver. The engine came to life and the truck lunged forward just as Ohanian, thinking that the hostilities were finished, left the protection of the Land Rover and ran towards Mike shouting: "Mike! Are you all right?"

But the truck had to pass close to Ohanian, and Selim, despite having got the crown and the jewel, had to vent his vindictiveness somehow. He reached down quickly to pick up the shotgun and fired both barrels at Ohanian.

"No!" screamed Mike, but Ohanian fell to the ground and lay still.

In a state of shock, Mike turned to the lamia and said: "My love, get back to the *car!*"

But despite the excruciating pain, the lamia said in a horribly distorted voice: "He killed our friend!" Her words sounded grotesque and her voice was dry, like that of someone who had not spoken for a long time.

Mike, tormented by the death of Ohanian, could only watch mutely at her lips. They no longer covered her gums and the pearl-white teeth were exposed. He tried to put his arms around her but she pushed him gently away: "Don't look at me, Mike," she rasped, "you won't like what you see!"

But as the truck accelerated past the Land Rover she reached into the pockets of the donkey jacket and pulled out the three *fruit-like things* she had been told would bring death when the little pins were pulled out. Was it Assyrian vengefulness? Did the ancients have a need for revenge in a measure that modern men and women have lost? Or was it the memory of something she had been taught as a child, that a queen cannot allow herself to die while she can still exact vengeance on those who had committed a great wrong?

Her whole body shook with the strength of her effort as she pulled out the pins. Then, standing at her full height, she threw the three grenades in quick succession at the rapidly receding truck. Her aim was admirable: The first grenade exploded at the back of the truck, tearing Selim apart and throwing the crown, the jewel and bits of Selim away from the vehicle. The second and third went off simultaneously beneath the truck, causing it to overturn and burst into flames. Her duty accomplished, the lamia's knees gave way and she crumpled to the ground. Mike covered her immediately with the donkey jacket just as Aisha ran up to help. She and Mike carried the lamia hurriedly to the Land Rover.

5

Dealing with the body of Ohanian was harder, and Aisha wept quietly as Mike, holding back his own tears, lifted the body of his friend and placed him gently beside Mukhtar.

"This was an unnecessary death," said Aisha as Mike started the motor.

"We must get to Mosul as quickly as possible!" Mike replied. He put the engine into gear and drove off.

Although Amalishah was now protected from the sunlight, she was in a frightful state. Aisha could not understand what had happened to her and asked "Will the tall lady recover, Professor?"

"I don't know!" Mike husked, as he tried to concentrate on his driving: "With enough care, perhaps." He felt numb and could not show any emotion. The death of Ohanian had wounded him deeply but Amalishah's life was in the balance.

"Then please, can you drive back for a moment and stop beside the burning truck?"

"Drive back?" asked Mike, as though in a daze. "Why?"

Aisha wanted to recover the crown and the jewel for Amalishah.

Part 3

Epilogue

52A

Obituary

Extract from an Obituary in the London Times:

Professor Sir Michael Townsend CBE, 67, and his wife, Amalishah, 45. Professor Townsend died of heart failure at Rockbridge Hospital, Hants., last Tuesday. He had begun his professional career as an engineer, during which time he amassed a considerable fortune and married his first wife Doris Wolfram, who was also an engineer. When Doris passed away less than a year later in a tragic car accident he left engineering and began a new career in archaeology. He became an expert on Assyrian and Babylonian history and was soon internationally renowned as an authority on ancient Assyria. He met his second wife, Amalishah, during an expedition to the Middle East and they were married in Mosul, Iraq, where they lived for about two years before moving to England. Amalishah Townsend was known as a gracious hostess to the family's close friends although she suffered from a rare dietary disorder and a skin ailment that made her shun sunlight. The funeral of Professor Townsend was attended by his son, Dr. Robert Townsend 27, and his daughter, Alma Townsend 18, as well as several dignitaries including the Mayor of London and the Chancellor of University College. Among Professor Townsend's numerous friends and colleagues at the funeral were Professors Carol and Bradley Weiss, who flew in from the U.S.A, Professor Leonard Ehrlich and General Hussein ElBalushi of the Iraqi Armed Forces, who came with his wife, Jehan.

Lady Amalishah Townsend died tragically a day after her

husband's funeral in a mysterious fire that ravaged the cottage at the end of their garden.

52B

LETTER TO ALMA

Dearest Daughter,

I write you this letter on the eve of your father's funeral. Tomorrow he shall be buried in the graveyard by the old village church he loved so much, in the shady plot beneath the bay tree. The funeral shall take place in broad daylight, or at least in as much daylight as an English Autumn can provide, and I will not be able to attend. But you and Robert shall be there, as will many of our closest friends, and your father's spirit shall not feel alone. When you and your brother return home I shall be in the living room with the curtains drawn, as is my wont, and perhaps you shall say, once again, that our home seems so empty now that your father is gone.

I did not shed tears when your father left us, but know that I have never felt as crippled by my condition as I feel now by my inability to attend his funeral. Not even when I was unable to play with you in the garden, or when I could not take you to school and pick you up. Not even when I could not share with you the little cakes you baked when you were six! My only solace is that you and Robert will never suffer from my symptoms. According to the experts your father and I consulted, whatever caused me to become as I am could not affect my genes and my condition will not be transmitted to my descendants.

I see in you an echo of myself, and when you were no longer a child I frequently thought of telling you a little about my life before I met your father. But during your early teenage years I was afraid that you might ask questions for whose answers you were not yet ready, and when you were older we never spent enough time together. Now that you are eighteen, and have begun your studies at Oxford, events have overtaken me and I must write a letter to say a very small part of what I wanted to tell you.

I hope that the hints this letter contains shall awaken your curiosity regarding my life before I met your father. You might find it an interesting story. If you wish to learn more about your mother's early years I suggest you begin by going over some of your father's later publications regarding the Assyrian goddess, Amalishah. Reflect upon the facts that the ancient goddess and your mother shared the same name and that the contemporaries of the ancient goddess believed her to be immortal.

I was not born with the inability to bear the sunlight or digest normal food. I only became how I am after a prolonged illness when I was still a young woman. There was nothing special about my illness, it was severe and terminal but it was just one of many illnesses that afflicted my people. It was not the illness that made me as I am but the cure. I was not conscious during much of my illness and do not know what the cure was, but soon after I felt healthy I realised that I was unable to digest normal food. Not much later, when I tried to go out in the fresh air, I discovered that sunlight burned my skin and destroyed the tissue beneath. It was evident that prolonged exposure to sunlight would kill me. There were other changes also, but they were not as important.

For a time I believed that my changes were temporary, but they were permanent and gradually dominated the way I lived. I became a creature of the night. Due to my social standing, the people around me had to adapt to my differences and their lives were forced to change, often drastically. In those days people were willing to accept what they did not understand because they knew that they understood very little. Everything was explained in terms of religion or superstition and so, for many years, I lived among normal people protected by religion and superstition.

Not long afterwards my ailments appeared I had to leave my home and live somewhere far from where I was born. In that new place conditions were harsh, but my needs were catered for and over the years my life gradually settled into a monotonous routine that, for me, was normality. For a long time very little of my world changed while I did not change at all, but then, in one terrible night, everything around me was destroyed in a storm of violence. All whom I knew perished, including those whom I loved, and much that was beautiful was lost during that night. Much that was ugly was lost also, but I was too young in mind to make the distinction and I suffered from the loss of those I loved as well as the loss of the beautiful and the ugly.

For a long time I lived on my own and knew only the crushing isolation of those who have lost everything but their lives. Yet although loneliness became my companion it also became my mentor. One can learn a lot during a long period of loneliness. It was loneliness that prepared me for what was to come, so that when I eventually met your father I was at first surprised, then I savoured the sweet taste of hope, and finally I found a happiness such as I had never imagined possible.

Your father and I lived as husband and wife far more blissfully than most, but it was not always so. When we first expressed our love for each other I knew that your father had doubts in his heart because of how I had lived long before I met him. I did not resent these doubts, for your father knew enough about my past to have good reason to question the wisdom of feeling love towards someone like me, but I hoped that he would come to see that the love of Amalishah was true and unblemished. Your father's misgivings were only laid to rest after we left the place where I had spent most of my life. But until then they awakened more than once, like a scorpion that stung his heart with venom, and every time his doubts were awakened I suffered deeply.

You must be wondering how dreadful my past must have been to make your father doubt me so. Some of my past was certainly dreadful, but it was never shameful. Your mother had always walked, as my people used to say, in the path of the lion, which meant that she always acted with honour and carried out her responsibilities dutifully. But the world in which your mother grew up did not have the softening influences of a society as interdependent and law-protected as yours. Even our religion did not encourage inner harmony, for we worshipped many gods and feared the demons that we thought were everywhere. We believed the gods to be whimsical, benevolent or malevolent without cause, always capricious and unpredictable, and if one believes that the gods can show malice without reason one always feels exposed and threatened. Such feelings harden the heart and enable one to act with unrestrained cruelty. Eventually my responsibilities imposed exigencies upon me that you would find abhorrent, as your father did, although they were far in the past. I shall not speak of what I was forced to do; suffice it to say that at first your father found it difficult to believe that someone who had lived a life like mine could love.

As you know, your father and I lived in Mosul for about two years before coming to England. On the way to Mosul I was exposed to sunlight and almost lost my life. Your father nursed me back to health and cared for me with single-minded devotion even though my burns had made me indescribably hideous. We got married soon after I was well and looked normal again, and while we lived in Mosul he taught me Arabic and English. He also taught me the rules and ethics of his culture, which were so different from those of mine. When we came to England he held my hand tightly and never turned away during the difficult period during which I struggled to fit myself into the society of an English academic.

It is now three months since your father's health started to falter and Robert came to live with us. I became aware that your father did not have long to live after he returned from a check-up at the hospital. As usual he told me everything, but although he did not mention the results of his tests and put on a jolly face in front of you and Robert, when you and I were alone you had said: "There is something very wrong with Dad!"

And I had replied "Yes, I know."

Then you had asked "How long has he got?"

And I had replied "Only the gods know!"

You had looked at me strangely and tears had come to your eyes: "The prognosis must have been very bad," you said, "You always speak of the gods when you're upset!"

When you uttered those words a darkness filled my heart, for I had to confront that which I had dreaded for many years. Your words made me aware, with a conviction I had never felt before, that your father, my Mike, was going to leave us and that the happy days I had spent with him were coming to an end. The darkness in my heart continued to grow as his health grew worse, but when he left us the darkness lifted and I found the strength to write you this letter.

The darkness lifted because of a promise I had made to your father when we first expressed our love for each other. It was late at night and we were alone in a moonlit grove near the place where I had spent most of my life. It was a magical night for me: the stars seemed to shine more brightly than usual, as though they had come closer the better to witness the pledging of our hearts. I do not remember the words your father spoke that night, but I do remember feeling that with this man, and this man only, I would find not just a remedy for my loneliness but also fulfilment. So although I had until then been as hard as a Hittite sword, when your father and I opened our hearts to each other I softened and my heart grew warm.

But there is also finality in fulfilment. If one has lived many years without purpose, and if one has previously lost everything one loved, when one finally finds someone who gives meaning to one's existence the prospect of living without that very special person becomes intolerable. And so, dearest daughter, in that moonlit grove so far from where I am *now, I promised your father that when he left this life I would follow.*

You might suspect that when I made that promise I expected to follow your father with reluctance. That was not so. I knew in my heart that he would be more than a husband, more than a teacher, more than a lover, more than a friend. I also knew that, when he left, the purpose and meaning that he had brought into my life would leave with him. So when you think of your mother know that she followed your father willingly. That is why I did not shed tears when your father left us.

The day after tomorrow I shall end my life in the little cottage at the bottom of our garden. The cottage will burn and I shall make sure that Amalishah will be reduced to ashes so that there will be no autopsy. Think of your mother's departure as a sacrifice to the dead. A willing sacrifice. Like everyone else, Robert will believe that my departure was an accident; I ask you to keep the truth about your mother's death a secret, even from Robert.

Your father has arranged that nothing in our home be disturbed while you pursue your studies at Oxford. You will have no material worries because your father leaves you and Robert a substantial fortune. I, dearest daughter, leave you two things that you shall find in the bedroom your father and I shared. In the locked wooden cabinet beside the fireplace you shall find a golden crown and a large red jewel. They were once mine; when I am gone they shall be yours.

Remains only to seal this letter and send it to our lawyer, Mr. Henderson, with instructions that it be given to you on your twenty-first birthday.

Your mother who loves you dearly,

Amalishah

Also from Oxford eBooks

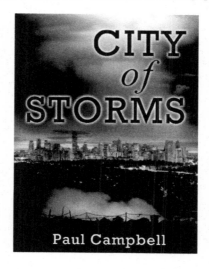

ISBN 978-1-908387-99-8 (Paperback)
ISBN 978-1-908387-97-4 (ePUB)
ASIN B00R893CEM (Kindle)

When top foreign correspondent Sean Brian flies into Manila in the Philippines as part of his Asian news beat, a typhoon and a political revolution are uppermost in his thoughts.

But what also awaits will turn his already busy life into a roller coaster of romance, adventure, elation and despair.

At the centre of this transformation is an infant boy child, born, abandoned and plunged into street poverty in the grim underbelly of an Asian metropolis.

This is the catalyst for a story ranging from the corrupt, violent world of back street city sex clubs and drug addiction, to the clean air of the Sulu Sea and the South Pacific; from the calm safety of an island paradise to the violent guerilla world of the notorious Golden Triangle and the southern Philippines archipeligo.

As we follow the child, Bagyo, into fledgling manhood, we can only wonder at the ripples that spread from one individual to engulf so many others – and at the injustice that still corrodes life on the mean streets of the world.

Lightning Source UK Ltd.
Milton Keynes UK
UKOW04f1525031117
312134UK00001B/19/P